THE CEREMONIES

THE CEREMONIES

T.E.D. KLEIN

THE VIKING PRESS   NEW YORK

LIBRARY OF CONGRESS CATALOGING IN PUBLICATION DATA
Klein, T.E.D.
The ceremonies.
I. Title.
PS3561.L374C4   1984   813′.54   83-47858
ISBN 0-670-20982-1

Portions of this novel first appeared in
The Year's Best Horror Stories: Series II in 1972,
under the title "The Events at Poroth Farm."

Printed in the United States of America
Set in CRT Devinne
Designed by Ann Gold

CHRISTMAS

The forest was ablaze.

From horizon to horizon stretched a wall of smoke and flame, staining the night sky red and blotting out the stars. Vegetation shriveled and was instantly consumed; great trees toppled shrieking toward the earth, dying gods before an angry gale, and the sound of their destruction was like the roaring of a thousand winds.

For seven days the fire raged, unimpeded and unquenchable. No one was there to stop it; no one had seen it start, save the scattered tribes of Mengos and Unamis who had fled in terror from their homes. Among them there were some who said that, on the evening of the blaze, they'd seen a star fall from the sky and crash amid the woods. Others claimed that lightning was the cause, or a queer red liquid bubbling from the ground.

Perhaps none of them were right.

Let it, therefore, rest at this: the events recorded here began as one day they would end—

In mystery

At last the flames were dampened by a night of steady rain. The morning sun rose upon a kingdom of ashes, a desolate grey land without a tree left standing or a trace of life—save, at its very center, the charred and blistered body of an ancient cottonwood, the tallest object for miles around.

The tree was dead. But crouched amid its branches, hidden by a web of smoke still rising from the earth, something lived: something older far than humankind, and darker than some vast and sunless cavern on a world beyond the farthest depths of space. Something that breathed, schemed, felt itself dying and, dying, lived on.

It was outside nature, and alone. It had no name. High above the smoking ground it waited, black against the blackness of the tree. Fire had ravaged its body; a limb had been devoured by the flames. Where once a head had been, and something rather like a face, was now a crumbling mass the form and color of charcoal. Still it clung implacably to life, as to the branch round which its claws were fixed. Survival was a thing of calculation; there was something it must do before it died. Now was not the time, but it was patient. It closed its one remaining eye and settled down to wait. Its time would come.

The planet spun; moons waxed and waned; vegetation returned, groping hungrily up through the ashes. The scarred place on the planet's surface was lost beneath a canopy of green, and once again the trees rose straight and tall to catch the sunlight.

Only in a small grove near the center was a difference to be seen. There the foliage was not so thick, and the trees themselves had grown back shorter, coarser, curiously stunted, like the life forms at the summit of a mountain. Others had taken on odd shapes, with trunks split into a hundred branching arms, or twisted, or swollen obscenely like the bodies of drowned animals. When a wind swept westward from off the sea, turning the roof of the forest into an ocean of waving leaves, no such movement stirred the shadowy confines of the grove.

The very earth there was changed. By night it seemed to glow as if a fire still raged beneath. At intervals thin wisps of steam would drift up from the ground, curling past the roots and leafless boughs, obscuring both the treetops and the sky.

The Indians seldom ventured near that part of the forest, and even avoided speaking of it after a woman gathering firewood described the thing she'd seen there, squatting in a dead tree in the middle of the grove.

For the thing, no word existed. But they found one for the grove in which it chose to wait.

Maquineanok, they called it. The Place of Burning.

A year passed. And another. And then five thousand more. The stars had shifted slowly in their courses. The sky looked different now.

So did the planet's face. The Indians were dead, and the forest land had dwindled to a third its size. Settlers had dotted it with homesteads; engineers had crisscrossed it with roads; farmers had cleared off a patchwork of fields for pasturing and corn. Villages had sprouted, townships spread; somewhere a city was being laid out that would spell destruction for another million trees.

Here and there some remnants of the former age survived: hidden knots of wilderness where man had never walked, and where the great trees still struggled as before, unchallenged and unseen. Such places, though, were few, and disappearing fast; soon, within the compass of a century, the forest and its secrets would belong to man alone.

Where the ancient woods were deepest, in the region that the Indians had called Maquineanok, five thousand years of quietude had already been breached. Months ago the grove had rung to the distant echoes of a hammer; now, at any moment, human footsteps might penetrate the silence and the gloom.

Still it waited.

The boy was not yet lost, but he was puzzled. He had wandered into this part of the forest by mistake, trying out the new snowshoes he'd received that morning, and suddenly he'd found himself unable to proceed, his left shoe mired in two inches of mud. Elsewhere the forest floor was blanketed in white, but here the earth showed through in great bare patches, and the grey December sky was reflected in puddles of melted snow.

Stepping back in search of firmer ground, he brushed a pale strand of hair from his eyes and tucked it beneath the hand-knit woolen cap. All afternoon he'd had a steady wind behind him, but now it had stopped; until this moment he had hardly been aware of it. Running a tongue over his chapped lips, he looked around him, ears straining for a sound. His own breathing seemed unnaturally loud in the winter silence.

There was something different about these woods. He saw it now. It was more than just the lack of snow. The trees were smaller here, and queerly formed; a ring of leafless branches, sharp as claws, reached yearningly toward his face, while many of the trunks and limbs were twisted into grotesque shapes, images from half-remembered dreams.

Pulling off a fur-lined mitten with his teeth, he stooped to unfasten the rawhide bindings of the snowshoes. It was growing late, and he was beginning to get hungry. At home there'd be warm eggnog waiting, and johnnycake made of cornmeal, and, in the huge cast-iron stove, a bowl of Christmas pudding. The older girls would be helping his mother in the kitchen; the others would be singing hymns, the younger children joining in as best they could. His two little sisters would be playing on the rug beside the chimney corner . . .

Around him the dark woods seemed to press closer, as if to cut off his escape.

He paused to wipe the dirt from his leggings and to retighten the laces. Standing, he slipped his boots from the muddy snowshoes and took a step backward, nearly tripping over the exposed roots of an old cottonwood. He reached out blindly, to steady himself—

With a cry he yanked away his hand. The tree had felt warm to the touch, like a living creature. Yet a glance assured him that it was merely dead wood: blasted by lightning, from the look of it, or scorched as from a recent fire.

Hurriedly he picked up the snowshoes and stowed them on his shoulder. With the cottonwood behind him he began to walk due eastward, the direction pointed by the lengthening shadows. He was just emerging from the grove, still uncertain of his way, when, prompted by some obscure impulse, he stopped, looked back, and saw it—the monstrous black thing staring at him from the tree.

He threw down the snowshoes and ran.

He ran all the way home—almost.

Just before he reached it, the boy slowed to a halt. Turning, he began to retrace his steps.

He believed he was going back for the snowshoes. He believed he would stay only long enough to retrieve them from where they had fallen, before dashing home to the safety of his family.

He was wrong. Across the miles of snow and ice, through the bleak December woods, a call had come.

He had been summoned.

The boy told no one of what he had seen. The next day he returned again, drawn back to the secret place to gaze aghast and wonder-struck at what lived there. Once again the thing rolled up its cold, unblinking eye to stare at him. And nothing moved, and not a word was spoken, and nothing broke the silence of those woods.

The next day was the same.

So was the next. And the next. And the one that followed.

On the seventh day, it killed him.

Afterward, it gave him back his life—but twisted now. Corrupted. Irrevocably altered. The boy fell prostrate to the mud and worshiped it.

He came to it each night throughout the spring and summer, to gaze and chant and sacrifice.

The last time that he came to it, it spoke to him.

It opened its fleshless black jaws and, just before it died, it told him, in great detail, exactly what it wanted him to do.

BOOK ONE:

PORTENTS

It has long been my conviction that, were an absolute and unremitting Evil to find embodiment in human form, it would manifest itself not as some hideous ogre or black-caped apparition with glowing eyes, but rather as an ordinary-looking mortal of harmless, even kindly mien—a middle-aged matron, perhaps, or a schoolboy . . . or a little old man.
　　—Nicholas Keize, *Beneath the Moss*
　　　　(Boston: East Side Tract Society, 1892)

MAY FIRST

The city lies throbbing in the sunlight. From its heart a thin black thread of smoke coils lazily toward the sky. April is almost thirteen hours dead; already the world has changed.

In a park above the Hudson the Old One waits, blinking his mild eyes at the sun. Insects plunge and dart around the refuse by the water's edge and buzz amid the grass beside the bench. But for their hum, the lap of oily waters, and the swish of passing cars, the park is still, the air hushed and expectant.

A cry from overhead breaks the silence: three long, tremulous notes . . .

And then the bird is gone. Leaves rustle softly, one branch at a time. The Old One sits forward and holds his breath. Soon it will happen.

A sudden breeze sweeps up from the river; blood-red blossoms scatter at his feet. The pages of an old newspaper shift and curl, revealing smudged bootprints, a naked leg, a jagged slash.

Above him trees hiss urgently in the wind. With a flash of green the leaves lift together and point toward the city. All the grass leans one way.

In the distance the coil of smoke whips back and forth, then twists in upon itself. Silently its black tip sways against the sky, splitting into a serpent's tongue.

The Old One licks his lips. It is beginning.

All the way from New York, as the bus sped through the gassy haze of the Lincoln Tunnel humming with Sunday-morning traffic, past the condos and diners and car lots that lined the highway, Jeremy Freirs had been thinking about the farm.

The ad had been enticingly vague: nothing but a three-by-five recipe card with a row of bright green vegetables printed along one side. It had been tacked to the bulletin board just above the table where he usually sat at the Voorhis Foundation Library on West Twenty-Third Street, as if left there for him alone. The handwriting had been neat and somehow girlish-looking:

SUMMER RENTAL
Private guest house on N.J. farm.
Fully electrified. Quiet surroundings.
$90/week inc. meals. R.F.D. 1, Box 63, Gilead.

At that price, if he could manage to sublet his apartment—a fourth-floor walk-up on Bank Street—he would actually make himself some money on the summer. And it seemed to him that "quiet surroundings" were exactly what he needed right now. It would probably mean a couple of months of celibacy, of course, but that wasn't much different from what he'd been going through this spring. It also meant he'd be able to forget the fact that he'd be turning thirty; there'd be no need to suffer through the celebration his friends were so keen on having, the lavish dinner at someplace expensive, followed by booze and slaps on the back. Well, he would just have to celebrate out there on the farm, away from civilization, like Thoreau. Probably be good for him, concentrate his mind on more important things. There was also his thesis to think about, The Something Something Something of the Gothic Imagination; he would figure it out eventually. Focus on the Participant Observer, maybe, or The Interplay of Setting and Character. Or, even more promising, Setting *as* Character . . . He was sure it would come to him; these things usually did. Meanwhile he'd be reading up on the subject—the primary sources, Le Fanu, Lewis, and the rest—making notes for a course he'd be teaching next fall and, who could tell, perhaps for years to come. To spend a summer among books: it was an appealing prospect.

So was the notion of escaping from the city this year: from the three flights of echoing stairs that, even after twice that many summers, left him panting and sweaty by the time he'd reached the top; from his claustrophobic little bedroom, the secondhand air conditioner churning endlessly in the window, blocking the view of the street; and, maybe most important of all, escape from the inevitable memories of a certain Laura Rubinstein who had shared that bedroom with him for so much of last summer and whose moving out at the end of it had been responsible for, among other things, the abandonment of a planned trip to England, the loss of a lucrative teaching assignment at Queensborough Community College (because of Freirs' erratic attendance and, as the department head had noted, "insufficient classroom preparation"), and the habit of stuffing himself with food as he sat up reading late into the night, alone in his apartment, resulting in a gain of twenty pounds by winter's end and the drastic alteration of Freirs' wardrobe.

He still missed Laura. For a while he'd actually believed she'd be his second wife, the one who'd prove that, whatever mistakes he had made in the past, this time around he'd get it right. There'd been a couple of other women since her, but no one he'd really cared about. Three weeks ago, on the day of Laura's marriage to an old boyfriend with a family house in Sag Harbor and tenure at NYU, Freirs had written to the box number in Gilead, asking for more information and suggesting today, the first of May, for a possible visit. He had already discovered that the town was too small for most maps of the state (except for one highly detailed Geological Survey map he'd found at Voorhis), but Hunterdon County Transport operated a twice-a-day bus service from the Port Authority which, upon request, made a detour to the town.

The reply had come less than a week later. It was written in the same girlish hand on lined yellow paper obviously drawn from a legal pad. Three photographs had also been enclosed.

Dear Mr. Freirs,

My husband and I were pleased to get your letter, and we'll be happy to have you come out on May Day and see our place. The Sunday bus arrives in Gilead shortly after two and will let you off across the street from the Co-operative. That will be closed when you arrive, but there's a bench on the porch where you can wait, and my husband will be by in the truck to pick you up as soon as services are over. You shouldn't have to wait long, and we'll see that you get back to town in time for the return bus.

The guest house is one of our outbuildings. It is newly renovated and electrified and, though you can't see it in the photograph, we will be putting new screens on all the windows. The left half of the building is used as a storeroom, but you should find the right half more than ample for your needs. There is a brand new bed, a wardrobe, a set of shelves, and a spare table you can use as a writing desk. (Your work sounds very interesting! At one time my husband and I considered teaching as a career.)

We are not fancy people, but I can promise you three square meals a day, well prepared, just as we ourselves eat. Our farm is not yet a fully working one (we purchased it only in November), but by this summer we expect to be eating our own produce. We are lifelong members of the Brethren of the Redeemer, a religious order with adherents all over the world, though most of its membership is concentrated here in Gilead, with other settlements in Pennsylvania and New York. Both my husband and I have attended college outside the community. We wel-

come the interest of those outside the faith and do not impose our beliefs on anyone.

We have no telephone, so if you cannot come to see us on May Day,
please let us know in writing as soon as possible. If we don't hear from
you, we'll assume you're coming, and Sarr will be there to pick you
up—but I see I'm repeating myself! So in closing, I look forward to
meeting you and hearing about life in New York.

Sincerely,
(Mrs.) Deborah Poroth

P.S. Jeremiah is our prophet, and so your name strikes me as a very
good omen!

Freirs had read the letter, with the rest of his mail, on the subway up
to Columbia. He'd found something charming about the woman's tone;
it was like getting a message from a pen pal in another country, complete with three exotic snapshots. Yet as he'd scrutinized the photos,
tilting them forward and back in the subway's glare, he'd felt a faint
twinge of nervousness.

The pictures were in color; but for that, they would not have been
out of place in some long-forgotten album of the past. The first showed
a dirt road bordered by woods, with pale winter sunlight slanting
through pine boughs and the leafless branches of an oak. In a clearing
on the left stood a small white clapboard house with an open porch in
front, nearly level with the road, and a line of thornbushes making
twisted shapes against one side. The porch was bare save for two narrow wooden chairs, one of them empty, the other occupied by a woman
in a long black dress, her dark hair tied back in a knot, her face masked
by shadows. On her lap rested something small and yellow, with a second at her feet; squinting at the photo, Freirs saw that they were kittens. The woman was sitting straight in the chair, staring directly
ahead. The whole scene seemed touched with the stillness and silence of
a Hopper painting.

Behind the house lay a tiny fenced-in garden, though neither flowers
nor vegetables were in evidence. The picture looked as if it had been
taken on a winter afternoon; Freirs hoped to find the place a good deal
greener now. He could see, beyond the trees, an open field broken only
by clumps of weed and sporadic knots of bramble. At its edge stood further pine and oak, rising in a dense forest.

The second picture showed another portion of the field, an arid patch
of reddish earth and stubble. A small brook glistened blurrily along
the distant edge. In the center of the picture stood a slim, bearded man,
somewhat Lincolnesque in appearance, posed stiffly with a rake in his
hand like a rustic in an ancient woodcut. By his feet crouched a fat
grey cat, glowering at the camera. The man was clean-shaven above a

fringe of dark beard; he wore a vest, homespun-looking black trousers, and a somewhat wrinkled collarless white shirt. He looked around forty. His face was pale and his expression somber, but Freirs thought he detected a hint of a smile at the corners of his mouth, perhaps for whoever held the camera.

The third photo was slightly darker than the others, as if taken when evening approached. At the edge of the picture stood the rear wall of the farmhouse, while squatting in the center was a low grey cinder-block structure reminiscent of an army barrack. It appeared to have two entrances, a glass-paneled door near each end. Freirs suspected that it was a converted henhouse.

Beyond its roof rose a dark line of treetops where the woods began. The building faced away from them, looking out upon the lawn; the grass grew right up to the doorways without a trace of path, as if, till now, no one had had occasion to approach it. Most of the brickwork in front was concealed beneath a dense growth of ivy, which had already spread over the rims of the windows. These were bare and very wide, allowing a view completely through to the back, where the trunks of massive trees cut out the light.

Even on the crowded subway, there'd been something about the scene that had disturbed him. He still wasn't sure what it was.

The photos, with their air of isolation, were like souvenirs of another world, removed in time or space: early settlers, maybe, or backwoods Maine. It was hard to believe that they'd been taken only recently in New Jersey, in a spot less than fifty miles from New York.

A month ago, his picture of Jersey had been compounded of a long-ago rock concert in the Meadowlands he'd let his wife drag him to, a disastrous interview in Newark during his leaner postgraduate years (to teach, of all things, Black English to inner-city youths), and several Metroliner trips to visit friends of Laura's in Washington. He'd always imagined the state as one vast slum, grey with swamp gas and pollution, populated by ghetto dwellers and gangsters. Somewhere beyond it, outposts of light, lay the monastic seclusion of Princeton and the boardwalks of Atlantic City, all taffy stands, convention halls, and casinos. Along its eastern edge, just across the river from New York, stretched a wasteland of oil tanks and marsh water, lit up redly here and there, deep into the night, by tiny sputtering flames.

But he'd been wrong. For the past weeks he'd been reading about the state, his interest piqued by the photos. It appeared that there was real wilderness out here after all, with deer, foxes, rattlesnakes, even a few bears. There were the Pine Barrens to the south, over a thousand square miles of them, where a man could walk all day without seeing a sign of civilization. The books told of places down there that outsiders never heard of, tiny little villages completely cut off from the rest of the state, with nothing but a church and a general store with one or two gas pumps out front. There were ghost towns, too, and towns with names like Hog Wallow and Long-a-Coming, and towns with dialects all their own. Some of them weren't even on the map.

To the west lay the Delaware Valley—there'd been a piece on it in *Natural History*—where, in a certain hollow just upriver from Philadelphia, one could still find relics of idols the Indians worshiped. In the hill country north of it rose Tackisaw Ridge, riddled with a network of hidden caverns. Hikers had found queer words and symbols carved into the rocks, but no one had managed to puzzle out their meaning, or even what language they were in.

Some of the towns were still just names to him—names like West Portal and Winterman and Vineland, which billed itself as "the witchcraft center of America." Others came complete with odd histories: Monson with its string of unsolved murders, and Redcliffe with its "devil museum," and Budd Lake with its reports, back in the forties, of a chanting heard on certain nights, echoing over the water. There'd been similar reports, ten years later, of a chanting near the Jersey City docks, and rumors of stone objects—"ancient ceremonial artifacts," the local papers called them—unearthed during excavations for the stadium in the Meadowlands.

And then there were the religious communities—pockets of ignorance, to judge by the descriptions: bearded men, black-robed women, and a polite fuck-you to strangers. It was astonishing that such places had survived, and on the doorstep of one of the biggest cities in the world.

But then, isolation, he'd come to realize, was also a state of mind, and an insignificant little village might easily be overlooked—except when, now and then, some journalist heard about it and decided it was quaint enough to warrant a photo and a few inches of copy. Freirs had read how, in May of 1962, the *Times* had "discovered" one such religious community near New Providence. Its existence had never been a secret; it had simply been ignored, until one morning New Yorkers had picked up their papers and there it was: a town that looked much as it had in the late 1800s, when it was first settled. The old religion, the customs, the special schools for the children, they'd all survived unchanged. Farm work was done entirely by hand, town worship was held every evening, women still wore long dresses with high collars— and all this less than thirty miles from Times Square.

These places were real. A few, it was said, had even had stone walls around them once—places such as Harmony and Mt. Jordan, and Zion and Zarephath, with round-the-clock Bible talk on the radio. Places such as Gilead, his destination.

*

Kenilworth, Mountainside, Scotch Plains, Dunellen . . . they themselves seemed far from Jersey: names out of Waverley novels, promising vistas of castles, highland waterfalls, and meadows dotted with flocks of grazing sheep. But the signboards lied, the books had lied, the *Times* had lied; the land here was one vast and charmless suburb, and as the bus passed through it, speeding west across the state, Freirs saw before him only the flat grey monotony of highway, broken from time to time by gas stations, roadhouses, and shopping malls that stretched away like deserts.

The bus was warm, and the ride was beginning to give him a headache. He could feel the backs of his thighs sweating through his chinos. Easing himself farther into the seat, he pushed up his glasses and rubbed his eyes. The scenery disappointed him, yet it was still an improvement over what they'd just come through. Back there, on the fringes of the city, every work of man seemed to have been given over to the automobile, in an endless line of showrooms and repair shops for mufflers, fenders, carburetors, ignitions, tires, brakes. Now at last he could make out hills in the distance and extended zones of green, though here and there the nearness of some larger town or development meant a length of highway lined by construction, billboards touting banks or amusement parks, and drive-in theaters, themselves immense blank billboards, their signs proclaiming horror movies, "family pictures," soft-core porn. A speedway announced that next Wednesday was ladies' night. Food stands offered pizzaburgers, chicken in the basket, fish 'n' chips. Too bad the bus wasn't stopping; he'd wolfed down an omelet two hours ago, standing in the kitchen of his apartment, but he was already hungry again.

With a sigh he turned back to his reading. He had brought a manila envelope bulging with photocopied articles from *Sight and Sound* and *Cahiers du Cinéma*, enough for him to fake his way through still another week's installment of the film course he was teaching at the New School. Luckily that bunch wasn't hard to stay ahead of: art students, mostly, on transfer from Parsons, satisfying their English requirement by sitting through a dozen or so old movies.

The bus was nearly empty, and he had a pair of seats to himself. No need to make halting conversation with some ignoramus who hadn't brought along a magazine to read. Around him all the other riders looked like Jersey types, blank-faced men and women in dowdy clothes, off on mysterious Sunday- afternoon errands. Farther forward sat two teenage boys cradling knapsacks and caps, a fat woman and her equally fat daughter clutching shopping bags, an old man chattering nonstop to the driver, and one lone young woman whose face betrayed nothing, probably on her way to meet a lover, he decided, or returning from some wild night in New York. Toward the rear a large black woman gazed impassively ahead, already looking out of place. White folks' country here. In the row in front of him a pale red-haired youth with an armed forces duffel bag was fiddling with his radio: not a suitcase-sized monstrosity like the black kids carried or the tinny little transistor Freirs himself owned, but a solid grey plastic thing, souvenir of some PX. A song by Devo had just ended in a burst of static, and a voice announced the time: twelve fifty-seven in WABC land. They were passing another industrial park now, its wide black lots deserted for the weekend: an electronics firm, a cannery, a forbidding-looking plant labeled Chemtex. To the west the sky was nearly cloudless, flooding the bus with sunlight. Hot for May; perhaps a promise of worse to come. The Poroths' ad had mentioned electricity, but would that include air conditioning? Unlikely. But he supposed it would be good to be a little warm. Sweat the pounds away.

He felt the bus slow slightly and saw a sign for Somerville approaching in the distance. He remembered the map he'd studied. They were halfway across the state.

Now, gradually, there was a change in the land. At first it was only evident in the stores along the road: a farm supply house with burlap sacks of feed and grain piled against the porch; a tractor showroom; a sporting goods outlet with advertising placards for guns and ammunition in the window. Then, here and there, an occasional well-tended farm set far back from the highway, the distant farmhouse seeming to turn slowly as the bus went past, the trees or fenceposts along the roadside flashing by in a blur. The land was greener now, the acres of asphalt and angry-looking rust-red earth receding into the east. He felt something in him quicken. On the radio one row ahead the electrified pastorale of Jethro Tull was fading beneath a shrill, insectlike buzz, and the youth twisted the dial to something else. "Then Jeremiah went forth out of Jerusalem," the radio said, "to go into the land of Benjamin, to separate himself thence in the midst of the people."

They were moving deeper into the country.

He had never spent time in the country before. Where he'd grown up, in Astoria, northern Queens, there'd been playgrounds, empty lots, little green patches of lawn, but nothing that hinted of real nature, nothing for a boy to explore. It was a neighborhood where Cub Scouts had learned to read subway maps, where the closest things to wildlife were pigeons and grey squirrels.

The only open land, besides La Guardia Airport to the north, had been Flushing Meadows Park and a cluster of enormous treeless cemeteries where various Freirs, Freireicher, and Bodenheim relatives lay buried. The park had been the site of two World's Fairs. It was mostly grass now, but a few of the pavilions remained, and Shea Stadium oc-

cupied its northern half. As a boy Freirs had spent hours sitting in a
favorite tree beside one of the artificial ponds, watching planes come in
and out of La Guardia. They'd come in all night as well, one every few
minutes until early morning. On summer nights, standing on the roof
of his apartment building, he could look to the right and see the
Bronx-Whitestone Bridge glowing in the distance, and the Triborough
to the left, with the lights of Manhattan behind it. A central Con Ed
power plant had stood just a mile and a half away, a monstrous thing
with five huge smokestacks, like some great beached ocean liner, and
he'd always believed that it made the electricity for all those lights.
The planes had been beautiful, winking in the darkness, and the noise
hadn't bothered him much; he'd grown up with it. Manhattan, when
he'd moved there after college, had seemed almost quiet by contrast.

Paradoxically, like so many other children in New York, he'd grown
up with the idea that what he loved best was the country. Phrases like
"the dark woods," "the forest primeval," and "the wide open spaces"
had made him shiver with longing. He'd felt an inexplicable nostalgia
at the pictures of farms and mountains in his schoolbooks; even a
poster of bland brown Smokey the Bear was capable of moving him. At
age six he had wandered through the parking lot behind his house
stamping out cigarette butts, convinced he was helping prevent forest
fires. Later, in junior high school, he'd been certain he wanted to be a
forest ranger when he grew up; so had nearly half the class. He had imagined himself sitting all day in some solitary tower, reading stacks of
books, gazing through binoculars from time to time, then slipping
down the ladder, beardless young Jewish St. Francis, to check up on
the bears and feed the deer.

Now, for all he knew, he was heading toward that very world, or at
least that world's domesticated neighbor, and he was beginning to feel
a little less certain of its rewards. The bus had left the highway back in
Somerville and had already made half a dozen stops in small towns
and roadside depots—Clover Hill, Montgomery, Raritan Falls: bas-
tions of silence and boredom where, on a Sunday afternoon in May, not
a soul was to be seen except the occasional tall scowling man or hard-
eyed woman in a pickup truck or station wagon, waiting for a passen-
ger to disembark. These were towns without drugstores or banks, towns
where the nights were for sleeping and homes went dark early. Kids
here, he supposed, would build backyard tree houses and fortresses in
the woods; they would join 4-H clubs, save up for their first rifles, and
spend their teenage evenings driving up and down back roads, following their headlights while the roadbed bumped and dipped beneath
their wheels.

He tried to imagine a place like Gilead, tucked away up one of those
roads, hidden in the less settled part of the county in a region of woodland and marsh. Unlike the towns he'd just passed through, it would be

truly self-contained, turned inward, its inhabitants wary of the shopping centers and uninterested in their rural neighbors. For the first time, he could see how such a place might survive, even in a county as fast-growing as Hunterdon. It would need little from the rest of the world, nor would it offer much. Outsiders would have no reason to visit, unless, like him, they deliberately sought it out. Those born into the community would never leave it; all their friends and relations would be nestled right there beside them. The land would thus be locked up tight, the area closed to newcomers—and, considering the religion practiced there, closed to new ideas as well. TV might be regarded as the devil's tool. Telephones, for all he knew, might also be proscribed; certainly the Poroths did without one. Yet even if they'd had a phone, how useful could it be if there was no one outside town to call? Lines of communication meant nothing if they weren't used; and these would not be. So Gilead would live on in its isolation, following its own peculiar paths until, in the course of time, it would simply be ignored, overlooked, and—he wondered if in fact this were already true—all but forgotten.

"I brought you into a plentiful country," the radio was saying, the words singsong as if from years of repetition, "to eat the fruit thereof and the goodness thereof; but when ye entered, ye defiled my land, and made mine heritage an abomination."

For the dozenth time he considered changing his seat. The youth one seat ahead of him, hunched glassy-eyed over the dials, had turned the volume down at Freirs' request, but the preacher still sounded as if he were speaking at the top of his voice. It was a Bible station out of Zarephath, and hot for Jeremiah. The town lay miles to the east, but the voice, though strident, had an unsettling intimacy about it, as if the man himself were crouched just inches from Freirs' face; he could almost smell the gamy breath and feel the spray against his skin. He'd had his fill of jeremiads, all this fire and spit and brimstone was beginning to give him a headache, but he felt curiously reluctant to ask the youth to turn the volume down again. Superstition, maybe; in a country of believers, you didn't interfere. And there was a kind of fascination to the rhythm of the words, even if their meaning was a mystery; it was like listening to a recording of one of Hitler's speeches. Besides, he liked the idea that people out here made so much of Jeremiah. He'd never cared much for his name before.

The Poroth woman had commented on it, the coincidence of names. He wondered what she and her husband would be like, and what they'd think of him. The woman, at least, sounded eager for company.

Reaching into the pocket of his jacket on the seat beside him, he withdrew the envelope containing her letter and the snapshots. He studied her face in the photo, holding it up to the sunlight streaming down beside him. It was hard to tell for sure, maybe it was just his lonely imagination, but she looked rather pretty, and younger than she'd first appeared. Maybe he should start thinking of her as Deborah.

The husband? Rather gloomy-looking. Not much humor there. But of course he was still little more than a cipher.

He looked at the third photo. This screened-in former chicken coop was where, quite possibly, he'd be spending the summer. It looked serviceable enough, yet there was something about it, he'd felt it from the start: something that disturbed him.

Perhaps it was the all-enveloping ivy, or the squat shape of the roof, or the way the shingled eaves hung low over the doorways. Or . . . yes, that was it—the windows. The windows in the back. They were too big, and too near the trees, and the trees seemed to press toward them in a way he didn't like. While the front windows looked out upon a comfortable expanse of lawn bathed by the pale rays of a late afternoon sun, those in back seemed to open on another world, a twilight of tangled branches and shadowy black forms. *They offer no protection*, he decided.

Later he would wonder what had prompted such a thought, and what there was to be protected from. But at this moment, with the photo before him and the bus bearing him toward that very scene, all such questions fell before a single overriding conviction: *It isn't right to build a house so close against the woods.*

Its outskirts had become the haunt of bargain hunters, a busy region of shopping centers and showrooms, but the town of Flemington was quiet on this Sunday afternoon, though cars still lined the parking lots of the churches at the edge of the business district. Farther up the street the bus stopped before a red-brick card and candy shop, New Jersey Lottery stickers on the window and commercial notices fluttering from a bulletin board by the door. Several passengers filed off, the youth with the radio among them; the lone attractive girl had long since disappeared into one of the small towns back down the road. With a hiss of air brakes, the bus continued on past the venerable white pillars of the Union Hotel; then a bakery, odd star-shaped loaves in the window; a real-estate office with its shades drawn; and the old county courthouse, beyond whose worn stone steps the killer of the Lindbergh baby had been tried. At the end of the street stood the offices of the local daily, the *Hunterdon County Home News*. Next to them a funeral parlor's awning reached toward the sidewalk.

The bus followed the main road as it curved westward, the stores and municipal buildings giving way to handsome suburban houses with gables, ornate shutters, and broad well-tended lawns, which in turn gave way to freshly plowed fields, pastures where cattle grazed, and occasional patches of woods. Abruptly the bus veered north, leaving the main road for a narrower one that twisted between tall hedges like the footpath it may once have been. It wound past small, shaded bungalows half hidden by trees and secretive little lanes where foliage blocked the view ahead. Down one of these the bus turned, branches scraping at its sides. The lane cut through a stand of cottonwoods and over a gentle, sparsely forested rise choked with ground ivy and brambles. Beyond it, winding away from each side of the road until they were lost amid the trees, ran what appeared to be the ruins of an ancient stone wall. As the bus passed through them, Freirs felt as if he were trespassing onto private ground.

The way continued through a lane of cottonwoods and maples that looked as if they'd been there for centuries. Behind them stood a succession of dark-shingled houses, three on one side, four on the other— dwellings without ornament, obviously old, with lawns trimmed neatly and glimpses of gardens in back. Just past them the road suddenly widened and came to an end at another running perpendicular to it, forming a T. Facing the intersection stood a rambling white clapboard building with a wide front porch and a POST OFFICE sign by the doorway. Behind it, and apparently attached, rose the tall rust-red pillar of a grain silo and the black gambrel roof of a barn, its weathered shingles curling in the sunlight.

The bus slowed as it came into the intersection and pulled noisily up to the building. In front of it Freirs could see three old-fashioned gas pumps and, along one side, what appeared to be a loading area, with broad ramps leading up to a garage adjoining the barn. By one of the doorways stood a dusty little tractor and a wagon piled high with bags of grain. An empty pickup truck was parked ahead, near the pumps, with another parked farther back, in the shadow of the barn. Both trucks looked decades old, like the car he'd noticed in a driveway down the street; their paintwork was dark, lacking all decoration and chrome.

No one was about. The porch was empty save for a straight-backed wooden bench; the front door was closed, the windows shuttered, the place as quiet and deserted an empty film set. There were no street signs to be seen, not even a sign above the building, and there'd been no words of welcome down the road. But Freirs knew, even before the bus driver turned and announced the name, that at last he'd reached Gilead.

The bus left him standing alone before the store, holding his jacket and his envelope of clippings. As Deborah Poroth's letter had warned there was no one to meet him, and as he turned to look around, he felt marooned. Across the street, set well back from the road behind a line of massive oaks, stood a building that he guessed to be a school—a square red-brick structure with a patchy brown playing field beside it and two lonely seesaws in front. At the opposite corner, on a piece of ground slightly higher than the rest, stood a little cemetery, old but obviously well tended, though here and there a tombstone was askew, like trees after a storm.

The sound of the bus's engine faded beyond the curve of the road, leaving a silence broken only by the buzzing of insects and the occasional cry of a bird.

Freirs hadn't really expected the town to be this small. He'd expected at least a town center, someplace for the populace to meet. Yet except for the schoolhouse back behind the trees, there appeared to be no civic buildings of any kind, not even a Grange hall or an American Legion post.

What surprised him most of all was the absence of a church. From where he stood he could see nothing but well-scrubbed houses bordering both sides of the road, and maples and oaks whose new foliage looked cool against the burning blue sky, the treetops receding into the distance toward a line of low green hills. The skyline was unbroken by either a golden cross or a slim white steeple. Perhaps services were held in some simple one-room tabernacle concealed behind a bend in the road.

Turning, with a sigh, toward the clapboard building—obviously the Co-operative mentioned in the letter, though for a store it was curiously bare of window placards and advertising—he climbed the steps to the front porch, wishing there were somewhere around to take a pee. The bench did not look comfortable, and wasn't. Above him, as he sat, he noticed a row of ominous-looking iron hooks protruding from a beam in the porch ceiling. Probably where they hung the sinners. He wondered, briefly, what sins lay on his own head.

He sat for a few minutes, savoring the silence. He was going to like this place, if the farm was as quiet as the town. Who knows, even boredom might be welcome. Tedium as Therapy: The Uses of Ennui. Time as a Function of . . . He was already beginning to feel drowsy. All those hours on the bus, and now this heat and solitude: it took a lot out of a body.

His bladder was full, though, and there seemed little likelihood there'd be a bathroom handy. Typical, that he hadn't thought to go back there on the goddamned bus. Opposite him, by the schoolyard, a line of oaks made patterns of shade along the roadside; inviting, but he'd be too conspicuous there. Past the farther corner the stone slabs of the cemetery stood bathed in sunlight; behind them rose secluded clumps of trees. That was the likeliest place. Besides, there might be some interesting old tombstones; do some rubbings there someday. At least it would help pass the time.

He strolled down the porch steps and across the street. Climbing the slope to the cemetery, he felt self-conscious. What if they didn't like strangers walking over great-granddaddy's head? That probably wasn't the case, though. People around here would be proud of these things, of how far back their families went.

Here was one, for example; he stood looking down at a small white headstone that the years had worn almost smooth. *Ephraim Lindt, who Died 1887 in the 63rd year of his Life*. That wasn't as far back as he'd expected. Obviously you couldn't go by the condition of the stone; the white ones tended to weather more.

Nearby he saw an older one that had held up better. *Johann Sturtevant, Call'd to His Maker 1833, Aged Fifty-One. His Dutiful Wife Korah, Join'd with Him in Heaven 1870, Aged Seventy-Eight*. Jesus, a widow for almost forty years, and in a place like this.

Farther back stood a small stand of willows and, behind them, a scraggly hedgerow. He approached them, unzipping his fly, and let loose a splattering yellow arc on the base of one tree. Insects circled round in protest. Off to the right he could see the assemblage of headstones regarding him like an audience—Buckhalter, Stoudemire, van Meer—but there was no one to see him but the ghosts of the dead, and surely they were tolerant. Envious, even. How long had it been since his citified cock had been touched by actual sunlight? Damn, but this place felt healthy! Zipping up and with nothing to flush, he wandered back to the graves.

Slowly he made his way through the aisles, stopping at intervals to read the inscriptions on the older stones. Their quietude, the sense of souls and bodies in repose, had begun to make him drowsy again. Many of the stones had faces on them, or angels' heads, or skulls; some of the more modern ones had willows, like the one he'd just watered. There were also smaller headstones, for children. Picturing the tiny wooden coffins, Freirs tried to imagine how parents must have felt in an era when half the population died in childhood. Maybe, in those days, they didn't mind so much.

Often married couples shared a single stone, but a number of others were in pairs, one for the husband, one for the wife, as if, in life, they'd slept apart and now saw no reason to change. Here lay the van Meers, Rachel and Jan, their gravestones side by side like bedboards. On hers, 1845 to 1912:

> *Such as I am,*
> *Thus shalt thou be.*

Just a cheery little reminder. And hubby, 1826 to 1906:

Let this to thee a Warning be:
Quickly thou must follow me.

Not something he felt like thinking about right now. Later, maybe. He moved farther down the row, wiping sweat from the back of his neck. Maybe it was the sun that made him tired. Butterflies flitted between the tombstones; bees poked among the tall grasses along the bottom of the hill. He looked once more toward the store across the street. The door was still shut; no one had returned.

Near the end of the row he stooped to puzzle out another inscription; the stone was of slate, and chipped almost beyond reading. Getting up again required too much effort. Dropping his jacket and envelope, he sat himself on the grass and stretched his legs, his feet merging with the shadow of the adjoining monument. It was the largest object in the row, a dark four-sided column whose top was jagged and oblique, yet obviously sculpted that way, as if to suggest that the shaft had been broken off. He craned his head back to read the words. The thing appeared to commemorate an entire family; a way of saving money, perhaps. You left a little space after the names, and, one by one, as the people dropped off, you added the years they died.

ISAIAH TROET   HANNA TROET
1839–1877   1845–1877

They had died the same year. Well, sometimes grief did that to people. Was it happier that way, or even sadder?

His eyes felt heavy. He lay back in the sunlight, cradling his head in the grass, and squinted up at the rest of the names.

THEIR CHILDREN
RUTH   1863–1877
TABITHA   1865–1877
AMOS   1866–1877
ABSOLOM   1868–
TAMAR   1871–1877
LEAH   1873–1877
TOBIAS   1876–1877

Odd. They *all* had died that year. Some sort of disaster, maybe. Plague, flood, famine in the land.

His eyes closed. Sunlight beat against the lids, while blades of grass brushed his cheek. For a moment he had a vision of long-lost souls with funnily spelled names.

Just as sleep claimed him, he recalled something else that had been odd: they had left out the death year for the one called Absolom. Idly, in a final thought, he wondered what it meant. Maybe Absolom had simply died the same year he was born.

Poor kid, he thought, and slept.

Wind sweeps in gusts across the Hudson, carrying the scent of oil from the Jersey shore: oil, and a burning, and the strange sweet far-off scent of roses.

No one has noticed—no one but the plump little figure perched unobtrusively at the end of the bench, a battered old umbrella by his side. No one else is watching; no one would understand. No one sees the patterns in the water, or smells the corruption beneath the flower scent, or hears the secret sound the grass makes when the wind dies.

Once more the air grows still. Small green moths flit among the weeds; hornets buzz thirstily around a barrel of refuse. No one could guess what is happening. The river rolls past the park, unobserved; the planet rolls through space, unsuspecting; the Old One's squat black shadow lengthens on the bench.

In the shadow, shielded from the afternoon sun, a baby sleeps peacefully, its tiny olive face protruding from a tight cocoon of blanket. A woman, presumably its mother, sits slumped beside it, head fallen forward, eyes sunken and shut tight, skeletal arms hanging like dead things at her sides. On the ground beneath her lies a crumpled paper bag from which the neck of a bottle emerges; the cap has long since rolled into the grass.

Except for the three figures on the bench, this area of the park is almost deserted. The only movement comes from near the trash barrel, where a pair of glossy yellowjackets rise and dip in ceaseless search for food. His face impassive, the Old One watches as one of the insects slips from sight behind the rim and falls greedily upon some rotting thing within. The other circles round the spot in ever-widening arcs until, having flown as far as the bench, it pauses above the paper bag, tiger stripes thrashing furiously beneath a blur of wings. Settling atop the bottle, it disappears inside.

Suddenly the air changes; he can feel it. Whispering the Second of the Seven Names, the Old One turns his gaze toward the river, the farther shore, and the shadowy hills beyond. Strange clouds have appeared on the horizon; part two of the sequence is almost complete. He sits poised, ready, rigid with anticipation. In a moment—In a moment—

A small green moth flutters past his face and comes to rest on the back of his hand. Feebly its wings open and close, open . . . close . . . then at last fall open and lie still. All movement ceases.

At the far end of the bench the woman's head falls back as if, in a dream, she has offered her throat to the knife. A small bubble of saliva grows and bursts at her lips. Her mouth opens like a rose.

High overhead a white bird wheels erratically in its flight and falls screaming toward the Hudson.

The signs are all about him now. It is time. The Old One sings the Death Song to himself and shivers with exultation. He has been waiting more than a lifetime for this—waiting, and planning, and readying himself for what he has to do. Now the moment is at hand, and he knows that the years of preparation have not been in vain.

Above the park the sky remains a blinding blue; the sun glares mercilessly down. With a metallic gleam the second yellowjacket lifts from its feast and comes spiraling toward the woman on the bench, to hover inches from her gaping mouth. From the empty bottle the other insect rises buzzing toward the baby's face. Mother and child sleep on.

The Old One regards them silently, watching the slow rise and fall of the woman's chest, the hollow cheeks and ravaged flesh, the infant in its mindless sleep. Here it lies, in all its glory: humanity.

He has plans for it.

And now, after a century's contemplation, he is free to act; the future is clear at last. He has heard the strange, piercing cries of the white birds circling overhead. He has read the ancient words chipped into the city's blackened brick. He has seen the foulness at the edge of a young leaf, and the dark shapes that lie in wait behind the clouds. Last night as he marked the birth of May, standing in solemn observance upon the rooftop of his home, he has seen the horned moon with a star between the tips. There is nothing left to learn.

Flicking the moth from his hand, he reaches for his umbrella, stands up from the bench, and grinds the tiny body into the earth. No longer shielded from the afternoon sunlight, the baby stirs, squints, and opens its eyes. A yellowjacket settles lightly onto its cheek; the other buzzes with interest round a frantically twitching eyelid.

Bound within the blanket, the infant struggles helplessly to free its arms. The little mouth opens in a scream. Oblivious, the woman sleeps on.

The Old One stands watching for a time. Then, with a wintry smile, he turns his footsteps toward the city.

The world had darkened. A deep voice was intoning his name. Freirs
jerked awake, grumpy and scared, to find his head in shadow; for a
moment he didn't know where he was. A figure was standing over him,
blocking out the sun.

"Jeremy Freirs?"

He managed a grunt of assent.

"I'm Sarr Poroth. My truck's down there by the road."

The man looked as tall as the monument beside him. The sunlight at
his back made him hard to see.

Still dazed, Freirs got to his feet and brushed himself off, then
picked up his jacket and papers. Yawning, he rubbed his eyes behind
his glasses.

"I think that bus ride knocked me out."

Wishing he were still asleep, he followed Poroth through the rows of
tombstones and down the slope toward an old dark-green pickup truck
parked at the edge of the road. The Co-operative across the street was
open now, he saw, with several more trucks and autos in the adjoining
lot. All were as somber in color, and most of them as antiquated-
looking, as the ones he'd seen earlier, like cars in old photographs. The
Co-op's windows were unshuttered now, with merchandise spilling out
the open door, and a balding man with glasses and a fringe of beard
was busily dragging straw baskets of sponges, axe handles, rubber
boots, and overalls from the doorway onto the porch. It looked like
moving day. The porch ceiling was already filled, garlands of clothesline, shiny metal farm implements, and kerosene lanterns dangling
like mobiles from the hooks that had looked so ominous before. A stocky
mechanic was bent beneath the raised hood of a car parked off to the
side of the gas pumps; Freirs could hear the regular iron scrape of
some tool he was using and, in the distance, the hum of a tractor.
Sounds of civilization. He blinked in the sunlight as he followed
Poroth toward the truck. His legs still felt stiff from his nap.

The screen door across the street swung wide and two young men—
brothers, from the look of them, and hardly more than teenagers—
emerged from the store carrying mesh bags stuffed with groceries.
They couldn't have been more than high school age, yet both, like
Poroth, wore beards without mustaches and dressed in black overalls
over collarless white shirts, making them appear almost elderly. They
had been talking together with some animation but fell silent as they
saw Freirs and Poroth descending from the graveyard across the
street. Poroth, ahead of him, raised his hand in greeting; they waved

back. The smaller of the two glanced at Freirs in surprise but quickly looked away, following the other down the steps toward one of the parked trucks. The strangeness, a feeling almost of foreignness, lay not so much in how they dressed as in how they moved: they walked closer together than boys in Freirs' world, and without the defiant swagger most of them affected. As they climbed into their truck, giving Freirs a last subdued glance over their shoulders, he had the impression that they'd have liked to stare longer but that it would have been rude, betraying an unseemly curiosity. Such restraint was somehow unnerving; he felt like one of the first Westerners to enter Japan must have felt, being received courteously and correctly but, it was clear, by people who considered themselves superior.

He wished he weren't wearing the chinos and blue workshirt, imitation L. L. Bean that here just looked phony and college-boy. Plus his goddamned gut hanging out. What Poroth and the others were wearing, that uncomfortable-looking black and white getup, a virtual uniform—was apparently what *real* country people wore. Beneath his shirt Poroth's broad back was probably as well muscled as any of the people Freirs knew who hung around $600-a-year health clubs or spent their leisure hours pumping iron at the Y. Though now that he looked at it closely, the shirt itself was sweat-stained and none too clean; was this the way the man attended church?

Poroth patted the metal flank of his beat-up green truck as if it were a farm animal. "She probably isn't what you're used to," he said regretfully. Freirs expected him to qualify this, to add some assurance of the truck's homely virtues, but the other merely swung himself up into the driver's seat and waited for Freirs to climb in beside him.

The pair of youths had just pulled out from the parking lot and disappeared up the road in their own truck, and once more the loudest sound to break the quiet was the regular metallic scrape from across the street where the mechanic labored over his engine. The man paused above some unseen part; then, as Poroth gunned the pickup's motor, he looked up, his face betraying neither friendliness nor interest. His beard looked somehow incongruous above the grease-stained overalls, a man out of the Bible attempting to pass for modern.

Poroth drove fast, either from a desire to impress or a simple impatience to be home. Thanks to the truck's height, Freirs enjoyed a commanding perspective of the road ahead. With every unevenness in the surface the two of them bounced on the springy black seat like cowboys on horseback; several times Freirs found himself reaching out almost surreptitiously to steady himself against the dented metal of the dashboard. He stole a glance at Poroth, whose skin, while rough, seemed surprisingly pale for one who spent most of his day working in the sun. Against the dark beard his face seemed all the paler. The beard, and the man's sheer size, made it difficult to tell his age. In the photo he'd looked as old as forty, but Freirs now suspected he was as much as a decade younger, perhaps as young as Freirs himself. He tried, in his imagination, to erase the beard from Poroth's chin and to do the same for the long, obviously home-cut hair. What sort of person would Poroth be in the city? Stick him in a three-piece suit, or on the subway with a briefcase beneath his arm, or sipping at a beer in some restaurant near Abingdon Square . . . No, it didn't work, he just wouldn't fit; he was too tall, too broad of shoulder, too obviously meant for outdoor labor. His very features were too stern, his brow thrust too far forward. There seemed no urban counterpart for him.

Poroth still hadn't asked him anything about himself, his interests, his impressions—none of the chat that Freirs would have offered a Sunday visitor. Had he done something wrong? Maybe Poroth had resented his snoozing in the graveyard.

"When you saw me resting back there," he said, speaking loudly over the sound of the truck, "I hope it wasn't also the resting place of some relative of yours."

Surprisingly, Poroth didn't answer right away, and he gave Freirs a quick, unsettling look. "Well," he said at last, "the fact is, pretty much everyone around here is related in one way or another. It's like a tribe —you know, a limited area with a few extended families. A sociologist would have a field day."

Freirs heard the complicity in Poroth's voice—he'd been speaking as one educated man to another—and remembered what Deborah had written: *Both of us have attended college outside the community.* Clearly Sarr didn't want him to forget it.

"Sounds incestuous."

Poroth shrugged. "No more than any other tribe. Our order's pretty strict. And there are also Brethren living outside of Gilead, so it's not as if we only marry each other. My wife's from Sidon, over in Pennsylvania—an even smaller settlement."

"You met at college?"

"No, we'd met years before that, at a Quarinale, a kind of planting festival. But we didn't get to see each other again till college. I was at Trenton, Deborah spent two years at Page. It's a Bible school." He paused. "We've only been back here for six or seven months. Deborah's still learning to fit in."

"Is fitting in important?"

"Very."

Freirs felt a stir of interest. "I guess she and I will have a lot in common, then."

Poroth darted him a glance. "In what way?"

"We're both newcomers around here."

The other mulled this over, frowning. "I guess you're right. There are some strong personalities in Gilead, and a few people haven't really accepted her yet. It's all a bit new to Deborah. At this point, she's still trying to get all the families straight. There are faces to remember, names and relations—"

"Yes, I saw a lot of those names on the tombstones back there. Sturtevant, van Meer . . ."

"That's right. And Reid, Troet, Buckhalter, a few stray Verdocks—"

"That was the stone I fell asleep by," Freirs said. "Troet."

"Ah, yes." Poroth kept his eyes on the road. "Actually, they were a distant branch of my mother's family. She's a Troet too. But that branch is gone now."

"They all seem to have died at the same time."

Poroth nodded. "Some kind of fire, I think. The Lord works in strange ways." He fell silent; then, as if realizing that this was insufficient: "Fire's always been a hazard in the country. These days, though, people around here live pretty much the way everyone else does, and they die of the same things other people do—heart attacks, cancer, an occasional accident . . . all the usual things. Of course, they may live a few years longer, what with working hard, breathing clean air, eating food they've grown themselves."

"Well, I plan to do plenty of hard work this summer," said Freirs, settling back, "but it'll be more the mental sort. Still, this looks like a healthy place to do it." He patted his belly. "Maybe I can even lose a little weight."

Poroth smiled. "I should warn you, Deborah's a good cook. I hope you're one who struggles against the temptations of the flesh."

Freirs laughed. "No better than the next man, I guess! You know what they say about the best way to get rid of a temptation." He laughed again and looked over at Poroth, but the other was no longer smiling.

They had already passed through a lane of brick houses, square and unadorned, notable only for the absence of children's outdoor toys, junked auto bodies, and whimsical lawn decorations that Freirs had seen in front of other rural homes he'd passed today. Many of the houses were bordered by plots of land in earthen rows, dotted here and there with little shoots of green. Children tended garden beside their elders; they waved to Poroth as he went by, eyeing Freirs uneasily. A house was under construction, bearded men clinging to the framework like sailors in the rigging of a ship. They, too, waved, their faces impassive.

"I see there's no restriction against working on Sunday," said Freirs.

"Far from it. We believe that labor's holy, and all days are sancti-
fied by it. 'For thou shalt eat the labor of thine hands: happy shalt
thou be, and it shall be well with thee.'"

"Amen," Freirs said automatically, though Bible talk merely bored
him, like words from a foreign text that had lost, in translation, some
essential meaning. But at least he'd found a reason for the state of
Poroth's clothes; every sweat ring was presumably a badge of honor.

They had been following the road over a slight rise of land, Poroth
gunning the motor to maintain their speed. Now, on the farther side,
they passed a sprawling red farmhouse and a barn that looked pegged
to the earth by the broad silo beside it. Cattle grazed up and down the
slope.

"Prosperous-looking place," said Freirs.

"Verdock's dairy," said Poroth. "More relations. Lise Verdock is my
father's sister."

The cattle all faced the same direction, as if in prayer. A few were
moving idly among the others in what seemed slow motion; the rest
were as immobile as creatures on a billboard. Freirs, smelling grass
and manure, breathed deeply. This stuff was supposed to save him.

"They stand tail to the wind," Poroth was saying, "so when they all
look east like that, it means good weather." He nodded toward a more
imposing house beyond the dairy farm, at the top of a long tree-lined
drive. "Sturtevant," he said. "Brother Joram has considerable influence in these parts."

"And does your father have a farm out here too?"

"No, he died ten years ago this fall. And he was never a farmer; he
ran the Co-operative. So did his father and *his* father. Now the
Steeglers run it—Brother Bert and Sister Amelia. Bert's mother was a
Stoudemire, which makes him . . . let's see, a third cousin once or twice
removed." He grinned. "See, it gets complicated."

"Maybe I should just regard everybody as one big happy family."

Poroth seemed to consider this a moment. "Yes," he said at last.
"Yes, happy." He nodded, though it seemed as much to himself as to
Freirs.

Freirs watched the scenery roll by, the dark fields corduroyed by
rows of early corn. So Poroth was taking to the land again after gen-
erations in town. That made him, in a way, as unfamiliar with farming
as Freirs was himself. It was somehow good to hear.

They turned right and continued downhill, a shade more steeply
now. At the bottom, Poroth swung the truck abruptly to the left, the
road following a shady, swiftly flowing stream half hidden from view
by trees along its banks. Through the open window Freirs could hear
the contented percolation of the water as it passed among the rock
with a sound like something singing to itself.

"Wasakeague Brook," said Poroth, raising his voice to be heard. "A branch of it runs past our land."

They kept to the brook as it wound by straggly orchards, cornfields, and an occasional ancient-looking farmhouse, the sort where strangers knocked on wintry nights and fires blazed within. It felt like a scene in some book from his childhood. "Boy," said Freirs, "I feel as if New York's a thousand miles away."

Poroth eyed him quizzically. "And is that a good feeling or a bad one?"

"Good . . . I think." Freirs smiled. "I'll let you know at the end of the day."

The road cut through a stand of beech and cottonwood. Branches snapped against the truck's hood; leaves flattened themselves against the windshield. Freirs moved back from the window as the foliage rushed past.

"As for me," Poroth said suddenly, "a thousand miles away's exactly where I like it." He sounded like a man with something to get off his chest. "Even two thousand would suit me just fine."

"Oh?" Freirs was still concentrating on the flashing branches. "Wouldn't that make getting in and out a little inconvenient?"

"Yes, I imagine it would! But you see, I don't *go* in and out. I saw the place for the first time around ten years ago, and I've never set foot there since."

Uh-oh. For a moment he'd forgotten where he was: among the apple-knockers, Garden State variety. These people voted against cities at election time and probably preached against them too.

"Sounds like you had a bad experience."

"Memorable, anyway. I'll tell you about it sometime."

"And how old were you then?"

"Let's see, I would've been . . . just seventeen."

So Poroth was actually younger than he. Hard to believe—and hard to believe a young man of normal curiosity could grow up so close to New York without ever hopping on the bus to see what it was like.

"It's a big world out there, Sarr. Don't you think you ought to give it another chance?"

Poroth shook his head. "I've already seen the world—as much as I want to see, anyway. I spent seven years out there. How many have you spent around here?"

"Why, none, of course," said Freirs, with a shrug. "It's hardly the same thing."

"I disagree," said Poroth. "You've only seen one side of the world. I've seen both. But I'm home now, and it feels right."

"Home for good?"

"Yes, sir! I intend to die right here in Hunterdon County."

"And Deborah," Freirs said carefully, "does she feel the same?" He already suspected that she didn't.

"No, Deborah's a bit more . . . adventurous than I am. And not so quick to judge, I'll grant her that. She's visited the city a few times, and I can't pretend she shares my feelings about it."

"I guess it was Deborah, then, who put the ad in the library."

Poroth looked blank. "What library?"

"The Voorhis, where I'm doing my research. That's where I saw your ad—on the bulletin board."

Poroth took his eyes from the road and turned a suspicious glance on Freirs. "You mean the notice that Deborah wrote out?"

"That's right. On some kind of recipe card, I think."

He shook his head. "Impossible. I put it up myself—at the bus depot over in Flemington. I wasn't sure, at first, that we'd want anyone from too far away."

"You mean, from New York?"

"At the time, yes. You see, we'd never done this before—it seemed safer to start with someone who already knew the area. The ad was kind of an experiment. I figured someone passing through Flemington might see it at the bus stop." He paused. "That's where I thought *you'd* seen it."

"Nope. I'd never been to Flemington in my life, before today." He was as much in the dark as Poroth but found something curiously enjoyable in the other's bewilderment. "All I know is, I saw it in New York. I guess somebody just decided to move it."

"Sure, but *who?*"

Freirs shrugged. "Some do-gooder, maybe. Or maybe it was fate. Unless you've got a better idea."

Poroth, staring distractedly down the road, fingers drumming on the steering wheel, said nothing.

He was still silent when, minutes later, the trees thinned out. Ahead of them the road forked to the right and led onto a crossing. Halfway up a hill above the opposite bank, guarded at the back by a line of aging cedars, stood a small stone cottage, squat, slate-roofed, and overgrown with vines. Battalions of flowers separated the house from the surrounding expanse of lawn. Additional rows had been planted in front, forming a series of terraced steps that led down to the stream.

Spanning the stream, and constructed of the same stone as the cottage, rose the arch of an old stone bridge only wide enough for one car to pass over at a time. Its railings were low and no doubt insubstantial, mere slats of wood; you'd hear them bend and crack before your car went off the edge, but they wouldn't keep you from falling. Freirs inadvertently held his breath as the truck rumbled across, but Poroth drove without pause or hesitation—perhaps, even, with a touch of bravado.

On the other side, unexpectedly, he slowed, following the road as it encircled the hill, the cottage from this vantage point looking like a kind of outpost meant to warn those farther inland of encroaching civilization. The flowers that surrounded it were sleeping sentries, ready at any moment to snap to attention.

"Nice-looking little place," remarked Freirs, as they were passing.

Poroth nodded. "My mother's. I expected to see her out in the garden. She's usually there this time of day." He scanned the yard, looking for a sign that she was home, and seemed vaguely troubled when he found none. Or perhaps that business of the ad was still on his mind.

"What are those things?" asked Freirs, nodding toward a trio of upright boxes on legs, like midget armoires, that stood in the yard on the side farthest from the stream.

"Beehives," said Poroth. "She even had 'em when we lived in town. My father and I used to get stung all the time." He shook his head, remembering.

As the road wound inland now, Freirs looked back. Just before the house was lost from view behind a wall of boxwood, he glimpsed something in one of the upstairs front windows—something that, for all the intervening distance, looked singularly like a face, frowning at them from the darkness.

Mrs. Poroth, more than nine years a widow, stood at the top of the stairs, watching the truck till it disappeared up the lane. Sunlight slanted through the small square windowpanes, setting in relief the rock-hard features, the strong, almost hawklike nose and masculine jaw, the tiny sharp lines where the corners of her mouth turned down as if with grief. And she had cause for grief. The vision had been confirmed; her prophecy had proven correct. Many a woman would have wept.

On a normal Sunday afternoon in spring she'd have been outside, silently absorbed over her lilacs and rosebushes. But today, after the hours of worship that had filled the morning, the songs and invocations to the Lord, offered up this week at the home of Brother Amos Reid, she had returned to her cottage and stationed herself by the window, waiting pale and troubled for her son's truck to pass, determined to see the visitor it would be bringing before he saw her.

And she had seen him.

Like one in a dream, she made her way with slow, unthinking foot-

steps down the ancient staircase and through the lengthening shadows
of the front room, moving absently toward the door. Stepping outside,
she gazed unsmiling at the garden. A haze had passed before the sun;
the countryside lay bathed in amber light. Honeybees poked drowsily
among the rows of blossoms spread across the south face of the hill.
Framed as she was within the doorway, her hair still black, though
touched of late with streaks of charcoal grey, and her shapeless black
dress reaching almost to the floor, she seemed the only truly dark thing
in the landscape.

There was too much to think about now, events too grave to contemplate; her mind refused, for the moment, to grapple with them and
turned instead, from force of habit, to the mundane concerns of earth
and leaf and weather. She surveyed the ranks of blossoms with a practiced eye, the flower beds extending down the slope past scattered
clumps of rosebushes and lilacs to the banks of the stream. The season
had, so far, been a warm one, just as she'd foreseen, and all the signs
now pointed to a summer of unusual severity. The tulips and hya-
cinths had already begun to wither on their stalks, and the lavender,
she knew, would be opening too early, perhaps within the week. She
would have to harvest it soon.

The lilac bushes, too, had blossomed early—a month ago, in fact—
though by tradition they should not have reached their fullness till
today, May first, the Beltane: sacred, some believed, to Baal's *teine*, the
ancient god's sacrificial fire. Legend said that, on this day, one who
bathed in lilacs' dew would be granted beauty for a year.

The legend held no charm for her. The time of her beauty was past,
and she was past mourning. it. There was no one on earth that she
cared about, not even her only son, Sarr. The lilacs' time was past as
well; soon they too would wither and turn brown.

Stepping from the doorway, the air around her humming with ci-
cadas and bees, she strolled morosely among the ordered rows of flowers. Their lives, though brief, had always been vastly more interesting
to her than people's. The crocuses and snowdrops were long dead and
the daffodils dying, but the peonies and baby's breath had just begun
to bloom, and a few other species were now at the height of their season:
the blue and purple columbines whose leaves, when grasped, brought
courage to the fearful; the delicate pink gillyflowers, sprung from
Mary's tears, whose petals could be used for divination; the lilies of the
valley—born, it was said, from the blood a saint had spilled fighting
dragons in the forest—whose cup-shaped blossoms, properly prepared,
were an aid to failing memory.

Not that she herself had need of memory aids, or courage, or divina-
tory powers. She forgot nothing, feared little, and foresaw far more
than she cared to. The Lord, in His harsh wisdom, had singled her out
from the rest. He had shown her shadows of the future, tormented her

with visions of the world to come. He had seen to it that, despite what good befell her, she would never be happy for long.

It had not always been this way. She had been born with certain "gifts," as the Brethren called them, a certain wayward talent for prediction or the lucky guess, for reading secret thoughts from people's faces; but such gifts were common to the women in her family. Others before her had known them.

They were a small people, the Troets, given more to scholarship than farming, which set them apart from the rest of the community; yet in some ways their strength lay far deeper than the farmers'. It had always been, curiously, a female's strength, expressed not in the usual human terms of opposition to nature, or in futile attempts to master or control it, but in a kind of day-to-day alliance with its laws. Nature had, in turn, rewarded them; the Troet women—one or two, at least, each generation—had been blessed with certain powers of intuition, as if they were in touch, more directly even than the farmers, with aspects of some fundamental process: rainfall and impending winds, vegetation's cycle, the changing of the seasons and the moon. Mrs. Poroth remembered her own maternal grandmother, a Buckhalter by name but a Troet by descent, who could read approaching weather in a cockcrow or a certain slant of light, and who'd speak familiarly of "little signs" that others had ignored. It had been a gift beyond her ability to explain; when asked about it—as, when still a child, her granddaughter had asked—the old woman would say simply, with an indifferent shrug, that there were "other ways of knowing."

Mrs. Poroth herself, it was believed, had inherited some of these powers; as a little girl she'd begun to understand, in a primitive way, how to let the world speak to her through the smells and colors of flowers, the shapes of leaves and clouds. But there'd been nothing truly exceptional about her talents—until that summer morning of her thirteenth year when, on the day after her grandmother's funeral, drawn by some unaccountable impulse to climb the stairs to the old woman's attic, she had discovered the Pictures.

They had been inside a folder tied with ribbon, crushed beneath a pile of dusty books in the darkest corner of the room. The renderings were crude, the sort of things a bright nine-year-old boy might have produced. They were drawn in luridly colored chalk on cheap rag paper, yellow and cracking around the edges and stiff with age. They looked at least half a century old.

Her eyes had widened as she sifted through them; she'd felt the sudden pounding of her heart. Crude though they were, the images had stood out from the cracked and yellowed paper with terrifying clarity. There were twenty-one drawings in all, each on a separate sheet and each, in its own way, filling her with inexpressible horror. There was a white birdlike thing with blood upon its breast, dying; a pool of dark

water, with the hint of something crouched beneath it; a pale yellow
book, fat and somehow repellent; a low earthen mound of odd proportions, and a red satanic-looking sun, and a cold oppressive moon, and a
round white shape against a black background that she first took for
another heavenly body, a planet or a moon, until suddenly, with a
shudder, she saw it for what it was, a great round lidless eye . . .

Some of the Pictures were so queer she couldn't tell what they were
meant to be. Like the slim black sticklike object; and the things that
looked like dogs, only so badly drawn it was hard to be sure; and a
pulpy thing that might be a coiled worm and might be smiling lips;
and another figure, small, dark, and shapeless, with the half-formed
look of dead things and decaying leaves, like a child's attempt to draw
some creature he had heard about but never seen.

And with each new image, impossible memories were stirring; even
the strangest of the Pictures, the three concentric circles with the red
slash down the middle, seemed somehow familiar, in ways almost painful to think about. And there were others even worse: a horrifying
scene drawn entirely in white, and another entirely in black; and a hideous thing that may have been a rose, except it had what looked like
teeth; and a tree with something in it, a thing that glared and beckoned.

She knew that it was beckoning to her. The room was tipping
forward; she was slipping, falling, the world spinning around her,
drawing her toward that terrible face in the tree . . .

Dizzy, she had somehow had the presence of mind to hide the evil
things, to shove them back beneath a stack of old papers before stumbling wild-eyed and delirious down the stairs.

When they found her minutes later, crumpled and unconscious on
the second-floor landing, it was believed she'd had a fall. She was carried into what had been her grandmother's bedroom and laid on the
dead woman's bed. There were some who felt uneasy about using the
chamber of one so recently departed, and a younger brother wondered
aloud if her fall hadn't perhaps been occasioned by a glimpse of the
grandmother's ghost, stalking the attic overhead. But the Brethren
were, above all, a practical people and not inclined to place much importance on such concerns. They knew they had nothing to fear from
ghosts.

She had lain all that day as if under a spell, barely breathing enough
to stir a goose-down feather held beneath her nose. Her face had become as rigid as a mask; when they peeled a lid back, they found the
eye turned up in her head so that little more than the white showed, as
if she were gazing at the inside of her skull. Her family feared for her
life and, having just buried one of their number, spent the hours in
prayer, begging the Lord to content Himself with the pious old woman

He had so recently taken to His bosom and to spare this unworthy child. But if He heard them, He made no sign.

The trance had continued through the night and into the following morning, a hot, windless day that turned the old house into a furnace. Brethren gathered on the first floor to mop their brows and pray for the girl's soul, many quietly preparing themselves for a second funeral. A few even wondered if this wasn't perhaps a judgment on the whole Troet clan and its strange contrary ways.

And so things had remained until evening of the second day, when suddenly the girl's eyes opened and she sat bolt upright, startling those assembled at the bedside with a scream that sounded like "The burning!" She was quickly declared to be out of danger; her dramatic awakening seemed merely to have been the culmination of a nightmare, and her family was relieved to discover that, despite her cry, she appeared to have no fever.

But the nightmare had been real, she'd been sure of it. She'd been flooded with visions, lying there, images of murder. Somewhere just outside Gilead a girl very like herself was about to die. There was light, and a tree, and an odd design with three concentric rings . . .

Her confused ravings were not entirely dismissed—the Brethren took such warnings seriously, aware that the Lord occasionally allowed men glimpses of events to come—but it was difficult to make sense of what she said. A tree? There were thousands of trees not half a mile from the house. A girl? It could be anyone's sister or daughter. And as for the design she'd babbled of, what were they to make of it? They could hardly be expected to act upon a prophecy so vague.

And in the end she had relented. Perhaps they were right, her family and the others; perhaps it had been a nightmare after all, brought on by her discovery of the Pictures—whose existence she'd been desperately anxious to keep secret.

Two days later a group of hunters had come upon the partially burned body of a girl from a nearby village, suspended from a tree in the part of the woods they called McKinney's Neck.

She had felt, in part, responsible for the death. A vision had been vouchsafed her, and she had failed to heed it. Never again would she allow this to happen.

That had been in 1939. Since then, over the years, she had sifted the Pictures many times, though always without joy, studying them at night by her bedside. She no longer had to see them all; merely staring at a few of the now-familiar images, drawn at random from the pile, was enough. Invariably the dreams would come.

She had never told a soul about the source of her knowledge. The community had no suspicion. The Brethren regarded her as a model of piety, and, after her first prophecy had been proved true, they ac-

corded her a superstitious respect not untinged with fear, coming to
her often for advice. She doubted they'd look kindly upon her use of
the Pictures.

She detested them herself; she knew what dreadful visions had inspired them. She knew the identity of the dark, formless creature, and
the terrible things it could do. She'd learned what the circular design
meant, and where it was to be used. And she knew—had always
known—who had drawn them all. Even in those first dreams in her
grandmother's house, she had seen in the Pictures the hand of her vanished ancestor, the boy Absolom Troet.

Over the years she had come to suspect, if dimly, what the boy's instructions might have been. And she trembled at them. For beneath
the dreams that the Pictures inspired loomed a great black certainty
that haunted every waking hour, a vision of the future which, as a
young girl, then a housewife, now a solitary widow, she felt powerless
to alter or prevent.

Though she knew she'd have to try. Surely the Lord expected nothing less.

In recent years, like one who leaves unread a message of bad tidings,
she had resorted to the Pictures less frequently—had avoided them, in
fact, preferring to leave them tucked safely inside the great leather-
bound Bible on the nightstand by her bed, as if to thereby make them
holy. She had no need to open the Bible; its every word was as familiar
to her as the images Absolom had drawn.

"And now, Lord, what wait I for? My hope is in thee . . ."

She frowned as she moved farther down the hill, troubled by what
she saw: the scattered clumps of rosebushes, the late-blooming teas and
early-blooming damasks and mosses that grew here and there above the
stream. They reminded her of something.

For just last night, aware that a visitor, an outsider, was due among
them this May Day, and knowing with dread that, exactly as prophe-
sied, a month with two full moons lay ahead, she had succumbed to curiosity and the demands of conscience. At bedtime she had opened the
Bible, slipped out the Pictures, drawn forth at random the images of
moon, rose, and serpent . . .

The dream, she recalled now, had been set right here, in this garden,
by that moss-rose halfway down the slope.

Darkly it came back to her.

She'd been walking here, just as she was now. Only it had been
night, and hot, and moonlit. One leaf on the moss-rose bush had looked
different from the others in the ghostly light: a single leaf half hidden
by the night shadows of the damasks, but her sharp eyes had picked

out from several yards away. There seemed to be—there at the tip—an odd, unnatural whiteness . . .

No, not just at the tip. She saw as she drew nearer that the entire leaf was edged in whiteness, the dark familiar greenness in retreat, as from a creeping frost or a cold invisible fire.

She ran her fingers over its surface; she was sensitive to plants, they spoke to her in a hundred furtive ways, and surely this one had secrets to reveal . . .

Her fingers, this time, told her nothing. Around her the air throbbed with the buzzing of unseen bees. Grasping the rose branch, she tugged lightly at the leaf. There was a sudden stinging pain, and with a cry she yanked back her hand. Protruding from the fleshy area just below her thumb was a pale green thorn snapped off jaggedly at the base. She pulled it out; it was curved, wicked-looking, nearly an inch long. How had she failed to see it in the moonlight?

The buzzing had grown louder, more insistent. As she brought her wounded hand to her lips, the blood flowing salty and warm, something occurred at the end of the branch just inches from her face.

A rosebud moved.

Her eyes widened. Why hadn't she noticed it before? The bud was fatter than the others, the skin moist and somehow pulpy-looking. It was clinging to the thin branch like a lump of rotting meat.

Warily she reached for it. It shifted at her touch. The air shrilled with an angry insect sound that clamored like a warning in her ears, and there beneath the radiance of the moon, in the heat of that rose-perfumed night, she felt a chill.

Torn from the branch, the bud seemed heavy in her hand. Her fingers probed the dark-veined leafy covering. One by one the leaves peeled back; like a piece of hollow fruit the skin split and fell away. Inside lay a pale, ropy thing curled like a length of intestine. As the moonlight fell on it, it stirred.

She saw now what it was: a plump white worm, thick as a baby's finger—a plump white worm that, as she watched, uncurled, raised its unwrinkled head, and glared at her. A plump white worm with a human face.

Grimacing, she dropped it to the ground. She was sure she heard the creature scream as she crushed it beneath her shoe: scream words at her as from a human mouth, human lungs, a human throat, words in some dark ancient tongue she'd never heard spoken aloud, but whose meaning, upon waking, she'd felt sure she understood.

And now, just this afternoon, she had seen the visitor, all plump and pink and innocent, arriving with her son. She had recognized something in his innocent face. The dream had not lied. The Pictures were real. For the first time in her life, she felt too tired to pray.

Absolom, the Old One, still lived: she'd known it all along, all her blighted life. She'd always known that one day he would make his move, assemble the performers—the man, the woman, the Dhol—and allow the process to begin. She had known that it would start the first of May and end the first of August, in a month with two full moons.

But she'd always believed she had at least a decade left to her. She'd believed she would have more time to prepare. She hadn't realized it would come so soon. This year. This May.

This summer.

His journey takes him south, where rows of skyscrapers reflect the westering sun and cast giant shadows up and down the avenue. An idle weekend crowd fills the sidewalks, strolling past the ranks of street vendors and spilling from the shops to join the mass that merges and splits and merges again into a living stream.

Unnoticed, the Old One walks among them.

A half-naked boy limps toward him, pale head swollen like overripe fruit, clutching a thumb-stained envelope. A blind trumpeter blares against the traffic from the doorway of an abandoned building. Someone stands hunched over a pay phone, mouth working furiously. On the corner a haggard woman waves a blackboard scribbled with names and exhorts the planet to save itself; humanity, she cries, has been judged and found wanting.

He knows that she is right. That judgment is his as well. Turning his back on the woman, he's confronted by his reflection in a store window: the short, plump figure swinging an umbrella, the blue serge suit gone baggy at the knees, the wide cherubic face beneath its halo of fine white hair.

It is the reflection of a little old man.

Once he had something in common with the figures crowding past him on the sidewalk; once, more than a century ago, he was one of them, part of the loathsome race that swarms over this planet. Now only the semblance remains, the organs, bones, and flesh. He has been washed clean of humanity; he feels no trace of kinship for these odious doomed beings, only a cold and unremitting hatred. As he passes down the avenue they part before him like stalks of corn.

Stoplights change from red to green and the crowd surges forward. A bus groans, lumbering away from the curb. Brakes screech as a taxi sounds its horn. Dark feline shapes crouch beneath a parked car, then dart into an alley. From the next block echo the cries of children and, from another part of the city, the wail of sirens. As the Old One turns westward once more, the sun is sinking toward the distant Jersey hills, toward the factories and the dumps and the oil refineries. Suddenly the land is touched with red and the refineries glow as if ignited, hills turning to flame. The river shines with fire.

The Old One blinks his mild eyes and smiles. Great events are imminent, and nothing that he looks upon will ever be the same. The crowds, the traffic, the hateful little faces of the children—soon, after the Voolas, they will trouble him no more.

But first there are a few more preparations to be made. There is not much time left, and he will never get another chance: five thousand years must pass before the signs again are right. He will have to act quickly.

He has already selected the man: some insignificant little academic with no family and no prospects. There are hundreds just like him in the city—all young, all hopeful, all doomed—but this one has been born on the necessary day, and (though the young fool doesn't know it yet) his interests lie in just the right direction. At this very moment he'll be out there on the farm, no doubt busily convincing himself that he likes it. He appears to be highly suggestible. He will do.

Now the Old One is faced with an even more important task, a task which has to be completed by Midsummer's Day.

He has to find a woman.

Not just any woman. The age has to be right. And the background. And the color of her hair.

And, of course, she will have to possess that very special qualification . . .

"Wonderful place you've got here." He was being just a little ingenuous, tramping through the undergrowth with Poroth. The farm looked better than it had in the photographs—greener, certainly—but it plainly needed a lot of work. Even Freirs could tell that, and the last farm he'd seen had been in *Days of Heaven*, with Richard Gere shoving a screwdriver into Sam Shepard. The Poroths had already cleared an irregularly shaped plot of land nearly twice the size of a football field, extending westward from the farmhouse's back lawn, past the barn and down to the meandering little brook that curved across the southern edge of the property, but there appeared to be many times this area still to be attended to, including a huge uncultivated section on the far side of the brook that Poroth had spoken of "saving for next year."

The place was much bigger than it had looked from the road—close to fifty acres, all told, though most of this was forest, or fields of weed too thick and high to walk through. Freirs reminded himself that the Poroths had moved in just last fall, and that, till then, the land had lain untended for seven or eight years. Perhaps this was why a young couple like the Poroths had been able to afford it.

He would have liked to ask Poroth how much the place had cost, now that the two of them were alone out here, lunch under their belts and the land stretching green and sun-soaked before them, but for most of this day—at least ever since they'd passed his mother's house, back there on the road—Poroth had fallen into some kind of mood, replying to Freirs' occasional polite questions with an air of gloomy distraction. Here was Brother Lucas Flinders' place, he'd said, barely nodding toward some tidy farmhouse they were passing. That one was the Reids'. Down this way lived Brother Matt Geisel . . . More than that he'd seemed disinclined to say. And then, toward the end, barreling down the three miles of pitted, unpaved road that wound through woods and brambles to the Poroths' farm, he'd barely talked at all, too preoccupied with keeping the old truck from going off into a ditch. Before them the road had seemed to buck and twist beneath their wheels like a wild thing, at times almost doubling back upon itself—"like it's trying to throw us off," Freirs had said, holding tightly to the door handle and wishing the other would slow down. What in hell was he trying to prove? Poroth had said only, "This sort of road's not meant for driving on," and hadn't so much as glanced in Freirs' direction.

He'd recognized the farmhouse from the photograph as soon as it came into view, a small grey-shingled boxlike affair, as tall as it was wide and obviously quite old, set close to the edge of the road as if eager to greet the few strangers who ventured out this far. The thornbushes along the side were green now, dotted here and there with dark red rosebuds. Deborah, Poroth's wife, had been standing there on the porch as they drove up, a pair of cats gathered like children at her feet. Even at this distance, Freirs could see that she, too, looked much as she had in the photo, dressed in homespun black from neck to ankle. She had waved gaily to them as Poroth spun the wheel and brought the truck around to the side of the house, where it came to an abrupt halt on a bare section of the lawn.

The first thing that had hit him was the silence. He'd noticed it as soon as Poroth shut the motor off. As he climbed out onto the grass, grateful to be on solid ground again, it was as if the whole world had suddenly come to a stop. Back in Gilead, standing alone, he had felt a similar quiet, but there it had seemed somehow less dramatic, a more fragile thing soon to be shattered by the inevitable noise to come, traffic noise and tractors and the intrusion of human voices. Here, though, he sensed that except for the small sounds of insect, bird, and wind in the trees, the silence was permanent, a central fact of life.

Deborah immediately came down from the porch to meet them. She was a handsome woman, even better looking than he'd hoped, with strong cheekbones and wide dark eyes beneath heavy unwomanish brows. Her mouth was large, the lips sensual and thick—not a puritan's lips at all; with makeup, in the right clothes, she would really be something to see. Her mass of black hair was obviously long and full, but she wore it swept back behind her head and knotted in a complicated bun with a severity that looked almost painful. He wondered what she'd look like with it down.

"I sure hope you didn't have to wait long," she said, after Sarr had introduced her. "Services always run so late at the Reids', the way Brother Amos can talk. I was afraid you'd get fed up and start walking back to New York."

Freirs smiled—in part to make up for Poroth, who, he saw, was scowling at his wife. Probably didn't like her putting down the neighbors. "Oh, I wasn't about to walk home. In fact, I had myself a little nap."

"I found him sleeping in the graveyard," said Poroth. "Right by that big stone of the Troets'."

Deborah laughed. "A good choice! They're Sarr's old relations."

"Yes," said Freirs. "I gather almost everyone is."

"And guess where he found our notice," said Poroth. "The one I put up in Flemington."

"Where?" She turned to Freirs.

"I found it on a bulletin board in New York," he said.

This news, he saw, had caught her by surprise. She looked from him to her husband, as if the two men shared a secret. "How did it get there?"

"That's what we don't know," said Poroth grimly. "Some kind of prankster, maybe."

"Or else a good Samaritan," said Deborah. She considered this a moment, then nodded. "Yes, it *must* have been, don't you see? Look how nicely everything's turned out. It just might be a sign from God." Eyes wide, she turned back to Freirs. "It's like your name—from Jeremiah. I'm sure that's an omen too." She grinned. "Maybe you'll turn out to be a prophet."

Freirs laughed uneasily. "I'm afraid I'm no relation. But then, you never can tell."

"I can tell," she said. "You were meant to come here, I'm sure of it. And I'm sure you're going to fit right in." Scooping up a cat, she began moving toward the house. "Now come on, both of you. I have lunch ready, and then Sarr can show you around. You two just better be hun-

gry. There's sliced ham and cheese, and fresh dandelion greens—"
Looking back at Freirs, she added, "Nothing from our own garden, not
yet, anyway—but there's a rhubarb pie from the Geisels right up the
road." To Sarr she added, "Brother Matt's coming by later. I think he
wants to meet our guest."

"Sounds like just what the doctor ordered," said Freirs, hurrying
after her. For a moment he caught a glimpse, in back of the house, of
the outbuilding where he'd be staying. It looked somehow less welcoming than the farmhouse. Maybe they didn't want to show it to him till
they'd softened him up. Well, that was okay; he could use a good lunch.
He followed Deborah up the porch steps, surreptitiously eyeing her
swaying hips encased in the black dress, the hemline sweeping barely
an inch above the floor. A wonder it didn't get dusty.

Behind them in the yard, Poroth sighed. The matter of the rental notice seemed to be closed. "I'll leave the truck out," he called, coming
after them. "We'll have to start back to town by five to make the bus."

While Deborah held the screen door open for Freirs, a pair of cats
dashed past her feet and into the house, closely followed by another
that Freirs hadn't seen. This could be a problem; he hadn't counted on
there being so many.

Inside, the house seemed cramped and dark, with an unmistakable
odor of cat; his nose tickled alarmingly. He heard Poroth's footsteps on
the porch behind him. The old floorboards creaked. "It's lighter in the
back," Deborah said, leading the way. They passed from a small front
hallway to what was obviously the living room, where a rocker and a
low, rather worn-looking couch stood facing a small fireplace. Beyond
it lay the kitchen, afternoon sunlight streaming through the windows
and a screen door in the rear.

It took Freirs a moment to realize what was missing. He looked in
vain for lamps, a light switch, television; there was nothing but a small
kerosene lantern on the mantelpiece. As he entered the kitchen, he saw
another on the shelf by the doorway. He cleared his throat. "I thought
your ad said 'Fully electrified.'"

"The outbuilding is," said Poroth, ducking as he came into the
kitchen. "I ran the wires in myself not two months ago. But in our own
home—" He shrugged. "We prefer to keep the modern world at a distance. Here, you see, we're independent of the city and its ways."

Freirs sensed, not for the first time, a hint of disapproval. Across the
room he noticed a huge cast-iron woodburning stove rubbing shoulders
with a shiny little Hotpoint. He turned to Deborah, who was busying
herself at the sink, cats milling at her feet. "I suppose that stove is
gas-powered."

"Correct," said Sarr. "We bought it secondhand from a man in
Trenton."

"Honey," Deborah said over her shoulder, "show Jeremy the tanks out back." Freirs watched her lay a platter of ham on the kitchen table and remembered how hungry he was.

"Here, look at this." Poroth pushed open the screen door and led Freirs out onto the back porch, where two more cats were lying on the dusty wooden steps. "Each one lasts about a month," said Poroth—but he was pointing to a pair of silver canisters standing like miniature spaceships against the rear wall of the house, surrounded by rose-bushes and weeds. "Ordinary propane. It heats our water and cooks our meals." Draping a long leg over the railing, he leaned back against the weathered wooden post and folded his arms.

"I don't get it," said Freirs. "You say you want to be independent of the modern world, but gas is just as modern as electricity. And probably just as expensive."

He thought perhaps he had offended Poroth, but the other seemed amused. "I know it doesn't sound very rational," Poroth said. "I don't pretend it is. The choices we've made have been largely . . . symbolic. Expressions of our faith." He smiled wryly. "Does that make any sense?"

Freirs shrugged. "I suppose so."

"Look," said Poroth, "we're not fanatics, Deborah and I. We have indoor plumbing. We own a truck. When one of us gets sick, we see a doctor. Some of the Brethren are stricter than that; others may think *we're* too strict. There's plenty of room for differences. You'd be surprised how open-minded the Brethren can be."

He would, all right. He hadn't forgotten the looks they'd given him in town. But he said politely, "You people must be a lot more liberal than I figured. I'd had you pegged as a New Jersey version of the Amish."

Poroth made a face. " 'Blackhats,' we call them. They're little better than tourist attractions, if you ask me."

"I guess I was going by appearances. I mean, you seem to dress the same as they do, except for the hats."

"It's true, we have our similarities. Certain customs, outward forms . . . This sort of thing." He pointed to his trousers. "See? No pockets. Pockets breed avarice. Give a man pockets, and pretty soon he'll want something to put in them. 'He that is greedy of gain troubleth his own house.' " Poroth smiled. "That's what I meant by symbolism."

"No kidding! I *thought* those pants looked strange." Wait till he told them about this back in New York.

"It's the same with the beard. See? Brethren don't wear mustaches because the military wore them—in Europe, anyway—and we refused to leave the farm." Abruptly he swung his leg down and stood; he was nearly a head taller than Freirs. "Electricity's a symbol too. You'll find a battery in our truck, another in our radio. We like to listen to the Bible broadcasts. But Deborah and I, we're not ones for labor-

saving and luxury. We have no interest in wiring up our home. As I
see it, an electric wire's a golden chain that binds a body to the city—
and that, my friend, is the citadel of corruption. When the city flickered, *we'd* flicker. When the city went dark, *we'd* go dark. That's a tie
we'd rather do without."

He started back inside. Freirs lingered a moment on the porch, gazing at the land that lay behind the house, at the outbuildings, orchard,
and fields, but thinking of the monstrous Con Ed plant back in Astoria
and how it had lit up the night sky like an ocean liner.

At last the view drew his attention. Where the fields ended, sloping
gently downhill from the farmhouse, his eye was caught by the distant
glimmer of a stream. The property was more extensive than he'd imagined, though its exact limits were hard to discern, for it merged gradually with the woods which, in every direction, formed a backdrop to the
scene. They were dark with shadows and, even at the height of afternoon, far from inviting. He realized suddenly how far he was from the
city, and felt a tiny shiver of excitement. This was the real thing.

The three of them ate in the kitchen, seated on heavy high-backed
chairs before an ancient wooden table that some long-dead Poroth ancestor had made. The farmhouse, he'd discovered, had no dining room;
it was simply too small—three rooms upstairs, two rooms down, and
rough plank floors with spaces often wide enough to see through. Deborah, smiling, had remarked that, when she swept out the kitchen, the
crumbs slipped through the cracks and ended up in the root cellar
below, where the mice ate them.

"And they, in turn, get eaten by the cats," Sarr added, as if com-
pelled to remind her of this. "All part of God's plan."

Freirs studied the two of them while Poroth said grace and the cats
prowled restlessly beneath the table. Except for the difference in
height—for even when he was seated, Sarr towered over them both—
and the fact that Deborah was, from what he could see, full-breasted
and wide of hip while Sarr was tall and rather willowy, the two looked
much alike, as if they'd stepped from the same faded tintype, represen-
tatives of some earlier generation. Despite their dark hair, both had
skin of a surprising smoothness and pallor, considering the time they
probably spent outdoors. It was already clear to him that Deborah was
the friendlier of the two; yet in moments of quiet like this one, as she
sat listening, eyes downcast, while her husband thanked the Lord for
His bounteousness and the guest He'd sent them today, Deborah wore
an air similar to Sarr's—a kind of guarded dignity. They seemed
brother and sister, in fact: two solemn-faced children raised in the wilderness, both of them on speaking terms with God.

By the time grace was over, though, Freirs had become distracted by a growing need to sneeze. "It's nothing to worry about," he explained with irritation when the two finally looked up. "I just happen to be allergic to a variety of things—cats most of all." He gritted his teeth and tried to smile as a pair of them, a yellow tiger-stripe and a charcoal grey, both obviously young, crowded closer to rub against his legs. He was as angry with himself as with the animals; he'd have been happy to reach down and pat them, scratch the downy hair behind their ears, but with each successive breath he could feel his nose becoming clogged, as if somewhere a mechanism had been triggered that he was helpless to control. The corners of his eyes had already begun to itch.

Sarr sat watching him in silence; maybe he saw such afflictions as evidence of weakness or of God's displeasure. Deborah appeared more sympathetic.

"I think it's a good sign," she declared, watching beneath the table as the cats, no doubt in an effort to leave their mark on a stranger, continued to rub themselves diligently against the bottoms of Freirs' pants legs. "I mean, the way they've taken to you. It shows you're welcome here. I guess we're *all* starved for visitors."

Sarr frowned. Clearly this sort of thing made him impatient. "Shall I put them outside?"

That was, in fact, precisely what Freirs wanted, but he was in no mood to make a scene; these animals were the closest things the Poroths had to children. Surely they could all work it out over the summer. "They're okay here," he said lightly, and launched into an elaborate cock-and-bull story—though who could say, maybe it made sense—about how the only way he'd ever get over the allergy was by exposing himself to the offending animals as often as possible. "It's just a matter of building up the right antibodies," he said, privately resolving to see a decent allergist as soon as he got back.

Deborah looked relieved. "Well, just remember now," she said, "if you ever have problems like this over the summer, there's always antihistamine in the medicine chest."

She sounded as if it were a foregone conclusion he'd be staying with them; and maybe it was. He already felt as if he knew them. Obligingly he marched off to the bathroom in search of the pills, grateful that she hadn't offered him some Brethren-approved medication like herbs or mud or some other crazy folk remedy.

The bathroom was a crowded little chamber just off the kitchen, with a small curtained window looking out upon the rosebushes at the side of the house. In the corner stood a bulky metal water heater apparently connected to the tanks out back and, next to it, a primitive sink with separate faucets for hot and cold. Freirs wondered why nobody'd had the sense to connect them; it only took a simple Y-shaped pipe. The room was dominated by a gigantic old claw-footed bathtub, big enough for two, that would probably take hours to fill. No showers for him, then, if he spent his summer here. He told himself that baths were more relaxing: reading classics in the tub, soft music on the radio—it might not be so bad.

The medicine cabinet was a revelation: dusty little plastic bags with roots in them, and colored powders, and things afloat in brown unlabeled bottles, side by side with a handful of prescription drugs for headaches, nausea, nerves—plus mouthwash and aspirin and scented bath talc, and, on the top shelf near the end, a half-empty package of strawberry douche. The Poroths must have an interesting marriage, he decided.

Back in the kitchen Deborah had set out a platter of cheese beside the ham and was busy slicing a loaf of thick brown bread, the kind he saw at German delis but that always seemed too expensive. She was wielding a bread knife that looked half as long as a sword, while Sarr sat watching her impassively, a king on his throne.

"Now *this* looks good," said Freirs, seating himself across from Poroth. He poured himself some milk from a ceramic pitcher and washed down the pill, some local version of Contac.

"Yesterday, I want you to know, that milk was in the cow," said Deborah. "It's from Sarr's uncle's dairy."

"Sure, I remember. We passed it on the way." He swallowed a large bite of bread and cheese. "And I'll bet this bread's homemade."

She nodded, pleased. "I haven't bought bread since we lived in Trenton. It's all baked right here."

"In that thing?" Freirs nodded toward the huge black wood-burning stove that stood beside the Hotpoint, already seeing pictures out of Norman Rockwell, Currier & Ives. "It looks at least a century old."

"It is," said Deborah. "It's as old as the house. But it's hard to regulate. We only use it for heating in the winter . . . and for certain ceremonial occasions."

"Does this place get very cold in the winter?"

"The attic needs work," said Sarr, obviously looking forward to it. "I'll have to put new insulation in this fall."

"It gets cold here all right," said Deborah. "You've heard people talk about three-dog nights, when you need all three dogs in the bed? Well, this January, Sarr and I had a couple of six-cat nights!"

Freirs winced, but not at the idea of such cold. His eyes were still red and he hadn't stopped sniffling. "God," he said, "I probably wouldn't survive the night! Though I guess on a farm like this six cats must have their uses."

"Seven," said Deborah. "You probably haven't seen Bwada yet. That's *his* cat." She nodded at Sarr.

"And where is he?" asked Freirs.

"She," said Poroth. "She stays outside all day—sometimes nights, too. She's more adventurous than the others. I've had her since she was a kitten."

Deborah added, "She's fat and just plain mean. That's why she sleeps by herself. Now, these are the nice ones, Jeremy—" And until dessert she proceeded to furnish him with detailed biographies of the other six, complete with ancestries. They all had names like Habakkuk, Tobias, and Azariah, names which sounded as if they'd been taken from obscure portions of the Bible and which Freirs immediately forgot. He was too busy thinking of Deborah. It would be heavenly, he imagined, to pile into that big soft feather bed they must have up there and lie beside her on a long winter night, slipping the flannel nightgown above her waist and breasts, feeling her warmth against the cold and darkness outside.

Dessert was a tart red rhubarb pie and a plate of lacy brown molasses cookies, the kind he bought at block fairs in the city. He wondered, over his second cup of coffee, if all the meals were going to be this elaborate. If so, he wasn't going to lose much weight out here, but he'd probably be content just the same.

Once coffee was over, Poroth wiped his mouth, pushed back from the table, and offered to show Freirs around. "You may as well see what you came for," he said, stretching as he rose so that his fingers bent back against the ceiling.

"You can see my garden from here," said Deborah, pointing out the window at a small brown fenced-in plot beside the house. "It doesn't look like much right now, but by summer there'll be squash, tomatoes, peas, cucumbers, carrots . . . We'll be eating well, I promise you that."

Clearly they were trying to sell him on the place. They must be counting on his ninety dollars a week.

"We're starting awfully late this year," said Sarr, as the two of them descended the steps from the back porch, Deborah having elected to remain in the kitchen. A pair of cats scampered out behind them just before the screen door slammed. "We'll probably just have enough for the three of us. But by next year we expect to produce enough to sell."

Even that prediction seemed somewhat optimistic. The garden looked far from flourishing, though there were small shoots where the carrots were coming up and green wooden stakes standing in hopeful rows above the young tomato plants. The adjoining lawn, by contrast, looked surprisingly hardy, as if the land's true destiny was to be one of the suburban estates that were already taking up so much of the county.

Across the lawn, and well off to one side, lay the weed-strewn wreckage of an old wooden outhouse, grass growing over the doorway. Freirs wrinkled his nose as they approached, but the air smelled of nothing but damp earth and pine. "You're free to use it if you like," said

Poroth, making one of his infrequent jokes. "I believe it's still in working order."

"Wonderful!" Freirs peered through the gaps in the planks. The bench inside was the double-seater sort, for the ultimate in rural togetherness. Welcome to Appalachia. He thanked God that the farm had modern plumbing.

Farther down the slope, its back to the surrounding wall of forest, was the low, barracklike outbuilding he'd be renting. It was the one he'd glimpsed from the front of the house; he recognized it immediately from the photograph.

"Am I right," asked Freirs, "in assuming that the place was originally a chicken coop?"

"True enough," said Poroth. "We've never used it as one, though. We keep our chickens in the barn."

The building looked somewhat more cheerful in the spring sunlight than it had when the photo was taken, though ivy now covered the walls more thickly and was curling over the edges of the windows, an ever-shrinking green frame.

"It's not completely fixed up yet," said Poroth, looking it over with a critical eye. "I still have to put up the screens. Still, I suppose we ought to go in."

Inside, the place was surprisingly dark, ivy blocking much of the sunlight. "I'll have all that trimmed away before you get here," Poroth said, snapping on a shiny new wall switch that turned on the overhead light. "If I did it now it would just grow back by summer."

There was nothing inviting about the room; the best Freirs could do, by an exercise of imagination, was to see it as a kind of monk's cell, unromantic but suited to the intellectual labors he hoped to perform this summer. It had a pale blue linoleum floor with a slightly uneven seam down the middle and was empty save for a sturdy-looking bed (room for just one, Freirs saw), a chest of drawers, and an oppressive-looking old wooden wardrobe standing like a watchman in the corner. There seemed to be only one closet. "Later this spring I'm going to build some bookshelves in here," said Poroth, eyeing one of the bare plasterboard walls, "and we can move in a table for you to use as a desk." He seemed happy to leave.

The other half of the building, with an entrance of its own at the opposite side, was being used as a storeroom. Its cement floor was packed haphazardly with lumber, battered-looking furniture, and dusty steamer trunks. The air smelled of mildew. Along the front windowsill, a row of dirty Mason jars collected cobwebs and dead flies.

"Deborah wants to fix this up too," said Poroth, "since we've already brought in the electricity. She'd like to turn it into another guest house."

Freirs was peering at a pile of old books, their covers warped a faded. *The Law of the Offerings. Footsteps of the Master. God's Providence and Gospel.* Religious tracts. "And how do you feel about that?"

The other paused. "I'd rather see how things work out this summer."

He turned to go, but Freirs had pushed past the furniture to a door in the far wall. "What does this lead to? A closet?"

"Open it and see."

Freirs pulled it open, then smiled. He was looking into the other room—*his* room. With surprise he realized that, in his imagination, he'd already taken possession of it. The familiar linoleum floor and narrow bed looked almost welcoming.

As they strolled outside, Poroth eyed him hesitantly. "So," he said at last, "do you think you want to rent the place?"

"Yes, I do," said Freirs, though he hadn't really made his mind up till that moment. "It seems to be just what I'm looking for."

Poroth nodded. "Good." He sounded, Freirs thought, as if he meant it, but he wasn't smiling, and there was uncertainty in his face. Freirs felt faintly disappointed. "And when do you think you'd want to come?"

"Probably right after my last class ends. There's a Friday evening course I'm teaching that doesn't get out till the twenty-fourth of June. I figured I'd come out here that weekend."

"All right. We'll try to be ready for you." Instead of turning back toward the house, he was moving in the direction of the fields and obviously expected Freirs to follow. "By the time you come out, I should have this land cleared off all the way back to the brook." He gestured toward the line of distant trees. "And it'll be under cultivation."

To the west a row of stumps showed where Poroth was engaged in cutting back a column of encroaching pine. Immediately ahead the land was bare, but marked by scattered mounds of ashes where great piles of underbrush and weeds had been burned. It looked like the aftermath of a battle.

"Of course, this place needs plenty of work," said Poroth, gazing around with apparent satisfaction. "That's what happens when land lies idle for so long. Deborah and I are already behind in our labors. Most of the Brethren finished planting weeks ago, beneath the last full moon."

"That sounds quite picturesque ,What do you people grow?"

"Corn. That's what this land is made for. 'Therefore God give thee of the dew of heaven, and the fatness of the earth, and plenty of corn and wine.' Of course, the Indian corn I'll be planting isn't what old Isaac had in mind."

"Ah. Hmm." What the hell was the guy talking about? "Are you people allowed to drink wine?"

"In moderation." He turned. "And you?"

Freirs patted his stomach. "Like I said before, my vice is food."

Poroth smiled, but only for a moment; then his face resumed its old preoccupied look, and he continued walking.

Before them rose the huge, sagging shape of the barn and, beside it, a gnarled old black willow with scales like a dinosaur, practically touching the overhanging roof, as if tree and barn had grown up together. Beyond it the still-uncleared land lay covered with the same ropy-looking weeds and homely little saplings that Freirs had seen in New York vacant lots.

The barn was where Poroth kept his truck at night. Flies buzzed over the ancient hay still scattered on the floor, though it had obviously been many years since livestock had sheltered here. Leaning against the wall lay a rusty collection of farm implements and, in the shadows at the back, an antiquated mowing machine that Poroth said he planned to repair. They all looked to Freirs like museum pieces; it was hard to picture anyone actually using them.

Along the left side of the barn, on a loft platform as high as Freirs' head and reachable by means of a trapdoor and a simple wooden ladder, Poroth had constructed a chicken coop. At the moment it housed only four fat hens, all recent purchases, and a pugnacious-looking black rooster who glared at Freirs accusingly, as if aware that under normal circumstances it would have been inhabiting Freirs' quarters.

"They're from Werner Klapp's farm right here in Gilead," Poroth explained. He shooed away a cat that was pawing the ladder. "They're not laying regularly yet, but by summer we should be getting all the eggs we need."

By summer. By summer. This was the Poroths' refrain. It was rather inspiring, how optimistic they were, as if the two of them, those earnest children, could make this place a paradise all by themselves. Freirs almost believed it might be possible. He knew *he* couldn't do it, couldn't repair houses, move masses of earth, apply the magic that would make the land yield its secret stored-up fruit. But these were rural people, country-born despite their lack of experience. Who could say what they'd be capable of?

Near the barn stood a small grey-shingled smokehouse covered with brambles and vines, its door hanging partially open. "I wouldn't go poking around there," said Poroth, giving it a wide berth.

"Why?"

"Wasps." He nodded toward a few black insects hovering like guards above the doorway. "They've got a nest in there, just below the roof. I mean to clean them out as soon as I get the chance."

Freirs peered inside as they passed. The ceiling, like that of the porch at the Co-operative, was arrayed with wicked-looking iron hook where probably, years before, hams and bacon had hung.

Down the slope from it lay the shallow brook he'd seen from the ba porch. Flowing past rocks and fallen trees, it curved out from

woods and ran a meandering course past the acres of stubble that
might some day be a cornfield, until it lost itself again in the swampier
woods to the west. Legally the Poroths' property extended far beyond
its banks, but all the area on the other side was forest now—a dense
wilderness of pine, oak, and maple that, in this century, at least, had
never known a woodsman's axe—so that the brook effectively marked
the southwest border of the land.

It also marked the limits of the afternoon's tour. Poroth, taking a
position at the water's edge, stood with arms folded, surveying the
brook's winding path as if he contemplated rerouting it. "We've got
minnows here, frogs, a few turtles," he said. "Still, it's no trout
stream."

"In that case I won't bring my fishing pole." Freirs stared idly into
the brook's clear depths. He was eager to get back to the farmhouse,
and maybe spend some more time with Deborah before returning to the
city. He glanced at his watch: nearly a quarter to five. They would
have to be starting back soon. Already the sun was sinking toward the
western pines. He thought of the work he'd meant to do by Monday
that would be waiting for him in the heat of his apartment.

Poroth had seen him check the time. "Well, there's really nothing
more to show you," he said morosely. "We may as well be—ah, *here* you
are!" He was looking down at a large grey cat by his feet. "This is
Bwada." He bent down and began scratching her head, an attention
the animal seemed merely to tolerate, for though her eyes closed momentarily as if in pleasure, she soon moved out of reach.

Freirs watched her uncertainly. She was fat and sleek, with fine
grey fur halfway between charcoal and silver. Placid-looking enough,
but you never knew about these animals. Hesitantly he reached out to
stroke her, but she backed away—mostly, it seemed, out of fear, though
as his hand drew closer she made a menacing sound deep in her throat.
He decided it was best to keep his distance.

"She's the oldest of the cats," said Poroth, "and it takes her a while
to get used to people. She's not even sure of Deborah yet." With a sigh
he squinted at the sun. "Well, we should probably be heading back. I
want to get you into town in plenty of time."

Freirs followed him up the grassy slope through the lengthening
shadows. Looking back, he saw Bwada crouched on the bank, eyes wide
as she followed the bobbing flight of a dragonfly above the stream.
Inching forward, she thrust out her paw and dabbed tentatively at the
moving water, as if testing whether the surface were strong enough to
walk on, then settled back again to watch and wait.

"She's found a way to cross the brook by some fallen logs over in the
woods," said Poroth, who had turned to see why Freirs had stopped.
"She's afraid to try and cross anywhere else. She really hates the
water."

His stride had an athlete's spring to it as he continued toward the farmhouse, rising up onto the toes of his boots with every step, arms swinging easily at his sides, as if drawing upon some private source of power. Strong ankles, too, no doubt. Freirs himself was beginning to feel bushed. It couldn't be just the walk, he told himself; he walked farther every day in the city. The antihistamine, maybe, or something to do with the country air. The air *seemed* healthy here, but maybe it was only an illusion. Though you had to admit those pines smelled sweet and good, down by the brook, nothing like the disinfectant pine smell he was used to, in aerosol and after-shave. You only smelled the real stuff in the winter, walking past a sidewalk stand of Christmas trees.

As they rounded the barn, they saw that a second pickup truck was parked in front of the house. Freirs felt a sudden rush of disappointment. "That's Brother Matt Geisel," he heard Poroth saying. "He and Sister Corah are our closest neighbors. They live up the road, just past the turn."

The man was in the kitchen with Deborah when they came inside, leaning stiffly against the counter as if his limbs were too long to fold into a chair. "Hello there!" he said in a gravelly voice, beaming from Poroth to Freirs. "We still had a few winter parsnips left over, and I thought you folks might find a use for 'em." He looked about sixty or seventy, his face lined and deeply tanned, like patches of leather stitched together.

"Matthew's brought us enough for a full-size family," said Deborah, nodding toward a pile of greens and pale carrotlike vegetables on the counter by the sink. She made a mock frown. "I wanted to give him some of these cookies, but he says he's getting too fat."

Geisel grinned broadly, displaying a mouthful of small stained teeth. "It ain't just me that says it. Corah, she says it too!" He blinked. "Anyways, we got ourselves a cellar full of parsnips from the winter, and with the weather like it is, pretty soon they won't be good for much. No sense wasting 'em."

"Brother Matthew," said Poroth, "I want you to meet Jeremy Freirs."

Solemnly the old man took Freirs' proffered hand. His grip was as steely as Freirs had expected. "You the fellow from New York City?" he asked, cocking his head and glaring at him with—Freirs had caught on now—the humorous gruffness that old codgers like this sometimes assumed.

Freirs nodded, playing the game. "Four fifty-two Bank Street, right in the heart of Greenwich Village."

"Jeremy's going to be renting our guest house this summer," added Poroth.

Deborah's face brightened. Casting a quick inquiring glance at husband, who nodded to confirm the news, she turned to Freirs grinned. "Good, Jeremy! I'm so glad." Freirs felt his skin grow warm; in less formal company, he'd almost have expected her to hug him.

But already her expression had changed. "Uh-oh, don't we have to get you back to town?"

"I'm just about to take him in," said Poroth.

Geisel ambled forward. "Well, I'm heading up to the Co-operative myself," he announced. "I'll be glad to give your young friend a ride."

"Thanks," said Freirs, and, seeing that Poroth appeared pleased, he added, "Yes, I'd appreciate that." He glanced at his watch. Nearly five o'clock. "But I think we're going to have to leave right now."

As they filed out to the porch and down to where the trucks were parked, he surreptitiously touched his wallet, wondering, suddenly, if the Poroths were going to hit him for a deposit.

"So it's all straight now, right?" he said, standing beside the trucks. "I'm aiming for the weekend I told you, the twenty-fourth of June. Of course, I'll get in touch before that. And you'll be able to pick me up again at the bus stop?"

"I'll be there," said Poroth. "Just let me know the time."

Geisel's old black Ford pickup looked even more beat up than the Poroths'. Geisel slapped its rusted fender. "A beauty, ain't she?" he said, grinning. He opened the door on the driver's side and climbed gingerly into the front seat. "I'll just slide my bones behind the wheel here . . ." Freirs climbed in beside him and waited as Geisel fiddled with the ignition and the choke, the other's solemnity genuine now, an old man operating something he still didn't quite believe in. The motor rattled, turned over, and caught. Freirs waved goodbye to the Poroths, returning Deborah's smile; they made a traditional-looking tableau as they stood waving back, the old grey house rising cozily behind them.

As the truck began to pull out, easing onto the bumpy surface of the road, Freirs looked back. Sarr was turning toward the fields, already preoccupied with some new task, while Deborah, still waving, had retreated to the porch steps, the late-afternoon sun shining almost directly behind her, outlining her full figure as she stood there, hips cocked, one leg on the higher step. As Freirs gave a last farewell wave, he couldn't help but notice that she didn't seem to be wearing anything beneath the long black dress.

Crack!

The axe blade bit deep into the wood, scattering chips of bark. The pine stood trembling; branches shook. The tree was part of God; he felt it testing him. But other matters occupied him now. He swung the axe back for another blow.

Crack!

He was thinking about the summer ahead—and about the visitor they'd had today, who'd be coming among them this summer with his books and clothes and city ways. He wondered if he and Deborah had done right.

Crack! Leaving the axe buried in the tree, he paused to smooth his hair back and wipe away the sweat. Pensively he ran a thumb along his fringe of beard. He felt perplexed. Lord knew they needed the money the visitor would provide, there was no gainsaying it; though it was hateful to ask payment for the things a proper Christian should have offered guests for free, he and Deborah were deeply in debt to the Co-operative, an institution his own father had once run (this is what stung the worst), and he wouldn't be able to hold up his head among the Brethren till all of it was paid. Oh, the money would certainly be useful. And yet . . .

He yanked the axe from the tree, hefted it in his hand, and swung it back.

Crack!

And yet somehow he had bad feelings about the arrangement. He'd had them from the start. He had been ready—eager, even—to return to the fold from which his family had strayed and to identify himself henceforth as a farmer, a tiller of the earth, a toiler in the vineyards of the Lord. It was the one truly worthy occupation he knew of, in God's eyes and his own, offering a life of piety and independence, a life close to nature. The souvenir plaque above his mantelpiece expressed it all: *A Plow on a Field Arable Is the Most Honorable of Ancient Arms.* And now—*crack!*—he was being asked to alter that dream. Though he only half acknowledged it to himself, at the back of his mind was the thought—unworthy, selfish, even snobbish—that he didn't want to play hotelkeeper. It wasn't right; it was degrading. It made him and Deborah little better than servants, peasants in the hire of a godless master . . .

Crack!

He was beginning to think he should never have let Deborah talk him into it. Taking in a lodger had been her idea; she was already pressing him to make room for another. It was she who'd persuaded him to convert the old chicken coop into a guest house; it was she who'd convinced him to bring in electricity ("You show visitors a kerosene lamp out there," she'd said, "and they'll turn right around and go home"); it was she who'd written the advertisement and gotten him to leave it on the bulletin board over in Flemington, despite the disapproval of the Brethren, who saw all forms of advertising as devil's work.

And now—*crack!*—was come the fruit of her endeavors. A stranger was due to enter their midst, an outsider, someone ignorant of their beliefs who could have but little sympathy for their chosen way of life. True, the man had seemed polite enough, but his godlessness was obvious in his every word, and he'd brought with him a reek of corruption from the city he was so determined to flee. He had already asked too many questions; he had already made too many jests. Of course, he'd sounded educated, in what passed for education among the worldly— was even a teacher, he had claimed—and doubtless it would be good for Deborah to have someone else to talk to. But—*crack!*—who could say where that might lead? Deborah was a fine God-fearing woman, but sometimes the woman in her nature seemed stronger than the fear of God. She was modest one moment, hot-blooded the next; there was no telling what she might do. What was it the prophet had warned? *The heart is deceitful above all things . . .*

Crack!

Deborah was inclined to wander from the path, that much he knew, and this smooth-talking teacher might prove a most dangerous influence. Claimed he'd spend the summer among his books . . . The thought made Poroth downright uneasy. Oh, he'd studied books himself once, far more than the Brethren would have wished, and he still owned a few. He had felt the magic in them, the lure of worldly knowledge, new notions, sweet-sounding words. But with the Lord's help he had put such things behind him; the Good Book was enough for any man. The rest were just invitations to idleness—and idleness was a sin that led to others.

Yes, the stranger would have to be watched; there was no telling what mischief he might get into. He had all but admitted, back in the truck, that he made it a practice to yield to whatever temptations lay before him. As if his stomach hadn't already revealed as much! And the way he'd looked at Deborah . . .

Crack!

With a groan the tree splintered and came crashing to the earth.

The old truck bounced noisily toward town, Geisel navigating her like a ship in a storm. He drove slowly, with his head thrust well forward, stretching his long, lined neck as he squinted at the road.

"Well, Mr. Freirs," he said at last, turning to face him, "what do you think of our little town?"

Freirs' mind had been on Deborah. Had it been his imagination, or
had she really been naked beneath that dress? And what if she'd known
he could see? With a sigh he turned to Geisel. Freirs had been deliberately avoiding conversation with him lest the old man turn the truck
over in a ditch while doing exactly what he was doing now, looking
away from the road. Just his luck to die here in the wilderness with
some old farmer he didn't even know.

"It *is* a little town," he said finally, keeping his own eyes straight
ahead. Maybe Geisel would take the hint. "I was surprised, in fact, how
tiny it really is. There's nothing in it but one big general store."

Geisel seemed to see that as a compliment. "Yes, sir, all a man needs
is right to hand. Mind you, there's also the Bible school across the
street, where they keep the town records. And don't be forgetting the
cemetery."

"I saw it," said Freirs. "Some nice old tombstones there."

The old man smiled. "Been lookin' at our ancestors, have you?"

"A few, anyway. It's interesting to see the local names."

The other gave a genial nod. "Yep, that's where they all end up
around here. You stay long enough, you'll end up there, too."

Freirs laughed uneasily. "Not *that* long, I hope! I'll only be here for
the summer."

"I know," said Geisel. "Young Brother Sarr's gone and fixed the
place up real nice. You should have yourself a mighty comfortable time. I saw how he and Sister Deborah even went and put in
electricity."

"I guess that's pretty unusual around here, isn't it?"

The old man scratched his head. "Well, none of *us* have it. Fact is,
some of the others here in town, some of the *old*-timers"—he said this
with a hint of smile—"they've had their differences with the Poroths
and their ways. They say the pair of them are too lax on some points."

Deborah without her panties, strawberry douche in the medicine
chest. Maybe the Brethren, too, had their generation gap. "And do you
agree?"

"No, sir, not me. Brother Sarr and Sister Deborah are neighbors of
ours, and we stick by 'em. They're good God-fearing folks, you'll find
out quick enough. See, that's the strength of our order. It don't look
that way to outsiders, maybe, but we like to think we've got room for
differences of opinion. The Lord wants for us to live His way, right
enough, but He knows we're all just children, and—well, He's always
been good to us."

He lapsed into silence. They were nearing the stream now, the dirt
road well behind them. Freirs was pleased to see that he already had a
sense of the distances involved, if not of the actual twisting route
they'd been following. The hedgerow-bordered lanes and snug farm-
houses seemed almost familiar, viewed in reverse from his trip out, and

the countryside somehow smaller, like a room remembered from childhood that one visits after the passage of years.

The road was winding gradually downhill. They rounded a wall of boxwood and abruptly Freirs saw, on the slope to the left, the small stone cottage where Poroth's mother lived.

"Now there," he said, "is one beautiful little place." He peered at the windows as the truck moved past but saw no face this time. "They don't build 'em like that nowadays."

"That house is"—Geisel did some figuring—"more than a hundred and sixty years old. It's always belonged to the Troets."

"I thought Mrs. Poroth lived there now."

"Yes, but she's one of them."

"Oh, that's right. Sarr mentioned it."

"Those Troets." Geisel shook his head. "They never were much for breeding, and most of the line's kind of died out over the years."

Gnarled hands gripping the wheel, he brought the truck around the base of the hill and onto the narrow stone bridge, which he took far more slowly than Poroth had. Freirs waited till they were across before he spoke again.

"I saw their monument back in the cemetery, a big granite thing. Sarr said they died in some kind of fire."

"Yes, sir. Back in the 1870s, it was. Even before *my* time." He didn't smile. "Wiped out one whole branch of the family."

Freirs tried, in vain, to imagine how all those people could have perished in a single fire. It must have been at night . . . But could anyone sleep that soundly? Mother, father, kids? Blackened bodies in the ashes. "It's strange," he said, "in that list of names, I remember one of them didn't have a date of death."

The old man rubbed his chin. "Well, you see, young Absolom Troet, he didn't die in the fire. Fact is, some folks say 'twas him that *set* it."

"What? You mean he killed his own family?"

Geisel shrugged. "Well, that Absolom, he was a queer one, so folks used to say. 'Twas quite a ways before my time, of course, and I ain't so sure of the details. But my old grandma, God rest her, she remembered him. Grew up with him, in fact. She said he was as sweet as can be, to look at him, with a face just like a baby. A likely little feller too, God-fearing as the next . . . And then one day, just about Christmastime, it was, seems he goes off somewhere, and when he comes back home he ain't quite right in the head. He was always up to some sort of mischief after that. Regular little devil!"

The wind is blowing steadily now, with the first hint of a chill. The sun is just a dirt-brown smear above the Jersey shore. Top halves of the taller buildings remain illuminated, glowing like pillars of fire. The lower parts are plunged in shadow.

The old man is tired, but at last his walk is ended. He has come to an area of tenements, ancient warehouses, and shops with foreign names. In the distance the oily river churns. He has reached his goal.

The cathedral looms above him, grey with soot. Around the great bronze doors at the top of the steps, saints and demons stand awaiting his arrival. On each of the twin towers a cross catches the waning sunlight.

White birds, the Gheelo, shriek high overhead. Their shadows vanish as the light fades, and the crosses retreat into gloom. The sky is dark as ashes.

Below his feet the pavement vibrates to the thunder of a subway. The stones of the cathedral tremble. Tucking the umbrella beneath his arm and whispering the Third Name, he starts up the steps.

Ahead of him, by the great doors, the blind eyes of the saints seem to widen in sudden understanding. The demons grin more boldly from their concrete resting place. A gargoyle laughs aloud.

Beyond the doors lies the hall of worship; beyond that, the convent. Here he will begin his search.

It will not be easy, he knows. He will have to be subtle about it. And persuasive. The sisters will be suspicious of a stranger's interest, and reluctant to confide in him.

He will have to win them over first. It is going to take time.

After all, he can't just walk into a convent and say, "I need a virgin."

JUNE TWENTY-FOURTH

C arol was staring out the window of the children's section when the little old man walked in. She looked up with surprise. Most adults remained downstairs, in the library's general reading room, and seldom ventured onto the second floor without a boy or girl in tow. Those who did were usually young mothers with a child home sick, or else had wandered up here by mistake.

But this man was far from young—he looked sixty at least, perhaps a decade more—and he appeared anything but confused. He made directly for where she was standing, a battered leather briefcase tucked beneath his arm and, peeping from it, the tip of a stubby little umbrella, even though there hadn't been a hint of rain all day. In his baggy blue suit, wisps of fine white hair catching the sunlight, he cut a rather comical figure.

Carol readjusted the shade and turned to meet him. She decided that he must be somebody's doting grandfather; from the way he gazed at the little girl who ran mischievously across his path, it was obvious he adored children.

Approaching the window, he brought his face close to hers as if about to offer a secret. Suddenly he smiled, an impish little smile that made his eyes twinkle.

"I think," he said, "you're just the person I've been looking for."

It was Friday, the ending of an uneventful week and the prelude to another empty weekend. She had spent the morning in bed, too tired to get up, lying naked on the sheets and staring lazily out her window. Beyond the padlocked grate that stretched across it, beyond the iron railing of the fire escape, she could see the dark bricks of the building next door, the topmost branches of a tree, a narrow ribbon of sky.

Lying there in silence in the gathering heat, she'd been daydreaming of a ballet she had seen the night before, the whole cast dressed in bright red leotards against a field of snow. How beautiful it had been!—and how unearthly! They had looked like whirling roses . . . She had started a letter about it to one of her older sisters, married and living in Seattle, but had put it aside before finishing the page; somehow, as if disturbing the waters at the bottom of a pond, the very act of writing had stirred memories of a different sort—not of the ballet, but of a dream it had inspired that same night. Not a good dream, either. Something about roses, something better left forgotten . . . And forgotten it had been; but all morning long a certain apprehension had remained, a flicker of unease, dancing in the shadows just beyond her reach.

With an effort she had roused herself at last, shaken off the dream, turned her thoughts to job and clothes and food. Her roommate had gone out after having eaten the one remaining orange and the last of the cottage cheese. The refrigerator was practically bare save for half a dozen eggs, and she'd recently begun to wonder if it wasn't wrong to eat even these; she had renounced meat while back at St. Mary's. Better not yield to the temptation; God, she knew, would reward her for her strength. She settled for a cup of instant coffee and a thick slice of Italian bread toasted on a fork over the top burner of the stove. Rochelle, she gathered from the emptiness of the refrigerator, was on one of her periodic diets; lately she had taken to calling Carol "anorexic" with undisguised envy. The girl could be impulsively generous and good-hearted, but Carol had begun to see signs of a selfishness beneath, perhaps even a growing resentment. They had been rooming together for less than a month. Carol suspected, occasionally, that it might have been a mistake to move in with her, and wondered what changes in their relationship the future would bring.

She herself had always been thin; her goal was to keep her weight just below one hundred, and the last time she'd checked it—old Mrs. Slavinsky, whose apartment she had shared until last month, had owned a scale—she'd been pleased to see that she'd succeeded: ninety-seven pounds. Food was, like so many other things in life, a test of will, something to steel herself against.

As she showered, she ran her fingers through her hair, trimmed almost as short as a boy's now, and felt a wave of relief. Until last week, reluctant to waste a quarter of her paycheck at one of the city's overpriced styling shops where rock music blared and dead-eyed young men and women chattered to one another over the inert heads of their customers, Carol had left her hair long, wearing it pinned up in a style she liked to think of as old-fashioned but which she'd realized, in the end, was just plain ugly. Her roommate had offered to cut it, more in the spirit of adventure, Carol suspected, than of friendship, but the thought of the slovenly Rochelle wielding a scissors over her was enough to discourage such experiments. Finally, one day last week, after returning stiff and sweaty from her dance class, she had gone and cut it herself. This, too, had been an act of will; her hair was, after all, her best feature. She knew that in other respects she was no beauty; she looked as if she might—and did, in fact—have an extremely pretty sister. Yet heads would turn to watch her, even in a crowd, for her hair was thick, silky, and strikingly red: as red, so her father had once told her, as sunset through a stained-glass window.

She missed her father. *Poor old man!* she sometimes thought, at odd moments in the day. Old he had been, as long as she'd known him, gaunt and white-haired, the pale skin hanging wearily from his bones. Old to have fathered five children: nearly two decades his wife's senior, and she herself had married in her thirties. That infant after infant had sprung from their loins seemed at once miraculous and obscene. Somehow together they had found the energy to create four daughters, Carol the third of them, until on the fifth try they'd produced a son. Here they'd stopped, presumably contented, but by then Carol's mother was herself a worn-out, shapeless woman with shadows beneath her eyes and hair that Carol had watched go grey; and her father, with the first demoralizing taste of surgery behind him and a series of operations on the way, was suddenly preoccupied with his own mortality. Until ill health had forced his retirement he had made an unsuccessful living selling advertising space on billboards; his only legacy, Carol sometimes thought in anger and humiliation, was an endless parade of ugly highway signs. He had died last December, shortly before Christmas, his energy exhausted. She remembered him in his final days, sitting transfixed before the television and, later still, lying spent in the hospital ward, waiting for death with what first had seemed stoicism but had proved in the end to be mere resignation, something close, even, to boredom, no strength left to be frightened, no strength to contemplate eternal life ahead.

Carol understood something of how he felt; she had seen it before. She had lived all but two of her twenty-two years in a drab little mill town up the Ohio River from Pittsburgh, and she knew what it was to be bored. She remembered her brother shooting endless solitary baskets at the hoop in their yard; and a neighbor's boy who spent each evening driving aimlessly up and down the highway; and her grandmother on her mother's side, solemn and alone in her room at the end of the hall, who'd told her why she always slept past ten: "Because if I get up any earlier it makes the day too long."

There'd been times, in her girlhood, when Carol had felt the same. But not often. Life had been too full of possibilities. She had been a princess from the fairy tales, blessed by an auspicious moon and accustomed to getting what she wanted. Inevitably a prince would come to marry her, and together they would accomplish great things. It was only a matter of time.

To this day she couldn't have said just how poor her family had been, but her years of girlhood in a tottering old two-family house near the railroad tracks had been comfortable ones, and she could recall

nothing she'd really longed for which, while her father was alive, she
hadn't received, save, perhaps, a milk-white stallion, a dragon's egg,
and, at one brief stage, the habit of a nun.

Like her two older sisters, she had attended St. Mary's, a large, well-
to-do parochial school for girls in nearby Ambridge, though by Carol's
turn the family had found it necessary to accept, not without shame,
some aid with the tuition. The two youngest children ended up in public school; once again Carol counted herself lucky—or even, perhaps,
blessed.

She'd survived the years at St. Mary's with her confidence intact,
though by then she'd come to think of it as "faith." God, or someone,
would look after her; God, or someone, always had. Not once had she
stopped to question what the future really held in store; she'd been far
too busy flirting with more agreeable ideas—ballet lessons, a film
career, a modern-day *Saint Joan*—and even, on occasion, with the
school's youthful priest (who'd been surprised to find himself mistaken
for a prince). She'd met few boys her own age except at functions with
other schools or at home in her neighborhood, and the ones she'd met
had seemed, without exception, ignorant and immature, their conversation limited to the local basketball standings and the cars they'd
someday own. Besides, she hadn't had the sort of figure that attracted
many of them; she'd reminded herself that the sophisticated beauties of
the future, the girls who turned out to be the professional models and
actresses, were frequently dismissed in their school days as awkward
and skinny. Most of her crushes had been confined to older girls in the
school, though she'd looked with interest at the boys her two older sisters brought home. The younger and more sexually active sister had
brought home a lot. One of them, a slim, quiet boy with long eyelashes
and poetic-looking long brown hair, had become, at a Halloween party
more than a year later, the first person other than a doctor that Carol
had allowed to touch her breasts. She had liked it so much she'd grown
flushed and almost dizzy, but she'd been slow to repeat the experience,
and hadn't allowed any touching below the waist; it wasn't hard to get
a reputation in a small Catholic town in Pennsylvania, even in the
1970s. She had heard the way people talked about her sister, who, parochial school notwithstanding, had lost her virginity by sixteen and had
been known to go driving with men in their thirties. Carol was
ashamed of this sister; it pleased her to be seen as the virtuous one.

She had never quite relinquished the desire to dance, to act, to be a
star, but in later years, as she dreamed her way through another St.
Mary's—college, this time—on a more-than-modest scholarship con-
veniently provided by the church, her world had grown more private
and less physical. Her hours now were occupied by Thomas à Kempis
and Tolkien, her mind by pastel visions: the Star of Bethlehem, Gan-
dalf's resurrection, Jesus preaching to the hobbits. She'd known little

of the doctors' bills and mounting debts at home, though that was where she still lived. Even when her father had been forced to quit his job, she'd been all but unaware of a change in their circumstances. Surely his condition would improve; perhaps it was a kind of test, such as so many of the faithful had endured. Having just completed a sophomore course in the Mystics, she wondered if she might not be one of them herself. She saw evidence of the Divine hand wherever she looked; all around her lay the City of God, with shining towers brighter than the sun. At times she half fancied she could see the angels who populated it, insubstantial creatures shimmering like snow. She sensed that she'd been chosen, though could not have said for what. But she knew if she was patient, God would tell her.

He had been curiously slow to speak. College had ended, the future was upon her, and nothing had changed. Her prince had not yet arrived; things, in fact, were growing worse. Her father was dying; her mother was being supported by relatives. The two older sisters had married—having a reputation hadn't mattered after all—and there was talk of selling the house. Carol realized that she'd been a fool; she had contributed nothing, she had cost her family much. How selfish she had been, and how blind!

One thing was certain: there was no place for her here. But perhaps there still was something she could do . . . Shaken, but with expectations undimmed, the fairy-tale princess had set off for New York.

The change, though, had not been a drastic one. For Carol it had simply meant replacing one saint for another, another set of walls, another world of earnest ceremonies and cheerful, well-scrubbed females. St. Mary's, St. Mary's, St. Agnes's: a school, a college, a convent.

The move, it's true, had not been undertaken lightly; she'd known no one in the city but a few contacts her school had provided—sisters and clerks and administrators, a list of Catholic names without faces to go with them—and New York had seemed, in her imagination, a terrifying place. But then, as it had turned out, St. Agnes's wasn't really part of New York, and there'd been little need to venture beyond its gates; she'd slipped quickly into the security of its daily routine as if she'd known it all her life.

And now even that was behind her. She was on her own at last, twenty-two years old and still lucky, happily ensconced in a new job without even having had to search for it. Clearly she was still among the blessed.

Yet in one respect she was worse off than ever, for she was almost totally without money; her pay, after taxes, was just $109.14 a week. And while a lifetime of poverty no doubt qualified one to walk the streets of heaven, it was depressing to think how many places in this earthly city were all but barred to her: the theaters, the clubs, the restaurants with their twenty-dollar meals, the dress shops where even a scarf or a belt was beyond her means. She was sick of avoiding such places, sick of abstaining from taxicabs, first-run movies, and hardcover books. Just once she'd have liked to be able to afford a good seat at the ballet; sitting in the back row no longer made her feel virtuous. Life was short, and she was getting too old for games like that.

Her job was less than a fifteen-minute walk, but the thought of those blazing sidewalks sapped her energy. Still, she was grateful for the work and knew how lucky she was to have gotten it, lucky that Sister Cecilia, God bless her, had phoned her when she did. Especially considering that she'd been out of St. Agnes's so long . . .

Work was, for her, the position of "junior assistant (part-time), circulation division," at the Voorhis Foundation Library on West Twenty-Third Street. She had been employed here since the middle of May and arrived every day at noon. Voorhis was one of the shabbier of the city's many private libraries and, like most of them, predated the free public system that Carnegie had built. Though it had fallen on hard times, it still maintained an extensive collection of nineteenth-century British and European literature, as well as ample general holdings and a children's section upstairs. Dues were sixty dollars a year, but there were special rates for students, golden-agers, and others, so that few members paid the full amount.

The library itself occupied a staid old building on the south side of the street, less than a block from the old Chelsea Hotel, with slate-grey walls and a line of high vaulted windows along the lower story. White paint peeled in jagged strips from the ceiling; two square pillars, tall and thick as trees, cast oppressive shadows across the floor.

She spent the first part of the afternoon maneuvering an overladen book cart through the maze of cabinets, tables, and display racks that filled the ground floor. The work was slow, undemanding, and dull, and she could be alone with her thoughts. No one so much as glanced her way. By midafternoon, as usual, many of the available seats were taken by scholars of various sorts who frequented the special collections: serious, bespectacled young men with dirty hair and ill-fitting suits, young defeated-looking women as faded as the building's plaster walls—aging grad students, most of them, down from Columbia or Fordham or City College or up from NYU. Their briefcases had to be searched carefully when they left; in the past, there'd been a lot of thefts. The remaining seats were occupied by elderly residents of the neighborhood: widowers, retired union men, social security pensioners—people with little money and lots of time.

There were always a few of them, she'd heard, waiting outside the doors each morning for the library to open, pacing impatiently up and down the sidewalk or slouched coughing in the entranceway. Once inside they'd take a newspaper from the rack, or a thumb-smeared magazine in its clear plastic binder, and for the rest of the day they'd hunched over it with what seemed intense concentration, moving only to turn each page. Others would select some book at random from the nearest shelves; laying it open before them on the table, they would fall asleep, head on their arms, until closing time. The same ancient faces reappeared day after day, except in the poorest weather; they came and left without speaking a word to anyone, not even a good morning or good night.

Carol didn't mind these solitary souls; in fact, she rather liked them. People that age were comfortable to be around. Here within the walls of Voorhis, amid the dusty sunlight and drowsing old men, the city seemed far away. The place, in its very routine, seemed a kind of fortress.

She took particular comfort in certain familiar sights and sounds that marked her day: the buzz of the fluorescent lights, the pale figures sprawled silent and motionless over their reading, the reassuring feel of her book cart as she wheeled it down the aisle, and the books themselves, symbols of order on their backs—young adulthood reduced to "YA," mystery reduced to a tiny red skull.

When she forgot the miserable pay and put all dreams of the future from her mind, Voorhis filled her with something close to nostalgia—as if, despite the years, she had never really left school. The high ceiling and the faded green walls, the solidity of the dark brown wooden shelves, the potted plants gathering dust on the window ledge, the shades above them glowing yellow in the sun and billowing like ships' sails at the smallest breeze—all were touched with a kind of holiness. Nothing, they promised, had changed. All her life she had been hypnotized by the same great metal clock that ticked off the minutes at the front of the room. When she crowded into the little glassed-in office and pulled up a chair before her battered wooden desk, running her fingers along the pencil grooves, the places where the varnish was worn away, the ragged green blotter marked with ring stains from the coffee mug, she felt a sense of permanence that revived the years of her childhood. Only the nuns were missing, and the crucifix on the wall.

Occasionally it occurred to her that, far from being out on her own, she had merely traded the school and the convent for another set of walls. So much for the expectations she'd had on leaving St. Agnes's . . .

She had spent more than six months there, but in January she had moved out, convinced that her vocation, her destiny, lay elsewhere; she still believed—though some might have mocked such pretensions— that she *had* a destiny. Someday she would look back on her life and see the reason for it all, shining through it like a golden thread that would draw her, in the end, headlong toward some brave and wonderful purpose.

Her first steps in this direction, though, had been hesitant ones and had ended in a rent-controlled two-bedroom apartment on West End Avenue and Ninety-third Street, where, fresh from St. Agnes's, she'd found work, of a sort, as live-in housekeeper and attendant to a tiny eighty-two-year-old Polish woman named Mrs. Slavinsky. Carol's expenses, along with $120 a week, had been provided by the woman's divorced daughter, who lived on the East Side and appeared delighted to have found, in this day and age, a well-bred young white girl to look after her mother. The arrangement had been, at the time, equally convenient for Carol, since it had spared her the necessity of finding a place of her own. Less agreeable was the fact that, though the job had been advertised as that of "companion," the old woman was in no shape to appreciate companionship, having but slight command of English. Worse, her hearing was failing, and seemingly with it, her mind.

Thus had begun four months of preparing kosher food and washing two sets of dishes (an observance Carol still found exotic), of vacuuming the worn Persian carpets and dusting the soot from the venetian blinds, of walking the old woman to the supermarket or the park or the toilet and remaining nearby while, through the winter and spring afternoons, she mumbled to herself or snored or squinted vaguely at the TV. The days had been monotonous. At least, Carol reflected, she'd had a bedroom and a TV of her own, luxuries she hadn't had at the convent; and two nights a week she had thrown herself into her modern dance class at a school twelve blocks south on Broadway, returning stiff and elated to the brightly lit apartment, usually to find Mrs. Slavinsky and her daughter, who came to sit with her those nights, engaged in some fierce and incomprehensible argument in Yiddish. The daughter also visited on weekends, allowing Carol to take the days off; but with few acquaintances outside her dance class and no other place to call home, Carol often found herself remaining near the apartment. She searched the want ads for interesting prospects, wondering where her talents lay, and resolved, come summer, to look into a course or two in dance therapy.

The second week of May, however, she had received an unexpected phone call. It was Sister Cecilia, one of the administrators from St. Agnes's; she had just heard about a job opening, assistant librarian at someplace downtown called the Voorhis Foundation, and, remembering how Carol had shown such a fondness for literature, always burying her head in a book, she had wondered if Carol might be tempted to apply . . .

Carol had been grateful, though somewhat puzzled; the sister had never shown this sort of interest in her back at St. Agnes's. The next day, leaving the house shortly after noon as if to go shopping—it was understood that, from time to time, the old woman might be left alone for an hour or two—Carol had taken the subway down to Voorhis.

The balding little desk clerk had raised his eyebrows with surprise. Why, yes, there *was* a job open in the circulation department, though it was rather strange to find someone already here inquiring about it, seeing as the officers of the library hadn't even agreed yet upon the wording of the ad they'd be sending to the *Times*.

"I heard about it from a friend," said Carol.

"Hmmm." The clerk had pursed his lips and eyed her skeptically. At last he'd given a little shrug and admitted that, since Carol had taken the trouble to come all the way down here, perhaps there were some people she might talk to. It was, he added, absolutely *perfect* timing on Carol's part; the boy who'd held the job till recently had simply not shown up one day last week, and even seemed to have disappeared from his apartment. All very mysterious. "And a shame," the clerk said wistfully. "He was a very sweet boy." He sighed; probably now he had no one to look nice for. "But Mrs. Tait seems to prefer a girl this time . . ." With a pout he had sent Carol upstairs.

Mrs. Tait was the circulation manager, and only one of the people who interviewed Carol that day; junior assistants were expected to fill in for any number of departments. Carol also talked to Mrs. Schumann, the children's librarian, Mr. Brown in acquisitions, and a sleepy-looking man in charge of maintenance. None of them seemed particularly curious about her background, or in making more than a few polite inquiries into her skills, and as the afternoon wore on it occurred to Carol that the job was hers if she wanted it; it was so lowly— only thirty hours a week, for the present, and paying even less than she made now—that the staff was obviously not inclined to waste time evaluating applicants. Besides, if they hired Carol, they wouldn't have to pay for an ad in the *Times*.

With all its drawbacks, Carol had felt inclined to take the job (surely it would lead to something better), and after the round of interviews it had, as expected, been offered. She'd realized, from the casualness with which the offer was made, that anyone who'd applied that day would probably have been hired; she'd simply had the luck to get there first. Once again she congratulated herself on her charmed life. But no sooner had Mrs. Tait invited her to start work the following Monday than Carol had had second thoughts—doubts about the salary, the sudden necessity of finding an apartment of her own, but also misgivings, now that the decision was hers, about her eagerness to abandon old Mrs. Slavinsky. She had requested, and been allowed, "a day or two to think things over."

The hour had been later than she'd realized; it was nearly five by the time she'd reached home. She had noticed an ambulance parked outside the building, and an empty police car, but her thoughts had been on other things. Upstairs, when the elevator opened, she'd heard men's voices; they were coming from the old woman's apartment. Suddenly fearful, she had unlocked the door. A policeman was standing in the front room, talking to Mrs. Slavinsky's daughter, while another spoke softly on the phone. Two black ambulance attendants were unrolling something near the entrance to the old woman's bedroom. All turned to look at Carol when she came in, but the only one who spoke to her was the daughter, who explained to her quite calmly, with little apparent grief and without a trace of accusation in her voice, how, sometime after Carol had gone out, she had phoned her mother, gotten no answer, tried again an hour later, still without success, and how at last she'd hurried over to find that the old woman, no doubt having returned to bed for an afternoon's nap, had somehow contrived to wind the blanket around her face . . .

She didn't seem to blame Carol. Later, after the men had left, bearing with them the shapeless thing in the bag, she had even offered to let Carol stay on in the apartment, at least until she was able to find a suitable place of her own. But Carol was in no mood to remain there; she was too horrified by the voices in her head, the guilty one that insisted it wasn't *her* fault, *she'd* done nothing wrong, and the one that reminded her how remarkably convenient the old woman's death had been. For now she was free to take the job at Voorhis; would have to take it, in fact. *Absolutely perfect timing . . .*

She reported for work at the library the following Monday and spent part of the first week in the Chelsea Hotel just up the block. But despite the place's legendary glamour and the furtive fascination with which Carol regarded the tenants and visitors who strolled its echoing yellow halls, the hotel was too expensive. A roommate service in a shabby second-floor office on Fourteenth Street had connected her with Rochelle, whose previous roommate had moved out. Carol was more than willing to take the tiny bedroom; it was private, at least. Rochelle, who slept on a sofa bed in the living room, had the run of the apartment. She was not the sort of person Carol would have chosen to live with, and in the month they'd been together they had not become real friends; but (Carol reminded herself) the girl could be quite goodhearted at times, and besides, with the situation as it was, Carol knew she couldn't be choosy. She was grateful for the roof over her head, grateful she could remain in the city. For a while she'd been haunted by visions of returning home to Pennsylvania a failure, to throw herself, like a child, back on the support of her family. Now, at least, she had a job; she could survive here after all.

At two fifteen today she'd been summoned to the first-floor office by the assistant supervisor, Miss Elms, a greying, harried-looking woman whose desk, opposite Carol's, was piled high with correspondence.

"You look as though you could use a change of scene," she said, regarding Carol dourly over the top of her glasses. "When you come back off your break, I'm sending you upstairs. Mrs. Schumann's got a four o'clock story hour—and since it's the last day of school, those kids may get a bit rambunctious."

Carol would have much preferred working downstairs, but told herself that, with the weather grown so warm these days, most of the children would probably be staying outside.

"Remember," the supervisor added, "you're not up there to read, and you're not up there to daydream. You're there to give Mrs. Schumann a helping hand."

Climbing the stairs, Carol wondered if Mrs. Schumann had been complaining about her to the supervisor. If so, it seemed unfair; she worked just as hard as anyone else. There simply wasn't very much to do on the second floor, short of helping fledgling readers with the harder words and keeping an eye out for the occasional fight. Yet she knew there'd been truth in what the supervisor had said; she had recently discovered that she preferred children's books to the children themselves.

All but the central desk upstairs was half-sized, a world in miniature: worktables like low wooden platforms rose just inches from the floor, and several of the chairs came only to her knee. Though she herself was slight of build and had small, delicate features, it was hard not to feel oversized here, like Alice down the rabbit hole or some invading giant from one of the fairy-tale books in the corner.

Mrs. Schumann, the children's librarian, sat placidly behind the desk. She was a heavy, slow-moving woman who perspired easily and who left her chair only with the greatest reluctance. Except for her, a pair of laughing little girls, and a dispirited-looking preschooler trudging glumly round the bookshelves with his mother, the floor was deserted, the air oppressive and still. Above the humming of four small electric fans that turned their heads from side to side, she could hear the chugging of the Xerox machine on the first floor, the *swish-swish, swish-swish* of the outer doors swinging open and shut, and the tread of footsteps on the stairs. School was out; soon the room would be filling up.

The footsteps echoed hollowly in the silence of the hall; a tiny face emerged above the banister. The child peered uncertainly around the empty floor like the first guest at a party, then slunk toward the central desk to confer in urgent whispers with the librarian.

Carol drifted toward the front window and stared idly down at the street. The buildings across the way were drab and dull, a large old residential hotel gone seedy, a furniture showroom, a warehouse with trucks lined up in front of it all day.

The rear windows held a better view. Here sunlight slanted down upon a tiny courtyard hidden between the buildings; overgrown by creepers, vines, and weeds, it had lain black and apparently lifeless all winter, she'd been told, but in recent months had flourished, until it presently resembled a transplanted patch of forest. During free moments of the day—and when, as now, she'd been assigned upstairs before the schoolchildren arrived—Carol liked to stand by the window, glad to find some glimpse of nature amid the bricks.

Below her a clump of thornbushes were irregular green blobs upon a darker field of undergrowth and earth. An oak and two young maples struggled upward toward the light, their trunks thin as walking sticks, while delicate green fernlike vines grew up the side of the opposite building, higher than the floor on which she stood. Through the glass she watched the fronds blow and tremble in the breeze, some of which passed over the top of the open window just below the ceiling. The shade stirred softly above her. Lifting its bottom edge, she felt the touch of cooler air upon her face; it carried the smell of soil and leaves and, from somewhere, the faintest, most elusive trace of roses.

Downstairs the outer doors went *swish-swish, swish-swish.*

Seen from this height, the view from the rear windows reminded Carol of a garden gone back to the wild, and she could never think of it without a queer, indefinable longing; given over entirely to plants, it hinted at some mystery far deeper than the mysteries in the books that lined the wall. She felt a strangeness in it, yet without the sense of dread that wilderness on a vaster scale inspired. No being had ever set foot back there, at least no one she had seen; she wasn't even sure that one could reach it, for the courtyard appeared to be surrounded by high metal fences. It remained forever beyond the windowpane, like a fragile green world preserved within a bottle.

Suddenly, in the midst of the green, something small and black caught her eye. It lay almost directly below the library window and half in the shadow of a thornbush, down among the ground vines and weeds. She leaned forward to peer more closely, pressing her forehead against the glass, but from this distance it was impossible to say just what it was, only what it appeared to be: an arrangement of small black sticks protruding from a shallow hole in the earth, forming a vague pattern, a circle bisected by a line extending slightly on both sides.

Carol sighed. So someone had been back there after all. Whether the objects had been dropped or buried, they were certainly a sign of human intrusion. Whatever their origin—some broken fragments of a plant, perhaps, a bit of machinery, or merely litter—it came to only one thing: her garden had been violated.

She was still bent dejectedly over the window, a little surprised at the strength of her reaction, when, from the hallway behind her, she heard the measured tread of footsteps coming up the stairs.

*

"I'm not a young man anymore," he was saying. "The doctors tell me not to make any long-range plans." He smiled wistfully and blinked his mild eyes. "But before I die I'd like to finish a little book I've been working on. A book about children."

They stood talking softly by the window, barely disturbing the stillness of the room. The little man's words didn't carry far, and they had a gentle, lisping quality which she found strangely soothing. His voice was high and quavery as a flute.

Though at first she'd half resented him for interrupting her reverie—why didn't he bother Mrs. Schumann if he had a problem, why had he come straight to her?—Carol had to admit that there was something rather touching about the man. For all his paunch and double chin he looked surprisingly frail up close, and a good deal older than she'd at first supposed, perhaps well along in his seventies. He was no taller than she was, with plump little hands, plump little lips, and soft pink skin with little trace of hair. He reminded her of a freshly powdered baby.

"This will be a book about your own children?" she asked, preparing herself for an onslaught of reminiscence.

He shook his head. "No, nothing like that. I've never been blessed with children." Again the wistful smile, all the more affecting in so droll a figure. "I do enjoy watching them, though. Like those two over there." He gestured toward the bookshelves in the rear. "Can you see what they're doing? My eyes aren't what they used to be."

Carol glanced over her shoulder. Behind the central desk, two small girls darted silently through the aisles of books. "Oh, them!" she said. She wondered if she should tell Mrs. Schumann, but the librarian was leafing through a pile of catalogues. "I'm afraid they're being rather naughty. They seem to be playing tag."

The little man nodded. "A game that predates history. Once upon a time the loser would have paid with her life."

From behind the shelves came a screech of laughter.

"That's the subject of my book," he went on. "The origin of games. And nursery rhymes, fairy tales, and the like. Some of them go back— oh, even farther than I do!" He cocked his head and smiled. "What I mean is, there's a bit of the savage behind even the most innocent-looking creations. Do you follow me?"

"I'm not sure I do." She felt a flicker of impatience; he still hadn't said exactly what he wanted.

He pursed his lips. "Well, take today, for instance, the twenty-fourth of June—traditionally a very special day. Magic spells are twice as strong right now. People fall in love. Dreams come true. Did you have any dreams last night?"

"I can't remember."

"Most likely you did. Young girls always dream on Midsummer Eve. The night just seems to call for it."

"But surely we're a long way from midsummer," said Carol. "The season's just begun."

He shook his head. "The ancients saw things a bit differently. To them the year was like a turning wheel, one half winter, one half summer, each with a festival in the middle. Winter had the Yule feast, summer what we're celebrating now—Midsummer Day. For us, of course, the year's been flattened to death on a calendar, and Yule is just another word for Christmas, but originally it had nothing to do with Christ. The only birth it marked was the birth of the sun."

"Wait, you mean . . . another Son?"

He laughed, a little louder than necessary. "No, no. Oh, *my,* no! I was referring to that big fellow out there." He nodded toward the window. "You see, Yuletide celebrates the winter solstice. Afterward, the days start getting longer. As of last night, though, we've come to the other end of the wheel. The days are growing shorter now. The sun's begun to die."

Carol found herself watching the sunlight as it streamed obliviously through the window, its radiance undiminished. How odd, with all the hot days still ahead—how odd to think of it cooling, dying, growing dark . . .

"Long ago," he was saying, "Midsummer was a time of portents. Rivers overflowed their banks or suddenly dried up. Certain plants were said to turn to poison. Madmen had to be confined, witches held their sabbats. In China dragons left their caves and flew about the sky like flaming meteors. In Britain they were known as drakes, serpents, 'worms,' and Midsummer was the time for them to breed. They say the whole countryside shook with the sound, and that farmers lit bonfires—in those days that meant fires of bones—in an effort to drive them away. There were other fires, too: fires, dancing, midnight chants to commemorate the passing of the sun. Even today there are places in Europe where children celebrate Midsummer Eve by dancing round a bonfire. At the end of the dance, one by one, they leap across the flames. It seems harmless enough, of course—at worst a burnt bottom or two!—but trace it back to the beginning and . . . well, I think you can guess what you'll find."

"More than just a burnt bottom, I suppose."

He laughed. "A *lot* more! A ritual sacrifice! Or take a more familiar example: an innocent little counting rhyme like 'Eeny meeny miny mo.' "

"Catch a beggar by the toe?"

"That's it. Except that twenty years ago, before they cleaned up the language, you would have said 'Catch a nigger by the toe.' And tw

centuries ago you'd have repeated a string of nonsense words: 'Bascalora hora do,' something like that. There are hundreds of varia-
tions. The one *you* grew up with, incidentally, puts you—hmm, let me
see . . ." He scratched his head. "Oh, I'd say somewhere around Ohio.
Am I right?"

"Hey, that's really incredible! I'm from Pennsylvania, right across
the border."

He nodded, not at all surprised. "A very pretty area. I know it well."
Turning, he gazed dreamily out the window, sunshine playing on the
little pink baby skull, the wisps of hair that glowed white with a touch
of yellow.

Carol watched him in silence as he stood before her, blinking in the
light. There'd been something in his tremulous old-man's voice which
hinted at considerable experience, but till now she hadn't been inclined
to take him seriously. Maybe it was his size, or his funny little lisp; he
was far too small to be threatening. No doubt his reference to Ohio had
been a lucky guess; still, she found herself oddly impressed.

Presently he turned. "I'll tell you what's even more remarkable," he
said. "You can trace that little rhyme of yours all the way back to the
Druids." He smiled at her look of disbelief. "Oh, I assure you, it's quite
true. Once upon a time, when Britain was occupied by the Romans, it
was a sacrificial chant. The Druids had a rather nasty habit, you
know—they liked to burn people in wicker cages!—and they used the
'Bascalora' method to choose a victim. 'Basca' means basket, and
'lora'—

"Isn't that Latin for 'straps'?"

His smile widened. "Well, bless me, you *are* smart! Binding straps,
yes. To tie the hands."

She was pleased to see the admiration in his eyes. "My one good subject," she said, and allowed herself a modest smile. Briefly another
thought intruded: the night sky, a mound aglow with flames, and a girl
very much like herself bound naked to a kind of altar. Something long
and white was emerging from the shadows. She pushed it from her
mind. "I've had a lot of practice," she said. "In Latin, I mean. And
your subject is—this type of thing? Childhood and primitive rituals?"

He nodded. "More or less."

Behind him three more children had arrived, and soon they'd be
asking for her help. She would have to cut this short. "It sounds absolutely fascinating," she said, "but you know, you're really in the wrong
place. The books we have up here—well, they're very basic, strictly for
pre-teens. You want downstairs, under Anthropology. Or you might
try looking through Child Development . . ."

He nodded genially. "Yes, I know, I've already been down there.
Voorhis has a very good collection." He patted the briefcase beneath
his arm. "Until this afternoon, in fact, I'd been looking for a certain

little book, a study of Agon di-Gatuan, the so-called 'Old Language.'
I'd searched the whole city, top to bottom, and this was the only place
that had it."

Carol was amused at how pleased he sounded with himself. "Oh,
really?" she said. "Top to bottom? You must be pretty thorough! The
city's an awfully big place."

"Not at all. Not when you know what you're looking for."

He smiled and took a step closer.

"And of course, the nice thing is, you get to meet such interesting
people. If I hadn't come up here, I'd never have made the acquaintance
of a charming young lady like yourself."

"Oh, now you're just teasing," said Carol, flattered and uneasy. She
had heard this sort of thing before; there were always one or two old
men who tried to flirt with her in a joking, grandfatherly way. "Maybe
I'd better say goodbye now. My mother always said that when a man
pays a compliment, watch out!"

"What? Watch out for a poor old thing like *me?*" He laughed and
shook his head. "I assure you, young lady, I'm perfectly harmless!"
His smile was so dazzling that she didn't stop to wonder if he wore
false teeth. "I'm nothing more than a—"

Suddenly he looked past her. Carol saw his smile fade into a frown
and, at the same moment, felt an insistent tug on her sleeve. She pulled
back, startled; a belligerent little white face was peering up at her.

"I have to have something on entomology," the boy demanded, still
gripping her sleeve. "With pictures." He seemed greatly put out by
Carol's hesitation. *"Insects!"* he hissed, and was duly directed one row
past Outdoors and Adventure.

When she turned back to the little man, he was staring out the window. She realized that he still hadn't explained precisely why he'd
come upstairs. No doubt he was just another lonely old pensioner
who'd lived too long and read too much and now wanted a chance to
tell somebody what he'd learned.

As if sensing her eyes on him, he turned. "Lovely garden," he said
softly. Behind him the topmost vines arched toward the sunlight. "I
wish I had more time for nature, but that's the one thing I don't have.
I'm busy every minute of the day."

In that case, Carol wondered, *why is he wasting time up here?*

"The truth is," he said, "there's job enough for two. I've been trying
to find someone at Columbia to work with me, some bright young student, but I didn't care much for the people they sent." He shook his
head. "No, I didn't care much for them at all."

He gazed absently toward the garden once more, then turned back to
her. "You know, when I was downstairs today I couldn't help noticing
all the scholars down there, looking oh so self-important as they pored
over their books, but not really knowing half as much as they liked to

think. And I suddenly asked myself, 'Why bother with people like that? Why not turn to a professional? I'll bet there's a children's librarian right here at Voorhis who'd be a lot more useful to me, and who'd probably be grateful for the extra work.' That's why I came up here. It was just a whim."

Carol's interest was stirred, but so were her suspicions. Was this funny little man about to offer her a job? Or was he merely looking for an unpaid volunteer? His project sounded interesting enough, but she was in no position to work for free. She hoped he wouldn't ask her.

"I've collected a huge amount of data over the past few months," he was saying, "and I expect to be acquiring more over the summer. You know the sort of thing: journal articles, newspaper clippings, dissertations, and so forth. More than I'll have time to read myself." He patted the briefcase again. "I'm an old man—at least that's what they tell me!—and frankly, I'm going to need some help." Laying the briefcase on the windowsill, he leaned toward her as if he had something urgent to confide; she noticed, with approval, that he smelled of talcum powder and soap. "What I'm looking for, you see, is someone to read over the material, pull out the important ideas, and, wherever possible, summarize them for me. Part-time, of course. Ten or fifteen hours a week." He stood back, hands on hips. "So, young lady, there it is in a nutshell."

"I see." She recalled the work she'd done four winters ago at college, the dark evenings at the library and the endless pages of notes. "You want a sort of research assistant."

"That's right," he said. "Someone I can depend on. Someone who's smart, who writes well, and who has an interest in the field." He paused a moment and regarded her quizzically; the wide, gentle eyes, level with her own, seemed to float in their sockets, taking in her surroundings, her features, her hair. "I feel certain that you meet my qualifications."

"Well, I—I do have an interest in the field," said Carol, not entirely sure what field he meant. She wondered if he'd mistaken her for a regular children's librarian, instead of just one of the downstairs assistants. Dare she tell him? And dare she ask him about pay?

"These articles," she said at last. "How would I obtain them?"

"Well," he said softly, leaning toward her again, "I rather like to do my own collecting." Idly he reached up to scratch at the corner of his eye, and Carol felt a wisp of breeze against her cheek. Above her the shades billowed and collapsed. "Sometimes I might ask you to locate a particular item for me, but that won't happen often. We'll meet each week, and—Whatever's the matter?"

"No, no, it's nothing. Please go on." For a moment she had felt a tiny stinging just above her left temple, but already it was gone. She smoothed back her hair and tried to look interested.

"Well, I was saying—Here, let me brush you off." His hand swept gently over her shoulder, and came away trailing several strands of her newly clipped red hair. "I was just saying that we'll meet wherever's convenient—here at the library or at one of our homes." He stepped back, slipping his hand into his pocket. "I live uptown, by the way, near the Hudson. It's an easy walk from the subway."

He paused as if awaiting a reply. Carol resolved not to give him her address, at least not for the moment. She remained silent.

He licked his lips. "None of this is important," he said at last. "It can all be arranged later. Each time we get together, you'll give me your notes and I'll give you the new material . . . along with your pay."

So there was to be money after all. "And this pay would be—"

He laughed. "I thought I'd mentioned that! I was thinking of twelve dollars an hour, plus expenses. Does that sound all right?"

"Twelve dollars an *hour?*" Hastily she tried to calculate. He'd said ten to fifteen hours a week; that would be anywhere from $120 to . . . She gave up; her heart was beating too fast. She only knew she wasn't worth that much.

He looked momentarily uncertain. "If you don't—"

"That sounds absolutely *fine,*" she got out. She hoped she appeared composed, but in her imagination she was already buying the outfit she'd seen in a shop on Greenwich Avenue, and a subscription to next season's ballet. Maybe even an air conditioner, too. God loved her.

"I'm glad it's satisfactory," said the little man, with the faintest of smiles. "It'll be off the books, of course."

"Off the books?" She wasn't sure exactly what that meant, except that it was something illegal. The ranks of dancers faded and the air conditioner stopped. The room grew warm again.

He nodded. Was there impatience in his face? "I assumed you'd prefer it that way. You won't have to give anything to your Uncle Sam."

"Yes, yes, of course." This was too good to be true. "You mean, then . . I could keep everything."

"That's right. You would, I take it, be interested?"

"Yes, absolutely. This is just the sort of thing I've always been fascinated by—fairy tales, and myths, and primitive religion . . ." She finished lamely, unable to recall if this was his intended subject; he hadn't actually said anything about religion, had he?

"Excellent," he was saying. "You sound like just the person I've been looking for. I need someone with an inquiring mind, who's not afraid of a little hard work." He unfastened the strap to the briefcase and began digging inside. "It may sound old-fashioned, but—Oh dear!" He drew forth a plump, pale yellow book and turned it over t examine it. There were catalogue numbers on the spine. "Oh, fe heaven's sake, look at this. I'm getting so *absent*-minded these days

seem to have walked off with someone else's book." He grinned sheepishly. "I'm afraid this must belong to that nice young fellow downstairs—the one with the glasses. Do you know him? At the table by the
bulletin board?"

Carol shook her head.

"Well, I'll just have to make sure to return it." With a sigh he laid
the book idly on the windowsill, then turned back to Carol with a dazzling smile. "Now, young lady, where was I?"

Downstairs, where rows of scholars frowned over texts, scribbled silently, or dozed, Jeremy Freirs reached for the yellow book and cursed
when he realized it was gone. It was a dog-eared old copy of *The House
of Souls* by Arthur Machen, bound in saffron-colored cloth, and it had
been lying on top of the pile on his desk. He searched the pile again,
but didn't find it. Damn! That pesty old queer must have taken it.

They had met, in fact, over that very book less than an hour before.
Searching for it through the labyrinth of Voorhis's open stacks, Freirs
had rounded an aisle in a deserted section of the library where bookshelves high as hedgerows blocked the sound from the street, and had
come upon the old man hunched over the volume as if tracing its words
with his finger. At Freirs' approach he had glanced up like a child
caught reading pornography—he was hardly more than child-size
himself, in fact—and then he'd snapped the book shut. Freirs had seen
him slip something hurriedly into his pocket. A pencil! No wonder the
old guy had looked guilty. He'd probably been writing in the margins.

There was something not quite right about the man. He didn't look
as seedy and dispirited as the other old-timers who frequented the library, yet he seemed far too elderly to be an academic. He looked like
the sort of man who'd play the kindly uncle in some saccharine 1940s
movie—not Freirs' style at all. Freirs had ignored him at first, but he'd
been unable to find the book he sought on the shelves. Behind him the
old man said softly, "Could this be the one you're looking for?"

He held the book out for inspection. Freirs glanced at the spine.
"That's it, all right. Are you using it?"

"No, no, I'm all done." Smiling, he handed over the book. "Here,
take it."

Freirs hefted the book in his hand. It was fat and heavy, damn it,
and he didn't have much time left to look through it all. He turned to

go, but a hand caught his arm. The old man was looking up at him. His voice was practically a whisper. "You're familiar with Machen? With his beliefs?"

"No," said Freirs, a little louder than necessary. "I've never read him. I just want to see if I *should.*" Once more he made as if to leave. If he stayed away from his seat too long, someone might steal his book bag.

"Oh, you should, you really should." The little man seemed not to care that he was detaining Freirs. "He knew a thing or two, our Arthur. You'll be well repaid for reading him, I promise."

Freirs nodded. "Good. I'm glad." Turning his back, he made his way up the aisles to his table.

He had a small square table to himself, in the rear, just beneath a bulletin board laden with clippings and notices like a brick wall overgrown with ivy. Throughout the spring it had been his usual place of work; the better tables, farther down the row, looked out upon the little patch of garden in back of the library, but he seldom arrived at Voorhis early enough to secure one. And just as well, too; if he'd had a window seat, he'd probably have spent all day staring out at godforsaken weeds instead of finishing his work.

Even without the distraction of a window view, he hadn't gotten quite as far as he'd expected over the past two months; he was still compiling a reading list for his projected dissertation, whose working title was currently "Hell's Abhorr'd Dominions: The Dynamics of Place in the Gothic Universe," though this now struck him as a little pretentious, even for Columbia. He added the Machen to the pile already on his desk, first transcribing the publication data—London, 1906—and a list of the book's contents, some half dozen stories. He was searching the literature at the moment, still uncertain of his dissertation's scope. Even the most unlikely books might be worth a footnote or two, if only as a way of dropping the name; the longer he could pad out his bibliography, the more unlikely it would be that the board of examiners would be able to check all his references.

He was leafing through the second-to-last chapter in a Gothic bibliography, alternately amused and aghast at the titles—*The Benevolent Monk, or, The Castle of Olalla,* 1807; *Deeds of Darkness, or, The Unnatural Uncle,* 1805; *The Midnight Groan, or, The Spectre of the Chapel, Involving an Exposure of the Horrible Secrets of the Nocturnal Assembly,* 1808—when someone cleared his throat. He looked up to see the old man standing beside his table, smiling down familiarly at him.

"I wonder if I can borrow Mr. Machen back from you for just one moment," the old man asked. "Would you mind terribly? There's a passage I really ought to check."

With a shrug Freirs tapped the yellow book at the top of the pile. "Be my guest. Just bring it back when you're done, okay?"

But after opening the book the old man showed no signs of moving; he stood riffling through page after page and peering at each with an almost comical fervor, head darting back and forth with the movement of his eyes.

"Ah, here we are!" he said at last. He nodded to himself. "Ah, yes .. yes."

Freirs sighed and returned to his own reading—*Gondez the Monk* ... *Phantoms of the Cloister* ... *Horrors of the Secluded Castle*—but moments later the old man began to speak. " 'We underrate evil,' " he said, his voice a portentous whisper.

Freirs looked up. "What's that?"

" 'We underrate evil,' " the man repeated, reading a passage from the book. " 'We have quite forgotten the awfulness of real sin. What would your feelings be, seriously, if your cat or your dog began to talk to you, and to dispute with you in human accents? You would be overwhelmed with horror. I am sure of it. And if the roses in your garden sang a weird song, you would go mad. And suppose the stones in the road began to swell and grow before your eyes, and if the pebble that you noticed at night had shot out stony blossoms in the morning? Well, these examples may give you some notion of what sin really is.' "

Finally he looked up from the book, face oddly transfigured, almost ecstatic. "Marvelous!" he said, all but smacking his lips. "What do you suppose the man is driving at?"

Freirs shook his head, reluctant to involve himself in a discussion, yet drawn to the game. Around them several readers looked up with curiosity or annoyance. "Obviously it's a kind of moral metaphor," he said. "Evil as a violation of normal physical law, an aberration—something like a disease. But the symbols he's dreamed up are unusual, to say the least."

The old man nodded. "Yes. Yes, I'm sure you're right. I can see that you're a very bright young man." He smiled slyly. "But then again, of course, they may not be symbols after all. For all we know, Machen may have meant them quite literally."

Freirs had been glad when, at last, he'd wandered away, no doubt to bother some other unsuspecting soul. But now the damned book was gone too; the man must have walked off with it. Freirs looked around the room but didn't see him; nor, despite the lost book, was he especially sure that he wanted to.

Anyway, the day was almost over. He had his final class to teach at eight and wanted to get home first to prepare for it, to go over his students' papers and brush up on his *Cahiers* and *Film Comments*. Celluloid, swish pans, *mises en scène*. Another world, that one, far from gloomy monastics and their Gothic battlements, farther still from flowering stones and singing flowers. Beyond the window several seats behind him, shadows were lengthening in the garden, doggedly climbing the bricks. He checked his watch: almost five o'clock. He'd press on to the end of the chapter, then get the hell out of this place.

Sunlight still streamed freely through the second-story windows, but suddenly the old man's eyes narrowed as if he'd seen a shadow cross the sky. Frowning, he glanced quickly at his watch.

Across the room, summoned by an impatient gesture from Mrs. Schumann (now reimmersed contentedly in the catalogues that covered her desk), Carol was leafing through a stack of books on dinosaurs for the benefit of a small boy and his mother, while a daughter awaited her turn. "He just can't get enough of 'em," the woman explained proudly, as her son studied pictures of steaming primeval swamps where monstrous reptiles preyed upon the weak, jaws tore flesh, and giant serpents struggled against batlike things with sharp-clawed wings and impossibly long beaks. None of it was real, Carol told herself; none of it had ever been real. Later, searching through Perrault and Andersen to find a fairy tale for the daughter, she stole a glance at the little man across the room. He was leaning against the windowsill, gazing idly at the book he'd carried upstairs. The sunlight from behind him made a nimbus of his hair. Suddenly, as if aware that she was watching him, he looked up and winked at her. His smile was radiant; even from the other side of the room it made her feel good.

So this, then, was to be her future employer. She still couldn't believe it was true. Nor could she believe that, for the duration of the summer, she would more than double her income. How could he afford to pay so much? He certainly didn't look rich; Carol recognized a cheap suit when she saw it. Was he a liar or a lunatic, and the job a hoax? Somehow she felt inclined to trust him. Perhaps he'd saved his money all his life, and now, reaching the end, found himself with no one else to give it to. She wondered how he'd made his living.

For her part, she reminded herself that she hadn't been entirely truthful with him. Thank God he didn't know that she was only an assistant here. As she read a page aloud, more to mother than daughter, she prayed she looked professional. " 'Whenever a good child dies, an angel of God comes down from heaven, takes the dead child in his arms, spreads out his great white wings, and flies with him over all the places which the child has loved during his life. Then he gathers a large handful of flowers—' " Lord, no! So depressing. She handed the woman a Disney Cinderella and made sure the little girl approved.

Over by the window, the old man was staring at her. He nodded reassuringly. "I see you have your hands full," he said, when she'd returned to his side.

She laughed. "Oh, today's one of our slow ones. You should come up here on a rainy afternoon. It's like a playground!" She smoothed back her hair. "I'm used to that, though. I grew up with three sisters and a brother."

"Ah, really." His smile was a trifle vacant. "I'm sure they're all very proud of you, coming to the big city like this."

"Well, I—I do hope to make something of myself," she said. Perhaps she should try to impress him, lest he change his mind about the job. "As a matter of fact, I'm planning to take some psychology courses next fall. In dance therapy." *If,* she added mentally, *I find the money.* "I may take night courses once or twice a week, up at Hunter."

He gave a courtly nod. "A fine institution. I know it well. This job should help you meet some of the expenses." He began to turn away.

"Speaking of expenses," she began, then regretted it.

"Yes?" His look was guarded.

"Well, you mentioned something about 'twelve dollars an hour plus expenses,' and I was just wondering"—she hoped she didn't sound greedy—"not that it makes the least bit of difference, of course, but I was wondering what expenses you meant."

He shrugged. "The usual. Paper, photocopying, typewriter ribbon . . . You do own a typewriter, don't you?"

"Oh, yes, of course. That is, I have access to one. It's my roommate's. She's almost never home." Some residual bitterness from the morning made her add, "And when she is, she's in no position to use it."

"A roommate, you say?" The little man pursed his lips. "Hmmm. A bit of a free spirit, is she?"

Carol nodded. "She thinks so, anyway. But—" She stopped herself; she really didn't mean to be unfair. "It's not that she does anything wrong. We just come from totally different backgrounds. She went to a big state university; I went to a little Catholic school. Girls only."

"And where might that be?" He didn't sound very interested. The shadows in the room shifted as a cloud passed in front of the sun.

"St. Mary's, in Ambridge." The little man blinked reflectively. "I'm sure you've never heard of it," she added. "There are at least twenty others with the same name." She looked past him, out the window. The fronds were tossing in the breeze.

He moved slightly, blocking her view. "Indeed I have. It's just above the highway, am I right? At the top of a hill?"

"You're thinking of the high school," she said. "I went there too." It was spooky, how much he seemed to know. "You have nothing against parochial schools, I hope."

"No, no, quite the contrary. They're the only places left that still teach proper English." He moved away from the window. "So you stayed within the fold, then. From St. Mary's to St. Mary's."

She nodded. "And then to St. Agnes's, here in New York."

"Another college?"

"It's a convent, actually. Over on West Forty-eighth Street." She waited to see his reaction. "I spent around six months there. I've only been out since January."

"You—a nun? Why, I never would have guessed it!" His eyes twinkled merrily.

"Well, not really a nun. I only got as far as my novitiate, in fact. I never even put on a habit." She noticed that, for all his professed astonishment, he didn't look particularly surprised. "It was just something I felt I had to try," she added. "I realize now that I joined for the wrong reasons—I mean, selfish reasons—but at the time there just seemed no place else to go. Things were really bad at home. My father was sick, and somehow I got it into my head that if I went and took the vows . . . well, that things might get better. Maybe my father would recover."

He nodded. He seemed to understand. "A kind of sacrifice," he said. "You made a very difficult choice."

"Yes, I suppose so. But for a while I had the feeling that it wasn't really my choice at all. I felt as if somehow I'd been *chosen.*" She shrugged. "I guess everybody feels that way at times: that they've been singled out for something special. I thought so, at any rate. It was a chance to give some direction to my life—which I thought I needed."

"Direction, yes." He appeared to consider this. "But you didn't stay very long."

"Well, you see . . . my father died."

"Oh, how *sad!*"

"And anyway, the whole thing just wasn't for me. I began to think about all I'd be giving up—meeting someone, falling in love, getting married—and when you start having doubts like that, you know you're in the wrong place." The memories returned. "Still, I was so sure that I'd been—"

"Chosen?"

She nodded.

"Well," he said, "who knows? Maybe you *have* been—but for something else. Something you never even dreamed of."

He *did* understand! She was going to enjoy working with this man.

"Anyway," he added, as if he'd read her thoughts, "*I've* chosen you . . . and I think it's going to be a very productive arrangement for us both." He paused. "I'm a little concerned abut one thing, though. This roommate of yours. You're sure she won't be too much of a distraction?"

"Oh, no, not at all. Rochelle and I get along fine. She goes her way.

go mine. If she's bringing somebody home and I have reading to do, I just go in my room and shut the door. We're different sorts of people, that's all. She thinks I ought to get more fun out of life."

He snorted contemptuously. "That's all very easy for *her* to say. She's obviously lost the most precious thing a young girl has."

For the first time that afternoon Carol thought she saw him glower, but perhaps it was a trick of the light; the room had dimmed perceptibly.

"Take my advice and stick to your guns!" he said, his voice no longer so gentle or so high. "I wouldn't have anything to do with the men that girl brings home. They're not for you."

Carol nodded dutifully, only half convinced. "You sound just like my father," she said. "He was very protective of me."

"Well, of course, of course. That's what fathers are for—to make sure their little girls don't overstep the bounds." He shook his head. "I'm sorry, I don't mean to be lecturing you. I'm sure you miss your father very much."

"Oh, yes. I just wish I'd known him better. But he was so old, even when I was a little girl, that I never really got very close to him. All I can do now, whenever I go home, is buy an occasional new wreath for his grave."

"Ah, yes, wreaths." The old man nodded sympathetically. "I'm half tempted to make them a chapter in my book."

She felt a tiny chill. "You mean they're more than just a decoration?"

He nodded once more, but now his face was somber. In the waning light the room had fallen silent, except for the queer singsong echo of a child reading aloud from a book of nursery rhymes. *"Frown thee, fret thee, Jellycorn Hill . . ."* The sky outside was almost grey.

"You can trace all burial customs back to ancient times," he said softly, "just like funeral rites. We put flowers on graves because—well, for the same reason a woman wears perfume. A corpse by any other name would smell no sweeter."

She bit her lip.

"No," he said, "it isn't very pretty, but this is the sort of material we'll be working on together. At bottom, most ceremonies are direct, distasteful, and utterly ruthless. Even the very notion of tombstones."

"I thought—" She stopped abruptly. Something had fluttered past the window, snowy white against the dark sky and the bricks. She'd glimpsed a flash of wings, as from a falling angel. Or an impossibly white bird. "I thought tombstones were simply to mark the grave."

"And also to weigh down the corpse," he said, his voice louder now. 'To prevent it from rising again." Taking the briefcase, he moved even ⸱rther from the window, and she had to turn to face him. Behind her ⸱ heard high, mournful cries; a flock of birds must be passing over the courtyard. She wanted to go to the window and look, but it would have been impolite.

> *"Mark thee, mind thee,*
> *Jellycorn Hill,"*

sang the thin, small voice of the child, echoing through the room.

> *"If Crow don't find thee,*
> *Mousey will."*

He was digging once more in his briefcase. He seemed to be in a hurry. "Here," he said, withdrawing a sheaf of papers. "You should find some interesting material in this batch, and you can consider it your first assignment." He handed them to her. They were photocopies of articles from various academic journals. She glanced at the top piece and frowned. *Celtic Heathendom. An Inquiry into the Epigraphy and Myth-Cycles of Fourth-Century Meath.* It looked rather formidable. So did the next. *The Ethnology of the A-Kamba.* East African, apparently.

"And I'm to summarize all this?"

"That's right. Just a page or two per article. You'll probably enjoy it."

Looking at still another piece, she doubted this. *Report of the Cambridge Anthropological Expedition to the Torres Straits, with Special Attention to—*

"Torres Straits? Where in the world are they?"

"The South Pacific." He grinned. "As you can see, I cast a pretty wide net."

> *"Scramble thee, scratch thee,*
> *Jellycorn Hill . . ."*

The last one seemed innocuous enough. *Notes on the Folklore of the Northern Counties of England and the Borders*—London, 1879. Maybe it wouldn't be so bad. She reminded herself of how much he'd be paying.

> *"If Mouse don't catch thee,*
> *Moley will."*

He cleared his throat. She looked up to find him holding an open checkbook, pen poised. "Along with the work, I think it's only fair that I give you some expense money," he said. "An advance, so to speak."

"Oh, that would be wonderful!"

"It won't be much. Just something to tide you over for the weekend." He winked. "Now, what name shall I put here?"

The question caught her by surprise. For a moment she had crazy impulse to give a false name, even though it meant the would be useless, but immediately she felt ashamed of herself. Rochelle was always making fun of her for being timid; now was the time to grow up. What was she afraid of, anyway? God would watch over her.

"Carol Conklin."

"Ah!" Beaming, he wrote it in. "A fine old *nederlandse* name!"

She nodded uncertainly. "But I think my mother's people came from Galway."

"Ah, yes," he said. "I know it well."

> *"Hide thee, haste thee,*
> *Jellycorn Hill,*
> *If Mole don't taste thee,*
> *Wormy will."*

He extended a plump little hand. "And my name's Rosebottom— spelled just the way it sounds. No jokes, please!" His old eyes twinkled merrily. "You can call me Rosie. Everybody does."

"Not Mr. Rosebottom?"

"Not Mister anything. Not even Aunt or Uncle. Just Rosie." He slipped the check into her hand. "I'll come by sometime next week and see how you're getting along."

With a courtly bow he moved off toward the stairs, swinging his briefcase. Momentarily she saw his little pink head flash between the banisters. Bobbing lower and lower, it disappeared from sight, still smiling.

The first thing Carol did, once the little man was gone, was to examine the check he had handed her. She could barely make out the *Aloysius Rosebottom* of the signature, for the letters curled like vines across the bottom of the paper, in contrast to the sedate A. L. ROSEBOTTOM printed at the top. Across the middle was written, *Thirty dollars even.* She wondered if she'd have trouble cashing it; the banks would already be closed.

It was only after she had slipped the folded check into a pocket, and was turning to see if anyone in the room might need her help, that she discovered the little man had forgotten his book. It was lying on the windowsill where he'd left it, a block of pale yellow in the waning light. Picking it up, she was surprised by its weight. It looked considerably older than she'd at first supposed, older than most of the books in the room. The cloth was worn in spots, but the front cover still bore traces of a design—imitation Beardsley, from the look of it—depicting what appeared to be the head of some fanciful animal; Carol could see long, supple horns (or were they antennae?) and great bulging heavy-lidded eyes. The book's spine, too, was ornamented with a Victorian-looking pattern of blossoms and leaves. Most of the title had been rubbed away, but she managed to puzzle out the words *The House of Souls*. The white library numerals inked at the bottom seemed almost a desecration.

"That old man left this lying on the windowsill," she told Mrs. Schumann, who'd been going through the offerings on the magazine racks for a group of patently uninterested children. Carol held up the book. "It's a wonder the binding isn't cracked, with workmanship like this. I'd better return it downstairs. Someone may be looking for it."

"I suppose so," said the older woman dubiously. For the first time, she looked put out. "You haven't done a heck of a lot of work here today. Who was he, anyway?"

"A friend of my father's." The lie was curiously comforting, as if speaking it aloud made it true. "He brought it up here by accident."

Mrs. Schumann blinked in slow comprehension, ignoring two small boys who were pawing through a rack of *Crickets* and *Ranger Rick* as Carol hurried from the room.

She examined the book as she headed for the staircase. It appeared to be a collection of stories by someone named Machen; she had never heard the name before and was not even sure how to pronounce it. She wondered how her new acquaintance—Rosie, how perfectly fitting the name seemed!—had managed to walk off with it. Had he thought it might pertain to his research? *Perhaps they're fairy tales,* she thought, and flipped through the book to see. It fell open at a story called "The White People." Someone—she hoped it hadn't been Rosie himself—had scribbled a few penciled notes at the top of the page. Skimming the opening paragraphs, an earnest, rather abstract dicussion of Sin, she gave up and snapped the book shut. This was no fairy tale.

The first floor was just as she had left it, crowded with figures pale and immobile as statues and as silent as the storeroom of a museum. Carol sneaked a glance at the clock above the front desk; she had a watch at home, a long-ago Christmas present, but it was broken and she'd never had enough money to have it repaired. *Till now,* she reminded herself.

It was nearly five fifteen, with still an hour and a half to go before Miss Elms flicked the light switch and announced closing time. For a minute or two there'd be no reaction except irritated sighs. Then one by one the statues would return to life. Among the grad students there'd be a faster riffling of pages; sleepers would lift their heads and shake off the hours of dream. Gathering up books and jackets, they'd shuffle grumbling and blinking toward the front desk.

A young fellow with glasses, Rosie had said. Sitting by the bulletin board. Carol looked around, and immediately recognized the one he'd meant: he was a frequent visitor to the library, a plump, distracted-looking young man with sandy hair cut squarishly short. He wore a faded plaid sports shirt open at the neck, its sleeves rolled up over thick, freckled arms. A blue seersucker jacket clearly in need of pressing was draped over the back of his chair, and a red cloth book bag, empty now, lay crumpled by his elbow on the table. He was squinting into an oversize volume, a directory of some kind from the reference section; a yellow pad beside it was covered with hasty-looking notes.

Approaching him, she cleared her throat. Up and down the aisle heads turned to watch her. "Excuse me," she whispered.

He looked up with annoyance, but on seeing Carol his expression softened. Perhaps he recognized her too.

She held out the yellow book. "I think this may be yours."

"Mine?" He peered uncertainly at the book, then nodded. "Oh, yes," he said, reaching for it. "Great." He kept his voice low. "Where'd you find it?" As he took the book from her, his eyes gave the tiniest flicker, and for an instant she felt his gaze drop to her breasts. It seemed almost a formality; she'd even known priests to do it.

"Someone brought it upstairs by mistake."

He smiled bitterly. "Yeah, and I'll bet I know who it was. That weird old guy I ran into today, over in the stacks."

She laughed. Once more heads turned. "You mean Rosie. He's very nice, really. He's working on a book." *And I'm helping him,* she wanted to add.

"Well, he's damned near kept me from working on mine. I was hoping to get through this by the end of the day"—he tapped the Machen volume—"and now I'm not going to have time. Am I allowed to check it out?"

"Not this one," she whispered, even before she'd glanced at the call numbers to make sure. "Special collection. It can't leave the library."

He scowled. "I was afraid of that. Maybe I can Xerox some things in it before I leave." He pushed back his chair. Carol saw herself about to be dismissed.

"Wait," she said impulsively, "I'll do it." The only alternative was to go back upstairs with the children and their mothers and the slowly growing wrath of Mrs. Schumann. "I have access to the copy room," she explained. "And I think the machine's free now." She hadn't heard it working, at any rate.

"Hey, that's really nice of you," he said. "Thanks a lot." He opened the book to the front and ran his finger down the list of contents. "Let's see . . . I'll probably just need 'The Great God Pan' and 'The Inmost Light.' " He peered speculatively at the titles. "And maybe the one that old man was going on about—'The White People.' " He handed her the book, then searched through his wallet and pulled out a ten-dollar bill. "I don't know what it'll come to. You can bring me change."

Everyone's giving me money today, thought Carol as she followed the line of shelves past the administrative offices toward the window-less little copy room in the rear. *My luck must be changing.* Taped to the dark wooden door, beneath a sign that said NO ADMITTANCE— STAFF ONLY, hung a sheet of paper reading *See Mrs. Tait at front desk for copy vouchers.* Inside, the air smelled of sweat and machine oil; a portable fan on a table in the corner did little to alleviate the heat. Mrs. Tait's aide, a furtive, narrow-shouldered old man who seemed as suited to the room as a hermit to his cave, was bent over one of the two silent machines, its immense glass-and-metal top lifted open like the hood of a stalled automobile.

"Oh, no," said Carol. "Is it broken again?" The second copier, she knew, had been out of commission for months; replacement parts seemed to be permanently "on order."

The man had looked up as she came in but was now bent back to the machine, tentatively prying at something with a screwdriver. He re-minded Carol of the witch in *Hansel and Gretel,* about to be swallowed up in the oven. "She was fine until an hour ago," he muttered, "but when I came back from my break—" He strained, grimaced; something came away inside with a clank of metal. "Well, she's on the fritz now, all right." Standing, he wiped his hands and regarded her suspi-ciously. "You catch anybody coming in here while I was gone?"

"No one I saw." Sighing, she filled out a mimeographed voucher and left the book atop a pile of others to be copied, paper markers dangling from them like prize ribbons.

"It's not your lucky day," she told the young man at the table, handing him back his money. "Both machines are broken down. Those copies of yours won't be ready till Monday at the earliest."

He cursed softly. "Oh, great! I'm leaving town Sunday morning, and I won't be back till the end of summer."

"Well, if you like," she whispered, as to a disconsolate child, "I could copy what you need and mail it to you with an invoice."

He looked up with surprise. "Really?"

"Sure. We do it for people all the time. After all, it's what you're paying for. You ought to get *something* for your money."

He eyed her appreciatively, as if, despite what she'd just told him, she had offered to do him a personal favor. "Yes," he said, his voice low, "that would be terrific. But you know, I'm not technically a subscriber. I'm here on an academic discount. Does that matter?"

"That's all right. Just tell me where you want it sent."

He folded the pad back to a fresh page. "It's an RFD out in Jersey," he said, writing it down. "I don't know the zip. It's such a weird little out-of-the-way place I'm not even sure they have one."

She felt a touch of envy. She'd be right here next week; he'd be off in the country. "Sounds nice to get away to."

"Yes, it's like going to an earlier century, completely cut off from the world. I can't believe I'll be out there this time Sunday." He smiled as he tore off the page and handed it to her. "I'll probably get culture shock when I come back."

RFD 1, Box 63, she read. *Gilead, New Jersey*. She handed it back to him. "You forgot to write your name."

He laughed, then looked sheepish as several nearby readers peered angrily up from their books. "Jeremy," he whispered, writing it down. "Jeremy Freirs." He pointed his finger at her like a pistol. "It's the kind of name that ought to have 'Occult Detective' after it, don't you think? Once upon a time it was Freireicher, I'm told, but somehow it got trimmed." He paused. "And what's yours?"

This time she hesitated only a moment, though she knew that this person, unlike little old Rosie, could potentially do her harm. "Carol Conklin. From an equally out-of-the-way place in Pennsylvania."

God, why had she volunteered all that? What was the matter with her? It wasn't as if this man was going to call her; by Sunday he'd be far away. And why would she even *want* him to call? He wasn't her type at all.

He was looking up at her with a little half smile. "Are you one of those farm girls I keep hearing about?"

She was wondering what sort of wise-guy answer he expected when, from the corner of her eye, she saw movement. At the front desk Mrs. Tait, the supervisor, thin and turkey-necked, with dyed blond hair, was staring in her direction. As Carol turned toward her, she made a gesture of impatience.

"Uh-oh," Carol whispered. "I've got to go."

He looked disappointed. "Well, anyway, here," he said, thrusting the sheet with his name and address at her. "You'll need this."

She was already preparing her story and trying to look busy as she approached the front desk. "He needed some research material," she explained, holding up the paper he'd given her. "He'll be away and wanted me to copy it for him."

"Fine," the supervisor said, not at all interested. "Let him fill out a request form before he goes. Now put that paper in your desk and come back out here; there's lots you should be doing. You don't get paid to stand around flirting with the patrons."

Blushing and annoyed, Carol deliberately avoided looking toward the young man's table as she hurried across the floor, past the magazine racks and reading section toward the office in the back. It was empty except for Mr. Brown, in charge of acquisitions, who looked up guiltily from his *Post* as she came in. He smiled when he saw who it was and continued to watch her, baggy eyes glittering with more than friendliness, as she slipped the sheet of paper into a clipboard she kept on her desk. She had suddenly begun to feel very resentful of Voorhis, of having to take orders from everybody in the place, and of the job itself, which had spoiled the one chance she'd had in—God, in *months*, it seemed, to talk with a man who seemed frankly interested in her. She felt the great grey mass of the library building overhead, a crushing weight bearing down on her shoulders.

Emerging from the office, she saw with surprise that the young man was gone; his seersucker jacket no longer hung over the back of the chair, and the desk was empty save for three or four library books that someone on the staff—probably Carol herself—would soon be replacing on the shelves. She felt a surge of anger, almost of betrayal; he had simply packed up and left, without even saying goodbye. She'd been no more than a servant to him, like a waitress or a clerk; just someone to mail him some research material. What an idiot she'd been to believe, even for a minute, that he was interested in her. And to think she'd actually gotten yelled at for it.

She was passing the high shelves and narrow aisles of the special collections, just beyond the card files, when she heard someone softly call her name. She turned. There he was, standing just within one of the aisles, like a fugitive loitering in an alley, reluctant to set foot beyond it. His jacket was tucked under one arm, his book bag by his side, as if he were about to make an escape. Grinning, he motioned for her to join him.

"Carol," he whispered—it was somewhat flattering to hear him speak to her so familiarly—"I was just thinking, since you, seem to have a country background and all . . ." She was about to correct him, she hadn't meant to give him that impression, but then she saw that he'd obviously rehearsed the next part. "I thought you might be interested in the film I'll be showing tonight. It's all about growing up on a farm."

"You're showing a film?"

"Yes, I teach down at the New School, one night a week. 'The Cinema of Magic.' Tonight's the last class. We're going to look at a film called *Les Jeux Interdits.*"

"Pardon?" He had switched languages so effortlessly that she hadn't followed him.

He leaned closer, as if imparting a password. *"Forbidden Games."*

"I've never even heard of it," whispered Carol. "Is it in French?"

He nodded impatiently, and she was afraid she'd sounded stupid. "It takes place on a farm during the Second World War," he said.

"Two little children form a secret club. They collect the bodies of animals—a beetle, a lizard, a mole—and bury them with elaborate magic rituals, using tombstones stolen from the local cemetery. The whole world is viewed through their eyes."

"It sounds interesting," whispered Carol. She was getting nervous about all the time this was taking; she was supposed to be reporting back for more work.

"Well, look," he said, "why don't you come tonight? You might enjoy it. And I can get you in free." He smiled. "Everybody else has already paid seven bucks for the privilege."

"Well, yes, that might be fun," she said hurriedly, thinking of the empty night ahead. "I could just walk in?"

"Sure. It starts at eight. Room three-ten, at the end of the hall. Just follow the crowd."

"You know, I just might. Only tonight's my late night. I don't get *out* of here till eight." She wondered if she might be sounding too eager. Unthinkable to let him see she had nothing to do.

He shook his head. "Oh, that's no problem. We never begin exactly on time. And the New School's what, only ten blocks south of here? That shouldn't take you long."

"I'll try to make it," she said. "I really will." She wasn't exactly sure where the school was, but she knew she could ask someone on the way. "Listen, I've got to go. They're waiting for me at the main desk."

"Oh, yes, of course," he said quickly. "I've got to go too." He slung the red bag over his shoulder. "Well, then . . ." He shrugged. "I guess I'll be looking for you tonight." Without waiting for an answer or giving her time to change her mind, he turned and headed toward the door.

She took another twenty-minute break. Afterward, allowed to remain downstairs by the grace or mere inattentiveness of Mrs. Tait, Carol found it hard to concentrate on her work—not that logging a stack of new acquisitions into the card file near the center of the floor required much thought. She was thinking about the evening ahead, wishing she had a chance to go home and put on something a bit more flattering than the blouse of her sister's she was wearing today. It was always that way: the important people came along when you were wearing hand-me-downs. Not that this would be a real date, of course, but it was the closest thing she'd have to one all weekend, and she'd have preferred to look nice for it. Her life had suddenly grown more complicated, richer in possibilities, a train back on the tracks and moving at last, building speed; between Rosie and Jeremy this had been a very special day, and she felt sure there'd be more like it ahead. When Mrs.

Tait reassigned her to the bookcase beneath the south window to arrange a bound and dusty set of *Natural History,* she took advantage of the solitude and lost herself in daydreams.

At last, knees aching, she stood up and smoothed down her skirt. Before her, just beyond the window, lay the garden, always wilder-looking at this level, a cool and silent world enclosed in glass and brick, the young trees swaying somewhere overhead in an unheard breeze; and wilder still at this hour of the afternoon, when surrounding buildings blocked the sunlight. It was like looking into the darkness of the woods; you could almost forget where you were.

And then, with a momentary chill, she remembered the small black shapes she had seen from the floor above. Rising on tiptoe, she leaned over the tops of the shelves and peered outside.

Yes, there they were, near the wall below the window, deep in shadow and half covered by earth. There was something familiar about the things. She squinted into the darkness, then gasped at what she'd recognized: the charred remains of some small animal.

A hand touched her shoulder. "I thought I sent you upstairs," said Miss Elms, the assistant supervisor, standing beside her.

"I had to return a book down here, and Mrs. Tait said I might as well see that these magazines—"

She paused. Her eye had been caught by a reflection in the window-pane. For an instant she thought she'd glimpsed a little pink face peering at her from the dim light of the hallway across the room. Could it be Rosie? Had the little man come back for her? She turned. The outer doors went *swish-swish* and the hallway was empty.

"Well, don't stand around here all day," said Miss Elms. "You seem to have this set put away, and there's a dozen other things you could be doing."

"I was just trying to get a look at what's out there," said Carol. She pointed toward the garden. "See? Below the thornbush?"

The woman adjusted her spectacles and glared suspiciously through the window. "Damned kids!" She shook her head. "How the hell did they *get* back there, anyway? That gate's supposed to be locked." She let the glasses fall around her neck. "Looks like someone's had themself a chicken dinner."

"Chicken?" The relief showed in Carol's face.

"Hell, yes," said Miss Elms. "There's a barbecue place over on Eighth Avenue. You know the one I mean." She checked her watch. "Now how about giving a hand up front? They'll be lining up with their books in a minute or two."

Carol followed her toward the desk. Behind them, unheard, the wind in the courtyard grew, tossing the vines and scattering leaves from the young trees. Something white danced past the window, blown from be neath the bush where it had lain: a clump of delicate white feathers stained red at the tip.

The sky is red and gold above the water, the water glows a darker red, and in each swims the pale shape of a half-moon.

Strolling southward along the river, the battered leather briefcase tucked tight beneath his arm and time like a toy in his hands, the Old One pauses just long enough to appreciate the symmetry: a half-moon in the early evening sky, its counterpart reflected in the ripples on the water—two halves of a shattered eggshell, with no chance it will ever be restored.

Here, indeed, is a sign, a token of the Moghu'vool. Soon the egg will be broken, the beast awake.

White shapes plunge and scream in the air above him; up and down the waterfront, soot-blackened rooftops echo with the sound. He turns and continues southward, smiling, heedless of the mournful cries. His legs are short and his progress slow, but he is in no hurry.

Shadows are advancing on the city to the left, and tiny lamplit windows are beginning to stand out on the dark shapes of the buildings. Higher windows still catch the reflected light. To the right the river glistens where golden columns of sunbeams pierce a band of cloud. Unseen in the distance, yet so palpably close he hears every breath, the community of farmers out beyond the low hills is now assembling for the planting, dutifully observing the customs of the clan, reciting their silly prayers, muttering hosannas to their silly god. Closer still, within his sight, silhouettes of oil tanks and factories rise along the farther shore, while above them the moon hovers just out of reach, alien, serene, and growing brighter with each passing minute.

A pair of lovers catches the Old One's eye, clasped obscenely on a slab of concrete above the water; then the ungainly figure of a jogger, and a small white dog that capers on the grass. He would like to lure it out onto the highway . . . But now, he knows, is not the time. He has a more important task ahead, and a destination waiting: imperative that he be hidden in the shadows when the man and the woman emerge from what will be their second meeting.

The woman—what a find she is, the greedy little bitch! It has been painstaking work, opening that library job to her and easing her into the slot, but it has been worth the effort. She is perfect. Perhaps (he smiles) he should send a contribution to the Convent of St. Agnes!

Of course, that man-crazy roommate may prove a problem . . . But
that is no great matter, in view of what he has accomplished today. Initial contact has been made, and the interview has gone according to
plan. The players have been chosen, the great wheels set in motion.

Swinging his briefcase there on the sidewalk, with the Friday-night
traffic rushing past him in a blur, he laughs aloud, an old man's high-
pitched cackle. "Eeny meeny miny mo" indeed! How easy it has been!

Freirs looked for the fifth or sixth time at his watch and at last yielded
to a bitterness he could no longer argue away. A quarter after eight,
and the thin redhead from the library hadn't shown up. Probably she'd
only been humoring him . . . But damn it all, she'd really seemed to like
him; and her interest had been all the more exciting because she'd
clearly been at pains to disguise it—unlike the young women in his
classes, whose seductive manner made him feel so old, even when their
ages were the same as his. The girl's very thinness had been alluring, as
if by some magic it could compensate for his own excessive bulk. Tonight's final screening had seemed like the perfect way to meet her
again. Yet apparently he'd misjudged her, she hadn't shown after all,
and the brightly lit double-size classroom was almost filled. Few of the
faces out there meant much to him. He was going to be in a bad mood
tonight.

Midway across the room one of the more ass-kissing students was
standing officiously by the light switches near the door, waiting like a
little soldier for his signal. Farther back, beside the pair of sixteen-
millimeter projectors, the T-shirted projectionist was eyeing him impatiently. Well, there was nothing he could do about it now; he
couldn't hold things up any longer. There'd always be a few latecom-
ers, of course, slipping in noisily and unapologetically half an hour or
more into the film—fully half the class were art students from Parsons
with no sense of time—but if he waited any longer the punctual ones,
the ones who wrote the long, carefully typed papers and raised their
hands in class and got themselves in a sweat over grades, would rightly
begin getting irritated. Already the students were beginning to forget
where they were, the conversation around him growing in volume.
Looking to the boy by the light switches, he gave a short nod.

The room vanished in darkness pierced only by a cone of white light
whose base was on the screen. Dust motes and cigarette smoke, for-

merly invisible, drifted through it like ectoplasm from the spirit world. Freirs turned and was feeling his way toward the nearest wall, preparing to stand for the first part of the film, then maybe slip out in the middle and read some journals he'd brought in his bag, when a soft, husky voice whispered urgently, "Mr. Freirs!" Donna, several rows to the right, curly-haired and full-breasted, her wide, heavily made-up eyes discernible even in the darkness, was gesturing at him and pointing to a seat next to her. One of the silver gypsylike earrings she always wore caught the projector light. There were one or two like her in every class: easy, aggressive, ultimately more possessive than one might have thought. He seldom let it get that far.

"Mr. Freirs!" she said again. She waved in invitation.

Ah, well, the thin girl from the library wasn't coming, and Donna was nice too. Kind of exotic, in fact, and by no means dumb. Careful not to stumble over the rows of protruding feet, he threaded his way toward her through the darkness.

The woods were a patchwork of shadow and light. Beside her flowed the river, sunshine dappling the reeds. Wide-eyed, obviously dazed, the little girl stumbled down an uncertain path, following the riverbank as it skirted the edge of the forest. In her arms she clutched something small, white, and limp—a teddy bear, perhaps, or some other nursery toy.

The angle shifted, and Carol leaned forward to see. This was no toy. In her arms the girl was clutching a dead dog.

No one around Carol seemed surprised. They looked amused, in fact, or passive, or bored. Several were whispering to their neighbors, barely watching the film, and down the row to her left an unshaven youth was slouched back in his seat, his eyes already closed. The woman one row in front appeared to be taking notes, but when, after five minutes, she'd failed to look up, Carol realized that she was writing a letter.

The room was hot from body heat and foggy with cigarette smoke. Because the floor was perfectly flat and the screen too low, it was hard to read the subtitles from the bridge chairs in the back; people's heads kept getting in the way.

Carol hadn't dared leave the library until work ended, and Jeremy must have misjudged the time it would take her, because even with good directions she'd arrived here nearly twenty minutes late. She was already beginning to regret that she'd come; she couldn't find Jeremy in the darkness and was feeling uncomfortable and alone.

On the screen the little girl and a young peasant boy were performing a kind of funeral ceremony for the dead dog, which they'd buried in the earthen floor of an abandoned mill. Placing a primitive wooden cross atop the mound, the boy clambered up to the loft and, reaching into an owl's nest built high in the rafters, removed the tiny body of a mole. This he buried beside the other grave; that way, he said, the dog would not be lonesome. When the little girl contributed her rosary beads, he draped them solemnly over the cross.

Watching distractedly, Carol still felt herself touched by the scene; it awakened memories of her own childhood, and of the secret religious rituals she'd enacted without quite knowing why.

The rest of the film, unfortunately, was dominated by the adults, a slack-jawed, clownish lot. They were caricatures, all of them, and impossible to care for. Carol's back began to ache from leaning forward in her seat, and she found her attention wandering even more. Down the row the unshaven youth was still asleep, the film's shifting light playing over his features like the shadows of a dream. This same light was reflected in the glasses of a stout young man several seats farther ahead, sitting bolt upright near the wall, his leg swinging impatiently back and forth. Was it Jeremy? Carol strained to see him more clearly, but in the darkness it was hard to be sure. For a moment, as if responding to her thoughts, he seemed to turn toward her, though his eyes were concealed by the glare from off the screen. But then a dark-haired woman sitting beside him leaned toward him to whisper something in his ear, and he turned away.

In the end, like lovers, the two children were parted, and Carol felt the customary lump form in her throat. The boy kicked over the crosses, trampled the mounds, and hid the rosary forever in the owl's nest, while, rigid with dread, the girl was led off like a prisoner and lost amid the crowds and confusion of a refugee center somewhere far away. Until this moment the story had been set within the rural isolation of a farm, and it had been easy to forget that, beyond the cornfields and the pastures, a modern world was speeding toward destruction.

She looked back at the young man near the wall—yes, she was sure now; it was Jeremy—in time to see him whisper something to his dark-haired companion. The woman turned to face him, smiled, and whispered something back. Her hand touched his shoulder familiarly. Carol felt a stab of disappointment so intense it made her catch her breath and look away. She saw that she'd been duped into coming here; she'd been a fool to have expected anything else. So much for her daydreams!

Moments later, at the front of the room, the screen was filled wit

Fin, like a gate slamming shut upon the characters' lives. By the time the overhead light came on, they had already receded into memory.

But Carol herself was already gone; she had gotten to her feet and slipped out the door before the film had ended.

She'd arrived at the New School with light still coloring the western sky. Departing now, she stepped outside and found herself in darkness broken only by the melancholy glow of streetlamps and a scattering of windows lit behind drawn curtains. Above the chimneys and the ventilator ducts a chip of moon looked small and far away.

After the heat and glare of the classroom, the cool night air with its solitude, its silence, brought a kind of relief. She walked listlessly, though, weighed down by a sudden feeling of fatigue and, beneath it, a dull unspoken loneliness. Several couples passed her as she made her way up the block—couples her own age, bound for a party, a disco, or a bar—and something in their voices made her feel painfully old. She was halfway to Sixth Avenue when, passing the doorway of an apartment house, she caught the smell of garlic, tomatoes, and cheese and remembered that she'd not yet eaten dinner. Her hunger had been forgotten for the duration of the film; now it returned with a rush.

Normally she'd have stopped at the all-night *bodega* at the end of her street to buy a package of spaghetti or a box of rice, but tonight the idea of cooking in that cramped, steamy little kitchen, with the ever-present roaches crawling just behind the stove, was too dispiriting to consider. When she reached the avenue, she paused. Tired as she felt, it was still too early to go home.

Home, in fact, seemed a rather dismal prospect, the more she thought about it. Rochelle would be up there with her new boyfriend tonight, the boisterous one who seemed so proud of his body and left coarse, dark curls in the sink and tub. The kitchen would be piled high with pots and dirty plates. The TV would be on—loudly, no doubt—but almost totally ignored; the two of them would be far more interested in each other. No doubt, too, they'd resent any interruption, though Rochelle would be more resentful than the boyfriend; he'd made one pass at Carol already. The television belonged to Rochelle and so did, in effect, the living room itself, since this was where she slept. Carol would be confined to her bedroom, trying to read or write letters above the sound of the TV's canned laughter and the less easily ignored laughter of the lovers.

Holding that image firmly in mind, she turned left on the avenue and headed toward the lights and crowds of Eighth Street, resolved that something good would happen to her before the night was through.

The night is growing dark now, but his mood is darker still. His wrinkled face is frozen in a scowl. From the shadowy recesses of an alley across the street he has seen the woman leave alone.

Something has gone wrong. Where is the man? The two of them are supposed to be together.

But perhaps it may still be arranged.

Stealthily he pads from the alley and into the street, moving toward the entrance of the school.

In the classroom on the third floor, Freirs and nearly a dozen of his students, some habitual sycophants, some who genuinely liked him, were still gathered near the front desk. After the film a far larger mass of them had surrounded him like a mob of petitioners, a few waving their late reports at him, their excuses loud and earnest, others eager to get their papers back and quarrel over the grade. It had taken him nearly fifteen minutes to get them sorted out and, as it was the final class, to write down the addresses of the students whose papers he would have to mail back over the summer. His red book bag was stuffed once more with work.

Now only the most loyal were left, clustered around him at the front of the room. Donna was among them, pretending to be interested in the topic at hand but fooling no one. Freirs took advantage of every opportunity to catch her eye; she was the best-looking thing in sight. "Listen," he was saying, half seated on the desk in a manner that allowed him to take the weight off his feet but still keep his head on a level with theirs, "a lot of you seem to think that superstition disappeared from the human scene somewhere between the talkies and TV." His eyes swept the group, daring them to look away. "I only wish it were true, but it's just not so. I mean, think hard. How many buildings have you seen lately with a thirteenth floor?"

One of the younger men smiled—a good-natured longhair, or so he'd always seemed, who all this semester seemed to have enjoyed feeding Freirs his best cues. Everyone liked a good straight man. "Oh, come on, Mr. Freirs, that thirteenth-floor stuff is just a joke nowadays."

"Believe me," said Freirs, "it's no joke. There are people in this country, even today, who think it'll rain if they pray hard enough. They're out there right now, happy as can be, brewing their love potions, warding off the evil eye, setting traps for demons. They tell time by the stars, just like their grandfathers did, and they still plant corn by moonlight." It was the Poroths he was thinking of, Sarr's gloomy frown, Deborah naked under that severe black dress.

The student was still regarding him with amused skepticism, probably putting on an act for Donna and the rest. Or maybe it just seemed funny to him that a pudgy city boy like Freirs should talk knowingly of old-time country ways. Freirs dug deep into his wallet and pulled forth a dollar bill. "You know," he said, "I can't resist this little test." He nodded to the younger man. "You're obviously one of those rare beings we all hear about, a totally rational man, and so I want to give you this dollar as a gift." He waved it theatrically in the air. Several of the onloookers turned to one another and grinned. What was old Freirs up to now? "All I want in return," he continued, "is a simple little note, signed and dated, selling me, for one dollar"—he leaned forward—"your immortal soul."

The others laughed, and Donna managed to get in a slightly too enthusiastic "Oh, Mr. Freirs!" The younger man eyed the money, smiling uneasily, but made no move to comply. "You want it in writing, huh?"

Freirs nodded. "That's all. Just a scrap of paper with your name on it, and the words, 'This is to certify that I sell my soul to Mr. Jeremy Freirs . . . forever.' "

The student laughed but shook his head. "Why take a chance?" he said, shrugging.

"Exactly! It's Pascal's wager in reverse." Freirs stood, looking flushed, and stuffed the dollar back into his pocket. He turned to the rest of the group. "So you see, kiddies, the old fears die hard. We're not out of the woods yet."

His thoughts were on the farm again, out there in the night across the river. Behind the smiling faces of his students, darkness waited at the windows like a living presence. "And now," he said, suddenly tired, "maybe it's time we adjourned for the summer. I've got a lot of packing to do."

"Hey, anybody up for a drink?" the long-haired youth asked brightly, as if it had just occurred to him. He glanced quickly around the circle, lingering an extra second on Donna.

Several of the others voiced an interest in going. Donna remained silent—leaving herself free, Freirs realized. He wondered how he could go off with her without making it too obvious. "Now if any of you still have problems with your papers," he said, "deciphering my handwriting or disagreeing with my comments, we can—Uh-oh, what's going on here?"

The lights in the classroom blinked once, then again. After the second time, only the light directly above them came back on. Freirs saw Donna reach nervously in his direction, then draw back her hand.

"Sorry, you folks. Gotta clear this room."

They turned. The voice, wheezy with age, had come from the shadows at the other side of the room. Dimly they could make out a small figure standing outlined in the doorway, silhouetted against the light from the hall. He appeared to be dressed in a shabby grey uniform several sizes too large. There was a pushbroom in his hand; he was holding it before him like a weapon.

"What's the rush?" said Freirs. "We've always stayed this late before."

The figure in the doorway seemed to shrug. "End of the year," he said softly. "Gotta clear the room."

Donna's lip curled. "Boy! These goddamned janitors think they own the school." She glanced at Freirs for support, but he was reaching for his jacket.

"Oh, well," he said, "I guess we've been here long enough." Gathering up a few remaining papers and stuffing them into the bag, he began moving toward the door.

Awkwardly the others filed out, brushing past the small grey figure, who had turned away and was busily dragging through the doorway a large brown trash barrel almost as big as he was. Its wheels squeaked unpleasantly behind them.

Outside, in the light, Freirs stood slouching in silence by the hall elevator, but several of the younger students headed for the stairs. "Come on," called one, "it's just two flights." With a sigh Freirs straightened up and moved toward the stairway. The ones remaining followed him—all except Donna, who reached worriedly to her ear. "Damn!" she muttered. Her left earring was gone.

The others had already started down. The hall was silent. Frowning, she searched the floor around her, then turned back toward the classroom. From its shadowed interior came a faint irregular squeaking, then silence again. Hesitating a moment, she strode through the doorway and disappeared inside.

"Do you mind putting on a light in here?" Her voice echoed in the hall. "I'm trying to find—"

There was a thud, a high-pitched little laugh, and then a protracted series of cracking sounds, as of the splintering of wood. Moments later came another sound: the crunch of compressed paper, as from an object being stuffed into a wastebasket.

With a snap the final light went off, and then a small grey figure emerged from the darkness pushing a laden trash barrel, its wheel squeaking rhythmically as he steered it down the hall. To this noise, as if softly in counterpoint, he was whistling a tuneless little song.

Outside, the group had begun to disperse. "There's no sense in wait-ing," said one of the women. "She's certainly not up there." The others followed her gaze; she was staring at the darkened windows on the third floor.

"Right," said a young man. "She must've gone on ahead."

They turned to Freirs; he looked puzzled and somewhat annoyed. "Well," he said at last, shrugging, "tell her when you see her that if she wants to talk about her paper, she'd better call me first thing tomor-row, because she won't be able to reach me after that." Slinging the bag over his shoulder, he nodded goodbye. "Maybe I'll be seeing some of you next fall. Have a pleasant summer."

Two of the students walked westward with him as far as Seventh Av-enue; but then, as Freirs turned south, they repeated their goodbyes and went their separate ways.

Smiling at what he's performed back there in the darkness, he slips from the doorway of the school, averting his face from the glare of the streetlamps. Beyond the glare, half hidden by the city's fumes, the night's first constellations glimmer faintly to the east, while before him, in the northern sky, Draco sweeps sinuously round an invisible pole star. To the west there are no signs at all save a lonely, broken moon.

He has no need for signs now. He knows where the stars tremble cold and unseen overhead, and where they did so fifty centuries ago and will do so five thousand years hence. No matter that the Milky Way is grey with smog, or that lamplight hides the familiar shapes of Gemini, Capella, and the Lynx. He knows just where to find them; knows, as well, their real and ancient names.

And he knows the land below them, knows it as a general knows ter-rain that's ripe for conquest. Far across the river, where the sun has disappeared, lie the dominions of the unsuspecting world. Beyond the dark horizon, men and women fight and scheme and struggle. Others toil in a field like figures in a biblical tableau, chanting as they work. He can almost hear their song.

They will be his special playthings, these farmers. They will suffer
first. His man Freirs—his fat, unwitting tool—will see to that. Soon,
soon . . .

Swift as death he moves along the block in their direction, noting, as
he hurries across the avenue, a paunchy, rumpled figure with a book
bag and a seersucker jacket—Freirs himself, one block farther south,
plodding gamely toward their common destination, unaware that he is
headed anywhere but home. One avenue west of him, nearer the water,
the old man turns southward too, jauntily swinging his briefcase, already eager to play his next part.

He pauses once in his journey to cock his head and listen for the
voices. Before him the sky is stained red with neon, but to the west it
shimmers with the whiteness of the moon. As he passes between the
buildings he can see dim lights on the river, the distant shore, and,
above it, the places where the stars will soon come into view. The stage
is being set; soon the fools will get what they deserve. Let them sing
while they can!

"Scramble thee, scratch thee,
Gillycorn Hill.
If Mouse don't catch thee,
Mole he will."

In the moonlight the women were planting corn. They labored side by
side, the seven of them, and in the gathering darkness they looked
much alike. All were young, all married; all but one had borne a child.
Their long hair hung down their backs loose and unadorned, but their
bodies were concealed, neck to naked ankle, beneath dresses of homespun black. From a distance only the burlap sacks they carried at their
sides were visible, and their pale white faces floating like will-o'-the-
wisps over the empty field.

Ahead of them walked the seven men, treading stiffly in their
starched white shirts, black vests, and high black leather shoes. They
moved together in silence, grave of expression, faces clean-shaven but
for the fringe of beard below each chin. As in a close-order military
drill they carried long wooden staffs sharpened at both ends, and with
every stride the men stabbed downward, making holes an inch deep
and a yard apart in the freshly turned earth.

Behind them the line of women reached deep in their bags and, stooping gracefully to drop three kernels into each hole, chanted another measure of the counting rhyme.

> *"Hide thee, haste thee,*
> *Gillycorn Hill . . ."*

Standing, they pushed loose soil over the holes with a scrape of their bare feet, then moved on.

Suddenly one of them laughed aloud—unaffected, childlike laughter that carried through the evening air. "I'm sure glad I didn't see what I just stepped on!"

The others giggled, causing a momentary break in the chant. "Oh, Deborah," said the one beside her, "there's nothin' out here but a few night crawlers, and I've been steppin' on them ever since the moon came up. I've just said nothin' about it." She took up the chant:

> *"If Mole don't taste thee,*
> *Worm he will."*

At the end of the row another woman stood and wiped her brow. "You'd best be right," she said. "I don't fancy the notion of tripping over a corn snake out here. 'Twouldn't do to have that kind of scare— not in my condition." She patted her distended stomach.

"Just listen to her!" Deborah laughed again. "Lotte Sturtevant's afraid her baby'll be born with a split tongue!"

"*Deborah!*" Her husband whirled to face her, eyes blazing angrily in the moonlight. "Have you forgotten yourself, woman? These good people came out here to *help* us."

He stood a little taller than the other men, wide shoulders tapering to a willow-thin waist, and despite the severity of his expression he was clearly a shade younger than the rest. His voice was stern and very deep, the voice of an Old Testament lawgiver, but it softened in one last urgent whisper: *"Please!"*

Just as abruptly he turned and caught up with the others; none of them had looked back. "My apologies, Brother Joram," he said to the older man who walked beside him. "She meant no harm. We both give thanks you're with us tonight."

"No need for thanks, Sarr." The man jabbed his pole into the earth and withdrew it with an expert twist. "We do what the Lord gives us to do. 'They helped every one his neighbor, and every one said to his brother, Be of good courage.'"

"Amen," said the others in unison, without looking up from their work, and the younger man chimed in quickly, "Amen." Behind them the women continued their chant, but more softly now, for they were listening. Their voices were no louder than the chirping of the crickets.

From a distance came the muffled sound of other voices where the old men had gathered at the edge of the field, their faces illuminated by a low cottonwood fire. It was their task to tend it, and from time to time a shower of sparks signaled that they'd heaped another log upon the flames. Nearby a cluster of children stood in dutiful guard over a bag of seed bigger than themselves. The fields, they knew, were filled with thieves: birds, and mice, and hungry yellow corn worms. To lose a single kernel meant bad portent for the crops.

Farther off the windows of the little farmhouse were ablaze with light, and from the kitchen, where the older womenfolk were busy with their special preparations, there came the sound of voices raised in hymn. Between the farmhouse and the field jutted the squat shape of the low cinderblock outbuilding, its windows dark. Close behind it, like an impenetrably black wall, rose the encircling woods.

Suddenly the air contained a new voice, a low and distant rumbling from the east. At first it had been barely distinguishable from the wind in the trees; now it was growing deeper, in lazy waves of sound, like the drone of some gigantic insect.

In the fields the women fell silent. The older men kept to their steady pace, eyes pointedly averted toward the ground, but a few of the younger ones surreptitiously scanned the horizon and found at last some small red winking lights that climbed among the stars. Miles above the woods and fields a shape like a great silver crucifix was streaking across the planet, heading westward.

The women stirred themselves. "We've got corn to plant," said the pregnant one. She peered into the darkened furrows at her feet, searching for a place to drop the seed. The others again took up the counting rhyme, but Deborah stared wistfully at the moving lights. Each Friday night the jet passed overhead, a jarring reminder of the world they'd shut out. "Wonder where it's going," she said, almost to herself. Her words were lost amid the chanting, the smell of moist black humus, the ancient and laborious routine. There was work to do, and her husband might be watching; she turned back to the corn seeds and the earth.

Ahead of her one of the men continued to gaze awestruck at the eastern sky. "So many stars up there," he remarked to his companions, "and so little light down here! You're a hard worker, Sarr, and a good God-fearing man, but I sure do wish you'd been ready when the rest of us were. Leastways we had a moon we could see by."

Poroth peered dolefully upward, aware that the other was right. Just above the trees the half moon reminded him of something damaged or broken, but the elders had assured him that, on the contrary, i' was a most favorable omen for the crops: waxing larger day by day, ' presaged an abundant growth and harvest. "It wasn't possible to ǥ these fields plowed by the appointed time," he said, hurrying to keep pace with the others. He remembered the weeks of backbreaking labor, struggling with a balky tractor rented from the Co-operative. "A month ago the ground we're walking on was covered by scrub and trees. This land hadn't been worked for seven years."

"We know that, Sarr," said the first man. "We know what this farm means to you, and what it must've cost. We respect you for it. 'Tisn't every man takes to the land so late." Coming to the edge of a row, he turned in unison with the rest and reversed his staff, using the alternate tip. "You're bound to make a few mistakes at first, but with the Lord's help you'll come out all right in the end. That's why we're here tonight, and why Brother Joram made his wife come along. She's sure to bring good portent."

There it was again, the omnipresent reverence for signs. A pregnant woman ensured good crops; a widow might bring disaster. Poroth knew that a cousin of his, Minna Buckhalter, was working in the kitchen side by side with women twice her age, his own long-widowed mother among them. Though Minna was strong enough for the outdoor work, she was considered unfit to bury seeds because last month she'd laid a husband in the earth.

Were the Brethren superstitious fools, then? Poroth didn't care. He'd had more education than the rest, and he'd lived for a while in the place that called itself the modern world—yet he was a believer, his faith unshaken. Fertile women meant fertile crops; their long straight hair meant long straight stalks of corn. Primitive symbolism, perhaps, but it worked; he was certain of it. Jets flew high above the earth, where angels played; there was room up there for both. Thunder was a collision of molecules, and also the voice of God; both might be true. The Lord was in His heaven, whatever name you called Him, as assuredly as there were demons here below, whatever faces they wore. Him you worshiped, them you wrestled; it was as simple as that. The only trick was not to lose your faith. The nature of the belief didn't matter, Poroth knew; what mattered was its intensity. He had a high regard for superstition.

"God's my witness," he said to the other men, "I know we've had our differences, but that's all past. Deborah and I are going to make you proud of us, you wait and see. You won't recognize this place!"

In the distance, light spilled from the kitchen doorway of the farmhouse; moments later came the slam of the screen door, echoing across the field.

"By Michaelmas," he went on, "I'll have every acre planted, clear back to the stream." He smiled at the thought. "You wait and see. This land's going to look like the Garden of Eden!"

The one called Joram paused and looked his way. If he was smiling, the darkness concealed it. "Mark you, Brother Sarr," he said softly, "the Gospels speak of another garden." They knew he meant Gethsemane.

From beyond the fire came the faint clanging of a bell. Joram held up his hand. "It's ready," he said. "Come."

They followed him from the field.

The Village was alive tonight. The shoe stores and overpriced boutiques that lined both sides of Eighth Street were already closed, their windows dim, but the crowds were out in force and the food stands and novelty shops were packed. Comic T-shirts, zodiac posters, pizza slices, frozen yogurt: there was something for everyone, and everyone had a gimmick on display. Carol passed a fat girl in dirt-farmer overalls; a goateed black with a gypsy headdress and an earring; a young couple with leather pants and shiny blue streaks in their hair, the girl wearing a wristband ringed with spikes.

Perhaps it was her mood, but she found herself disliking almost everyone she saw. It did no good to narrow her eyes and view the world through a veil of lashes; the faces still swam at her out of the shadows, only now they were distorted, as in a waking dream. From a doorway a dark figure made explicit sucking sounds and hissed something at her in Spanish; a group of heavy-set blond boys staggered past, football types from the suburbs, drunk already and raining blows on the one in front, nearly shouldering her off the sidewalk. Dodging a black selling incense and a party of teenagers arguing where to go next, she slipped into a bookshop just off Sixth Avenue and killed some time by leafing through the fashion magazines. They had foreign editions of *Vogue* here, and photo annuals from Japan. Glossy sullen-faced women in shiny dark lipstick pouted across the pages. She tried picturing herself as some of them, and for the first time the idea didn't seem so farfetched. St. Agnes's seemed far in the past; or maybe it was just the prospect of more money to spend and her close brush with the young man at the library.

Leaving these fantasies on the rack, in magazines selling for five dollars or more, she journeyed back out onto the sidewalk, up the block, and around the corner to the relative quiet of MacDougal Street. It was less noisy here; ahead lay the darkness and trees of Washington Square, as if she'd come to the edge of the city. It was time she got some food in her.

That was not going to be easy, unless she was willing to stand at a counter eating vegetable tacos or falafel or a greasy wedge of pizza. She had only seven dollars in her wallet, with perhaps two more in change. This might well have to last her till Monday; Rosie's expense check was useless for the moment, and—if her supermarket refused to cash it—would remain so all weekend. Her roommate never had any money either; she got men to pay for everything. It was an arrangement that, at this point, Carol would have welcomed.

With a hand on her pocketbook and an eye peeled for strangers she wandered farther south, lingering a minute or two before a shop off the park, where she stared pensively at a slinky blue dress in the window and tried to imagine herself in it. Afterward she considered a more modest transaction—treating herself to cappuccino and a croissant in one of the coffeehouses along Bleecker Street—but a dollar eighty-five seemed a foolish price to pay for a cup of coffee. Besides, all the seats were taken in every place she passed; couples waited morosely by the open doorways, peering inside for vacancies, while others sprawled over tables set up cafe-style on the sidewalk. Movement here was only partially impeded, but farther west the sidewalks were completely blocked by street musicians. Standing behind open guitar cases or hopeful-looking upturned hats, they played wherever the crowds were thickest. From every side their music filled the night.

Carol fought her way past the crowd surrounding a Jamaican steel drummer and felt her exhaustion returning; somewhere soon she would have to rest. She was just crossing the street to avoid an even larger mob near the corner, flute music issuing from its midst, when, among the knot of spectators, their backs to her, her eye was caught by a bit of movement and a flash of red. It was a red canvas bag, swinging back and forth at the end of an all-but-unseen hand. Regularly it swung out from the crowd, then was lost again from sight, like the pendulum on an overwound clock—or the leg she'd seen swinging in the darkness of the classroom.

It was him, of course: Jeremy, the young man from the library. Even from behind, she recognized the book bag, the stocky build, the rumpled seersucker jacket that hung from one plump shoulder. He seemed to be alone. And as she watched the bag appear and disappear, appear and disappear, she was struck by the crazy, not unpleasant notion that, like an engineer flagging down a train, fate was giving her a sign.

Her first impulse was to hail him, but she stopped herself in time; she didn't want to seem too aggressive. Crossing the street once more, she slipped to the opposite side of the crowd and wormed her way up to the front.

At first she could see nothing but the encircling faces; they were gazing toward something on the sidewalk. She looked down. At her feet squatted a diminutive old man with shiny black skin and grimy turban, piping frenziedly upon a wooden flute. Beside him lay a battered black umbrella. Between his knees he gripped a basket filled with loose change, from the middle of which rose a pale, serpentine thing that swayed before his face.

Carol blanched. For an instant she had taken the object for some grotesque phallic joke, but now she realized what it was: a stick of wood carved to resemble a rearing snake, moved by pressure from the flautist's knee upon a metal rod. From a distance the illusion might have been effective; here on the sidewalk in front of her it just looked silly.

Suddenly the man's eyes widened as he turned toward someone in the crowd. His pudgy black fingers curled more fiercely over the stops, his cheeks puffed in and out, and the music climbed to a shrill tremolo, just as a dollar bill fluttered like a dying moth into the basket at his knees.

Who was throwing dollars away? Carol looked up—and recognized Freirs at the same moment he recognized her. He was standing on the other side of the circle, his tie slightly askew, jamming a wallet back into his pants pocket. Street light was reflected in his glasses. As he turned and saw her, his face brightened; he signaled to Carol to wait where she was. Pushing his way through the knot of people, he made his way to her side.

"So it's you again," he said. "The elusive librarian!" He seemed quite pleased to see her. "There's just no missing you—that hair of yours really stands out in a crowd. It's like a flag." Behind him the piping grew faster, as if in celebration. "I looked for you in class tonight. It's a shame you didn't come."

Carol shrugged. "I had to stay late at work," she heard herself say. "Maybe next time."

"There won't be a next time," he said, looking pleased at the fact. "At least not till next fall." He glanced doubtfully up the block, at the head shops and frozen-custard stands. "Don't tell me you live around here. This is no place for anyone who works at Voorhis."

"Oh, no," she said, "I was just taking the long way home."

"Really?" He appeared to consider it a moment. "Feel like stopping off for a drink? A cup of coffee maybe?"

She felt a queer thrill of triumph out of all proportion to the question. Absurd, of course, but there it was: a tiny voice that whispered, *Anything can happen now.* It was almost as if he had asked her to marry him.

Within the stone circle the flames snapped ravenously, demanding still another log. Insects danced and died amid the smoke, which, rising in a slender column, twisted among the stars and was lost in the surrounding darkness.

At the edge of the firelight the children crouched impatiently by the bag of corn seed, their eyes drawn past the flames to the tables that the older men had brought from the house and were now busy setting up: a folding bridge table, a sewing table, and the small square wooden table from the Poroths' kitchen, arranged in a row and, as the children watched, draped with a dark cloth to form one long platform. The screen door slammed again, and four women could be seen hurrying across the yard like stretcher bearers, hauling something heavy in a sagging white bedsheet. Behind them emerged others, arms laden with large brown thermos jugs which they placed by the fire. None of them spoke, and none were smiling; the only sound now was the distant clatter of pans from within the kitchen and, regular as a pulse beat, the slow and steady cadence of the crickets.

Suddenly, for the second time, the night was split by the clanging of a large brass dinner bell brandished by one of the elders. Setting it down beside him, he reached for a hand-hewn limb of cottonwood and added it to the fire. It fizzed and crackled like a living thing.

Nearby the women had lifted the bedsheet onto the tables and were crowded alongside, backs to the firelight, busily molding a flat, straw-colored mass that lay inert upon the cloth. They had been working since sundown, gathered around the huge cast-iron stove, measuring out the cornmeal, the molasses, the shortening, milk, and eggs. With practiced fingers they had scraped the separate portions still hot from the pans, fitting them together into the prescribed shape, using icing as mortar. Now at last it was ready, arranged hot and smoking by the fireside, awaiting the workers' return from the fields.

The younger women struggled in behind the men. Theirs had been the harder job, as tradition dictated; man's work would come later, with the cultivation and the harvest. All were tired and hungry, in no mood for surprise; but all of them stopped short, men and women alike, when they saw what lay upon the bedsheet, burnished by the flickering light.

It was the size that astonished them; it was longer than a man and covered most of the combined tabletops. In shape it resembled an immense five-pointed star, its entire surface studded with an intricate pattern of currants, nuts, and glistening sweetmeats. It smelled of corn and fruit and molasses, and everything about it spoke of holidays and feasting. Only its name, born of long custom, was ordinary: cottonbread, they called it. Ceremoniously they filed around the tables.

"I didn't think I'd be seein' this again so soon," said one of the men, wiping the dirt from his hands. "It's a sight bigger than the loaf we had last week, wouldn't you say, Rachel?"

"That's because we don't have so many mouths to feed," said his wife.

A heavy-set man grinned and nudged the first one in the ribs. "Not yet, anyways!"

The men around them chuckled—all but Poroth, the youngest here, who stood a little apart from the rest, silent and uneasy. He wasn't one for joking, especially about matters such as that. Children were holy, a gift from the Lord; a woman's body was His sacred instrument.

He glanced anxiously at his wife. She was hunched beside a little girl, whispering something in her ear to coax a smile. It wasn't right that she herself was childless. Just as soon as they were out of debt he would make a mother of her; he knew she was impatient for that.

How beautiful she looked with her hair down—far more beautiful than the local wives. If only she would learn to hold her tongue! After all, this was his land and these people his guests. Even though other hands had prepared the food that lay before them, he'd refused their offers of charity and had paid for it himself. It had put him even deeper into debt; but then, first planting was a once-in-a-lifetime occasion. He prayed that nothing would mar it.

Behind the friends and townspeople assembled by the tables, behind the knots of children and old men, he noticed the spare, severe-looking figure of his mother. She was talking with his Aunt Lise and Lise's widowed daughter, Minna Buckhalter, both of them a full head taller than she was, their jet black hair drawn tightly in the back. Lise had been his late father's sister, and she and Minna bore an almost haunting resemblance to him. It was a look perhaps more handsome in a man—the wide and sturdy shoulders, the thin ascetic lips, the stern, deep-set brown eyes—though it lent them an undeniable air of strength.

His mother's back was turned to him, as it had been so often these past years—ever since, with Bible school behind him, he'd made his impetuous decision to leave the community. In time he had returned to it, with much learned and no regrets, but there was still a coolness between them. What little love there'd been had proven difficult to restore, like corn that wouldn't grow in played-out soil.

But then, he remembered, he had himself to blame: for when he'd returned, he hadn't been alone. He'd had a wife with him—a stranger who, while of their faith, came from outside the area and, more important, seemed to make little effort to adapt herself to local ways. Her morals were, of course, beyond reproach, her training as strict as his own; he wouldn't have considered marrying any other kind. Still, there were those who thought her frivolous, high-spirited—dangerous, even. And then there'd been the question of the ceremony itself, that hurried little song-and-dance performed by an assistant college chaplain, with none of the parents in attendance ... Yes, it was a lot for a mother to forgive, especially one who had no other child. Though he couldn't help but wish she were a little less reluctant to so much as speak Deborah's name.

Lately he'd begun to wonder if this hardness of his mother's wasn't somehow connected, in some mysterious and fundamental way, with the very things that made her so special in the community—her supposed "gifts." He himself felt no particular reverence for them; what good had they ever done him? What good, for that matter, had they ever done *her?* Sometimes, in fact, it seemed as if this special knowledge was all but wasted on her; it apparently brought her not a moment's pleasure. She was like one who, shown a magic window to the future, yawns and looks away. Throughout her life she'd seen things, heard things, felt things coming—bitter winters, summer droughts, births and deaths and storms—but none of them had ever seemed to matter. Nothing had commanded her attention, nothing moved her: nothing, at least, within the bounds of the visible world. "'Tisn't right to get attached to things," she liked to say. "The Lord don't mean for us to love one another too much."

She had baffled him even in the early days, before his father's death. There'd been times when she appeared to lead an almost secretive existence apart from the family, nor had she ever shown the slightest interest in its affairs. She had shared none of her husband's devotion to business, the doings of the town, the rise and fall of others' crops or the fortunes of his own beloved store, the buying and selling of grain and supplies, the faithful nightly entries in the ledger, the bedside prayers for guidance as he balanced his obligations to God and the community with the same care he brought to balancing his books. Instead, even then, she'd been prone to moods of distance and distraction, as if listening for faraway voices or preoccupied by some half-remembered dream.

It had been clear, even then, that the Brethren felt uneasy in her presence, though they were loud in the praise of her piety. Many of them still clearly regarded her as something of an oracle, and she was popularly reputed to have second sight. As to the actual extent of her powers, Poroth himself couldn't say; he only knew that he had inherited no such powers himself—for which he supposed he was glad. Still, watching her as she stood there in the darkness, her face, as always, turned away from him and the moonlight so cold on her hair, he found himself recalling all the things this night represented and longing for some small token of encouragement from her, some word of benediction.

But that, he knew, would have to come from somewhere else.

Nor was it long in coming. The others, he saw now, had fallen silent. They were watching a grey-haired woman, Sister Corah Geisel, who stood at the head of the table. Her hands held something out of sight.

"We're plain folks," she began, gazing into the familiar faces around her. "And I'm no good at speechmaking. You all know that this farm's been standing empty for too many years, ever since Andy Baber gave up working the land, and so we're all real glad to see it under cultivation again. But probably no one's half as glad as we are, Matthew and me. You see, livin' where we do, just over on the next road, we've always felt kind of on the *edge* of things out here, and . . . well, it's good to have some company again!" The others laughed and nodded. "So, bein' as we're their closest neighbors, and since there's no one likelier to do them this service, we wanted Sarr and Deborah here to have our chaplet." She held up a dried and withered garland of corn: two ears, the husks, and a shaggy mass of leaves. "It's from a good crop—the Lord was bountiful last summer—and you all know it just wouldn't be right to plant without one. We're hopin' it'll get these young people off to a proper start." Solemn as if she were crowning a queen, she placed the garland upon the uppermost point of the star-shaped loaf.

Faces turned toward him expectantly, his mother's among them; Poroth realized he would have to say something. He cleared his throat. "Brother Matthew and Sister Corah do us a real honor, and I know the Lord'll bless them for their neighborliness. We give thanks for the bread we're about to eat, and thanks for those who prepared it. It's made from store-bought cornmeal, but next year, thanks to you good folks, we'll be using our own."

"And next year we'll be planting on time!" Deborah had added that. She'd replaced Sister Corah at the head of the table and stood clutching a long, serrated bread knife, its blade gleaming redly in the firelight. The brightness was reflected in her eyes.

"And now," he said quickly, "let us bow our heads together in silent prayer." He stood biting his lip, eyes closed, but the only sound he heard was one of the children driving some predator from the corn seed.

At last he looked up. He had been distracted, annoyed at his wife; there had been no prayer in his heart. He wondered if somehow the others had seen, but they were staring pensively at the cottonbread as if lost in recollection. Only Deborah herself stood watching him now— and, just beyond the firelight, seven pairs of wide unwinking eyes. He hadn't noticed them till this moment.

"How did *they* get out?" he whispered, nodding toward the cats as he moved beside his wife.

She shrugged. "I never locked 'em up."

"Of all the dumb—" Once more he dropped his voice. "You *know* how Brother Joram feels."

"Oh, honey, don't be angry with me. 'Tisn't anything important. Joram will just have to watch his step." She reached once more for the knife. "Are we ready?"

He nodded curtly. "Ready."

Metal flashed. She brought up her hand and, with a smooth stroke, sliced off the topmost point of the star. It remained lying before them, still decorated by the cuttings from last year's crop.

Just beyond the firelight the seven pairs of eyes followed every movement, missing nothing. Silent as shadows, two of the animals rose and padded back to the house. The others crouched nearer the flames, purring softly.

Corn fragrance hung above the table, reminding those assembled of their empty bellies. With the first clean slice the spell that held them had been dissipated, replaced by simple hunger. They murmured in anticipation.

"Brothers, sisters," said Poroth gravely, "let us break bread."

The command was, this time, a literal one. Crowded round the bread loaf, the celebrants broke chunks off with their hands. They were polite, even deferential; the pieces they took were not large. Still, the star's smooth contours soon looked ragged, and before long, limbs devoured, it had been reduced to a shapeless yellow mass. The severed portion, a triangle nearly as large as a kite, was brought past the fire to the children, who greeted it with shouts of pleasure. It had been garnished with extra sweetmeats, including three plump candied crab apples and a slice of glazed peach; they fell upon it eagerly. The garland of corn had been removed beforehand and left in a prominent place at the head of the table, where it presided over the destruction of the loaf.

Like corn bread it was dry, crumbly, and provoked an immediate thirst. Cups were handed around; the thermos jugs were emptied, disgorging strong hot coffee brewed with chocolate. Older children trooped forward for their share; the younger ones sang planting songs, or dozed, or fought over the sweetmeats. Men were lying full-length on the grass; benches were not part of this occasion. Some of the married couples sat together in the darkness, washing down the last of the bread while they searched the zenith for meteors; others remained standing, sipping their coffee as they gazed dreamily into the flames. In the warm reddish light their features were drained of detail, taking on the ageless look of masks. Here and there a lightning bug glowed and dimmed above the lawn, and in the sky beyond the cornfield the Sickle rolled serenely toward the western horizon. Children chased a buzzing june bug from the bag of seed; overhead Draco and the Queen

wheeled in an endless chase around the pole star, the Dragon's tail
directly overhead. In its tip shone Thuban, pole star of the ancients,
once a herdsman's beacon and the light to which the pyramids aspired,
stony angles pointing toward its gleam. Since that hour five thousand
years had flashed and died like sparks; the heavens had shifted. But
not until this present spring had the world really changed.

At night the city seemed immense. The sidewalks looked as wide as
streets, the streets like highways; in the absence of traffic the avenue
resembled a dim, empty arena, its spectators all gone home. Cars
passed only at intervals now, in groups of two or three, and could be
heard from blocks away. Carol's voice sounded loud amid the silence.

"Jeremy, I can't keep *up* with you!"

"Sorry," he said. "I guess I'm still upset about that bag."

The two of them were walking north toward Chelsea, their footsteps
slapping heavily against the pavement. Freirs no longer had his book
bag. Earlier that evening they had stopped to eat in a crowded little
Italian restaurant on Sullivan Street, Freirs slipping the bag beneath
his chair, and later when he'd reached for it, it had been gone—stolen,
most likely, though Freirs still clung to the hope that it had been taken
by accident and might eventually be returned; it had contained nothing but books and student papers.

The loss of the bag had spoiled what had been, until then, a happy
evening, though for Carol the incident was already receding into the
haze of the past. The two of them had shared a bottle of chianti over
dinner; she'd had nothing to eat since her afternoon break, and that
first glass had immediately gone to her head. Later, after coffee, he'd
convinced her to join him in a brandy. It had never taken much to get
her drunk, and tonight she'd been especially susceptible. Despite the
coffee, she was beginning to feel drowsy and, in her imagination, was
already staggering into bed and pressing her body in sleep against the
cool sheets. She could think about the day's events tomorrow morning.

It was now well past midnight. A mile to the north the red, white,
and blue lights that illuminated the Empire State Building throughout the July Fourth season had gone dark, with only the wink of a red
warning beacon left to mark the top, while up and down the avenue the
lights of the deserted shops glowed pallidly behind steel security gates.
In the shadows of a butcher's window, hanging carcasses and the

goose-pimpled body of a turkey pressed against the metal bars like creatures in a cage.

She walked slowly, aware that she'd eaten too much. Still, hadn't it been nice of him to take her out like that! It was something she missed, here in New York, where most restaurants were beyond her means, places to pass without entering. Today, though, her luck seemed to have changed. All evening she'd been thinking of Rosie's check, carefully folded in her handbag, and of how she was going to spend it. Two benefactors on the same day—it was almost too much to believe.

"I feel like I've eaten enough to last the whole weekend," she said, hoping she sounded sufficiently grateful.

"I wish I could say the same." As he walked he stared gloomily down at his paunch, as if surprised it was still there. "I've really got to get in shape this summer. If I don't lose around twenty pounds . . ." He shook his head.

They were passing the open doorway of a barroom, its patrons concealed by darkness; the sounds of salsa music and argument spilled out into the night. Carol hurried after him.

"I don't think you look so bad. Honestly."

"Well, thanks." He stood a little straighter. "But you should have seen me a year ago, during my diet. I was positively *lean* then. Like you."

She shrugged, though she knew she'd been complimented. "My two older sisters have really full figures. I was always the skinny one."

"Not me," he said mournfully. "When I was growing up I was a regular little tub. My parents had to send me to a weight-watchers' camp in Connecticut." He slowed, briefly, for her to catch up. "You know, come to think of it, that was just about the only time I ever really got out into the country. That, and a temple youth-group trip, and a few weeks at a tennis camp on Long Island. Pretty provincial, huh?"

"Oh, I wouldn't say that." She wondered if he'd been kidding. "I'll bet you think it's the *rest* of us who are provincial."

He grinned. "I don't deny it! But then, that's what comes of being a New Yorker all my life." With an easy sweep of his hand he took in the nearly deserted street, the lights of distant traffic, and, it seemed to her, the whole titanic nightscape of the city, the dark alleys, silent buildings, and the millions around them now dreaming in their beds.

She envied him his growing up here. It was a world he knew well enough to thrive within, and one he might help her know better—something, anyway, worth hoping for. For a moment, as she walked up the avenue with him, Freirs already ahead once more, it seemed to her that she was on a different street entirely, one that, if only she didn't stumble, would lead her to a future in which all things were possible.

"I can't help wondering," she said at last, "what you'd make of *my* town."

"I'm sure I'd like it."

She laughed. "Don't be. It isn't very interesting."

"Well, you know—Pennsylvania and all." He waved his hand vaguely to the left. "I expect it's pretty scenic out there."

She glanced at him skeptically. "You sound as if you've never been west of the Hudson."

"Oh, don't get me wrong," he said. "I've done my share of traveling. L.A., Chicago, Miami . . ." He waited till she'd drawn beside him. "My parents moved down to Florida a few years ago. Horrible place! And after college I spent some time in Europe. But as for good old country living in the good old U.S.A.—you know, going to sleep with the chickens, getting up with the hogs, or whatever it is they do out there . . ." He shrugged.

They were approaching another bar now. Carol moved closer to his side. She couldn't explain why, but she felt quite safe with him, despite the fact that he himself was plainly somewhat tense. Both of them had been sobered by the loss of the book bag, and the night had sharpened her senses when she'd first stepped from the restaurant, but now her giddiness was returning. Perhaps it was Jeremy, or perhaps only the drink. Love stories always made her weep when she read them late at night, whether or not they were really sad; she trembled at mysteries after too much black coffee, even when their plots held no terrors. It was hard to tell for sure.

Normally she might have been a great deal more apprehensive. Although they were nearing her own neighborhood in Chelsea now, she was unaccustomed to being outdoors at this hour, when every stranger was potentially a threat: the sleepy-eyed schoolboy who shuffled past them, hands plunged deep into his pockets, might be secretly caressing a rosary down there, or his own nakedness, or a knife. Faces which would have been ignored by day now took on a peculiar cast, and she was acutely aware of figures in the distance, coming toward her through the empty streets. Even their footfalls were audible; she could hear them, and anticipate the encounter, from several blocks away.

At this moment the view ahead held only a bored-looking householder walking his dog. From the sidewalk behind came the voices of a couple speaking rapidly in Spanish and, across the avenue, the echoes of a small, lumpish figure staggering after them upon a black cane, a tattered parcel clutched beneath its arm. Newspapers swept like ghosts through the foyer of an abandoned movie theater near the corner, its marquee blank, display case bare of posters; wind stirred the heaped-up trash against the doors as the two of them hurried past, reminding Carol of the rustle of dead leaves.

"You know something?" she said. "I think the country will be good for you."

"Really?" He sounded as if he cared. "I sure hope so, because I keep suspecting I've been missing something."

"Well, *I* think you have. Of course—"

She stumbled slightly and felt his hand reach out to steady her. He seemed to hold her longer than was necessary.

"Of course, I don't know you very well," she said, pulling away slightly. "You may get bored. What are you going to do if you're unhappy out there?"

"Unhappy? What do you mean?"

"Can you just come back here to the city if it turns out you don't like it? I hope you haven't paid the whole thing in advance."

"No, I haven't paid anything yet," he said. "But I told the Poroths I'd stay the summer, and they're expecting me to, so I guess I have a certain commitment."

"Still, that's hardly the same as a contract."

"Maybe," he said, glancing at the figures behind them. "But I feel my word to the Poroths is just as binding as a contract. It's the way those people operate. And anyway, I did sign something with the other couple, the ones subletting my apartment. They wanted the place till September, and I gave it to 'em. They wanted the whole thing in writing, and"—he shrugged—"I gave it to 'em. So I just made my mind up: I'm going to stay the whole summer and that's all there is to it. You won't find *me* coming home crying!"

For a moment she thought she'd heard real self-pity in his voice, but then, screwing up his face, he made a mocking little sound like the sobbing of a baby, and she broke into laughter. Soon he was laughing with her—but only for a moment; clearly the doubts she'd raised were still on his mind.

"Jesus, I *hope* I don't get bored out there," he said. "I certainly don't expect to. My dissertation alone should keep me busy round the clock. If you could see the size of my reading list . . ." He shook his head. "God, I'm still so pissed about that book bag. There were things in there of my own, aside from all those papers. You wouldn't believe the catching up I've got to do. There's a course I'm teaching next fall that I'm completely unprepared for, a night class at Columbia—"

"I thought you taught at the New School."

"Sure, but nobody's going to pay the rent on *that.* You've really got to scramble for the jobs these days. You've got to take whatever comes along and hope that someday someplace gives you tenure. Me, I admit it, I'm a bit of a hack. I'll go wherever they pay me and teach whatever they like."

She felt a trace of envy. "The pay must be good at Columbia."

"Well, it isn't actually the college I'll be with, it's the General Studies program. But it's the best I can do right now. The course itself is partly my idea . . ."

The rest of his words were drowned out when, beneath their feet, the pavement trembled like the roll of a hundred drums. In an instant they were engulfed by a cavernously deep rumbling, as if something vast and invisible were bearing down upon their lives. Through the subterranean corridors below them an IND express hurtled noisily uptown, leaving only silence in its wake.

Silence . . . but broken by a certain sound behind them, a queer irregular thump-and-scrape from somewhere down the block.

"What will it be on?"

"Pardon?" He was peering over his shoulder, but quickly turned back to her; one didn't stare at cripples. In the distance the little figure with the cane, head bowed, continued its laborious progress up the sidewalk. The emptiness and the night seemed to press heavily upon it.

"Your course," she said. "What'll it be on?"

"I'm calling it 'The Gothic Imagination.' That's the kind of title they go for up there. I told them I'd start with Shakespeare and work right up to *Absalom, Absalom,* and believe it or not, they bought it. They must think—"

"Wait a second! Since when did Shakespeare write gothics?"

He paused. "Well, there's always *Hamlet.* You know—ghost on the battlements, lost inheritance . . . But that was just part of the sales pitch. The same with the Faulkner; I threw them in for the names. The truth is, I'll mainly be reading a lot of crazy old horror stories, the sort of stuff I should have read ten years ago. I've been faking it all this time, and now's my chance to find out what I've missed." He turned to look at her, smiling. "Should be fun, eh?"

She felt a tiny urge to needle him, for there was something about his enthusiasm that irritated her—the same smug faith in good fortune, perhaps, which she occasionally recognized in herself. Or perhaps it was just that he seemed so blithely prepared to leave her.

"And what will you do out there," she asked, "if you get sick of ghost stories?"

"Oh, that shouldn't be a problem," he said. "I'm pretty good at keeping myself busy. One thing's for sure, I'm not going to spend the summer sitting on my ass. I'm going to get myself in shape, maybe even do a little jogging. Establish a routine and stick to it. Bran and yogurt at breakfast, dental floss at night, shoes on the shoe trees before going to bed . . ."

She noticed with some amusement that, as he spoke, he was swinging his arms more forcefully and holding his head up straighter.

"And in the evening," he said, "who knows? I might try to teach myself astronomy. That's something you can't do in the city—stargazing. I'm bringing out a book with all the maps. It'll be nice to learn what' actually up there."

The two of them looked upward as they passed along the block, b

by now the city sky was almost starless. The moon had vanished behind
the buildings to the west; they saw it shining low over the cross streets
and the vacant lots.

"If things get too boring," he added, "I suppose I can always get a
lift into Gilead. What there is of it, anyway." He shrugged. "And, of
course, if worst comes to worst, I can always try bird-watching, I hear
that's fun, or go for walks in the woods. In fact—now, don't laugh!—
I'm bringing out a whole slew of those little illustrated field guides. I
mean, let's face it, I don't know a hell of a lot about campcraft—I'm
like the guy in the joke: the last time I tried rubbing two sticks together was in a Chinese restaurant—but there are quite a few things
I'd really like to learn: like mushroom hunting, and animal tracks, and
the names of some of the flowers. Round-lobed hepatica, Dutchman's-
breeches"—the names rolled off his tongue—"bachelor's button, touch-
me-not . . ."

She nudged him with her elbow. "You sound just like the nature
counselor at B.C.Y.C."

"Oh, yeah?" He stopped and faced her. "And what, pray tell, is
B.C.Y.C.?"

"Beaver County Youth Camp."

His mouth opened in an incredulous grin. "Beaver County? Is that
where you're from?"

"Uh-huh!" She burst into giggles.

He laughed, too, with something like relief. "The girl from Beaver
County . . . What a find!" It was as if a wall between them had been
broken. They leaned against one another, rocking with laughter. "And
what a great title for a film! We'll get—"

Suddenly he caught his breath. She felt him stiffen.

"Jesus! How does that guy keep *up* with us?" He squinted into the
darkness. "I've never seen a cripple *move* so fast."

She turned and looked, but the sidewalk behind them was empty, the
streets hushed but for the wail of a distant police siren, rising and falling, rising and falling, like a hungry baby screaming unheeded in the
night.

The time of idleness was drawing to an end. Away from the others,
near the rosebushes at the side of the house, the Poroths lay drowsily in
the long grass and the shadows from the kitchen light, resting beside
one another. They were alone here but for a trio of their cats, two

stretched in sleep between them, another curled purring on Deborah's stomach. With the murmur of voices so distant and the bonfire out of sight behind the house, Sarr felt sorely tempted to roll over and hold her in his arms—they were used to making love among the animals, outdoors as well as in—but he forced the desire from his mind. Not for another full day; not until the planting was complete. Sunday, though, was going to be special. Sunday after services . . .

"Just a few more hours of this, Lord be praised," he said. "But I can't say as I look forward to tomorrow night, with just the two of us. I'll bet we end up working straight through to Sunday morning."

Deborah made a sympathetic noise. "I sure hope I don't doze off again the middle of the sermon. They've never let me forget it!"

"Don't worry," he said sharply, "I'll make sure you stay awake. But as soon as we come back here, I'm going to sleep for the rest of the day. And you're going to be right there beside me, naked as Old Mother Eve, so that when I get up—"

"Oh, no, I'm not, honey. And neither are you." She reached over and ran her fingers through the dark hair on his chin. "Don't you remember? We've got a visitor coming on Sunday."

Sarr made a face in the darkness. "I forgot all about him." With a sigh he sat up, dislodging a cat about to seat itself on his chest. "Well, at least it'll bring in some money. Lord knows we can use it." He turned and looked across the lawn at the outbuilding, a squat black form against the night sky.

"We'll have to get the place fixed up tomorrow," said Deborah, as if reading his thoughts. "Put up the screens and get the ivy off those windows. And I don't intend doing it all myself."

He grunted noncommittally.

"We'd best do it early," she went on. "We'll have more planting at night, and Sunday'll be too late. 'Twould be awful if he came out here with all his goods, took another look at the place, then turned around and went home." She paused, speculating. "I sure hope he doesn't mind a few bugs."

He got to his knees and began brushing the dirt from his pants. "Well," he said, "you never know about those city people." Yawning, he stood and sniffed the air; the wind was blowing off the marsh, but he could smell the fragrance of the freshly planted field, the moist soil and vegetation. "All right, woman!" He prodded her gently with his toe. "High time we got back to the others."

"Sure wouldn't want old Joram to squawk!"

"No, wouldn't want that." He smiled in spite of himself, but the felt a surge of anger. How dare she talk that way? And how dare he her? Troubled, he turned from her to stare into the distance. As ways, the view calmed him. He was simply going to have to make understand. But not now, not on such a night . . .

There was a faint glow in the eastern sky, past the outbuilding and the woods. The wind was blowing from behind him and went hissing through the tops of the trees; they nodded together as if sharing a secret. As a boy, on nights like this, he'd used to pretend that, if he stood on tiptoe, he could see truck depots, railroad yards, and glimmering lights—the lights of New York City, not fifty miles away.

Rejoining the others gathered around the cottonwood fire, they savored the last quiet moments before their return to the field. Here and there a knife blade rose and fell in the ruddy light as the younger men sat sharpening the ends of their staffs. Two acres had already been planted; before they departed tonight they'd have completed two more. A fifth would still remain, but after dark tomorrow Poroth and his wife could see to that themselves. "'Twill keep 'em out of mischief on a Saturday night," joked one of the men. "We'll see 'em stagger into worship next morning with corn seed in their hair!"

Poroth made no answer. He was crouched in the shadow of the table and, as tradition demanded, was busy binding last year's garland to the top of the staff. The dried husks and withered ears dangled from the wood like talismans atop a spear.

Some of the more flirtatious wives stood near the men but talked among themselves, flaunting their long, unfettered hair. As a rule it was worn pinned up in a severe and deliberately unbecoming style, to be let down only at bedtime before one's own husband. During the yearly planting, however, this rule was relaxed.

"Like a pack of spoony schoolgirls!" came a low, laconic voice from the darkness. " 'Father, turn away mine eyes from beholdin' vanity.' "

Deborah's youthful figure broke away from the others. "Why, Rupert Lindt, is that all you can say after staring at us half the night?" She took another step forward and, with a toss of her head, struck a mock-seductive pose. "You better go back and read the second half of the book: 'If a woman have long hair, 'tis a glory to her.' "

From the darkness came the man's embarrassed laugh and an automatic chorus of *amen*'s. The one called Joram frowned and looked away. Among the Brethren it was considered unseemly for a woman to speak to a man other than her husband, and they took an equally dim view of those who quoted scripture back and forth in argument; for a people so conversant with the Bible it was far too easy to do. "Sarr," he said at last, turning to the younger man, "you've come back to us like a prodigal son, and we rejoice in it—just as we rejoice in the wife you've brought back. The Holy Spirit's in her, we all know it is, but there's still much she'll have to be taught. 'Tisn't a night for jests. 'They that sow in tears shall reap in joy.' I think you know the rest."

"I do," said the other, aware of the correct response. " 'He that goeth forth and weepeth, bearing precious seed, shall doubtless come again with rejoicing, bringing his sheaves with him.' Don't worry, Brother Joram. I'll teach her to weep."

Beside him came a muttered "Amen."

From the west a breeze gathered, carrying the scent of marsh water and rotting pine; it ruffled their beards and stirred the rosebushes at the side of the house. The night was cooler now, and the work sweat had dried on their bodies. They turned to face the fire, the men in their vests, the women in long dresses. Bats flitted through the darkness above them like the shadows of small birds; moths clustered around the dancing flames where the old men stood talking. Across the lawn bustling shapes moved to and fro in the light of the kitchen. The screen door opened, and a line of older women emerged from the house bearing small metal lanterns to help with the clean-up. The door slammed shut. Low in the sky the half-moon seemed close enough to touch, God's oppressive thumbnail poised just above their heads.

Joram stood. "Up, brothers, sisters," he called softly, striding toward the fields. "We've sore travail before us." Passing the knot of children, he bent and addressed the smallest of them, all but dwarfed by the bag of seed. "Now mark you don't let varmints eat a single one," he warned. "'Twould be bad portent!" With his face turned away from the firelight it was impossible to tell if he was smiling.

Soundlessly the others followed. The time of rest was over.

By now the tables had been cleared of the last scraps of food and of the cloth that had covered them. A lantern had been placed upon the one in the center, and in its beams a younger woman stood folding up the bridge table, her hair knotted back like that of the elders in the kitchen. Moving past the tables, Poroth set down his staff and approached her.

"I want to thank you, Cousin Minna," he said, putting a hand on her shoulder. "It was good of you to come tonight. I only wish you could've been out there with the rest of us."

The other nodded gravely. Above the glowing lantern, her homely face looked prematurely aged. "Piet wouldn't have wanted me to stay home and mope. You know how he loved a night like this, with all the folks gettin' together underneath the stars. I can feel his spirit with me right this very minute, standin' by my side. It's with me all the time, these days. I expect you feel it too."

"I do," said Poroth—and in a way he did. Or maybe it was just a passing breeze. "I swear he's almost close enough to touch."

Hearing a faint movement behind him, he turned half eagerly to look and found himself facing his mother. She was carrying one of the empty brown jugs back to the kitchen.

"Here," he said, "let me help you with that." He took it from her and started toward the house, expecting she would walk beside him. But moments later, looking back, he saw that she hadn't moved. She was standing perfectly still, as if the shores of some vast and invisible ocean were stretched before her feet, and she was watching him with an expression which, in the dim light, he found difficult to read.

"You go on," she said. "Your Aunt Lise is in there washing up."

"I know she is," he said, puzzled. "So are all the rest. Aren't you coming?"

She shook her head. "I've got to be getting along. It's later than I thought." Poroth heard a certain weariness in her voice. He was about to return to her side, but she stepped away from him and held up her hand. "No, don't worry about me. Ain't nothing more I can do to help around here. You'd best be getting back to the field. The others'll be out there by now."

"I don't plan to keep them waiting," he said. "But first I'd like to hear just how you think you're going to get home."

She shrugged. "The Lord gave me two good legs, and I'm not too old to use them."

Somehow he had known that that was what she'd say. There was really no arguing with her, once her mind was made up, though he felt it his duty to try. "Mother, with all its turns that road's a good six miles long, and it's at least another mile to your house. That's quite a ways to walk."

"You don't have to tell me how long it is," she said. "I've been down that road before."

"That was during the day. This time you'll be walking in the dark."

"You know what they say. 'Tis only dark for them that will not see." She began moving away.

"I don't understand," he said. "What's all this hurry for? You came with Aunt Lise, and now she'll be expecting to take you home. Or if you don't mind waiting a spell, you can go with Amos Reid. He and Rachel brought their car tonight. So did lots of others."

She shook her head again, looking vaguely troubled. No, not troubled, exactly. It was something about her eyes, a kind of resignation. "I haven't time to wait," she said almost mournfully. "The night's got me thinking, somehow, thinking about what's coming and what's past, and how there's something I should be doing that I'm not. I just can't seem to shake it, the thought of what's ahead . . ." She muttered something under her breath.

The young man strained to hear what she had whispered; it had sounded like "the Voolas." He had never seen her quite so bad before. "Now just hold on a minute," he said. "You've gone and got yourself in a state. And there's no cause to, not tonight. Tonight's a time for rejoicing. After all, just look at me!" He threw wide his arms. "Here I am, all set up now, back where I belong. On our own land."

"Don't go talking foolishness, son. The land ain't ours. You know very well that Andy Baber owned this place, and so did Andy's father, and his father before him."

He scowled. "Well, it was ours a hundred years ago—which means that we came first. That's the whole reason I bought this farm. I figured you'd be pleased, seeing as how your people were the ones who built it."

"They weren't my people. It's a big family, you know that. They were just another branch."

"They were Troets."

She nodded bitterly. "And you remember what happened to them."

He felt a chill pass over his shoulders. Why had she brought *that* up? Was she trying to spoil this night for him?

But she had already begun to apologize. "Don't pay me no mind," she was saying. "I'm just a useless old woman. Fact is, it's done me good, seeing you here in a house of your own, the seeds in the earth, the bread on the table. The night's been blessed, so far, and I'm sure the crops'll do just fine. I just wish there were something I could do for you and Deborah, but . . ." She paused, as if remembering. "But now it seems it's later than I thought."

With a brief dismissive wave she turned and moved off across the lawn, passing between the outbuildings and the farmhouse, heading toward the road. For a moment, walking through the squares of light spread on the grass beneath the kitchen windows, her figure seemed to grow larger and, somehow, almost fierce; then she'd passed beyond them, becoming once again as dim and insubstantial as a wraith on some forlorn moonlit errand. Circling around the side of the house, she slipped into its shadow and was gone.

He remained standing there, watching for her to reappear among the trees that lined the road, but after a minute or two he turned away. Setting the jug back near the foot of the table, he stooped to retrieve his staff and walked bemusedly toward the fields to join the other men. The night was indeed turning out to be a blessed one; his mother's private sorrows were already forgotten. At long last she had mentioned Deborah by name—surely that meant something!—and the crops, she'd said, would do just fine.

He felt like singing.

Behind him, past the fire, the younger women had replenished the sacks they'd carried at their sides, leaving the huge burlap seed bag only a quarter full. Huddled nearby, their features drawn and fatigued, the children sat watching intently for every kernel spilled— but no more intently than the four remaining cats, who crouched u seen in the shadows beyond the ring of stones, eyes aglow like coa

As the women shouldered their now-heavy sacks and trudged slo back to the fields, the smallest of the children dipped his hand into the bag and brought up a streaming fistful of seeds. Wagging a finger in solemn imitation of his elders, he admonished the corn in a grave whisper:

"Mark thee, mind thee,
Gillycorn Hill . . ."

Stooping amid the plowed furrows, the women took up the chant and repeated the same traditional warning:

"If Crow don't find thee,
Mouse he will."

As they straightened up, one of them groaned and rubbed her stomach. The woman beside her smiled. "What ails you, sister? Too much cottonbread?"

The other nodded. "That star was big as a barn door, and I think I ate half of it! Don't know why they call it cottonbread—it's heavy as a stone."

Deborah paused to push back a lock of hair. "My husband knows all about that sort of thing," she said, "but he seems to want to keep it to himself."

The moon was settling into the treetops. They peered ahead into the gloom, where the seven men were a row of moving shadows. "That was stone-ground white flint cornmeal," Poroth was saying. "I had to send all the way to Tipton for it. The man who sold it to me—a blackhat from the Barrens—said it'd been milled by waterpower."

One of the others shook his head. "Probably charged you double for it!"

A few of them laughed, but the younger man pretended not to hear. "It was made of the same seeds we're planting tonight," he went on, "the same white flint corn that the Indians grew. Just the thing for a start as late as this. They say it has the shortest season."

"Let's hope it's not too short," came a stern voice from the down the row. "Short the life of man, and soon the harvest."

"Now let's be fair, Joram," said another. "You said yourself it made a real nice cottonbread."

His wife, walking several paces behind them, had been waiting for this moment. "Amos," she called, "will you ask Brother Sarr something for me?"

The chanting died. In the sudden silence her words rang across the field.

"Ask him why they call it cottonbread."

The young man didn't wait for the question to be repeated. "I thought everybody knew that," he said quickly, without looking back over his shoulder. "It's because they used to cook it over the cottonwood fire. Tasted real good, I'll bet!" As if to put an end to the subject, he slammed his staff with special vehemence into the earth. The crown of corn leaves rustled fiercely.

The question had come as a surprise; he hoped he'd sounded convincing. Obviously Deborah had been talking again. Would she never learn? Back there by the fire Brother Joram had practically told him to take a stick to her, and he, for all his college education, had found himself agreeing. She was getting to him, that woman, in more ways than one . . .

He paused a moment and turned to watch her slip three seeds into the hole he'd just made. Her hair swept loosely past her face, the way it did as she climbed into bed beside him each night. Standing, she covered the hole with a careless scrape of her bare foot, and as she looked up their eyes met. She smiled. It was a loving smile, and a knowing one.

He looked down, biting his lip. He was hungry for her, and she knew it. All week he had avoided her embrace, hoarding his pent-up energies for the planting; it would help ensure a bountiful crop. But now the sight of her moving another pace closer and bending toward the earth, deliberately thrusting out her hips, so aroused him that he had to turn his face away or he'd have cried out. Savagely he plunged his staff into the furrowed ground and gave it a violent twist; several leaves were shaken off and lost in the darkness. If only he hadn't made that vow . . . He thought of her round body, the softness of her skin beneath the rough dress, and wondered, as he rejoined the ranks of the men, if he dared hoist that dress and enter her tonight, with all the corn seed not yet sown.

Nudging the woman beside her, Deborah nodded toward her husband. "Did you see the way Sarr was looking at me?" she said in a low, husky voice. "As soon as you folks leave, I swear he's going to take me right here in this field!"

The image was a scandalous one, but credible nonetheless. They burst into delighted laughter.

Poroth heard the laughter, but not what had provoked it. "Like a pack of spoony schoolgirls," Rupert Lindt had said, and he'd been right. How deliciously innocent they were, Deborah no less than the rest. And how shocked they'd be if he told them the truth about what they'd done tonight.

> *"Hide thee, haste thee,*
> *Gillycorn Hill . . ."*

He had stumbled upon it, quite by accident, in German class; a book in the college library, confirming his suspicions, had hinted at still darker things, older than the pyramids, older than recorded history. He'd read of pre-Christian nature worship and how, each spring,

tribesmen had once sacrificed their gods in human form. The rest he'd
figured out for himself. Beneath his neighbors' sobersided piety he had
glimpsed the painted face of the savage; behind this evening's quaint
observance he had seen a blood-stained altar and a figure stretched
naked upon it like a five-pointed star. He had witnessed the ritual
slashing of the throat, the rending of the limbs; while his friends enjoyed their moonlit meal, he'd had a vision of frenzied hands tearing at
a thing without a head, while, just beyond the firelight, children
fought greedily over what looked like a face. Though their food now
bore a deceptive modern name, it had formerly been known as *Gottin*
bread, symbol of what they'd once devoured—the flesh of the Goddess
incarnate, her hair the garland that now crowned his staff.

> *"If Mole don't taste thee,*
> *Worm he will."*

All such goings-on, of course, were safely in the past; there was no
harm in them today. Perhaps he'd read more history than the rest of
the Brethren, and perhaps he'd seen more deeply tonight, but his faith
remained as strong as it had always been. The origin of everything was
dark, no doubt, but blood spilled long ago had long since dried. Time,
he knew, made all deeds respectable; some people even ate their god
each Sunday. For him all gods and goddesses were one, aspects of an
all-encompassing Divine; and after tonight's sacrament, followed by
his mother's benediction, he walked with the confidence of one who'd
been truly blessed.

Behind him, appropriately, the women had reached the final, optimistic verse of their chant:

> *"Fly thee, fleet thee,*
> *Gillycorn Hill . . ."*

Forcing his thoughts from the altar, the naked victim, the memory of
his wife, he raised his voice with theirs in an exuberant shout:

> *"If Worm don't eat thee,*
> I will!"

There was a sudden splintering of wood. The point of his staff struck
something hard and wriggling. From the earth before him rose an
angry sound like fat sizzling on a fire, and something thrashed convul-
sively, almost wresting the staff from his grasp. An ear of brittle corn
snapped off and fell silently at his feet. In the distance one of the cats
leaped up and went streaking across the lawn.

Lifting the staff, he squinted closely at its tip, but the moon was almost gone and he could see nothing. The wood felt cracked and pitted
ear the end; it was sticky to the touch, and oddly cold.

His stomach now unsettled, he pressed the staff once more into the ground, turning it against the clean soil. He said nothing to any of the others, and by the time the third acre was planted he had driven the incident from his mind.

It was then that it happened. The hour was late; the crickets still sang, but the lightning bugs were dimmed, and the moon had long since disappeared behind the scrub pines to the west. Suddenly, by the faraway blaze, a child cried out in dismay.

She was standing over the bag of seed, pointing to something at her feet. Soon she had been joined by a group of the older men. "'Tis nothing!" one of them called hoarsely. He waved the laborers back to the field, but Poroth and his wife continued hurrying toward the fire. In its light, amid a milling crowd of children and elders, they saw the seed bag lying on its side, looking slightly more shrunken than they'd remembered it. Gaping from the bottom was a small circular hole through which spilled a steady stream of corn seed.

"'Tis nothing," repeated the old man. "We'll get it all." Around him his comrades were already gathering up the individual kernels that lay scattered in the grass.

But what none of them spoke of was the other hole they had seen and quickly covered over—a hole that, before the bag rolled on its side, had lain just below the first, twisting sinuously into the earth.

Carol was sorry when at last they reached the front steps of her building, where tattered aspidistra struggled against cellophane bags and candy wrappers in two soot-covered boxes on either side of the doorway. The place, which till now had seemed a haven, somewhere she could actually afford, suddenly looked very shabby to her; she was glad it was night and that the nearest streetlamp was several houses away. Freirs acted as if he didn't notice, but she was afraid he was only being polite. He had to be richer than he pretended, she was certain of it, one of those self-confident New York Jewish boys who'd grown up with all the advantages and didn't realize how lucky they were. Or if he wasn't rich, he was at least generously supplied with money and would soon be relaxing in the country while she'd still be here working all summer. For their entire walk together she'd been acutely aware, with every block they passed, that he'd be leaving the city on Sunday; and though she reminded herself that the day had been an extraordinarily good one—blessed, practically—she couldn't help feeling that, at the same time, God was being curiously cruel: no sooner had she met some-

she might truly fall in love with than he was being taken away
from her.

Freirs himself, she'd noticed, had begun to grow inexplicably jumpy
as their walk drew to an end. He'd become skittish as a greyhound, in
fact, seeing shapes in every shadow, certain they were being followed,
and some of his tension had rubbed off on her. Only a few yards from
her house he had frozen without warning in his tracks and seized her
arm, yanking her back as if before a chasm and gesturing wordlessly at
a thing the size of a pea pod that had scuttled across their path. Carol
had let out a little cry before she'd realized it was only a waterbug.
How in the world was a person like this going to get along in the
country?

She paused at the bottom of the steps, not sure whether to ask him
up for coffee or to say goodbye. "Well, Jeremy," she said, "it sounds
like you're in for a great summer. I envy you, I really do. I just hope
you'll give me a call when you get back to the city."

"Hell, we can do better than that. How about coming out to visit me
sometime? It would do you good, get you away from the dusty old
books and little old men. You could come out for the weekend"—his
confidence seemed to slip—"or else just for the day, whatever you
like."

"Oh, Jeremy, I'd love to!"

"Gilead's just a couple of hours by bus," he went on. "It's a nice scenic ride, really not bad at all. Or you could take the express to Flemington, around twelve miles east of it, and save yourself almost an
hour. Either way, I could come pick you up. The Poroths have a truck
they'd let me use."

"That sounds wonderful," she said. "It would be lovely to get away
for a weekend." She wanted to ask where she would sleep if she stayed
over, but didn't have the courage. Surely the farmer and his wife must
have a spare room she could use.

"Great," he said. "Then it's settled." He already had a scrap of
paper pressed against his knee and, with his foot on the bottom step,
was scribbling down her house number from above the doorway. "I'll
write you when I get out there and let you know everything's okay."

Standing with him on the sidewalk, she followed his gaze, then
looked up past the tiers of dirty brick and plaster to a row of windows
on the fifth floor. They were dark. Maybe Rochelle had gone out with
her boyfriend, and for once Carol would have the place to herself. More
likely, though, she was in bed, and certainly not alone. "If you'd like to
come in for coffee," Carol said, making up her mind, "we'll have to be
very quiet. My roommate's probably asleep already."

"Oh, that's okay." After the triumph of getting her to agree to see
him, he seemed disinclined to press his luck. "It's late, and I've got a
ton of books to pack tomorrow."

"Just don't forget to take along those nature guides," she said, starting up the steps. "I want you to be an expert tracker by the time I come out."

She heard him hesitate, then follow her. When she turned he was standing beside her, smiling. "I was hoping you'd come out a good deal sooner than *that,*" he said. "Maybe even next weekend."

He held the outer door open while she reached into her handbag for her keys. "Well," she said, a little surprised, *"maybe* I could . . ." She searched her mind for doubts, objections, other plans—and realized, feeling suddenly foolish, that she had none. She had no plans for the entire summer. "Yes," she said, "that might be very nice. I think I can probably get away."

"Okay, then. I intend to write you as soon as I get out there. And you'd better write back!" He tapped her nose with the tip of his finger. "Remember, I'm depending on it."

"Don't worry. I've got two married sisters plus my mother, and I never miss a letter." She paused, fitting the key into the inner lock; it was time to make her goodbyes. "Well, I've had a wonderful evening, and I really want to thank you for—Oh, no! Look at this." She withdrew the key and pressed against the door. It swung open at her touch. Something had happened to the bolt.

He bent to examine it. "Looks like somebody unscrewed the little metal plate," he said, poking at the pitted wood with his finger. "I wonder if anything's been robbed." He shook his head. "This fucking city."

She stared uncertainly into the dim light of the hallway. "It's sort of scary."

"Look, would you like me to come up with you? I'll just see you to your door, I don't want to come in or anything."

"Could you, please? I'm sure there's nothing the matter, but just in case someone's inside there . . ." She swallowed.

"Glad to. I'll go first."

Frowning, he stepped into the hall. She followed him. The passage was a narrow one, and silent at this hour; their feet scraped audibly against the yellowing white tiles that climbed stained and broken halfway up the walls. At the farther end a thick black metal door concealed an elevator scarcely larger than a closet, lit by only one bare bulb that dangled from wires in the ceiling. It trembled as the two of them crowded inside, and again when the inner door slid echoingly shut.

With a *whirr* of distant gears the car gave a lurch and rose slowly up the darkened shaft, their shadows flirting back and forth with the swinging of the bulb. They watched the shadows, the curls of paint around the emergency button, and the numbers sliding past the small glass porthole in the door. Through it, as each new floor came into view, a pale circle of light winked open and shut like an eye, then disappeared below them. They said nothing, both of them hushed, listening.

The car slowed, sighed, and came shuddering to rest at the fifth floor. Peering through the glass before Freirs pushed ahead of her, Carol could see that there was no danger after all. The hall was empty.

She walked beside him to her door and slipped her key into the lock. It was an awkward moment; maybe she should plead with him to come in.

"Well," she heard herself say, "thank you once again. I had a really lovely evening." She hoped he could see that she meant it, and wondered if he felt the same. At the turn of the key the door swung inward; beyond it the front hall was dark. She dropped her voice to a whisper. "And it was really sweet of you to come up here like this. I only wish it weren't so late." Quickly, before she lost her nerve, she encircled his neck with her arm and pressed a kiss to the side of his mouth. He seemed to take it as his due.

"Amen," he said. "See you in Jersey."

"I'll be waiting for your letter." She stepped into the darkness; he raised a hand in farewell and turned away. Shutting the door, she heard the clang of the elevator and, moments later, the churning of gears as it started down.

The apartment smelled of garlic and fried meat and, from the doorway of the living room, men's after-shave. Rochelle and her date had not gone out, then; there'd be no dawdling in the kitchen tonight, and no light to guide her to her room. Half feeling her way, Carol tiptoed through the hall; the only illumination came from beneath the bathroom door at the other end. As she passed, it swung silently open. In its light stood the boyfriend, staring at her openmouthed, olive-skinned and hairy. He jumped back when he saw that it was her, his sex jiggling; she tried to look away. The light was snapped off, and she heard a low chuckle. "Thought you were Shelly!" he said. There was toothpaste on his breath.

"No, it's only me." She could feel the nearness of his body as she brushed past him; she groped blindly, nearly stumbling, toward her bedroom. There was the sound of breathing behind her, then a pause, and she heard him pad slowly down the hall.

Once inside the room, she closed the door tightly and switched on a small lamp by her bed. The dancers on the posters seemed to leap out from the wall, arms outstretched in welcome—Merrill Ashley, Baryshnikov, Karen Kain as the Swan Queen—but it was hard to turn her mind from that figure in the bathroom, the damp and shining hair . . .

She forced herself to think of Jeremy, hoping he was really going to send for her, reminding herself, lest she be hurt, how little she really knew of him. How strangely nervous he had been at the end of their walk here, furtively watching for criminals—and cripples!—yet never for a moment losing that special New York cockiness of his. Maybe she should have insisted he come in; she wished he were here beside her, to hold her all night in his arms, but by now he would be downstairs, perhaps back on the street. She went to her window to see.

Parting two slats of the venetian blind, she peered outside. Yes, there he was, trotting briskly down the front steps, his body foreshortened from this angle. He seemed to be moving fast, his stride lengthening; she hoped it came from feeling good about tonight, and not from any eagerness to leave. Within seconds he'd reached the dying maple that stood halfway up the block, leaves trembling in a final ray of moonlight. Soon he would be past the corner, out of sight.

She was just about to turn from the window when, from the shadows somewhere beyond the row of tenements to her left, almost at the edge of her vision, she thought she saw a small white shape drop soundlessly to the sidewalk and go scurrying after him, waving something in its hand as if it were a wand. Midway to the corner it made a queer, mincing little pirouette and disappeared behind a line of cars parked beneath the tree.

This was no cripple; it looked as plump and agile as a child, though surely no child could be out at such an hour. Tugging at the cords along the end, she readjusted the blinds for a better view. The slats tilted open; parallel bands of street light flooded the room. She peered outside again, but it was too late: the moon had set, the street was still, the tree dark and unmoving against the sky. A trail of mist was rising in ghostly tentacles from the sidewalk. Both figures were gone.

JUNE TWENTY-FIFTH

A very special day indeed! Dawn has broken over the horizon like the lifting of a vast, immeasurable curtain, and the sky is rosy with promise. At ease upon the rooftop of his building, he settles back in the dusty canvas deck chair and blinks contentedly at the heavens, his face aglow with early morning sunlight. The air up here is temperate, with just a hint of blossoms beneath the street smells and the scent of roofing tar. Birds cry raucously overhead; breezes stir the pale wisps of his hair. Behind him lies the dark river, sweeping past hills still mottled by shadow. Before him, eastward, stretches the city, its towers like an endless line of tombstones, black against the brightening sky.

The Old One lies back, yawning, and allows himself a smile. He has had a full day of it, and a full night. There has been much to do: roles to play, rituals to perform, the theft of a minor belonging. He has spent the greater part of the night observing the man and the woman; later he narrowed his attentions to the man and stood watch in the street below his window—a squat, shabby little figure hovering just beyond the lamplight, patient and alone, standing huddled beneath the black umbrella, unmoved by the rain that broke the stillness, or the stillness that followed the rain.

At last the window had gone dark, like the woman's a mile away, and, noting the time with a satisfied nod, he'd begun his journey homeward. Even then he was busy, preparing lines of future conversation, reciting certain chants, whispering a word in a long-forgotten tongue. Years of calculations have waited to be verified within the compass of a single sunrise; there have been readings to be taken from the shadows it produced—from the winking red and yellow lights of an unknown vessel passing silently up the Hudson, from reflections of a fading star in the puddle at his feet. His figuring has had to be precise, his timing flawless. In this way, and no other, can the final sites be chosen for the Ceremonies.

Now he is tired, too weak to do more than turn his head from side to side and contemplate the clear, unclouded sky. Yet still he has not slept; nor will he, until the thing he's planned is done. Of human needs, food alone remains, and the occasional dose of sun to warm his bones. As for the absurd routine of sleep—the head mashed to the pillow, the face relaxed or clenched, the mind unmoored, eight hours adrift, lost among infantile fantasies—he has put all that behind him long ago, as easily as a serpent sheds its skin. As for dreams, they have not troubled him for more than half a century.

Not that he would sleep now, in any case. He is far too pleased with the progress he has made. In every act, her every word, no doubt her every thought, the woman has proven herself suitable—positively eager, in fact. She has come through her first day splendidly: after a certain delay, quite inconsequential and in no way her own fault, she has gone on to establish a really promising emotional relationship with the selected man. Final contact is complete.

The man himself is perfect, right down to the date and the hour of his birth nearly thirty years ago. Perfect, too, that he's a solitary soul, lonely and suggestible—the sort who'll pose no problems if correctly used. And used he will be, that much is certain. After all, what else are tools *for?*

The roommate is another story. Something is going to have to be done about her. "Free spirit" indeed! Why, she's nothing but a common whore! He isn't going to have her tempting his little virgin. Not a chance!

Yes, something will definitely have to be done—and soon. He isn't sure what method he will use, but he has never lacked for ideas.

The ascendant sun is dazzling now, making rainbows in his eyes. The Old One blinks and looks away. Beside him, arrayed upon the low brick wall that runs along the edge of the roof, lies the simple apparatus that will occupy his day: the jelly jar, still empty, and the bag, quite full, and—resting on a musician's practice book to keep the pages from turning in the breeze—the shabby leather flute case with the black plastic handle. Common objects, all of them. There will be nothing strenuous for him today, but he will not be idle.

Taking the bag by its cloth straps, he hangs it on a nail projecting just inside the wall, where it dangles heavily, suspended a few inches above the surface of the roof. The leather case is next; from its velvet lining he withdraws a stubby white flageolet that shines like polished ivory. Before putting it to his lips, however, he lays the music book upon his lap, opened to Exercise Seven: Atonal Syncopations. He has, in fact, no interest in music and no intention of wasting time on such a composition, but the seventh exercise bears a vague resemblance to the complicated patterns he'll be playing, and any other tenant who chances upon the roof today will see only a harmless little man, lips puckered, lunch stowed on the wall beside him, laboring earnestly over an unmelodic series of minors, trills, and dissonances. It is good to be prepared.

Already the air has begun to grow warmer; the breeze is soothing at this height, with the occasional fragrance of early summer foliage from the park a dozen floors below. He breathes deeply. Holding the flute in both hands, he blows three notes, soft and low, that fade into silence. The air grows still. Eagerly he looks toward the bag.

Inside it, something stirs.

The touch of a smile crosses his face; he blows the notes once more. The bag stirs violently now, as if something inside it were struggling to be free. It gives a sudden jerk, almost dislodging the brick on which the jar rests.

Carefully placing the jar at his feet, he begins to play.

There is no rhythm to his playing, and no tune. The patterns are impossible to discern. To any listener, it would seem—but for a certain exotic quality in some of the phrases—little more than a succession of random tones, like a man punching typewriter keys in an unknown language. And yet the notes, in fact, form a song. The Death Song.

Which, curiously, is a song about birth.

The gleaming white tube sways erratically before his face; his fingers scuttle like spiders up and down its length. Above him the air trembles with the sound, and whirlwinds sweep invisibly toward the heavens.

It is a moment of awakening. The bag rocks back and forth. All nature is stirring now—the river, the trees, the dancing air—and something outside nature, deep beneath the earth, where rock grinds slowly against rock. He can hear it stirring, and is glad.

Raising his eyes from the now-blinding sun, he goes on playing, gazing into a sky so blue it looks as if it were ready to shatter into a million pieces, like the rending of an egg.

It is going to be a beautiful day.

All morning he plays softly upon the flageolet, his small pink head bobbing in elusive time, the flute sound competing with the cries of the birds. At intervals he pauses to watch the movement in the bag; the thing inside thrashes wildly, nearly tearing through the cloth. Whenever he sees this, he smiles.

Once the sun has wandered to the other side of the sky and is settling toward the western hills, he plays his last three notes. They are the first three he played, but in reverse order. Laying aside the instrument, he pronounces a certain word and pushes himself up from the chair. Five hours or less till midnight: his present work is all but done.

By sunset he is ready. The chair is folded and in place beside the elevator tower, the music tossed away; the flute case and the jelly jar, now full, he takes downstairs.

Behind him, in the center of the roof, lies the aftermath of his day's labor: a glistening pink cruciform of entrails, tied with a stolen red hair.

And spread beneath it, torn as if by razor claws, lies the empty canvas bag, glowing scarlet in the sunset—a bag that, till this day, has held no more than books.

Darkness finds him crouching on the walkway by the river's edge, his dim white form reflected in the water, making certain languid motions with his hand in the space between the concrete and the railing. From the distance of the park he would seem a vulnerable little figure, like a child crouched before a mud puddle, absorbed in some grave and private task. His hand flicks downward, and a cascade of small bright objects, jagged shards as white as bone, falls glimmering in the moonlight to vanish beneath the waves. Here and there a feather, like a speck of cloud, is carried by the wind.

All that remains is the Libation, the offering of the Orh'teine. Formula calls for a beaker or a flask; the jelly jar, he knows, will do as well. With a flourish he empties it into the river. In the instant before it is lost from sight, it stains the waters a cloudy black—though by daylight they may well have shown up red.

Clutching the rail with both hands, he climbs to his feet and stands facing the river. Across it lies the Jersey shore, and beyond that rolling farmlands, the plowed earth cooling now and plunged in night. A few tiny lights flicker like campfires in the dark hills.

To this the man is bound. Tomorrow, with the morning, he'll be speeding toward the countryside, his head stuffed full of ignorant romantic nonsense, his bags weighed down with piles of books—books of just the right sort. How useful he is going to be, once he comes of age and, in the moonlight, reads the passage from the storybook . . .

The old man speaks the Fourth Name, whispers three more words, and smiles. A chilling breeze from off the river stirs the pale wisps of his hair. Watching the stars sweep majestically toward the horizon, he thinks of all that is to come.

The woman is to play the major part, but the man's role will come first. The blind fool doesn't know it yet, but there are going to be some changes made amid those distant hills—changes beyond dreaming.

And on the night that he turns thirty they will all begin with him.

BOOK TWO

POROTH FARM

"Surely," I said, "there is little left to explore. You have been born a few hundred years too late for that."

"I think you are wrong," he replied; "there are still, depend upon it, quaint, undiscovered countries and continents of strange extent."

—Arthur Machen, *The Novel of the Black Seal*

JUNE TWENTY-SIXTH

Dear Carol,
    Greetings from the sticks! I've been here all of four and a half hours and already my voice has taken on a colorful rustic twang. By this time tomorrow I expect to be walking around with a straw hat over my eyes and a wheat stalk dangling from my lips. Amazing what this country air can do.

Actually, the air here *is* quite nice, and it makes me wonder what in God's name I've been breathing for the last twenty-nine years. (I just hope it doesn't give me one of those legendary country appetites.) Outside in the yard you can really smell things growing. Which, for this guy, is something of a novelty.

Everything out here is ridiculously green, and so silent I'm tempted just to sit still and listen to it. No traffic noise, no subways or construction gangs or psychos. And no more jangling telephones, thank God! Believe me, it's every bit as quiet as the library. You'll feel right at home.

I came out today on the afternoon bus, lugging two monstrous suitcases stuffed with books, papers, and a few changes of clothes. Sarr met me in Gilead with his truck. He's just like I described him. He comes on a bit solemn at first—gloomy, even—but underneath it all I believe he's just shy. You'll like him.

You'll probably like Deborah even more. She's already filled me in on all the local gossip. (Gilead, it seems, is not composed entirely of saints; though I noticed she didn't bring this up till her husband was gone.) She also insisted on telling me the complete, unedited life histories of each of their seven cats. I'll spare you the details; you'll probably get an encore when you come out. She's fascinated by New York City, incidentally, which I gather she hasn't visited since meeting Sarr.

So here I am, ensconced in my rural retreat, sitting at an old wooden table which I've set up as a desk. There's a small bookcase right beside it which Deborah found in the storeroom, and another one next to my bed. My books are all unpacked now, and I've spent the last couple of hours getting things tidied up a bit, patching a few holes in the screens, etc. The windows let in lots of sun, and the place is much more cheerful than I probably made it sound. You'll see when you get here (which, needless to say, I hope you'll do next weekend). I certainly don't anticipate any problems.

Well, I suppose I ought to get busy with some work of my own. I hope to devote myself to the Three R's while I'm out here—reading and 'riting, with 'rithmetic to help me figure out how to crowd a year's worth of the first two into a single summer. (To keep track of my progress I intend to start a journal, but somehow doubt it'll rival Thoreau's.) Earlier today I found some old lawn chairs in the store-room on the other side of this outbuilding, so I guess I'll take one of them outside and read till dinnertime. There's only an hour or so of daylight left, and I may as well take advantage of it.

See you soon, I trust. Write and let me know.

XXX

Jeremy

P.S. I'm enclosing a Fleminton bus schedule. You have to tell the driver in advance that you want Gilead; otherwise they bypass the place.) You could come out Friday after work and be here before dark.

Horace Walpole, *The Castle of Otranto* (1764). Chapter one. "Manfred, Prince of Otranto, had one son and one daughter: the latter, a most beautiful virgin, aged eighteen, was called Matilda. Conrad, the son, was three years younger, a homely youth . . ."

No one can accuse Walpole of beating around the bush.

Essay topics: Show how the techniques of stagecraft are used to en-hance suspense. Gothic fantasy as literature of setting, mystery as literature of plot, science fiction as literature of ideas.

Why the Gothic is inherently conservative. Sexual nature of grief.
Sexual nature of fear.

After dinner, chapters two through five. " 'I would say something more,' said Matilda, struggling, 'but it would not be—Isabella—Theodore—for my sake—oh!' She expired. Isabella and her women tore Hippolita from the corpse; but Theodore printed a thousand kisses on her clay-cold hands . . ."

Somehow this stuff doesn't really grab me. Castles, monks, giant hel-mets . . . Maybe I shouldn't have started so far back.

Or maybe it's just the glare from this goddamned desk lamp. Mus get a proper shade for it next time I'm in town, otherwise I'll go blin Would walk back inside & ask the Poroths for one, but don't thi

they'd be much help, since—bless their masochistic hearts—the two of
them seem determined to make do with gas lamps & kerosene lanterns.
(Something I deliberately neglected to mention in letter to Carol.)

Anyway, thank God for Thomas Edison.

Nighttime now. The Poroths already have their lights off, & a million moths are tapping at my screens. One of them's a fat white fellow
the size of a small bird. Never saw one like it. What kind of caterpillar
must it have been?

Jesus, I hope the damned things don't push through the wire.

Wonder if the dampness brings them out. There's a line of hills not
far away, but here the elevation's low & the night air smells of water.
Already I've noticed a greenish band of mildew around the bottom of
my walls.

Bugs, too. Lots of them. This place is really infested. (Something
else I neglected to tell Carol. Ditto dampness, musty smell, wasps near
smokehouse, etc. etc. Why turn her off the place before she comes?)
Seems to me the Poroths might have taken a bit more time to clean it,
instead of waiting till I got here; I had to go over the entire room twice
after Deborah'd left, & each time I found new ones. God know what
they were. Sure as hell don't care to look them up in the guide.

Worst of all are the spiders, esp. near the screens. Think I got most
of them by now, but had to use up half a roll of paper towels squashing
the bastards. Must buy more the next time I'm in town, & a can or two
of insect spray.

Killing spiders is supposed to bring bad luck—

> "If you wish to live & thrive,
> Let the Spider walk alive"

—but I'll be damned if I'm going to sleep with anything crawling
around in here. Anyway, too late now: I'm already a mass murderer.
They can add up the total in heaven.

Still hard to know just what to make of the Poroths. Everything
they do seems to have a special meaning that outsiders can't begin to
understand. Even the farm itself has a kind of religious significance.
It's supposed to bring the two of them closer to God—here they can be
"in the world, but not of it," Sarr says—& they're supposed to find satisfaction in the day-to-day labor, rather than in the money it might
bring. That's why they have no restrictions against working on Sunday, & why progress is such a dirty word to them: it means escape from
toil.

Deborah seems to work as hard as Sarr does. She was cleaning up in
here when we arrived, on her knees scrubbing the floor. Something
curiously erotic about a woman in that position, exerting herself while
you're at your ease.

Sarr tried to pitch in & help for a while, but finally he excused himself & left. He was probably relieved to get back to the fields; he's sure not much on small talk. At dinner tonight he gave me a blow-by-blow chronicle of this morning's service—apparently the whole community meets each Sunday in someone's back yard, with the Poroths' turn coming up next month—& then launched into a long, earnest explanation of the various theological differences between the Brethren & the general run of Mennonites, differences he claimed were extremely deep. (For a silent type, he really talks a lot when he gets going.) He lost me after the first minute or two. As far as I'm concerned, they're all just fundamentalists & they all wear funny clothes. I've even noticed an occasional 'tis or 'twasn't creeping into their conversation, esp. when they're going in for Bible talk. I gather the townfolk are even more prone to it.

Made my first mistake at dinner tonight. Sat down & started to eat, then heard Sarr saying grace. Hastily apologized, of course, & waited till he was done, but I find that such things don't embarrass me the way they used to. Maybe that's because I'm nearing thirty.

(Shit, only one goddamned week left. Somehow I dread that moment. Better not to think of it.)

The food, at least, was even better than I'd hoped: chicken, peas, & baked potato, with spice cake for dessert. Homemade, too. Deborah obviously likes to cook.

I'll bet she makes Sarr a damned good wife. He kept reaching out to touch her every time she passed where he was sitting. I guess planting makes people horny. Can't say I blame him; I felt almost the same this afternoon, when she was scrubbing my floor. Not that she makes the slightest attempt to be seductive.

I'd like to see her with her hair down. Still can't get that picture of her out of my head, standing there waving goodbye to me, naked beneath that long black dress.

She seems to be the perfect Bountiful Housewife: full breasts, wide hips, always filled with energy. Looks as if she'll bear a lot of children.

Right now, though, those damned cats are the closest thing they've got, & they fuss over them as if they were real children. One of them, Sarr's cat, may be a bit of a problem. She's the grey one, the oldest of the lot. She also happens to be the meanest. Maybe she's jealous of the rest, or maybe she was just born with an evil disposition. All I know is, she's the only cat that's ever bitten anyone—various friends & relations, including some local bigwig named Brother Joram—& after seeing how she snarls at the other cats when they get in her way or come too close while she's feeding, I decided to keep my distance. Fortunately, she seems a bit scared of me & retreats whenever I approach.

Probably best to keep away from all of them, in fact. Sneezing, itching eyes, whenever they're around. Should have gone to that allergist when I had the chance.

The Poroths seem pretty catlike themselves. Interesting case of people resembling their pets. Sarr is inclined to be morose & somewhat taciturn—a solemn, slightly suspicious tomcat—while Deb is bubbly & talkative, as animated as one of the kittens. Clearly a case of opposites attracting, despite the similarity of appearance.

At dinner Sarr said that some of the locals still use "snake oil" for whatever ails them. Asked him how the snakes were killed, slightly misquoting line from *Vathek:* "The oil of serpents I have pinched to death will be a pretty present." We discussed the wisdom of pinching snakes. Learned there may be a copperhead out back, over near the brook. Somehow the Poroths neglected to mention this on my first visit. Will watch my step. (Though according to my field guide, far more people die each year from bee and wasp stings than from snakebites. Insect venom is more toxic.)

Supposedly there are frogs & turtles out there too. Have yet to see any. Maybe they only come out at night.

Over coffee, Sarr talked of the house he hopes to build someday, when the two of them have children. He'll build it out of stone, he said, "three floors high & three feet thick." Then he shut up, & I had to keep the conversation going through dessert. Hate eating in silence: animal sounds of mastication, bubbling stomachs. Didn't some Balzac character claim talk aided digestion? Probably true.

By this time they both looked ready for bed (though I doubt if sleep was the only thing on their minds), so it seemed wise to get out of their way. Brushed my teeth—not forgetting dental floss—& took the usual vitamins, just in case.

As soon as I left their place & came back here, I began to feel sort of lonely. Still some light left in the sky, but the lawn behind the house was already swarming with fireflies. Never saw so many. Knelt & watched them for a while & listened to the crickets. That's one sound the city doesn't have. Too bad Carol isn't here; she'd appreciate it.

Wonder if she'll actually come out. Hope my letter made the place sound inviting; hope I didn't lay it on too thick. Maybe I should have been more honest with her. Just as well I didn't mention how narrow my bed is, though—really no more than a cot. That's the sort of thing she can discover on her own. (Also, incentive for losing a bit of weight this week.)

Must remember to get a haircut, if I can get into Flemington. May be my last one for quite some time.

Later: After making it through *Otranto* (not the most auspicious start), wasted nearly an hour arranging my books. First tried putting them in chronological order, since that's the way I hope to read them; t copyright dates can be ambiguous with the older works, & too many authors get broken up. Then tried chronologically by date of author's birth, but I didn't know most of these, & no way to find out. So back to boring old alphabetical order by author, with anthologies bringing up the rear. (After much deliberation, decided that the works of Saki had to be placed under M for Munro.)

Why am I so neurotic about my books?

Anyway, they look damned nice, lined up on the shelves.

Ann Radcliffe, *The Mysteries of Udolpho* (1794).

Sat up late pushing through volume one. All the elements of classic Gothic romance. Heroine passive but resourceful; hero/villain dark, mysterious, & cruel—predating Byron and Brontës. Lots of spook effects. (Understand they're all explained away "scientifically" at end of volume two; if so, a bad mistake. M. R. James speaks of her "exasperating timidity" in this regard. Check reference.) Plot dated, but loved the descriptions of picturesque scenes, esp. Udolpho itself, rugged Apennine castle. Would be nice to put book on curriculum, but only one student in a dozen would read it. Too damned long.

Long for me too. In fact, had to keep remembering to slow down, be patient, let myself unwind. After twenty years of school, I've gotten into habit of skimming everything, as if novels were newspapers. Tried to put myself in frame of mind of eighteenth-century reader with plenty of time on his hands & no distractions.

Certainly no distractions here. No TV or movies, no goddamned Sunday *Times,* no friends to call or drop by ... Nothing but the insects batting themselves mindlessly against the screens.

What was it Emerson said in his journal? "Thank God I live in the country!"

Suppose it's time I got some sleep. Wish to hell there was a bathroom in this building. Poroths said they'd leave the kitchen door unlocked for me, but I sure as hell don't feel like stumbling all the way back there without a flashlight & maybe waking the two of them up. Looks so goddamned *dark* out there. Where did all the fireflies go?

Maybe I should get a hollow metal oil drum to pee in & lift it for exercise each day as it fills, like the guy who started out lifting a calf every morning &, by the time it grew up, was strong enough to lift a full-grown bull.

Guess I'll water the grass in front of this building: pissing beneath the stars, just like my ancestors. Very romantic. (Though God knows what'll be crawling up my ankles.)

At least the crickets are still there to keep me company

*

Back inside now. Felt vulnerable, standing there against the night, but must say the sky looked spectacular. I don't think I've ever seen so many stars & can't remember the last time I actually saw the Milky Way. That's something else the city doesn't have. (Though, typically, my first thought on looking up was, Jesus, it's just like the Planetarium!)

Anyway, stood there gawking till my neck got stiff.

But the real shock was the view I got of this building. The lamp on my desk must be the only illumination for miles, acting as a sort of beacon, & I could see dozens of flying shapes making right for the screens. When you're inside here, it's like being in a display case: every eye can watch you, from the woods & fields & lawn. But all you see is darkness.

It wouldn't be so bad if this room weren't open on three sides— though I suppose that does let in the breeze. Wish the trees didn't crowd so close to the windows by my bed. The middle sections of their trunks are all lit up where the light falls on them; between the undergrowth and roots, there's not even enough space back there to walk.

Two A.M. now, and a few moths are still hovering outside the screens. A little green one must have gotten in when I opened the door. It's flying around this lamp now, along with several gnats too small to kill.

Lots of noise out there, too. How could I have said this place was silent? Trees moving, branches snapping, sounds of breeze & running water. Frogs now, croaking somewhere in the distance, with the crickets coming in behind them.

This is what I wanted, I suppose.

Just saw an unpleasantly large spider scurry across the floor near the foot of my bed. Vanished behind the footlocker. Must remember to get that insect spray, & a flashlight.

Wonder what Carol's doing now.

JUNE TWENTY-NINTH

Dear Jeremy,
  Greetings from the Apple! I'm glad to hear you're enjoying
yourself, and that you haven't fallen down any cisterns or caught poison ivy or been eaten by a bear. We'll make an outdoorsman of you yet!

You really deserve a nice long reply, but this one's going to be short,
as I'm writing it on my break, with half a dozen people in this tiny office breathing down my neck. I just wanted to let you know that,
thanks to good old Rosie, I'll be able to see you more easily than I'd expected. It turns out Rosie owns a car, and he told me I could borrow it
this weekend, as he has some "very important business" (he pursed his
little lips, and looked oh so stern as he said this) which will be keeping
him in New York.

The only drawback is he needs the car on Monday for some Fourth of
July affair, so I won't be able to take advantage of the three-day weekend. Still, it'll be nice to get out of the city, and we'll have some time
together. I hope to get an early start Saturday morning, so if all goes
well I should be there by noon. I wish I had some sort of map, but Gilead sounds like one of those little towns where everybody knows everybody else, so once I get there I'm sure I'll find someone to give me
directions to the Poroths. I don't expect to have any trouble; remember,
you're dealing with the third runner-up in the B.C.Y.C. Senior Girls'
Pathfinder Competition.

Rosie's really done a lot for me, I must admit. He's a very dear person and treats me just like his own daughter—or, rather, granddaughter. He says he doesn't think I'm eating right, so tomorrow, before I
come to work, he's taking me out for a champagne brunch at some
fancy place on Twenty-first Street. Now that's the sort of life I think I
could get used to—a glass or two of bubbly in the morning and I'll be
floating all day! And yesterday he brought me a bottle of wine from, as
he called it, his "private cellar" (which is probably just a cupboard
above the kitchen sink). Maybe I'll bring it out with me as a house gift
this weekend.

I've also been working very hard, believe it or not. I want Rosie to
feel he's getting his money's worth. Last Saturday I really buckled
down and went through all those articles he gave me, so I could have
the summaries ready for him when he dropped by here on Monday. I

think that really impressed him, at least I hope so. I charged him for twelve hours' work (actually it took me close to sixteen), and he gave me a check for $144 right there on the spot. He took me completely at my word. After the way some people treat me in this stupid library, I really appreciate decency like that.

By the way, rather than go to the trouble and expense of Xeroxing those stories you'd requested, I'll simply bring you the entire book this weekend. It'll be a lot easier, and anyway, Rosie's convinced me that things like that are much more fun to read in the original. I'll sign it out before I leave work today.

Rosie's just amazing when it comes to books—I mean the things he's learned. You'd be surprised, he's really quite good company, for a person his age. He's been all over the world (mostly doing some kind of heavy research in linguistics), and he tells the most incredible stories. I had him up to my apartment last night, just for coffee and cake, and he talked to me in something called Agon di-Gatuan, which means "the Old Language." He's teaching me a chant in it and promises I'll be able to speak it fluently by the end of summer. It's like nothing I've ever heard.

Well, my break's just about over, and I'd better end now if I want to get this in today's mail. See you on Saturday.

XXX

Carol

P.S. Rosie gave me something for you. I'll be sure to bring it with me. He just loves to give presents. He's also very keen on order, decorum, *rules,* things like that, and is always telling me how "old-fashioned" he is—"and proud of it." I don't think he quite approves of Rochelle. Last night, just as he was getting ready to leave, she walked in with a few of her friends, and one of the guys made some kind of joke about "older guys stealing all the best girls." It was meant to be funny, and Rochelle said I should take it as a compliment, but poor old Rosie looked *very* upset.

JUNE THIRTIETH

O n some days he gives way to rages.

Morning finds him on the beach, walking back and forth along the water's edge, the battered old umbrella tucked uselessly beneath his arm. He pays no attention to the flocks of bathers, to the cries of children braving the assaults of the surf or playing on the rubbish-strewn sand, or to the oily, sun-warmed bodies of their elders lying inert upon blankets with radios and picnic baskets by their heads. Humanity, for the moment, is forgotten, its noise and filth and ugliness ignored. He is far too busy studying the patterns of the waves and, at other moments, squinting directly upward into the blinding blue dome of the sky.

To those on the beach, should anyone chance to be watching, this awkward little figure trudging through the wet sand in a baggy blue suit and soggy overshoes which more than once become soaked as a wave breaks over his ankles might seem a tourist from some other era; as he peers up and down the beach, he might well be in search of some seaside vista fit for the amateur painter or photographer. Or perhaps he'd be mistaken for some confused but harmless octogenarian who's wandered out from one of the old-age homes that line the avenue across from the boardwalk.

But the concerns of art and freedom are, in fact, far from his mind. More urgent matters have brought him to the shore today: matters of geography, sand formation, tides.

He is scouting locations.

Suddenly he pauses, grows rigid. Something up the beach has distracted him: a pair of lovers lying together, body to body, in the boardwalk's striped shadow.

Rage sweeps over him like a wave. Jerkily he begins moving toward them, lips tightening, color surging to his face. He can feel, in his fists, the pumping of their loathesome hearts; the air before him rings with ancient voices screaming for a kill. Oh, to perform the Voola'teine! To drown the pair, to burn them where they lie, to climb the boardwal' and drop knives upon their flesh through the cracks between t' planks. In a vision he sees thrashing young bodies buried bene: waves of smothering sand . . .

He calms himself in time and turns away. The day is young. H other sites to visit.

*

That afternoon he spends walking jauntily through the park, swinging his umbrella, making silent calculations with the figures he discerns in the branches of the trees. As the sun slips behind a horn-shaped cloud, he spies a group of people coming toward him up the path: a slim, be-spectacled man and his pale, wide-eyed wife, their little girl in her red sunsuit, and a baby recumbent in a stroller.

And like the sudden waning of the light, his rage returns.

His eyes narrow; his face goes dark; his little hand tightens on the umbrella. Trembling, he whirls and follows them, his face fixed in an amiable smile.

The family turns eastward toward the zoo; he follows, drawing closer. As they stop to exclaim at penguins, hippos, bears, he eases himself beside them, nodding fondly to the parents, watching benignly as they're drawn on toward the panther curled within a spot of shade, the lion dozing grandly in the sunlight, the tiger pacing madly in its cage . . .

He sees the air vibrate around the tawny form, feels its baffled hunger, shares the beast's longing to leap and slash and rend. Blinking before the cage, smiling at the children, he loses himself in a reverie of death: how he would love to press that vile infant through the bars! to lacerate its flesh! to crush its throbbing neck with his own hands!

And he could do it, too. Though he dares not. Not now.

But for one brief moment, while the gazes of the other three are turned toward the cage and the infant's gaze toward him, he allows his mask to slip. The grin disappears. Eyes go hard. Teeth show in a tiger-ish snarl . . .

Smiling once more, he strolls onward, momentarily relieved. Behind him, to the astonishment of its parents, the infant explodes into wails of terror.

North of the zoo, just off the path, rises a small stand of dogwood and magnolia bushes and, hidden behind them, a tiny patch of dark ground that shelters wildflowers. He stands poised in the middle of it now, fea-tures contorted as before, swinging about him with his umbrella. *Swoosh!*—foliage lies slashed to pieces. *Swoosh!*—heads of flowers are sliced off clean. Knuckles whiten on the umbrella; his complexion grows red; his breath comes in furious gasps between clenched teeth. The air around him shrieks with mangled leaves and tattered blossoms.

The episode lasts but a minute. Afterward, calm once more, the smile back in place, a fragile pink magnolia in his buttonhole, he slips back to the path, umbrella at his side, and heads jauntily for home.

JULY FIRST

The letter was waiting for him in the kitchen. Freirs read it over lunch. He looked up to see Deborah watching him intently from across the table.

"Remember," he said, "I mentioned something about having guests out?" Deborah nodded, while Sarr continued eating. "Well, I hope it's not going to be inconvenient, but believe it or not, this friend of mine is thinking of driving out here tomorrow. I know it's a little early in the summer, but—"

Deborah silenced him. "Now don't go worrying yourself. That'll be just fine." She stood and began clearing away some of the dishes. "We like having guests out here, don't we, honey?"

Sarr nodded without much enthusiasm. "Mmm-hmm. Be glad to meet him."

"Well, actually, it's a girl. Name's Carol. Someone I know from the city."

Sarr looked up from his dessert with a tiny flicker of annoyance—and perhaps something else. "She'll be staying overnight?"

"I think so." Freirs fell silent, reluctant to say more.

Sarr's mouth made a thin straight line. "We'll put her in the room upstairs."

Deborah, moving past him, touched his shoulder. "Honey, isn't that for Jeremy to say?" It drew an angry look.

"Upstairs will be fine," Freirs said hurriedly, disinclined to make an issue of it. Let them go ahead and prepare a room for her; she wouldn't have to stay there. "She should be getting here around noon tomorrow. Somebody's lending her his car. I was just wondering about the food situation. If you like, I could drive into town and pick up a few extra things."

Sarr pushed his chair back from the table. "No, no need of that. 'Tis a blessing to have guests in a home, and she'll be welcome here." Wiping his mouth with the back of his hand, he stood. "Well, guess I'd best see to those cuttings out there, before the worms do." He turned and left the kitchen, his heavy footsteps echoing on the porch. Moments later they heard him descend the back steps and set out toward the fields.

Freirs waited till he'd gone. "He didn't look all that pleased, did he?"

"Oh, he's not one to show it, but he's pleased, all right. He likes when strangers come and look the place over. Reminds him that he really belongs here—that he's back where his roots are."

"Roots?" Freirs laughed. "You know, he mentioned something about that the first time he was showing me around. I thought he was kidding."

Deborah shook her head. "My husband doesn't jest. This farm's real special to him."

"But I thought you bought the place just last winter."

"We did—but Sarr's family owned it a long time before. They were the first to settle here."

"You mean the Poroths built this place?"

"No, it was on his mother's side. The Troets. They're another one of Gilead's old families."

"Yes, I remember. A group of them died in a fire."

"And this is where they lived."

"You mean the fire was right here? On this site?"

She nodded. "It was a long time ago—a hundred years or more. Sarr told me about it. He says the house we're in now is the second on this spot, built on the old foundation. The first burned right down to the ground, with naught left but the chimney and this old thing." She gestured toward the squat cast-iron stove. "I forget how many people died. Six or seven, I think. Mother, father, babies—the whole family."

"Except for one," said Freirs. "The young boy that people think set it. Matt Geisel told me about him."

"Well, whatever the cause, it was a tragedy." She turned back to the dishes.

Freirs nodded, then reached for the pudding bowl. "Must have happened at night, while they were asleep. Otherwise you'd think they could've gotten out."

"Yes . . . Yes, it must have been at night." Deborah stood at the window, gazing absently into the sunshine. It was barely noon. Freirs sat contented over dessert. Outside lay her garden, the cornfields, the barn, distant hills—familiar things, all of them, the constants of her life; yet it seemed, at the moment, that they hinted at a terrible impermanence. She turned away, busying herself with the washing, but her thoughts were on something else entirely, something madly out of place on so bright and fair a day: the image of a cold black sky and, beneath it, reddening the night for miles around, a pyramid of flame.

She heard a spoon scrape against the bowl. "Come on, Jeremy," she said, rousing herself. "I want to see you finish up that pudding."

"A real smart choice," the man is saying. In the sunlight flooding through the open doorway, the smile lines around his mouth show as lines of fatigue. "It's always a pleasure to deal with someone who knows what he wants." He marks several spaces with an X and slides the forms across the battered desk. "Now all I need from you is your John Hancock, there at the bottom of the page . . . Uh-huh, and there too . . . That's right, very good. Thanks a lot." Gathering up the papers, he pushes back his chair and stands. "Now if you'll just wait here a minute, Mr.—uh, Rosebottom, I'll get these things taken care of for you right away."

"You're very kind."

Outside, in the lot, sunlight gleams from the silent rows of cars. A line of red plastic pennants flutters overhead. Seated by the doorway of the office, the old man hums a tuneless little song and watches the afternoon traffic speed obliviously past. He feels the building vibrate to the rumbling of the trucks and smells the gasoline fumes and the smoke from the exhausts. Here, on the outskirts of the city, the world lies locked in concrete, but his thoughts are far away, where tiny shafts of green push through the soil and small houses sleep in the shadow of the woods.

Out there, among the farming people, the visitor will now be settled in: reading, or dozing, or engaged in some half-hearted exploration of his new surroundings. Perhaps he has already had his first discouraging taste of loneliness or boredom, unwilling as he might be to admit it. Another day should bring him around—just in time for his birthday and the delivery of the book. When the moment comes, he will be ready.

And as for the woman . . .

"She's all yours now, mister. Here's the ownership. Your keys are in the car." The salesman has returned; together they start across the lot, past grill and chrome and windshields bearing scrawled white prices. On one of them the price has been erased. "Well, here she is. You can drive her right out of here." He pats the polished metal of the hood. "She'll give you years of service."

"Years?" The old man blinks distractedly.

"No question about it! G.M. built these things to last. You can't go wrong buying American." The hood reverberates hollowly beneath his fist. "Registration's in the glove compartment, along with your warranty. Like I said, any problems, you got all the coverage you need. It's good up to one year or ten thousand miles, whichever comes first."

And what if neither comes? the old man wonders, but he is barely listening.

He is thinking of the farm, and of the woman who will visit it this weekend. Her position is much clearer than the man's, her motives quite transparent; her behavior can already be predicted—and provoked. Once a few small tasks are successfully behind her, her education can begin in earnest. She will make a willing pupil.

But there is still another visitor to come—though nobody will think of it as one. At least not till it stands revealed . . .

"And don't forget," the salesman is saying, "there's a free tank of gas waiting for you, right over there at the pump." He holds open the door. "Take it from me, mister, you got yourself a lot of car for your money. She'd make it clear around the world."

The Old One smiles. "Oh, she won't be going quite that far. Just to New Jersey and back."

BOOK THREE

THE CALL

12. CALLING IN THE DHOL.
Only the player holding the Book may call in the Dhol, and
only at the designated time.
— Instructions to the Dynnod

JULY SECOND

The heat in the little Chevy had grown oppressive, but rolling down the window meant she couldn't listen to the radio. No matter, she'd had her fill of Honda ads and reports of what a great weekend it was going to be. Silly to get your hopes up . . . But maybe it *would* be great. Carol turned her head from side to side as she let the gusts of wind from off the highway cool her scalp; once again she found herself thanking God she'd had her hair cut short. Did men feel this cleansed, this free, all the time? The Voorhis Library back there in the city seemed like a prison on the other side of the world.

She had lost track of the time, and with it her sense of direction. She knew only that she was extremely late. Despite her intentions of starting out at ten, she had put in too many hours last night over the week's work for Rosie—papers on a certain Ozark nursery rhyme, a fertility ritual in North Africa, and something called the Mao Game, though it wasn't Chinese but Welsh—and she'd overslept this morning despite the sunlight streaming through her blinds. Rochelle, who'd been supposed to wake her, had gone out—shopping for shoes, she'd said, returning just as Carol left—and obtaining the car from the uptown lot where Rosie kept it had taken the better part of an hour. It had been almost one by the time she'd left the city, and the last news report she'd heard had said one forty-five. Now the radio was drowned out by the wind.

On the seat beside her the reassuring bulk of Rochelle's red canvas tote bag, borrowed for the weekend, bobbed up and down with the motion of the car. Inside, pressed against her nightgown and a sweatshirt she probably wouldn't need, lay the wine Rosie had brought her—a home brew, white, in an unlabeled bottle—and a slim little package wrapped in white paper that he'd given her for Jeremy. It was a pack of cards, he'd said, "an amusing variation on the old tarot deck." Leave it to Rosie to think of everyone. Alongside them were the three books she was taking to the farm. Two were for herself, just in case she found the time: a dog-eared paperback of *The Bell Jar* and an early Teilhard de Chardin, copiously underlined by the fellow novitiate from whom she'd borrowed it long ago. The third book—the Machen—was for Jeremy, and bore special instructions from Rosie. "Now for heaven's sake don't just hand it to him when you get there," he had told her, old eyes twinkling. "Save it for Saturday night. It's the sort of tale you've got to read at bedtime; otherwise it simply doesn't *work!*"

One thing about Rosie, he sure took his literature seriously.

Freirs sat in a deck chair on the lawn outside his building, squinting in the glimmering sunlight and heat, attempting to concentrate on his book while brushing away two small flies that kept buzzing around his head. He would have been glad to move back inside to the cool shadows of his room, but he was hoping to work up a last-minute suntan before Carol arrived. He wished that despite Deborah's good cooking he'd made more of an effort to diet during the past week, but at least he'd forced himself to take a few minutes' jog along the road this morning (followed by a long soak in the tub) and afterward had made a real attempt to brighten up his room; there were clean sheets on the bed, a poster of Resnais's *Providence* tacked to the wall, and a vase of fresh-cut roses from the bushes beside the house. His books and papers were in order. He had even trimmed the ivy vines that surrounded his windows.

The day was at its hottest now, the heat soporific, and, despite the persistence of the flies, it took some effort of will simply to remain awake. He was beginning to feel slightly guilty, sitting there reading, daydreaming, drowsing, shifting position only to unstick his perspiring skin from the back of the chair, all in plain sight of Sarr and Deborah laboring in the nearby field to the beat of some monotonous little chant. It was clearly hard work—a lot harder than turning the pages of a novel, and a hell of a lot more boring. But he made no move to help them, nor did he retreat inside. *Whatever they may think of me,* he told himself, *I'm paying good money for this reading time and I'm damned well entitled to enjoy it.*

He was, in fact, enjoying it. *The Monk,* the Gothic he was immersed in, was proving far more lively than the others he'd read—and, as he'd been pleased to discover, unrelievedly dirty-minded, even by modern standards. He could imagine the sensation it must have caused back in the eighteenth century.

But he was growing impatient and uneasy. Where was Carol? What could be keeping her? She had told him she'd be there by noon, and it was already a quarter past two. Maybe something had come up and she'd had to bow out of the weekend. For once he wished the Poroths had a phone; it was frustrating to have to rely on the mail. He had left a forwarding address with the post office back in New York, but so far he'd received nothing except Carol's letter, addressed directly to the farm, and a few birthday cards, hollowly cheerful things congratulating him on entering his fourth decade, a doom which in fact would befall him tomorrow. He had carefully hidden the cards away in the top drawer of the bureau, deep among his notebooks and his stationery, so as not to be reminded of the day. He wondered if tomorrow's mail would bring a card from Laura or his ex-wife. He rather hoped it would not.

God, could it really be tomorrow? How had it come so soon? He felt like Doctor Faustus, with his one bare hour to live. Of course, turning twenty had been even worse; it had seemed so tragic, somehow, to kiss his teenage years goodbye, with all their arrogance and special privileges, that sense of glorious future possibilities . . .

He felt the book fall shut. His head was growing heavy; his mind was slowing down. He was dozing off again, drifting back into a purple world where dreams and half-dreams mingled, heated by the sunlight that flamed against his eyelids. Carol sat nearby, stretching her arms in the warmth. With a languorous movement she rolled toward him, mashing her hips against the back of his hand, and instantly he knew that she was naked beneath her skirt; he could almost feel a wisp of hair against his fingertips. But the hair, he saw now, was not Carol's, it was Deborah's, thick and dark as fur, and at his touch she rose and stood before him with Deborah's full hips, Deborah's full breasts. He saw her glaring down at him, saw her mouth fall open as if she were about to speak, and suddenly the place his fingers touched was wet.

He awoke with a gasp. The Poroths' old charcoal cat, Rebekah, was pacing back and forth in the grass beside his chair, butting her head softly against his outstretched hand and looking up at him. As he watched, her pink tongue darted out to lick his fingertips.

Backs aching from the hours spent stooped over the furrowed ground beneath the burning sky, Sarr and Deborah were planting pumpkin seed between the bare rows where soon tiny corn sprouts would dot the field. Less than fifty yards away their visitor sat nodding over his reading, brushing sporadically at some invisible flying insect. From time to time Deborah would look toward him and smile, but her husband only shook his head and kept his gaze upon the ground.

Whenever the mood struck them, they would sing one of their planting songs—a different song this time, simpler, more in keeping with the present task:

> *"One for the blackbird,*
> *One for the crow,*
> *One for the cutworm,*
> *And three to grow."*

Suddenly Deborah paused in the singing and poked her husband in the ribs. "Look," she said, lowering her voice and grinning. "Look him."

Over by the outbuilding Freirs had dozed off again. The book lay open on his lap, the pages turning slowly backward.

Sarr frowned and looked away. He could usually convince himself he loved this labor—hellfire, he really *did!*—but it was harder with Freirs so near and so disconcertingly idle. In truth, he would much rather have been asleep right now himself, or at least lying up in the little bedroom on the cool sheets, while Deborah, in the kitchen, made him something cold to drink. Then she would come upstairs to him with two tall glasses on a tray, the ice cubes clinking as she walked, the long dress swishing softly around her legs . . . He shook his head to clear it of this vision and stomped some dirt over a clump of seeds with the heel of his boot.

"Wouldn't be surprised if he got twenty hours of sleep a day!"

Deborah smiled. "Now, honey, that's not fair. You know how late he stays up every night, and I've seen him up real early in the morning, doing his exercises. He didn't see me looking."

Sarr snorted derisively. "Exercises! That's a laugh! And then he spends all morning soaking in the tub—as if he's even worked up a sweat! Let me tell you, if he really wanted to build some strength he'd be out here helping us. Lord knows there's plenty of work to be done." Laying a line of seeds along the furrow and pressing each into the earth, he straightened up and rubbed his back. "I'll give him all the muscles he wants. I'll bet he's never done a day's work in his life. Not real work, like this."

He noticed that his wife was making a face at him. "What's so funny?" he demanded.

"You are," she said, nudging him with her hip. "You act like you've been doing this ever since you were a little boy. You forget who you're talking to! I've seen where you grew up, and the nearest you ever got to a field was that playground out behind the school. I remember you at college, only a few years ago. You didn't have a callus on your hand! In fact, I remember now, that's just what I liked about you. You had the softest hands I'd ever seen."

He had to laugh. She really took him out of himself, this woman. She was good for him. "Lord's my witness," he said, "*any* hands would seem soft to you after some of the clodhoppers you took up with. I was probably the first man you ever saw who didn't have dirt all over his face and manure on his shoes!"

Playfully she tossed a lump of dirt at him. "Well, you sure do now, mister!"

He reached for her and would have thrown her down beneath him, he knew she expected him to, but at that moment a small cloud drif across the sun and shadows darkened the field. His smile fa abruptly; he drew away his hand. "There'll be a time for this later said. "Right now we've work to do." He bent back to the rows.

Responding to his mood, she pulled away. She was used to these changes in him. "And not even much time for that," she said. She wiped a sleeve across her sweating forehead. "If that girl of his is coming today, I've got to get back inside soon and start dinner."

Sarr nodded silently, busy grappling with the earth. Deborah's mention of the girl had reminded him of something that had been troubling him. He felt like a fool, now, for having carried on so with her. There was something more important on his mind.

It really was a shame, Carol decided, that she wasn't going to sleep with Jeremy.

She would have liked to. And under different circumstances she might actually have done it. Surely God would have understood (though the farmer and his wife might be shocked). She'd never pretended to be a saint, she told herself; if Rochelle could sleep with all those men, it wouldn't hurt for *her* to sleep with one. High time she got it over with, in fact; this maidenhood of hers, this blessed virginity, was fast becoming a burden and a bore. While once it had seemed worth preserving, setting her a cut above the rest of the world, now it seemed little more than a souvenir of the convent, separating her from her friends, her own sisters, most of all from Rochelle. She was sick of being different.

But now was not the time to change. After twenty-two years of holding onto something, you didn't just give it away to the first halfway acceptable man who came along. Especially not tonight, on what amounted to their second date, in a glorified henhouse with stern, religious, disapproving strangers all around. She hoped Jeremy didn't expect anything more, and assumed he'd had enough sense to make provisions for her to spend the night inside the farmhouse.

Not that there was anything wrong with Jeremy; as soon him as anyone else. It was all very well to remind herself that, considered critically, he was not the first man she would have chosen and that her interest in him derived, in part, from that most humbling of predicaments, his being, at least for now, the only game in town. Still, the choice was more than just pragmatic. He genuinely appealed to her. He made her smile.

All this past week he'd been much on her mind. She had found herself pausing in her homeward walk down Eighth Avenue to stare expectantly at the western horizon, as if to catch a glimpse of distant marvels—in Jersey, of all places! She'd also found herself inventing entire conversations with him, conversations which, however playful or earnest, invariably ended with a mutual declaration of love. *I must be crazy*, she told herself for the dozenth time. Was her life really so empty that she'd fall for the first halfway intelligent man who showed

an interest in her? And did it really take so little—a drink, a cheap
Italian meal, a walk home in the dark? Surely there was more to her
life than that.

FLEMINGTON, the sign said. KEEP RIGHT.

Moving back into the slower lane, she took a moment to count her
blessings. There was her family, of course, though scattered now, and
Rochelle, and the sisters she still talked to at St. Agnes's, and evenings
at the ballet every week or two, and maybe an occasional fancy meal
this summer with Rosie, and the endless rows of library books that
stretched before her, thirty hours a week . . .

Surely that was enough for any girl. More than enough.

But a contemptuous little voice inside her head whispered, *Who do
you think you're kidding?*

So be it. She spun the wheel and pressed her foot against the gas
pedal. The Chevy swung onto the exit ramp and sped across the waiting world toward Gilead.

Freirs put down the book and checked his watch. It was almost a quarter to three. He looked to the right, squinting at the sun. Sarr and
Deborah were still at it, both of them bent almost double, moving
through the plowed field with the seed bags at their sides, chanting as
they went. They reminded Freirs of a pair of huge black insects de-
positing endless rows of eggs. Behind them sunlight glimmered from
one of the homemade scarecrows that Sarr had erected—really just
aluminum-foil pie plates with strings through one end, dangling like
limp kites from the tops of a row of stakes so that, at the smallest
breeze, the plates would swing and flutter back and forth, banging
softly against the stakes with the sound of far-off temple gongs.

How strange and picturesque it all seemed. He felt as if he were in a
distant country. It was easy to forget that the two of them out there
were human beings, people he sat down to eat with, people like himself.

He hoped Carol would arrive soon; the day seemed to be passing so
quickly that, even with the sun still high, he could feel the chill of evening, the day already lost. A fly settled boldly on his cheek and he
struck at it, knocking his glasses askew. Quickly he adjusted them,
hoping the Poroths hadn't seen. Where in God's name was Carol? In a
little while he was going to get angry, or worried, or both. He plunged
despondently back into the novel, trying to lose himself again and
speed her coming.

Sarr was thinking about the girl while he counted out the seeds, and he
was troubled. He wondered if he'd done the right thing, allowing
Freirs to have her out this weekend. Maybe his mother was right.

He had seen her at her house the previous night, where, offering some fresh eggs and a bag of early peas from Deborah's garden, he'd gone to seek his mother's advice on how best to deal with the members of the Co-op, to whom his debt was about to fall due. Thirty-seven hundred dollars for the mortgage, and another thousand for repairs—he would owe them, by August, nearly five thousand dollars. But there were a few grounds for hope, including a modest family trust left by his father that might, in emergencies, be drawn upon . . .

When he'd mentioned, in passing, that Jeremy Freirs had a girl coming on Saturday, his mother had seemed shocked. No, more than shocked. Dismayed, almost, like one who's learned an enemy has breached the gates.

"Son," she'd said at last, "I wouldn't open my door to her."

"Now, now," he'd said, "the two of them aren't going to spend the night together. I wouldn't allow such a thing on my land." He was already beginning to feel sorry he'd brought it up, and guilty about having acquiesced so easily to Deborah's argument that what Jeremy and Carol did was none of his business. Of *course* it was his business; everything that went on under his roof or on his property was his business.

The evening—so agreeable, at the start, perhaps because he hadn't brought Deborah, always a source of tension—had ended in the sort of unforgiving argument, neither yielding an inch, that he hadn't had with his mother since he was a boy. Even as he'd left, she had still seemed uneasy. "No," she kept saying, "the woman shouldn't come. She shouldn't be here at all."

"Well," Sarr had said at last, "it's too late now. I can't stop her from coming; I can't go back on my word. At the very least, I have to offer common hospitality. Don't worry yourself, Mother, there'll be no sinning on my land."

But she hadn't appeared comforted.

And now, as he labored in his fields, Sarr couldn't get the matter off his mind. Maybe, in some dark way he didn't yet understand, he had made a mistake.

He wondered if he would have to pay for it.

Mrs. Poroth grimaced beneath the beekeeper's veil. Grey wisps drifted past her face from the nozzle of her smoker, a teapot-shaped metal contrivance packed with smoldering rags and fanned by miniature bellows. Every few minutes she would shake her head uneasily, as if trying to clear it of some indigestible thought. Earlier, as she'd gone ·bout her Saturday chores, pruning the hydrangea on the south side of ·e house and, with veil on, examining the upright wooden frames of · beehives for the day's accumulation of honey, she'd considered, half seriously, the possibility of setting up a roadblock on her lane. Anything to keep away the visitor.

Of course, maybe this was just some idle girlfriend of Freirs' and not the woman whose coming she dreaded; there was no way to be sure. Still, she hated to take chances. Stationing herself by the third hive, lowest on the hill and closest to the roadside, she waited for the visitor's car to pass.

If the woman turned out to be the one she feared, what should she do? Killing her, of course, would be a sin, and the Lord punished such acts, even when committed for good ends, though she was half prepared to accept the sin and the eventual punishment. Besides, she reflected, killing was probably the kindest thing she could do for the poor girl.

No, she couldn't do it. She would have to play by the rules. The Old One would be playing by them too.

There was nothing to do for now but find out all she could. Adjusting her veil and once more directing the smoker into the hive so that the insects, reacting as if to a fire and gorging themselves on honey, would grow sluggish, she lifted the flat unpainted lid and withdrew one of a dozen wooden frames acrawl with bees. Transferring the honey-laden frame to a storage chamber above the hive, she stood once more and prepared herself to wait for the passing of the car. If the chosen woman was in it, she would recognize her—by her hair, if nothing else. It would be red. It would have to be. That, too, was a rule.

Gilead at last. There was no mistaking the tidy little crossroads and the general store, obviously the Co-op that Jeremy had spoken of. He had also said something, Carol recalled, about "high walls" surrounding the town, but no doubt he'd exaggerated; the only walls she'd seen were low stone ruins back at the approach road, stretching from each gatepost and winding off among the trees. She might not even have noticed them if she hadn't been told to look.

But perhaps, she mused, there were walls here of a different sort. The place seemed different from other towns: neater, certainly, to judge by the well-tended lawns she'd passed coming in, and more decorous in other ways as well. Across the street from the Co-op, where a red-brick schoolhouse glared through a line of trees at the grassy playing field in front, a group of little children played quietly on seesaws, neither shouting nor laughing, as subdued as children in a century-old woodcut, and all without a sign of adult supervision. Nor were there the usual small-town idlers gathered in front of the general store.

Parking in front, just beyond the untended gas pumps, she climbed the steps and entered. The store appeared uncommonly well stocked and smelled, in the dim light inside, of spice and old apples. It was most like entering a cave. The beams in the ceiling were heavy with merchandise—everything from sausages to snowshoes, from bulbous white garlics to lamp wicks, frying pans, and coils of rubber hose. A tall white metal cooler hummed serenely near the back, stocked with cheeses, ordinary-looking cans of soda, and things wrapped in wax paper. Low shelves near the front displayed cellophane-packed cupcakes, barbecue chips, and beef jerky. A huge jar of pickled eggs stood beside the cash register on the counter.

The woman behind the counter was talking with another woman; both were elderly and dressed in black. While pushing through the screen door, Carol overheard references to a Brother Joram and a Lotte Sturtevant, who was apparently growing quite enormous lately, but the two women fell silent and turned to her as soon as she came in. She asked directions of the one behind the counter. "I'm trying to reach the Poroths' farm," she said.

"Well, now, Sarr and that wife of his, I believe they bought the old Baber place."

The other woman nodded gravely. "My Rachel was out there last Friday evening. They're the ones that planted late."

Farther back, in the shadows, Carol saw an alcove with another wooden counter, almost the mirror image of this one, and a wall lined with shelves and cubbyholes, in some of which leaned dusty-looking white envelopes. This, then, would be the local post office. It looked little used.

"You want to head out along the granary road," the first woman—no doubt the postmistress—was saying. She stepped from behind the counter and, holding open the screen door, gestured in the direction of the retreating maples and the line of distant hills. "Keep goin' straight past Verdock's dairy—it's just around that bend—and there you turn right and go along for half a mile or so." She launched into a lengthy, detailed account replete with references to gullies, washed-out crossings, and lanes that dipped up and down like greased pigs, with particular attention to a mill road ("'Course there ain't no mill there nowadays, it's all fell down since I was a girl") and a fork ("Don't go turnin' off on the little old road that splits off it on the left, 'cause that's goin' to lead you to the Geisels, and Matt and Cora like visitors so much they ain't goin' to let you leave before suppertime"). Carol found herself nodding politely, eagerly, but forgetting everything as soon as it was spoken. *Right past Verdock's dairy,* she remembered that much. She would find the place, no fear. She thanked the two of them and left the store.

"And be sure to say hello to Sister Deborah," the woman called after her. "Tell her we'll be lookin' for her at worship tomorrow." The other woman tittered.

Parked in front of the store like a reminder of the world she'd left, the small cream-colored Chevy was one of the brighter objects in sight; the only other vehicles she'd seen since entering town had been dark unornamented cars and pickup trucks at least a decade old. Driving down the road in what seemed the suggested direction—it was, at least, the way she'd been heading anyway—she proceeded slowly at first, studying every passing farm and homestead for signs by which she might distinguish it later, if she had to return this way; then, as she realized that there were relatively few turnings to choose from, with more confidence. On impulse, more from the memory of something Freirs had told her than from anything the woman in the store had said, she turned right when the road branched after the large dairy farm and found herself heading downhill toward a small, swiftly running stream whose sound echoed in the fields and thickets through which she was passing.

She drove for what seemed several miles along its winding banks, avoiding a narrow stone bridge—had the woman said anything about a bridge?—and coming at last to a clearing where a cluster of shanties stood huddled at the edge of the woods. The road she'd been following curved back uphill among the trees, branching just before the houses into an unsavory-looking pitted dirt road that she prayed was not the Poroths'. Three large, nondescript dogs raced up to the car and yapped fiercely at its wheels. A man in shirt sleeves—not bearded but unshaven, and with a hillbilly's long, straggly hair—looked up from a rusting automobile he'd been scraping, his dark little eyes peering suspiciously toward her car. In the weed-choked yard several pale, moon-faced children in T-shirts and shorts paused in their playing to watch her pass. They looked surprisingly ragged for this area, almost Appalachian. She drove past quickly, determined not to ask for directions here, and with sinking heart followed the road back uphill, taking the first opportunity she found to double back in the direction of the stream.

This time the way felt familiar; when she came again to the stone bridge, she turned left with more confidence and drove over it. The road wound steeply uphill once again, curving past a small stone cottage, a cozy-looking place set well back on a rounded hill, the yard around it overgrown with flowers.

She was so busy admiring them as she drove by that she almost didn't see the tall, faceless figure looming darkly at the edge of the road. With a little cry she swerved to avoid it, the car speeding around the bank of earth and shrubbery as if under its own volition, carrying her past. The road climbed farther, curving now in the other direction; she wasn't inclined to look back. It was only later, when the house would have been concealed from sight behind the bend, that she realized what she'd seen was a woman in a long black dress and the odd, shroudlike mask of a beekeeper.

*

"She's going to be here soon," Deborah was saying, "and I mean it, honey, the least you can do is drive to the Geisels and get us some of that rhubarb wine."

"I heard you the first time," said Sarr. "Don't worry, I'm going." He wiped the sweat from his forehead. "But I don't intend taking out the truck for a task like that. *Some* of us still know how to walk!" He cast a pointed glance to where Freirs lay dozing. "You've got the room all ready for her?"

Deborah nodded. "If she's really going to use it." This had been designed to get a rise from him, and it did.

"She'd damned well better!" he said, exasperated. "'Tisn't a whorehouse I'm running!"

"Oh, easy, honey, it's not for us to decide. Don't forget, they're not our people." She paused, musing. "Wonder if she'll be pretty. It's hard to picture what Jeremy likes."

"I can tell you what he likes," said Sarr. "Have you ever seen the way he looks at you?"

"What he does with his eyes is his business." Still smiling, she raised her fist. "But let me tell you something, mister. What you do with *your* eyes is *my* business! Now get along down to the Geisels and buy that wine! She ought to be here any minute—should've been here hours ago. Get moving!"

He pretended to cower before her, the sight all the more comic because of his huge size. "I'm moving," he said. He loped off toward the house to get his wallet. The screen door slammed.

I wonder what's keeping her, thought Deborah. *Probably overslept herself. A good match for Jeremy.*

She looked at him. He was no longer asleep. She smiled; he smiled back.

The screen door slammed again, and Sarr emerged. With a wave he disappeared down the road.

The road was proving difficult to follow. It gave another twist, a living thing, hostile to the tires digging into its dusty back, and she had to wrench the wobbly steering wheel to keep the car from going off onto the shoulder or even crashing into the thick underbrush. The front wheels suddenly dropped into an unseen gully with a jarring clang of metal. Applying the brakes, she proceeded more slowly, fearful lest the dust and the bumps and the potholes damage Rosie's car. She pictured herself explaining how it had happened, Rosie's baby smile turning amber, and the empty way she'd feel if he dismissed her. How had she er gotten herself into this? It was like a carny ride one couldn't get off. Grimly she continued down the road, jaw set, imagining with something close to hunger the comfort of the bed that awaited her at the farmhouse.

Her eagerness to see Jeremy had long since yielded to a certain resentment. What a fool she must look, to have gone to so much trouble just for him! Better to assert herself from the start; if he thought she'd driven all this way simply for the privilege of cuddling up to him, the boy was in for a surprise. Did he take her for one of his horny little students? She would show him just how wrong he was.

On the radio a man was prophesying fair weather; it seemed like magic that his voice remained so steady, so unaffected by the pounding and the bumping of the car. The time, he said—"Bible time"—was four thirteen.

God, she was late! And perhaps there was no one on this back road after all; perhaps it would simply grow narrower and narrower until it finally disappeared amid the undergrowth and swamp. What if she was simply getting deeper into wilderness and would never be able to get out without abandoning the car? *Everything's going to come out okay*, she repeated to herself. Meanwhile the radio was whispering the far less sanguine words of Jeremiah: "And I will appoint over them four kinds, saith the Lord: the sword to slay, and the dogs to tear, and the fowls of the heaven, and the beasts of the earth, to devour and destroy."

She was almost ready to turn the car around when, up ahead, half obscured by dust and the waves of rising heat, she saw a dark figure stalking grimly toward her like a moving shadow.

It circled the car warily as she slowed to a stop. She saw a gaunt, rather handsome face staring down at her, eyes wide and shy above the fringe of beard. She knew immediately who it was. "Sarr," she said, almost breathless with relief. "At last!"

Mrs. Poroth put the beekeeper's mask back in the closet and sat herself morosely on the narrow bed. She was worried. She had seen the woman. It was her, the one whose coming she'd dreaded. She had recognized the red hair and the intense, almost ascetic face, like that of an unwitting Joan of Arc. A holy victim.

Removing from the drawer in her night table a tattered yellow pile pressed flat between two sheets of cardboard, she untied the ribbon that held the sheets together and gazed down once again at the Pictures. Hesitantly she reached for the one on top—a landscape draw entirely in white upon a grey background—and turned it over. S sifted through the rest of the pile, not shuffling them, proceeding w no established order, merely allowing her mind to roam free as scanned Picture after Picture. Her gaze fell immediately on the i of the book, an obscene fat yellow volume, covers bulging, bloated, almost, as if barely able to contain the mass within. The moon drawing, too, caught her eye; but the moon that would appear in the sky tonight, she knew, would be nothing like the cruel, slim crescent shape in the Picture, with the star trapped between its tips. The one that shone tonight would be full.

Laying aside the Pictures, she closed her eyes, fell stiffly back on her bed, and tried desperately to think of a connection.

The hum of insects was beginning to drive him to distraction. His ears tingled to the buzz of a mosquito, it seemed about to pierce into his brain, and yet behind it he could hear the reassuring drone of the hornets and bees and those flies with heads like jewels. What *was* there in that sound? He cocked his head to listen, and, for a moment, believed he understood: it was the hum the world made as it went about its work, serenely preoccupied, all gears meshing smoothly, the mechanism utterly dependable.

Now there was another sound behind it, another motor—and in the distance a small white Chevrolet came lurching slowly up the dirt road toward the farm. Out of the corner of his eye he saw two kittens padding across the lawn to investigate, tails eagerly aloft. He got up from his chair and walked hurriedly around the side of the house to the driveway, just as Deborah was emerging from the back door. She joined him at the bottom of the steps, and by the time the little car had pulled up next to the house, he and Deborah were waiting side by side, cats gamboling at their feet, as if the two of them were the farm couple and he Deborah's lawful husband.

Carol had arrived at last, but more than four hours late, and he could see, even through the dusty windshield, that she was in a bad mood. Well, he would just have to hold her awhile and make her feel better. Turning the engine off, she wiped a hand across her shining forehead and climbed silently from the car. For Deborah, now rushing forward to welcome her, she managed a smile, but it looked forced, strained; and for him, hanging back, there was no smile at all, not even a hello—though he got a greeting he would not quickly forget.

"I swear I could strangle you!" she said, slamming the door shut as the kittens fled back across the lawn. "How could you tell me this place was only an hour or so away?"

*

His first reaction was simple embarrassment that she should speak to him that way in front of Deborah. Her mood also unnerved him; it was going to be that much harder now for the two of them to get romantic—which was presumably what they both wanted. Hesitantly he reached in through the window for the tote bag on the seat. "Here, I'll get this." It was heavier than he expected; he felt the awkward weight of a bottle and some bulky parcels.

He was about to start for the outbuilding, but she took the bag from him. "That's okay, I've got it," she said, already calming down. She turned to Deborah, who, behind her back, had been giving her a cool, appraising glance. "I'd really like to go wash up. I feel like I've just run a marathon."

"Come on inside, then. The bathroom's just off the kitchen." Deborah led her up the back porch steps, the two of them chattering about the unseasonable heat. Seen together like that, buxom brunette and slim redhead, they looked like some Victorian allegory of darkness and light. After all those nights alone on the farm, he was glad that one of them was his.

He drifted back to his room, casting his eye over it one more time before she saw it. The roses on the night table were a nice touch, he decided. Too bad the windows in the back didn't let in more light.

Finally, bored, he walked back up to the house. Voices came from the second floor, but not, as usual, from the Poroths' bedroom. Dismayed, he hurried upstairs to find the two of them, just as he'd feared, in the small spare room in back intended eventually for a child's bedroom. They were talking about the pictures that covered the walls—a series of nursery rhyme cutouts and lithographed Bible scenes chosen with the room's future occupant in mind. Deborah was holding a wrapped-up bottle. Carol's tote bag already lay upon the bed, a fresh towel beside it.

"Jeremy," said Carol, beaming, "do you know, this is just like the room my sister and I had when we were growing up! I swear, I had some of these same pictures."

"Oh, really?" He stood in the doorway, hoping that his face didn't betray his disappointment. "I guess all that's really needed is a crib."

Deborah was watching him closely. He couldn't tell if she was gloating or feeling sorry for him. "Well," she said, "call me if you need anything. I've got to get back downstairs now—there's something in the oven." She held up the bottle. "And thanks again for the wine."

"Carol," he said when she was gone, "you don't really intend to stay *here*, do you?"

Her eyes widened. "Where else would I stay?"

He sighed. Already things were going wrong. Out there, beneath the sun, the world was turning serenely, yet inside here a piece of it had

turned away from him. "The fact of the matter is, I thought that you'd be staying out there with me."

"That's certainly not what *I* had in mind," she said. "And I don't think the Poroths would approve of an unmarried girl spending the night back there with you."

"Their opinion doesn't matter."

"Of course it does, Jeremy. We're guests in their home."

"I'm not a guest. I'm paying rent."

"Yes, but *I'm* a guest," she said firmly, "and I wouldn't want to offend them. And anyway, though it probably sounds silly to you, I just don't do that sort of thing."

He'd deserved that, he realized. There was nothing dumber than trying to argue a girl into bed, and that's exactly what he'd been trying. Now she had blown him out of the water. "It's okay," he said. "I understand." Maybe he could still change her mind.

"And look," she said, "I'm sorry about that little outburst of mine, back in the yard. I didn't mean to take it out on you. I guess I just got nervous driving Rosie's car."

He shrugged. "Didn't bother me. Honest. I'm just sorry you had such a rough trip." Glumly he eyed the room's low ceiling, the wide plank floorboards covered by a throw rug, the shallow, smoke-stained fireplace taking up most of one side. How could she actually think of staying here? It was so damned claustrophobic. Around him shapes were thumbtacked to the pale blue papered wall: faces grinned from the ramparts of a cardboard castle, a white-robed priest made solemn gestures before an altar fire, a cow danced dreamily round a startled moon. He waved his hand toward the room at large. "Well, anyway, welcome to the Land of Nod."

"It seems very comfortable."

He sniffed. "A little stuffy, though." Frowning, he went to the other side of the room, where a tiny dormer window looked out upon the yard. Just inside the panes, hanging by a length of string from a hook above the lintel, a hollow, ruby-red witch ball of hand-blown glass revolved slowly in the sunlight. Large as an overripe apple, it was designed to keep evil spirits at bay; inside it lay a sprig of angelica, the herb beloved of the Holy Ghost. Across the room, from a trick of the light, a glowing disk the size and color of a rose appeared to float upon the wall above the bed.

From behind him came the muffled sound of a zipper. He caught his breath and looked around, half expecting to see Carol stepping lightly out of her jeans, but she was busy rummaging through the open tote bag; a hairbrush and a pair of slacks already lay upon the bed. Inside the bag he glimpsed a fat yellow book with ornamental covers but failed to recognize it. She reached inside for the volume, then seemed to think better of it and shoved it back among the clothes. *God,* he thought, *she's even brought some kind of prayer book!* With a sigh he turned back to the window. Unfastening the latch, he pushed open the two sets of panes, letting in a breeze from the yard. The leaves of the apple tree whispered with it just outside the window, and the witch ball stirred lazily on its string. Past the garden the dusty white Chevy sat dozing in the driveway. In the distance he could see his own building, the afternoon sunlight shining fiercely on the shingles of the roof, and, beyond it, the smokehouse and the old black willow that grew against the barn. She would have a pleasing view if she stayed up here tonight—a better view than he would have from down there on the lawn.

And he would be alone down there.

But she still might reconsider, the optimist in him decided. In fact, he felt confident that she would. Far from discouraging him, her behavior back in the yard had made him feel curiously protective: here she was, supposedly a resourceful corn-fed country girl, yet she'd apparently managed to get herself lost two or three times on the ride out and had obviously had trouble navigating the final stretch of road. Whatever she liked to fancy herself, she was certainly no pathfinder. He realized that in the short week he'd been living here, he'd begun to feel at home.

"Come on," he said, "let me show you where I live."

Their footsteps clattered through the hall and down the stairs, the floorboards echoing as they passed.

Behind them in the little room, deserted now, the ball of ruby-red glass spun like a planet in the sunshine. The image it cast on the opposite wall was aglow with rosy light, its center filled with swirling bands of red.

Gradually, hour after hour, the sun would settle earthward; the rosy light would travel ever higher up the wall. At last, trembling with the final rays of sunset, it would strike the lower corner of a Bible lithograph, then a line of badly painted foliage, a rock, a patch of moss, a bit of long white robe . . . until, like some intense supernal spotlight, it would shine directly on the center of the picture, on a bright configuration with the contours of a star: the altar fire.

Inevitably, for a moment, the star and rose would merge.

Afterward, the sun would settle further; the spotlight would move on. Yet for that single moment, beneath its rays, the fire would have flickered, glowed, and come to life. For an instant the flames would leap higher, burning with a vastly deeper hunger, now shifting, now spreading, devouring picture, planet, all.

Lazy clouds drifted above the tops of the surrounding trees; wisps of shadow swept the grass. Freirs sat slouched next to Carol on a rock by the banks of the stream, beneath the shade of one of the willows that grew along the side.

To his uneasiness the two of them had once more fallen silent, and now barely stirred except to brush away an occasional fly or flip a stone or twig into the water—water so clear that it was impossible to tell the depth. Along the opposite bank, where the woods began, the pine trees shifted restlessly in the afternoon heat, but the water here beside them was nearly cold enough to freeze one's fingers.

Carol leaned over, trying to see her reflection, but the current was too swift. Sunlight glimmered from the water's surface, picking out dead leaves and bits of debris being carried downstream. In the shadows one could see other things, smooth and pale and snakelike, twisting among the rocks at the bottom.

She seemed preoccupied. Freirs watched her out of the corner of his eye with a yearning he couldn't quite remember feeling since the days before his marriage. He wished she were staying more than just one night; he hadn't realized, till now, how lonely he had been. It was something of a surprise, in fact: she looked so wonderfully *right* sitting here beside him in her old plaid shirt and slim-legged jeans, her skin so pale in the sunlight, her hair so red against the grass.

And she herself hadn't been immune to the feeling. By the time the two of them had left the farmhouse, she'd seemed very happy to be here with him today. Deborah had been singing in the kitchen. Outside, the air had grown cooler. Butterflies were dancing on the lawn.

"God," she'd said, "it feels like coming home!"

But something had unaccountably changed her mood; without warning she had suddenly become less friendly, just when he'd begun to feel close to her.

It had happened in his bedroom. A silence had seemed to fall between them, there among his books and papers. Somehow she had had a change of heart. He had seen it when she'd first walked through his doorway; he'd seen a vague expression of distaste come over her—had she actually wrinkled her nose?—and a certain wariness when she'd looked from bed to rear window and window to bed, as if measuring the distance.

He had tried to keep the conversation going, something he was usually adept at, but maybe in the past week he'd gotten out of practice. They'd talked about a hike they hoped to take, and where to search

for animal tracks, arrowheads, edible wild plants. But it had been no
more than filling in the blanks. She'd seemed restless and distracted
the entire time and was soon suggesting that they go back outside. She
hadn't even wanted to sit down—had flatly refused, in fact, to sit beside him on the bed. You'd have thought she was a virgin, the way
she'd behaved.

He wondered if maybe the fault lay with the bed itself: with its presence, its very concreteness. Women, he knew, were practical at heart—
quite ruthlessly calculating, some of them, certainly the one he'd married—but there were always a few romantic souls who managed to
forget that making love was also a matter of bed space and damp sheets
and where to put the elbows. Maybe Carol was one of these, her head
spinning round and round with flower-scented fantasies until, with a
jolt, she stumbled against the hard physical reality of his narrow iron
bed. Maybe she preferred to think they'd do it in the air, like angels.

He'd given it one try, at least. He'd felt fat and dull and sweaty, but
he'd kissed her just the same, leaning toward her as she looked at the
woodcuts in a paperback *grimoire* and planting a firm kiss at the side
her mouth. She'd been surprised, of course—her eyes had gone wide
and she hadn't exactly fallen into his arms—but she hadn't pulled
away.

But then, like a kid on his first date, he had failed to follow it up.
Instead, he'd made some lame remark about the Brethren and their at-
titude toward sex—"very Old Testament," he'd said—and the two had
lapsed back into awkward conversation. The moment had been lost.

Afterward, more tense now, and with more blank space to fill, they'd
strolled aimlessly around the farm, Freirs pointing out the various
outbuildings and fields just as Sarr had done for him and, beneath a
demeanor almost as reserved, watching her reactions with the same
anxious curiosity.

She had not been impressed. At first the place had seemed, paradoxically, both novel and familiar, but her initial enthusiasm had apparently worn off, and she was no longer moved by the mere sight of
rural landscape. Casting a critical eye at the broad, uncultivated lands
beyond the stream, the old wooden outhouse rotting beneath its tangle
of vines, the mass of the encroaching woods, the farm machinery rusting in the barn, the north field overgrown with weeds, she had pro-
nounced the farm "in very poor repair."

She'd been right, of course, yet somehow the comment had irritated
him. What did she expect? After all, this was Sarr and Deborah's first
year here. He realized that he'd come to feel a certain loyalty to them.

How to change the mood? How to bring them closer once again? He'd
wondered about it all through the remainder of their walk—and now,
sitting here beside her on the sun-warmed rock while streams of
shadow spread across the lawn, he still wasn't sure what to do. Drop

his pants? Recite a poem? Whip out some maginary pocketknife and carve their initials on the nearest tree? A directly physical approach was out of the question—he could hardly just reach out and grab her, here among the insects and the rocks—and he'd long since run out of things to talk about. What, after all, had he been doing with himself for the last week, except sitting on his ass and taking notes? He had already tried to describe for her the Gothic excesses of *The Monk*, but though she'd seemed interested enough—"My God," she kept saying, "to be so afraid of nuns!"—the novel's horror had quite suddenly and unexpectedly begun to pall on him. Subterranean dungeons, inquisitors, and chains all seemed rather foolish and insubstantial out here in the sunlight, with dragonflies dipping innocently above the stream and the smell of pine trees wafting from the woods on the opposite bank.

And anyway, Carol was beginning to seem distracted. "I hope he'll understand," she said abruptly. "Sarr, I mean. I should have offered him a lift. I didn't know he'd be away this long."

Freirs shrugged, just as happy that Carol hadn't gone off alone with Sarr before reaching the farm. That would have made her even later, and . . . well, he didn't like the idea of the two of them sharing anything without him. Anyway, why bring him up now?

"He mentioned something this morning about buying wine," Freirs said. "There are some people over on the next road who make it out of rhubarb and dandelions and things." The thought reminded him of dinner; he looked back to the house—just in time to see Sarr himself walking up the back steps, a large jug swinging heavily from his arm.

He turned back to Carol without mentioning it, but she too had been looking toward the house. She stood, brushing off her jeans. "He's back," she said. "They'll probably be getting dinner ready soon. I'd better head on over to the house and wash up."

Freirs stood and followed her slowly back across the lawn, past his own ivy-covered building. Somehow it looked quite unlovely now. "Do you still want to see that field guide?" he asked hopefully. "The one that has the recipe for cattails?"

"After dinner," she said, not even turning. Suddenly she laughed. "Speaking of cats . . ." Beside them, attracted by the direction of their walk, loped two of the younger cats, an orange male and a tortoise-shell female, perhaps anticipating dinner.

"Where are all the others?" asked Carol, crouching to extend her hand toward the female. With the usual feline ambivalence it dodged her attempt to pat it on the head, remaining just beyond arm's reach; but the orange male crept warily up and, tail lashing, permitted her to stroke its neck.

"The older ones tend to go off by themselves," said Freirs, watching Carol's fingers sliding through the animal's silky hair. *Lucky little bastard.* "They spend all day creeping through the long grass like tigers on the prowl. One of them's a big silver female—you'll see her tonight—who actually roams around in the woods, just like a wild animal. Sarr says she eats what she kills there."

At that moment, up ahead, Deborah appeared at the back door and stepped out onto the porch, her apron white against the long black of her dress. She was carrying a large ceramic bowl. At her side a thin, wicked-looking bread knife hung like a ceremonial sword. Crouching, she set the bowl carefully beside a smaller one at her feet. The dangling bread knife touched the floor and caught the sinking sun. Brushing back a lock of hair, she stood and waved a greeting to her guests, then tilted back her head and yelled what sounded like a single mystical demon-name: "Bekariabwada! . . . Bekaria*bwaaaa*da!"

From the long grass behind them three blurred shapes, a charcoal, a tiger-stripe, and a silver grey—Rebekah, Azariah, and Bwada—streaked across the lawn and up the back steps. And sure enough, one of them, Freirs noticed, bore something small and struggling in its teeth.

The city feels deserted this evening. It is the start of a three-day weekend, and even some of the poor have managed to escape. The rest sit in their doorways and curse the heat.

The Old One doesn't mind the heat. In fact, he is in an extremely good mood. As he waits outside the building where the women live, he hums a little song.

The sun sinks toward the river like a dying rose. Lines of jagged shadows creep farther down the sidewalk. One by one, as the darkness descends, he flexes his pudgy little fingers.

"Honey, are you sure Matthew gave you your money's worth?"

Sarr looked up from the astrological column in that day's *Home News:* Full moon tonight, and unexpected sights beneath it. "Huh?"

"Matthew Geisel. Did that old man try to cheat you?"

"That's no way to talk about Brother—"

"Because this thing's not even full," Deborah went on. "See? It's five or six inches down." She pointed to the wine jug that stood upon the table. Suddenly her expression changed; she looked at him suspiciously. "Hey, have you been into this?"

Scowling, he went back to his paper. "And what if I was? It's hot out there."

She sighed and shook her head. "Gonna get yourself sick, you are, walking in the sun with a belly full of wine. It's a wonder you left any for the rest of us."

He grunted noncommittally, already looking forward to finishing off the jug at dinner, along with the wine that Freirs' skinny red-headed girlfriend had brought out. The Brethren didn't hold with drunkenness, but as sins went it was a minor one. No sense getting into an argument over a few tart swigs of rhubarb wine. He looked up. "Want me to rinse off those greens?" he asked. "Or feed the cats?"

She was having none of it. "All that's been done," she said. "Dinner'll be ready in a minute. Go see where they are."

"Last time I looked, they were still out there trying to make friends with Zillah and Toby. She seemed to give up on Zillah—without getting scratched, praise the Lord—and then she started in on Toby. Picked him up just like a baby."

"And he let her?"

"He seemed to like it."

Deborah shrugged and began methodically slicing a tomato. "Probably thought she was his mother, with that hair of hers. You don't suppose that's the real color, do you?"

Sarr smiled. He was tempted to say something about women and cats, but held his tongue. "Oh, I don't know," he said. "Here she is. Why don't you ask her?"

He was amused to find the subject dropped. While Carol, then Freirs, filed into the bathroom to wash for dinner, Deborah busied herself at the stove. Suddenly she paused and turned to face him.

"By the way," she said, "aren't you forgetting something?" She nodded toward the porch. "May as well get it over with before you wash up."

Sarr winced. It was time for the body count. He had almost forgotten. With a sigh he heaved himself from the chair. "Ah, yes. 'Twouldn't do to neglect the dead."

Pushing through the screen door, he stood with hands on hips and watched the cats gathered round a bowl heaped with dry commercial cat food mixed with last night's table scraps; a water dish stood nearby. Moments later the two remaining kittens, charcoal Dinah and coal-black Habakkuk, came scampering up the back steps to join the other five. Bwada raised her silver-grey head to glare at them as they crowded in beside her. She gave a warning hiss, but they ignored her and, purring softly, proceeded to gobble up as much food as they could in dainty but determined bites.

While they ate, he went grimly about his task. It was not a pleasant one, even when blunted somewhat by the drink. Each evening around mealtime, now that summer was here, the cats had taken to bringing in dead things, corpses of animals they'd caught during the day: field mice, moles, shrews, birds—even, once, a slender green garter snake. It was doubtful that they saw those creatures as food (though Bwada, on occasion, had been known to make a meal of one—as if she weren't fat enough already). Usually they just laid the bodies out upon the kitchen steps for the Poroths to see. Sarr believed the offerings were meant as tribute—a kind of ceremony.

Tonight, thank the Lord, they had returned with relatively little plunder: he saw only two mangled field mice and, almost out of sight within the shadows by the wall, the not-quite-lifeless body of a young robin, one delicate brown wing still trembling.

A good thing Deborah hadn't seen this. How she raged and carried on about the birds! Frowning, he stooped to pick the mice up gingerly by the tails. With his other hand he grasped the robin by the legs and walked down the back steps to a pair of garbage cans that stood beneath the porch. His head was swimming slightly from the wine, but he knew his intoxication only brought him nearer to the essential mystery. Placing the bird on the hard ground and looking away, he crushed its skull beneath the heel of his boot. As he did so, he thought he felt a tiny soul flutter past his face and up to heaven.

Wrinkling his nose, he lifted the lid from the nearer can and was immediately sickened by the foul odor of rotting flesh that welled up from its depths. Quickly he dropped the three bodies into the can and clamped the metal lid back on. It was a process he'd had to repeat, with little variation, nearly every night, but he still had not grown used to it.

Before returning inside, he paused a moment, leaning against one of the square white posts that supported the roof and gazing out at the farmland as it stretched away past the outbuilding and the brook to the distant line of woods. He spent a lot of time here on the porch, especially at the end of the day, staring alone and silent at the land. It was a sight that never failed to move him; familiar as it had become, he still felt like a stranger.

It was a paradox, really. During the day, at the height of the sun, while he sweated over some intractable root or turned the soil of some outlying pasture, though the land resisted him with all its strength, he nonetheless felt himself its master. But at moments like this—at dusk, when the world was at peace and he could survey his domain in lordly comfort from the back steps of his house—it somehow seemed to him that the land wasn't really his at all and that, with no human figure to mar the landscape, the farm reverted to what it had always been: a living thing, belonging only to itself. The waving grass and newly planted fields seemed to keep their own counsel; there was a consciousness at work in the lengthening shadows by the apple tree, outbuilding, and barn. True, he had purchased all these himself only last fall; the deed, signed, dated, and notarized, lay upstairs in a desk drawer. But how foolish he'd been to think that he could actually own this land, land which had been here so long before him and would be here so long after his body had crumbled beneath it. He was just another visitor, though thankful even for that; enough that he'd been given tonight's scent of roses and marsh water and pine, the faint evening breeze that even now brushed his face, and the darkness stealing leaf by leaf over the great trees.

Suddenly, disturbingly, another scent was mingled with the roses: the scent of decay seeping up from the garbage cans, a reminder of what lay waiting for everything that walked or crept upon the earth. Turning away, he hurried back into the house.

When he emerged from the bathroom after washing and rewashing his hands—faintly troubled, as he was every night, by the inevitable thoughts of Pilate—the odor of death seemed to linger in his nostrils, gradually mingling with the smell of roasting meat that filled the kitchen. Deborah was still at the stove, stirring one large black pot while keeping watch on a smaller one. The others were already seated, Freirs, as usual, toying with his napkin ring. The wine had been opened, the four glasses filled. It looked tawny and sweet; Sarr wished there were more.

"It's lovely, the way you've fixed this place up," Carol was saying. She ran her hand appreciatively along the smooth, age-stained wood of the little dining table, set with four straw place mats. It was the same table that, a week before, had borne the star of cottonbread. "This kitchen's around ten times the size of the one in my apartment, and I'll bet it's twenty degrees cooler in here."

Bending over the stove, Deborah called back, "There's a certain person I know who believes the city's hotter because it's so much closer to you-know-where!"

Sarr forced a smile, but he felt a flicker of annoyance. "Oh, I wouldn't put it like that, exactly," he said, crossing the kitchen, "but Lord knows there's precious little comfort there." He pulled back his chair and sat down heavily. "It's a matter of science, I suppose—something to do with the pavement and the brick. Hardly the sort of place *I'd* care to live."

There, the gauntlet was thrown; no use blaming it on the wine. He hadn't meant to speak out that way, but it was too late to take it back. He suspected he was going to have an argument on his hands, because Freirs had stopped toying with the wooden ring.

"Sure," said Freirs, "it *is* a bit hotter in the city. But that's why God gave us air conditioners."

Sarr heard the laughter of the two women, and his smile vanished. He had always been uncomfortable with jokes, especially jokes about the Lord. He began to frame a reply, but paused, for Deborah had come from the stove carrying a large, steaming bowl of barley soup. Placing it on a hand-painted tile in the center of the table, she seated herself and clasped her hands piously before her. It was time to say grace.

He took a breath. "Dear Lord," he said with sudden vehemence, clasping his own hands and dropping his gaze, "as we, Thy servants, prepare to enjoy the richness of Thy bounty, we give thanks for the two good people who have come to share it with us—"

He glanced up to see their reaction. Freirs, as usual, was merely inclining his head, staring pensively at the soup bowl, as if to prove that, while polite, he was not about to buy any of the Poroths' beliefs; but Sarr was pleased to see that Carol's fingers were locked in fervent prayer, her eyes shut tight, her expression rapt. She looked almost angelic.

"—and thanks to Thee, O Lord, as the source of all well-being and content."

"Amen," they murmured, even Freirs. Perhaps he was going along for Carol's sake.

Carol—she was an odd one for Freirs to bring out here. He wouldn't have thought she was his type. Not that she wasn't attractive; she was, and Sarr was honest enough with himself to acknowledge the feelings she'd inspired in him ever since he'd met her out there on the road this afternoon.

It was good to have her so close now; he suddenly realized that it had been years since he'd sat down to dinner with an unmarried woman from outside his family, especially one with Carol's strange mixture of independence and submissiveness, her soft uncallused skin, her clean-looking red hair cut so curiously short, so unlike the women's here in Gilead. He couldn't help picturing her climbing into his bed, so thin and pale and trembling; and he knew that tonight, as he made love to his wife, his thoughts would stray unbidden to this new woman, at least until he forced himself to think of holier things.

Deborah was speaking, lightening the mood, drawing the visitors in while she poured the rhubarb wine and served them their soup. She was so much better at that than he was. "I wouldn't trade the country with anyone," she was saying, "but there are times I miss the city something awful. If I hadn't gotten myself married I probably would have tried to live there for a few years. I still think about going back someday, just for a visit."

Freirs made a mock bow. "Just remember," he said, "whenever you're in town you'll always have a place to stay. Not exactly the Waldorf, maybe, but comfy enough." He raised his glass. "To travel, and the broadening effects thereof."

The others raised theirs. "To country virtues," said Carol, smiling. "And to those of us who still remember them."

Deborah giggled. "And to city vices!" She took a sip of the wine. "Mmm, good."

Sarr watched uneasily, wondering if Freirs and Deborah were flirting with one another. Unable to think of another toast, he brought the wineglass to his lips and took a large swallow, almost without tasting it. The lines, he realized, were shifting, setting him and the new woman against his wife and guest. He alone remained consistent. The thought made him feel stronger and at last encouraged him to speak.

"Deborah," he said, choosing his words carefully, "I know you've got a longing for the city. I've heard you talk of it before. And it's just as I told you when I made you my wife: you're free to do as you please. I'll not stand in your way." He took another drink and wiped his mouth. "As for me, though, I'll never set foot in that citadel of godlessness again. It's a place of corruption, and its people are swollen with envy and greed. Even the very best of them are infected. I hear it in their voices: the obsession with luxury, money, and the things of the world."

He looked from face to face. He could see that they knew he was serious. Freirs, though, was eyeing him skeptically. No doubt he resented not being the center of attention—how like a schoolteacher!—and would take any word spoken against the city as a personal attack. Probably he would try to assert himself in the eyes of the women. Yet to so so would only be natural; it was God's way that men must compete. Sarr understood and forgave.

"That's why I'm so glad the two of you are with us here tonight," he went on, nodding to Carol and Freirs. "Lord's my witness, I truly believe you'll both be the better for this. At least you're out of danger, at least for now."

"Danger?" said Freirs. "You mean like street crime?"

Sarr shook his head. "It isn't criminals I mean, nor dirt and noise. I mean a danger to the spirit. I see the city as the prophets did, a place to rival Babylon. Everyone is buying and selling, and everything's for sale. Even their own souls have a price."

Freirs smiled. "I'm not so sure about that," he said. "I've tried to buy a few lately, and no one's selling. In my film class I asked someone—"

But Sarr wasn't waiting for his explanation. "Perhaps you should have offered more," he said. "Remember, you're competing with the devil, and he's got the city in his pocket."

He was still feeling, he realized, rather light-headed. Too many hours in the sun. It would be good to get some food in him.

"Mind you," he added, almost apologetically, "I didn't always think so. When I was growing up here, I used to dream about running off to see the Empire State Building, and at night I'd pretend that I could see it brightening the sky. I used to think that, if light was good and darkness evil, then God must love the cities best. I knew He'd made man and man had made the city, so I thought that was where He must live." He paused, suddenly remembering. "I don't think so anymore."

"I gather you had a less than delightful visit," Freirs said lightly, with a look toward Carol. "What happen, you get mugged?"

"No, not that. I may have been a bit too big for that, even then. I've heard they prefer old ladies."

"They'll take whoever they can get. How old did you say you were?"

Sarr rubbed his chin. "It was Christmas of your senior year in school," said Deborah. "That's what you told me."

Sarr nodded. "That's right. I'd just turned seventeen. My father'd died that fall, God rest his soul."

"My father died then too," said Carol. "I mean, in the fall. It'll be a year this November."

"Really?" He regarded her with new interest. "Then that's another thing we have in common."

Freirs looked up, quick to catch a hint of conspiracy. "You mean, aside from your both being country people?"

"No, I meant aside from our both being religious. We talked about it when I met her on the road."

"I had a Bible program on the radio, that's all," said Carol. She sounded irritated, but it was hard to tell at whom. "As for our respective fathers . . ."

"We've both experienced loss," said Sarr. He was about to add a biblical observation on the ephemerality of man, but Deborah cut him off.

"I'll bet *her* mother took it a whole lot harder than—"

Sarr silenced her with a look. "My mother bore her loss with dignity," he said, with another glance at Deborah. "She's always kept pretty much to herself and doesn't let on how she's feeling. But I knew what was in her heart—I knew that the feeling was there—and I thought, If only there was something I could give her, something that would *interest* her, it'd pull her away from . . . well, all the things that were on her mind. So one Saturday morning I put on my father's old sheepskin coat—"

Deborah nodded grimly. "Like a lamb to the slaughter!"

"—and I hitched a ride to Flemington and climbed aboard the bus to New York. I thought I'd bring her back some sort of gift. A jewel, maybe. Something precious." He shook his head. "It was a long time ago."

"And your mother," said Carol. "She didn't mind your going?"

He looked pained. "I told her I'd be in Flemington till after dark, trying to find a part-time job. It was probably the first time I ever lied to her. Not that she was fooled."

"Nothing fools her," said Deborah. "She knows everything."

"But she never seemed to care too much *where* I went," said Sarr. "So I yielded to temptation and set off."

He sat back, pulling himself almost physically from the memory. At the same moment he became aware of a scratching at the door, where four owlish little faces were peering through the screen. It was the younger cats; he still tended to think of them as "the kittens." As he rose to let them in, he saw Carol turn and look questioningly at Freirs, who shrugged in acknowledgment. "It's okay," Freirs said. "They're in here almost every night. I think I may be getting used to them."

As always, no sooner was the door opened for them than the cats seemed to grow undecided about whether to enter, even though Sarr stood waiting by the doorway. Bwada pushed impatiently from behind them and bounded beneath the table, but the others hung back as if making up their minds; and when at last the four slipped past his feet into the kitchen, it was with a kind of wary indifference. Their parents, Rebekah and Azariah, remained outside, pacing like tigers back and forth along the steps, and soon disappeared into the long grass at the edge of the yard.

Sarr returned to the table to see Deborah ladling out more soup and the cats grouped like disciples at her feet. Freirs looked up from his bowl as Sarr resumed his seat. "So there you were," he said, "speeding toward Gotham and God knows what iniquity. Then what?"

Sarr smiled uncertainly. "Well," he said, "it's a long story."

"No doubt," said Freirs.

Carol added, "You can't just leave us on the bus, you know."

"I'm afraid that Deborah's heard it all before."

"And more than once," said Deborah. "Still, you'd best tell them, honey, now that you've a proper audience."

He had meant, as the host, to hold his tongue, the way he usually did, but somehow this whole meal had started wrong. Perhaps it was the wine.

"Well . . ." He took another swallow. "All right, then. Perhaps you'll even learn from my mistakes. I remember I reached the city a little after noon. The first thing I did was just stand there in the bus station and look at all the people. I'd never seen so many in one place, nor yet so many shades of skin. 'Twas like looking into an anthill, only this one was going on all around me and I was in the middle. I was bigger than most everybody else, and I know there's always Someone up there watching"—he pointed toward the ceiling—"so I'm not the kind to feel scared. But if I was, that's the time I would have felt it."

"It's hard to believe you'd never been to New York before," said Freirs, as if already regretting he'd given up the floor. "Let's face it, you're only a little over an hour away." He glanced guiltily at Carol. "Okay, maybe two hours, if the traffic's bad."

"The Brethren don't see it like that," said Sarr. "Just because a place is an hour or two away doesn't mean they'll want to pay it a visit. I'd say half the folks in this town have never been to New York." Beside him Deborah nodded. "They read about it in the *Home News*—"

"The ones who aren't afraid to read a newspaper," she added. "Some of 'em around here think it's a sin to read anything but the Bible."

"And some don't," said Sarr firmly. "A few of them see it on the TV, if they have one, or even at the drive-in up in Lebanon. They know all about New York. The point is, they just plain don't want to go. My mother's never been there, and never will. But I was curious, and I don't scare easy. So there I was, in the middle of the anthill, plowing my way toward the street.

"The first thing I saw when I got outside was this little fellow in a red getup, standing there on the sidewalk and ringing a dinner bell. He had a beard as white as old Brother Mogg's and twice as long, but I could see it was just lamb's wool. I knew who he was supposed to be, of course—you can't walk a mile out of Gilead, that time of year, without seeing an electrified Santa Claus on some fool's lawn—but I sure wasn't expecting to see a grown man dressed up that way in public.

"I stood and watched him for a while. It turned out he was collecting for some sort of charity, and I figured I'd best give him something. I had the money with me I'd saved up from working in my father's store. Looking back now, it doesn't seem like much—less than forty dollars—but it was all I had. I reached down in my pocket to dig it out, and that's when I found out it was gone.

"I can still remember how I felt. It was like somebody'd poleaxed me, it near made me dizzy. I went stumbling back into the bus station, searching every stranger's face, trying to find out which one could have done this to me—as if I'd know just by looking in his eyes. And I'll tell you something: everyone I passed looked like he could have done it. Maybe it was just the way I was feeling, but I swear there wasn't an honest face amongst 'em."

The room had grown silent but for the purring of the plump grey cat as it pressed itself against the foot of his chair. He realized with a flush of embarrassment that the others had long ago finished their soup and were waiting for him to do the same. "Here," he said, pushing the bowl roughly toward his wife, "take it! I've had my fill." As she collected the bowls he frowned and turned away, reaching down to stroke the grey cat's head.

Carol was watching him expectantly. "How awful," she said at last. "To lose all your money like that! And it always happens to the ones who need it most."

"I assume you took the first bus back to Flemington," said Freirs. There was a shade less sympathy in his voice.

Back at the oven, Deborah laughed. "Then you don't know Sarr." She swung back the oven door and reached inside with the potholder; something bubbled and hissed, and the smell of roasting meat grew stronger. "He's a stubborn one, he is. He's not one to give up without a fight."

Sarr smiled. "I'm stubborn, all right. And also a damned fool! I could have come home, because I still had my return ticket, right there in the pocket of my shirt. But that would've been too easy. I was out for justice. Maybe God had meant it for a sign, but I thought He was giving me a test. So what I did was, I went back out to the sidewalk and just stood there goggle-eyed a while, staring at the crowd. I had this crazy notion that maybe I'd see some other fool's pocket getting picked. I didn't, of course—no thief's *that* stupid—but I did get some advice. I felt a kind of tugging at my coat sleeve, and when I looked down, there was old Santa Claus peering up at me. His face was covered by the beard, but I could see his eyes, and they were sad. 'I saw them take your money,' he said. His voice was real soft, like an old flute. 'It was two black boys with coats like yours. They ran up there.' He was pointing north, past a row of bars and pawnshops and movie-house marquees. Way off in the distance I could see a line of trees, as if that was where the city came to an end. I thanked him, and he wished me luck, and I headed up the street."

Sarr paused as his wife returned to the table with a platter topped by a sizzling brown leg of lamb. It was followed by potatoes, his Aunt Lise's homemade mint jelly, and Deborah's own garden-grown beans. He saw Carol eye the meat dubiously and assumed she must be worrying about how much it had cost them. Well, it hadn't been cheap, especially for a man already in debt, but there were certain obligations to a guest that couldn't be evaded.

"Sure wish I'd had a meal like this when I started on my walk," he said, sliding the platter toward him. He took the carving knife Deborah handed him and sliced off a thick slab of meat. "Unfortunately, I'd nothing but a few cents change tied up in a handkerchief—just enough to buy myself a bar of—chocolate." He speared the meat and turned to Carol. "Here, pass me your plate."

She shook her head. "Thanks, but no. I don't eat meat."

He felt a spark of irritation. *So that's why she's so skinny.*

Deborah looked upset. "Why didn't you say anything, Carol? I could have made something else tonight."

"It's really okay," said Carol. She seemed embarrassed. "There was no need to go to any trouble. I've been a vegetarian since college, and I'll manage perfectly well on what you've got right here."

"But Jeremy, why didn't *you* say anything?"

Freirs shrugged. "I didn't know. We've only had spaghetti together. Carol, you never even told me."

"I'm sorry," she said. "I guess I never got the chance. Honestly, it's no big deal. I'm happy with the beans and potatoes."

"Well," Deborah fretted, "as long as that's enough . . ."

"It will be," said Carol. Poroth could see that she wished the subject had never come up. "Now poor Sarr, here, all he had to eat was a bit of chocolate."

"Well, that wasn't till later," he said, grateful she'd remembered. "At the time, all I wanted was to find my money." Carefully he served the others, then himself. "I suppose it was foolish of me to try."

"Naive, at any rate," said Freirs. "How'd you think you'd recognize the thief? There are a lot of sheepskin coats in New York."

"I expected the Lord would give me a sign. He's never failed me, you know."

Freirs looked skeptical. "Really? Another sign?"

Sarr nodded. "He doesn't fail believers. And with that knowledge in my heart, I kept on walking north. 'Twas a sour, cold day, I remember, with grey skies and a wind up, but there was no snow on the ground. It must have been a good deal hotter down below, because clouds of steam kept rising from holes in the pavement, and everyone in town seemed to be out of doors, rushing from one shop to the next, studying the goods behind the windows. Most of the goods looked awfully shoddy, with nothing special to them but their prices. I can't for the life of me see how anybody could afford them. Even if I'd had my money, it wouldn't have gotten me much. And yet everyone I saw seemed to have a package or two under his arm. Not a person was smiling—there wasn't a happy soul amongst 'em—but they sure must have wanted the things in those windows, like pigs fighting over a pile of garbage. I guess that's how they celebrate Christmas over there. It's a wonder they don't hate it."

"A lot of them do," said Freirs. "The rate of crime and suicide goes up that time of year. But it sounds like you're saying it's just what the people deserve." Sarr saw Carol's look of annoyance, but Freirs went blithely on. "You think they're all wicked, don't you?"

"No, I don't," said Sarr. "I think a lot of them are wicked, but a lot of others are nothing more than victims, and it's up to us to punish the first and save the second. Sometimes, I'll grant, it can be hard to tell the difference, but still I don't condemn them all. Not even the women who tried to stop me on the street, the ones who called out to me as I passed. I didn't understand, then, what it was they wanted, but I had a sense of it—I saw as how they weren't dressed for the cold—so I made no answer and walked on." He had added that for Deborah's sake; he couldn't let her get the wrong impression. "I know about them now, of course. They said they wanted love, but they really wanted money. 'Twas all right there in the Bible, though I never thought I'd see it for myself. Some of them were wicked, all right, 'an abomination unto the Lord.' But some, I'm sure, were just the victims of the city."

Deborah eyed him with amusement. "Come on, honey," she said. "Tell them what you did."

"I am," said Sarr. "What I'm saying is, there were all *kinds* of temptations in that city· places I could have entered, things I might have done. But I passed them by."

Freirs grinned. "You were broke!"

"No, sir," Sarr said gruffly, "I was strong. The Lord was with me. I passed the tempters by and kept on walking. I walked until I came to the line of trees I'd seen from down the street. They began just past a low stone wall. It was a bit of greenery at last, the edge of Central Park. I'd heard about it. A dangerous place, that's what I'd been told, but when I looked over the wall I could see there were people all through it that day, out for a stroll, eating roasted chestnuts or just sitting on the benches with their hands stuffed in their pockets. The street ran right alongside it, but I followed my instincts and walked on up the path toward where the woods looked deepest. I suppose I thought God was going to lead me to the thieves who stole my money. But He had other plans for me . . ."

A breeze lifted the flowered muslin curtains in the window by the sink. Night was coming on. The sporadic clatter of their knives and forks now rose above the faint rhythm of crickets.

"At first the park was real ugly," he went on. "Everywhere you walked you could hear the sound of traffic, automobile horns, people yelling at each other . . . And everywhere you stood you could see buildings in the background, just behind the trees. Maybe this time of year it would have been different, with leaves to cover up the view, but when I saw it the branches were bare. Besides, the place just didn't seem real. Not to me, anyway. It was supposed to look like you were in a forest; I could see how they were hoping to fool you with the rocks and the brooks and that winding little path going up and down over the hills. Yet wherever you looked there was garbage on the ground, and the trees were black with soot.

"But as I kept on heading north, the place began to draw me in somehow. It was so *huge* for a city park, it just went on and on—"

"It's supposed to be twice the size of Monaco, in fact."

"Oh, Jeremy, hush!"

"—and I began to lose the sense of being in a city. I could still see buildings far away, behind me and on either side, but the place seemed quieter now. I could actually hear the wind in the branches, and there weren't many people anymore, just a few strange, lonely-looking old men out for a winter's walk. All of a sudden the trees thinned out—I hadn't been expecting that—and I came to the edge of a great flat meadow. Most of the grass there was dead, with bare patches showing through everywhere. Underneath that dark grey sky it all looked very sad. There were two or three figures in the distance kicking a ball around, but I wasn't interested in them, so I moved off to one side, still keeping to the trees. After a while they began getting thicker again, and the ground got hilly. One minute I was walking over a little stone bridge, the next I was moving through a tunnel. On the other side I couldn't see the meadow anymore. I couldn't even see the buildings. I was inside a tight little ring of trees—a perfect circle, the limbs actually *touching* one another, like children playing ring-around-the-rosy. And I was in the middle all alone, with not a sound or a sight to distract me. Why, I could have been in the center of a forest, the deepest forest on the face of this planet, with no one there to see me but the Lord.

"I knew at once it was a holy place, God's own preserve in the very heart of wickedness. And I don't mind telling you—" He gripped the edge of the table and leaned forward, talking especially to this new woman who had come among them, who seemed to have some of the Holy Spirit in her. "I don't mind telling you that in that lonely place, myself a stranger of just seventeen years, I got down on my knees and said a prayer. I said, 'Father, make me a vessel of Thy cleansing light and deliver me from evil. And if Thou pointest the way, I shall follow.' That's what I said, and I started to get to my feet.

"And just then, out of the corner of my eye, I thought I caught a flash of movement somewhere outside the circle. By the time I turned, I'd missed it, but then there it was again, only far off to the side now, like a pair of dark shapes flitting past the trees. 'Twas only a glimpse, mind you, and then they'd moved away out of sight, but I was sure somehow that God had led me to the black boys I was after, the ones with coats like mine. I was wrong, though, I must have been, because when I ran across the circle and into the woods there was no one around. And the woods were so thick thereabouts, what with creepers and puckerbrush and all, that I didn't see how two people could've run through that way anyhow, one right beside the other, and I thought that what I must've seen was one man running with his shadow, or the shadow of a bird."

Freirs looked as if he were about to ask a question, but Deborah spoke up first. "Honey, you're gonna have them thinking you were drunk!" She lowered her eyes. "'Course *I* know you'd never touch a drop."

He grinned briefly. "I'll not claim that! But I'll grant I was feeling pretty light-headed by that time. Remember, I'd had nought to eat since morning, and had a long ways still to walk."

"You mean back to the bus?" said Carol.

"No, I kept on heading north, at least until I got out of the park. When that was behind me I took to the cross streets and started working my way up in a kind of zigzag fashion, wandering from one side of the island to the other. I actually believed I could cover every block. The streets up there were even dirtier, and there didn't seem to be as many people as before. There were the same holes in the ground, though, and the same steam coming out, as if the whole town had been built on top of a volcano. My own breath was steaming too, like a dragon's, and when I walked through a steam cloud I couldn't tell which part came from underground and which came from me. I was hungry and tired by then, and little by little I could feel the day get colder as the sun began going down, even though there were still a few hours left of afternoon. Most of the faces around me were black or foreign-looking now, and by the time evening came I felt like I'd wandered into a completely different country. But I put myself in the hands of the Lord and kept right on walking.

"The farther I walked, the more black faces I saw. Everybody'd watch me as I passed, at times just with curiosity, at times with something more. I saw a few people smile, like they knew some joke against me, and a lot of others glared at me with hatred in their eyes. At one point a group of kids tried to stop me from going up their road. They formed a line across the sidewalk and told me that if I wanted to get past I'd have to give them all my money—just like the kings of Jerusalem asking pilgrims for a toll. But like I said, I'm not a one to get scared off. There were a lot of them, but I was bigger, and I knew the Lord was with me. I turned out the pockets of my pants to show them I had nothing and just kept on walking. No one tried to stop me, and I never looked back. My pockets stayed turned out for the rest of the night."

"For the rest of the—" Freirs stared with disbelief. "What'd you do, spend the night in Harlem?"

Sarr shrugged. "Can't say. I just kept moving, that's all, and I wasn't much aware of the passage of time. I even forgot to worry about what my mother'd think. I just knew that the night was coming early, I didn't have my money, and everything around me was godless and ugly and mean. The houses—well, they were a horror, they looked as if they'd been deserted for years, like the ruins down the road from here, only there were lights coming on in some of the windows. And the shops were foul and dingy, though their prices were just as high as all the rest. Even the churches made me wonder, they looked so much like shops, with doorways along the sidewalk and billboards in front. There was one place, the Church of the Dog . . ." He shuddered.

"And the people I saw! If only I could forget. The ones in the alleys, or sitting on the curb, or lying in the street asleep with bottles by their heads ... It was almost night now, freezing cold, and they should have been indoors. So should I, though I didn't pay much heed to it till the sky turned really dark. I managed to find a few faint stars up there, but not a great many—nothing like out here. And then the streetlights all came on, up and down the blocks without a sound. They made everything seem even darker, and the stars were blotted out. That's the time I felt the loneliest, I think. I found myself looking into every window I passed and wishing I could join the folks inside, black as they were. It seemed so warm and light in there, especially from out on the street with the homeless ones and half-starved dogs and frozen-looking cats."

Idly he glanced down at Bwada, who was curled beside his chair, preoccupied with licking one fat grey forepaw, toes spread and gleaming nails extended. In the sudden silence she paused a moment and looked up, then turned her attention back to the paw.

"You'd think she was just a sweet-tempered old lady," said Deborah, "but it's all play-acting. I saw the way she tore open Joram's hand."

"'Twas nothing," Sarr said quickly, noticing Carol's look of uneasiness. "She meant no harm, nor Brother Joram either. A misunderstanding, that's all it was. A clash of spirits." Still, the city was momentarily forgotten, and the deep-rooted old affection he'd been feeling—almost a reflex now, whenever he thought of the cat—was pierced by the memory of that bellow of pain, the small grey shadow fleeing toward the woods, his own stammered apologies and the other man's furious, accusing glare as he yanked back his hand and watched the upturned palm fill quietly with blood.

The heart is deceitful above all things, and desperately wicked: who can know it?

How right Jeremiah had been! How eternally mysterious the world was, and all the beings in it.

He realized, with a start, that Carol was asking him something about the city and that his head had begun to throb uncomfortably. The drink was wearing off.

"There's not much more to tell," he said, "not that much I actually remember. I recall a fight outside a barroom, with one man spitting teeth, and some children throwing dice against a playground wall, but what sticks out more is the line of police cars I saw parked along one lonely street with the lights out and the motors running, and the men in their uniforms sitting together inside, talking and laughing as if they were waiting for something. After I was past them I stopped to look back, and I saw one of them come out of a building and another going in. And farther up the block a boy about my own age, sitting on his stoop, made an angry face at me—I guess he supposed I was one of the police—and asked me if I'd gone and had myself a piece. That's just the way he put it. He pointed to the building I'd passed and said there was a fourteen-year-old girl in there, living in the basement. Her mother'd run off to Puerto Rico, and this afternoon they'd put her father in jail, and now the girl was all alone and the police were taking turns with her."

He fell silent for a moment, surprised by the vividness of his own memory and wondering what impression it had made on Carol. Somewhere inside him, where his thoughts were darkest, he felt the first unwelcome stirrings of a reawakened lust, but fought them down.

Carol had stopped eating and was frowning in his direction. "I can't believe a thing like that could happen around Christmastime. It's just too sick! Where were all the decent people hiding?"

"They must have been inside," he said. "I only saw the ones left out in the cold. And everyone was crazy, and no one seemed to care. Everyone was talking to himself, or singing like a drunk, or making odd gestures in the air, or shouting his lungs out at things I couldn't see. I remember a huge black man, big as a bear, who stumbled past me carrying on a conversation with himself in two different voices. And then behind him came this skinny old white man, the only one I saw up there, tagging after him like someone in a clowns' parade, laughing and pointing and making the madman sign, as if to tell the world, See, this man is crazy!" Sarr twirled his finger beside his head. "I think the second man was as far gone as the first.

"And everything was ugly, and everything was crazy and corrupt. I kept telling myself that the whole city wasn't like this, *couldn't* be like this, but it's still the only part I really remember. I hadn't eaten all day, nothing but a little bitty candy bar, and I was high—dizzy, almost—by the time I reached the river at the top of the island. There was another stretch of woods up there, and a field for sports. It was as far north as I could go, so I turned around and started walking back. I could never do a thing like that today—all those miles on an empty belly, without a thought of sleep—but I was younger, then, and inclined to extremes."

He looked past the others, past the sink and the curtains and the window screens, into the remembered darkness.

"The night I'd picked was very long, the longest of the year, and I began to wonder if I'd ever see another morning. Whenever I came to a cloud of steam I'd walk right through the center, hoping it would warm me up a little, but by this time my teeth were chattering so hard I thought they'd break like china, and the wind seemed to go right through my coat and gloves. I felt like I'd been walking forever past those eyes looking out at me from windows and doorways and alleys, those sad dark faces saying things to no one in particular.

"Finally, though, the sky began to brighten some, and when I was two or three miles to the south I realized that the streetlights had gone off. Things somehow looked a little better then, and for the first time I wondered if maybe I'd been too hard on everyone, too quick to judge." Out of the corner of his eye he saw Deborah give an almost imperceptible nod. "I told myself that if the people I'd been among seemed godless, 'twas only because they'd never been taught the truth, and that just because a few of them acted crazy, it didn't mean they all were.

"And just then, as if to prove it, the steam parted and I saw a really distinguished-looking coffee-colored man walking toward me up the block. He was getting kind of old, I could see, but he stood erect and tall, and he had on a long grey winter dress coat with a scarf tucked in at the neck, and a fancy creased hat, and he was swinging a long black umbrella with a shiny wooden handle. The sun was just beginning to come up, and I finally remembered the day—'twas Sunday morning— and I said to myself, 'See, here's a good sort of man, probably on his way to church. There are still a few decent people left in this city.' And then, as he got closer, I saw that he wasn't looking at me. His eyes were glassy and fixed on something just in front of him, and he was *snarling* to himself, words I wouldn't repeat even in anger.

"I knew right then exactly where I was, and where I'd been all night. I knew that the Almighty had vouchsafed me a vision. Those frozen streets, the sky without stars, the ground steaming under my feet . . . There are spots in the world where the hellfire peeps through, and I'd just had a tour of one.

"It was meant as a warning, of course. I put aside all thoughts of my money, made sure to keep the river on my right, and kept on moving south.

"Well, even the longest night's got to end eventually, that's one thing I've learned, and by the time the sun was up above the buildings and the day had gotten warmer I was halfway back to the bus station. I figured I was in the normal world again, I thought I'd put all that wickedness behind me, and so when I passed an open area with statues and iron gates and big Greek-looking buildings—Jeremy's old university, it turns out—I decided it was finally time to sit down awhile and maybe put my feet up. I'd seen the river gleaming at the end of the cross streets, with a thin green park beside it sloping down toward the water, and there seemed to be plenty of benches I could rest on before heading back. By that time my wandering was beginning to catch up with me, and rest was what I craved.

"There were a surprising lot of old folks in the park that Sunday morning, walking dogs or just watching the river, and they all looked nice and peaceable and happy with the world. I knew I was among my own kind now. God's my witness, it was really a relief. A few of the benches were already pretty well filled, but way up ahead, past the others, I saw one that was empty except for a little old man sitting by

himself, all bundled up in an overcoat and muffler, with just his little
pink head peeking out like a baby's, and fuzzy white hair on the top.
He had a brown paper bag on his lap, and I figured he was fixing to
have lunch. But when I sat myself down at the opposite end, he pulled
up the bag and stood, as if he hadn't wanted company. Well, that was
all right with me; I was suddenly so tired I could hardly keep my eyes
open. I remember, though, how he stopped to look down at me as he
walked past, and how his whole face lit up when he smiled. Reminded
me of my grandfather, or maybe even my father in one of his better
moods, like just after worship. I think I may have dropped off then, at
least for a second or two, because when I opened my eyes he was still
standing there, looking sort of concerned. But when he saw I was okay
he just nodded and gave a sort of wink. Then he stuffed the bag into a
trash can and strolled away, humming some peculiar little song."

"I hate this part," Deborah said abruptly. She got up and went to
the stove for the last of the vegetables.

He ignored her. "I can still see that wink, and the careless, almost
contemptuous way he stuffed that bag in among the garbage . . . Afterward I must have gone right back to sleep, because I don't remember
anything else. I recall I had a dream about a man with snow-white
wings, I thought it was my father come back as an angel. I don't know
exactly how long I slept, but it must have been for some time, because
when I woke up I was shivering, my hands were clenched like fists inside my pockets, and the day had gotten darker. I'd thought it was a
child's cry that woke me, but there weren't any children in the park,
and not many adults left either. It was late afternoon. I shook myself
awake and hurried from the bench. Lord, how my body ached! Just
after I passed the trash can, I heard a tiny little cry, so faint it
sounded miles away. But something made me stop. I looked around,
and sure enough, 'twas coming from the bag.

"Well, Deborah knows the rest. Inside there were the remains of a
sandwich—wax paper with some icy crusts of bread, a bit of meat—
and six or seven newborn kittens. Dead. Frozen, I believe, though a
couple looked broken like—"

"Honey, please!"

He nodded, the vision fading. "I'm sorry, Deb. You're right. I'm acting like a fool. Enough to say it was a sight not fit for Christian eyes.
But then I noticed a bit of movement, and I reached down and found
that one of the bodies, a little grey thing underneath the others, still
had a tiny breath of life left in it. I picked it up—it was so small I
could hold it in one hand—and very softly it began crying, crying . . ."

The sound of it came back to him, and the chill from off the river. He
could feel once more the stiffness of his limbs, the pain of the wind
against his numbing fingers, the exhaustion of that journey. Suddenly
he felt very tired.

"The shops there were still open," he said at last. "That's just about the only thing we have in common, the people of the city and the Brethren, we're none of us too proud to work on the Lord's day. But the shopkeepers in that hellish place had hearts like flint, and nary a one would give me a penny's worth of milk—not that I could have paid for even that. So I asked God for forgiveness and took the milk anyhow, a carton from a supermarket shelf. I saw to it that the creature got nourishment, warm from my own mouth. No one was looking, or if anybody was, no one seemed to care. Except for me. I cared. And I cried. God help me, that's the only time in my life I've ever stolen anything—that Sunday in that city of yours. Ten years it's been, and then some, and I've yet to set foot there again.

"They say the Lord works in mysterious ways. I'd hoped to bring a jewel home, and now somehow I'd found one—the last innocent thing left amidst all that corruption. I kept her inside my shirt, pressed up against me, all the way back to the bus station and all the way to Flemington. She was almost dead by the time I got her home, but I knew my mother'd nurse her back to health."

Carol lay down her fork. "And did she?"

"Sarr's mother can do anything," said Deborah, returning to the table with the salad. "She has the healing gift."

"I won't deny it," said Sarr. "She can make things live and grow when she's a mind to."

"So the story has a happy ending after all." There was relief in Carol's voice. "And the kitten?"

"Haven't you guessed?" Sarr bent forward and lifted Bwada onto his lap. Squatting there uncertainly with her ears bent back, claws digging into his trouser leg, the animal looked fat and sullen and dangerous, but as soon as Sarr began to scratch the silver fur between her ears she blinked contentedly—and relaxed, settling herself on his lap with an almost inaudible purring.

The others looked on, grinning; even Deborah seemed pleased—Deborah, who had heard the tale before and who bore little love for Bwada, the one cat of the seven that was Sarr's alone.

But Sarr himself shared none of their content. Now lapsed into reverie, he was years away and thrice as many miles, remembering in Bwada's purr the susurrus of wind as it raced beneath a frozen grey sky through that desolate circle of trees; and as the cat sound swelled and deepened, taking on what almost seemed a note of warning, he heard once more the old man's peculiar little song.

I'm among loonies, Freirs was thinking. *These people are all insane! Every time somebody farts they think God is giving them a sign.*

All through the story he'd been watching Carol's face. She'd been listening with rapt attention, and at certain points—whenever Poroth had prayed or called on God—she'd gotten positively starry-eyed.

But maybe it wasn't God that made her starry-eyed. Maybe it was Poroth.

Well, what else did I expect? he told himself. *He's a hell of a lot bigger than I am, and in a hell of a lot better shape, and that soft, low voice of his would probably make any woman think she's a little girl again being tucked into bed by her daddy.*

He wondered if Poroth talked so much whenever a new woman was around. Or perhaps it was the influence of the wine; that home-brewed stuff had been surprisingly potent. His own head was still swimming with it.

And of course there was that brooding quality he had—something, Freirs knew from experience, that women seemed to like. It was so easy to mistake for real depth.

Maybe this was all a bad idea, he told himself. *Maybe I should never have asked her out here in the first place. Clearly Sarr's the master here. This is his world.*

"No, I'll not deny it," he was saying to Carol. "I still feel the attraction of the lights. But I'm a wiser man today—I know it sounds prideful, but it's true—and I know the path we've got to follow. We've got to give up the ways of man and the ways of the city: the corruption, the idleness, the love of worldly gain. And you should too. You should come back to the only constant things: the land . . . and God."

That bastard! thought Freirs. *He's using God to make time with my girl!*

"Now I'm not saying we have it easy here, Deborah and me, and I'm not saying we have a lot of anything but work. But we're living the way the Lord wants us to, living just like people in the Bible." Poroth's hands took in the kitchen, the farmhouse, the fields and woods beyond. "Our only aim, really, is to abide by what the prophet said: 'Stand ye in the ways, and see, and ask for the old paths, where is the good way, and walk therein.' "

Carol nodded as if she understood. "Yes," she said, "that's Jeremiah. I kept hearing passages from him on the radio today. He must be big in these parts."

Deborah seemed to find this irresistibly funny. Her husband did not. "He's the prophet of our sect," he explained.

Freirs spoke up. "And a good thing, too. I sometimes think that's the only reason they let an unbeliever like me stay here—because they liked my name."

Carol barely seemed to hear; her eyes were still on Sarr. "The one thing I don't understand," she said, "is where you're hiding your church. I drove all over Gilead and didn't see a single one."

"Oh, we don't go to church," said Deborah, getting to her feet. "We hold our meetings in the Brethren's homes. Later this month we'll be holding one here, and you're welcome to come out and see for yourself."

"We take our call from the Gospels," added Sarr. " 'Where two or three are gathered together in my name, there am I in the midst of them.' "

Carol nodded. "I see. That's Matthew, isn't it?"

"Hey," said Freirs, surprised, "you're pretty good!"

She looked slightly embarrassed. "Didn't I tell you? I went to parochial school for twelve years."

Freirs' eyes widened. "No kidding! I knew you were Catholic and all, but—well, I guess I'd always pictured you as just a nice corn-fed country girl from some little red schoolhouse in the sticks." He tried to remember if she'd said anything about parochial school over dinner the previous week. Probably he'd done so much of the talking that she'd never had a chance.

"There's a *lot* you don't know about me, Jeremy," she said. She turned to Sarr. "You see, I may go about things a bit differently, but I've tried to live in the Lord's way too."

Freirs regarded them sourly. *They sound like they're on speaking terms with God,* he thought. *But I'm not so sure I'd want to meet the Poroths' version on a dark night.*

Leaning back in his chair, he peered out the window above the sink. It was certainly dark enough out there tonight. The moon seemed to be hidden behind a cloud, with only a pale streak above the trees to mark its presence. A line from a poem came back to him: *On the farm, the darkness wins.* Though no doubt the Brethren would argue that the darkness here was the darkness of God.

Beside him Deborah was clearing away the salad plates; the Poroths ate their salad European-style, just before dessert. "Hey," she said, nudging him gently on the shoulder, "come back and join us. I went to a lot of trouble over what's coming."

It proved to be a steaming Indian pudding which had lain nearly three hours in the stove. Made of cornmeal and molasses, it was served with thick fresh cream from the Verdocks' dairy in town. "Now, Carol," she said, "I sure hope you'll have no objection to *this.*"

"Not the slightest," said Carol. Her eyes widened as Deborah ladled out a generous serving for each of them. "God, it's a wonder the two of you can even stand!"

Freirs nodded ruefully. "I'm still trying to figure out how they stay so thin."

"I have to watch that man like a hawk!" said Deborah, laughing. "He'd eat everything in the bowl if I let him."

Pensively Poroth licked the spoon clean and looked up. "They warned me about that when I married you," he said. "They told me, 'Sarr, that woman from Sidon's going to starve you!' " He eyed her with affection. "But the truth is, we work hard, Deborah and me. We're at it all day, seven days a week. Keeps a body from getting fat. We don't believe in sitting on our duffs."

There was a moment of silence; Freirs decided that Poroth had been speaking to him. He forced a smile. *Keep it light.* "Oh, physical labor's all right, I guess, if that's what turns you on. But as the philosopher said to the farmer, 'While you're feeding your hogs, sir, you're starving your mind.' "

He glanced sidelong at Carol for approval and caught a smile. Maybe the night was still salvageable.

"By the way, have I told you about the exercises I'm doing?" While Deborah set aside the jug and brought out Rosie's wine, he launched into a description of his daily routine: the sit-ups, the pushups, the stretching motions for the back. "I've also done a little jogging," he heard himself say. "It's more interesting here than in the city, and a lot more private. Maybe I'll explore the other end of this road, or hike in the direction of those hills . . ."

He listened to himself talk on aimlessly, inconsequentially: perfect New York small-talk. Yet perhaps he'd overplayed his hand, for Carol, he saw, had turned back to Sarr, who, all the while, sat silent and unsmiling. *They're sharing something I can't touch,* he decided.

Deborah was smiling at him sympathetically. "Sounds okay to me," she said. "A lot more fun than washing dishes." She got up from the table and began collecting their bowls.

Carol seemed to shake herself awake. "Oh, can I give you a hand with that?"

"Won't say no!" Deborah tossed her a towel. "You can do the drying up."

Neither Poroth nor Freirs made any move to help. Freirs had offered a few nights ago and had been politely rebuffed by Deborah; such work, she'd said, was "women's work." It had shocked him at the time to hear her say such a thing, but he'd been content to let her have her way. If she was so big on tradition, he sure as hell wasn't going to dissuade her.

He seized the opportunity of being alone with Sarr. Digging into his wallet, he extracted a ten-dollar bill. "For tonight's dinner," he said in a low voice. "Thanks a lot. It was great."

Poroth smiled wanly and shook his head, not even looking at the money.

"Go ahead," said Freirs, "take it. I want to reimburse you. It's for Carol. I mean, let's face it, she's not your guest, she's mine."

Poroth did not appear to take the hint. In fact, Freirs thought, he looked hurt. Maybe he'd been more sincere all evening than Freirs had realized.

"Put away your money, Jeremy," he said quietly. "It's well meant, I know, but I can't accept it. Our hospitality's for everyone; your guest is also ours. Truth is, I sore regret every cent we've had from you already. I like to think of you as a guest here, and I only wish we could treat you as a guest deserves."

God damn it, thought Freirs, *isn't that just like a Christian! Just when you've decided that you hate his guts, he goes and makes you feel guilty about it.*

Drying her hands with the dish towel, Carol yawned and realized how tired she was. She would probably fall asleep as soon as her head touched the pillow. And with the thought of bed, she remembered the present Rosie had given her for Jeremy, and the book she'd brought out for him. It was meant to be read only at bedtime, the old man had emphasized, and surely bedtime would not be long in coming. She turned to Deborah at the sink beside her. "I'm just going upstairs for a moment," she said, lowering her voice, though at the table the men were still talking. "A friend of mine gave me a little gift for Jeremy."

She saw him look up as she left the kitchen. He looked concerned, probably afraid she wasn't coming down.

"I'll be right back," she said.

The living room was small and low-ceilinged, with simple oak furniture grouped around a braided rug. Several not-very-clean-looking farm implements lay scattered on the floor beside a wooden bench, patches of metal gleaming from their rust, as if polishing these tools was the usual evening's pastime. In the corner near the stairway stood a tall grandfather clock whose ticking, when all else was silent, could be heard throughout the house. A narrow wooden writing desk stood in the opposite corner, its dusty bottom shelf stacked with books, many of them college texts; Carol noticed a *Fundamentals of Social Change* and a volume of inspirational verse. It was apparent from their position that they were never removed, yet clearly Poroth had been unable to bring himself to throw them away or store them in attic or cellar; perhaps they were a source of pride, perhaps one of temptation.

By the other wall a corn-husk broom and iron tongs leaned against the stones of the fireplace. There was a smell of wood and lemon oil in the room and, behind it, one of charcoal; though the fireplace must have stood empty for some time now, it had obviously seen much use during the winter months. Venturing closer, Carol stopped to read the crude wooden plaque that hung by the chimney, with a motto from someone named Cowley burned into the wood: *A Plow on a Field Arable Is the Most Honorable of Ancient Arms.* On the mantelpiece below it lay a garland of dried flowers, a group of china cats (several chipped or broken), and a little wooden weather house with the man out in front. He looked a lot like Sarr.

Taking a lamp that stood burning on a table in the corner, she hurried upstairs. In the flickering light the Man in the Moon gazed down at her benignly from the wall as she rummaged through her tote bag for the parcel and the book. Outside the window, the real moon lay hidden by a cloud. Pressing her face to the glass, she tried to pick out the long, low guest house and the barn. They were hard to find. She'd forgotten how dark it got in the country once the sun went down.

Jeremy would be out there alone tonight . . . Well, it simply couldn't be helped. There was no way she'd dare offend the Poroths by sneaking off with Jeremy, on whatever pretext. Besides, she was far too tired to contemplate sleeping with him now, tired from the drive out, the wine, the tensions of their silly conversation. She had felt Sarr's eyes boring into her all evening and had felt herself, for a moment at least, the more desirable woman in the room. Jeremy had suddenly seemed too abrasive, too eager.

But in fact, her mind had been made up all afternoon, ever since she'd seen that awful grey-brick building he was living in. The thing was ugly even for a chicken coop; it reminded her of something abandoned by the army. Jeremy had tried, of course, to brighten it up a bit—the blankets had been folded, the furniture polished, the books all put away—but somehow that had only made it more depressing. A vase of roses he'd placed by the bed had failed to disguise the pervasive smell of mildew (her nose wrinkled in recollection) and a hint of insect spray; and just outside, their shadows falling across his pillow, a group of trees had stood peering in at them like spectators waiting for a sacrifice. Just as well she'd be spending the night here in the farmhouse.

Downstairs the two men were still slouched at the table over the wine, Sarr fiddling with a worn-looking pipe while Deborah mopped the counter by the sink. Both Poroths looked tired, though Jeremy sounded awake and animated as always. Well, not as always: she'd noticed, earlier tonight, that his leg no longer swung nervously beneath the table, as it had back in New York. At least the country was having some effect.

"—or that line of Butler's," he was saying—God, he never

stopped!—"about how 'I'd rather buy milk than own a cow.' And let's face it, there's some truth to that. For instance, speaking for myself, I'd rather rent a room than own a house."

"On the other hand," Deborah called back, giggling, "I'll bet you'd rather have a wife than—"

They looked up as Carol came in.

"Jeremy," she said, "I just wanted you to know that I didn't come here empty-handed today." Smiling, she stood beside his chair. "In fact, I have two things I'm supposed to give you: this book you wanted"—with mock gravity she laid it on the table before him—"which, according to my instructions, you're to open at bedtime. And this gift from Rosie"—she placed it beside the book—"which you're to open now."

Deborah came to the table. "Oh, Jeremy," she said, "lucky you!" She ran her fingers over the book's embossed yellow covers. "They sure made them nice in those days."

"What book is it?" asked Sarr. He made no move to touch it.

"Oh, I remember now," said Freirs, unwrapping the small package. "It's a story collection, that's all. I need a couple of things in it for my project."

"I borrowed it from Voorhis," Carol added. "I'm supposed to take it back with me tomorrow."

Deborah picked it up and examined the spine. "Oh, I see," she said, "it's a library book. *The House of Souls.*" She smiled at Freirs. "This looks like it'll send you off to dreamland, all right!"

Freirs had undone the white paper and was examining the slim cardboard packet inside. " 'Dynnod,' " he read, puzzling out the ornate gold letters on the front. He opened the flap at the end. "Hmmm, it's a set of cards of some kind."

"Rosie says they're like the tarot deck," explained Carol, peering over his shoulder; she'd never actually seen the cards before. "Dynnod's Welsh for 'images', he says. They're supposed to correspond to the twenty-two whatever-you-call-'ems—picture cards."

"The Greater Arcana," said Sarr.

They all looked at him. "You know what these are, honey?" asked Deborah.

"I know the tarot, yes. But not these." He eyed them dubiously. The card on top bore a round yellow face and the words *The Sun.* "Or at least, I'm not sure. I'd have to look them up."

"Sarr has read more weird old books than any twelve people," said Deborah, seating herself beside him. "He knows almost as much as his mother."

He shook his head.

"I'll bet you do, honey," she said. "It's just that she gets it all without reading."

"I've never heard of this sort of thing," said Freirs, who had been studying the box. "It doesn't say 'Welsh' on the label. It just says 'Made in U.S.A., Crystal Novelty Co., Cranston, R.I.,' and 'Instructions included.' But there don't seem to *be* any instructions." He showed them the empty box.

"God, how annoying!" said Carol. "Isn't there anything printed on the back?"

He turned it over. "Nope. Nothing except 'For entertainment purposes only.' " Looking to the deck, he slid the top card off; the one below it showed a crescent moon. "I guess they mean it's not supposed to be used for gambling."

"Well, of course not," said Carol. "It's for fortune-telling. Isn't that right, Sarr?"

He shrugged. "Maybe. What did your friend say?"

"You mean Rosie? He didn't say. But isn't that what a tarot deck's for?" She sat down and reached for the moon card. The pale crescent shape was faceless against the purple sky. Between the two horns gleamed a star.

"A tarot has seventy-eight cards, though," Sarr said guardedly. "This only has—did you say twenty-two?"

"Let's see," said Freirs. One by one he began going through the deck, counting each card as he came to it while Carol, beside him, read the title at the bottom.

"The Sun."

The face, she decided, was mysterious and cruel—anything but sunny.

"The Moon."

"Look," said Deborah, "look where that star is. Isn't that impossible?"

"There's something like that in the *Ancient Mariner,*" said Freirs, with a whispered *two* to himself. "At one point he looks up and that's what he sees."

"But it isn't natural."

"It's not supposed to be natural."

"The Book."

"Gee, it looks just like *this* one," said Deborah, pointing to *The House of Souls*. The book in the picture was fat and mustard-colored. It bore no visible title.

"The Bird."

A graceful white shape with a splash of red at its breast.

"The Watchers."

"It's just a group of pussycats," said Deborah.

Carol studied it a moment. "Hmmm, you're right. I wonder why they give it that title."

Freirs revealed the next card. "The Moth."

It looked more like two green leaves stuck together, Carol decided. She was still disappointed by the oddness of Rosie's present—which, in a way, had become *her* present. The illustrations weren't very pretty, just rather lurid lithographs; and what was the point, anyway, seeing as they'd forgotten to include the instructions?

"The Wand."

Black as ebony, and shiny-looking.

"Odd," said Freirs. "It seems to have holes along the side."

"The . . . Dhol."

"The what?" Deborah craned forward to see; Sarr squinted at it suspiciously. The thing on the card was dirty black and had four legs; beyond that it looked ragged and half-formed, a papier-mâché mouse.

"It must be a misprint," said Carol. "For mole, maybe. Or vole."

"Honey, maybe you can look it up later."

"The Serpent."

A pale, snakelike thing. Funny, thought Carol; she'd have expected a typical red Welsh dragon.

"The Mound . . . The Lovers."

A man and woman, smiling.

"The Eye."

A single staring eye amid the branches of a tree.

"The Rose."

It was hard to say why the picture was so disturbing, thought Carol. Perhaps it was the inner row of spiky petals that looked so much like teeth.

"The Marriage."

Odd, the thing standing beside the woman looked like the molelike creature from the earlier card.

"The Pool."

Greenery all around . . .

"The Tree."

"It's the same picture we saw before," said Deborah. "It's 'The Eye.' "

"You're right," said Carol, more disappointed than ever. "It must be another misprint." The deck was unusual, all right, but obviously rather cheap.

Freirs slid up another card.

"Hmm," said Carol, "this one doesn't even have a title."

The card bore a simple design of three concentric rings slashed by a vertical red line.

"Maybe it's like the Joker," said Freirs. He turned another card.

"Spring."

The card showed a landscape, but done entirely in white.

"This is *weird*, " said Carol. "White's supposed to be for winter."

"Summer."

A landscape all in green.

"Fall."

All in red.

"Ah, here it is. Winter."

The land was black, like the aftermath of a fire.

"Here's the last one," said Freirs. "Twenty-two."

"The Egg." Carol made a face. "Is this supposed to be some kind of joke?"

The picture was of a globe of the earth, the familiar continents clearly visible.

"Well," said Freirs, as if trying to inject a note of heartiness, "your friend Rosie comes up with some pretty unusual presents. I'll have to write him a nice thank-you." He tapped the edges of the cards against the table, lining them up evenly once more. From the one on top the sun's face glared toward the ceiling. " 'A gaze blank and pitiless as the sun,' " said Freirs. "Does anyone want their fortune told? I have no idea what these damned things mean, but maybe I can improvise something."

"No thanks, for me," said Carol. "I'm really exhausted after all that driving. You know how it is when you get away from the city." Pushing back her chair, she stood up. God, she really *was* exhausted! "And I think I had a little too much wine. I guess I'd better just go on up to bed." She saw Jeremy's smile fade.

"We're pretty tired too," said Sarr. "We'll be up in a few minutes."

Carol stood looking down at Jeremy, feeling awkward. She handed him the yellow book. "And don't forget this," she said, trying to cheer him up. "I've got to take it back with me tomorrow." He stared at it miserably, as if it were his own death warrant.

"Oh, yeah. Thanks." He didn't look up.

"Well, then—" She made her goodnights to them all, and, on impulse, leaned over and kissed Jeremy on the cheek, wondering as she did so what he'd think of it and, more, what Sarr would think. *Nonsense,* she told herself, *surely these people can't disapprove of that!* She felt Sarr's eyes on her as she turned to go but couldn't tell what he was feeling.

Jeremy, though, was no mystery. Looking through her bedroom window when she got back upstairs, she saw him leave the kitchen and walk dejectedly across the lawn, the book tucked beneath his arm. For a moment he was outlined in the kitchen light; then the night closed over him like a shroud.

If Rochelle hadn't had that second glass of wine and the remainder of a joint, she might have taken more notice of the fact that the lock on the door of her building was broken again for the second time in a week. The door swung open as she leaned against it, and closed behind her with an echoing of metal up and down the tiled hall. The hall itself appeared more dimly lit than she remembered; two bulbs at the other end had been removed—stolen, probably—since she'd come through here earlier today, leaving the passage to the elevator obscured by shadow.

But it was late. She was in no condition to recognize signs such as these, and in no mood to heed them. Shrugging off the darkness that had settled upon the street, she pushed her way inside and moved wearily down the hall.

She felt cheated. Buddy had not shown up tonight, nor had she been able to reach him by telephone. The party had proved enjoyable enough without him—she had known most of the people there and had given her phone number to one of the host's friends who'd been eyeing her all evening and had come up to her near the end—but afterward, on the cab ride home, she had grown depressed again, weighed down by a vague sense of betrayal. Carol was away for the weekend, all excited over some guy she hadn't even slept with, and for the first time in months she and Buddy could have had the apartment to themselves, without the need to keep their lovemaking out of Carol's sight or to endure her lonely envy. Instead, she was coming home alone; the night was all but wasted.

The streetlamp by her doorway had been dead almost a week. The moon had long been lost behind the rooftops. Her mind still fogged by alcohol, she had overtipped the driver and stumbled from the cab, bruising her knee as she stepped down. She paused now in the middle of the hall to rub it, then walked blindly on. Something shrank within her as she remembered what awaited her upstairs, the dark and silent rooms, the emptiness beside her in the bed.

Turning toward the elevator, she nearly tripped again over a shapeless bundle of rags that, hidden by shadow, had been heaped up against the rear wall. She mouthed a curse. Just as soon as she got the money together she was going to move out of this rat hole. She'd had enough of garbage in the halls.

As she pulled open the elevator's scarred black metal door, the bundle rose and followed her inside.

She turned, her stupor lifting, to find a gaunt and wrinkled old woman beside her, filthy-looking and impossibly stooped, the back bent almost double. The face, too, was averted, as if in deference or fear, but by the light of the one bare bulb that dangled from the ceiling Rochelle made out a mass of stringy hair, deep creases and discolorations in the skin, and, clenched as if praying, a pair of plump little hands. It was the hands that bothered her most.

Pressing the button for her floor, she edged away. The metal door slid shut. "Do you belong here?" she heard herself demand. Her voice was harsh within the little car.

The figure made no answer. But as the car jerked upward, something stirred beneath its rags.

"I asked you a question!" snapped Rochelle. "If you don't belong here—"

She gasped. The figure had turned toward her and was beginning to straighten up. Overhead, with an almost audible *pop*, the bulb in the ceiling winked out. There was time for one brief, desperate scream that echoed through the blackness of the car—and then the plump little hands closed over her throat.

The night was filled with the sound of crickets, a vast and mindless machine grinding without end. Lightning bugs gleamed above the grass. Bats darted under the eaves of the barn. In the light from the kitchen the apple tree's branches were bright against the darkness.

Freirs looked disconsolately toward the sky, wondering, now that it was too late, if he should have asked Carol to come out for a stroll. But it was not a time for strolling; the night was dark and unpleasant, the moon half concealed behind clouds. And anyway, how obvious it would have been to resort to such a ruse, and how humiliating if she turned him down.

No, there'd been nothing he could say or do—not in front of the Poroths. There was no way he could have invited her out. It would have seemed too much like pleading.

Brooding over the patronizing little peck on the cheek she'd given him, he slunk back to his room.

Somehow I didn't think I'd be writing this tonight. I suppose I had visions of Carol with me, beside me, all night long ... Instead she's up there in the farmhouse right now, about to sleep the sleep of the virtuous in that tacky little room, while I'm alone out here, scribbling the night away in this goddamned journal & trying to lose myself in the dubious consolations of prose.

It's probably my own fault. She was probably embarrassed to do anything in front of the Poroths, & I didn't encourage her enough. And maybe she really was tired . . .

If only I'd asserted myself more. If only I hadn't behaved like such a goddamned gentleman, she'd be here beside me now. Wish to hell she didn't have to go back to the city tomorrow.

And now I've also got a headache, thanks, no doubt, to Rosie's wine. Damn

He took out his anger on the bugs. He spent half an hour going over his room, spray can in hand, looking for them.

He found them, too. As many times as he'd gone over the room—the corners by the ceiling, the spaces around the window frames, the cracks beneath the sills—he always found new ones. There was no keeping them out.

Whenever he saw an insect, he blasted it with the spray. Spiders, doused with it, curled up like men in despair, clutching their knees; he almost could have felt sorry for them, if only their brown legs hadn't been so hairy and their eyes so cruel. He blasted some large beetles that were clinging to the screens, trying to push their way in; they convulsed and dropped away, disappearing. He watched a lot of daddy longlegs curl up and die, and fat, bloated caterpillars wriggle. He tended not to kill the moths out there—they seemed so vulnerable, so hopeful, like humans, striving toward the light beyond the screen, bodies pale against the surrounding darkness—unless their banging annoyed him.

The ones he really liked, however, were the fireflies; he felt a little sorry when he sprayed a few by mistake as they clung to the wire. When he sprayed them, they'd glow, and that cold light wouldn't wink off, it would just keep glowing, glowing much too long, till at last it faded away.

That's the only clue, he decided. *The dead ones don't wink.*

At that moment, the singing began. He could hear it from the farmhouse, coming faintly through the night. The Poroths were going through their hymns.

He had heard them do this before: their evening devotions, they called it. But he'd never heard them singing as late as this, and never with such intensity. They must be atoning for the glass or two of wine, he decided. Big sin!

"Marvelous grace of our loving Lord,
Grace that exceeds our sin and our guilt,
Yonder on Calvary's mount outpoured,
There where the blood of the Lamb was spilt."

The rug had been rolled up; Sarr and Deborah were on their knees on the bare plank floor, watched by three of the cats. Their hands were clasped before them; their eyes were shut tight. They seemed to be beseeching something they could see inside their heads.

"Dark is the stain that we cannot hide,
What can avail to wash it away?"

Their voices rose louder and louder as they worked themselves into the song.

"Look! there is flowing a crimson tide;
Whiter than snow you may be today."

Briefly Sarr thought of Carol in the next room; her crimson hair would be pressed against the whiteness of the pillow.

"Grace, grace, God's grace,
Grace that will pardon and cleanse within . . ."

He threw himself into the song, singing all the louder to regain the feeling that was gone.

"Grace, grace, God's grace,
Grace that is greater than all our sin."

Carol had been almost asleep when the singing started. She roused for a moment, but she was so tired—curious, she couldn't *remember* the last time she'd been so tired—that moments later she was slipping again into sleep, incorporating the words of the hymn into her dream.

"There are days so dark that I seek in vain
For the face of my Friend above . . ."

Jeremy's face . . . Sarr's face, his dark probing eyes . . . a black thing watching from a tree . . .

She started awake, thought briefly of the Dynnod, and drifted back to sleep—

"But tho' darkness hide,
He is there to guide
With the touch of His hand and His love."

—back to sleep, with Sarr's hand, Jeremy's hand, the hand of God on hers.

*

The room smelled faintly of insecticide. He had put away the can and decided to call it a night. Now he sat morosely on his bed, listening to the voices drift across the lawn to the outbuilding. They made him feel even lonelier. The others were all there, together in the farmhouse, and he was alone out here, exiled till dawn.

He wondered if Carol was singing with them. He doubted it, though it was hard to make out individual voices; she was probably already in bed. *Wonder if she's thinking of me. I'd give anything to be inside there with her ...*

Suddenly the singing stopped. He could picture the two of them climbing into bed and envied them, their warm familiar bodies pressed together, the mattress sagging softly beneath them. All was silent now, except for the crickets.

Unfortunately, he wasn't very tired. In fact, he was still restless and on edge. The sick feeling left by the wine had finally worn off.

Maybe a dip into someone else's mind would do the trick. He undressed and got into his bathrobe. Glancing around for a book to read, his eye fell on the faded yellow covers of the one Carol had brought him. Seating himself at his desk, he ran through what he knew of its author. Machen had been a Welsh minister's son who went to London and lived alone for many years, nearly starving, haunted by fantasies of weird pagan rites and longing for the green hills he'd left behind. Lovecraft, in a survey of the field, had praised him highly.

Freirs flipped through the yellowed pages, searching for the story the old man had recommended, "The White People." It was near the center; the book fell open easily to it. Someone—perhaps old Rosie himself, hadn't he been scribbling something that day?—had written in pencil just above the title, *Only effective if read by moonlight.*

Too bad the moon was blocked by clouds tonight; it might almost have been worth a try. Just for fun, of course. By way of experiment he snapped off the desk lamp. Surprisingly, moonlight was now streaming into the room, falling onto the bed and a strip of the floor with a radiance far brighter than he'd imagined, though the table he was using as his desk was still in shadow. Peering out the window, he saw that the clouds had begun to part; the moon was shining down now unimpeded.

Leaving his chair, he seated himself on the edge of the bed and laid the book on the windowsill. He discovered that, by squinting, he could just make out the words. It might be amusing, he decided, to try and absorb the story this way. Maybe it would ease him into a dream.

Holding the book open to the moonlight, he began to read.

*

His eyes were moving faster. They felt as if they were darting back and forth as rapidly as insects, yet his vision seemed glazed, as if he were no longer reading the words but was instead being read by them, carried along like the beetle he'd seen kicking in the swiftly flowing stream, borne by the current . . . toward what rapids?

The story's prologue, a framing device, had confused him, with all its high-flown talk about the human soul and the Meaning of Sin, and he wasn't even sure exactly where the tale was set—somewhere in the countryside, that's all he could be certain of, with a big house near a forest, and secret places, hills and pools and glades.

But the main portion of the story, the extract from a young girl's notebook, was staggering, overwhelming. It was as if it spoke to him aloud.

"I looked before me into the secret darkness of the valley, and behind me was the great high wall of grass, and all around me were the hanging woods that made the valley such a secret place . . ."

He couldn't read it rapidly enough: the air of pagan ecstasy, the rites one doesn't dare describe, the malevolent little faces peering from the shadows and the leaves. It was, he felt certain, the most persuasive story ever written. He found himself whispering the lines as he read them, the words coming faster and faster—

"I knew there was nobody here at all besides myself, and that no one could see me . . . So I said the other words, and made the signs."

—and by the time he'd finished he was half convinced he heard another voice, one softer and more ancient than his own, whispering an even stranger story in his head, a story in a language he seemed dimly to remember.

He had no idea how much time had elapsed. It might have been days. His head was still spinning from the rush of words, or maybe it was only from the effort of reading in so faint a light. A pair of flies, trapped in the darkened room, were crashing into the window screens around him; the crickets droned their song; frogs piped madly by the brook, but he no longer heard them. Still in the story's spell, he felt himself slip off the robe and walk slowly across the room, opening the door to the lawn outside and stepping into the darkness.

But it wasn't dark. It was a different night he stepped into, one almost as bright as a stage. Every rock was visible, every blade of grass; every object cast a shadow. The clouds had rolled back, the sky had opened up, and the full moon now shone forth onto the yard with all its power. Pale light seemed to pour from the sky, revealing things not meant to be seen, the secret night side of the planet. He felt the wet grass beneath his feet, and small wet things that moved, and things both hard and sharp, but he didn't pull away. He felt himself drawn like a dancer across the lawn, past the back of the farmhouse and the line of dark rosebushes standing like sentries along one side, the house itself sleeping in the moonlight, its windows dark. And still he was drawn back, toward where the bubbling stream made sucking noises at him, back toward the massive shape of the barn, the moonlight so strong now he could see his own shadow floating over the grass, floating toward the gnarled old willow that grew against the barn. And his own shadow yearned toward the shadow of the tree, and he watched it and felt himself follow, past the corner of the barn, moving inexorably toward the dark branches. And at last his shadow touched the other, merged with it, was absorbed in it; and still, not knowing what he did, he followed.

Deborah caught her breath in wonder. Beside her, two of the cats looked up and regarded her curiously, then settled back to sleep.

She too had been asleep, but she'd been awakened by the shift in the clouds and the bright moonlight which had suddenly flooded the room. There were no curtains on the windows; their people didn't hold with them, feeling it correct to get up with the sun. Unable to go back to sleep, she had been sitting up in bed and gazing absently out the window, head still spinning from the wine and the pictures of the Dynnod, when suddenly Freirs' door had swung open, down there in the yard, and now Freirs himself emerged into the light, his body pale against the lawn.

Her eyes widened. He was naked.

His expression was strangely preoccupied as he stepped onto the grass. She felt excited, watching him pad farther from the building, like a child watching something she shouldn't. She hadn't seen a naked man, aside from her husband, in—she couldn't remember how long it had been. But here were Jeremy's smooth white buttocks, his thighs, his sex . . . She caught her breath.

Where was he going at this hour? *He must be off to have himself a pee,* she thought. *But why's he heading clear across the lawn?*

At no time did he glance up toward her window (not that he could have seen her in the darkness anyway, she told herself, and he without his glasses); and he couldn't have known, as late as this, that anyone was watching. She wasn't sure of the time—the only clock was downstairs, the big grandfather clock Sarr had inherited; she could hear its regular ticking—but she thought it must be close to midnight.

He was walking slowly, like a sleepwalker. Maybe he *was* sleepwalking, she thought; Jeremy wouldn't walk barefoot like that, he was far too squeamish about bugs! worms! night crawlers! Yet there he was, across the lawn and disappearing in the shadow of the barn.

Perhaps she should stop him. If he was sleepwalking, could there be any danger? She dismissed the thought as soon as it occurred. Why embarrass him? If he wandered off into the long grass or the forest—

well, he wouldn't be hurt, the Lord watched over sleepers; and if he found himself on rough ground, why, he'd simply wake up. She thought of calling to him through the open window, but she was already too excited. She could feel herself breathe faster now and was suddenly aware of her hand beneath her unbuttoned nightgown, cradling and squeezing her breast.

With a little sigh she lay back, deliberately jarring the bed, hoping to awaken Sarr, his face pressed to the crumpled pillow. He stirred, clutched the pillow tighter, and slept on.

She shifted closer to him, so close that she could feel the warmth of his body. He, too, wore the traditional nightgown, but as her hand explored beneath the sheet, she could feel that it had worked its way above his waist. Her fingers caressed the familiar contours of his hips and slid into the soft, girlish hair. Gently yet urgently they closed over his penis.

He groaned softly, still asleep, and turned toward her, eyes closed. She tugged more insistently, and in reflex he twisted his hips to be nearer her, snaking his arm along her body, at last finding her breast. Carefully keeping her breath slow and silent, she rolled herself on top of him.

In the smaller room, Carol slept on, outlined in the moonlight, her arm thrown over her eyes. Her regular breathing grew faster; suddenly her hand clutched the edge of the sheet, her other hand formed a fist, and a tremble shook her body like a fever. Her leg straightened, then pulled back; her form seemed to grow heavier, pushing into the mattress, as if she were retreating, in her dream, from some unwanted approach. Soundlessly her mouth formed words. Above her, in the pale light, the cardboard nursery shapes stared indifferently down.

He felt the rough bark against the soles of his bare feet and sensed dimly that he was climbing the gnarled old black willow that grew beside the barn. The branches bent beneath his weight but did not snap. He felt himself climb upward, unerringly as a squirrel, as if he had done it many times before and knew exactly where to place his hands and feet.

Attaining the upper branches, he made his way out onto one of the thicker limbs, let go with both hands, and, precariously balanced, stepped lightly onto the barn roof just before the limb began to give way, the old wooden shingles curling wet beneath his toes. He continued climbing, bathed in moonlight now, the moon's face just above him, whispering him on.

At the apex of the roof he unbent and slowly stood upright, one leg

on each sloping side, one foot planted east and one foot west, straddling the center line. The moon, gazing down at him, was close enough
to touch. He raised his hands to it.

Deborah eased the sleeping Sarr onto his back, rose on her knees, and
straddled him. Reaching down, she grasped him and put him inside
her. He slid in easily.

Hands raised as if in supplication, Freirs felt himself make over-
tures to the moon, gestures and faces that no one could see, no one
would ever see, no one had ever seen before. Perhaps some ancient force
was in control, but there was no thought of explaining what he did, or
why. Past and future did not exist. There was nothing real but his own
movements. The shingles, he sensed idly, were rough against his feet.
The ground seemed far away, but he had no fear of falling. From this
height the land below him, the distant farmhouse with its little black
windows like eyes, its outbuildings and its garden, seemed almost lu-
minescent in the moonlight, with the trees a dark ocean around it.

Sarr awakened and looked sleepily up at Deborah, her face pale
above him, eyes half shut. He reached out and caressed it, then slipped
the nightgown up and off her shoulders so that her breasts hung down
heavy and full above him. Briefly he tasted a dark nipple. Slowly, then
faster, lifting and lowering her body, she began to pump.

Freirs tried to touch the full moon's face, and shaped his lips toward
it, and heard someone whisper to it, words he'd never heard before and
didn't know the meaning of and instantly forgot. Beneath his feet the
fireflies were like shooting stars, and a silver mist was rising off the
field. He smelled roses; he could taste them on his tongue. Listening to
the chanting in his ear, he waved his arms and made the faces and did
the gestures with his fingers, looking like a madman's shadow as he
signaled to the moon and to the dark woods spread below.

The moment came. He wriggled his head, arched his neck, threw his
chest out in the night air. Sarr kissed the breasts before his face and
arched his body into Deborah, who leaned forward to widen herself
just as Freirs threw his arms wide and Sarr pushed himself all the way
in so that Deborah gasped and they trembled, all three, and Deborah
made a moaning sound just as Carol cried out in her sleep and Freirs
heard the whispering and chanting louder now inside his head and
realized that the sounds he'd heard were coming from himself.

Abruptly he stopped singing. The trance left him; the dream fled.
He was standing on the barn roof, weary and gasping and suddenly
exhausted, as if he'd just finished a race, dance, and a struggle, all in
one. He looked down, lost his balance, almost fell. He was astonished at
where he was standing, and at his own nakedness. Carol, for the first
time that day, had been out of his thoughts, yet there on the rooftop,
with the planet at his feet and the taste of roses in his mouth, he looked
down at himself and saw he was erect.

*

The dream. Those mad, twisted trees, and the eyes.

Carol was still shuddering from it, trying to throw it off, as she lay breathing heavily in the tiny bed, the damp sheets clutched to her throat. Moonlight seemed to filter into the room like poison, seeping into her brain, making everything she looked upon seem strange and menacing: the shiny little cardboard figures with their evil, knowing smiles, the gaping black fireplace, the pale red witch ball hanging in the window like the child of the moon.

The moon—its very brilliance was disturbing. She remembered the story she'd read long ago, about the sailor who fell asleep on deck, lying on his back with the full moon shining brightly on his face, and how, rising from a dream in which an old woman clawed him by the cheek, he awoke to find that his face had been permanently drawn to one side . . .

She was suddenly aware that something had changed. Something was missing. Without realizing it she had been breathing in time to the old grandfather clock downstairs, whose loud ticktocking could be heard throughout the house, through the spaces in the floorboards, the thin walls and doors. And suddenly the clock had gone silent.

Ah, there it was again, with a pair of faster beats thrown in as if to make up for the missing ones. No doubt a broken spring. Well, everything had to run down eventually, after years and years . . .

She drifted back to sleep, her face smoothing, her breathing growing slower, the dream dissipating like smoke from an altar.

The spell was broken. The magic didn't work anymore. He almost slipped three times as he crept down the side of the slippery roof, ass in the air, fearfully clutching at the shingles. When he groped for a branch of the willow, it broke off in his hand.

Somehow he was able to grasp a limb and hoist himself back to the tree, and at last, with much difficulty and a badly skinned elbow, he climbed down to the ground. He realized he was trembling from exhaustion.

Jesus, he thought, *what the hell was in that wine?*

Slipping timidly around the side of the barn, he covered his nakedness, an Adam after the Fall, and dashed across the wet grass to his doorway. He winced with every step, feeling dozens of wriggling living things, some imaginary, some less so, beneath his bare feet. He prayed no one was looking.

When he was back inside he stood shivering by his bed. *A great way to catch a cold!* he told himself; these nights out here were damp, and his feet felt clammy. His skin, he noticed, was covered with mosquito bites; he itched all over as he slipped his robe back on. His eye fell on his wristwatch on the stand beside the bed. Just past midnight.

He shook his head and sat down on the bed. *Of all the schoolboy stunts!* he thought, wiping his feet off and scratching at his ankle. *Whatever possessed me to—*

He paused. Something odd had just occurred.

While he'd been sitting there, trying to reorient himself, he'd been half-consciously aware of the crickets in the yard outside. The regular cadence of their chirping had been soothing, like the sound of a well-oiled machine. It had been making him drowsy, in fact, lulling him to sleep.

But for a moment just now the crickets had seemed to miss a beat. They'd been singing steadily, ever since he'd left the farmhouse, yet all of a sudden they'd simply *stopped,* a break in the natural flow—and then moments later they'd begun again, only out of rhythm for a beat or two, as if an unseen hand had jarred the record.

Well, they were back on the beat now. It was nothing to worry about, probably something to do with a temperature change.

He turned back to preparations for bed: locked the door, put the Machen on the table, closed his journal for the night.

It was only when he'd opened the top drawer of the bureau to put the journal away that he saw the brightly colored greeting cards he'd shoved to the back and realized, with a sudden burst of sadness, that it had happened without his remembering it; the moment he'd dreaded had come and gone. It was his birthday.

And in her stone cottage on the hill above the stream, seated at her bedroom window with the moon swimming full above the hedges by the roadside and the Pictures scattered at her feet, Mrs. Poroth, hearing the crickets break rhythm, looked down from the moon to the image of the yellow book, and from that to the one that lay beside it—a shapeless black scribble with a hint of stubby legs—and realized, at last. whv the woman had come out today.

BOOK FOUR

THE DREAM

Think ye that the lot of them—the Worm, the Virgin, and the rest—are but Symbols of Corruption and Purity? Then think ye again . . .
—Nicholas Keize, *Beneath the Moss*

JULY THIRD

Carol opened her eyes, shut them tighter against the brightness streaming through the unshaded window, then opened them again and stretched languorously. She had not slept well; bad dreams—or, rather, one bad dream—had troubled her throughout the night. Now she was glad to be awake. Yesterday the room had had a musty smell, but this morning it was filled with sunlight and the scent of things in bloom. From outside the window came the raucous cries of birds; aside from that the world was silent, no sound of breakfast dishes or of singing in the kitchen.

Dressing in jeans and a clean shirt and running a hand through her hair, she peered out the window. No one was about; the farm seemed deserted. Then she remembered: it was Sunday. The Poroths would be at services, at one of the Brethren's houses, and would probably be away till past noon.

Going downstairs, her footsteps on the wooden treads breaking the morning stillness, she saw, by the clock in the living room, that it was not yet eight. But perhaps the clock was wrong; she suddenly remembered that late last night she had heard it wind down. Or had that too been part of the dream?

Her eye fell on a portable radio standing by one of the kitchen shelves. Hoping it might give her the correct time, she switched it on. The sound of singing filled the room: a hymn, like the ones Sarr and Deborah had been singing last night, only here there were dozens of ecstatic voices backed by an organ. She stood listening to it a moment, then snapped it off. They reminded her, those voices, that she herself should be in church this morning. Well, she would make sure to drop in and say a prayer this afternoon, just as soon as she got back to the city. God would understand.

The silence in the kitchen was oddly oppressive, but outside the cries of the birds held a note of invitation. She pushed through the screen door and out onto the back porch. The sunlight was intense, and the land in back, stretching down toward the distant stream, looked beautiful, but there was a smell of dampness in the air. Two of the younger cats—an orange one and a tortoise-shell, she didn't know their names—lay washing themselves in a small patch of sunlight, but when she started down the back steps they both rose and trotted after her.

The grass was wet around her ankles as she strolled toward Freirs' outbuilding. She walked to the front and peered through the screen, a little nervous. Yes, there he was, a pale shape lying twisted in sleep on the bed. The shape stirred, and she saw, with embarrassment, that he was naked. Hastily she stepped back and began moving away, hoping he hadn't awakened and seen her.

She continued down to the stream. Schools of tiny silver fish darted back and forth in the shadows of the rocks. It looked so inviting that she could almost imagine herself going for a swim; she reminded herself that, after all, she hadn't bathed this morning. She would leave her clothing there on the rock and step gingerly into the water. It would be chilly, of course, as it climbed her legs. And perhaps while she was naked and so occupied, Jeremy would awaken and, walking silently down behind her, would surprise her, there in the warm sunlight. He would reach for her hand—

This was no way to behave on Sunday morning! *Besides*, she thought, *the water's only a foot or two deep, and the bottom must be covered with sharp stones.*

With a sigh she sat herself on the rock and gazed at the pine trees across the stream, trying to pretend the place felt holy. Jeremy could get up when he pleased.

Woke up later than I'd wanted to, feeling stiff & hung over. Carol & I went for a ride in Rosie's car, me at the wheel. Told her, as we drove, about its being my birthday; she was properly solicitous, I was gloomy. Telephoned Mom & Dad from a shopping center outside Flemington; they seemed worried about my allergy ("you mean they have *seven* cats?") & whether the seclusion's good for me.

After lunch in Flemington, Carol insisted on buying me a small birthday cake to take back with us. Spent the afternoon driving through the countryside, past endless miles of farmland, shopping malls, new suburban tracts. This area is changing fast.

Had a somewhat unpleasant encounter in town . .

Gilead wore a soberly festive air as they drove up to the crossroads. A dozen cars, most of them black and all of them at least a decade old, were parked along the main street, and there were dark-clothed figures talking in small groups on the open land that adjoined the general store. Several turned with undisguised curiosity as the car approached, but their faces seemed friendly enough.

"Let's stop," said Freirs, pulling up beside the store. "I want to buy more bug spray."

The front door was open now, barrels of goods crowding the porch.

"This place is a co-operative, you know," Freirs whispered as they walked inside past boxes of cutlery and rolling pins. "All the Brethren own it and all share in the profits. Karl Marx would have been pleased." After so much time on the road, it took Carol a few moments for her eyes to adjust to the store's dim light. She looked for the woman she'd talked to yesterday, but there seemed to be no one behind the counter. Three men were standing near the back, by a passage that led to the grain warehouse. All of them had beards that curved from ear to ear; all were gaunt and solemn-looking, with faces that looked as if they'd been carved out of the same unyielding wood. They had been talking about someone with a drinking problem—"a scandal to the community," one of them was saying, "and I hear tell his boy Orin's a-takin' after him"—but they fell silent when Freirs and Carol entered. The man in the middle turned toward them.

"And what might you be wantin'?" he said. There was a wariness in his voice, but Freirs appeared not to notice.

"I need a can of insect spray," he said. "Something good and powerful."

The other stared at him a moment, as if he'd recognized Freirs and was trying to recall where. Suddenly he nodded. "Ah, yes, well, you *would* be havin' some trouble with the bugs, now, wouldn't you? I mean, 'tis that time o' year." Carol saw him dart a quick glance to the others. "Now let me see what I can rustle up for you."

He led Freirs over to an aisle along the wall, and the two of them disappeared behind a pegboard; Carol heard them talking and the clink of cans. She was left facing the other two and feeling awkward. Awkward for them too, apparently—they stared silently at the floor, not even acknowledging her presence.

Suddenly she heard feet tramping up the wooden porch behind her. In the doorway a heavy-set figure stood silhouetted against the light. "Steegler, if you tell me you've no more sandpaper," he called out, "I swear I shall—" He caught himself. "Ah, Adam! Werner!" He came forward, a dark bear of a man, nodding to the other two. He turned to Carol, and his eyes narrowed with interest. "And who might this be?"

"I'm just visiting," she said timidly. "With him." She made a vague gesture toward the other aisle.

"Be right with you, Brother Rupert!" came the voice of the storekeeper. He rejoined the group, followed by Freirs, who was carrying a hefty-looking metal canister.

The larger man ignored him. "Ah, yes," he said, as soon as he saw Freirs. He looked from him to Carol and back again. "You'd be the one from the city, yes? The one who's stayin' with Sarr Poroth?"

"That's right," said Freirs, his voice level. "I'm the one. And you are—?"

"Rupert Lindt." He stuck out a beefy hand which swallowed Freirs' up whole; but if his grip was painful, Freirs made no sign. "And this here's Adam Verdock and Werner Geisel."

Freirs shook both their hands as well. "I've been drinking your milk all week," he said to Verdock. He turned to the third: "And judging from your name, you must be related to our neighbor."

"I guess you're right," said the other. He was the oldest in the room, his head nearly bald, his beard shot with grey. "You know my brother Matthew, do you?"

"Sure," said Freirs. "He lives just down the road from us. In fact, you might say—"

"And then again you might not," said Lindt. "Fact is, those Poroths are off on a road by themselves—like they are in a few other ways, as well. Matt Geisel is on the other branch, the one that doesn't run so far from town. 'Tis a good—oh, what would you say, Werner, a mile or two closer?"

The other nodded uneasily.

"Lord knows why they bought it," Lindt continued. "Old man Baber hooked himself a proper one when he sold that place to Poroth. 'Tis a ways too far from the rest of us, if you ask me."

"And a ways too close to the Neck," added the storekeeper, ringing up the purchase on the cash register.

Freirs looked startled. "What neck?"

"McKinney's Neck," said Geisel. "You don't want to go pokin' your nose around there. The ground's treacherous this time o' year, and you're liable to get yourself drowned."

Lindt seemed to find this funny. "Heck, nobody's gonna drown in a little bitty patch of mud, leastways nobody whose mama taught him to walk right." He cast a cold eye on Freirs, then a warmer one on Carol. She felt her heart beat faster. "You goin' for walks in the woods with this fellow?" he demanded, nodding toward Freirs. "Or you come out here to give that Deborah woman a bit of competition?"

"Now come on, Rupert!" It was Adam Verdock who spoke. He was the tallest and thinnest of the men, the one with the gravest expression. He'd been the one speaking when the two of them had entered the store. "Brother Rupert's only jesting with you," he explained. "I was talkin' to Sarr and his woman only this morning, just after worship—he's my nephew; as you young folks may know, I married his pa's sister—and he says everything's goin' just fine, you're the best guests a man could want. Says he'd like to put up a whole string of guest houses, if he could."

Lindt snorted derisively. "Sure, and maybe get himself outa debt!"

Freirs took the spray can—Carol was afraid, for a moment, that he was going to aim it at the larger man's face—and slipped his hand protectively in hers. "Come on," he said, "let's go."

She held back a moment; she had a sudden vision of herself and

Jeremy up to their necks in quicksand. "Tell me," she said nervously, turning to Geisel, "just in case we do decide to take a walk in the woods, should we avoid that McKinney section you mentioned?"

"Well, like I say," the old man answered, "it's a little treacherous out there in the Neck, especially for a stranger. And there are some"— he cast a sidelong glance at Steegler—"who say the place is haunted."

The storekeeper stepped from behind the counter. "Now, now, Werner," he said testily, "I don't claim that. But you know perfectly well the place has a mighty peculiar history."

"What's this about haunted?" asked Freirs. Carol could almost see his ears perk up; this was probably just the sort of thing he'd come out here for.

It was Lindt who answered, looking somewhat amused. "I believe they found a girl hanged out there, back before the war." He nodded to Carol. "A nice young girl, she was, pretty much like yourself. Ain't that right, Werner?"

The older man nodded. "'Twas in the thirties, I recollect."

"Suicide?" asked Freirs.

"Not likely. There was talk of other things that had been done—"

"Beggin' your pardon, all of you," said Verdock, looking pained, "but I don't think this is a fit subject for a Sunday."

"You're right," said Freirs hastily, to a chorus of nods and *amens*. "Anyway, we've got to go. Sarr and Deborah have a nice dinner ready for us . . . debt and all." He glanced quickly at Lindt. "Mr. Verdock, Mr. Geisel—a real pleasure." As he took Carol's hand and began walking out, he called over his shoulder, "And Rupert, next time you're in New York, be sure to look me up."

She was glad when they were back outside on the street.

They didn't go right back to the farm, though. Freirs was now excited. He dragged her across the street toward the line of massive oaks and, beyond them, the schoolhouse.

"Come along," he said, "I've got a sudden yen for local history. Let's look up that murder."

"But where are we going?" asked Carol as she followed him across the dusty brown playing field.

He nodded toward the red-brick walls of the school. "The town library. It's supposed to be here in this building."

Carol laughed. "This is turning into a busman's holiday!"

"Oh, don't expect this place to be like Voorhis. Sarr says it's hardly more than a school library—and Bible school, at that. He warned me about the place, in fact. He told me, 'You'll not find the shelves filled with pornography, the way they are in New York.'" Freirs shook his head. "Good old Sarr! He really thinks we're next door to Gomorrah."

The library proved to be on the first floor of the building, and, true to the Brethren's work ethic, was open even on a Sunday. Poroth, they soon discovered, had not been exaggerating about its contents. As the two of them surveyed the narrow room with its meagerly stocked shelves, they saw nothing that would have corrupted the most innocent schoolchild. There were cookbooks, books on farming, and books of household hints, but the bulk of the works were religious, and most of them appeared to have been written in the days when people still drove Model T's to church. An entire shelf was devoted to refutations of Darwin; another bulged with temperance literature, most of it written before the start of Prohibition.

"Sarr was right," said Carol. "There's certainly nothing here to make the blood race."

"Yeah," said Freirs. "Too bad!"

Carol looked in vain for a librarian. There appeared to be no one around, nor even a desk or a counter where one would have worked. Voorhis seemed very far away. The only other person in the room was a short, portly woman who was fanning herself vigorously as she peered through a section of inspirational novels.

"I've read every one of 'em once or twice before," she confided, after they'd walked over to introduce themselves, "but I like 'em even better when I know how the story comes out." She explained that, in fact, there was no librarian on duty—"leastways not summers, when the school's closed down. Folks just come in, take what they please, and bring the books back when they can."

"No kidding," said Freirs. "What's to stop somebody from just walking in and stealing all the books?"

The woman seemed surprised. "The sort of folks who come in here ain't the sort who steal," she said, regarding him with suspicion. "And the sort who steal ain't the sort who come in here."

Freirs, having sized up the woman as a regular, explained what he was looking for. She led him and Carol to an alcove near the back where floor-to-ceiling shelves sagged beneath the weight of thin brown books the size of atlases, piled flat. They were bound volumes of the *Hunterdon County Home News.*

"Perfect," said Freirs.

"Back before the war," Rupert Lindt had told them. The two scanned the shelves for the volumes from the thirties, and found them in a pile near the floor. From the way the books stuck together from the heat when Freirs pulled out the one marked *1937,* Carol guessed they were rarely consulted.

He flipped through the volume. The newspapers were yellow with age and smelled like a damp cellar. Over the years many of the bindings had loosened. Most were missing corners; here and there whole sheets were torn in half. The *Home News* had, in those days, been a weekly, with few issues more than eight pages long, but it was obviously the only source of local news; Gilead had never had a paper of its own.

Carol watched as Freirs turned the pages. What struck her immediately about the stories she saw was their violence; rather than the sedate era she'd imagined, the newspapers conjured up an age of lawlessness, freak accidents, and sudden death. A local dentist, speeding from Flemington to Sergeantsville, had injured his best friend in an auto crash and had promptly committed suicide: ARRESTED AS DRUNKEN DRIVER, said the headline, HE GOES TO OFFICE AND INHALES LAUGHING GAS. A man in Pennsylvania had been shot down by a fellow hunter in an argument over a deer. A Baptistown man had been stung to death by bees.

Other news was more frivolous and bespoke a happier time. A convention of dance teachers in Atlantic City had proclaimed the end of jitterbug ("People are tired of the jumping dances such as the Shag, Big Apple, and other athletic steps," explained one), and railroads still ran everywhere: a special train had been initiated, running from Flemington to the New York World's Fair, whose admission price had just been raised to fifty cents. A New Haven Railroad ad suggested SLEEP ON THE TRAIN—WAKE UP REFRESHED IN MAINE. Clearly some conveniences had vanished since then.

It took them nearly half an hour to work through the 1937 volume and the subsequent one before they came upon the article Freirs sought, in the issue of August 3, 1939. It had been an otherwise happy summer week, the populace keeping busy with a round of local fairs, auctions, and church socials. The weekend's weather had been hot; temperatures had run to 96 degrees during the day, 81 at night. The moon had been full. Amid the welter of other news the report of the murder near Gilead—"SLAIN GIRL'S BODY FOUND IN WOODS"—would have gone virtually unnoticed if the two of them hadn't been looking for it.

The article was a brief one; no doubt many of the details had been suppressed. The girl, one Annelise Heidler, twenty, had been reported missing on the evening of July 31 by her father, a prominent Flemington attorney. Two days later a party of deer hunters had discovered her corpse suspended from a tree in the woods outside Gilead. It had been partially burned and bore markings "of an obscene nature" made with black grease. "Although police refused to speculate," the article added, "elderly residents of the town have opined that the perpetrator or perpetrators may have been imitating a similar crime committed on July 31, 1890, in the same location."

Freirs' eyes widened. "Jesus," he said, turning to Carol, "it seems the murder had a precedent."

"Somehow that makes it even more horrible."

He nodded, not really listening. "Let's see what the paper said." Replacing the volume, he searched for the one marked *1890.*

"There it is," said Carol. She pointed to an upper shelf. Freirs had to reach for the book on tiptoe and tug to pull it out.

It was well that, this time, they knew the exact date of the article they sought, because finding it in this early volume would have been difficult. The *Home News* had changed greatly in the intervening half century, and the version they were looking at now contained far fewer photographs; the typeface was smaller, the front page more cluttered, and the headlines, true to the practice of the day, maintained an almost enigmatic reserve: A FATAL ARGUMENT, THE CLOSING OF A BREWERY, UNFORTUNATE ACCIDENT IN HIGH BRIDGE.

Freirs leafed quickly through the book, watching the county's history pass in review. Mills had been erected; people had made fortunes in the railroad; a Baptistown farmer had set a state record with a squash that weighed 118 pounds.

He came across the article he wanted in the first issue of August. The county then had been suffering an unusually hot summer. The week's average temperature, the paper said, was 98 degrees in the shade. Ads recommended Hood's Sarsaparilla as "an excellent remedy for summer weakness during the oppressive, muggy weather of the dog days." A West Portal boy had gone blind from picking strawberries in the hot sun; eleven celebrants at the Hunterdon County Harvest Festival— "the biggest gala in the history of the county"—had had to be treated for heat prostration.

The article in question was a relatively brief one, crowded out by optimistic pieces on the fair. TRAGEDY REVEALED, it said.

Gilead, August 2.— Authorities here report the death of Lucina Reid, 16, daughter of Jared Reid of this town. She had been missing since the evening of July 31. Her body was discovered by searchers in the section of outlying woods popularly known as McKinney's Neck, the full moon aiding them in their task. Positive identification of the body was difficult, abominations having been practiced upon it, though further reports indicate that death was due to strangulation. Authorities are searching—

She heard Freirs catch his breath. For some reason, she didn't know why, she felt her own heart pound a little harder as she read the passage again.

Authorities are searching for Absolom Troet, 22, of the same town, believed to be the last to see Miss Reid alive.

*

For Freirs, it was like seeing a familiar face in the middle of a night-mare: it made the nightmare worse. *So here the trail ends,* he thought. The evil led back to Absolom Troet, the boy with the devil in him. Freirs recalled the blank space on the tombstone and, even in the heat of the library, felt a shudder.

"This is the guy who set fire to the farmhouse that used to be on the Poroths' land," he said to Carol, knowing there was too much to ex-plain. "He was some kind of distant ancestor of Sarr's, and when he was a little kid he killed his whole family, burned 'em in their sleep. And now it seems he must have gone right on murdering."

"God!" said Carol, shaking her head. "I thought things like that only happened today."

There was nothing about the crime in the following week's paper, but two weeks later a brief notice appeared to the effect that Absolom Troet, "wanted in connection with the killing of a Gilead girl," was still missing. "Authorities have been unable to locate him," the notice said. "It is believed he has taken his own life." There was no further mention of the crime.

"Well," Freirs said, "there's just one more item to search for." Shov-ing the book back onto the shelf, he withdrew one still earlier, marked *1877.*

It was a curious sensation, looking through these volumes in reverse. Time was running backward, and Hunterdon County grew younger. New Jersey, he saw, had been a rather wild place in '77; he read of cat-tle rustling, stable fires, and hunting accidents. A Milford boy had died in February from the attack of a "mad bull," another from the bite of a snake. In Flemington in March one Deto Turo, described as "an Italian bootblack," had stabbed three men in a bar. In June a Moses Rehmeyer, four years old, had fallen down a cistern and drowned, and a man had been sentenced to twelve years' imprisonment for horse stealing. One of the lead stories in July, DIED FROM DRINK-ING TOO MUCH MILK, told of a cook "employed on Gen. Schwenck's large dairy farm" who'd drunk herself to death after having become, in the words of the article, "very fond of fresh milk." He wondered what the temperance crowd had made of that.

There were dozens of reports of fires—civilization in those days seemed to have been one colossal tinderbox—but it wasn't until he saw the notice TRAGIC FIRE IN GILEAD, near the end of the volume, that he knew he'd found what he'd been searching for.

"Here it is," he said.

The report was a brief one, buried near the bottom of the page.

Gilead, Nov. 1.— The farm of Isaiah Troet, 38, was the scene of a terrible tragedy last night when sparks from a wood stove ap-parently ignited combustible material in the kitchen. Eight of the family are believed to have perished in the conflagration that destroyed their home. Among the dead were Troet, his wife Hanna, and six children, all of whom were apparently asleep when the fire broke out. The volunteer fire brigade arrived too late to save the unfortunate family. Authorities from Annandale and Lebanon picked through the charred remains this morning and attributed the fire to "an act of God." The only survivor, nine-year-old Absolom Troet, had been outside at the time of the blaze, attending to a sick calf in the barn. Authorities say the boy will live with relatives.

"Can't we go now, Jeremy?" whispered Carol. "This tiny print's beginning to give me a headache. Or maybe it's just thinking about all those poor people."

"Sure," said Freirs. "Sorry for taking so long." He slipped the book back on the shelf and wiped the dust of the old paper from his hands.

He thought about Absolom Troet all the way back to the farm. And he kept wiping his hands.

Sarr and Deborah were in the house when we got back. They were all fired up & full of the Holy Spirit; even when I was out here in this room, I could hear them clattering through the kitchen, humming little snatches of hymns. I suppose that when you don't have any Broadway shows around, or movies or TV, you take whatever entertainment you can get.

They both told me over & over how "exalted" they felt, but as far as I'm concerned they might just as well have said "exhausted," since they'd apparently spent the last four hours praying on their knees, rising to sing, kneeling, standing again . . . Good preparation for planting seeds, maybe, but not the sort of religion *I'd* choose.

They were both very nice about my birthday, though—why hadn't I told them, Deborah would have baked me something special, etc. etc. She actually kissed me on the side of the mouth. (Could feel her breast brush against my arm. I don't think she wears *anything* beneath that dress.) Sarr put down the wicked-looking scythe blade he was honing & contented himself with an earnest shake of my hand.

Wish I knew how Carol felt about him. Of course, nothing could have gone on between them last night (notwithstanding a few fantasies I had when I came out here), but I still sense a certain interest there, at least on Carol's part. As for Sarr, I'm now convinced he has his mind on God and eyes for no one but his wife. But who can say? Who can say what's in another person's head?

I twisted Carol's arm a bit, & she agreed to stay for dinner, despite lots of moaning & groaning about the drive back to New York. It was a nice meal, one that Carol, this time, could eat: cheese omelet, garden salad, & that cake of Carol's for dessert. She & I finished off the Geisels' wine from last night; both Poroths declined. I guess one night of transgression is enough for the weekend.

Deborah, as usual, spent the meal laughing & carrying on & generally having a good time—she obviously craves company—but Sarr tended to withdraw a bit as the evening wore on. He sat there like one of his own cats, getting all silent & brooding & inscrutable. Maybe it's because I made the mistake of asking him about those murders . . .

"God's my witness, Jeremy," he said, "you know more about those things than I do. I'm just plain not interested. I wasn't around in 1939, and I certainly wasn't around in 1890. I've heard my mother had some sort of premonition about the one in '39, but I'm not really sure. She was a young girl then. I told you about the gift they say she has."

Freirs nodded. "Obviously in this case the gift didn't help."

"I guess not," said Poroth. He sounded somewhat downcast. "My mother seldom speaks of it. I expect it's troubling to her."

"What intrigues me most," said Freirs, "are the legends these things give rise to. I gather people claim they've seen ghosts in the woods where the murders occurred."

Poroth shrugged. "Some claim that. Personally, I don't hold with such tales. I believe they're probably in error. Still, there could be something to it. It's not for us to say."

Freirs decided that he liked the idea of having a haunted place so nearby. It was just the sort of thing he could take back to his classes, evidence of modern superstition.

Carol was gazing at Poroth sympathetically. "You don't believe in ghosts yourself, then?"

"On the contrary," he said. "I know full well that they exist, as sure as there are eggs and fireflies and angels. I just don't think they stay out there in the woods."

Freirs decided that he hoped they did.

Carol wanted to leave before eight, to give herself plenty of daylight to navigate the dirt road & the way back to Gilead, but the Poroths' clock has gone off & I'd left my watch inside here, so she probably didn't start till close to nine, when it had already begun to get dark. Hope she makes it okay; she was really nervous about the goddamned driving.

Was sorry to see her go. Never really got as close to her as I'd wanted to, & don't know when she'll have another chance to come out here.

There's a kind of genuineness in her I don't find in most New York girls; she makes me feel like a teenager again, which isn't really as bad as it sounds, esp. for an old man of thirty.

"Oh, come off it," says another voice. "You jusy want to get laid."

Could be. (Sigh.) Maybe I'll try to see her in the city next time, in my own environment, rather than out here on someone else's turf.

Came out here after she left & tried to do some work. Started on *Melmoth the Wanderer* by the Rev. Charles Robert Maturin. Powerful stuff, but after the Lewis book I'm getting a little sick of all the Catholic-baiting. No doubt it's great fun for the connoisseur of atrocity scenes—still more mothers clutching the wormy corpses of their infants (a Gothic staple, I suspect), starving prisoners forced to eat their girlfriends (that's a new one on me)—but the Inquisition's over now, the villains dead & gone, & all a book like this can do is put you in a rage. Fine for getting me through tomorrow morning's pushups, no doubt—a drop of adrenaline works wonders—but otherwise quite useless.

Hmmm, never thought I'd find myself sticking up for the Papists. Must be Carol's influence.

Afterward, wished I'd taken some notes on that story "The White People," which Carol took back with her. Already seem to have forgotten most of it, and what I do remember seems oddly confusing & repetitive. I did locate, in one anthology, another Machen piece, about a London clerk named Darnell who has mystical visions of an ancient town & woods & hills.

> Our stupid ancestors taught us that we could become wise by studying books on "science," by meddling with test-tubes, geological specimens, microscopic preparations, and the like; but they who have cast off these follies know that the soul is made wise by the contemplation of mystic ceremonies and elaborate and curious rites. In such things Darnell found a wonderful mystery language, which spoke at once more secretly and more directly than the formal creeds; and he saw that, in a sense, the whole world is but a great ceremony.

The writing was beautiful, with a real magic to it—yet somehow my mind began wandering. When I was halfway through I looked down & saw something squatting sticklike on my pillow, just beneath my nose, something like a cross between a cricket & a spider & a frog, & as I watched the thing began to chatter; it pranced & chirped & shrieked at me & shook its tiny fist, & then I woke up. The story was still where I'd left it, & a huge white moth, horned like the devil, was tapping at my window

Must be midnight now, & the coldest night so far. Strange, really: it was hot all day, but with evening comes a chill. The dampness of this place must magnify the temperature. Carol complained that it gave her bad dreams last night, but she wouldn't talk about them.

Yes, past midnight; I just checked. Thirty years behind me now, another birthday gone. Where do the damned things go?

JULY FOURTH

You'd never have known it was a holiday. The morning hung damp and overcast when Freirs staggered from his bed and began his morning ritual of exercises. He had skipped them yesterday, and somehow they didn't come easy; instead of doing one more pushup than the time before, he could barely do one less.

He spent most of the morning on *Melmoth,* but by noon he'd had his fill of corpses and his head was spinning from the novel's convoluted plot, stories within stories within stories—perfect for class assignments, he decided, but exhausting en masse. He was glad to put it aside and break for lunch. Deborah was working in the garden, accompanied by several of the younger cats, but she'd left a meal for him; he sat eating egg salad, gingerbread, and a tall glass of milk while leafing through the seed ads in the *Home News.*

When he left the kitchen, he saw that the sky had cleared and that a strong sun was beating down, drying the morning's dampness. The temperature had climbed. Absently he searched his room for a distraction. The vase of roses caught his eye, the dark red blossoms vivid as a flame against the pale green of his walls.

Blossoms . . . It seemed as good an idea as any. Putting on his sneakers, he picked up his *Field Guide to the Wildflowers* and went for a walk.

He decided, as he turned his steps down the slope of the back yard, to follow the little brook and see where it led; he recalled that, after the water wound north through the abandoned field, it seemed to disappear into the woods, making it a good point for exploration. At the water's edge he saw dozens of little silver fish, several dead ones floating upside down or washed up in the mud. As for the frogs he heard each night, he still could not find one. No doubt they slept all day—a habit he hoped he'd never fall into himself.

At the brook's first bend he heard the sound of thrashing. There in the distance stood Poroth, tall against the sun, head thrust forward, jaw set, swinging a scythe as he cleared the field of scrub. He reminded Freirs of some extra from an Eisenstein film. Or maybe the Grim Reaper, Freirs decided.

He looked up as Freirs approached. "Hello there," he said. "And where might you be off to?"

"Just going for a walk."

Poroth grinned. "You sure you don't want to try your hand at this?" He held the scythe out in either invitation or challenge.

Freirs sighed. "Oh, why not?" he said. "Might as well see what I've been missing." Making his way through the tall grass, he took the tool from Poroth's hands.

"You hold it like this," said Poroth, twisting the blade around so that it was poised to cut, "and you swing it like"—he demonstrated with his hands—"this."

Feeling as if he were gripping a bicycle, Freirs aimed for a clump of weeds and swung. The long curved blade, gleaming in the sunlight, swished harmlessly past them and almost caught him in the leg.

"You're trying too hard," said Poroth, concealing whatever amusement he may have felt. "Don't twist your body so."

Freirs tried again; the tool still felt awkward in his grasp, but the blade caught the bottom of the weeds and whipped right through.

"You keep this thing pretty sharp," said Freirs, staring at the blade with new respect.

Poroth reached into his back pocket and drew forth a thin grey rectangle of stone. "Sharp as a razor," he said. "I whet the edge a dozen times a day. But mind you keep the blade up there, or you're going to strike against a rock, and 'twill be of no blessed use to me then. I've yet to clear this part of the field."

Freirs brought the blade higher, but it was a more difficult position to maintain, putting more strain upon his shoulders. By the time he took a few more swipes, his shoulders ached.

"God!" he said, his pleasure draining away, "they ought to make this thing smaller, with a lighter blade. I don't like the way this one's designed. You can't swing it without whirling yourself around."

Poroth smiled. "My friend, they've been using that design for a thousand years or more—without a change. What you want's a sickle. It's a smaller tool, for a single hand to use. I've got one back at the house."

"Fine," said Freirs, rather dubious. "That can be my next lesson." He handed the scythe back to Poroth. "Now I've had enough of playing farmer for the day. I think I'll play explorer." He waved and began moving off.

Poroth watched him go. "Mind you watch out for copperheads. They say the woods are thick with 'em this year. Brother Matt says he saw a pair last week, around three miles downstream. Don't go sticking your foot in any holes or clumps of brush, and don't go turning over rocks."

Freirs stopped walking and looked suspiciously at the ground. "What happens if I get bitten?"

Poroth shrugged and brought the scythe back up into position. "You won't die," he said. "But you won't like it." He began swinging the blade in a determined rhythm.

Freirs headed downstream, with considerably less enthusiasm. He was aware that Poroth took pleasure in doomsaying, perhaps even in unnerving a visitor from the city, but the lure of exploration had diminished.

The worst thing, he discovered, was the mosquitoes. They hadn't been so bad up by the house, but down along the brook the air was thick with them, and he found he was continually fanning them away with every step. There were caterpillars, too, fat green ones that burst if you stepped on them, and little yellow ones that hung from every tree on invisible filaments of silk. Several times he found himself forced to take off his glasses when bugs and bits of leaf got caught between the lenses and his eyes.

For a hundred yards or so it was hard to tell where the fields left off and the woods began. He had to stick close to the brook, following an indistinct little trail that ran along beside it, for elsewhere the undergrowth made walking difficult. He was glad, at first, that he'd brought the field guide with him; here and there he stopped to look up various flowers—at least the ones he hadn't already squashed underfoot.

Crouching down, he identified the buds of a swamp rose mallow, which he remembered from *Forbidden Games,* and something called a great St.-John's-wort, which the book rather unnecessarily warned him not to eat. A lot of things, it seemed, were poisonous in these woods. He was careful to memorize the three-leafed shape of poison ivy. At one point, noticing a large, exotic-looking flower, he half wondered if he'd stumbled upon some rare black orchid out of *Tim Tyler's Luck,* but it turned out to be nothing more than skunk cabbage. Soon afterward he began encountering massive clumps of the stuff; there was a moral here somewhere, he decided.

By this time he had lost interest in looking up any more names. The woods were getting thicker, with tall trees arching overhead, blotting out the sunlight. As he moved still deeper into them, attempting to follow the stream's path through branches that impeded his progress and snapped in his face, he discovered that he'd have to get his feet wet, for the trail had completely disappeared and the underbrush grew right down to the water's edge. Rolling up his pants, he hesitantly dipped one sneakered foot in, then the other. It was like stepping into an underground spring, and made him think of caves of ice deep beneath the earth. He gritted his teeth and walked on. Soon the cold seemed to go away; either he was getting used to it or his feet were numb. Ahead of him, like a bridge across the stream, rose a low archway of decaying boughs and vines. He ducked under it and continued forward, his sneakers sloshing in the water.

On the other side of the arch he saw that, as the stream curved west, it had formed a small circular pool with banks of wet sand surrounded by statuesque oaks, their roots thrust below the surface. Obviously a watering place, he decided; there were animal tracks in the sand— deer, no doubt, and what may have been a fox or perhaps some farmer's dog. He wished he'd brought his tracking manual with him; it was going to be difficult to check such things from memory.

The place, as he moved forward, seemed surprisingly familiar, but he wasn't sure just why. Had he dreamed of it?

He waded toward the center of the pool, the water rising past his ankles. Everything was silent but the birds, and they were few, calling to each other in the trees overhead. The air around him echoed with the sound.

Somehow he felt soiled here, impure, as if he himself were the impurity, the thing that made the birds cry out. He was suddenly conscious of his body: of the oily juices flowing from his pores, the noisy rush of air in and out of his nostrils, the foulness of the city that clung to his hair, the foulness of his flesh, the foulness deep within him. He had no business being in this place; his mind—a human mind, any mind at all—did not belong here. This pool was not for those who thought; thought defiled it. He felt the alien shoes upon his feet, the canvas, dye, and rubber, the filth of the city that had spawned him. And he looked down at himself, and saw the water lapping round his ankles, and his own reflection . . .

For an instant the two beings stared at each other, forest man and city man. And during that instant all sound, all movement, ceased. And he laid himself full length in the pool.

Afterward he stood, freezing water dripping from his shoulders and his hair. He heard the birds once more, singing with fury or joy, he couldn't tell which, and he saw the sunlight lancing down between the leaves in shimmering gold bars. A longing gripped him: he felt a strange pull to the west. And when, like the needle of a compass, he turned in that direction, looking westward from his fixed point in the center of the circle, it was as if the trees had opened. He could see the brook stretch endlessly ahead, shining into the heart of the forest like a thin silver line, pointing toward places only the birds and the animals knew. When he saw this he yearned to go farther, and dreaded to go farther, and was suddenly so tired that he turned and went running up out of the pool and lay exhausted in the sand.

As the afternoon drew on, the sky became overcast again. Rain hung like a promise in the air. He breathed deeply, found his feet, and took the homeward path, realizing, as he left it, where he'd seen the place before. It was in the Dynnod, on the card marked *The Pool*. The resemblance was uncanny.

The sky remained overcast all day, but the rain did not come. At night the sky was cloudy, and all the stars were hidden.

*

At dinner I was famished, thanks to the day's exertions, & found myself agreeing to a second helping of pie. So much for willpower!
Wouldn't be surprised if I put on a few extra pounds before the summer's over.

Sarr and Deborah seemed a bit jumpy; I think we all felt Carol's absence. Or maybe it was the weather, that feeling of tension you get before a rain, a sense of something holding back. I certainly never saw
them lose their temper at a cat before, as Deborah did tonight. For the
past week she's been trying to convince Sarr to put bells around the
cats' necks—she feels sorry for the mice and birds they kill—& so tonight, when Toby showed up at the door with feathers sticking out of
his mouth & a tiny yellow leg among them, she almost had a fit; she
snatched up the bread knife & chased him down the steps and halfway
to the vegetable garden before she turned around and came back, looking very ashamed of herself. I thought for a second she would really
run him through.

"Happy Fourth of July," I said, but that didn't go over well. They
regard the day as primarily a war holiday, a celebration of the military
& an excuse for people to avoid work. You certainly get no feeling of
the holiday out here; nothing to distinguish it from any other day, except for the saying Sarr quoted glumly, "Fourth of July, corn knee-
high." Alas, since he planted so late the corn isn't even up to my ankle!
No wonder he was in such a sour mood.

Managed to brighten things up a bit, I think, by telling them of my
"day's adventures," i.e., my little outing. In fact, they seemed eager to
hear all about it, like parents asking what I did in school. I'm sure
they've both been down that exact same path dozens of times, since it
cuts right through their property; but then, I always get a kick out of
hearing visitors describe their first day in New York, & I suppose it
was the same pleasure for them: familiar surroundings seen through
unfamiliar eyes. So I tried my damnedest not to disappoint them:
played up my hatred of the bugs, nervousness at being alone in the
wilderness with snakes & wolves & quicksand pits, etc. May have over-
done it a bit, but I think they were amused.

Or at least Deborah was. She told me that next time I go for a walk I
should carry a sprig of pennyroyal behind my ear, as somehow this
prevents the female mosquitoes from knowing I'm around. (The females are the ones that bite.) She said she'd clip me some; she grows it
in her garden.

As for Sarr, I'm not so sure he realized when I was kidding about my
day's exploits, & for all I know he may have felt secretly contemptuous—though I suspect his main feeling was one of concern. He told me,
with great seriousness, that it's just as well I stopped where I did

today, at that bend in the stream, since if I'd followed it a couple of miles deeper into the woods I'd have ended up where the stream empties into a marshy backwater & it's easy to get lost. Just beyond the marsh, he said, is a place where on certain nights you can actually see clouds of steam & swamp gas rising from the ground, & will-o'-the-wisps, and trees that, in these parts, you don't expect to find. It's the place the men were talking about in the store yesterday, where those two girls were killed—the place they call McKinney's Neck.

When I think about it now, the whole afternoon seems almost as unreal as a dream. Glad I'm back inside again, four walls keeping out the night, with bed & books & lamplight here beside me. At times like this the farm seems like a precious little island, & no one but a fool would venture out into the darkness where they don't belong.

Feel too stiff now, & a hell of a lot too sleepy, to sit up writing anymore. Time to put away this journal & turn in. Carol's probably going to bed now too, never knowing how lucky she is to be surrounded by all that concrete & brick, those noisy, well-lit streets . . . Manhattan may be just another island, but it's nothing like this place. Ten to one I dream of it again tonight—so arrogant, so massive, & so safe.

                                                            Fourth of July
Dear Jeremy,

Well, it looks like you're not the only one who'll be spending the summer in isolation. When I got back here last night I found my roommate gone, along with most of her clothes. She'd typed me a note saying she was going off on a trip with one of her boyfriends (I've never been able to keep track of them), and that I should hold her mail and water her plants while she's gone. She didn't even say where she was going. I can't understand it, for her to just pack up and leave like that without giving me any kind of warning—it seems so inconsiderate. But I guess it's the sort of thing I should have expected from her. She's always been extremely irresponsible. She did leave me her share of the rent, though, thank heaven, enough for the entire summer, right down to the last penny, in two neat little piles of cash labeled "July" and "August."

Incidentally, in case it wasn't obvious to you, I had a wonderful time this weekend. I really did, you know, it was just what I needed. I'm going to write the Poroths a little bread-and-butter note as soon as I finish this. They were both extremely nice to me, in every way possible, and I do hope I'll get a chance to see them again before too long. They're so different from some of the people you meet in this city, you just can't imagine.

Believe it or not, the ride back to New York took only an hour and a half, and I had no trouble at all in that parking lot uptown. I guess it was because of the holiday weekend; the whole city seems deserted. It was depressing to come back, that's for sure, but I kept thinking about the Poroths, and the countryside, and you and all those cats.

Rosie came down here tonight and insisted on taking me out to dinner. He pointed out how I really ought to be happy for the extra room I'll have now, and for the peace and quiet, not having Rochelle's awful friends running around all the time. I know he's right, and in a way I suppose I *am* just as happy she's gone, but I still can't help feeling a little bit abandoned. I miss her. Who knows, I may even miss you . . .

JULY SIXTH

Had she meant the letter as bait? In retrospect Carol was forced to admit that perhaps there had been something slightly calculating about it. But then, she'd merely hoped to be invited back to the farm before the end of summer. Never for a moment had she expected that Freirs himself might show up in the city—and only two days later.

"I thought I'd go by that restaurant again," he began, telephoning her at work, "just in case that goddamned book bag turned up." And then, as if it were an afterthought: "Anyway, you sounded like you might be in the mood for a little company. So here I am."

He was calling from the Port Authority bus terminal; it was nearly four o'clock on a hot and muggy Wednesday afternoon. He had gotten a ride to Flemington that morning, shortly after reading Carol's note, and had taken the early bus out. Though he'd be stopping down on Bank Street first, to search his apartment and talk with the new tenants, this evening he expected to be free. Would she care to meet for dinner? He would pick her up at seven thirty.

Two hours still remained before she could leave work, and Carol spent them thinking of what lay ahead. Freirs hadn't said anything about where he planned to stay that night. No doubt he planned to stay with her, in her bed. The thought was a disturbing one, yet undeniably attractive; she turned it over and over in her mind.

What struck her first was his presumption. Did he actually believe that, having put him off once—or twice, if you counted their first date—she now *owed* him this night? Yes, quite likely he did; for, considering how methodical he could be, how stiff-necked and precise, it wouldn't have surprised her if he were one of those conscientious souls who proceeded according to schedule: first date a kiss, second something stronger, third a night in bed.

But wait, maybe even here she was being old-fashioned. Maybe she was living in the past. After all, Jeremy had been married once, and perhaps for him the usual three days' expectations had long since been compressed into a single busy evening. In which case, Carol realized, she was already in his debt twice over—though it scarcely made the prospect more inviting; she'd be damned if she was going to give herself to him simply out of social obligation. When she took a lover it would have to be someone special, not just an impatient man exacting his due.

And yet . . . And yet by the end of their weekend together, she had been resigned—no, more than resigned, she had been determined to sleep with him, if not there at the farm, then somewhere else. She'd known it ever since that first evening together: that he would be the one. She had been ready then—and she was ready now.

And how pleasant it would be to lie with him tonight, knowing he was there beside her in the darkness, keeping her company in the suddenly empty apartment; to feel his naked skin pressed against hers, warm between the cool of the sheets. Neither of them would have to get up early tomorrow. They could sleep together late into the morning.

The day had so far shown no signs of drawing to a close. Light continued to stream into the room around the tattered edges of the shades; the shades themselves glowed yellow in the sun, and heat had made a prison of the unmoving air. As she knelt to steady the contents of her book cart, Carol felt herself perspiring beneath her blouse, while through her ran a tiny flicker of foreboding. If it was this bad so early in July, what would the rest of the summer be like?

She piloted the overloaded cart through a delirium of aisles and shelves and tables, her mind far from the routine tasks, her footsteps keeping time to the regular squeaking of the wheels. Entering the little glassed-in office to complete a series of subscription forms, she thought that at any moment she might faint: the air conditioner was still broken from last September, and with three desks crowded side by side the room seemed even smaller than it should have, and twice as cluttered. Her own desk lay buried beneath a stack of old *Library Journal*s and an assortment of damaged paperbacks; its lower drawer was stuck fast, its wooden surface clammy to the touch. Carol ran a hand through her damp hair and slumped back in her seat. It was going to be a warm night for making love.

Later, bringing an armload of returned books upstairs to help fill in the hour left of work, she passed between the ranks of children's classics and inspirational works that lined an aisle near the doorway: *Little Women*, retold for younger readers; *King Arthur and His Merry Men*, with Victorian illustrations; *Great Teens in History*, a girlish Joan of Arc on the front. Dog-eared and skinny, with brightly colored covers and ragged spines, the volumes seemed repositories of a kind of innocence that, after tonight, she'd be unable to share. She paused beside the reference desk to study the photos on a Girl Scout poster, relic of some long-ago recruiting drive, and found herself face to face with a racial mix of laughing little girls. They, too, seemed inhabitants of another, more innocent world, a world already receding into the past. She wondered if they'd laugh for her tomorrow.

Enough! she told herself. She must keep things in perspective. What, after all, were a tiny patch of skin and a few drops of blood to St. Agnes's beheading, Catherine on the spiked wheel, Ursula ravished by the Huns, Marcus stung to death by wasps? Why pretend the thing she'd do tonight had any mystical significance?

Moving toward the front of the room, the day's heat at last beginning to lift, she deposited her books on a return table by the window sill. Downstairs this area was where the ten-cents-a-day bestsellers lay piled; up here the books were sooty, and faded by the now-departing sun, but a scattering of gold Newbery medallions gleamed among their covers like symbols of purity.

Purity! Once more it rose in her, that absurd feeling of regret. This was a world she'd be leaving tonight. She felt like one condemned to death, gazing upon all she encountered as if for the last time.

Around her children were reading aloud to themselves, mouths laboriously shaping the words, while others puzzled in silence through the more difficult books or roamed up and down the aisles in a temperature-induced torpor, pulling out volumes at random and putting a few of them back. Most of the children, absorbed in their reading or daydreams, took little notice of her or Mrs. Schumann; those who were bored made it obvious, unlike their elders downstairs, leafing impatiently through picture books or disputing with their friends. Still, the second floor was quiet at this hour, the atmosphere unusually subdued, and there were few real fights to settle; the room echoed with a soft gabble of voices punctuated only by laughter and the occasional high-pitched complaint. Carol found it a curiously restful sound.

Just before closing time, she was about to replace a handful of books on a shelf at the back of the room when, turning down the farthest row, she came upon a pale, skinny little girl, underpants below her knees, in the act of lifting her dress above her waist. Two small boys who'd been crouching in front of her jumped to their feet and dashed noisily up the aisle, disappearing around the other end. Carol heard the patter of their footsteps as they raced across the room. One of them made straight for the doorway and vanished down the stairs; the other paused only to snatch up a baseball cap and glove before hurrying after him.

The girl, however, was frozen guiltily to the spot, her eyes wide. She'd had time to yank the underpants up over the crumpled pink of her dress but was still clutching the waistband with both hands. Abruptly she let the elastic snap free, attempted to smooth back the dress, and cried, "Didn't do nothing!"

Nor had she, of course. There was certainly nothing to punish her
for, and though Carol couldn't resist giving her a brief, whispered reminder on How Some People Take Advantage of Other People's Innocence, she said nothing at all when, a few minutes later, the girl's
irascible-looking mother came to claim her.

In fact, though she was slow to admit it to herself, Carol was
amused—and in some dim, disreputable way, even somewhat aroused.
She couldn't get the sight out of her mind: the child's brazenly hoisted
dress, the sunlight on her legs, and the two boys hunched like worship-
ers before that frail, hairless little tuck of skin no bigger than a fortune
cookie. There was a kind of power in it. It reawakened memories of her
own, playing doctor with the neighbors' boy, and body magic in the loft
above the garage, and—was it a painting she'd once seen? That group
of men who stared in fearful wonder at the bound and naked body on
an altar: had she seen it in a picture book? Maybe it had only been a
dream.

Only a dream. But in the shower that evening, as she prepared herself for Jeremy's arrival, the vision remained, and she stood with head
thrown back, the hot spray beating sharp against her skin, obscurely
stirred as she felt the water on her, and the eyes.

Jeremy arrived more than half an hour early, muttering about the heat
and noise outside and the trash in the hallway downstairs. The restaurant hadn't found his book bag, nor had it been returned to his apartment, and the couple who were subletting the place had treated him, he
said, "like a stranger in my own home." He'd met a friend for drinks,
but the conversation had quickly turned boring. He looked at Carol
expectantly, as if waiting for her to set things right.

She was fresh from the shower and still in her robe, her wet hair
wrapped in a towel. She'd been rather put out that he'd come so much
sooner than planned, and after buzzing him in downstairs she had
struggled into a bra and panties and had raced through the apartment
gathering up loose clothes and flinging them toward a closet, wiping
the crumbs from the kitchen table and her hair from the tub, and
squinting at her features in the steamy bathroom mirror. She'd
thought she looked disconcertingly pale, though it was hard to tell in
the bad light; just to be safe she'd pinched her cheeks the way Scarlett
O'Hara used to do before meeting a beau.

But Scarlett O'Hara had never found herself parading around in a
terrycloth bathrobe and turban, and no beau of hers had ever shown
up with sweat stains on his shirt and liquor on his breath. The whole
evening seemed to be getting off to a miserable start—at least that's
what she'd thought—until, settling himself on the living room couch,

Jeremy eyed her up and down and said, "You know, you look damned nice right now."

She waited for the derisive little smile which was often the only way he signaled he was joking; but his mouth, and his eyes, remained serious.

Nervously she tightened the sash. "I suppose I'd better get dressed."

"Hey, don't go doing that for *my* sake!"

She laughed. "I thought you wanted to go out for dinner."

"Of course I do, but what's the rush? Come on, sit down here a minute." He slapped the cushion beside him, then pulled away his hand, as if surprised at his own audacity.

Surprised at hers, she sat.

They were silent for a time, as if each were pondering the implications of this new development. Carol heard her breathing coincide with his. Seated so close to him, she was exquisitely aware of how little she had on beneath the robe. Her skin still tingled from the shower; he would find it clean if, by some chance, he were to reach out and touch her right now.

At last, with something like a sigh, he reached out and scratched his knee. "Jesus," he said, "remind me never to drink on an empty stomach."

"Do you want me to make some coffee?" She was already getting to her feet.

"No, no, sit down, it would just make things worse. One cup and I feel like I'm in the Boston Marathon." He patted his heart. "And after the second I'm awake all night. Even without it, these days, I seem to be staying up later and later. My whole schedule's screwed up."

Carol nodded. "Mine too. I guess I'm still not used to having this place alone."

She watched the final minutes of sunshine inching steadily up the wall and was struck by how shabby the apartment looked even in the waning light. The living room still smelled faintly of Rochelle, especially by the couch where they were seated. Rochelle had slept on it whenever she was home; unfolded, it became a bed considerably wider than her own. Carol thought of all the men this couch had seen; she had already decided that this was where the two of them would sleep tonight.

"My roommate was one of the noisiest people I've ever met," she said. She wondered briefly why she'd used the past tense. "Sometimes, just as I was turning off my light, I'd hear her snoring. And when one of her boyfriends was over . . ." She made a face. "I could hear them even with my door closed. I guess that's why the silence feels so strange. Lately I just can't seem to get to bed before two or three in the morning."

"Oh, really? You sure went to bed early enough that night at the farm."

His voice was edged with resentment. *God,* she thought, *how ridiculously selfish he can be!* But at least he still seemed interested.

"I was tired from all that driving," she said. "And I didn't get much sleep there anyway."

"Yeah, I remember. Nightmares, you said. Hell, I'd get nightmares too, with all those Bible pictures hanging over my head! Next time, why not stay out back with me?" He gave her a sly look.

"Who knows?" she said. "Maybe I will." She saw that she'd surprised him and felt an urge to laugh. "That is," she added, "if you promise I won't have any more bad dreams."

He shook his head. "I only wish I could. But I promise I'll be there when you wake up."

"You don't say!" Smiling, she leaned closer to him. "And just what good do you think that'll do?"

"Oh, I don't know. I'll be there to talk to you, comfort you a bit. And I can always do this."

As he put his arms around her, her nervousness returned with a rush. She couldn't understand it; she was proud of her slim body. This was supposed to have been a time of letting go, of shedding inhibitions; her natural passions were supposed to take control. Soon she would lie back and become the woman she wanted to be, and Jeremy her true lover; the walls were about to be breached, the mystery revealed. Yet instead she could feel herself grow rigid against him, her heart pounding furiously, her hands beginning to tremble. What in heaven's name was the matter with her?

It wasn't as if she hadn't had time to prepare for this; she'd had nearly a quarter of a century. She knew perfectly well what would happen now, or at least what was supposed to: the things he was going to do to her, and how she was expected to respond. It was like knowing all the answers without ever having been asked any of the questions.

"Come on, now, Carol, please don't tighten up," he said, his voice close to her ear. She'd never heard him sound so gentle before. "Just sit back and relax. I won't hurt you, honest. I won't even budge." His hand came to rest above her hip; she felt it pressing lightly against her robe, like a living creature that moved when she moved, breathed when she breathed. "Come on," he whispered. "Talk to me."

"What should I talk about?" Her voice dismayed her; it sounded so breathless and frightened that she barely recognized it.

"Talk about anything you like. Tell me a secret. Or tell me a dream."

She willed herself to relax. "I save my secrets for confession," she said. "And I never remember my dreams."

"Except the one at Poroth Farm . . . Remember?"

"A little, yes. Not all of it."

"It doesn't matter." He drew her closer. The towel loosened from her hair and slipped softly to the couch. "Go on. Tell me."

"I'm sure it all had something to do with those weird cards Rosie gave you," she said. "I couldn't get some of those images out of my head." Reluctantly she cast her mind back. "I remember being in a kind of jungle—an awful place. The undergrowth was all ropy and thick, and the air was steamy hot and hard to breathe, and in the distance I could hear wailing flutes, and drums just hammering and hammering away without a stop. It was night, I'm sure of that much, but all around me everything was shining like it was on fire."

She felt his hand stir almost imperceptibly.

"I didn't know who I was," she said, "or what I looked like. Maybe I was dead and no more than a ghost, because I seemed to be floating over the ground, gliding between the trees. The vines and bushes somehow opened up for me, and I passed right through without a scratch. The farther I went, the louder the flutes and drums kept getting, and the thicker the trees, but just before the end I began to see a kind of clearing up ahead. For the first time, I caught a glimpse of the sky. The moon was out, and ..."

"And what?"

"It was shining like a spotlight on the center of the clearing."

"All the better to see with." Gently his hand slid toward her breast. She pressed it closer with her own.

"I wish I hadn't looked," she said. "It wasn't nice at all. In the center, all alone, stood a tree, and these men were gathered beneath it, watching something on the ground. Then they moved back, and I saw that at the foot of the tree was a kind of altar. There was a body on it—the body of a girl."

"And then, I suppose, you saw that the girl was you. And woke up with a scream." He was touching her breast, caressing it.

"No, it was nothing like that. It was worse. Much worse." She could feel her heart racing again; she wondered if he felt it too. "I woke because I heard something fall onto the body, and lying there in the moonlight was this long white slippery thing, curling and uncurling ... And then suddenly, as I watched, it arched up from the body and began to sway, faster and faster, and I could see that somehow it was *dancing*, heaving itself up and down to the music, like a great blind snake—"

"Uh-oh, you know what that means!"

She nodded and pulled away slightly. "Yes, yes, I know. But this time I'm not sure it applies. Anyway, why does a snake always have to be a phallic symbol? What if it was simply—a snake?"

"It's possible, I guess." She felt his hand slip beneath the robe. "As a matter of fact, there's this crazy Bram Stoker novel—"

"Wait, Jeremy, what are you doing there?"

"Nothing."

"That doesn't feel like nothing."

"I'm not going to hurt you. Just lift yourself up a minute."

"You mean . . . like this?"

"Mm. Do you have to keep both legs so—there, that's better."

She watched what he was doing, still held passive by the dream.

"Try to relax," he said. "Tell me about the way it ended. About the altar, and the nonsymbolic snake. I'm not going to do anything you don't want me to."

Her eyelids felt heavy. She took a deep breath and let it out. "You don't understand," she said. "It turned out to be something else entirely. Something more. I only saw a part of it, I think—the part above the altar. I remember how the creature rose up and down to the music, in time with the drumbeats and the whistling of the flutes. The other end seemed buried in the ground, there was just no telling how far under it went. Somehow I sensed that it was attached down there, that all I was seeing was the tip. And then I"—she caught her breath, half curious as to what Jeremy was doing, half reluctant to think about it—"I realized that the drums must be coming from the same place, from somewhere far below me, deep inside the earth . . . And suddenly it occurred to me, with absolute certainty, that all the things I'd been seeing—the altar, the clearing, the whole entire jungle—were a part of something else, something huge and hateful and alive."

She could feel her panties being tugged down over her thighs, and liked the feeling, the fact that there was nothing she herself had to do. She could let her mind wander, back to that night . . .

"I knew, then, beyond a shadow of a doubt that it was there and all around me, stretching from one end of the night to the other, a single monstrous creature half as big as the world. The sound of the flutes was the sound of its breathing, and the drumming was the beating of its heart. That horrible white snake that thrashed back and forth on the altar was just a tiny artery, pulsing with its blood. But hanging from the tree was the most hateful thing of all, because that's where it sat watching me, the eye and the face and the brain—"

She was jerked upright by the sound of the buzzer. Someone downstairs was ringing to get in. Yanking up her underwear and closing the robe, she hurried across the room and pressed the intercom button. "Who is it?" she called. Her voice was trembling.

There was no reply; the intercom hissed with ghost winds roaming up and down the empty halls. Freirs stirred impatiently on the couch.

She called again, louder this time. "Who's there?"

Something crackled tinnily, and at last, from the emptiness, came a faint, familiar voice. It was Rosie.

He prays he isn't too late. Yet as he stands there panting in the entranceway, waiting for the woman to admit him, his patient little smile never wavers; and no one who's been watching him from the street could possibly realize that it masks a howl of blind demonic rage.

All day he has plotted the man's progress toward the city; he's traced him every mile of the way. He has charted the woman's reaction, has catalogued her every mood and sigh, down to the tiniest flutter of her heart. Nonetheless, he has been careless; in all his calculations he's neglected to take one small factor into account. The air is warmer, ever so slightly warmer, than he's anticipated: less than a degree, perhaps, but enough to make a difference. He knows that even on a cooler day, when men and women are brought together—human beings being human—anything might happen. What the two of them upstairs might regard as consummation will, to him, mean catastrophe; a lifetime of planning may come to nothing in the space of a single gasp, a sudden cry of pain. And possibly that very thing has already occurred.

In which case, of course, the two will have to die.

But even if he has arrived in time, there is a second problem, no less urgent, created by the unexpected heat: a problem, in a sense, of waste disposal . . .

It hadn't seemed important at the start—merely a question of temporary storage—but thanks to the weather it is now approaching an emergency. He cannot put it off any longer; there is no more time to lose. He simply has to get the man and woman out of the apartment. If they chance too near that couch . . . well, it might prove rather nasty for them all.

Nasty indeed. That's just how he is feeling at the moment. But after the woman has buzzed him inside and he's passed through into the hallway, his face remains frozen in its customary smile. Even here, someone may be watching; you can never be too sure.

Only when he finds himself within the familiar confines of the elevator, safe amid the privacy of its battered metal walls, does he allow the mask to slip. As the door scrapes shut and the little car lurches skyward, the smile drops away and his lips curl back in a snarl of animal fury. Teeth gnashing with a sound like grinding stones, features contorted almost beyond recognition, he shakes his tiny fists in the air, and all the evening's pent-up rage comes bursting out of him in a frenzy of noise and spit and flying limbs. Like one possessed he flings himself about the car, fists lashing out to beat against its walls; walls and floor reverberate with the pounding of his shoes, and the little car rocks back and forth as if a swarm of maddened bees were trapped inside.

At last, on the fifth floor, when the car has come to rest, its doors slide open on the plump, unassuming figure of an old man. He stands there looking cheerful and composed, if a trifle winded, and his eyes twinkle with impish good humor as he steps into the hall and makes for the apartment at the end. Mopping his brow with a small white handkerchief, he blinks amiably at the heat, fixes his smile in place, and rings the bell.

Voices are coming from the living room. He cocks his little head to hear and sniffs the air that flows beneath the door. No, there is no question about it: he will have to get them out of there, away from that accursed couch, and soon—before they open it and find what is hidden inside. Flesh, even when suitably prepared, does tend to smell so in warm weather.

I was going to answer the door, but Carol beat me to it. Never saw a girl get dressed so fast.

In her own screwed-up way she probably felt guilty about my being there, because she proceeded to make a totally unnecessary fuss over Rosie—what a wonderful surprise this was, how much she'd been wanting to get the two of us together, etc., etc.

Can't say I was especially pleased to see him again, considering his rotten timing—in fact, I spent several minutes silently cursing him—but I have to admit the guy seems inoffensive enough (though I could do without the lisp and the mincing little walk). He was all smiles, from the moment he waltzed through the door, & despite his age he appeared to be constantly in motion, sniffing around the room like an overgrown pink puppy; you could almost see him wagging his little tail.

I thanked him, of course, for that crazy deck of cards—hadn't yet gotten around to writing the thank-you note, and now I won't have to—& must admit the old guy showed a rather flattering interest in my work. Exchanged chitchat about film courses, grad school, the plight of Ph.D.s, but I got the impression it was mainly for Carol's benefit. He seemed pathetically attached to her; in fact, the only time he looked a little hurt was when Carol said she was surprised to see him. He just couldn't understand it; had she forgotten about their dinner date tonight? Apparently she had, or at least that's what she claimed. She acted very embarrassed, apologized & all, but behind his back she shrugged at me and shook her head. Maybe Rosie's the forgetful one.

Anyway, we decided to make it a threesome for dinner. Playing the proper hostess, Carol asked us if we wanted to have a glass of wine before going out. I certainly could have used one by that time, preferably ice cold, the way I was feeling, but Rosie said he was famished and seemed eager to get away.

Outside, it was already dark—one of those hot, smelly New York nights when the streets echo with mambo music & drums. There was violence in the air, even more than usual, & everyone seemed to be out on the sidewalk dancing or drinking or waiting for something to happen. On nights like that, in Puerto Rican neighborhoods like Carol's, you can almost imagine you're in the tropics. The sound makes you impatient, it's hard to concentrate on things. Not such a bad feeling, really, though it has its scary side. I can see why so many people I know retreat to Fire Island or the Hamptons for the summer; I can also see why, if I were a bit younger & poorer, stuck in the city with nothing to lose, I'd be tempted to bash somebody's brains out with a tire iron. As it was, my impulses were somewhat more humane: I felt like pulling Carol out of the glare of the streetlamps & making love to her all night. I'd even have been willing to go back up to that stuffy little apartment with the roaches & the heat.

Must admit, there's something about her poverty that appeals to me. It's sort of a turn-on to think that, little as I have, I could really be a help to her financially.

It took us some time to decide on a restaurant, since Rosie kept suggesting all sorts of obscure, outlandish places on the other side of town. Maybe he was trying to impress us. Finally we settled on Harvey's; it's just a few blocks east, & they never rush you. Carol & I made do with omelets—with her crazy notions about food, she seems destined to remain a cheap date—while old Rosie wolfed down a filet mignon half the size of his head.

Dinner was excellent, though we were interrupted in the middle by a very brief brownout; Carol says New York's had a lot of them this year. All of a sudden the entire room went dark, but it only lasted a few seconds before the lights came back on. Still, I was grateful for the candle on the table.

I'm not sure just why, but Carol excused herself right after that, & when she sat down again she was looking sort of distant & hardly spoke for the rest of the meal. I wondered if somehow she'd been rattled by the lights going out, or if it was something I'd said, but I think now that she was probably just feeling a touch of embarrassment—& maybe even, in some weird Catholic way, remorse—over what had gone on back in the apartment. Only natural, I guess; when you've opened up too much to another person, you sometimes tend to backtrack a bit as compensation. Just the same, I do wish she hadn't turned quite so cold.

Rosie offered to foot the bill, as I knew he would, but he & I ended up splitting the total between us. Which meant that I sort of got taken. Afterward I expected him to call it a night, & was looking forward to some time alone with Carol, but no such luck; it seems our Rosie is something of a night person. He insisted Carol and I accompany him to this old West Chelsea bar he knew about—drinks on him, at least— & it turned out to be way the hell over on Eleventh Avenue, practically knee-deep in the Hudson. At the rate he walked, with his stubby little legs, we must have killed a good half hour just getting there.

The place wasn't anything special, but nevertheless we stayed for a couple of rounds. Toward the end Rosie started getting all sentimental over his childhood out in the country somewhere, & we more or less let him run on. Hard to picture him as a farm boy.

We didn't get back to Carol's till after midnight. By this time, I think, Carol would've been as relieved as I'd have been to see the last of Rosie, but he mumbled something in this pitiable little voice about being "close to exhaustion," & quick as a catechism she was asking him up for coffee.

As soon as we stepped out of the elevator, Carol said she smelled something funny, & after a moment I smelled it too. We all braced ourselves as she unlocked the door to her apartment, & sure enough, that's where it was coming from. Held my breath & ran into the kitchen, where I noticed that the pilot light had gone out & that the rusting old hulk of a stove in there was hissing like a snake. It had probably been leaking for hours, & the entire apartment was filled with gas. If any of us had lit a match the whole place would have gone up.

Rosie & I opened all the windows while Carol went downstairs to wake the super. He turned out to be a grumpy old Cuban who acted as if the entire thing were Carol's fault. He took one look & said a pipe had broken somewhere above the shutoff valve. He'd have to get some men to fix it in the morning.

Rosie insisted on putting us up at his place. So there we were, piling into a taxi at one thirty A.M. & heading uptown, Carol fussing about her stove but maybe just as relieved that everything had worked out this way, & me cursing to myself, while Rosie, all unaware, beamed at us from the front seat.

He lives in one of those ugly old buildings off Riverside Drive, way up in the hundreds near Columbia. The apartment itself is really much too big for him—two huge bedrooms, high ceilings with plasterwork and ornamental molding—& thanks to rent control the old bastard probably pays next to nothing for it. He told us he'd been living there for more than thirty years, but he certainly hasn't done much with the place. The kitchen was pleasant enough—all chinaware, teacups, & painted little trays, like the haunt of some dotty old lady—but the rest of the place barely looked lived in. Nothing on the walls but a few framed art prints—calendar stuff—and a crude, obscene-looking kid's drawing he said was by a little boy he knew. For someone who's traveled as much as he claims, he doesn't seem to have acquired anything very interesting; you certainly can't accuse him of being a materialist. The only books I came across were the usual bestseller-type things—*I'm OK, You're OK, How to Be Your Own Best Friend*—& a few dusty Victorian sets that you see in old ladies' parlors & no one ever looks at anymore. Carol seemed a bit disappointed; I guess she'd been expecting a museum.

Rosie apologized for the place's looking so "spartan" & said something about not being home much. Until a year or two ago, apparently, he spent most of his time abroad or in the library—"sometimes both," he said. I kept picturing libraries & reading rooms all around the world, and in each of them, somewhere in the corner, that same wizened little face.

By then the two of us were close to dropping off, & I could see exactly what was coming; in fact, I should have seen it the moment that buzzer sounded back in Carol's apartment. Somehow, without meaning to, I had cast myself in the dumbest role of all: I was the horny but thwarted lover in one of those exasperating Howard Hawks comedies, condemned to spend the night alone. And sure enough, Rosie proceeded to stick me on a sofa in the anteroom adjoining his, with Carol in the spare room & his own fat little self parked neatly between us.

So I had to go to bed celibate again, with a premature hangover, a bad mood, & a useless hard-on. I couldn't get my mind off Carol—the sight of her half out of those flimsy white Woolworth's panties, looking like a skinny little farm child with her small ass & slim white thighs & solemn expression, but also incredibly sexy. Boy, do I want her badly.

Somehow, despite it all, I slept without a single dream & got up feeling just as lousy. Rosie was puttering around making breakfast & whistling some tuneless little song—he looked awful; I think he'd taken out his false teeth—but Carol was more distant than ever. Later, as we rode downtown together on the subway, she seemed preoccupied with her apartment & her job. Clearly it was time to say goodbye. So I got off at Forty-Second Street, sat through half a porn film called *The Coming Thing*, & took the bus back here to Poroth Farm.

BOOK FIVE

THE WHITE CEREMONY

Then there are the Ceremonies, which are all of them important, but some are more delightful than others.
—Machen, *The White People*

JULY SEVENTH

J ust as well that Jeremy was gone. Carol needed time to get her thoughts in order. That he'd had her so worked up last night, that she'd been naked, exposed before him, and so obviously excited, ready to yield—somehow it all seemed far more intimate than if they'd actually gone to bed together. And to think that, the entire time, he'd had his own pants on! The whole thing was just too embarrassing. It almost made her angry.

It also made her angry to return to her apartment and find the gas still on. "Couldn't the men fix it?" she asked the superintendent, who stood grumpily in his first-floor doorway with a Spanish station on the radio behind him and something spicy frying in the kitchen.

"They comin' round this afternoon sometime," he said, impatient to return to his meal. "These guys, they're very busy. You come back tonight, everything be fixed."

"You mean they haven't been here yet?" said Carol. "That's funny, *somebody's* sure been up there."

Back upstairs, careful not to breathe in the vicinity of the kitchen, she looked around. No, she had obviously been wrong; she could find nothing out of place, nothing missing or stolen (not that there was anything worth stealing, she reminded herself), no real sign that anyone had been here since last night. The sunlight streamed harmlessly through the open windows; the apartment still reeked of gas, and she was reluctant to stay more than a minute or two. Idly she straightened up the stack of papers in her bedroom, more of Rosie's articles to plod through. *Myths of the Cherokee* (Washington, 1900). *Description of a Singular Aboriginal Race Inhabiting the Summit of the Neilgherry Hills* (London, 1832). They would be here when she got back; it was nice not to have to look at them now. She would change her clothes, go off to work, and try to forget everything that had happened last night.

Holding her breath, she entered the kitchen, rinsed out a few glasses—no sense letting the repairman think she kept a dirty house—and wiped off the counter. In the living room she fastened back the curtains, wondering if it was safe to leave the old TV set unguarded, and decided that no one would want it anyway. If those workmen took anything, she could report them somewhere. She noticed several strands of black hair on the rug near the foot of the couch. *There's al-*

ways something of Rochelle's here, she thought, as she picked them up between two fingers and released them out the window. They drifted downward on the summer breeze, floating like a spiderweb.

The library, despite the heat, was unchanged from the day before; she felt as if she'd never left. There were fewer grad students this time of year, but their elders, those pale wraiths who haunted the long tables and magazine racks each day, took no notice of the season; they had no beaches or resorts to flee to when the weather grew warm. There were the usual piles of ragged-looking books to put away, and she did so silently for most of the afternoon, but her mind wasn't on her work. She was thinking of her apartment: of the super—how rude some men were, they certainly did what they pleased!—and of Jeremy, who'd made her feel so vulnerable. Was he laughing over her right this minute? Did he think of her at all? Maybe to him she was just another conquest. And she was, she told herself, there was no sense denying it; she had been conquered last night. She thought of Rosie—and quickly pushed the thought from her mind. He was the one man who treated her kindly; she didn't want to think about what she had seen in the restaurant last night, it was too ugly . . .

Later, as she patrolled the aisles of the children's section, she was almost able to put the restaurant incident from her mind. Mrs. Schumann was reading Hans Christian Andersen fairy tales to a story group at the table in the corner. Carol passed by from time to time on her rounds and caught the tale in snatches: "The Girl Who Trod on a Loaf." No doubt the little monsters had specifically asked for that one. It was the most repellently bloody-minded of the lot: a little girl who pulled the wings off flies, and her bizarre punishment, standing helpless and frozen while these same insects crawled over her face and body.

She was glad to see that two little boys, at least, were having no part of such sick fantasies. They were crouched before the bottom shelf of the biology section, a shelf that, Carol knew, contained some junior-level health and medical texts. Strolling round the floor, she passed them twice; they appeared to be engrossed in an oversize anatomy book, their small, intense faces studying something hidden by its covers. Carol surmised, from the way one of them glanced guiltily over his shoulder at her the second time she walked by, that the two were searching for nude pictures; it was a common preoccupation among the children who used the library. The bank of fans atop the bookshelves hummed, and Mrs. Schumann's voice continued to drone across the room, echoing like a memory.

On Carol's third round she noticed that the thinner of the two boys was sitting cross-legged on the floor, the other kneeling. She was debating whether to direct them to chairs—their pants were going to be filthy when they got up—when suddenly the larger of the two made a

little dip of his head and fell forward onto the other boy, clutching him
in a furious hug. In a second they were rolling over on the floor, grunting with exertion and tearing at one another's faces, the book tossed
aside. Carol was bigger than they were—as the assistant supervisor
had once reminded her—but not so much bigger that she was able to
tear the two apart. She ran for Mrs. Schumann, who stood up from the
reading circle like some great plump monster rising from a pool, and
together they managed to separate the two combatants. They were
brothers, it turned out, fighting not over the volume on the floor but
over a small pocketknife which each claimed as his own. The fight
ended with the knife in Mrs. Schumann's desk drawer, permanently
confiscated, and the two boys warned not to set foot inside the library
again without a note from their mother—a note which, both women
knew, would never be produced.

It was the knife that brought the memories back, memories of the
previous night, the incident at dinner . . .

She had been so happy as they'd all sat down, happy that Rosie and
Jeremy seemed to be hitting it off; happy, in a way, perhaps, that Rosie
had arrived in time to stop her from doing something irrevocable;
happy just to be spending a summer night in the company of two men
she liked, in a comfortable candlelit restaurant with good food and an
air conditioner that worked.

She remembered how Rosie, smiling fondly, had been talking to her
of her future; how all his words had gone to her head, all his talk about
courses and openings and opportunities. "You're an unusually tal-
ented young lady," he'd been saying, exuberantly waving his steak
knife. "I expect great things from you!"

Then suddenly, like the ending of a dream—she felt a chill even now
as she remembered it—suddenly the lights had flickered once, twice,
and gone off, leaving only the candles on the table.

It had all happened in an instant. Seconds later the power had come
back on; once again the air conditioner's hum had filled the room, and
with it movement, conversation, laughter. But in that frozen moment
of shadows and silence, with only the candle on the table for illumination, she had seen Rosie regarding her—and it had been like seeing him
for the first time. In the altered light, that instant, everything had
looked different: the old man's face had been hard, icy, cruel. He had
held the knife poised in her direction, and his tiny eyes had glittered
like razors in the candlelight.

The bed was wide and almost filled the little room. They lay naked, the
two of them, drugged with the heat of the evening, staring at the lantern light that flickered from the table by the wall. Deborah's hair, unfastened, was spread beneath her like a cape, black against the
whiteness of the sheet. Around them lay their seven cats: Dinah and
Tobias by Deborah's head, Habakkuk, or "Cookie," at her feet, Zillah
with her face buried just behind Sarr's ear, 'Riah and Rebekah on the
corner of the bed, and Bwada half beneath it on the wooden floor, yet
well within reach of Sarr's caressing hand.

They lay silently, listening, waiting for Freirs to leave for the night.
They could hear him downstairs in the bathroom, noisily brushing his
teeth, rinsing his mouth, zipping up his toilet kit, and blowing out the
kerosene lamp. The thin wooden door opened with a rattle, followed by
footsteps in the kitchen directly below them. Deborah leaned from the
bed and watched his progress; through the chinks in the wide-plank
floor, with its warped and tilted boards, she saw the faint gleam of
Freirs' flashlight moving toward the back door. The door opened,
closed, the latch clicked shut, and they heard footsteps descending the
back steps. There was silence, broken only by a faint muttered "God-
damn!"—he had stepped on something in the grass—and then they
were left alone with their thoughts.

"He was in a bad mood tonight, wasn't he?" whispered Deborah. "I
think it was over Carol. Every time he spoke of her his face got angry."

Sarr half closed his eyes, settling back against the hard mattress as
if it were of down. "It's only what he deserved," he said slowly. "He
went back to the city for one reason, and you and I both know what it
was. His heart was filled with lust, and the Lord made him suffer
for it."

"He *misses* her, honey, it isn't any more than that. He's courting
her, just the way you courted me."

He appeared to consider this a moment. "Well, maybe it's only natural to follow after someone your heart's set on . . . But he should never
have followed her to *that* place!" His face had become hard again; he
looked like the faded photograph of his father which glared sternly
from atop the bureau.

"He was only going home."

"He was leaving all the things we've offered him here, leaving it all
behind like it meant nothing to him, like *we* mean nothing. And for
what? For a mess of light and noise and show. 'Twas a mistake, going
back there."

Deborah was silent a moment. "I guess so," she said. "But you know, honey, this place is quite a change for him. He's not used to our ways yet. He likes having people around." She paused. "Can't say I blame him, either."

"Oh, I see." A hint of smile played about his lips; without turning his head to look at her he reached over and cupped a breast in his hand. "You're saying I'm not man enough for you anymore, is that right? And you want him instead?"

She giggled and edged closer to him, dislodging two of the cats. "That's right," she said. "I'm getting sick of the likes of you. I'm thinking I'll take me a lover." She rolled over and pressed her body next to his. He ran his fingers through her hair, brushing it away from the pale skin of her shoulders.

"Guess I should have listened to my mother," he said, planting a kiss on her mouth. He looked into her face, then smiled. "Glad I didn't, though."

The cats moved out of the way, reluctantly, as they made love. The old bed creaked and trembled.

Afterward, even while still inside her, his eyes still closed and his breathing heavy, he was reaching out for the Bible on the nightstand. He slipped out of her just as his hands closed on the book's worn leather binding.

She sighed. "You know, honey, this is the last night we can do this for a while."

"Hmmm?" He lay on his elbows in the bed, already thumbing through the dog-eared pages, squinting at the columns of print in the flickering light.

"I said we can't do this for a while—'less you want another mouth to feed."

He stared at her a moment as if weighing the matter. Then, shaking his head, he returned to the Bible. "There'll be time for such things," he said. "We owe so much now, you and I, and have so little ourselves . . ." He paused again. "Well, maybe the prophet can guide us."

He handed her the heavy book and got up from the bed. Silently he walked to the corner of the room near the fireplace where the wall faced inward toward the house, unadorned with pictures and unbroken by a window. Moving the simple hand-braided rug out of the way, he knelt facing the wall, his bare knees upon the planks.

"Let's begin," he said. He closed his eyes.

Deborah sat upright in the bed, feeling the hard wooden headboard against her back; it seemed only fitting, the hardness, when she held the Bible on her lap. It was open to Jeremiah, as was usual when they performed the ceremony known as "drawing the sortes," though occasionally Sarr would test himself by substituting a less familiar chapter. Deborah raised her gaze to the opposite wall, where below a

tattered Trenton State banner hung an ancient crocheted design, the
Bird of Paradise in the Tree of Life. Keeping her eyes upon the green
and gold foliage, she flipped through the chapter at random and poked
her finger toward the bottom of the page.

"Twenty-nine three," she said.

He remained silent, rigid.

She read over the text and raised her eyebrows. "'Fraid I started off
with a mean one," she said. " 'By the hand of Elasah the son—'"

"—the son of Shaphan, and Gemariah the son of Hilkiah, whom Ze-
dekiah king of Judah sent unto Babylon to Nebuchadnezzar king of
Babylon . . .' "

"Right." She looked away, flipped the pages again. "I wonder if
Jeremy's been using those cards Carol gave him"—her finger stabbed
downward—"to tell fortunes with, the way we use the Bible. Eight
fifteen."

" 'We looked for peace, but no good came; and for a time of health,
and behold trouble!' Frankly, I think Carol swallowed a white lie
about those cards. The Dynnod's not for telling fortunes."

"How do you know, honey?"

"I read about it back in college. One of my religion courses."

"I thought the cards were just a game invented by some novelty
company."

"The cards are, yes. But the pictures on them are a whole lot older."

"What are they for, then?"

"They're supposed to bring on visions."

Deborah stared blankly at the ceiling while her fingers selected another passage. "Hmmm. Well, I guess Carol didn't know any better."
She looked down. "Forty-four seven."

" 'Wherefore commit ye this great evil against your souls, to cut off
from you man and woman, child and suckling . . .' "

"Right." She chose another. "Thirty-seven four. Speaking of suck-
lings, Lotte Sturtevant's belly is so big now that all of us think it's
going to be a boy. Twins, even. Now, if I were to have a son, say—"

" 'Now Jeremiah came in and went out among the people . . .' "

"—he could help me with the housework when he was little, and you
with the farm work by the time he was half grown. You've been saying
you could use another hand. And there's—" She looked down. "Um,
eleven six. There's just no end of things that need doing around here."

" 'Then the Lord said unto me, Proclaim all these words in the cities
of Judah, and in the streets of Jerusalem, saying, Hear ye the words of
this covenant, and do them.' "

"Right." She flipped farther back. "I expect all that rusted machinery in the barn is going to have to be cleaned or sold or—forty-nine
sixteen."

" 'Thy terribleness hath deceived thee, and the pride of thine heart, O thou that dwellest in the clefts of the rock, that holdest the height of the hill: though thou shouldst make thy nest as high as the eagle, I will bring thee down.' "

"And have you noticed how the caterpillars have gotten under those eaves? There's a regular mess of them, last time I looked, and the other day Jeremy complained they're nesting in his building. Five thirty. And the woods by his windows need clearing—"

" 'A wonderful and horrible thing is committed in the land.' "

"The land, yes. All that land's just going to waste right now. Ten twenty-two."

" 'Behold, the noise of the bruit is coming, and a great commotion out of the north country, to make the cities of Judah desolate, and a den of dragons.' "

"Uh-huh." Deborah smoothed back a lock of hair and stared reflectively at the ceiling. "You said those cards are supposed to bring visions? The ones she gave Jeremy?"

"That's right."

"Do they really work?"

Sarr nodded, still facing the corner. "Of course they do. All magic works."

"Maybe we ought to tell Jeremy."

There was a pause. "I don't think the Lord means us to interfere. Consider it a part of his spiritual education."

"I wouldn't say—"

Sarr glanced impatiently over his shoulder. "Come on, Deb, let's get on with this."

"All right. Just one more." She leafed blindly through the pages. Her finger stabbed toward the words. "Five thirty."

" 'A wonderful and—' Wait a minute, we just did that."

Deborah peered at the words. "My Lord, you're right! That's funny." She turned to another passage and looked toward the ceiling, her finger poised above the page.

At that moment a staccato drumming echoed from somewhere above them. The sound seemed to start at one corner of the room and, like Freirs' footsteps earlier that night, to pass above their heads and beyond the farther wall. The cats looked up and growled, tails lashing.

"Oh, no!" groaned Deborah, laying aside the Bible. "Not again."

They'd been hearing it for the past few nights: the sound of tiny feet magnified by the reverberation of the wooden boards. Mice were up there, young ones, born just this spring and thriving in the past month's unseasonably warm temperatures; but as they ran across the attic floor, feet thumping on the floorboards, they sounded huge as weasels.

Sarr, still on his knees, was gazing toward the ceiling. He shook his head. "We'll have to let the cats get at them. There's nothing else to do."

"Oh, no, honey. I'll not have it! I'll not have them killing things." Protectively with her hands she reined in Dinah and Toby, drawing them toward her, but both continued to look longingly at the ceiling, making little sounds of eagerness and hunger deep in their throats.

Sarr got to his feet and came over to the bed. "Look," he said gently, "you don't want those creatures to keep you awake all night, do you? They'll just multiply, you know."

"Then you and I can go up there and put them out—give them a way to get outside, where they'll have more to eat. I'll not have any murdering in my house."

She closed the Bible and laid it back on the table, then settled down in bed, face turned toward the wall. Clearly this was to be her last word on the subject. Sarr, sighing, climbed in beside her and blew out the light just as another series of footsteps rattled overhead.

Soon, despite the occasional noise, both he and Deborah were sleeping soundly, chests rising and falling in a common rhythm. But all night long the seven cats looked up toward the ceiling, eyes wide, and growled.

Rosie came to see her that night. He seemed positively cherubic, all chuckles, winks, and smiles. It almost made her forget about what she'd seen in the restaurant the evening before.

"I just dropped by to see if they'd gotten that awful *gas* under control," he said, shaking his little head. "Frankly, young lady, I was worried about you."

He had brought her a gift in a large, flat cardboard box—*it's some kind of clothing,* thought Carol eagerly—but he wouldn't let her open it till after they'd talked. "First," he said, "I want to see those summaries you've been doing for me," waggling his plump finger with mock-schoolmasterly concern; but when she handed him her notes on the Cherokees and the aborigines he barely seemed to glance at them.

"Excellent, excellent," he said distractedly, shoving the papers into a folder and withdrawing a slim grey book. "It's clear to me now that you're ready to go deeper, young lady. High time I started giving you some language lessons."

*

Ghe'el . . . ghavoola . . .ghae'teine . . .

He gave her the lesson in her bedroom, Carol having invited him in; somehow the living room held bad associations for her now, and Rosie himself seemed just as happy to escape it. The two of them sat sipping iced tea, Carol on her bed and Rosie propped like an animated rag doll in the high-backed chair.

For more than an hour he read to her from the book he'd brought, an old, flimsily bound language text entitled *Some Notes on Agon di-Gatuan or "The Old Tongue," With Particular Respect to Its Suppression in the Malay Subcontinent. Appendiced with a Chian Song Cycle and Primer.* It had been privately printed in London in 1892, and the binding was now held together with black electrical tape. Rosie, face half buried in the book, would read a string of words aloud in a strange high singsong voice, and Carol was expected to repeat them with the same accent and intonation.

Riya migdl'eth . . . riya moghu . . .

"It's actually the only way to learn a language," he assured her. "The way a baby does—by imitation and constant repetition."

He seemed convinced that he was right, and surely he knew what he was talking about. But the words she repeated were meaningless to her, like catechisms in an alien religion; for the life of her she couldn't remember a single one only seconds after repeating it, and she couldn't understand how familiarizing herself with some obscure phrases from a long-dead native dialect was supposed to help her in her reading. What possible good was all this going to do her? What was this Old Language, anyway?

"It's rather special," Rosie explained, looking up from the book. "It's the language people speak when they speak in tongues."

This didn't sound right at all, but she didn't have the heart to argue with him. "I don't think I understand," she said, hoping he wouldn't lose patience with her. "What do the words mean?"

Rosie smiled. "It's a song about angels," he said. "One of the Dhol Chants."

"Dhol?" The word was somehow familiar.

"Yes, like in the Dynnod. You remember."

"But I thought that was Welsh," she said, thoroughly confused now, and already weary of it all. Maybe it was the heat; the iced tea didn't seem to be helping much. "How can something be Welsh and also Malayan and also be spoken in tongues if it's not—"

"Carol," he said gently, shaking his head, "the important thing is simply that you memorize this little rhyme." He returned to the book.

Migghe'el ghae'teine moghuvoola . . .

Carol struggled to say the words. They seemed formed for other mouths than hers, other tongues. Yet somehow Rosie didn't seem to mind; he just kept nodding and smiling and watching her with satisfaction in his eyes. The alien sounds reverberated in the room, as if every word she'd uttered were hanging in the air, filling the space around her like incense, softening the edges of things and making her so dizzy she couldn't think straight. Later she recalled Rosie patiently explaining something about "who the Vodies are," and wondered if she'd heard right; and there'd been something he'd said about "things hidden behind the clouds"—had she been dreaming?—and she vaguely recalled his promising to teach her the rules for ancient games, contests, dances, and she herself thinking how this, at least, would have a bearing on her work, maybe she could teach them to the children in the library . . .

"And next time," he added, "I'll teach you something special, the real names for the days of the week."

She wanted to ask him what he meant, why he was filling her head with such strange impossible things that made no sense at all, but he had gotten to his feet and was already opening the box on the night table.

"Because you've been such a good pupil," he said, eyes twinkling. He sliced the ribbon with a surprisingly sharp fingernail and lifted the lid. Inside, something pale lay covered by tissue paper. He reached down and withdrew a white silk short-sleeved dress that glimmered in the light.

She heard herself gasp. "Oh," she said, "how beautiful!"

She got up from the bed and felt the cloth; it ran like water in her hand. There was, she saw, no label in the back, or else it had been removed; maybe Rosie was embarrassed about where he'd bought it, or maybe he was ashamed of how expensive it was. She held it next to her body. The style was old-fashioned and a little full for her, yet it was cut rather short, almost embarrassingly so, in fact; she would have to keep her legs well together when she wore it. But oh, how lovely it was!

"I can't wait to try it on," she said.

Rosie shook his head. "I don't want you to. I'm sure it'll fit well enough." He flashed a sheepish grin. "Actually, I have to tell you, this dress originally belonged to a friend, but she only had a single opportunity to wear it, and, well"—he shrugged—"I wanted you to have it. You may find it a trifle large, but I think it will do fine. I've taken the liberty of having it altered."

"I'm sure it'll be perfect," said Carol.

"What I was hoping was, maybe, if you had some time, you could wear it this Saturday night. We could make an evening together, you and I—unless, of course, you have some nice young man to look after you, someone a bit more handsome than an old thing like me."

"Why no," she said, grateful for something to do, "that would be wonderful. I have no plans at all. Honestly, it's so sweet of you, Rosie, giving me something like this. You know, I've been *needing* a summer dress; I had absolutely nothing nice to wear."

He was nodding. "Good," he said. "When I saw that dress I immediately thought of you, because you see"—he smiled—"it's your natural color."

On his way home that evening, as he sits on one of the old folks' seats on the northbound bus, blinking at the passing lights and smiling at the occasional passengers who jostle him as they climb aboard, he thinks about the snow-white dress, the woman he's just left . . . and remembers the first time.

The first woman to wear that dress had been a farmer's daughter. Strong, better muscled than the slips of girls these days. And tediously pious. And trusting.

Like all first times, it hadn't gone very well.

The groundwork had been boring but necessary, exactly the sort of stupid sentimental story she'd been brought up to believe. He had told her he was going to marry her; he'd said he had great plans. He intended, he'd said, to make something of himself in the town. They had gone for long walks together, along country lanes and over the fields and through the woods.

Especially through the woods.

How she had enjoyed it, dreaming of the future with him! She had probably enjoyed it right up till the end.

He had tied the rope too tightly, that was his mistake. She'd been heavier than he'd thought, which had tightened the noose even more. And her struggles, once he'd gotten the dress off her, had made it tighter still, cutting off her wind before he'd gotten more than halfway through the other things he was supposed to do.

Oh, he had chanted the right words, and had drawn the necessary pictures in the earth below her as she struggled, and he'd even anointed her body with the black powder, in the special way the Master had prescribed . . .

He had tied that rope much too tightly, though. That had been his big mistake. She had died far sooner than he'd intended.

But then, he had just turned twenty-two, and this had only been a dry run, an experiment. He was still young. He would practice.

Next time, he vowed, he would get it right.

JULY EIGHTH

Good to get up in the country again: warm breeze, sunshine, sound of birds outside. Lay in bed listening to them late into the morning. Sarr was off clearing brush from the area just beyond the stream, & every so often I could hear his scythe ring out as it struck against a particularly thick branch. Deborah was closer by, just behind the house, hanging laundry on the clothesline. (Must remember to give her these pajamas of mine, maybe also the bedsheets. The dampness around here makes it harder to keep things clean.) Later heard her working in her garden; from time to time she'd call out to one or another of the cats, scolding them for going after birds.

Trouble getting out of bed; actually, slept poorly last night, awakened from time to time by what must be mice running across my ceiling. (*Hope* it's mice, anyway, & not rats!)

Don't know exactly what time it was when I finally got up, but I felt famished & really had to force myself to do my exercises. Guess it's because I missed another day. Somehow I only managed to do twenty-seven pushups, though I was supposed to do forty. I'm slipping back—better watch that.

Managed all of Le Fanu's "Carmilla" before lunch. Wonderful allusions to forbidden books: *Magia Posthuma, Phlegon de Mirabilibus, Augustinus de cura pro Mortuis,* and something called *Philosophicae et Christianae Cogitationes de Vampiris* by John Christofer Harenberg. Oh, for a peek at such stuff!

Eggs for lunch, from our hens. Still can't say I taste any difference, though Deborah seems to take it as an article of faith that country eggs must taste better than week-old city ones; so I humor her & smack my lips & tell her that there's simply no comparison. I'm beginning to think that country people have to have it confirmed, every so often, that they've made the right choice.

After lunch, hit the books again. Started *Tales of Hoffman* but put it aside; ugly, disturbing, & a hell of a long way from the Nutcracker Suite. Next, prompted by that odd phallic image in Carol's dream & by something Sarr mentioned at dinner last night about there being an unusual prevalence of snakes around here this summer (just my luck!), took down Stoker's *Lair of the White Worm,* about some legendary monster surviving beneath an old Derbyshire castle.

At first it made a welcome change of pace: not too subtle, I suppose, but I liked the references to local history & to a place the author called "Diana's Grove." (Cf. "Lucky's Grove" in the Wakefield tale, sacred to the evil god Loki.) After a few chapters, though, my attention began to wander; I got tired of waiting for the goddamned Worm to show up & was put off by the uninspired prose. Dutifully the book brought in the whole supernatural grab bag—the Druids, the rites of ancient Rome, even a discussion of African voodoo—but there was somehow no magic in any of it, & no real feeling.

So I occupied myself out here till dinnertime with scissors & a can of insect spray, cutting away the ivy that's grown across my windows. Those little green shoots fasten themselves onto the screens & cling like drowning men, practically ripping out the wire when I pull at them. Something almost frightening about their tenacity—all that mindless, unshakable will. The spiders living among them seem timid in comparison, scrambling frantically for cover in the leaves. I only killed a few that seemed inclined to stand their ground; & now, here at this rickety old table, with the windows dark & nothing but the screens between me & what's alive out there, I'm teasing myself with Hammer Films visions of how the survivors might take their revenge. Wish, now, I hadn't killed any—or else had killed them all . . .

Beef with noodles for dinner tonight, praise the Lord, & apple pie for dessert. Drifted into the kitchen a bit early; didn't know what time it was, but knew I was hungry & smelled something good. So did the cats. All seven of them were assembled by the back door waiting to be fed, milling back & forth with tails swishing, Bwada growling at the others, & I had to push my way through them to get inside (stepping over the usual assortment of bloody mice & moles which they'd laid out for inspection & which I was careful to avoid looking at). Deborah was humming some sort of hymn; she seemed glad to have me around.

Just then there was a chorus of miaows from outside the door, followed by the clank of an overturned garbage can & the sound of little claws scrabbling down the back steps. Above all this I could hear Sarr swearing—words I'd never heard him use before—& a few moments later he walked into the kitchen clutching his hand to announce, with some amusement, "I've just been bitten by a corpse!"

At least he'd thought it was a corpse.

He had just come back from the fields, hungry for his dinner and for human company. The cats had been waiting for him there on the porch, purring and rubbing up against his ankles as they displayed their day's catch—all the luckless little animals they'd pounced on in the grass.

Listen to them purr! he thought. *They're just natural-born killers.*
Yet the Lord must love them more than He loves a sinner like me . . .
He stooped to pick up the nearest body, a tiny brown field mouse.
Good-natured Azariah, striped like a plump tiger, purred and butted
his head against Poroth's arm. "Away with you!" he muttered, cuffing
the cat lightly with the back of his hand. Gingerly he picked the mouse
up by the tail and tossed it into the garbage can.

A young goldfinch was next—a good thing Deborah hadn't seen!—
and then another mouse. Stooping a fourth time, he paused. The one
remaining body looked different from the rest.

At first he'd taken it for the remnant of some larger animal—a fox's
paw, perhaps, the stump of a severed limb—until, crouching down to
get a closer look, he saw four legs, like little sticks or twigs, and exposed
along one end, a row of tiny yellow teeth.

The thing was black, burned-looking, with the texture of dirt and
dead leaves; it looked like a child's clumsy attempt to fashion an animal. He realized, quite suddenly, what it must be: the dried and swollen body of a shrew. It appeared to have been dragged across the
ground, or even buried; no doubt, too, it had been well mauled by the
cats, for the mouth was all askew, nearly vertical, in fact, and there
was soil and mold still clinging to its fur. He looked in vain for eyes,
and for a tail to lift it by. Grimacing, he was forced to grasp the thing
tentatively around the middle. It felt odd to the touch, like picking up
a crumbling clod of earth.

Suddenly it moved. He felt it twist in his hand and bite him on the
thumb. With a yell he dropped it and watched it patter off into the
grass, with Bwada and the rest in frantic pursuit.

"Come back here!" he called, but the cats paid no heed. It was nearly
the end of dinner before they returned, with nothing to show for their
chase.

" 'Twasn't dead at all, you see." He scooped himself a final helping of
salad. "Must have been just feigning, like a 'possum."

"Well, I just hope you don't go getting rabies," said Deborah. "You
never know in the summertime, and it's a death I wouldn't wish on
Lucifer himself."

"I'm not dead yet," said Sarr, extending his hand. "See? It didn't
even pierce the skin."

"Looks okay to me," agreed Freirs. "I hope you're not going to start
foaming at the mouth right here at the dinner table!"

Deborah shook her head. "I don't know," she said. "I hear flittermice
in these parts carry rabies—"

"Bats," explained Sarr, to Freirs' puzzled look.

"—and who knows what other things might be infected. This is one time I'd feel safer if a doctor were around." She was still fretful as she began clearing away the plates.

"Hey," said Freirs, "do you suppose house mice can get rabies?"

"Why?" Sarr was absently examining his thumb.

"Because I think I've got mice living up in my attic back there."

"You too?" said Deborah, from the sink. "This sure seems to be the season for them."

Sarr nodded. "Yes," he said, "we've been hearing them too." He glanced at Deborah, then dropped his voice. "Want me to let the cats up there?"

"I heard that," said Deborah, "and the answer's no! Jeremy will just have to learn to make friends with them."

Freirs smiled. "Sure," he said, "I'll fit 'em out with little sneakers." He turned to Deborah. "But I hope they're not going to keep it up all summer. It's going to make it hard to get to sleep."

Sarr was regarding him somberly. "Just make sure you don't sleep on your back. And if you do, make sure you don't snore."

"Why's that?"

"So if one of them gnaws through the ceiling, he won't fall in your mouth."

Freirs laughed, until he saw that the other wasn't smiling. "I think that'd be a lot worse for the mouse than for me."

"Don't be too sure," said Sarr. "I once read about a man who was killed by a mouse that ran right up his arm and jumped into his mouth. Somehow it got wedged in the man's throat and almost bit its way right through."

From the sink came an exasperated "Honey!"

"What happened?" asked Freirs.

"Both of them suffocated, man and mouse." Sarr saw the expression of disbelief on Freirs' face. "It's a true story," he said. "There was even a picture. I'll never forget it." He could still see, in the crude Victorian illustration, the terrified face of the man's wife, and the man's wide-open mouth and staring eyes as the small dark thing leaped toward him.

"I think it served him right," said Deborah, returning to the table with a bowl of fresh fruit. "He was probably trying to kill the mouse, when he could have just turned it out of doors." She nudged Freirs with her elbow. "Bet you didn't know he was such a one for tall tales, did you?"

"Say what you like," said Sarr. "*You* believe me, don't you, Jeremy?"

Freirs laughed. "Well, frankly, no. But just the same, I think I'll sleep with my mouth shut tonight."

*

There's one of the little bastards right now!

Lying here in bed, listening to sounds above my head. A moment ago it was one of my little friends in the attic; just before that was an airplane, the first I've heard all week. It seemed to pass directly over the farm; I can still hear the roar of its engines receding in the distance. Such a familiar sound, once upon a time—& now it seems like something from another world!

Sounds in the woods, too. The trees really come close to my windows on one side, & there's always some kind of stirring coming from the underbrush, below the everpresent tapping on the screens. A million creatures out there, probably. Most of them insects & spiders, I guess, plus a colony of frogs in the swampy part of the woods, & maybe even skunks and raccoons. Depending on your mood, you can either ignore the sounds & just go to sleep or—as I'm doing now—remain awake listening to them.

When I lie here thinking about what's out there, & how easily I can be seen, I feel vulnerable, unprotected, like I'm in a display case. So guess I'll put away this writing & turn off the light.

Darkness fills the apartment—darkness and the weary droning of an air conditioner, as if the two were coterminous, the droning the sound of the darkness itself as it settles like a veil over floors and furniture, stretching across doorways, masking books on shelves and pictures on the wall. The droning muffles other sounds; the apartment is an isolated cavern, cut off from the world and beyond the reach of time.

Outside, twelve floors down, the weekend has begun. Friday night has reached its zenith, dawn is still five hours away, and the streets are filled with noise: music, voices, distant sirens. The planet rolls serenely into blackness, the stars hidden by haze. Overhead a yellow gibbous moon, one day wide of half, glares down upon the city like a cat's eye.

Within the apartment an occasional band of light reflected from the headlights of some passing car sweeps the high ceiling and slides down a wall, picking out a small framed picture, crude as a child's, done on yellowed paper cracked with age—the picture of a naked girl standing side by side with some tiny black animal. Below it an older hand has written simply, *Marriage*.

Otherwise the darkness is unbroken, save for a single cone of yellow light, a candle flame within it, falling from the gooseneck lamp upon the table where the old man sits working.

He sits crouched forward, staring intently at the instruments before him on the table: the straw mat, the bone needle, the pliers, the little bowl of amber fluid, the guttering candle in its brass candlestick, the shard of metal. His own face is painted like a savage's, streaks of color emanating from his eyes and mouth and a heavy black line down the center of his forehead where he's rubbed the holy powder. He looks like a lion, a sunburst, a flower as big as a man. Around his neck, on a knotted leather thong, he wears something resembling a pendant, something curved and yellowing and hard: an index finger—human, female—that, one short week before, pressed the buttons of an elevator downtown.

He picks up the metal shard in the pliers and holds it in the flame. His old-man's breath is audible as he waits for the metal to grow hot, smoke, turn red . . . When it is glowing he places it upon the straw mat before him and, with the bone needle, scratches the first sign into its surface. Picking the shard up once more with the pliers, he dips it in the bowl of amber liquid. The liquid bubbles and hisses; a little puff of foul-smelling steam rises up the cone of light. The old man croons a certain word and smiles.

He smiles because the sign has taken; the ceremony will not be in vain. Counting to himself, he turns toward the window beside him in time to see a single star glimmer in the night sky. He watches it float-ing just beyond the window, centered in the topmost pane. Then, as the count is repeated, it dims and disappears behind a wave of mist. The old man expels his breath and turns back to his work.

The visitor is out there now, somewhere in the Jersey hills—he can feel it. All week long he has seen the evidence of its arrival, felt the changes, read the signs. Now he can be sure. It has come.

Once more he holds the metal shard within the cat's-eye of flame that sputters atop the candle; once more the shard grows smoky, blackened, and turns red. He lays it on the straw and scratches another sign.

Another step. There are always steps to follow, rules to be observed. Funny, that he of all people should have to play by the rules. The visi-tor must find it funny too. The Old One has not seen the visitor, not for more than a century, but he knows what must be happening: some-where in the Jersey hills the process has begun. It will continue now, advancing ever more quickly, ravenous as a flame.

The flame spreads outward and licks against the metal. He holds it forth again. The signs he's scratched so far are intricate and tiny— tiny like the visitor, seemingly insignificant, easy to overlook.

But tomorrow at this time, once he's gotten the woman to perform the Ghavoola, the White Ceremony—why, then the thing will be free to advance a step up the ladder . . .

He places the metal shard back on the mat, whispering another word as he scratches the third and final sign. It is hard to repress a smile.

Even though he knows how it all must end, he feels a certain excitement at what is to happen now. Already the woman has performed a useful service; she has played the proper messenger. But now it is time for her to garb herself in white, step forward, and assume her rightful role.

The metal is still hot, still glowing. Smiling, the paint streaks curving on his cheeks, he picks it up with the pliers and touches it to the tip of the severed finger hanging around his neck.

The finger twitches, as if recoiling from the heat.

He pulls the metal away and examines it, turning it over and over before him. The shapes scratched on its surface gleam evilly in the lamplight.

He whispers the Fifth Name. The blade is ready.

JULY NINTH

He arrived at seven that evening, exactly when he'd said he would. More than an hour of daylight still remained, but the sun was hidden behind a row of buildings and the avenue was dark beneath their shadows. "I'll wait for you down here," he shouted into the intercom. "I've got the car tonight."

The car? Then perhaps they'd be driving somewhere outside the city—what a relief that would be, on a night as hot as this. Crossing her fingers, she hurried down the hall toward the elevator.

Behind her she was leaving an apartment full of work. She had meant to spend all day on Rosie's project; she'd been absolutely determined to complete the task today, for earlier this week he'd provided her with a formidable array of new journal articles and reports with a host of arcane-sounding titles—*Seventeen Years among the Sea Dyaks of Borneo* (London, 1882), *Holiday Customs in Malta, with Sports, Usages, Ceremonies, Omens and Superstitions of the Maltese People* (Valletta, 1894)—but it had been so enervatingly hot in the apartment, even with the windows open, that she'd lain in bed as if drugged until afternoon and had put off starting work till just a few hours before. Hours of reading still awaited her tomorrow; she'd have to spend all day catching up.

Somehow, despite the pay, her initial enthusiasm for the project had waned. The papers had proven to be less interesting than she'd hoped, and Rosie, too, had continued to show surprisingly little interest in her summaries, barely glancing at them except to praise them mechanically and make out her paychecks, never once quizzing her on the material. The entire project had begun to seem more and more like busywork.

It felt good to escape the stuffy apartment, just as it was going to feel good to get out of the city. The thought of escape was so welcome, in fact, that it almost made her forget how unwell she'd been feeling all day. But as she pressed the button on the wall and waited for the elevator to ascend, the throbbing weakness in her legs reminded her that she would have to make this an early night. She'd been having stomach cramps since morning, and now it seemed as if a metal band were tightening round her head. Her period was due, and as she stepped into the elevator she felt the familiar heaviness, a fullness in her stom-

ach, breasts, and thighs. A good thing the dress Rosie'd given her was
so loose. It was too loose, in fact, obviously fit for someone with a bigger
frame than hers; though whoever'd altered it had made the hem awfully high. *Still,* she told herself, *I have to wear it, I simply couldn't
say no; after all, it was a gift . . .*

Rosie wasn't waiting for her in the hall, nor was he on the front steps
when she emerged. She looked in vain for him until a horn sounded farther up the block. She recognized the car and, dimly, the little pink
smiling face inside. He was waving.

As she neared the car he jumped out and ran around to the other
side to open the door for her, just as if the old Chevy were a coach and
four and she the princess he'd been waiting for all his long life. He
himself appeared rather dapper in a blue-and-white seersucker suit,
though she believed she noticed an odd little streak of red just below
his ear. It looked like lipstick; perhaps the old scamp had a woman
somewhere.

"You look absolutely ravishing, my dear," he said, eyeing her up
and down. "That dress suits you perfectly. I only wish I were forty
years younger!" His eyes twinkled. "And I'm glad to see you wore
your nice white shoes, that's very sensible of you. I *knew* you were a
sensible girl."

He's being silly, she thought, but she felt a rush of pleasure at the
attention. "Actually, the shoes belong to Rochelle," she said. "I'm surprised she didn't take them with her. They're a little too big for me. I
had to put tissue paper in the toes."

"That's my girl!" He beamed. "I'm sure Rochelle won't mind. And
just look at you, you're a vision—a vision all in white." With a mock-
courtly bow he took her arm, about to help her into the car, but suddenly he paused, just as she was bending to get in. "Uh-oh," she heard
him say, "this will never do."

She straightened up and saw that he was frowning. Though he
quickly averted his eyes, she realized he'd been staring at her hips. He
was obviously embarrassed. She studied herself nervously, already
worried about her period. Clearing his throat, he leaned toward her
and spoke in a near whisper. "I think, Carol, that with a dress as thin
as that one, you might be better advised to wear, shall we say, under-
garments of the same color."

She looked down and blushed. He was right. The pink panties she
was wearing showed clearly through the thin fabric of the dress.

Even as a voice inside her said *And what if they do? They look sexy,*
she heard herself stammering apologies to him as if she'd committed
some terrible faux pas. "I'll run up and change right now," she said.
"It'll only take a minute."

She hurried back toward her apartment, hot with embarrassment,
aware of his eyes watching her as she climbed the front steps. Upstairs

in her bedroom, feeling like a little girl who'd been naughty and didn't know why, she removed the panties and slipped on a pair of white ones from her drawer. *There,* she thought, standing before the mirror, *now I really* am *a vision in white . . .* She checked once more in the mirror, half afraid that the delta of red hair below her stomach might be showing through the filmy cloth; but no, she was pale as a statue.

He was still standing by the car when she came back down the steps and seemed so genuinely pleased to see her that her mood brightened again. He hadn't really meant any harm, she told herself, he hadn't meant to embarrass her; it was really her own fault. And he hadn't been looking at her lecherously, not at all, he was just a prissy old grandfather type who wanted her to look her best.

"Wonderful," he said, "that's a considerable improvement. Now I know that I can take my little girl *anywhere!*" He helped her into the car and began to close the door. "Whoops, watch your fingers now. Don't want you to lose any!"

She tugged her dress down as she sat waiting for him to get in. She hoped there'd be no more remarks about her clothes and was determined to change the subject. *I can take my little girl anywhere,* he had said; perhaps it would be someplace fancy. She would love a fancy place tonight, with white tablecloths and roses, dark red roses, a vase of them on every table.

"Are you going to tell me where we're going," she asked, as he climbed in beside her, "or will it be a surprise?"

He turned the key, and the engine sputtered to life. "As a matter of fact," he said, a little smile playing about his lips, "we're going someplace special tonight, in honor of our first fortnight together."

"Oh?"

"Yes," he said, watching her out of the corner of his eye as he pulled out into the street. "Tonight I'm taking you to Coney Island."

He had been joking, of course, at least in part. As soon as he'd seen the uncertainty and disappointment on her face—disappointment she hadn't been able to hide—he'd laughed and explained that, in fact, their destination was a charming little Scandinavian restaurant near Cobble Hill in Brooklyn, where he'd already made reservations.

But afterward—after a delicious meatless meal with homemade chocolate cake shared between them, and nearly half a bottle of Rosie's nameless wine that he'd produced from a cooler in the back seat and brought into the restaurant with him—he turned to her and said, "Now it's time to keep my promise. Next stop, Coney Island!"

It sounded like fun, now that dinner had been such a treat. She had heard of Coney Island ever since she'd been a little girl, but she'd never been there. "Isn't it sort of—you know, dangerous?" she asked, as they made their way along the quiet sidewalk toward the car. Brooklyn was different from her own neighborhood; now that it was night she heard the faint sound of crickets, and the city seemed far away. She found that it made her think of Jeremy.

"Dangerous?" he was saying. "You mean lots of blacks and Puerto Ricans?"

"Well . . . yes, I guess so."

He smiled reassuringly. "There's nothing to worry about. There are lots of people there, people of all types, but they're all just interested in having a good time, you'll see. Besides, I keep telling you—tonight's a special night. I'd never put my little girl in any danger!" The smile widened. "Or myself, either! Just between the two of us, I intend to live forever!"

He snapped on the headlights and spun the steering wheel, and they set out through the darkened streets. Rosie had insisted that she wear her seat belt and shoulder harness and wore his as well; like other old people he was an awkward, hesitant driver who tended to go too slow. He was so short he had to crane his neck to see over the wheel, and he kept peering back and forth at every cross street, proceeding with extreme caution as if unsure of the way.

"Are you looking for signs?" she asked.

"What? *Signs?*" He darted her a nervous glance.

"For Coney Island."

"Oh!" He laughed. "No, no, not really, I just want to get us there safe and sound. You can't be too careful, that's what I always say." He patted the dashboard. "Never was fond of these contraptions."

She soon saw that she'd been wrong; he did know the way, even in the darkness through the back streets of Brooklyn. Once she even saw him looking up through the windshield rather than at the road, as if he was navigating by the stars. Within a few minutes they were rolling down Shore Parkway, the water on their right with the lights of tankers reflected in it, a warm wind rushing through the open windows. Faster traffic passed them by. Behind them, across the water, she saw Staten Island and the glowing form of the Statue of Liberty; ahead stretched the Verrazano Bridge, a spiderweb of cables and lights. The highway passed beneath the nearest arch, an immense gateway, and as the little car moved through it, she felt the bridge pass over her like a wave. It was like entering a new country or, on a certain midnight, a new year, feeling the change wash through her every cell; she felt invigorated now, as if breathing cleaner air—as if her cares, her loneliness, her poverty were in that other world behind her.

In the distance ahead of them, across Gravesend Bay, gleamed the lights of the amusement park. One tall structure, shaped like a palm tree, stood out above the others.

"The parachute jump," said Rosie. "I think we'll pass it up. There's so much else to do."

She was looking toward the lights, enjoying the pleasures of expectation, when the car passed a group of running shapes on the stretch of grass to their right—late-night joggers? fleeing fugitives? It was impossible to tell, they'd gone by so fast, but somehow the vision had been unnerving, those heaving brutish shapes . . .

Moments later she felt a little bump beneath the car. Looking back, straining against the constricting web of her shoulder harness, she could see the dark, humped form of some small animal dead behind them on the highway. Rosie appeared not to notice. They hadn't killed it, she told herself, it had obviously been dead a long time. Still, her mood of expectancy was dimmed.

It was dimmed even more when, after Rosie had pulled into a commercial parking lot on Neptune Avenue near the boardwalk and they'd gotten out, she heard the roll of distant thunder.

"Maybe we'd better stay close to the car," she said, eyeing the sky uncertainly. It looked clear enough now, though, the half moon almost supernaturally bright, and she could see stars up there she never saw in Manhattan's hazy skies.

Rosie, she saw, was shaking his head and smiling, not even bothering to glance up.

"Don't worry," he said, "I heard the report. The rain'll hold off for a while yet. We'll have time to do one or two things, I promise you." He reflected a moment. "In fact, we'll have time to do *three* things, three delights: the ferris wheel, the beach, and"—he cocked his head—"and a surprise."

Ahead of them ran the dark length of the boardwalk, dividing the beach from the amusement area. The ferris wheel rose gaudily in the distance, twirling like a great jeweled pinwheel. As they drew closer, the crowds increased—young people mostly, brown and black and white, a few in beards and yarmulkes, couples and groups of boys and, even on a Saturday night, many families with children in strollers or carriages. The air was filled with a cacophony of music and voices: disco piped from a dodgem-car emporium near Nathan's, salsa from an all-night *cuchifrito* stand, rock songs sounding hard and tinny from hand-held radios, calliope music from a carousel on the next block, screams from the roller coaster rumbling overhead with CYCLONE outlined in colored lights on its side, the cries of food vendors selling pizza, Italian sausages, clams on the half shell, saltwater taffy, cotton candy, buttered corn on the cob. Young men in colorful booths hawked games of skill and chance, as if this were some electrified Arabian bazaar. Carol heard the whoop of an occasional siren, maniacal laughter from a loudspeaker outside the funhouse, wild animal sounds from the

safari ride, the buzz and grate and clank and rattle of a hundred attractions that, all around them now, were flashing with lights, constantly in motion—a whole new world of movement, of strange,
gargantuan machine shapes whirling and spinning and bobbing and
dipping like a factory gone mad.

An area devoted entirely to kiddie rides reminded her of the children's section at Voorhis, fond parents grinning at offspring who rode
miniature fire engines round and round in endless circles, and racing
cars, dune buggies, helicopters, pony carts, old-time autos, boats that
churned slowly through a shallow ring of water, spaceships that
echoed the huge silver Moon Rocket looming beside the boardwalk, a
scale-model kiddie roller coaster (*That's the only kind they'll ever get
me on,* thought Carol), a half-sized Tilt-a-Whirl, a serpentine caterpillar ride with wide eyes and broad grin, a beleaguered-looking merry-
go-round, music issuing from it, with mirrored panels and peeling
paint and horses that looked somehow gaunt and starved.

"I'm dizzy," said Carol, "this place is like a dream," instinctively
drawing closer to Rosie as he threaded his way through the crowd. She
felt particularly vulnerable in her white dress, which stood out from
all the clothes around her and which she feared would be stained by ice
cream or mustard or a spilled glass of orangeade. Food and drink were
everywhere, carried in every hand, forever underfoot; the smell of fried
things and spices and the sugar smell of cotton candy hung in the air.
She thought of her period again and wondered if her headache would
come back. The wine they'd had at dinner was already making her
sleepy.

"We'll try the ferris wheel first," said Rosie, turning to her and raising his voice to make himself heard. "Maybe it'll help us get our bear-
ings." He nodded toward the immense structure now ahead of them, a
hundred fifty feet of steel and light bulbs called the Wonder Wheel.
The seats were enclosed within metal cages lined with wire screening;
the outer cages had the better view, while an inner ring of cages
slipped back and forth, swinging wildly on short metal tracks.

Carol looked around and lost sight of Rosie, then saw his diminutive
form by the ticket booth. He returned to her bearing two yellow tic-
kets. "Come," he said, "we'll take an outside car. You're not scared,
are you?"

Carol hesitated. "Well, I've been on ferris wheels before, at county
fairs . . . but never anything this big."

He chuckled. "Don't worry," he said, ushering her into a waiting
car, "it's no more dangerous than going up in an elevator."

The car was large. Half a dozen people were already inside, seated on
two small wooden benches. She and Rosie took their seats on the third,
Carol making sure the seat was clean before sitting down. An attendant slid the door shut, enclosing them all within the wire cage.

There was a sudden vibration; the great wheel began to turn. The car
gave a lurch and was airborne. On the bench behind them a couple
began talking urgently in Spanish; on the farther seat a small, nervous
child asked its parents, "When's it gonna stop?"

The car did stop, halfway up the side of the circle, while down below
two more cars were filled. Just outside the cage glowed a row of bare
light bulbs, with thousands more ringing the wheel, illuminating the
thick iron cogs, the peeling turquoise paint, the rusting chicken wire
that stretched like a spiderweb between the metal braces, as if warning
that, up close, the material world was but an insubstantial thing, with
gaps yawning wide.

Carol turned and looked behind her, at the grotesque illuminated facade of Spook-a-Rama, with its strange twenty-foot-tall monster grinning at the onlookers and the walls polkadotted with signs: SEE
DRACULA'S SCREAMING HEAD CHOPPED OFF! SEE FRANKENSTEIN
SPEAKING FROM THE GRAVE! SPECIAL TODAY: SEE THE INVISIBLE MAN.
She smiled and was going to bring the last to Rosie's attention when
the car gave another lurch and once more began to rise. Signs advertising Bat Woman, Cat Woman, Screechy Nell, and Coffin Nanny
flashed past, come-ons for Meatless Bony Sam and Skully the Ghost
Head dropped away beneath them, and, with a chorus of *oohs* and *ahs*
from the other seats, they found themselves in the air, nearing the top
of the wheel, the car rocking gently with the motion.

Once again it slowed to a halt as more people climbed on, but now
the whole amusement park was laid out at their feet, a wilderness of
lights, the rides below them twisting along their miniature tracks like
children's toys beneath a Christmas tree, others spinning like beach
umbrellas. Behind them came terrified, delighted screams from the
roller coaster. Across Surf Avenue, before a wall of housing projects, a
BMT subway train rumbling along its elevated track looked like just
another ride, as if the entire city out there to the west were merely one
vast amusement park.

"It's beautiful!" said Carol.

Rosie looked up and blinked distractedly at the scene; he had been
peering at his watch. "Yes," he said, "I knew you'd like it." He
hummed a little song to himself and sat back in the seat, staring not at
the world below but at the sky.

On the right, in the distance, she could see the outline of the Verrazano Bridge. Nearer, to the left, stretched the expanse of boardwalk
and dark sand and, beyond it, the darker ocean, with rows of lights reflected in the water, miles off, where freighters lay mysteriously at an-
chor. A combination of sounds drifted up to her, music and voices,
machines and distant waves, like a flood of all the memories in the
world.

Another lurch; the car began its descent, the great wheel fell away, and they seemed to be settling downward without apparent support, slipping toward the sound and lights and the dark walls rising up to block the view.

They went around a second time. Once more the boardwalk, beach, and ocean dropped into view, Carol wondering what lands lay beyond the dark horizon. She felt a sudden tickle on her hand and looked down to see a tiny six-spotted ladybug crawling diligently over her thumb, like a shiny little red plastic toy from the amusement park below. "Hello, bug," she said, "are you coming for a ride with us?" She held her hand out to Rosie, who smiled wanly.

"When this is over," he said, "we'll take a walk along the sand, how'll that be?"

"That will be fine," she said, looking back toward the beach.

As the wheel turned, the car on the inner track ahead of them rolled clatteringly toward their own. Carol gave a little gasp of alarm but felt foolish when, to a chorus of screams within it, the other car swung away just before it hit them. Rosie smiled, and Carol looked down to find the bug was gone. Scared off, she supposed.

On the next ascent, Carol felt the same excitement as the car rose to the top of the wheel and the scenery lay spread out below, and the same inevitable disappointment as the car moved onward, back toward the ground. The view had become precious to her because of its very transience, a glimpse from a moving platform. Sometimes her own life, too, seemed as fleeting.

"I wonder if we'll get another time around," she said.

"Hmm? Oh, no, I imagine this will be the last," said Rosie. He seemed preoccupied; he'd been staring with rigid fascination at the light bulb that glowed just beyond the window of the car. She peered at it just in time to see a small red dot with black legs mashed burning against the heated glass of the bulb, but then the car scraped noisily along the exit track and an attendant was hauling open the metal doors and urging people out. She followed Rosie toward the passageway, feeling disturbed but unable to express it. Her head had begun to ache again.

"Come," he was saying. "Let's see what it's like down by the water."

They walked up a nearby ramp to the boardwalk, continuing on it past a line of food stands, tattoo parlors, and fortune-telling booths. From the space below their feet came the sound of soul music and salsa; dimly she heard voices. Ahead of them another ramp led out onto the sand, which stretched away toward the shifting black line of surf.

The beach looked mysterious in the moonlight, dotted here and there with shapes that could have been dreamers or driftwood or corpses. She followed Rosie out onto the sand, feeling it give beneath her shoes, making walking difficult. She took the shoes off and held them in her hand, walking barefoot, the sand deliciously cold between her toes.

Rosie turned and watched what she was doing. "Be careful," he said, with a hint of disapproval, "there's a lot of broken glass around here."

Behind them, in the darkness beneath the boardwalk, she could make out the shapes of teenagers smoking, listening to radios, or embracing in the sand. She turned away, the sound of the music receding as she moved slowly toward the water. To her right a black couple stood and kissed in the middle of an empty stretch of beach, like a tree standing alone on an arid plain. Beyond them she saw the lights of a steel pier extending into the water; past that, much farther past, she could see the lights of ships. On either side of her, jetties of huge boulders thrust deep into the surf.

As she and Rosie drew closer to the water's edge, the sound of radios, the music of the carousels and games, was lost behind the steady roar of waves.

"Follow me," said Rosie, a touch of urgency in his voice. "Let's get far away from everybody else." He began walking along the edge of the water, away from the lights. Beside them the waves seemed to make an angrier noise, though in the darkness their height was difficult to judge. Once again Carol heard the distant roll of thunder and wondered how long it would be before the rain came.

They walked along the water, saying nothing. Gradually they came to a stretch of beach where the garbage seemed less plentiful and where Carol could find no other people, unless there were couples crouched unseen in the sand making love. The only shapes on that stretch of beach were the seagulls, scattered over the sand like ghostly white statues. The birds made no sound at all, nor did they take to the air when the two of them walked past; they simply turned and watched the pair, as if waiting.

Abruptly Rosie stopped and looked down at the water. "I think we've gone far enough," he said. "Let's go back now." He walked a little way, then stopped. "Funny," he said suddenly. "Come over here right now and I'll show you a trick."

He was pointing to a certain spot at his feet where the ocean had just gone out. Nearby, up from the water's edge, lay a curving line of clam shells, like ashtrays half filled with sand; they reminded her somehow of the dead animal they'd passed on the highway. "If you stand right here with me," he said, "and hold my hand real tight, I guarantee you won't get wet."

Carol moved next to him. "You'd better take your shoes off like I did," she said. "The next wave's going to soak your feet up to the ankles."

But he was putting his finger to his lips. "Sssshhh," he whispered, "you have to know the trick. Just close your eyes and try not to move."

She did as she was told, and heard the hiss of the oncoming wave. She shut her eyes tightly, expecting to feel the chill of water sweeping

by, but felt instead old Rosie throw his arms around her, and heard the
sudden raucous cries of seagulls screaming up and down the beach.
She was so surprised that she opened her eyes; Rosie was gazing
fiercely up at the moon, and just in front of them the wave was parting, sweeping past them without so much as touching . . .

She shut her eyes again and felt the old man relax his hold. "Sorry if
I scared you," he was saying gently, his voice soft, almost intimate.
"You can open your eyes now."

She looked down. "Rosie, that was wonderful!" she said. "How did
you do it?"

He was already ambling away. "Just a question of finding the right
spot," he said over his shoulder. "It's a game we old-timers know.
Nothing to it, really."

He began to whistle. Above him in the blackness the half-moon
floated over the beach like an alien presence, holding something unnatural in its geometries. She trudged after him through the sand, her feet
as dry as if she'd stayed indoors.

The music and the screams were louder now. They were passing
through a line of arcades below the boardwalk, ignoring the entice-
ments of the vendors. SHOOT THE RAPIDS! SHOOT THE HOOPS! proclaimed the billboards. They passed the peeling facade of the World in
Wax Musée but didn't stop to go inside.

Rosie, in fact, seemed to be rushing her. He had actually taken her
hand as they'd walked up from the beach, mumbling something about
"rain coming soon, time enough for one more ride," and he'd persuaded
her, shamed her, into going on the one thing she'd vowed she'd never
do. They were heading toward the roller coaster.

Next to it loomed the entranceway of the Hell Hole, a giant red
Satan in front holding a pitchfork obscenely from his crotch. ALL YE
WHO ENTER HERE, ABANDON HOPE, a signboard read. Satan seemed
to leer as they passed.

"I think he's trying to warn us to go home," said Carol, nervousness
constricting her chest.

"What? Who?" Rosie seemed distracted again; he had been looking
up at the stars.

"Satan," said Carol. "I think he knows where we're going."

Rosie let out a sputter of laughter. "Satan? Who's he?" She felt his
grip tighten on her hand; he was leading her toward the ticket booth.
"Come on," he said, "the line's moving now, I think we'll make this
run."

The open red cars were filling up quickly. Carol was about to slip
into one of those in the middle, but Rosie steered her toward in the

rear. "It's better here," he said. "I mean, you won't find it so frightening, your first time. Trust me." The hand tightened on hers once more.

"Okay," said Carol, swallowing. She felt a chill sea breeze on her neck and, sitting beside him, removed a light blue kerchief from her purse and tied it around her throat; it was going to get colder when the ride started. Rosie was looking up again, but then he turned to her and frowned.

"What's the matter?" asked Carol.

"That kerchief," said Rosie. He was reaching for it. "It's *much* too nice. I really don't think you ought to wear it here. It might blow away, and then you'll go blaming poor old me! Here." He unfastened it and handed her a clean white handkerchief from his jacket pocket. "Put yours away and wear this. If you lose it, it won't be any loss. Come on, now, Carol, the ride will be starting in a moment."

She fastened the handkerchief around her chin and huddled down beside him. Her heart was pounding so hard she could almost hear it above the thunder of the other cars and the screams of the riders. Or perhaps it *was* the thunder she was hearing . . . A burly attendant came down the line at last to fasten them into their seats with leather waist straps.

"Don't *worry* so," said a small voice close to her ear. Rosie was smiling at her, eyes merry. "Just repeat that angel song I taught you and you'll feel better. Come on, now, you remember. Sing with me." He began chanting the tuneless little rhyme he'd had her repeat that evening in her room. *"Ghe'el, ghavoola, ghae'teine . . ."* She knew the words were in the Old Language, but their meaning had long ago been lost to her, and her mouth refused to shape the syllables.

"You're not trying," he said. "Believe me, Carol, it's an excellent way of calming down. Come on, now, let's try again. *Riya migdl'eth, riya moghu . . ."*

He sang the words, and she sang them back to him. With a grating of metal and a chorus of excited screams from the passengers in front, the car began to slide forward on the track.

"Sing," Rosie commanded. "Don't think about where you are. *Sing!"*

Carol closed her eyes and sang the words. *"Migghe'el ghae'teine moghuvoola . . ."* They did help, somehow, just like Rosie said they would—they helped even though she didn't know what she was singing. Or was that what made them so powerful? She tried not to think about the vibration of the car, the steep climb that threw her back against the seat as they ascended the first rise. She gripped Rosie's hand and shut her eyes and sang the song to herself.

She opened her eyes when the car seemed to be slowing down, and gasped, for ahead of her the other cars seemed to be spilling into an abyss—and then they too were hurtling downward, faster than they'd

have fallen, faster than she ever thought she could go, and screams
were in her ear and her eyes were shut tight again and she felt Rosie's
hand on hers and once again she sang the words as if they were a
prayer.

It was not so bad with her eyes closed. She even managed to open
them before the final run, for she thought she'd felt a raindrop on her
cheek. They had just reached the top of the last peak, the highest one;
the car climbed slower and slower and almost stopped, until for a moment it seemed poised, balanced between the two worlds, ready to slide
forward but equally ready to slide back. And just as they were tee-
tering on the edge, with the whole park spread below them—the ferris
wheel, the beach, the dark ocean—she thought she saw a wisp of fog
along the ramp ahead of them. For a moment she thought it might be
smoke from a burning bulb, or some trick of the moonlight . . . and then
in the next instant they were hurtling downward, ahead of them people were screaming, she was holding onto Rosie with all her might, and
they were dropping with such speed she thought the straps would
break and she'd be thrown right out of the car, into the darkness.
"Sing, Carol!" he commanded, and she sang, together they sang, raising their voices above the roaring and the screams. And suddenly, like
a vision, there was a huge white bird before them, hanging angelically
in the air, and Rosie was reaching up—protecting her, she knew—and
batting at it with something in his hand, something that gleamed in
the light, his hand moving so fast she couldn't see, and he must have
broken its neck, because the next moment she felt its body smash
against her, then fall away behind, and it left a bloody stain all over
the front of her new white dress.

Later, as they stumbled from the park, Rosie comforting her and
dabbing ineffectually at her dress, she felt, almost in sympathy, a
trickle of her own blood at the juncture of her legs. By the time they
reached the car, the sky had opened up and it began to rain.

On rainy evenings, after Bert Steegler had locked up the Co-operative
and bolted the huge sliding doors of the barn that served them as a feed
and grain warehouse, and after his wife, Amelia, had closed the books
for the night, having carefully recorded the day's entries for parsnips
and soybeans and peas, the two of them would hurry across the street
to their house by the schoolyard, share supper with their eldest daugh-

ter and her family, and then don their old raincoats and go back outside. They would take the long way around the square, avoiding the
mud near the school and continuing past the cemetery to the home of
Jacob and Elsi van Meer.

When the weather was warm, a few of the old-timers would already
be gathered on the van Meers' front porch sipping mint tea with
chunks of ice in it from the freezer at the Co-op, the men with their
pipes, the women crocheting or knitting. They would sit and watch the
rain come down, talking of crops and the Scriptures. When a vehicle
went by on the road that wound past their front yard, an event that
occurred only rarely, they would speculate on who was inside and
where he was bound. When the iced tea ran out and the women were
yawning and the men had smoked their last pipeful of tobacco, they
would stretch, get slowly to their feet, exchange goodbyes, and head for
home.

They didn't always feel the need to talk; sometimes they just sat together in silence, listening to whatever sounds the night made. They
craved no entertainment. They were content.

Or most of them were. Adam Verdock, who'd just arrived from his
dairy down the road, recalled a relative of his up in Lebanon who'd
yielded to his wife—not one of their sect—and had had his home wired
for electricity. "'Twas hard to stop, after that. First he bought the
woman an electric steam iron, then he bought one of them things with
blue lights that kill the bugs, and finally he went and bought himself a
television set, just like young Jonas Flinders."

There was a general sighing among those assembled, and a rueful
shaking of heads. They knew what was coming; most of them had heard
the tale before.

"Well, he had that thing put in, right in his living room where he
could watch it all the time, and at first he thought it was something
really special. But then his little ones took to it, and I hear it turned
their heads right around. They got to scanting their dinner and their
chores so they could sneak in and watch, they'd be asking for every
frippery they saw, and his oldest boy near got himself thrown out of
school for the way he was acting 'round the girls. That was enough for
him; he took that contraption and buried it out behind his hog wallow.
Now he does penance for two hours every night, staring at a blank spot
of wall right where that thing used to sit. He says it's to remind him of
his sin."

More headshaking, sounds of assent, another round of tea. Bethuel
Reid got up and walked noisily to the bathroom; Jacob van Meer continued rocking in his favorite chair; Adam Verdock filled his latest
corncob pipe.

Finally van Meer cleared his throat. "Wouldn't be surprised if that nephew of yours decided to buy one of those things, just to please that woman of his."

Verdock let that sit a while, puffing ruminatively. "No," he said at last, "that ain't what she wants. What she wants is company. She's from a big family, you know, one of them New Church clans up in Sidon, and she's used to havin' lots of folks around. I think she won't be happy till she's got herself some little ones—and that ain't up to her, it's up to Sarr. Right now he ain't ready to raise a child, and he knows even less about raisin' crops." He paused. "Ain't that right, Lise?"

His wife didn't look up from her knitting. She was a Poroth and, consequently, inclined to be more sympathetic. "Seems to me Sarr's doin' all he can with that place," she said, "and I think he's doin' right by his woman. At least he's agreed to take in a boarder."

"Yes, I saw the fellow at the store," said her husband. "You remember, Bert, 'twas last Sunday. Fat fellow, kinda soft lookin', but he seemed likely enough. Got a little insolent with Rupert."

Steegler nodded. "Struck me that way too. Young Sarr seems to speak well of him, though. Brother Rupert, now, he's got little good to say for a fellow who doesn't earn his keep." He paused. "Of course, Rupert would talk that way, wouldn't he?"

"Now don't be unchristian," said Amelia. "We're goin' to be guests at Brother Rupert's house tomorrow morning, don't forget."

There were nods all around. Worship that week was going to be held at the Lindts'. The following Sunday would see it at Ham Stoudemire's, and then would come the Poroths' turn.

Elsi van Meer looked up. "You suppose Lotte Sturtevant will be there? She's gettin' awful close to her time, from the look of her."

"She's got a few weeks yet," said Amelia. "But I'll grant she's sure swelled up. Never seen the like. It will be a son, I'll wager—and a mighty big one."

"She ain't due till the end of the month," said Lise Verdock. "It may well take till August."

Van Meer paused in his rocking. "Let's hope so," he said. "Let's hope it goes past Lammas Eve."

"Amen," they all said hurriedly, and nodded. "Amen," said Bethuel Reid, who had just come back out to the porch. He shuffled across to the old wicker couch and sat heavily beside his wife.

Van Meer resumed his rocking. His wife shooed a bug from the pitcher of iced tea. Lise stared meditatively at the rain falling in thick cascades from the eaves of the porch. In the distance came the sound of thunder.

"Really comin' down," she said. "Funny how nobody predicted it. 'Twasn't the sort of day for rain." She paused. "'Bout time we had some, though. Corn's been needin' it."

The others turned to stare out at the night. Once again they heard the rumble of thunder. Past the farther side of the house, beyond the line of trees, they could hear the rain beating against the tombstones in the cemetery.

"Amen," Reid said again.

JULY TENTH

Sarr and Deborah were going to spend the whole day at worship; they had walked toward Gilead hours before Freirs woke up. He was left to share the farm with the animals: the seven cats, four hens, and rooster, the birds that sang unseen behind the leaves, bugs that whirled frenziedly in the heat. The sun itself was hidden behind a lowering grey sky; the ground was still damp from last night's rain and had a stagnant smell. On days like this the earth seemed capable of breeding insects, like the carcasses of horses were once believed to do.

From the window he could see Bwada and Rebekah chasing after something near the barn, the grey cat in the lead despite her greater age. Lately they'd taken to stalking grasshoppers, which swarmed around the cornfield in abundance.

Foregoing his exercises, he went into the farmhouse and made himself some breakfast in the kitchen, leafing gloomily through one of the Poroths' religious magazines, and then returned to his room out back for some serious reading. He picked up *Dracula*, which he'd started the night before, but couldn't bring himself to scribble more than a few lackadaisical notes.

Tried to settle into the Stoker, but that soppy Victorian sentimentality began to annoy me again. The book begins marvelously, on a really frightening note—Harker trapped in that Carpathian castle, doomed to be the prey of its terrible owner—but when Stoker switches the locale to England & his main characters to women, he simply can't sustain that initial tension.

For that matter, what's so bad about becoming a vampire if it means you live forever? Wish one would come & bite me. I'm sure I'd develop a taste for blood eventually.

Besides, the story's spoiled for me: I keep picturing Carol in all the female roles & find myself wanting her. Dear Carol, weather is lousy, wish you were here . .

With the Poroths gone he felt lonely and bored. He found himself staring at the cobwebs in the corner of the ceiling, the mildew on the walls, the dying roses drooping in their vase. It was hard to concentrate. Though he'd brought shelfloads of books to entertain him, he felt restless and wished he owned a car; he'd have gone for a drive, visited friends in Princeton, perhaps even headed back to New York . . . But as things stood he had nothing to do but take another walk.

He picked two sprigs of pennyroyal from the garden where Deborah had shown him and stuck them behind the earpieces of his glasses. They tickled as badly as the mosquitoes they were supposed to ward off, and even with no one to see him he was conscious of how silly he must look. When he reached the stream he tossed them in the water.

He followed the stream's twisting path back into the woods. Even though he'd seen it only once before, the way already seemed familiar. Ducking once more beneath the arch of vines and branches, he winced as he prepared to get his feet wet. To his surprise the water seemed less cold this time. Thin wisps of greenish scum floated here and there on the surface.

The pool, though, when he reached it, was as clear as he'd remembered. There were some new animal tracks in the wet sand. Ringed by oaks, the place seemed strangely beautiful, yet even here, somehow, he felt bored. Again he waded into the center of the water and looked up at the sky through the trees. In the center of his vision, directly overhead, a flock of gulls were heading westward, their great wings extended. He could almost hear them shrieking.

The gulls passed. Feeling himself alone once more, he recalled the excitement he'd felt that night on the roof of the barn and, by way of experiment, made a few of the same gestures with his face and hands . . . but his memory failed him, the moment had passed, and these halfhearted movements seemed awkward and unaccountably robbed of their power. Standing there up to his ankles in water, he felt foolish.

Worse, upon leaving the pool he found a bloated red-brown leech clinging like a tumor to his right ankle. It wasn't large—a long way from the "cluster of black grapes" that some Faulkner hero he'd read about had found dangling from his groin—and he was able to scrape it off with a stone; but it left him with a little round bite that oozed blood and a feeling, somehow, of physical helplessness. The woods had once again become hostile to him and, he was sure, would forever remain so. Something had ended.

Listlessly he followed the stream back to the farm. When he reached the edge of the woods he heard, once more, a distant shrieking overhead and saw another line of gulls, if that's what they were, sweeping high across the sky. *How can gulls be all the way out here?* he wondered. *We're so far from the sea.*

When he looked down, he saw, out of the corner of his eye, a familiar grey shape. It was Bwada—but Bwada as he'd never seen her before. She was crouched on the other side of the brook among the rocks and

weeds, frozen like an animal in a museum diorama caught just before it springs. Her eyes were wide, glazed, and somehow astonished-
looking, as if she were staring at something directly in front of her
but seeing nothing. All at once her body gave a tiny jerk, a kind of hiccough, and Freirs saw strands of pink foam at the corners of her jaws.
He realized, suddenly, that she was hurt.

He remembered Deborah's warnings about rabies, but dismissed
them. Rabies didn't take effect so fast; he'd seen Bwada racing through
the grass only an hour before. More likely she'd simply eaten something that had disagreed with her.

He stood watching the cat for a moment, uncertain what, if anything, he should do. Insects buzzed around him in the stillness; from
the cornfield behind him came the shrill cawing of crows. "Are you
okay, girl?" he said at last, with a warmth he didn't feel. "You all
right?"

She continued to stare directly ahead of her, the empty gaze never
wavering. He saw with surprise that her claws were extended; they
were gripping the rock she clung to as if at any moment it might rise
up and shake her loose. Abruptly she gave another hiccough, and her
body seemed to tremble.

Bwada was the only cat he actively disliked, the only one that regularly hissed at him, but with the Poroths gone he felt responsible for
her. Frowning, he walked to the water's edge, picked out a flat rock in
the middle of the stream, and in two long strides was standing on dry
land beside her. Hesitantly he reached out his hand. The animal's gaze
remained turned away from him, but suddenly her lip curled back and
he heard, above the murmur of the water, a low growl building in her
throat. Instantly he yanked back his hand. He was just about to turn
away when in a fleeting moment of sunlight he noticed, for the first
time, a dark, glistening stain on the rock where her body pressed
against it.

Warily he circled her to get a better view, keeping his distance. The
animal's growl became louder, higher in pitch. Suddenly he saw it, on
the side that had been turned away from him, almost hidden by fur: a
rose-red gaping hole in the flesh beneath her ribs. Around this wound
the skin was folded back in small triangular flaps, like little petals. It
was clear, even from several feet away, that the wound had been made
from the inside.

He remembered Poroth's story of the mouse caught in the man's
throat and recalled a kind of slug he'd read about that, when eaten by a
bird, will bore its way out through the bird's stomach. But he'd never
heard of such things happening to a cat.

More likely, he decided, she had impaled herself on a tree branch or
the sharp end of a root—something that, as she'd disengaged herself,

had tugged the flesh out with it. He was surprised there wasn't more blood.

One thing was certain: there'd be plenty of blood—his own—if he tried to pick her up. In her condition she would probably try to scratch his eyes out. Still, he would have to do something; the Poroths would expect it. After all, the damned animal was like one of their own children, especially to Sarr. He thought, briefly, of trying to contact the two of them, but he had no idea where they were today. Even with a phone, it would be almost impossible to locate them; they could be at services at any house in the community.

It occurred to him, suddenly, that there was one thing he might do: find himself a pair of gloves—surely Sarr must have work gloves somewhere—and use them to carry the hurt animal back to the house until the Poroths returned. Yes, that was it. He cleared the brook in two strides and hurried up the hill toward the farmhouse.

The slope was more tiring than he'd expected, and proof of how out of condition he was. He felt thoroughly winded by the time he reached the house and pounded up the steps of the back porch, where two of the younger cats eyed him with alarm. Once inside, he realized that he didn't know where to look. *This is crazy,* he told himself as he dashed up the stairs. *She'll be dead before I get back.*

He checked the low cabinet in the upstairs hall, but it contained only linen and blankets. Entering the Poroths' bedroom, where the creaking of the floorboards made him feel like an intruder, he stood panting in the center of the rug. Where would Sarr keep his gloves? There was a Bible on the nightstand by the bed, a kerosene lantern on the dresser. He peered at the shelves that ringed the crowded little closet, but found only hats, shoeboxes tied with twine, a painting set, a sewing box, two old cast-iron banks, and various dark folded clothes of Deborah's that he was nervous about searching through. The dresser contained neatly folded clothes and, in the top drawer, a tidy stack of deeds, diplomas, loan receipts, and a few old photos, including one of a severe-looking bearded man with Sarr's jaw and brows.

By the time he'd decided that the gloves must be in the workroom above the barn, he was certain it was already too late. Anyway, he'd had enough of this. Tiredly he ran downstairs, hurried out to his own room, and tore the frayed woolen blanket off the bed. If the damned animal were still alive, this would serve as well as gloves.

He trotted back down the slope to the stream, the blanket beneath his arm. Even before he reached it, he could see that the rock on which the cat had perched was now bare.

Probably dragged herself off into the woods to die, he thought, disappointed more at his own wasted efforts than at the loss of the cat. He eyed the pines across the stream; there'd be no finding her in there.

He wondered what he'd tell the Poroths when they got home; bearers of bad news were always blamed, and, after all, he'd been left in charge here today. He could picture their anger as he told them of the hurt animal and of his own failed efforts to help her. If he hadn't taken so long up at the house, she might still be alive. Maybe his own shirt would have sufficed, instead of a blanket. Maybe he'd been a coward not to have used his bare hands. Sarr would never have hesitated.

Glumly he walked back to his outbuilding and threw the blanket on his bed. Better to say nothing, he decided. Better to pretend he'd never seen the cat. Let Sarr discover the body himself.

He spent the rest of the afternoon reading in his room, pushing through the Stoker. He wasn't in the best mood to concentrate.

Sarr and Deborah got back after four. They shouted hello and went into the house. When Deborah called Freirs for dinner, neither of them . had been outside.

All six cats were on the back porch, finishing washing themselves after their evening meal, when he walked up to the house.

"Have you seen Bwada?" asked Poroth, as Freirs pushed through the screen door, the cats filing behind him into the kitchen.

"Haven't seen her all day."

He had done it; the lie was told. There'd be no going back now.

"Sometimes she doesn't come when I call her in for supper," said Deborah. "I think it's because she eats the things she kills."

"Well," said Sarr, " 'twill still be light after supper, and I'll go look for her."

"Fine," said Freirs. "I'll help." Perhaps, he decided, he could lead the other down toward the stream. Maybe the two of them would come upon the body. Resignedly he sat down to eat.

And then, in the middle of dinner, came a scratching at the door. Sarr got up and opened it.

In walked Bwada.

What a relief! Never thought I'd see her again—& certainly not in such good condition.

She was hurt badly earlier today, I know she was. That wound in her side looked fatal, & now it's only a hairless reddish swelling.

Luckily the Poroths didn't notice my shock; they were too busy fussing over Bwada, seeing what was wrong. "Look, she's hurt herself," said Deborah. "She's bumped into something." The animal did move quite stiffly, in fact; there was a clumsiness in the way she held herself. When Sarr put her down after examining the swelling, she slipped when she tried to walk away, like someone walking on slick ice instead of a familiar wooden floor.

The Poroths reached a conclusion similar to mine: that she'd fallen on something, a rock or a branch, & had badly bruised herself. They attribute her lack of coordination to shock or perhaps, as Sarr put it, "a pinching of the nerves." Sounds logical enough, I suppose. Sarr told me before I came out here for the night that if she's worse tomorrow he'll take her to the local vet, even though he'll have a hard time paying for treatment. I offered to lend him money, or even pay for the visit myself; I'd like to hear a doctor's opinion.

Maybe the wound really wasn't that deep after all; maybe that's why there was so little blood. They say animals have wonderful restorative powers in their saliva or something. Maybe she just went off into the woods & nursed herself back to health. Maybe the wound simply closed.

But in a few short hours?

I couldn't continue dinner & told the Poroths my stomach hurt, which was partly true. We all watched Bwada stumble around the kitchen floor, ignoring the food Deborah put before her as if it weren't there. Her movements were awkward, tentative, like a newborn animal still unsure how to move its muscles. When I left the house a little while ago, she was huddled in the corner staring at me. Deborah was crooning over her, but the cat was staring at me.

Killed a monster of a spider behind my suitcase tonight. That new spray really does a job. When Sarr was in here a few days ago he said the room smelled of it, but I guess my allergy's too bad for me to notice.

I enjoy watching the zoo outside my screens. Put my face close & stare at the bugs eye to eye. Zap the ones whose faces I don't like with my spray can.

Tried to read more of the Stoker book, but one thing keeps bothering me: the way that cat stared at me. Deborah was brushing its back, Sarr fiddling with his pipe, & that cat just stared at me & never blinked. I stared back, said, "Hey, Sarr? Look at Bwada. That damned cat's not blinking." And just as he looked up, it blinked. Heavily.

Hope we can go to the vet's tomorrow, because I want to ask him how a cat might impale itself on a rock or a stick, & how fast such a wound might heal.

Cold night. Sheets are damp & the blanket itches. Wind from the woods—ought to feel good in the summer, but it doesn't feel like summer.

That damned cat didn't blink till I mentioned it.

Almost as if it understood me.

BOOK SIX

THE GREEN CEREMONY

And my heart was full of wicked songs that they put into it;
and I wanted to make faces and twist myself about in the
way they did . . . So I did the charm over again, and touched
my eyes and my lips and my hair in a peculiar manner, and
said the old words . . . and I was so glad I could do it quite
well, and I danced and danced along, and sang extraordinary
songs that came into my head . . . songs full of words that
must not be spoken or written down. Then I made faces like
the faces on the rocks, and I twisted myself about like
the twisted ones, and I lay down flat on the ground like
the dead ones.

—Machen, *The White People*

JULY ELEVENTH

The sky above the city is the color of dirty water, the air heavy with humidity. An occasional drizzle smears the windows of the massive grey building near Riverside Park and runs in sooty patterns down the bricks. Inside, the apartment smells of old rugs and furniture, and of an old man who only bathes when he has to.

The Old One doesn't care. As he enters the front hall carrying a brown paper bag of groceries and, on top of them, his day's mail, shakes off his umbrella in the bathroom and leaves it open in the tub to dry, then sits down on the stained lid of the toilet and carefully slips off his galoshes, he pays no attention to the place's shabbiness or smell, or to the pleasures of coming home. Repairing to the kitchen, he stocks the sparsely filled refrigerator with groceries and removes the tape and tissue paper from the bag; the mail he throws away unopened, except for two bills. Tugging out his false teeth, twin strands of saliva stretching from the ends, he deposits them in a water glass in the bathroom. He spends the next half hour at his desk, balancing his checkbook and writing out checks for the rent and electricity, delicately licking the stamps he keeps in a cigar box in the drawer and affixing them with care to the envelopes. These he leaves on the table in the hall for the next time he goes out. Then, idly scratching his nose, he walks to the bookcase in the living room and stoops before a set of drab brown Victorian volumes gathering dust on the second shelf from the bottom.

How amusing, he thinks, as he withdraws one of them—amusing that a key to dark and ancient rites should survive in such innocuous-looking form.

A young fool like Freirs would probably refuse to believe it. Like the rest of his doomed kind, he'd probably expect such lore to be found only in ancient leather-bound tomes with gothic lettering and portentously sinister titles. He'd search for it in mysterious old trunks and private vaults, in the "restricted" sections of libraries, in intricately carved wood chests with secret compartments.

But there *are* no real secrets, the Old One knows. Secrets are ultimately too hard to conceal. The keys to the rites that will transform the world are neither hidden nor rare nor expensive. They are available to anyone. You can find them on the paperback racks or in any secondhand bookshop.

You just have to know where to look—and how to put the pieces together.

There are pieces in an out-of-print religious tract by one Nicholas Keize. And in a certain language textbook which, in its appendix, transcribes nursery rhymes in an obsolete Malaysian dialect surprisingly like Celtic. And in a story, supposedly fiction—but not when read at the right time—by an obscure Welsh visionary who barely suspected why he'd written it, and who regretted it in later years and died a fervent churchman. And in the pictures on a cheap pack of novelty cards based on images from unguessed-of antiquity. And in a Tuscan folk dance included in a certain staid old dance book which, along with pliés and pirouettes, has the dancer make a pattern called "the changes."

The pieces are there, simply waiting to be fitted together into what, from the start, they were meant to be: a set of instructions for the Ceremonies.

Carefully the Old One wraps the book in tissue paper and tapes it closed. He leaves it on the table in the hall. He will send it off tomorrow, in the box he's prepared.

He hopes that Carol likes his little gift. Dancing is supposed to be her specialty.

Bwada's walking better now, seems more affectionate than ever toward the Poroths—even lets Deborah pet her, which is something new—& has an amazing appetite, though she seems to have difficulty swallowing. Some minor mouth infection, perhaps; she won't let anybody see. Sarr says her recovery demonstrates how the Lord watches over the innocent; affirms his faith, he says. Quote: "If I'd taken her to Flemington to see the vet, I'd just have been throwing away good money."

Later this week he'll have his mother over to take a look at her. She healed Bwada once before, & maybe she can do it again.

But even without her, the swelling on Bwada's side is almost gone. Hair growing back over it like mildew growing up my wall, spreading fast.

Mildew. I'm all too familiar with it now. Every day it climbs higher on the walls of this place, like water rising; glad my books are on shelves off the ground. So damp in here that my note paper sags; books go limp, as if they're made of wet cloth. At night my sheets are clammy

& cold, but each morning I wake up sweating. My envelopes have been ruined—glue's gotten moistened, sealing them all shut. Stamps in my wallet are stuck to the dollar bills. When I wrote a letter to Carol today, I had to use the Poroths' glue to stick the thing together.

Spent a lot of my afternoon in here rereading "The Turn of the Screw," which I hadn't looked at since my undergraduate days. Seem to be alone in finding it the single most pretentious & overrated ghost tale ever written (though perfect for the MLA crowd); Clayton's film version, which I showed in class this year, is ten times as effective. Searched in vain amid the psychological abstractions for an authentic chill & found only one image that moved me: his description of a rural calm as "that hush in which something gathers or crouches . . ."

Outside, another drizzly day. Soggy-looking slate-grey skies, gloomy evening, thunder. Hasn't let up since Saturday night, & depressing as hell, like something out of *Cold Comfort Farm*. One huge cloud seems to have settled over the landscape like a bowl. A few pale shapes—seagulls again?—high overhead, but no other birds around, & no sign of the sun.

Wandered around the farm late in the afternoon, bored with sitting still. The Poroths were out pulling weeds among the shoots of corn & were blessedly silent for once. Was tempted to join them but didn't feel like getting my hands dirty, much less spend an hour or two bent almost double.

Rainy night. After dinner, reluctant to come out here & be alone again so soon, hung around the farmhouse with the Poroths, earnestly squinting through *Walden* in their living room while Sarr whittled & Deborah crocheted. Rain sounded better in there, a restful thumping on the roof; out here it's not quite so cozy.

Around nine or ten Sarr went to the kitchen & hauled out the radio, & we sat around listening to the news, cats purring around us, Sarr with Azariah in his lap, Deborah petting Toby, me allergic & sniffling. (My "total immersion" experiment isn't working.)

Nice to have a radio, though, & feel that tenuous contact with the world out there. Even Sarr must recognize the attraction. Remember hearing how, up in Maine, some poor families spend each Sunday sitting in their car parked in their yard, listening to the only radio they own.

Guess I'm just not cut out to be a modern-day Thoreau.

Halfway through some boring farm report I pointed to Bwada, curled up at my feet, & said, "Hey, get her. You'd think she was listening to the news!" Deborah laughed & leaned over to scratch Bwada behind the ears. As she did so, Bwada turned to look at me. I wonder what it is about that cat that makes me so uneasy.

Rain letting up slightly. I'm sitting here slouched over the table, trying to decide if I'm sleepy enough to turn in now. Maybe I should try to read some more, or clean this place up a bit. Things soon grow messy out here, even though I don't have much to keep track of: dust on windowsills, spiderwebs perennially in corners, notes & clippings & dried-up rose petals scattered over this table.

I think that the rain sound is going to put me to sleep after all. It's almost stopped now, but I can still hear the dripping from the trees outside my window, dripping leaf to leaf &, in the end, to the dead leaves that line the forest floor. It will probably continue on & off all night. Occasionally I think I hear a thrashing in one of the big trees down in the direction of the barn, but then the sound turns into the falling of the rain.

JULY TWELFTH

Carol staggered into the apartment, fanning herself with a creased copy of *Spring:* "Start Fresh with Our Three-Part Summer Makeover." Her Tuesday-evening dance class had been exhausting, and the ride back downtown no better: twenty-five minutes on a crowded bus with inadequate air conditioning.

Here there was no air conditioning at all. *As soon as I have the money I'm buying one,* she reminded herself. *It must be a hundred and ten in here.* No sooner had she locked the door behind her than she was unbuttoning her damp clothes, dropping them to the floor in a heap as she made for the bathroom.

She felt a little better after showering. She brought in the cheap Woolworth's fan from her bedroom and planted it by the TV. Switching both of them on, she settled back naked on the couch, eyes half closed, and listened to the reading of the news.

Except for the weather, it had been a normal day. The city was closing another hospital; vandals had defaced a statue of Alice in Wonderland in Central Park; blacks were charging police brutality in the arrest of a so-called "voodoo priest"; the mayor had presided at a fashion show; a girl's head had been found in a trash can near the Columbia campus; and Con Ed was warning consumers to "go slow" this week on the use of air conditioners. The catalogue was curiously soothing, a meaningless litany. It was almost enough to sleep to.

"Firemen in the Brownsville section of Brooklyn battled a six-alarm blaze that took the lives of at least seven persons, all but two of them children. And now—"

Behind her the buzzer sounded. She roused herself and went to the intercom.

"Package from a Mr. Rosebottom."

She buzzed him in and, stepping into the bedroom, wrapped herself in her bathrobe. A minute later the doorbell rang; she turned down the TV and went to answer it.

"Sign here, please," said the delivery boy, handing her a flat grey cardboard box, then a slip of yellow paper and a pencil. He seemed bemused at finding an attractive girl in her robe waiting for him and looked as if he were struggling to think of something clever to say. She felt his eyes on her as she scribbled her name, and pulled the bathrobe tighter. "Thanks, honey," he said, a flicker of a smile. "Enjoy it."

She saw, when she'd gotten the box open, that Rosie had sent her another dress. It was old-fashioned looking, cut similarly to the first—maybe if she felt ambitious she could take it in a bit—but the color, this time, was dark green. *Consider this a replacement,* he had written in a note. *At least this one won't show grass stains!*

In the box with it, wrapped in tissue paper, he'd enclosed a second-hand book, a slim brown antique-looking volume whose spine had long since been rubbed clean of lettering. The title page read, *The Ridpath Dance Series, Volume IV. On the Folk-Dances of Umbria and Tuscany. Newly translated into English. New York, 1877.* Idly she flipped through it. There were several crude line drawings of peasants dancing in various ungainly costumes, faces utterly expressionless, but most of the book was filled with diagrams, a mass of footprints and black arrows. She thought she recognized a few simple steps —there was one promenade that seemed right out of "The Cunning Vixen"—but it was difficult to imagine what most of the others must look like. She put the book aside; probably Rosie would know.

Once again the dress bore no label—*Wherever does he find these things?* she wondered—and, as before, the material felt like silk. Shrugging off her robe, she slipped the dress over her head and examined herself in the mirror on the closet door, pressing the cloth against her belly, breasts, and hips. Like the first dress, now safely packed off to the cleaners, its hemline was cut rather high, and she realized that, once more, she was going to have to keep her knees tight together when she wore it. Maybe Rosie found her legs exciting; or else he just didn't know the length young women were wearing their skirts these days.

She would have to call him to thank him—*he's really spoiling me,* she decided—but she was feeling too tired now. Still in the dress, she returned to the couch. The cloth felt smooth and cool against her bare skin; there was something a little bit sinful about it. She lay back and stretched her legs. The TV, with its volume down, was practically inaudible.

"Unprecedented temperatures," someone was saying. "Freak storms . . ." She ran her hand inside the collar, touching her neck. "Warm air masses over New Jersey . . ."

New Jersey. Visions of the countryside, the peaceful blue skies of the farm, came back to her in the breeze from the fan. She remembered tiny silver fishes darting in the stream, the fields of young corn, Sarr and Deborah and the kittens.

"Reports of thunder," the TV was saying. "Changes in the atmosphere . . ." She ran her hand deeper beneath the dress, closed her eyes, and thought of Jeremy.

Thunder last night, but heard no rain. Wonder if the weather's affected the stream, because walking by it today, I noticed it's becoming clogged with algae.

Chicken & dumplings for dinner. Had three helpings. Deborah didn't seem to mind.

Northanger Abbey, Jane Austen, 1818, chapters one through seven. Not the parody I'd expected—the mock-Gothic bit obviously isn't central to the story—but witty nonetheless. Fun to picture Deborah in the leading role.

Love stories tend to bore me, but this one's proved quite bearable so far.

Bwada seems to be almost completely healed now, at least outwardly, though still may have some sort of throat obstruction. When she miaows there's a different timbre, a kind of huskiness. Sarr's mother is coming tomorrow to look at her.

Read some more Le Fanu in bed. "Green Tea," about a phantom monkey with eyes that glow, & "'The Familiar," about a staring little man who drives the hero mad. In neither case—cf. de Maupassant's "The Horla"—is the hero sure just why he's been singled out.

Not the smartest choices right now, the way I feel, because for all the time that fat grey cat purrs over the Poroths, she just stares at me. And snarls. I suppose the accident may have addled her brain a bit, or perhaps she somehow blames *me* for it, or has forgotten who I am, or something . . . Can a cat's personality change like that?

Petted Toby tonight, the little orange one—my favorite of the bunch, the one I like to play with even though my nose gets clogged & my eyes tear. Came away with a tick on my arm which I didn't discover till I undressed for bed. A tiny flat thing, paper thin, like a squashed spider; it was dull red, no doubt from having made a meal for itself on my blood. As a result, I can still feel, even now, imaginary ticks crawling up & down my spine.

Damned cat.

JULY THIRTEENTH

Another poor night's sleep. Awakened sometime shortly before dawn by thunder, not so distant now. Once or twice I swear it shook the ground. No sense to it at all; the weather had been mild enough when I went to bed, & it's just the same right now, with not a sign of rain. Maybe the noise was caused by "heat lightning"—you sometimes read about such things; but though I sat up for half an hour last night peering through the screens, I saw no lightning.

I did hear someone singing (or trying to) very late, out toward the farmhouse and the road. Possibly just an old tramp out on some night-time excursion, but it didn't sound like one. It's hard to tell, though, when you're half asleep; maybe it was only Sarr or Deborah gargling in the bathroom.

I've been thinking a lot about Deborah lately—about how little Sarr seems to appreciate her. Sure, he grabs her all the time & obviously likes having her around, but I wonder if he wouldn't feel the same way toward any woman within reach. Still can't decide if anything went on between him & Carol.

For that mattter, I wonder just how much Deborah really cares for him. He's tall & powerfully built, sure, if you happen to like that type. (And I guess most women do.) But guys like that can sometimes be so goddamned boring . . .

Of course, Deborah might not *mind* being bored. Anyone who could spend all day shelling peas, or shoving seeds into holes, or praying on her knees, obviously has a pretty high boredom threshold. Still, I can't help thinking that Deborah's interested in me. She's certainly attentive enough, giving me all that good food, taking my side against Sarr whenever disagreements arise. And she certainly is looking good these days, the more I see of her. That long black dress may cover her up to the neck, but the cloth is thin (thank God for summer!), & I'm sure she wears nothing beneath it.

I know it's wrong to have these thoughts, no doubt the loneliness is getting to me, but I can't help wondering if Sarr ever goes off by himself in the evening—a night out with the boys, maybe. I sure wouldn't mind being alone with Deborah some time . . .

This morning, though, all three of us were together, up in the work area Sarr's constructed in the attic of the barn. The two of them were

cutting strips of molding for the extra room upstairs, and I was helping, more or less. I measured, Sarr sawed, Deborah sanded. All in all I
hardly felt useful, but what the hell?

While they were busy I stood staring out the window. There's a narrow flagstone path running from the barn to the main house, & Toby &
Zillah were crouched in the middle of it taking the morning sun. Suddenly Bwada appeared on the back porch & began slinking along the
path in our direction, tail swishing from side to side. When she got
close to the two little ones she gave a snarl—I could see her mouth
working—& they leaped to their feet, bristling, & ran off into the
grass.

Called this to the Poroths' attention. They claimed to know all about
it. "She's always been nasty to the kittens," Deborah said, "maybe because she never had any of her own." (I thought she sounded a bit
wistful.)

"And besides," said Sarr, "she's getting old."

When I turned back to the window, Bwada was gone. Asked the
Poroths if they didn't think she'd gotten worse lately. Realized that, in
speaking, I'd unconsciously dropped my voice, as if someone might be
listening through the chinks in the floorboards.

Deborah conceded that, yes, the cat had been acting a bit odd these
days, ever since the accident. It's not just the kittens she fights with;
Azariah, the adult orange male, seems particularly afraid of her.

Sarr was more helpful. "It's sure to pass," he said. "We'll see what
my mother thinks."

Mrs. Poroth arrived while they were eating lunch. The three of them
had been seated at the table, talking about the general store. "It wasn't
always a co-operative," Sarr was saying. "Years ago, before my father
ran it, it was owned by just two families, the Sturtevants and the van
Meers. It did quite well in those days, so I've been told, but then there
were several bad years in a row. The rain was poor, some crops around
here failed, and the price of corn fell off. 'Twas just a streak of bad
luck. Nobody was at fault, and nobody could have predicted it—"

"Some folks could."

They turned to see the hard, unsmiling woman standing in the doorway to the hall.

"Mother," said Sarr, rising, "how did you—"

"I let myself in through the front door," she said. She walked into
the kitchen and looked around. "The animal's outside?"

"I'll get her," said Sarr. He walked out to the back porch. They
heard him hurry down the steps.

"Mrs. Poroth," said Deborah, "this is Jeremy Freirs. Jeremy, this is
Sarr's mother."

"Glad to meet you," said Freirs, standing.

The woman nodded, barely looking at him.

"Jeremy here's from New York City," added Deborah. "He's our summer guest."

"Guest?" The woman eyed him coldly. "I thought he was a tenant."

Freirs flinched, but Deborah did not. "We've come to think of him as a guest," she said. "He's been a big help to us. Why, just this morning—"

At that moment Sarr came through the back door carrying Bwada. The cat lay cradled sleepily in his arms, but its eyes were wary as they surveyed the people in the room.

Freirs looked from the cat to Mrs. Poroth. He'd been surprised by the woman's behavior—and was just as surprised now to see her regarding the animal with an almost ferocious intensity. She seemed to be staring directly into Bwada's eyes.

At last she shook her head. "This isn't the kitten I nursed."

"Well, of course not, Mother," said Sarr. "That was ten years ago. You've seen her a hundred times since."

"That ain't what I mean." She came toward him, reaching for the cat. "Give her here."

The animal seemed to grow limp in Sarr's arms; its eyes closed further, as if it were about to fall asleep. But Freirs thought he heard, from deep within its throat, a low, forbidding growl.

Mrs. Poroth's hands closed firmly around the animal. Freirs was sure he heard that growl now—it had grown higher, more menacing— but the woman appeared not to notice, or at least not to care. She picked the cat up and held it in the air before her face.

And suddenly the animal exploded. With a howl of rage it twisted in the woman's grasp and slashed out at her face. Deborah screamed. The woman's hand went to her cheek. The cat dropped to the floor and raced shrieking round and round the kitchen, while Sarr and Deborah jumped back in alarm.

Freirs glanced at Mrs. Poroth. To his astonishment the woman appeared to be smiling. There were four bloody lines across her cheek, but she no longer seemed to notice. With a single swift movement she stepped to the screen door and yanked it open. In an instant, like a silver-grey projectile, the cat disappeared through it and down the back steps. Through the window they saw her racing toward the woods.

How impressive Deborah was this afternoon! The way she stood up to that bitch.

After hearing Deborah's description of her early in the summer, I suppose I'd been expecting a sort of backcountry witch, filled with homilies and spells and homespun wisdom. Instead, I got a nasty old hag. Still can't get over how rude she was; she obviously didn't take to me at all. Probably hates New Yorkers. Anti-Semitic, too, I'll bet.

I almost have to laugh, now, the way that goddamned cat attacked her. Though at the time it wasn't quite so funny . . .

They searched for her everywhere. All of them were white-faced and shaken except, oddly, Mrs. Poroth herself. She appeared almost calm.

"I've seen what I came to see," she said to her son. She didn't appear to mind the deep, painful-looking scratches on her face and declined to stay. "'Tis just as I thought. There's a spirit in that animal, something that's against all nature. There's naught I can do, though, for I know you'll not heed what I have to tell you. The animal's yours, and you're the one that must destroy it."

He didn't say anything until she'd left, but he was obviously troubled. "No," he kept saying to himself, "no, I couldn't do a thing like that. This time she's wrong."

"Of course she's wrong," said Deborah, tight-lipped. "She was just upset about what happened."

Sarr nodded, but he seemed unconvinced.

They strolled around the property without managing to find the cat. In vain they searched the smokehouse and the barn. "Sometimes she gets under the front porch and won't come out all day," Deborah recalled, but the cat was not there. Finally they gave up.

"She's off in the woods," Sarr said. "She'll come back when she's ready."

"In a better temper, I hope," Deborah added.

Freirs left them, still despondent, at the house and walked back to his room. He noticed, as he approached, that the door on the other side of his outbuilding was slightly ajar. It might easily have been left that way by Deborah or Sarr—because that half of the building was used as a storeroom, the two of them were always bringing things in and out—but he wondered if the cat might possibly have slipped inside. He was tempted to go back up to the farmhouse and tell the Poroths, but he didn't want to seem afraid, especially in front of Deborah. Besides, he'd be embarrassed if they came all the way out here and found nothing. He told himself that he had nothing to fear; it was only a cat, after all. And if he found her he'd be a hero.

Stepping inside, he closed the door behind him and switched on the light. The room smelled heavily of mildew and mouse droppings. It was piled high with lumber, bottles, old furniture, carefully folded seed bags, and dusty footlockers, some of which obviously predated the Poroths and had, no doubt, been moved down here from the attic in the farmhouse.

Crouching, he peered nervously beneath an old sofa which sagged beneath the weight of four overstuffed valises and a cardboard carton filled with empty jars. From behind him came the buzzing of horseflies as they slammed themselves against the windowpanes; the sills below were littered with their bodies.

A dead wasp lay among them, probably one from the swarm in the smokehouse, lying just inches from the tiny space at the bottom of the pane by which it probably had entered. Freirs imagined it battering itself against the glass and wondered if, as it lay dying, it had seen the hole at last and realized the futility of its efforts.

In one corner, almost at eye level atop the slashed and pitted surface of a table, an ancient steamer trunk caught his eye. It was decorated with faded ribbons and appeared to be some remnant of the previous century. Upon it lay several piles of moldy-looking books. He picked them up gingerly, one by one, holding them away from his face lest they be crawlng with silverfish and worms. They proved to be religious tracts, and as boring as most of that genre. *Heaven's Messengers*, he read with distaste. *Bible Themes for Busy Workers. The Shepherd and the Sheep*. He tossed the books aside and raised the lid.

Inside there were more of them, and some badly folded old clothes. So much for his fantasies of stereoscopes, antique postcards, jewels ... The clothes, though moth-eaten, might have had a certain value—he noticed a woman's black dress with large cloth-covered buttons down the front, a dress which, though severe, might have fetched a good price in some Village boutique—but he wasn't very interested in such things. The books here were even worse: *Aids to Believers. Handfuls of Help. Beneath the Moss. The Footsteps of the Master*.

At the bottom of the pile, however, against the trunk's age-discolored lining, lay what appeared to be a stack of magazines. He lifted them out, hoping for a cache of old *Munsey's* or some ancient *Harper's Weeklies* from the Civil War days, but they proved to be something more unusual: yearbooks. *Spring Street Bible School*, the covers said. *Gilead, New Jersey*.

There were almost two dozen in all, in no particular order, ranging from the early 1880s up to 1912. The covers were of paper, cracked and yellowing, with several separated from the bindings; the yearbooks themselves—mere pamphlets, actually—were only thirty pages long. Most of them bore names at the top, written in childish hands: Isaac Baber, Rachel Baber, Andrew Baber ... This was the family, he recalled, that had previously owned the farm.

Picking up the most recent issue, he flipped through it back to front. Student essays filled the pages, essays with titles in old-fashioned gothic letters on such subjects as "The Duty of a Christian" and "Living in the Way of the Lord." There was also a selection of song lyrics: not alma maters but hymns: "Reapers of Life's Harvest," "Blue Galilee," "There Is a Power in the Blood."

To the work! to the work! there is labor for all;
For the Kingdom of Darkness and Error shall fall;
And the name of Jehovah exalted shall be,
And we'll shout with the ransomed, "Salvation is free!"

In the front of the book were four group photos: male and female students, male and female faculty; obviously the sexes had been segregated. There appeared to have been fewer than sixty students in the entire school, and half a dozen teachers. They were a solemn-looking bunch, sitting stiff and unsmiling as they gazed up at him from that bygone day as if through a sepia mist. He scanned the captions; a welter of familiar names greeted him. P. Buckhalter, J. van Meer, several Lindts and Reids and Poroths. Most, he realized, would be dead by now. The name Baber had been carefully underlined wherever it appeared. In the first row, among the youngest boys, he was amused to notice a pale, earnest little face labeled M. Geisel.

Suddenly his eye was caught by the name V. Troet. There were an R. Troet and an S. among the girls, he noticed, and a B. among the female faculty. Deborah had said it was a large family.

What of the branch that had been wiped out in the fire, the branch that had lived right here? Were any of them represented? No, he checked again; the books only went back as far as 1881. They'd all be dead by then, dead and in their graves.

All but one . . .

He turned to the earliest book; the boy would have been around thirteen then.

Yes, there he was, in the middle row, crowded in with the rest: A. Troet.

He held the book up to the light, peering more closely at the tiny, blurred figure that stared at him from the page. The figure was short, with a wide, honest-looking face, but beyond that it was indistinguishable from the rest. Perhaps—was it a trick of the light?—perhaps there was the tiniest hint of a smile at the corners of the lips, a lone smile among all those grave little faces . . .

No, it was just his imagination.

He looked ahead to the next book, 1882. There he was again, A. Troet, still slightly shorter than the rest. He felt a tiny, inexplicable chill. This time there was no doubt at all. The figure was smiling.

There was no mention of him in the following year's book, or in any of the others. No doubt he'd dropped out of school and out of the world—until he'd struck again in 1890 . . .

Well, his photo would make an amusingly ghoulish little pinup for the wall above Freirs' desk. Portrait of the Devil as a Young Man. Tucking the collection of yearbooks beneath his arm, he piled the other books back inside the trunk, laying the clothing on top. He hoped he hadn't piled them too high, and that the trunk would close. Reaching up, he pulled the lid down—

He jumped back. Bwada was crouching behind the trunk only inches from his face, eyes unblinking, burning into his. A hissing sound escaped her throat, and her body seemed to swell. Spreading her claws, she prepared to leap.

Suddenly, for no discernible reason, she appeared to think better of it. She settled down, licked her lips, and purred.

"Nice cat," said Freirs, backing out of the room. "Nice cat." There'd been something about the way she licked her lips, something not quite right, but there was no time to worry about it now. "You just sit there, and I'll be right back with your friends."

Slamming the door, he ran for the farmhouse.

She walked home, musing, following the dusty road as it wound its contrary way through the forest and fields. She paid no mind to her torn cheek; there were nine ways of making pain go away, and she knew them all. Besides, she had more important matters to occupy her now.

The visitor had come. It was here among them. When she'd looked into the cat's eyes she had seen it glaring out at her, as if through the eye holes of a mask.

Lucky that she'd seen it while it was still so weak. Proof, no doubt, of divine Providence—for she knew how to fight the thing. Her boy, Sarr, was useless, but she knew what to do.

Yes, that was a possibility old Absolom hadn't counted on—that one of the Brethren would know and be prepared.

She had been prepared for more than twenty years. She had known that it would happen like this; it was just as her visions had shown her.

She set her jaw, thought of the struggle that lay ahead, and continued down the dirt road with a more determined stride. She felt vindicated. She'd been right after all. On her cheek the blood was dry, the wound already healing.

Rosie was waiting for her when she got off work at seven. He'd stationed himself at a table by the window of the shabby little coffee shop next door, biding his time with a chocolate malted and a slice of pound cake until she emerged. He knocked on the window as she walked past and waved her inside.

"Just let me pay the bill," he said, making greedy little sounds with his straw as he sucked up the last of the malted. He stuffed the final crumbs of cake into his mouth. "May I walk you home? I want to talk."

Carol had talked with Rosie on the phone just last night, when she'd called to thank him for the new dress, but she was happy to see him again. Voorhis had been hard to bear today; Miss Elms, the assistant supervisor, had wounded Carol with a caustic remark, early in the afternoon, about her lack of enthusiasm—"When you came to work here we all thought you were going to amount to something, but so far you haven't"—and there'd been hints from one of her superiors, oily Mr. Brown in acquisitions, that he and Mrs. Tait were considering reducing her hours still further during the summer lull. *They aren't even paying me a living wage* now, Carol had thought, but she'd been too cowed to say anything.

Rosie's smiling face made a welcome contrast to the librarians' sour ones, and strolling downtown with him, laughing at the excited way he'd peer into every store window they passed as if he just might buy whatever was inside, be it a baby toy, a side of beef, or a maid's uniform, was the perfect way to unwind.

"Have you looked at that book I sent over?" he asked, as they waited for the light to change at Twenty-first and Eighth. "The one with all those country dances?"

"I've only had time to glance at it," she said. "Some of the steps certainly look complicated."

"How'd you like to try one with me?"

Carol shrugged. "Sure, if you like. Any particular reason?"

He looked hurt. "Don't you think it might just be fun?"

"Oh, of course, Rosie," she said hastily. "Of course it'll be fun. I only meant, did you send the book over as part of our research, or simply because you know I like dancing?"

He stuck his hands in his pockets and moved closer to her as they walked. "As a matter of fact, young lady, that book is extremely germane to what the two of us are studying. The steps peasants once danced in tiny, isolated North Italian villages were the same ones

312 T.E.D. Klein

children danced in Elizabethan England—and are still dancing in modern-day East Africa."

"No, it *can't* be!"

"Oh, yes. And strictly *entre nous*, yours truly is the first to have discovered the connections. So you're going to be involved in some pretty important research, young lady—original research that ought to cause quite a stir. You may find yourself with a very nice little career, by the time we're done."

"Wow, wouldn't that be incredible!"

She reminded herself that the old man was probably just trying to impress her, or else he might simply be mistaken. But what if he was right? Wouldn't it be wonderful to make a real contribution to scholarship, to be respected at last as an authority on something, her work studied by the sort of earnest souls who came to Voorhis every day? That institution's miseries were temporarily forgotten; she was thinking, instead, how the tedious little summaries she prepared twice weekly for Rosie, the abstracts of papers and journal articles, might be worthwhile after all.

By the time they reached her house, he was mopping his forehead repeatedly with a large white handkerchief. "Lordy," he said, "I can't *remember* when it's been so hot."

"It is pretty awful," she conceded. "I hate to think of what's still in store."

"Do you think I might come up and cool off?" He dabbed wearily at his throat.

"Oh, of course you can. I'll give you some iced tea. I have to warn you, though, it's probably hotter up there than it is here on the sidewalk."

Rosie smiled. "Well, I'll take my chances."

He continued to smile mysteriously as they rode up in the elevator. By the time they'd reached the door to her apartment, she'd begun to grow uneasy.

Unlocking the door, she pushed it open. A wave of cool air bathed her face. From the living room she heard the soft churning of a motor. She turned to him, eyes widening. "Rosie, did you—?"

He nodded, chuckling. "Had it installed this afternoon, while you were at work."

"Oh, Rosie, this is the nicest surprise I've ever had!"

She rushed into the living room. There, fitted into the window, was a glossy white Fedders, two round vents regarding her like eyes.

Rosie followed her in and stood grinning at his handiwork. "It should make the place a bit more livable, don't you think?"

"God, will it ever!" she said. "But how in the world did you get *in* here?"

He shrugged. "Your super was very understanding."

Carol breathed deeply of the cool air and let the chilly breeze caress her face. She wished there were some way to repay him, or at least to show her gratitude. "Well," she said finally, "it's certainly going to be more comfortable to read in here, thanks to you. I'll be able to work twice as hard now."

"You know, I do believe you have a point. In fact"—he surveyed the room—"there's something the two of us could work on tonight. Here, give me a hand with this." He began tugging the coffee table toward the wall.

"What are you doing?" she asked, already coming forward to help him.

"Clearing away some of this furniture," he said, grunting with exertion. "It'll give us more room."

"Room for what?"

Rosie smiled. "Why—to dance, of course!"

But it was only Carol who danced that night.

Opening up the book of folk dances seemingly at random, he chose one near the back. "Here," he said, handing it to her, "this one looks interesting."

"Il Mutamentos (The Changes)," she read. "Of unknown origin."

> This dance is said to mimic, in symbolic terms,
> the transformation of a worm into a butterfly.
> It may be performed either singly or in pairs.

"It looks a little monotonous," said Carol, studying the diagrams. "All this spinning . . ."

"Nonsense," said Rosie, "just give it a try. You'll find it more fun than you imagine. Here, I'll play shaman, and you can be the nubile native girl." Clapping his hands, he began singing in a frail old-man's voice, softly at first, as if to himself, but then with growing enthusiasm.

"*Da'moghu . . . da'fae moghu . . . riya daeh . . .*"

Shamans? Native girls? What was the old man talking about? "Wait," said Carol, trying to hear the beat before taking a step, "that sure doesn't sound like Italian."

"A dialect," said Rosie, still clapping his hands and nodding. "From Tuscany."

"Oh." Carol peered over his shoulder at the book, still hesitant to begin. "Look, couldn't we do some of the others, instead? The ones near the front look like more fun."

Rosie smiled patiently and stopped clapping. "Don't worry, Carol, we'll get to it. We'll get to all the others, if you like." Gripping her shoulders in a fatherly way, he moved her into the center of the floor. "But this is the one I think you should try now. Just a practice run."

"But—"

He raised his hand for silence. "Believe me, Carol," he said, "it's your dance. It's for you."

And he clapped his hands again, and cocked his head, and sang. And in the center of the little room, to the interminable churning of the air conditioner, she danced.

JULY FOURTEENTH

Taking a bath at Poroth Farm was a three-step operation, and Freirs had become adept at it. First it was necessary to turn up the flame on the modern gas-powered hot water heater—a round white tubular affair nearly as tall as a man, which took up much of the bathroom—while simultaneously twisting a faucet in the unit's side, releasing more water into the tank. One then waited half an hour or more, doing chores or checking through whatever assortment of seed catalogues and Bible tracts the postman had brought, or, as was usual in Freirs' case, celebrating the end of morning exercises by snacking on some likely morsel discovered in the cool of the root cellar, where most of the perishables were stored. When the water supply was hot and ready, one returned to the bathroom, turned down the flame and the water, and opened the spigots in the huge old bathtub, stained with age and big enough for three, which stood beside the heater. Finally, after another wait, one could climb into the tub and enjoy a long-overdue soak. It was a somewhat tedious process, but an ultimately rewarding one. Freirs went through it almost every day.

It was half past ten and he was about to perform the first step in the operation. The day was hot and overcast, and as he trudged across the yard toward the farmhouse, his towel around his neck, he found himself wishing once again that he had a car at his disposal—something to take him away from the confined, landlocked atmosphere of the farm. *Maybe it's ridiculous to think of spending the entire summer out here,* he told himself, not for the first time. *I'm clearly not cut out for it.* But where, then, could he stay? He couldn't just kick that couple out of his apartment; they had it, by rights, till September. And the Poroths were depending on his ninety a week.

The two of them were singing—chanting, praying, he couldn't decide what function it actually served—while they weeded the narrow field adjoining the road. They didn't see him go by. Two of the younger cats and the older tiger-striped male, Azariah, were curled like spectators in the grass, watching them. The field itself, bare when Freirs had first arrived at the farm, was now well covered by a tangle of cucumber vines. "These are fast growers," Poroth had told him confidently. "I figure they'll be ripe by the end of August—just in time to put 'em in your salad."

Well, maybe he'd still be around then. He would see . . .

He climbed the steps of the back porch and entered the kitchen. Across the room, one of the wooden chairs was propped against the bathroom door. Without thinking he moved the chair away and pulled the door open.

There was a scrabbling sound. Out of the corner of his eye he saw a grey shape dart past his feet and across the kitchen floor. It was Bwada.

For an instant he deliberated whether he should try to catch her—he knew how wicked those claws could be—but then, to his amazement, the cat dashed herself against the screen door, throwing it open. Moments later she had vanished outside. *Jesus!* he said to himself, *that's a trick she didn't know yesterday.*

Sarr and Deborah were standing ankle-deep among the broad leaves of the cukes when, behind them, they heard a commotion. An orange blur was zigzagging through the grass with a silver-grey shape streaking just behind it. Suddenly Azariah came tumbling toward their feet with Bwada practically riding on his back in a frenzy of clawing. In less than a second the two had become a snarling ball of orange and grey, spitting, screaming, with an occasional glimpse of flashing claws and teeth.

A few seconds more and Sarr was upon them, screaming with a rage as great as theirs. A brawny arm stabbed down, and Bwada was hauled twisting and struggling into the air, gripped around the neck. Sarr stalked back toward the house with her, brandishing the animal before him like a trophy of war.

"For God's sake put her down," cried Deborah. "You're *strangling* her! You'll crush her neck!"

He looked back, eyes wild, the veins standing out in his head. Only moments before she had been pleading with him to watch out for the claws, and, moments before that, to stop the fight.

"If I kill her," he said between his teeth, "God's my witness, I'll not shed a tear!"

The animal had long since ceased struggling and now hung limp in his grasp, seemingly lifeless except for periodic hissing sounds that came from deep within her throat.

Marching up the steps and into the kitchen, Freirs sheepishly holding the screen door for him, Sarr yanked open the bathroom door and hurled the animal inside. He slammed the door shut, propping the chair back in place before it.

"Sorry," said Freirs. "I'm the one who let her out."

"It's all right now," said Sarr. Wearily he sprawled onto one of the kitchen chairs, his hand and wrist a mass of lacerations. He was breathing deeply. "It's all right." He paused, composing himself. "Have you already turned on the water?"

"Uh, no, I was about to, but I—"

Sarr shook his head. "Don't. Put off your bathing till the end of the day. I want to leave her in there for a spell. God's my witness, I swear my mother was right. The devil's in that animal."

Deborah had come into the kitchen and now stood behind him, caressing his neck. "Can you imagine?" she said to Freirs, "she just attacked poor 'Riah for the second time today."

They had put her in the bathroom last night, after she'd been located among the trunks and old books of the storeroom in Freirs' building. She had been strangely tractable at the time, nestling in Sarr's arms, making no protest as he'd closed the door on her. "I almost hate to do it," he had said, "the way she's acting now. But when I think of what she did to Mother—" He shook his head.

This morning, when they'd come downstairs at seven, she'd been gone. Apparently she had learned to turn the knob on the bathroom door by swatting at it with her paw. She had still been in the house, though, for, in addition to the screen door, the heavy wooden kitchen door was closed. As Sarr and Deborah had descended the stairs, followed by the six cats who'd shared their bed, they had seen Bwada race up from the root cellar and pounce on Azariah.

"And now she's gone and done it again," said Deborah, with a shudder. "Make sure that chair's braced tight against the door."

From the bathroom came a disconsolate miaow.

"You're staying in there!" Deborah shouted angrily. "We'll see how you like it!"

A miaow again, but drawn out this time into a long, ugly caterwauling that sounded disconcertingly like human speech.

The three eyed one another uneasily.

"She's not been sounding like herself lately," said Sarr. "There's a kind of—hoarseness. At first I thought it was the accident. Now I'm not so sure."

Freirs nodded. "Yesterday, when I found her in the storeroom, there was something funny about her."

"Funny?"

"She licked her lips—you know the way an animal will do—but it looked like she had something in her mouth."

Sarr shrugged. "Maybe she did. That place is full of mice."

Deborah laughed. "Or maybe she's got a frog in her throat!"

"I don't know," said Freirs, shaking his head. "I'm not too familiar with cats, inside or out, but I'd say she's got something in there. Something wrong. A tumor, maybe, a growth of some kind. I'd take a look at her, if I were you."

"I'll do that," said Sarr, "as soon as we let her out tonight. I'm even thinking of taking her to that vet over in Flemington. There isn't much else I can do." He stared gloomily at his hands and fell silent. At last he looked up. "Well, there's one thing. I wonder if you'd excuse us for a few minutes, Jeremy. I want Deborah here to join with me in prayer."

"Oh, yes, of course."

"And you know," said Sarr, "maybe when we're done I should give a look to her mouth. No reason to wait till tonight. Better to get to the source of the trouble right away."

Freirs wandered into the living room and leafed boredly through an *Old Farmer's Almanack* while Deborah sat down across from her husband. The two of them propped their elbows on the table and clasped their hands. Freirs looked in at them once; they were silent, their eyes tightly shut.

He drifted back into the living room and waited, listening to the ticking of the clock.

Was there another sound?

Yes, he heard it now. A low, grating sound was coming from the other room.

It came again, followed by the frantic scrape of chairs and Sarr's angry swearing. Freirs rushed into the kitchen in time to see Sarr yank open the bathroom door.

"The window!" Deborah cried, pointing. Its screen gaped outward, crisscrossed by two wide slashes.

The room was empty

She wasn't in the storeroom this time, or in any of her usual hiding places. Sarr & I searched the workroom in the barn & the chicken coop too, on a platform six feet above the floor. Plenty of dust & fat buzzing bluebottles, but no sign of the cat. Even took a peek into the old smoke-house, as much as the wasps there would let us. We looked for her till dinnertime, in fact, but she was gone without a trace.

It began to rain during dinner & I hung around the house till it stopped. When I got back here I attempted to relax by reading Algernon Blackwood's "Ancient Sorceries." One of his lesser tales, perhaps, but I found it anything but relaxing. It's about a town inhabited by a band of feline witches—were-cats, I guess you'd call them—& it's done unpleasant things to my imagination.

Close to midnight now, & despite the day's heat, the coldest night we've had so far. Think I'll have some trouble getting to sleep; tonight the whole atmosphere seems weird, worse than ever I recall. Thunder coming regularly—more rain on the way, no doubt—& lightning with it, obviously close by. But why, then, is there so much more thunder than lightning?

A bright flash that time—I felt the whole room shake, right down to the floor. Wish I were inside the farmhouse tonight. Wish I weren't sleeping alone.

Can hear the two of them in there singing their nightly prayers now. A rather comforting sound, I must admit, even if I can't share the sentiments.

Maybe I'll be able to fall asleep if I pretend—

He looked up. There'd been a rustling at the window by his bed, the one that faced the woods. He turned to look, but he was blinded by the desk lamp beside him, and the window was a great square of blackness.

Suddenly a flash of lightning lit the sky. Freirs shouted and drew back. A humped grey shape was pressed against his screen, outlined in the light. The eyes were wide, unblinking, cold as a snake's. The mouth hung partly open. There appeared to be something crouched inside it . . .

All this he saw in the flash of lightning, while the pale little face of Absolom Troet smirked down at him from the picture on the wall. An instant later the darkness returned. He heard something drop heavily from the screen and pad off into the underbrush, to the echoing rumble of thunder. The next time lightning flashed, the view held only the forest.

JULY FIFTEENTH

Iwoke up to the sound of Sarr's axe. You could probably hear it all over the farm. He was off among the trees at the edge of the property, chopping stakes for Deborah's tomatoes.

Went out and joined him for a while. I told him about seeing Bwada last night, & he said that she hadn't come home. Good riddance, say I. Helped him chop some stakes while he was busy peeling off bark. Christ, that axe gets heavy fast! My arm hurt after three lousy stakes, & Sarr had already chopped fifteen or more. Obviously what I need is more exercise, but think I'll wait till my arm's less tired.

I left Sarr to his business & went up to the house. Guess I got there a bit earlier than usual, because Deborah was still running her bathwater, & just as I came up out of the cellar with a jug of milk she walked through the kitchen with nothing but a towel wrapped around her. She jumped; so did I. Don't know which of us was more surprised. I took one look at those creamy white shoulders, which I'd never actually seen before, & those beautiful white legs & thighs, and my cock gave a little leap. Like a fool I immediately averted my eyes, & she hurried into the bathroom, but she was laughing as she closed the door.

I could hear her shut the water off & settle into the tub. Sarr's axe still rang out from time to time from over near the woods. I waited a little while, then I went to the door & called—with a jokiness I didn't really feel—"You sure you don't want me to scrub your back?"

She didn't say anything for a second; maybe she was actually considering the idea. Then she said something about Sarr's not liking it.

"He's half a mile away," I said, giving it the old Freirs try. I really would have loved just to *see* her . . . She laughed again, I think, & then—alas!—she said, "Not today."

Well, so much for *that* dream. If she wasn't up for anything then, I'm sure she never will be. Moments like that don't come very often.

Oddly enough, she was extremely friendly—almost affectionate, really—for the rest of the morning. After she got dressed she made me some delicious wild-blueberry pancakes (with berries she'd picked herself), & it seemed plain that she liked having me there while she puttered around the kitchen.

Today, she informed me, is St. Swithin's Day—whoever the hell he was—& she recited a little rhyme:

"If rain on St. Swithin's Day, forsooth,
No summer drouthe,"

or something like that. Apparently the day's weather is supposed to determine the weather for the next forty days. All very scientific, like that business with the groundhog. I looked out the window, but the sky was so changeable that I found it hard to decide exactly what kind of weather we were having then & there, much less *going* to have. The clouds were moving fast across the sun, with a huge grey one looming just above the horizon. So as I see it, we're in for forty days of sun, clouds, nastiness, & fog, with just a touch or two of rain.

Sarr came in around lunchtime, looking troubled. Seems he'd accidentally killed some kind of thin white snake that had been crawling along one of the branches. He'd sliced it in two with his axe, & the thing had had babies inside.

"It was a milk adder," he told Deborah, as if that signified something of great importance. She asked him if there'd been much blood. "Yes," he said. "But it was white."

He explained to me that milk adders are supposed to get their sustenance by sucking the milk out of cows' udders. Maybe this one had been on its way back from the Geisels'. They're the closest ones around here who own cows.

I said I thought all that was only a legend.

He nodded. "So did I."

He had buried the thing immediately, before the cats saw it. The babies had gotten away.

Later he fell to talking about some other local legends—about the Hop Ghost, that hops behind you when you walk past a churchyard at midnight, and the Magra, a sort of unwanted companion, and something known as the "Jersey Devil," the thirteenth offspring of a Mrs. Leeds, who'd cursed being pregnant again. In the end, Sarr said, she'd given birth to a horrible half-man half-bird thing which flew up the chimney & disappeared.

He also told me about dragon beetles, supposed to be as big as a man's fist, & screwworms, which can breed in people's nostrils, & hoop snakes, that swallow the end of their tails and roll along the ground behind their prey.

I was curious about the last; it sounded like a variation on the old Uroborus myth, the dragon with its tail in its mouth. The alchemists had used it as a symbol of eternity, unity, the all-in-one, or some such blather. Maybe there was something to it after all.

Actually, I've always had a yen to read that Eddison novel, *The Worm Ouroborus*, but I'm told it's impossible to get through. Waded through some poems in *The Ingoldsby Legends* before dinnertime, & that was punishment enough.

Omelet for dinner with home-grown herbs. Damned good. The hens have been laying well lately.

At night the wind blew from the north & the sky got very clear. I spent close to an hour sitting out back in the deck chair with my *Astronomy Made Simple* & a flashlight. There was no moon out, but so many stars that I could almost read the book by their light. I picked out the Eagle, the Swan, the Plowman, & the Bear, & sat & watched the Dragon chase the Virgin. I'll forget all the names in a day or two & don't intend to learn them again, but it was nice to have done it once. Saw at least eleven shooting stars, then I lost count.

The Park West Institute of Dance was one of the few places in the neighborhood not yet gentrified, although the old two-story building it occupied on the west side of Broadway now housed a joggers' shop and a fancy new women's boutique. Carol had been coming here for nearly six months and had begun to feel like a regular. Until this summer she had had to content herself with a single weekly dance class on Tuesday nights, but now, thanks to Rosie, she could afford to take an additional class when she was in the mood; and she was in the mood tonight. It was Friday, and her datelessness weighed more heavily upon her than usual. Tomorrow, at least, she had something to look forward to—Rosie would be taking her to an evening concert in Central Park—but tonight she knew she couldn't bear to go home immediately after work to sit alone in her apartment reading Rosie's articles, air conditioner or no air conditioner.

As she slipped on her leotard in the noisy little locker room, she wondered how many of the women around her had husbands or boyfriends waiting for them at home. Not that many, from the look of them. They were an older, unhappier-looking bunch than the Tuesday-night crowd, women who were filling some gap in their lives or who'd suffered too many disappointments; they were taking it out here, throwing themselves into an activity where they need depend on nothing but their own bodies. She was pleased to see that, as usual, she was one of the thinnest in the room; she told herself she would look young for years and felt no envy for the woman to her left, cursed with huge breasts that were already starting to sag. There were a lot of plump thighs and soft-looking stomachs. Dance, for some women, was probably no more than a pleasant way of dieting.

The main room stretched for half the length of the building, occupying the space above three stores. One wall was lined with floor-to-ceiling mirrors whose silver backing, here and there, had flaked away. Windows ran along the opposite wall, above a barre worn smooth by years of ballet students. Carol had not taken ballet since college. She regretted that she hadn't continued with it, and didn't pretend that the modern dance classes at Park West accomplished anything more than keeping her limber.

There were sixteen people in tonight's class, including three slim, amiable-looking young men she immediately assumed were gay. The teacher—not the one she had on Tuesday—was a wiry little woman in her late thirties with tight black curls and a drill sergeant's voice that belied her height. She, too, seemed less than happy to be here tonight.

The first half hour of the class was given over to mat and barre work, stretching arms and shoulders, twisting necks, and raising legs in modified pliés, all to the softest of calypso tunes played on the tape deck in the corner of the room. Outside the dirty windows she could see the lights of the buildings across the street, a starless black sky overhead. There was no sign of a moon.

The teacher clapped her hands for attention. "All right, let's review the combinations we learned last time." For this part of the instruction the class moved onto the polished wooden floor in ranks of four across, following the teacher's moves while a disco beat, louder than before, now rocked the room. The steps were familiar to Carol from her Tuesday-night class and she was good at them; although she would be learning nothing new, she was pleased to be singled out several times for demonstrating the correct form. "Watch the redhead," the teacher said more than once; it took Carol a moment to realize the woman meant her. As she danced, twisting her torso and letting her arms swing free, she watched herself reflected in the mirrors on the one side and the glossy blackness of the windows on the other. She liked what she saw.

With twenty minutes still to go the teacher switched cassettes again, the disco music giving way to a reggae group Carol had never heard before. Once more the volume was raised; the rhythm grew faster and harder to resist.

"All right, people," said the teacher, "it's time for improvisation. Back against the wall in groups of four, and come out when I call you." Dividing up the class, she motioned for the first group to come forward. Improvising was something Carol had never done before; immediately her pride gave way to nervousness, as if she'd been asked to speak in public on a topic yet to be announced.

Still, the music was persuasive; she found herself tapping her foot and rocking her hips to the beat while watching the first group of four women take the floor. "Get in tune with your bodies," the teacher called, without noticeable effect. "Don't watch anyone else. Just let

your body follow the music, let it come naturally." Only one of the four
was any good, Carol thought, a haughty-looking dark-haired girl who
tossed her shoulders and shook her head as if she were actually on some
Caribbean beach surrounded by a dozen obliging black men. Carol
wondered what she was going to do when her turn came.

"Next four," the teacher called, and two women and two of the
young men stepped forward, the previous group having retreated back
to the mirrored wall. "Don't watch anyone else, I said," the teacher
cried a little testily at the two men, who seemed to be blithely dancing
with one another. "Close your eyes if you have to." The four did so,
with predictably awkward results.

A gesture from the teacher indicated that Carol and her group
would be next. At the woman's command they moved out onto the
floor, Carol, two older women, and the remaining man. "Close your
eyes," the teacher said, "and feel the music. Let it move your body."

Carol tapped her foot self-consciously, trying to do what the woman
had advised; but though she liked the music, it was nonsense to think
that it could really move her. It wasn't fair, she told herself; she'd
never wanted to be a choreographer.

It occurred to her, suddenly, that she might do the Mutamentos, the
Dance of the Changes she'd practiced two nights ago. It was a slower,
more sinuous dance, and didn't really go with the lively black music
she was hearing, but it consisted of only nine simple movements, and if
she did them in the right rhythm she might be able to fill up the time
till the next group was called out.

Shutting her eyes, she tried to remember. There were two different
spins, and a side step and a back step . . .

Yes, that was it, she'd got it now; the trick was remembering the odd
movement of the hands, and where it came. It felt strange to be doing a
folk dance here in class; she wondered if she looked foolish. No doubt
the other women would be performing some wildly expressive modern
dance routines or some reggae steps they'd picked up. Hoping the
teacher didn't think the less of her, she opened her eyes.

She found herself facing the mirror, the teacher's image reflected in
the glass. For some reason the woman looked amazed; she was staring
back and forth between Carol and the two other women, her eyes growing progressively wider. Carol sneaked a glance at the others and
gasped: they too appeared to be performing the Changes. Their eyes
were shut tightly; they looked rapturously happy. The man, eyes also
shut, was a little way off, doing disco numbers by himself.

Carol felt somewhat chagrined; obviously the two women had
cheated. They'd opened their eyes while hers had been closed and copied Carol's steps. Perhaps they meant to mock her; perhaps they too
hadn't known what else to do.

Looking back toward the teacher, Carol saw that, if anything, the woman's astonishment had increased—for she was now staring at the man. Carol whirled to look at him. He too was performing the folk dance, keeping time with her and the others, though his eyes, at the moment, remained closed. *It isn't fair!* Carol thought, suddenly indignant. This was her dance, and the others were imitating it.

The four of them, in fact, were moving in unison now, pounding the wood floor with their feet at the same time, spinning at the same time, the others with their eyes shut tight, the huge room echoing to the sound of their feet. It was almost uncanny. She noticed with embarrassment that the bulge in the young man's tights had grown larger, and wondered who in the class had aroused him.

Just then the teacher stepped forward. "Did you people rehearse this?" she cried. "You've got it down pat." Without giving anyone time to answer, she signaled for the final group to take the floor.

The other three moved back toward the mirrored wall, but Carol, lagging behind them, found it hard to stop dancing; she was still caught up in the rhythm. Dimly she heard the others talking. "I just did what the music *told* me to do," the young man was explaining to his friends. She noticed in the mirror that the four new women seemed to have picked up the dance merely by watching their predecessors: they too were performing the Changes now, and in the same perfect unison.

She wanted to speak to them, to ask them how they'd learned the dance so fast, but she was too busy watching her reflection, watching her hips jerk, her head toss, the motions of her hands—when suddenly, with a crack like a gunshot, her image in the mirror splintered into thousands of pieces. There was a crash at her back. She turned to see one of the tall windows shatter and fall. Someone shouted; behind her the crowd was backing away from the shards of broken mirror. Abruptly the four dancers stopped and opened their eyes, staring at one another in confusion. The teacher hurried over to the tape and shut it off.

"Maybe some kid with a slingshot," she heard one of the men say.

"Is it a sniper?" someone cried. Women screamed and retreated toward the doorway. Carol followed, though even as she ran she wondered how a sniper could have done it. It had all happened so quickly . . . yet it seemed to her that she'd heard the window shatter an instant *after* the mirror had cracked.

"I think we'd better call it a night," the teacher said. The students followed her off the floor and into the locker areas.

People were still talking excitedly about the incident as Carol dressed and moved toward the doorway. As she left the studio she saw the dance teacher in conversation with a large black man in janitor's overalls. The two of them were standing at one side of the dance floor, pointing up toward the corner of the room near the ceiling where a complicated spiderweb of tiny cracks covered the heavy masonry. Carol hadn't noticed them before. As she walked past, she heard the man saying, "We lost a window downstairs too."

She paused, nervous again. "Is there really someone shooting out the windows?"

The man shook his head. "Naw, nothin' to worry about, lady. Ain't no sniper out there. The old place is just settlin' a little, that's all."

"Oh, what a relief!"

Nonetheless, she was glad to get away; as she walked down the hall and the echoing stairway, she was sure she heard tiny cracking sounds.

The night was clear and cool, with a panoply of stars. The others were already on the porch, their faces ruddy in the lamplight, when the Verdocks pulled up in their truck.

"How is she, Brother Adam?" called Jacob van Meer, seated in his rocker as if it were a throne.

Verdock shook his head. "Not so good, I think." He and Lise came up onto the porch and pulled up chairs. "We must try to remember her in our prayers tonight. She'll need 'em."

"We left Minna with her, to tend her till the morning," said Lise. She was talking to everyone on the porch but, as was customary, directed her words to Elsi van Meer and the other women. "Minna's made her comfortable, and she'll see to it the garden's looked after till Hannah's got her strength back."

"*If* she gets it back." It was Rupert Lindt, who had joined them that night and was taking up a good portion of the couch.

"Now, now, Brother Rupert," said Verdock, "the Lord looks after those that keep the spirit."

The other shrugged. "Maybe so, but the spirit and the body's got to part some day. I can't say much about Hannah's spirit, but her body's gettin' old."

Hannah Kraft was a widow of limited means and solitary habits whose health had been poor for decades, although never so poor as she'd painted it—at least not until now. Now, in her eighties, she seemed to be dying in earnest. The Verdocks had visited her earlier in the evening with their widowed daughter, Minna, and had left Minna there to spend the night with the old woman in the little three-room house off the back road.

"She takes on something fierce about the weather," Adam was saying. "A good thing it's so mild tonight. She told Minna she can't get a wink of sleep anymore, what with the thunder and the rain."

"Well, Hannah will go on," said Bethuel Reid, perhaps the closest to her in age. "I remember—years ago, it was—when she wouldn't let you get a word in edgewise and you couldn't make sense of a single thing she said."

They nodded, all of them, but Lise Verdock raised her voice to add, "She says there's noises pretty nearly every night now. A rumbling, she calls it, like something's moving out there."

"Well, sure," said Bert Steegler, "it just stands to reason, you stay down by the Neck and you're goin' to hear noises at night."

Van Meer looked skeptical. "Oh, a few frogs, maybe, a whippoorwill or two. And maybe the Fenchel boys up to their usual mischief. But I trust you're not holdin' with all those stories about spirits."

"Well, maybe I am, maybe I ain't. All I'm sayin' is, there's holes in those woods, there's underground springs, there's pockets of gas in the swamp . . . Such things'll make a bit of noise, as I'm sure Brother Rupert remembers."

Lindt nodded, pleased to be singled out. He was the youngest man there, and the largest; he had a habit of saying disagreeable things, often in a booming voice, but these people had known him since his boyhood and tolerated his ways. Any time they needed help, they knew they could count on his strong shoulders.

"I grew up near the Neck," he said, "and I know the sounds the swamp can make. But this time I ain't so sure. I've heard the thunder too, and it ain't the same. I think it's a sign. Just like all the snakes we've had this summer."

Van Meer paused in his rocking. "What are you drivin' at?"

Lindt shifted uneasily in his seat. "All I'm sayin' is, let's look at what we got. We got us a new influence in the community—a snake in our bosom, so to speak—and I think you all know who I'm talkin' about."

"I follow you, all right," said Adam Verdock, "but I think you're makin' a mistake. I met the boy too, that day in the store, and I liked him all right. Seems to me he's got a good name, too; it honors the prophet."

"Or mocks him," said Lindt.

"I asked Sarr about him," said Bethuel Reid. He drew deeply on his pipe. "Sarr says he just reads books all day."

There was a round of head-shaking. Idleness was sinful when there was land to be worked.

"Ever see the fellow's hands?" said Lindt. "Soft as a baby's. Any fool can see he's never done a day's work in his life. Must have a lot of money stuffed in his pockets—like all those city people."

Reid nodded, glad he had no pockets of his own. "Yep. That's their trouble."

Steegler nodded too, and grinned with a sidelong glance at Lindt. "All I know is, he had some young woman out here the other week. He must be doin' more than just readin'."

"Well, you know those city folks," said Lindt. "They don't believe in marriage anymore."

Lindt's thoughts had turned more than once to Carol since he'd first seen her. He himself was married and unhappy; he spent little time with his wife and had come alone tonight.

"And when they do get married," he added, "they don't stay that way for long. Some day, you mark my words, that city's gonna be smote with fire, like the Cities of the Plain."

There was a chorus of assent, with several abstentions.

"Well, I spoke to Sarr about it," said Verdock. "'Tain't as if I didn't try reasonin' with him. I told him—I said it just ain't proper, takin' a man's money and callin' him a guest. But Sarr, well, when he makes up his mind he's hard to change."

"That ain't it," said van Meer. "'Tain't proper to bring someone like that into our little congregation, someone who don't fear the Lord and don't know our ways."

"Our Rachel was talkin' about that just the other day," said his wife. "She says Amos don't want his children exposed to such people."

"I don't think it makes much sense to worry 'bout such things," said Lise. "Not now, anyways. All we can do is say our prayers, trust in the Lord, and keep watchful."

She waited for the amens, but they were slow in coming.

Minna walked slowly from the kitchen, carrying a broad wooden tray whose hand-painted rose border had almost entirely peeled away. She ducked her head as she passed beneath the low beam of the doorway.

"Here we are, Hannah. This'll get you off to sleep quick enough."

The old woman was sitting up in bed, her head turned toward the open window in the wall behind her. She didn't look around when Minna entered, and turned only when she felt the tray placed upon her lap, to stare fretfully at the bowl of oatmeal and the cup of steaming milk.

A cool breeze blew through the window, bearing the smell of damp earth and summer leaves and almost masking the odor of sickness and decay that hung about the room. Insects wandered up and down the screen. Minna heard the night sounds of the forest, the sound of things calling to each other, the chant of the crickets and frogs.

Scowling, the old woman tried a mouthful of the oatmeal and took a sip of the warm milk. Suddenly she slammed the mug down and shook her head.

"No," she said, waving away the food, "I can't get to sleep! If it ain't one thing, 'tis another. First there's the thunder, it made my head ache—and now this! 'Tis too damned quiet."

Minna smiled stiffly. "Quiet? With all that commotion out there? You just listen to those crickets for a spell and have yourself some o' that milk—there's honey in it—and you'll be sleepin' like a baby in no time."

"Hmph," grumbled the woman. "More like the dead!"

She took a few more swallows of milk, then set the cup back down and turned around on the bed to stare once more out the window.

"Watch out that don't fall now," called Minna, pointing to the tray balanced precariously on the old woman's lap. Ducking through the doorway, she went into the kitchen.

There were plates to wash. The little house had no running water, and Minna took the bucket that hung by the washstand and walked outside, down the front path to the pump. She gave the pump handle a few vigorous strokes, her arm strong as a man's. Above her a shooting star streaked across the sky.

From the house came the crash of falling crockery. *I knew it*, Minna thought, cursing herself as she hurried toward the bedroom.

Fragments of the shattered bowl gleamed amid a pool of oatmeal. The cup lay overturned on the rug. Minna noticed these things before she saw the woman twisted half off the bed—her mouth stretched wide, eyes bulging, hands clutched stiffly to her throat. From the gaping mouth came the last spasmodic moments of the death rattle.

Minna was a strong girl and had seen death at close hand before. She did not scream. She jerked the woman by the shoulders, shook her, slapped the dead white face, listened for a heartbeat. There was none.

"Dear Lord," she whispered, "take the soul of Sister Hannah to Thine everlastin' mercy. Amen."

Methodically she laid the body straight upon the bed, pulled the blankets up over the face, and bent to clean up the shards of crockery, the spilled oatmeal and milk. Only then did she scream—when, lifting the overturned cup, she saw what had lain curled beneath it: the tiny white shape, thin as the finger of a child, coiling and uncoiling on the rug.

Three A.M. The building is asleep. Outside, in the darkness, a chilly rain drums against the pavement. A streetlamp on the corner makes oily reflections in a puddle. Lampposts in the distance are obscured by mist.

The lobby is deserted, the light dim. Barefoot, dressed in baggy shirt and pants and clutching his little bag of tools, he tiptoes down the stairway to the basement. The corridor winds before him like a maze, its turnings illuminated by bulbs in metal cages, its ceiling just a foot above his head, as if pressed down by the weight of the building. From somewhere comes the hum of huge machines.

His teeth are out; his mouth hangs slack. The concrete floor is cold beneath his feet. He hurries past the steel-grey doors of the laundry room, the storeroom, the room where the superintendent keeps his mops and pails. Here it is at last, a battered metal door marked No ADMITTANCE. Impatiently he slips a strand of wire into the lock and gives it a twist. The door swings open.

The room is dark; from the darkness comes the hum of a machine, louder than before. Reaching inside, he switches on the light. Beneath him, down a flight of iron steps, stands the furnace.

It is huge. It fills the room like a monstrous metal tree, a vast tangle of pipes arching from its central core and spreading like branches across the ceiling.

Shutting the door behind him, he rushes down the steps and crouches like a supplicant before it, emptying his tool bag on the floor. A screwdriver tumbles out, then a wrench, then a pair of thick asbestos gloves.

It takes him but a minute to remove the boiler plate midway up the side. Within, the gas burns a bright and steady blue, and the roaring it makes is like a waterfall. The flame is not high now—in summertime the furnace only heats the building's water—but its force is still intense; as he lays aside the metal plate, his face is scorched by blasts of burning air. In the firelight, the black streaks on his skin look like a sunburst.

Stepping back to where the heat is less intense, he takes a stub of blue chalk from his pocket and hurriedly scrawls the circles on the floor, and then the circles within circles. The design is crude, simple, totally unlike a cabalistic star or tetragrammaton. It has eyes, a tongue, and claws. It resembles, in fact, a kind of beast: something primeval-looking, serpentine, coiled with its tail in its mouth.

The design is ready. He climbs the steps and switches off the light.

Now the only illumination in the room comes from the mouth of the furnace, aglow with dragon fire.

Standing just outside the chalk line, he shrugs off the loose-fitting shirt and drops his baggy pants. Naked, he steps into the circle, his soft pink body hairless as a baby's. Closing his eyes and taking a deep breath, he begins the dance.

His movements are awkward at first, then more certain. Suddenly he flings his arms wide and hops from foot to foot in an ever more complicated rhythm. From his toothless mouth comes a low ecstatic crooning and a string of unintelligible words.

"Da'moghu . . , riya moghu . . . riya daoh . . ."

Round and round he dances, eyes shut tight, hands weaving ancient shapes above his head. Faster and faster move his fingers and his feet, faster comes the stream of words. Sheened in sweat, his body glows eerily in the flickering blue light that bathes the room. He bows, he leaps, he spins, pirouetting girlishly but turning ever faster till he's whirling like a dervish, his tiny withered penis flopping up and down, his plump breasts sagging and jiggling like a woman's. The crooning grows in volume, turns into a ululation, then a high-pitched wail.

"Riya moghu . . . davoola . . . DA'FAE!"

And suddenly with a cry it is over. The vision has come. Exhausted, he sinks to the floor and lies flat on his back with his head in the center of the circle, body still trembling, limbs still twitching from the dance. His eyes, opening, roll back to stare at the fire, but he sees far more. He sees all that he has to.

The Dhol has come at last. It is out there now.

And it is free.

JULY SIXTEENTH

Sun's been warm today. Blue sky, fleecy clouds, refreshing summer breeze, all that rot. The sort of day that's supposed to make you feel good to be alive. Would have been perfect except for the bugs.

Got up reasonably early. Butterflies on lawn, cats playing tag. Bwada never came back, which is also nice. Sarr repairing leaks in the barn roof & knocking down nests of caterpillars from beneath the eaves; Deborah weeding in her garden, pruning rosebushes, hanging out sheets to dry. They do keep busy, these rural types.

And I should keep busy too. I've been here three weeks now & have yet to write a word on the dissertation. Slipping in my exercises, too. Didn't do them yesterday, and haven't done today's yet, either.

God, three weeks! Hard to believe. Even out here the time goes fast, when you stand back & look. Half of July's already gone, & I can almost feel August's hot breath on the back of my neck, something huge & angry waiting for me beyond the next hill . . .

From his rooftop, with the hot afternoon breeze at his back, he surveys the great doomed city spread before him in the sun. He hears, floating up to him, the hum of traffic, people's voices, the hiss of wind from off the Hudson. Children's cries reach him from the playground on the next block; he leans over the wall for a better view. Two of them down there are fighting. The larger boy has the smaller one down and is kneeling upon the other's shoulders, slapping at the face below him, slapping, slapping . . .

Elbows resting on the parapet, head resting on his hands, the Old One smiles as he waits for the tears to start. There; he has seen the gleam. His smile widens, spreads across his face. For a moment, as a wisp of cloud obscures the sun, the shadows change, his skin looks chalky pale, and he becomes a thing of stone, a gargoyle.

The gargoyle moves, dissolves. He raises his gaze from the playground to the dark green line that slices through the center of the city.

He has business there tonight—he and the woman. He is prepared. She will be, too, when the time comes: for tonight she'll wear the second victim's dress.

Last night was his turn to dance.

Tonight will be the woman's.

Night, now, & tired. Spent a lot of time in the sun this afternoon with *Arthur Gordon Pym.* The flies made it pretty hard to concentrate, but figured I'd get myself a tan. Probably have a good one now. (Hard to tell by looking in the mirror, though; light's too dim.)

But it suddenly occurs to me that I'm not going to be seeing anyone for a long time anyway, except the Poroths, so what the hell do I care how I look? Deborah had her chance; no sense trying to look good for her anymore.

No moon tonight, which works to the advantage of the stars.

One thing rather troubling: When I came back here after dinner I felt like reading something light, to counterbalance all the claustrophobic horrors of the Poe book with its pirates & corpses & cannibals—so I reached for the Saki collection.

Now I *know* I shelved that damned book under H. H. Munro, where it belongs. I specifically remember doing it, & I'm equally sure it was that way last night, because it gave me A.N.L. Munby on one side with *The Alabaster Hand* & Oliver Onions on the other side with *Widdershins,* all three books in fancy old bindings & looking quite handsome together. I remember sitting here admiring them.

But the Saki wasn't there tonight. I found it under S.

It's just a little thing, of course. Utterly trivial. Nothing else in here is out of place, that I can see. Nothing's missing. But it means that somebody must have been in here today—somebody who went through my books (maybe my other things as well) &, not knowing Saki was Munro, misfiled it.

Can't believe it was Sarr or Deborah. They've always been respectful of my privacy here, and anyway, when could they have come in? I can't remember a time today (except dinner, of course) when I wasn't here, either in this room or right outside the door.

Oh, well, maybe I'm wrong; maybe the heat's getting to me. I suppose I might have stuck the book back in the wrong place myself, late last night when I was sleepy, or when I was working today.

Just to play safe, though, I'm going to start hiding this journal. There are too many things I wouldn't want either one of them to read—I mean, all those stupid daydreams about Deborah . . .

I can hear them at their prayers right now, over in the farmhouse; until just a few minutes ago they'd been singing hymns. Comforting, to hear sounds like that on a night as dark as this.

But when I think about them poking around in here & then not telling me, it gets my dander up.

Meant to write a letter to Carol tonight, after putting it off for several days, but now I'm just too tired. I'll probably have trouble getting to sleep, though; my eyes itch & I can't stop sniffling. Must be the dampness.

He was waiting for her at the subway stop in front of the Dakota, a picnic basket on the ground beside him. He brightened when he saw her. "Carol," he said, waving his hands for emphasis, "you look like a dryad come to life."

"A what?"

"A wood nymph, a tree maiden."

She laughed. "Thank you. I feel like I just stepped out of 'La Sylphide.' Or maybe the Saint Patrick's Day parade!"

She was all in green tonight—in that beautiful green dress he had bought her, beautiful even if the fit was a little too loose and the hem a little too high, with green shoes she'd discovered in Rochelle's closet, and even a green scarf at her throat. The scarf she had thought of herself, just before leaving the apartment, knowing that Rosie would be pleased. She was beginning to anticipate his taste.

Of course, she had white on underneath. But even the most puritanical man in the world couldn't object to *that;* absolutely nothing showed through the tightly woven material of the dress. In fact, she had been a bit daring tonight and hadn't even put on a bra; it was all in perfectly good taste, of course, it wasn't as if anyone could actually *see* anything, but when she breathed she could feel the dress rub ever so lightly against her nipples, so that they stood out against the cloth. She had never walked around this way before. It felt good, now that she'd done it. It felt good to know that men would be watching her, wanting her, good to know that she was desirable to them. *Slowly but surely,* she told herself, *I'm coming along . . .*

"Come," he said, "we want to get a good seat." He reached for her hand. He had already picked up the basket, an old-fashioned wicker one with a blanket folded over the top and the handle of his umbrella peeping out in front. Together they crossed the street to the park.

Crowds of people were already streaming in the same direction, moving up the paths toward the Great Lawn. Most of them, like Rosie, were carrying baskets or tote bags or blanket rolls.

"I've never been to one of these before," said Carol, as they passed beneath the trees. It felt strange, to be walking through what was virtually a forest in the midst of all these people.

"You don't know what you've been missing," said Rosie. "This is the way music's meant to be heard, underneath the stars."

She looked up. There were no stars yet—the sun would not be going down for almost an hour—but behind the canopy of branches the sky was already growing dark.

"They're up there," said Rosie. "Take my word for it."

The trees suddenly gave way, and before them lay the broad expanse of the Great Lawn, acres of it, already covered with human figures. She couldn't remember ever having seen so many people gathered together, except in pictures of Woodstock. *It's like a religious event,* she thought, with a feeling of excitement, and she was suddenly very happy about being here, among all these people, not just in the park, but happy about being in New York where special things like this could happen, happened all the time.

"Do you want to sit up close," Rosie was saying, as they picked their way among the people and the blankets, "or is halfway back okay?"

"Oh, this is fine," she said.

He stopped at the first open spot of ground and, with a flourish, laid out the blanket. Reaching into the basket, he began to pull out paper plates and silverware.

"Wait till you see the dinner I've packed!"

There was French bread, and goose-liver paté, and deviled eggs, and cold chicken, and Rosie's own sweet golden wine, and strawberry tarts for dessert. It was absolutely perfect, like a dream, almost, to be sitting here on Rosie's blanket among this happy crowd (some of them surely envying her right now, it was such an extravagant dinner), with the food spread out before them and the band shell in the distance and, behind it, the towers of Central Park South glowing gold in the sunset.

They were still eating, finishing the last of the wine, when the orchestra began to take its seats. She could hear it tuning up, one instrument at a time, then increasing in volume and complexity until the sound swelled into a wave.

Suddenly applause swept the crowd, and heads turned; the conductor had appeared. There was an interlude of silence—and then the music began, a gaily seductive piece that made her want to sway her body in time. "It's Dvořák," Rosie whispered. " 'Slavonic Dances.' Afterward I'll play you something even nicer."

"On what?"

He smiled. "You'll see."

It was dark now, with the only light coming from the band shell and the distant buildings. She looked in vain for a moon.

"Sorry," said Rosie. "No moon tonight." She hadn't realized he'd been watching her.

"That's a shame," she said. "I would have liked a full moon overhead. It would have been just the right touch."

He shrugged. "This month has two full moons, one at the beginning, one at the end, which makes it pretty special. Right now you'll just have to make do with starlight."

The stars had come out—the brighter ones, at least, that could penetrate the haze—by the time the orchestra reached the second half of the program.

" 'The Rite of Spring,' " said Rosie, as the haunting tones of a bassoon floated in the air.

"I know," she said. "I love it. I've always wanted to see the ballet but never had the chance."

"The inspiration for it was the image of a naked girl dancing round and round before the elders of her tribe—round and round until she died."

Her heart beat faster. "Yes," she said, "I can picture it."

The night grew even darker as the piece progressed; the crowd was stilled and silent. Lying back on Rosie's blanket and gazing up at the sky, Carol found it easy to forget where she was, and where the strange, discordant music was coming from, with its undertone of menace and ancient evil. At times she almost imagined it was directed at her alone.

Toward the end, as the woodwinds became strident and the kettle-drums pounded like a pulse beat, he turned to her again. She sensed him looking down at her in the darkness.

"Carol, you're not tired yet, are you?"

"No. Why?"

"I just thought, since you're lying down . . ."

"No, honestly, I was just enjoying the music." Had she somehow offended him? She sat up.

"Then you're not tired?"

"Not at all."

"Good."

Suddenly, with a drumbeat and a blare of horns, the music ended. The meadow echoed with applause, and then people around them were standing, folding blankets, and pushing slowly through the darkness toward the paths out of the park.

She and Rosie picked up their things and followed, moving with the rest. On the outskirts of the crowd, vendors were selling hot dogs, ice cream, soda, and white plastic hoops that glowed in the dark. Rosie disappeared for a moment and came back with a hoop, which he fitted over her head like a necklace.

"There," he said, "it's your halo."

Around them now the crowd was splitting up, half streaming toward the paths to the east, half to the west. Carol began following the second group, but Rosie stopped her.

"Let them go," he said "I have a better idea." He took her hand and they began walking north, away from the crowds.

"Wait," she said, suddenly afraid. "Where are we going?"

He turned to her and smiled. His grip tightened on her hand. "Don't worry, it's a special place I know. You'll love it."

They went on, cutting across paths and down a slope toward a low wooded area. Soon they had left the crowd far behind them.

"But isn't this dangerous?" said Carol, in a near whisper. The trees were so thick now that she could no longer see the lights of the buildings that bordered the park.

"You're safe with me," he said. "Honest. Trust me."

She still felt nervous; she had heard so many frightening things about this park that she'd even been uneasy walking in it earlier with him. She remembered Sarr Poroth's story about wandering through the park that winter day. He had come out safely enough, but he hadn't been here at night and he wasn't old and frail like Rosie. Though Rosie's grip on her hand was anything but frail.

They were walking blind now; she had lost all sense of direction and was relying completely on him.

"I don't know," she said, trying to control her nervousness with a joke, "I sure hope you know karate."

She heard him chuckle as he pulled her along. "I don't need karate. I've got God on my side."

A few steps farther on, at the entrance to a foul-smelling little tunnel that ran beneath a footbridge, he stopped.

"Look, remember that little rhyme I taught you? In the Old Language?"

"You mean the one we sang together on the roller coaster?"

"That's right. It made you feel braver then, and it'll do the same now."

"But I've forgotten all the words."

"I haven't. Come on, I'll teach it to you again."

As they started through the darkness of the tunnel, their footsteps loud against the cobblestones, he whispered the words, and she repeated them, and the echoes in the tunnel repeated them again. And he was right: it was happening just as before, the fear was leaving her like a dream, a dream that on waking she would never be able to remember.

They emerged from the tunnel and left the path, moving through a densely wooded thicket where the ground was rocky and she nearly stumbled. Ahead of them loomed an archway of branches . . . and suddenly she found herself in a grassy clearing, a nearly perfect circle surrounded on all sides by trees so close their branches seemed almost intertwined. She knew she had never been here before, or even near it, but the place seemed somehow familiar—*like a fairy ring*, she thought—and she knew that here, at least, she was safe.

He had let go of her hand and was searching in the basket. "Ah, here we are. I knew I'd brought this old thing along."

It was a stubby white flageolet of polished wood.

"Oh," she said, "I didn't know you played the flute!"

He beamed at her. "Let's just say I've taught myself to play one or two songs."

He brought it to his mouth, but paused.

"Wait a second," he said, "before I go gumming it up, why don't you have a try?" He extended it toward her. "Don't worry, it's clean."

"But I don't know how to—"

"That's okay," he said, holding it out, "just give it a try."

She stepped back—he was practically shoving the thing into her face—but she didn't want to hurt his feelings and he seemed so eager that at last she took it and put the end in her mouth. Touching her fingers to the holes, she played a few notes. The sound was jarring, strident, but the fact that she had tried it seemed to please him.

"Good," he said, taking the instrument from her. "I can see you've got real talent!" He laughed.

"Very funny," she said, oddly humiliated. "Now it's your turn."

"I'd be delighted," he said, with a courtly bow. "But only on one condition—that you dance for me."

"Here?" She searched his face in the darkness, trying to see if he was joking. "What kind of a dance?"

He cocked his head. "The one we've been practicing, of course!"

"I'm still a little stiff from a class I took last night," she said. "And I'm not so sure I'd feel right doing it here . . ."

"Come on now, Carol," he said, smiling, "this is absolutely the perfect place. You've always wanted to be a dancer. Now's your chance!"

Maybe it would be best to humor him. Besides, it was so dark no one would be able to see her.

"Oh, all right, why not? I'll pretend I'm a—what did you call it?— a dryad."

She stepped forward into the circle and waited silently, trying to recall the steps from last night. There were just nine of them, she knew, repeated over and over in a complicated sequence: a step here, a back-step, a spin . . .

He was already raising the flute to his lips, and now he began to play—a slow, measured series of low notes, not exactly a melody, but the notes seemed to belong together, flowing into one another like the music a snake charmer played. Concentrating on the rhythm, she began to dance, slowly at first, in time with the music, but then faster as the music picked up speed. She had started out feeling somewhat self-conscious, even after her practice it was hard to think of where to put her feet, but gradually, as she let the music take her, she began not to think about the steps, they began to be second nature, maybe it was the wine; she simply let her feet and hands and head move the way they wanted to and felt wonderfully free and not afraid at all.

The song ended. She found herself standing in the center of the cir-cle, thoroughly winded but, like last night, eager for more. She took a few deep breaths; her head was spinning.

"That was wonderful!" said Rosie. He walked out toward her. "It was like watching the music come alive."

"Oh, really, I was awful." She shook her head but was pleased. "It's a wonder you could even see me. There's practically no light here."

He smiled. "I could see that necklace of yours whirling in the dark."

"You mean my little plastic halo!" She could feel it encircling her sweaty throat. Her hand went to it. "I'll have to remember to dance with it again some time."

He checked his watch. "As a matter of fact, we have more time right now. It isn't very late, and there's something I'd rather like to try. Something special."

"A different dance?"

"No, just a different song."

She shrugged. "All right. Sure. It might be fun to try out a new song."

"Actually," he said, "it isn't new at all. In fact, it's very very old. But I think you might enjoy dancing to it." He didn't give her time to reply. Laying out the blanket, he sat down and crossed his legs. "Ready?"

"No, wait." She ran a hand through her hair and loosed the top but-ton of her dress. "Ready."

The new song was even more beautiful than the first—more exotic, yet she almost felt she'd heard parts of it before, and wondered where. No matter, she was busy now, concentrating on the steps: *The back-step, the spin, the lift of the arm, the faster spin . . .*

The rhythm was different this time, it took her a while to get accus-tomed to it, but then she saw that, in fact, it was far more suited to the dance than the first song had been.

The lift of the arm, the faster spin, the special signs the hands made with the next spin ... And then the step, the spin, the spin ...

And suddenly she was into it; the music was inside her now and the stars were whirling overhead. It felt lovely, she had never known dancing could be like this ... And the steps were suddenly easy, they came to her so naturally that she didn't even have to think about them, she could watch the trees surrounding her like guards, their arms entwined, all black and green in the starlight.

The spin, the spin ...

And the night was heating up around her, and the grass was soft, and the tune he was playing was indescribably beautiful; she let it move her as it willed, stepping when it called for her to step, and spinning when it called for her to spin, and her body grew warm as she whirled round and round in her silky green dress with her flame-colored hair forming the center of a great green flower and her head spinning and her hands making the signs ...

The special signs the hands made with the next spin, the step, the spin, the spin ...

And her body was hot now, her feet were on fire, she paused to kick her shoes off beneath one of the trees and then whirled back into the circle, barefoot now, the music lifting her again, whirling her round and round until her head was spinning faster than the stars and the green dress was swirling round her legs and her necklace was twirling in the dark and her body was burning, burning ... And she knew what to do; while Rosie played and didn't see, she spun behind a tree and slipped off her underwear, leaving it a little splotch of white on the dark grass, and then she spun back into the circle, Rosie would never know, she whirled and danced for him and felt the music lift her as before, the grass alive and hot beneath her feet, her dress swirling around her waist now, her legs and body bare against the night, the night air on her body as she spun.

The spin, the spin ...

The trees danced round and round her and her body was on fire, and she knew she would have to dance faster till the burning went away, and dimly she knew, as she danced even faster, that her dancing was forming a pattern within the circle of trees, tracing a picture so monstrous and huge that no one in a million years could ever possibly imagine what it was ... And the stars were a part of the dance now, whirling with her as she moved about the circle, and dark green things were stirring in the grass, rising from the earth and fluttering around her, tiny green butterflies with wings like leaves, or maybe they were leaves that moved like butterflies, creatures from a deck of magic cards, and even the trees were moving to the song, and things in the trees, the faces in the leaves and the branches and the air, and she danced and danced until she felt so hot that she thought she would burn up, and she knew she was the native girl who'd dance until she died, and her body was on fire, and the fire was all around her, and she collapsed in a heap in the middle of the circle just as the song ended.

She could hardly remember how she got home. She had dim memories of Rosie pulling her after him into a cab, and of riding up in the elevator with him, her feet still bare, the floor painful beneath them, painful and dirty and cold . . . And then he was gripping her hand tightly and saying goodbye at her door, just as if he were a proper young gentleman and she his date.

And the next thing she knew it was Sunday morning, she was still in her green dress, the cloth all damp and sticky now and wrinkled from the bed, and her hair was matted and greasy and there was a silly white piece of plastic around her neck.

She was stiff and aching all over, but her feet hurt the worst. They were raw and blistered, as if instead of dancing last night on some grass in the park, she had been walking through a desert.

It was then she realized she'd forgotten the shoes. She'd left them, and the panties too, somewhere beneath those trees. They were probably still there.

There was no way out of it. She would simply have to go back uptown and get them. After all, they were Rochelle's shoes, not hers; Rochelle had probably paid forty or fifty dollars for them, and she wouldn't want to come back and find them gone.

The park was filled with joggers and radios and dogs that day, and angry voices arguing in Spanish. Blacks in headbands and earrings were playing conga drums by the fountain which, last night, had echoed to Stravinsky. She noticed litter everywhere; she didn't remember its being there last night, but perhaps it had been too dark to see.

It took her almost an hour to find the clearing where she'd danced, and by then her legs were aching so much she wished she'd never come.

The clearing, seen in daylight, was a terrible shock. She'd remembered it as being like something in a dream, a vivid dream of green leaves and cool air and music beneath the stars, but by day the place appeared completely different. The trees were burnt and blackened along the inside of the ring, and the grass where she'd been dancing was lifeless, charred quite black in spots. The very air that had smelled so sweet last night now reeked of burning. *What a shame,* she said to herself as she looked around, *there's just no place for nature in a city like New York.* She looked at the trunk of the nearest tree; it was completely scorched, right up to the leaves. *These trees are all going to die,* she realized. *It's those awful Puerto Ricans with their campfires.*

She walked around the ring of trees several times and combed the blackened earth, but she never found the panties or the shoes.

BOOK SEVEN

THE ALTAR

22. OBJECT OF GAME.

. . . In each round the player acting as Dhol must attempt to gain power points in the prescribed manner. When sufficient points have been obtained, players may proceed to next round.

Play continues until Final Round, when, of course, the object changes and the rule no longer applies.

—Instructions to the Dynnod

JULY SEVENTEENTH

Had a bad night last night. Even though I was tired I had trouble getting to sleep because my goddamned nose was so clogged. And no sooner had I finally drifted off than I was awakened again by a noise.

It sounded like something in the woods just outside this room. Smaller than a man but, from the sound of it, on two legs . . . It was shuffling through the dead leaves, kicking them around as if it didn't care who heard it. There was the snapping of branches & every so often a silence & then a bump, as if it were hopping over fallen logs. I stood in the dark listening to it, then crept to the window & looked out. Thought I saw some bushes moving, back there in the undergrowth, but it may have been the wind.

The sound moved farther away. I could hear, very faintly, the sucking sounds of feet slogging through the mud. Whatever it was must have been walking directly out into the deepest part of the woods, where the ground gets soft & swampy.

I stood by the window for almost an hour, & finally all was quiet except for the usual frogs. Had no intention of going out there with my flashlight in search of the intruder—that's strictly B-movie stuff, I'm much too sensible for that—though I wondered if I should call Sarr. By this time, though, the noise had stopped & whatever it was had obviously moved on. Besides, I tend to think Sarr'd have been angry if I'd awakened him & Deborah just because some stray dog had wandered past the farm.

Went to the windows on the other side of the room & listened for a while. Out in the yard everything was peaceful. It was extremely dark, & I could barely make out the shapes of the smokehouse & the barn, but I could hear those pie-plate scarecrows off in the cornfield, clanking whenever the breeze stirred them.

I stood at the window a long time; my nose probably looked crosshatched from pressing against the screen. Then I lay in bed but couldn't fall asleep. Just as I was getting relaxed the sounds started again, much farther off now: a faint, monotonous hooting which may have been an owl, though somehow it didn't sound like an owl, or any other kind of animal, for that matter. And then, as if in answer, came another sound—high-pitched wails & caterwauls, from deep within the woods. Can't say whether the noise was human or animal. There were no actual words, of that I'm certain, but nevertheless there was the impression of *singing*. In a crazy, tuneless kind of way the sound seemed to carry the same solemn rhythms as the Poroths' prayers earlier that night.

The noise only lasted a minute or two, but I lay awake till the sky began to get lighter. Probably should have gotten through a little reading but was reluctant to turn on the lamp.

Must have been around noon when I got up. Took my towel & went up to the farmhouse for a bath. Didn't see Sarr & Deborah anywhere around & expected to find them in the kitchen eating lunch. But the house was empty, except for a few cats on the back porch, and the farm seemed very lonely.

Only then did I realize it was Sunday, & that the Poroths were off somewhere at worship. I'd been sure it was Saturday . . .

Interesting, how you can lose track of time out here. I suppose in some ways that's healthy, getting away from the pressures that were on me in New York, but it's also a little disorienting. At certain moments I feel positively adrift. I've been so used to living by the calendar & the clock.

Sat soaking in the tub till I heard the Poroths walking up the road; they'd been over at some farm near the Geisels' & had worked up a good appetite. So had I, even though I'd done nothing all morning but sleep. Over lunch (eggs with thick slabs of bacon, home fries, & blueberry pie) we talked about the wildlife around here, & I mentioned the noise last night. Sarr suggested that the shuffling sounds weren't necessarily related to the wailing. The former may have been those of a dog, he said; there are dozens in the area, & they love to prowl around at night. As for the wailing . . . well, he wasn't so sure. He thought it might have been an owl or—more likely, he said—a whippoorwill. Apparently whippoorwills can make some very weird sounds, & they tend to do so at night. (Lovecraft had them waiting by the window of a dying man & singing gleefully as they made off with his soul.)

I wonder, though, if the wailing might not have come from the same stray dog that shuffled past my window. I've heard recordings of wolf howls, & I've heard hounds baying at the moon, & both have the same element of *worship* in them that these sounds did.

I didn't broach the subject of the Poroths' coming in my room while I was gone, the misfiled book, etc. Just didn't quite know how to bring it up. Deborah's fairly easygoing, but you never know when Sarr's going to take offense at something.

After lunch he got up to start work, while I, as usual, lingered in the kitchen with Deborah. A minute or two later we heard him calling us from the yard, to come quick and see "the sign from heaven." Through the window we saw him pointing at the sky.

We hurried outside & looked up. There, way up in the clouds, a thin green line, like a living thread, was streaming across the sky. We watched as it passed slowly over the farm. Hard to tell how long it was; at one point it seemed to stretch from horizon to horizon.

"What *is* it?" Deborah asked.

"A sign from God," said Sarr. But he had to have it both ways: "—and also a migration."

He was right, the second time at least, because just then a few flecks of green drifted down toward us, carried on the breeze, & we saw that they were tiny moths the color of leaves. Above us the line was passing onward, snaking away into the distance, moving west. Eventually it was lost from sight.

Sarr was exultant—"the Lord has vouchsafed us a vision, a promise of good harvests," etc., etc.—but I found the sight oddly disturbing. Came back here to the room & looked it up in my *Field Guide to the Insects*. Apparently some butterflies—the monarchs, for one—actually do migrate, even across whole continents; but there was nothing in the book about these little green ones, & I couldn't even find out what they were.

Deborah finished stacking the dishes and wiped the crumbs from the table. Lifting the old pewter milk pitcher, she carried it into the hall, where she lit the little oil lamp that hung from a hook beside the stairway. With the pitcher in one hand and the lamp in the other, she started down the narrow steps.

The cellar was the most primitive area of the house, with a floor of hard-packed earth and stone walls lined with crude wooden shelves. The ceiling was low, like the roof of a cave—too low for Sarr to stand upright—and the air, redolent of vinegar and spices, was noticeably cooler than anywhere else in the house. Raising the pitcher, Deborah poured the leftover milk back into a large metal canister near the foot of the stairs and refitted the lid. On a shelf against the nearby wall—above a row of empty pickle jars which she hoped, by summer's end, to fill—lay a cardboard egg carton. Down here, in the cool darkness of the cellar, hens' eggs remained fresh for weeks; each day she'd add new ones to the carton and take the older ones for meals. Today, she noticed, there were only three eggs left on the shelf; she had used the rest for lunch. But with the hens laying as well as they had been, she knew she could count on four more by dinnertime.

Back upstairs, taking the little basket that hung on the porch where the cats played, she headed toward the barn, Zillah and Cookie trotting at her heels. Sarr, sleeves rolled up, was bent over a thick growth of weed at the margin of the cornfield, slicing at it with a sickle. Freirs was back in his room, seated at his writing table; she could see him dimly through the screens. It was a shame, she reflected, that someone as smart as he was spent so much time on spook books and showed so little interest in religion; in all the weeks he'd been living here he'd never once asked them how services had gone. Well, next week he'd be able to see for himself, because they were going to be held here at the farm, right outside his door.

This morning's worship had been a satisfying one. True, they'd had to hold it in the hot sun; Ham Stoudemire's trees were lately so infested with tent caterpillars that anyone standing in the shade risked getting one down his neck. (She would have to make sure Sarr checked all their own trees this week, as well as the eaves of the barn.) And a few of the Brethren had made some rather odd remarks about "the stranger" they were harboring here—how silly! (Just as well, probably, that she and Sarr hadn't told the others he was a Jew.) And, too, there'd been the memorial prayer for old Hannah Kraft—that, of course, had been a sad note; poor Minna Buckhalter had been so upset . . .

But Deborah had been pleased to see that stuck-up Lotte Sturtevant looking so red-faced and puffy; she wouldn't look that way when *she* was with child. (And why had the woman insisted on coming at all? Perhaps that awful Joram had made her.) She had also enjoyed the singing; the morning's heat had brought out the spirit in everyone.

> *"Saved by the blood of the Crucified One,*
> *Ransomed from sin and a new work begun . . ."*

Swinging the basket in time, she rounded the corner of the barn and walked inside. Sunlight slanted on the pitted metal surface of the truck parked just within the doorway. A pair of fat bluebottles with heads like gemstones buzzed in the light. Along one wall the line of antiquated farm implements rusted on the hay, their spiked wheels and jagged iron jaws giving them the look of medieval instruments of torture.

> *"Sing praise to the Father and praise to the Son,*
> *Saved by the blood of the Crucified One."*

The hens were quiet today. Usually when she entered all four of them glared impatiently down at her from the high chicken-wire coop, squawking for their food bucket, but today only one of them peeped through the wire. She could see the dark red rooster pacing agitatedly behind it.

Climbing the heavy wooden ladder up to the platform where the coops lay, she reached above her to unfasten the latch at the side.

She froze; it was already unfastened. Around her head the bluebottles buzzed crazily.

Lifting herself to the platform, she saw, in an instant, the reason for the quiet: amid a small mound of feathers at the back of the coop, their yellow legs thrust at odd angles in the air, lay the plump and headless bodies of three hens.

Deborah maintains that Bwada did it. As she points out, the cat was known to be adept at turning handles, latches, etc., & just because she's run off, there's no certainty she's dead. "Remember," Deborah said, "she's used to eating what she catches in the woods."

That's where her argument breaks down—because the hens had not been eaten. They would certainly have made Bwada a succulent meal, yet their bodies had scarcely been touched. Only the heads had been taken.

Sarr claims he's heard of weasels doing this & came up with a dozen stories to prove it. While only a few days ago he was ready to believe that Satan had entered the cat, now he refuses to believe that his beloved old Bwada could have done such a thing. "She may have fought with the other cats," he said, "but that was out of jealousy. She'd never stoop to this."

I'm willing to suspect anything right now. Having just read some Frederick "White Wolf" Marryat this afternoon, I'm not even so sure I'd rule out wolves, were- and otherwise, as a possibility. My *Field Guide to North American Mammals* lists both red & grey foxes & even coyotes as surviving here in New Jersey. No wolves left, the guidebook says. But of course it may be wrong.

Why would any animal—Bwada, wolf, or weasel—make off with heads like that? Simply out of sheer meanness? It just doesn't seem natural.

As if she were out to convince me just how nasty she really is, Mother Nature had one more shock in store for me. When I came back here to this building tonight, after talking long into the evening with Sarr & Deborah, I reached out in the darkness, closed my hand over the doorknob—& crushed three fat green caterpillars. They left a foul-smelling whitish liquid on my hand.

"Guess what I have in my hand." Rosie, grinning, held something concealed behind his back. Across the room the air conditioner fought a
noisy war against the summer night.

"Is it for me?"

His grin widened. "Now I ask you, have I ever come here empty-
handed?"

"Is it something to wear?"

He shook his head. "Uh-uh, no more clothes, young lady! You're better off choosing your own."

"Is it something to read?"

"In a way. But don't be misled, it's not a book." He paused. "Give
up? Here. Something to play with."

He drew forth an object wrapped in brown paper. Tearing that off,
Carol saw that it contained a small cardboard box and recognized the
green and gold design on the front. *Dynnod,* the letters said, in swirls
of acanthus leaves and roses.

"Oh, of course. They're the same cards I took out for Jeremy. Gee,
thanks, Rosie. They're beautiful!"

Actually, she was rather let down; she'd been hoping he'd brought
her jewelry. And she seemed to recall that there'd been something a
little unpleasant about these particular cards.

"You never explained how these work," she said, slipping the cards
from the box and once again looking in vain for some instructions.
"They're for telling fortunes, right?"

Rosie nodded. "Only you tell them through a kind of game," he said,
"and the winner gets his or her wish. Here, sit down. I'll show you how
to play."

The rules were confusing. There were only twenty-two cards, but in
order to win the game it was necessary to memorize them all, since the
object was to guess which cards were held by one's opponent. Carol
found her gaze returning again and again to the smiling man and
woman on the card marked *The Lovers,* and though she tried her best
to concentrate, her thoughts kept straying to Jeremy.

"You're not paying attention, Carol," Rosie said for the third time.
"You have to study *all* the cards. Now this tree's the *da'fae* because
green is *daeh,* and we call the fire *tein'eth* because *teine* means red . . ."

"I'm trying," she said, already tiring of the game. There didn't
really seem to be much point to it: it was difficult to score because each
card held a different value which also had to be memorized, and so far

as she could understand there was no clear way to tell when the game
ended and who had won.

"The cards," he kept saying. "You have to keep looking at the
cards."

At the end of an hour Rosie simply laid down his hand, announced,
"It appears you've beaten me, young lady," and proceeded to read
Carol's fortune in the cards that she held. As fortunes went, it seemed,
in part, too bland—prophecies of friendship, hard work, a second visit
to the country—and, in part, too silly: "There's a test in your future,"
he said, studying the card marked *The Mound*.

"A test of what?"

He tapped the card and looked up, grinning. "A test of will. Can you
move mountains?"

No, Carol decided, she just couldn't see the point of it all. It wasn't
the sort of game she'd care to play again.

The room smelled of perspiration and roses. Lying on the bed with her
hand over her eyes, oblivious to the night sounds outside her window,
Mrs. Poroth breathed deeply and let her mind drift, skimming lightly
over sleep as if upon the surface of a pool. Around her on the coarsely
woven sheets lay nearly a dozen of the Pictures, their lumpish figures
glowing in the lamplight like paintings on the rough walls of a cave.
The others lay scattered where they'd fallen, on the floor beside the bed.

Gradually her breathing slowed and her face softened, the harsh an-
gular lines at each side of her mouth smoothing slightly as she left familiar thoughts behind and let herself fall into darkness, deeper now,
where other presences, indistinct but real, hovered expectantly around
her as if summoned. The rose scent was here too, but at the center of it
she heard the click of teeth; she felt the brush of earth against her
cheek, and something moist, and fur; there was a slow, distant heartbeat, vast and heavy as a continent, and the stir of giant leaves, and
the sound of something wormlike, probing for her in the darkness as if
seeking to enter her skull . . .

A tiny doubt touched her, and still with eyes shut she awakened,
struck suddenly by a fear she'd thought long buried, the fear that she
was alien in this world, even in this stony little room she had known for
the long years of her widowhood. What was she doing here, after all?
What was her real purpose, and why was she so sure that God had chosen her to be the instrument of His will?

The thought of God brought a hardness back to her face, and a resolve. Fear was a weapon of the devil. There was something, she knew, that would have to be destroyed, and soon. It was only a matter of finding where it lay hidden—that would not be hard—and of fending off a possible attack. All she needed was the strength.

Again the doubt assailed her, the futility of it all. *This is wrong,* she thought, *it's foolish. I'm not a young woman; I shouldn't have to carry such a burden by myself.*

But even as she gave the thought words, she rejected it. She knew there was no one who could help her, no one else as capable as she.

Calmer now, she felt a new claim on her attention, drawn like a compass needle by something just beyond the bed. Opening her eyes, she sat up and scanned the room. On the floor where her gaze came to rest, she saw it staring from the Picture—the crude jagged lines of the tree, a scribble of waxy green crayon with a hint of eyes amid the lower boughs. She stared back at it a moment, then suddenly looked down at her right hand. The fingertips lay lightly upon another of the Pictures, one she recognized dimly from her dream. It was a dark, humped shape, swelling in the center of the paper like a mound of earth.

JULY EIGHTEENTH

Morning. Despite the heat, he switches off the air conditioner by his bed and raises the window overlooking the river. A warm breeze bathes his face and brings the scent of roses. The air is clear at this hour; he can see figures moving in the glass and brick apartments on the opposite shore, and, farther west, the wavering green line of low hills.

Out there, beyond the Jersey hills, the thing is thriving. All this past week it has performed the special Ceremonies of its own: the required rites and, at certain times, the necessary sacrifices. Gradually, as the week spiraled toward its conclusion, it has honed its skill and gathered its murderous strength.

Its moment is approaching—and so is his own. There are special preparations he must make. Concentration is essential; the darkness and the heat will not bother him, but the room must be silent. Shutting the window and pulling down the shades, he lies back naked on the bed, intones the Sixth Name, and prepares himself.

Tonight, when it is time to act, he will be ready.

Thanks, no doubt, to my recent decision—No More Asking For Seconds At Dinner—woke up feeling half starved this morning, after a crazy dream in which I was eating everything & everyone in sight: Carol, the Poroths, the cats, the cornfield, whole continents . . . As I recall, it ended with my swallowing my own foot. Jeremy Freirs, the human Uroboros.

Carol—God, it's been at least a week since I've written to her. Better do so before she loses interest in me. Must get around to it before tomorrow's mail.

Squeezed in a second helping of corn bread this morning, telling myself it was to make up for the lack of eggs. We won't be seeing many omelets around here anymore till Sarr & Deborah get around to buying a couple of new hens. That one poor bird that's left doesn't look like she's going to be much good for anything for a while.

After breakfast, sat on the front porch reading some Shirley Jackson stories, but got so turned off at her view of humanity (everyone callous & vicious except for her put-upon middle-aged heroines, with whom she obviously identifies) that I switched to old Aleister Crowley when I came out here to my room. His *Confessions* look too long to read all the way through & are obviously untrustworthy as hell, but at least he keeps a sunny disposition.

Inspired by Crowley's jovial satanism, took another walk in the woods, hearing for the first time since I've been out here the distant barking of dogs & thinking about hounds of the Baskervilles, Tindalos, Zaroff, & the rest. Didn't Lovecraft have a hound as well? Weather so inviting, despite the mosquitoes, that I walked all the way back to the pool at the edge of the marsh, where the brook bends. But the pool was covered by a layer of greenish scum, with something dead floating in the middle of it. I turned around & ran back to the farm.

Maybe these things are normal out here, as we move toward the height of the summer.

Sarr was working his way along the border of the cornfield, clearing off bunches of weed with a stubby little sickle. "Little," he agreed, "but razor sharp. You want to try it?"

I'd had such bad experiences with his other tools that I wasn't too keen on taking up a new one; but then I figured what the hell, with any luck this'll probably be the only time in my life I ever get the chance to play with one of these things, & I may as well make the most of it. I took the sickle from him & hefted it in my hand—hard to believe the Russians actually put this thing on their flag; it's like making a coat of arms out of a meat hook or an ice pick—then I took a few tentative swings, & to my surprise it sliced right through the thickest stalks & branches, pretty as you please. It's a lot smaller than the scythe & a lot less unwieldy; you hold it in just one hand. And unlike the axe, it was easy to lift.

"Very good, Jeremy," said Sarr, "I think you've found your talent at last."

The dogs were proving difficult to walk with. She had three of them to deal with, two easily distracted young males and a female not yet come into her first heat. True to their shiftless master, they had never known an ounce of proper training and were used to roaming at will. They were friendly enough, but as free-spirited as wild things. Mrs. Poroth felt the daylight wane; shadows were crossing the forest floor, darkness creeping steadily up the trees. She realized that she still had far to go.

She herself had gotten an early enough start, up, as usual, by five, just before dawn, to tend her bees and complete whatever weeding her garden required, but the Fenchels, where she'd stopped hours later to pick up the dogs, were accustomed to staying up most of the night hunting what game they could, whether or not in season, drinking whatever was available, and no doubt scavenging what they thought they could get away with from their neighbors' land. None of them but young Orin ever rose before ten. The elder Fenchel, Shem, was the one she'd had to talk to, and as luck would have it he'd been sleeping off a bender until well past noon.

Not that she'd expected any problem borrowing the three dogs. Shem Fenchel was obliged to her for too many kindnesses—the boils she'd lanced on Orin's neck, the painful shingles on his own hand she'd ministered to, the birth she'd attended when Sister Nettie Stoudemire had been called away—to begrudge her the use of his hounds for the afternoon, or even to ask her the reason. He assumed that she was using them for tracking.

He was wrong. But as she'd set off with the dogs that day, leaving behind the Fenchel clan's collection of shanties at the fork in the road and disappearing into the forest, the animals jerking eagerly at their lead ropes and pulling her in every direction, she looked as if she were on the track of game.

In fact, though, she was not relying on the dogs to lead her. She knew quite well where she was going, and the fastest way to get there. The dogs were simply for protection, weapons of defense. She herself was sharp-eyed and wise, but she was getting old as well; alone, she would be no match for the teeth and claws and catlike stealth of the Dhol in its present form, especially if it caught her unawares with the source of its power so near.

That source would be somewhere by McKinney's Neck, of that much she was sure. But she was making slower progress than she'd counted on, the dogs tugging at her arm and baying excitedly at every scent they passed, stirring up birds and insects and small scuttling things that fled their path as the three dogs bounded noisily through the underbrush. The Neck was still miles away, and the light was growing dimmer. She prayed she'd reach the place before sundown, even though she would not perform her work till after dark. There would be only the thinnest sliver of moon tonight, but it would be sufficient.

She said another prayer, as well: that the place would not be guarded.

But it might be, she told herself. It was, after all, a key part of the plan, enabling the Demon to plot and learn and grow. Destroying it would not destroy the evil, but it would buy time.

She tightened her grip on the ropes and let the plunging dogs drag her onward. Already she was wondering if the altar she sought would be as small as she imagined, and as easy to obliterate. She didn't know exactly what it would look like, but that part didn't worry her. She would know it when she saw it.

Unseen by human eyes, it lay in the woods north of the stream, just beyond the marshlands and the swamp, between the clawlike roots of a lightning-blasted cottonwood whose fall had left a clearing in the trees—a clearing through which one might view, unobstructed, the sky, the stars, the moon.

Even from a few feet away the thing looked scarcely different from a rather large molehill: a low mound of mud and sticks and foliage, a bit too regular for a product of nature, perhaps, but by no means conspicuous enough to excite attention. If not for the ring of small standing stones that surrounded the thing like a row of miniature menhirs, a Stonehenge built to child's scale, no one would have suspected that it was, in fact, an altar—an altar which, though scarcely one week old, had already seen much use.

Only from up close would one have noticed the intricate patterns scratched in the surface of the mud, the circles within circles within circles. And even then, unless one happened to observe the polished shards of white and yellow protruding here and there, one would have missed the most interesting structural detail of all: the carefully packed layers of tiny skulls that formed a pyramid just beneath the mud.

All the skulls were empty now, picked clean of flesh by paws not fitted for such delicate work—and by teeth and a tongue that were. There were mouse skulls at the bottom and the middle, with curved yellow incisors, giant eye sockets, little room for brain; and there were three new acquisitions at the top: larger, more primitive, and beaked.

A quiet night. We made some popcorn after dinner & sat around the living room with the radio on, watching the antics of the cats & listening to some crazy station out of Pennsylvania that plays a mixture of country-western & Bible-belt gospel. Neither kind of music has ever been high on my list, but it seemed sort of appropriate tonight. It's like the Gothics I've been reading, I guess—either you like that sort of thing or you don't, simple as that.

Quiet out here now, thank God. I'm sick of playing front-row audience to every bit of local fauna that decides to march past my window. Sat up reading—or trying to—"The Jolly Corner." James seems so goddamned labored. (M. R. James of Cambridge, now *he* had the touch. Why so little fuss about him?)

Normally that sort of reading would have put me right to sleep, but my damned nose is so clogged again that it's hard to breathe when I lie back. Usually it clears right up as soon as I leave the farmhouse & come out here. I've used my little plastic spray bottle a dozen times in the past hour, but after a few minutes I start sneezing & have to use it again. Tried to read some more James so that I could get him out of the way, or at least fall asleep, but found my eyes too irritated, watery.

Maybe it's the mildew. The stuff continues to grow higher on my walls in a dark, greenish band. Tomorrow I really ought to take a damp rag & give this place a cleaning . . . & also trim the ivy that's been spreading over the outside of this building. It's already begun to block the light. If I wait too long, I may not be able to get out the front door.

Silently it watches, crouched on the wardrobe in the corner, muscles bunched like cables beneath the steel-grey fur. The eyes narrow, focusing intently, missing nothing, while the long hooked claws slide out like stilettos. Poised, ready, motionless except for the faint spasmodic twitching of its tail, it waits for the right moment and prepares to spring.

Below it, one short leap away, the man sits hunched over the table, absorbed in his writing, his breathing harsh in the quiet of the room. Near his head several gnats and a tiny green moth dart round and round the lamp. The man is soft, plump, and white, like the grubs it has sacrificed in the forest this morning. But when the claws rip through his flesh, the white will turn to red.

Kill him! he shrieks silently. *Why doesn't it* kill *him?*

The apartment is stifling. The shades are drawn, the windows shut, the little room locked tight. Transfigured by the deepness of his trance, the Old One lies soaking and exhausted on his bed, wet with urine, perspiration, and an amber fluid oozing from his plump half-open lips. His eyes are wide, unblinking, seeing nothing, seeing all; his body twists and twitches on the stained and wrinkled sheets; his brain throbs with rage. The White Ceremony is complete; the Green, too, is behind him, performed precisely as it had to be, precisely as the Master dictated. The necessary words have been spoken; the required signs have been made; the forces have been released. The Son is awakening . . .

So why, why, won't the thing out there kill him?

The altar was an obscenity, and larger, incredibly larger, than she'd expected. Even the dogs avoided it, after sniffing avidly at the muddy skulls, and now they stood waiting beside her in the darkness, tied to one of the great tree's upthrust roots. She heard them shift tensely among themselves, making occasional low growling sounds deep in their throats.

Mrs. Poroth gripped a heavy broken limb and squinted at the moon through the space in the trees. She was bone-weary, her arms stiff from the hours of trying to control the dogs, her palms and fingers blistered from the ropes. She dreaded the walk back in the darkness.

She willed herself to relax and watched the sky. She let her mind go free.

The moment came. The dogs fell silent. Raising the broken limb, she muttered a short prayer and brought it down against the swollen black shape before her. There was a crunching sound, as of breaking china, and she felt the limb sink into the crumbling mass. She brought it up again and smashed downward. Dimly she could see white shapes tumble toward her feet.

She worked for a few minutes more, knocking away the clods of earth and mud until only an irregular low mound of earth was left to mark the spot. Taking up the limb one last time, she scattered the remainder of the tiny skulls and pounded them to dust.

It watches without blinking, moving not a muscle. It senses that its waiting is almost at an end.

Abruptly, below it, the man pauses in his writing. He takes a white cloth from his pocket, blows his nose, curses softly. With a jarring scrape of metal he pushes back his chair and stands. Yawning, he switches off the lamp.

The thing on the wardrobe twitches, jerks forward a fraction of an inch. Now would be the best time: the man will be blinded by the darkness while it can see perfectly. It steels, tenses, arches itself to spring—

But suddenly it is confused. Something is holding it back. Something new. A hitherto unknown cautiousness—a sudden sense that, even now, it lacks the requisite strength, as if the very source of its power were now dim and uncertain. The man is soft, but he is also large; he is vulnerable, achingly vulnerable, but there is still a chance, a tiny chance, that if it tries to kill him tonight, it will fail. And even that tiny chance cannot be taken; too many things are hanging in the balance.

It watches as the man below stumbles into bed. In a few minutes he is asleep, his breath coming sonorous and slow.

Noiselessly it drops to the floor, leathery pads breaking the fall, four limbs yielding easily to absorb the shock. As it moves along the bedside, the man's face, stupid with sleep, is only inches from its fangs. It will be good, when the time comes, to tear that face.

But such pleasures must wait; there are suddenly new calculations to make and further rites to perform. It will have to grow still stronger, gather its speed, hone its murderous skill. Tonight, to bring itself one step closer to the necessary strength, it will add a new trophy to its altar in the woods.

Silently it pads across the room and pauses at the door. Slowly, with claws aching to become hands, it reaches toward the knob, grasps it, twists . . .

On the bed the man stirs, turns, and sleeps on. The door opens softly

on the night, where the lawn lies shining beneath a sliver of moon.
Something soft and grey slips outside. Slowly the door closes, clicks
shut.

Quietly, implacably, it moves across the lawn toward the farmhouse.

Sarr slept soundly, his right arm encircling Deborah's waist. The six
cats shared the bed with them, curled by their feet or nestled in the
space between their bodies. Outside the uncurtained windows, the crescent moon floated through the dark skies like a question mark.

From downstairs came the sound of the screen door opening, followed by the inner door. Sarr slept on, but Deborah stirred sleepily in
his grasp. Vaguely it came to her that Freirs must be entering the
house to use the bathroom; it was understood that he was free to do so.
Odd, though: he'd always gone outside, so far as she knew . . .

She listened, half dreaming, for the fall of his footsteps in the
kitchen below. Instead she heard a soft tapping noise—as if (and she
was to remember this later) the hard plank floor down there were being
touched, ever so lightly, by four tiny rakes.

A sound. Had that been a bump on the stairs? She stirred herself
awake for a moment, then lapsed back into dream. Dimly she sensed
Azariah, the older orange male, wriggle out from his accustomed place
by her feet to investigate.

Silence. The dream reclaimed her. There was a warming fire encircling her, warm as Sarr's brawny right arm. But the fire grew louder,
it *hissed* at her, and she knew that it was the breath of some great
beast . . .

And then skinny old 'Riah came scurrying back up the stairs and
buried himself beneath the bedclothes, trembling like a frightened
child. She could feel him, and she wondered what could be wrong, how
could anything tremble so when there was fire all around?

Now, from the stairs, came another sound—a low, insistent purring—and later she would remember thinking, as she listened to that
sound, *How could there be a purring from the stairs? Weren't all the
cats in bed with her and Sarr?*

The purrs continued, steady, almost seductive, reaching from the
darkness of the hall. Suddenly, as if in response—as if, for cats, the
sound held a note of beckoning—she felt two soft balls of fur dislodge
themselves from somewhere near her legs, drop upon the rug at the foot
of the bed, and pad into the hall.

There was an audible swish, like the sound a springy young sapling makes as it snaps back into one's face . . . A swish—followed by two bumps.

And then she and Sarr were waking, sitting up confused and frightened and horrorstruck, for they were hearing a sound coming from below, a sound they'd never heard before, the sound of cats screaming.

Before she knew what was happening, Sarr had leaped from the bed and was pounding downstairs. He reached the bottom in time to see Toby, Azariah's little orange double, give a final twitch of his limbs and, faintly in the moonlight, the slim black tail of Habakkuk disappear out the kitchen door.

Toby was dead by the time Deborah came downstairs. Neither of them ever saw Habakkuk again.

JULY NINETEENTH

Dear Carol,

Sorry I haven't written in a while. It's easy to lose track of time out here, and I've really been pushing myself to get through that summer reading list. There's also been some trouble with one of the cats—that heavy grey female, you may remember her, the old one who originally belonged to Sarr. She'd been acting very wild, and last week she ran off into the woods. We thought she was gone forever, but it seems that last night she came sneaking into the house and *murdered* two of the kittens, one of whose bodies she seems to have made off with.

Toby, the little orange one, was my favorite of the bunch. (Remember how he liked to have you pet him?) The other one, Cookie, was the smallest and, I suppose, probably the easiest to carry away.

The Poroths seem to be taking the two deaths like the deaths of children. Sarr woke me around half an hour ago, tapping on my screen and calling gently, "Jeremy . . . Jeremy . . ." He was carrying his axe like a sidearm and sounded very grim—almost shell-shocked, in fact: his voice was deep, subdued, filled with grief and confusion. He informed me, in all seriousness, that in a few minutes they're going to be holding a funeral service for the two cats and they'd like me to be there.

I tell you, Carol, this summer started off like Currier & Ives, but it's ending up like Edward Gorey. I don't know which is more bizarre: what that damned Bwada did last night, or the Poroths' sweetly crazy notion of holding a full-scale funeral for a couple of dead cats, or the fact that I, here just for the summer and relatively unaffected by all these goings on, am already wondering what I ought to *wear* to the goddamned thing.

Anyway, I don't want to be late and hurt their feelings, so will end this and try to get it in the day's mail. Do come out again—*soon*. I mean it. I want you here to help keep things sane.

XXX

Jeremy

He lies rigid on the bed, staring sightlessly at the ceiling. The sheets have dried now, the sun has come up, and his limbs no longer tremble. He has lain here unblinking for almost twenty hours; for the final ten of them he has not moved a muscle, save for the nearly imperceptible rise and fall of his belly. The room around him, the street outside, the formless living mass that is the city, all these are forgotten. He is not here. He is across the river now, belly to the ground, moving through the forest on all fours.

Contact has finally been attained.

Contact!—a linkage of the minds, just as, so long ago, the Master promised. He sees through *its* eyes now, feels the roughness of the forest floor through the pads of its feet, listens with ears more acute than any human's for the rustle of small creatures in the leaves. He smells the scent of pine boughs, marsh water, putrefying flesh; he feels his muscles ripple like a tiger's. Its body moves now to his will.

He feels the creature's fury, shares the memory of last night—the discovery of the ruined altar, scattered pebbles, shattered skulls—and shares, too, the hunger for revenge. They will pay, the race of men.

That, too, the Master has promised.

Stealthily he presses through the undergrowth to the forest's edge, slips through the long grass bordering the stream, and swims across with a confidence and ease no cat has ever felt. Selecting a likely maple on the other side, he lopes easily up the trunk; it is as effortless as running on the ground. Creeping out along an upper limb, he settles down to watch.

The three of them are gathered in an empty field, their figures ungainly and stiff as they stand intoning words out of a book. Before them lies a freshly dug hole and a small blanket-wrapped form.

For the first time in ten hours there is a flicker of movement on the Old One's wrinkled face, a nearly infinitesimal twitching at the corners of the lips.

And that same moment, as it gazes upon the proceedings from its perch in the tree, the animal's mouth widens into an almost human smile.

Unpleasant day.

Cats' funeral went off well; proved, in fact, to be rather touching, even to my jaded & allergic eyes. It was held out beyond Deborah's garden. Sarr had dug a small hole for the body, which was wrapped in black cloth. The other body—well, God knows what Bwada's done with it.

The Poroths, too, were dressed in black, but that's normal for them. I wore my best shirt & pants, the ones I'd first arrived in, & did my best to seem concerned: when Sarr quoted Jeremiah and asked, appropriately, "Is there no balm in Gilead? Is there no physician there?" I nodded with all the gravity I could muster. Read passages with them out of Deborah's Bible (Sarr seemed to know it all by heart, Deborah almost all), said amen when they did, knelt when they knelt, & tried to comfort Deborah when she cried. Asked her if cats could go to heaven; received a tearful "Of course." But Sarr added that Bwada would burn in hell . . .

What concerns me, apparently a lot more than it does either of them, was how the damned thing could have gotten into the house. Deborah said, with real conviction (though I don't think she'd believed it until this incident), "The devil taught her how to open doors." Sarr nodded solemnly & added, "She was always a smart cat."

He reminded me of an outlaw's mother, still somehow proud of her baby.

Yet after lunch he & I looked all over the land for Bwada so that we could kill her.

Took the same route we'd gone over twice already: barn, storeroom, beneath porches, even down among the pines that grow on the other side of the stream. He called her, pleaded with her, & swore to me she hadn't always been like this.

We could hardly check every tree on the farm, unfortunately, & the woods must offer the perfect hiding place for animals even larger than a cat. So of course we found no trace of her. We did try, though; we searched all the way to the old garbage dump at the far end of the road.

But for all that, we could have stayed much closer to home.

We returned for dinner, & I stopped by my room to change clothes.

My door was wide open.

Nothing inside was damaged, everything was in its place as it should be—except the bed. The sheets were in ribbons right down to the mattress, & the pillow had been torn to shreds. Feathers were all over the floor.

There were even claw marks on the blanket.

At dinner the Poroths tried to persuade me to sleep downstairs in their living room; they said they'd lock all doors tonight so that not even a human burglar could get in. Sarr believes the thing is particularly inimical, for some reason, toward me.

It seemed so absurd at the time. I mean, nothing but a big fat grey cat . . .

But now, sitting out here, a few feathers still scattered on the floor around my bed, I wish I had taken them up on their offer. Wish I were back inside the house. I did give in to Sarr when he insisted I take his axe with me.

But what I'd rather have right now is simply a room without windows.

I don't think I want to go to sleep tonight. I'll just sit up all night on my new bedsheet, my back against the Poroths' extra pillow, leaning against the wall behind me, the axe beside me on the bed, this journal on my lap.

The thing is, I'm rather tired from all the walking I did today. Not used to that much exercise. Slacking off too much lately.

I'm pathetically aware of every sound. At least once every five minutes some snapping of a branch or rustling of leaves makes me jump. And who'd have believed that mice could make so much noise as they patter across my ceiling? They may be small, but they sound like veritable behemoths.

How did that line go from the funeral today? From the Book of Jeremiah?

Thou art my hope in the day of evil.

At least that's what the man said.

JULY TWENTIETH

A dream of dragons. Woke up this morning with the journal & the axe cradled in my arms. What awakened me was the trouble I had breathing—nose all clogged, sneezing uncontrollably. Down the center of one of my screens, facing the woods, was a huge diagonal slash . . .

BOOK EIGHT

THE TEST

"What we did was no harm at all, only a game . . ."
—Machen, *The White People*

JULY TWENTY-FIRST

The dawn was grey and overcast. The sun was lurking just behind the tops of the surrounding pines, yet there seemed no end to the night. It was like one of those short, chilly winter days when darkness extends far into the morning—the sort of day when all a man's instincts rebel at getting up, and when the thought of rising as early as five thirty seems scarcely to be borne. Yet five thirty was when the sun rose; and with it rose Ham and Nettie Stoudemire.

There was, beyond the darkness, another reason for Ham's reluctance to face the day: this year had been, for him, a year of troubles. If it wasn't a late frost that had stunted the roots of his young saplings, it was the fruit tree blight, or worms in the tomatoes, or tent caterpillars that nested in his maples just when he and Nettie had played host to the assembled Brethren.

And now, after splashing some cold water on his face and sipping a pre-breakfast mug of coffee with Nettie—who, as the local midwife, seemed better able to cope with getting up mornings—and after stumbling from his house into the semidarkness, now Ham discovered what appeared to be some new trouble over at the pigpen.

The animals were gathered in one corner, snorting and pawing at something on the ground. Only one thing will disturb a pig that way, and even as he hurried toward the pen Ham imagined exactly what, in fact, he found: a garden snake, thick and black and harmless, which had somehow wandered into the pigs' territory and had been stamped to death by their hooves.

Climbing nimbly over the fence, he gave the animals hard whacks on their sides. To them it was like a caress; they moved apart to let him pass. He took the dead, mashed body, still quivering from nervous contractions, and hurled it sidearm toward the woods, past the northern edges of the field.

A bad omen, he thought to himself, this early in the morning. A bad omen for the day.

Ten minutes later, as he strode out to the cornfield, a hoe upon his shoulder, he saw the next snake. It was small and slim and green, and was moving slowly down one of the planted rows. Such snakes were beneficial—they fed upon the rodents that fed upon the corn—and he let it go by, though not without the shadow of a frown. Watching as it passed timidly down the furrow, he turned to follow its course—and, turning, saw another snake, less small, less slim, and darker green.

Briefly he recalled something he'd heard at the worship last Sunday: a chance remark, prompted by the news of Hannah Kraft's death, about this season's having seen more reptiles in the woods than any time in recent memory . . .

Ignoring his growing uneasiness, he pushed between the waist-high stalks of corn into the next row. To his relief it was empty, empty except for the brown tilled earth and the green of the stalks and the yellow where the ears of corn peeped through—

And where the foot-long yellow corn snake slipped easily around a nearby stalk and glided up the row in search of food.

He turned and walked purposefully toward the house, keeping down the impulse to run. A garter snake was unwinding from the bushes that grew in front of the basement window. Wait—there were two more just behind it.

"Nettie," he called. "Nettie!"

The door opened and she stood upon the back steps, studying his face. "Ham? What's the—" She looked past him. "Oh, sweet Lord!"

He turned. For a moment it looked as if the cornfield was alive with snakes, each row a river of cold squirming bodies.

"Lord," she said, "'tis like the plagues of Egypt!"

He looked down at his feet; the very ground on which he stood seemed to breed them. As he watched, three small dark heads appeared only a few yards away, three small heads with eyes of shiny black, heads that grew like ground vines and that, slipping from their holes, crept forth to wriggle upon the earth.

He pointed, wide-eyed, to where two more scaly bodies were emerging from the ground. "Something down there is forcin' 'em up."

In the shadow of the outhouse writhed a veritable Medusa's coil of them, strands of which were detaching themselves and moving toward the woods. How could the earth hold so many? It was as if they'd been planted like seeds a moon or two ago and had now begun to ripen.

Retreating to the back steps, he stood beside his wife and surveyed the things that crept across his land. "What does it mean?" she kept asking—asking herself, or him, or God. "What does it mean?"

Others were asking that same question. At Abram Sturtevant's a beloved old pony suddenly turned vicious and bit one of the children on the neck; Hildegarde Troet watched with horror that morning as a family of mice came dancing out of their holes beneath the kitchen and ran round and round the floor; Adam Verdock's cows had, for the past two days, been giving sour milk, and a hen in Werner Klapp's henhouse had just laid its third double-yoked egg. One of Shem Fenchel's dogs, the younger male, snapped at the female and had to be locked up. Shortly after noon Rachel Reid's canary sat stock still in its cage, its beak gaping wide, and uttered strange, piercing cries.

What was happening? Were they living under a curse? At first they asked individually, but as they learned, throughout that day, that others, too, were suffering the calamities, they grew more frightened and asked it of one another. What was happening? they asked. What did it mean?

A fourth day has dawned, a fine layer of dust has settled on his eyeballs, and still he has not moved. He does not hear the radio blaring salsa music in the street below, or the sound of children's voices in the playground down the block, or the urgently repeated ringing of the telephone. He is far away, far across the river. He has not broken contact.

He will see this thing through till the end. To do otherwise would be unthinkable.

He intends to be in on the kill.

Freirs counted his change and tried to get his story straight as he stood contemplating the pay phone that jutted from the rear wall of the Co-op, just inside the passageway to the grain warehouse. Surely, he told himself, Carol wouldn't turn him down—it wasn't as if he was asking so much, just a night or two of simple hospitality—but just the same, it was best to be prepared.

He had decided, this very morning, to leave the Poroths; had awakened, in fact, with that resolve uppermost in mind, having spent the previous night camped in the farmhouse, sleeping on a mattress in the middle of the living-room floor. He had gotten up shortly after daybreak in a sour mood, eyes itching and nose running, his skin covered with cat hairs. This was no way to be passing the summer, hiding in a cat-infested farmhouse while another feline, downright homicidal, lurked somewhere nearby. The whole thing was turning into a bad dream. He wanted out.

The Poroths, unaware of his intent, had been nothing if not solicitous. They had moved aside all the living-room furniture to make a temporary bedroom for him and had made sure that the doors to the house were firmly locked, both front and back. Yesterday, on their way back from Werner Klapp's chicken farm, where they had purchased four new laying hens, they had stopped off in town to buy new screening for Freirs' room and a latch to bolt his door from the inside. Sarr had rigged up a simple wooden floor lamp for him from an old clothing rack and some spare parts found in the storeroom. Obviously the two of them were sorry that events at the farm had taken such a turn; obviously they wanted him to stay for the rest of the summer. *It's probably my money they want,* he told himself.

He hadn't yet said anything to them about leaving, though no doubt they sensed the possibility. He wasn't sure just how to bring it up, and besides, there was one thing he'd have to arrange first in private: finding a place in New York where he could stay until his own apartment was vacant. Perhaps Carol would be willing ... He would have to propose it as a temporary measure, of course—just until he found a summer sublet. He could ask if he might simply use the couch for a few days; and then, if things developed as he hoped they would ...

Getting into town to phone her had seemed a problem. The Poroths would hardly be driving in again, having made the trip just yesterday, and he hated to ask to borrow the truck, especially when he'd have to make up some innocent-sounding pretext for needing it.

It had looked, though, as if he'd have no choice. He'd been seated on the front porch, preparing himself to walk down to the cornfield where Sarr and Deborah were working and ask them for the keys, when from up the road had come the sound of an engine, followed by a cloud of dust the same grey as the sky. Moments later a square yellow van had rattled into view with HUNTERDON OIL & GAS in large red letters on its side. Sarr had hurried back from the field in time to help the company's driver replace one of the tall silver cylinders that stood behind the house with a new one and to stow the empty cylinder in the back of the van. Afterward, with an apologetic smile—as if this were a betrayal of the Poroths' trust—the driver had presented them with a printed receipt and, attached to it, the bill for last month's gas. The first Sarr had slowly and conscientiously signed, but the bill had left him scowling and shaking his head.

Freirs, seeing his chance, had asked the man if he'd be driving toward Gilead; there were things he needed at the store.

The Poroths had exchanged a glance. "You should have told us yesterday," said Deborah, "when Sarr and I went in. We'd have been glad to pick up something for you." Sarr, meanwhile, had been looking gloomily away, as if he knew that Freirs might be leaving them soon and was resigned to it.

"I need more bug spray," Freirs had said. "Something a bit more powerful."

"But how will you get back?" Deborah had asked as Freirs climbed into the van. "Should I—"

"He'll find a way," Sarr had cut in. "Come on, woman, there's work to be done." He had turned his back and started off in the direction of the fields.

"I'll get a hitch," Freirs had yelled, as the van came to life with a roar. "See you by dinnertime." Soon they'd been rolling down the road, the farm receding behind them, Deborah's forlorn figure still watching them go, Sarr's already lost behind the house.

He still felt faintly guilty, standing here now before the phone. He was going to betray these people. Deborah, in particular, would be hurt.

He forced himself to think of the city as he slipped a dime into the phone and dialed Carol's number. The memory of New York's hot and sticky streets was beginning to seem almost attractive. There'd be movies to catch up on, and restaurants to try, and Carol—

"Please deposit seventy-five cents," said an unfamiliar voice.

He thumbed in the contents of his back pocket, fixing his face in a smile to help put himself into the proper mood. *Okay,* he thought, *here goes nothing.*

Where was Rosie? What could he be up to? She hadn't heard from him in *days.* This wasn't like him at all.

Carol reached down from the bed, picked up the phone, and dialed again. She let it ring for almost a full minute, her ear pressed close to the receiver, as if, by listening with all her might, she could hear the ringing echo through the corridors of his apartment, the sound of morning traffic in the street below his window, the regular faint whisper of the old man's labored breathing . . .

No, it was no use. No one was going to answer. She hung up the phone and wondered what to do.

There was really nothing to get excited about, of course. Rosie was probably out of town, attending to business or visiting friends. He would be back this weekend, she was sure of that, because he'd promised to take her to the ballet Saturday and he always kept his promises.

But then, he'd also promised to call her sometime this week, and here it was Thursday and she hadn't heard from him. That was unlike the old man; he usually phoned her every day, often twice, and sometimes even took her out to lunch at one of the Cuban Chinese restaurants in the neighborhood. She had come to expect his little calls, to look forward to them. Perhaps, in a way, she depended on them.

His sudden silence worried her. After all, he was so old and frail; he'd never actually told her his age and she'd never dared ask him, of course, but the more she'd seen of him the more she'd begun to think that he must be eighty at least.

What if he was lying dead, right this minute, on the floor of his apartment? That sort of thing happened often in New York, she'd read about it; there'd been a poor old man in the Bronx who'd died of a heart attack and had lain for *months,* an entire summer, in fact, his body decomposing, swelling, bloating with maggots and gas until it seeped through the ceiling of the apartment below.

Or what if he wasn't dead but simply in a coma, unable to hear the phone? Or perfectly conscious but simply unable to *reach* the phone? How horrible she'd just been, then, to let the phone ring for an entire minute; she could almost picture the old man lying there paralyzed, listening to the rings, helpless to stop them, praying that someone would help him. . .

She swung her legs off the bed and hurried to get dressed. Maybe nothing would come of this, she was probably just being silly, but she wouldn't be able to go to work this afternoon until she'd satisfied herself that he was all right. She had to do *something,* anyway. She owed him that much.

The phone rang nine, ten, eleven times without an answer.

"Damn!" said Freirs. It was almost noon. Maybe she was on her way to work. Well, he would wait around for a while and try her again at the library. Having gone to so much trouble to get here, he wasn't about to leave without talking to her.

He wondered how he'd kill an hour or so, and wished he'd had the sense to bring a book. He'd thought general stores were supposed to stock magazines or at least the local papers, but the Co-operative had none. He was surprised how much he'd begun to miss the *Times.* The cemetery across the street held no interest for him in all this heat, the dusty headstones baking in the sun. Briefly he thought of the corpses beneath; at least they'd be cool down there.

His shirt, he saw, was sticking to his back, and there were already sweat stains beneath his arms. With a sigh he rubbed the perspiration on the back of his neck and walked into the main room of the store.

Too bad the Brethren seemed never to have heard of air conditioning; the only trace of refrigeration in sight was the cooler near the back. Bert Steegler, carefully marking catalogues at the front counter, looked up with as little friendliness as he'd displayed when Freirs had entered. Steegler's wife was across the corridor in the post office section, filling out a pile of official-looking forms. Freirs wandered down the nearest aisle, smelling the clean, cozy scent of spice, coffee, and floor wax. One aisle up from the passage leading back to the warehouse stood three large burlap sacks of grain, the first of them open at the top. *I wonder whether you plant this stuff or eat it,* he thought, running his hand through the kernels.

"Is there somethin' you want?" Steegler had come around the counter and was peering down the aisle at him. Freirs dropped the grain and pointed to the cooler.

"I think I'll get myself one of these hero sandwiches." He took the largest, with a not-too-cold can of diet cola. "And I'd better pick up some insect spray," he added, suddenly remembering his lie to the Poroths. A dark red can labeled Chemtex caught his eye; this brand looked even stronger than the first. *For Outdoor Use Only,* the label warned; probably that just meant it was powerful.

Steegler eyed the can dubiously and seemed reluctant to ring it up.

"Don't worry," said Freirs, grinning. "I'll make sure I point it away from me."

But as the other looked up, Freirs saw the hardness in his gaze, the set of his mouth, and realized he'd misread the man's expression.

"You fixin' to stay out here much longer?" asked Steegler.

Freirs flushed guiltily. Had the other read his mind? "What do you mean, 'out here'?"

"I mean here among the Brethren."

"Oh, I don't know," said Freirs. Across the corridor Steegler's wife had paused in her writing and appeared to be listening. He chose his words with care. "Sarr and Deborah are expecting me to stay until the end of the summer. Why?"

Steegler shook his head. "Nothin'. Just wonderin', that's all." He totaled Freirs' bill with pencil and paper, a small drawer serving to hold the cash. "You tell Brother Sarr I said hello, all right?"

"Oh, sure," said Freirs. "Sure thing." Taking his purchases, he walked quickly from the store. He was confused. Why had Steegler been so hostile? It was almost as if the fellow wanted him to leave town . . .

Not until he'd seated himself on the hard wooden bench on the Coop's front porch and was unwrapping the sandwich on his lap did an explanation present itself. *Of course!* he decided. *He must have heard me over by the phone and figured I was calling New York. He's probably afraid I'm running out on the Poroths.*

Freirs felt better now. Yes, that must be it. It wasn't that Steegler wanted him to leave town—quite the opposite. The fellow wanted him to stay!

Ever since he'd first laid eyes on him that warm Sunday in May, Bert Steegler had never forgiven the outsider for sleeping in the graveyard. Oh, he'd seen him, all right, up there in the shadow of the Troet monument, snoozing away the afternoon with his fat belly in the air, just like those were his own people up there and he had a right to lie amongst them. Steegler and his wife had family buried there—poor little six-week-old Annalee, Lord rest her soul—and he took it amiss to see this sloppily dressed stranger lying on top of the departed like they were so many clumps of earth. He had seen Brother Sarr Poroth climb the low hill to the monument that day, had seen him wake the city fellow and take him down to his truck, and had heard how the Poroths had opened their home to him. Brother Sarr didn't seem to mind the outsider; but then, Brother Sarr didn't seem to mind very much about a lot of things: the proper respect the community was due, to say nothing of his own mother, the boy up and going off to get his education in some other town, then trotting back home like the Prodigal. And now he was flouting the Co-operative itself—which, was, after all, really no more than the community of Brethren anyway, as they existed on paper—to which he owed—what was it now? Why, it was over $4900, the last time he'd checked. How did the boy think he was going to pay that off? A good thing his father wasn't alive, Lord rest his soul; the old man wouldn't have taken kindly to a son so deep in debt to the Co-op.

Steegler craned his skinny neck and peered out the window. Yes, he was out there, all right; he knew he hadn't heard the fellow walk down the front steps. There he was, sitting fat and lazy on the bench, young enough to work, certainly, and probably strong—folks who carried a lot of weight usually had the muscles to go with it—but preferring to remain there in idleness, swallowing his sandwich and staring out at nothing, with Lord knows what sinful thoughts in his head. Brother Rupert Lindt was right about the fellow: that sort expected others to work for them but wouldn't do a lick themselves. It set a bad example, him being there like that, with his bulging pockets, in front of the store that was the symbol of the community. He should never have listened to Amelia, he should have taken that bench away years ago; he'd warned her it was an invitation to the idle, but she'd maintained that old folks needed a place to rest their bones. As if old folks had nothing better to do this side of the grave than sit and stare at the street. For all he knew, the fellow was discouraging trade.

From across the room the glass door to the cooler didn't look completely shut; it would be just like the outsider to leave it hanging open, wasting the propane gas whose price had just gone up another dollar twelve a tank. Steegler hurried down the aisle to check and saw, with a tiny edge of disappointment, that the door was in fact closed. He turned lest any of the cornmeal livestock feed had spilled from the sack the fellow had been running his hands through. That's when he saw the worms.

The corn was alive with them. There were dozens—no, hundreds, he suddenly realized, as his eye took them all in: squirming little yellowish things nearly the color of the corn, slipping in and out amongst the kernels like the inhabitants of some satanic city.

And even as Steegler told himself that it couldn't be the stranger's fault, that the worms must have been breeding there for weeks, that the unusually hot weather was to blame, or whoever'd sold him the corn (hadn't it been Brother Ham Stoudemire?)—even as these thoughts occurred to him, the association was formed: the stranger spoiled things just by touching them. It was like the Bible said: at his touch sprouted vermin.

He couldn't wait to tell Brother Rupert about this. He could almost see the other now, the slowly widening eyes, the deepening scowl, the angry clenching of his huge fists.

Bert Steegler was no fool. He had a good idea what was behind Lindt's dislike of the outsider: it was that thin redheaded girl, the one'd he'd had with him that Sunday right here in the store. Steegler had seen the larger man glance her way and glance again, and he'd sympathized; everyone knew Sister Anna led Rupert a hard life.

Still, he could appreciate the truth of what Lindt said. The fellow out there on the porch just didn't belong here. He had come amongst the Brethren bearing the taint of the city; he was a gateway for sin. Gilead would need a cleansing to rid itself of him.

The subway uptown was almost empty in the late morning heat except for a pair of Columbia summer-termers, one of whom kept eyeing her over his paperback, and a group of black youths with baseball caps and duffel bags. Two of them were looking past her and giggling. Pretending to wipe the sweat from her forehead, she turned and saw a tattered blue sign pasted to the window just above her, bearing a cross and the printed slogan, IT'S A BLESSING TO BE A VIRGIN. Below them someone had scribbled, *But you got to give Great Head.* Quickly she looked away. She was glad the next stop, 110th Street, was hers.

She walked south until she recognized the ancient grey brick building just off Riverside Drive. From eight till six a doorman was on duty, a sleepy-looking Hispanic whose only uniform was a T-shirt and brown slacks. He seemed confused as to what she wanted of him and, after she'd explained herself, reluctant.

"No," he said, shaking his head slowly, "I can't open no door for nobody."

"But he may be in there *dying,*" Carol pleaded.

His expression suggested that he found this unlikely. "Look, lady, I ain' got no key. The super, he the one with the key, but he gone out now. You wanna come back tomorrow, you talk to him, okay?" He looked away, his face impassive, as if she weren't standing there in front of him.

"Well, can I at least go up there and knock on his door?"

He nodded, still not looking at her.

"Thanks a lot." She walked past him to the elevator and jammed her thumb onto the button marked 12. A minute later she emerged on Rosie's floor. His apartment was at the end of the hall, behind a dull green rather shabby-looking door from which gleamed three brass locks of formidable size. The old man was worried about thieves.

"Rosie?" she called, holding her finger against the buzzer beside the door. "Rosie?" She could hear the buzzer's muffled ringing within the apartment. She pressed her ear to the door. There was no other sound.

She knocked now, softly at first, then harder, putting her ear once more to the door.

Nothing.

She shrugged, began to walk away, then stopped and went back. "Rosie," she called, putting her mouth to the crack, speaking as softly as she dared because she was somewhat embarrassed to be doing this, "Rosie, this is Carol. If you're in there, listen to me. I can't get in the apartment, but I'm coming back tomorrow and I'll have the super let me in. So try not to worry. I'll be back."

More than an hour had passed, and he still couldn't reach Carol. There was no answer at her apartment, and the woman he'd spoken to at

Voorhis said that Carol hadn't come to work today. "No," Freirs had told her, "no message." He hung up, troubled, almost indignant, at this unexpected absence of someone he'd regarded as reliable. Where the hell was she, anyway? Who had she gone off with?

Well, he would call her in a day or two, when he got back to New York. He certainly wasn't going to wait around here any longer; he had already wasted enough time. Gilead's main street had been dull, with cars passing but rarely and those inside them regarding him with little warmth; and the library, where he'd thought he might spend the afternoon, had been unaccountably closed. He had drunk too many cans of soda, there on the porch, and eaten too many potato chips. Now, as he got to his feet and moved slowly down the front steps, the heat made him feel dizzy.

It was a long way back to the farm. He walked for more than twenty minutes down the road that curved past Verdock's dairy and the Sturtevant home, hoping for a ride, but the only car that passed him was an antiquated Ford, black as a hearse and traveling in the opposite direction. The elderly couple inside, also in black, regarded him with stony disapproval as they went by, giving him a taste of their exhaust.

He watched the car recede slowly up the narrow road until it rounded a bend and disappeared, the faint hum of its engine lingering a moment or two afterward. Once again the air was still, but for the sound of a distant tractor and the echoes of an axe; not a thing was moving save the cows eyeing him suspiciously in a field to the left, the butterflies hurrying from flower to flower, and an occasional green snake that wandered onto the pavement and slithered back into the grass at his approach. The oak trees' shadows lengthened perceptibly with the passing day, as if reaching back toward town.

Five minutes later, just as he was descending the hill that ran past Ham Stoudemire's farm and stepping past the dark, motionless form of a garden snake coiled in sleep at the edge of the pavement, a rusty blue pickup truck appeared up the road, two black-garbed figures inside, a sparsely bearded boy at the wheel and beside him a plump, snub-nosed girl. The truck bore swiftly down upon him. He stuck out his thumb and flashed a hopeful smile.

Far from slowing as it neared him, the truck increased its speed and made a sudden swerve to the right. The garden snake woke just in time and slipped into the grass. Freirs jumped back to avoid being run down.

"Assholes!"

He hoisted an angry finger at them as they went by, hoping, at first, that the two had seen the gesture and then, on reflection, that they hadn't. No sense getting into fights with the townspeople. Teenagers, he supposed, were teenagers everywhere, even among the Brethren. Anyway, for all he knew they'd just been aiming at the snake.

It wasn't until he'd descended halfway to the brook, the road ahead now crisscrossed with shadows of trees, that he encountered a genuine samaritan: a leathery old farmer with a truckful of garbage, on his way to the town dump half a mile past the Geisels' north field. "I almost didn't stop for you," he said, eyeing Freirs warily through eyes whose whites had turned as yellow as corn. "Thought you might be one o' them gangsters."

Freirs laughed and assured him that he was as honest as the next.

The other nodded gravely. "You're the one who's stayin' at the Poroths'."

"How'd you know?"

"Figured that's who you'd be, soon as you opened your mouth."

"It must be hard to keep a secret around here. Everybody seems to know everything that's going on."

"Pretty much."

It occurred to him, after they got under way, that the man might be a resource. "For a town this small," he said, "there seems to be a wealth of family history."

The other was shaking his head. "There ain't too much wealth in *this* town, son. We don't hold with gatherin' up the goods o' this world like some folks do."

"No, no, I mean, a wealth of memories, a sense of identity based on family background." God, he sounded like a textbook! "Like Sarr Poroth moving back to his ancestral farm after more than a century. That's pretty amazing."

The man shrugged. "It was for sale at a good price, and someone was bound to settle there by and by. The Babers never did do much with it—not as much as some folks might."

"I suppose the land's not all that fertile down there."

"No, sir, there's nothin' the matter with that land. It's just a matter of clearin' back the trees from time to time. You've got to have the will to see it through." He paused. "Less'n you fancy livin' in the woods, like some around here."

"You mean families like the Fenchels. I've heard Sarr speak of them."

He nodded. "Folks like that."

"And the McKinneys," said Freirs. "They must live out there, too, even deeper in the woods."

The other looked puzzled. "Never heard of anyone by that name, leastwise not around here."

"No? What about the place they call McKinney's Neck? I figured it was named for someone in the area."

"I expect you're right. But I sure ain't never heard of no McKinneys. Not in these parts."

Freirs tried to remember his stroll through the cemetery. Now that he thought of it, he couldn't recall seeing any gravestones with that name.

"At any rate," he said, "I mean to hike through that region someday. Maybe I'll even run into a few ghosts."

The man didn't take the bait. "Don't see why a ghost would pass his time out in the Neck. Ain't nothin' there but swamp water and mud. You just be careful you don't go sinkin' in."

"Still, I hear some pretty strange things have happened out there." He watched for the other's reaction. "Even a couple of murders, I hear."

The man's expression barely changed, save for a certain impatience. "I remember somethin' like that, but it was years ago. 'Twould be well before you were born. And beggin' your pardon, it seems to me that when it comes to killin', the place you're from has the rest of us just about beat."

"I won't deny it," said Freirs. He tried to look properly contrite. "But the killings I'm thinking of were a bit unusual—both on the last day of July. I don't suppose anything special happened last year on that date, did it? Or maybe the year before? Some sort of violent crime, or someone missing? An unexplained death, maybe?"

The man drove a while in silence. "Nope," he said at last. "Not so's I remember. Summer's pretty quiet around here. Why?"

"Oh, nothing," said Freirs. "Just a thought."

July 31, 1890, and July 31, 1939 . . . Why those two dates nearly half a century apart? There had to be something special about them, something that separated them from all other July thirty-firsts . . .

"Fact is," the farmer said, breaking into Freirs' reverie, "that time o' year's amongst the holiest, August commencin' as it does with the Feast o' the Lamb and closin' on the harvest festivities."

"Really?" He was slightly disappointed. "I guess your year must be filled with all sorts of holy days."

"Well, we try to live in the way o' the Lord. For instance, only last Sunday, at worship, Brother Amos turned to me and said . . ."

But Freirs' mind was already back at the farm, going over the preparations to be made before leaving: the explanations that, tomorrow morning, he would have to give the Poroths, the shelfloads of books to pack away . . . And through it all his thoughts kept returning to the faded old photograph that he'd taped to the wall above his writing table—the photo of that curious little white face, smiling at him from the past.

It was the leg of mutton that prompted his question—the mutton which, upon Freirs' return, lay roasting in the oven for the night's dinner, its smell filling the little kitchen.

"Deborah, what's the Feast of the Lamb?"

She shrugged. "Just another one of our observances. Why?"

"The man who gave me a lift here mentioned that it comes at the beginning of August. I'd never heard of it before."

"Honestly, Jeremy," she said, laughing, "you haven't even tasted tonight's meal and you're already hungry for more!" She turned back to the cucumbers and tomatoes she was slicing for the salad. "What else did he tell you?"

Freirs thought back. "Nothing very interesting," he said. "I don't think he knew that much. I asked him about McKinney's Neck, but he'd never even heard of anyone around here named McKinney."

"Come to think of it, neither have I," said Deborah. "Honey, was there ever a McKinney family in these parts?"

Poroth looked up from the previous day's *Home News*, which he'd been frowning over. "None that I recall."

"So where'd McKinney's Neck come from?" asked Freirs.

The other shook his head. "Couldn't tell you. But I'll see what I can find out." He returned to his reading.

"If you're interested in the Feast of the Lamb," said Deborah, "you could join us at the Geisels'. That's where we'll be having it this year. Sister Corah's a wonderful cook, but I warn you, there'll be a lot of praying."

"I take it I'm invited."

"I don't see why not. Honey, can't Jeremy have the lamb with us at Matt and Corah's?"

"He'll be welcome," said Poroth. "If he's still here."

Freirs flushed. "I certainly *hope* I am."

"And why wouldn't he be?" said Deborah, busy taking out plates and saucers. "Put away the paper, honey, it's time to eat." She glanced at Freirs. "Nobody's going to leave meals like *this* behind."

"How could I?" Freirs said, with a heartiness he didn't feel. Eyeing the food she was already laying on the table, the bright reds and greens of the salad, the cold pitcher of milk, the beans fresh from the garden, he wondered what the Poroths had been saying about him today.

*

The subject of his leaving didn't come up again. But after dinner, as the two men stood on the back porch watching darkness settle over the land and listening to Deborah singing hymns as she worked in the kitchen, Sarr returned, if only indirectly, to an earlier subject.

"You know," he said with obvious deliberation, "God answers to many different names, and He's worshiped in strange ways. But He's always the same God."

There was a pause; Freirs felt the other's eyes on him. "That's true," he said at last, wondering what the man was driving at. "I'm sure it doesn't matter what you call Him."

"It doesn't," said Poroth heatedly. "The words may be different, but the spirit's always been the same. At Trenton the professors talked about 'other systems of belief,' and so did all those books in there"—he nodded toward the house, where his few remaining college texts stood gathering dust in the living room—"and at first I was troubled, I don't mind telling you, at how many different forms God seemed to take. But in the end I found I was able to return to the fold with even more faith than I'd started with, because I came to see how, even when He had different names, He was the same God I knew."

"I once read a story," Freirs began, "about how the people in Tibet have nine billion names for Him . . ."

"You don't even have to go that far away," said Poroth. "There was a little village down in Mexico that the Catholics were wonderfully proud of. The Indians in the area had all been converted, you see— they'd been Christians for at least a hundred years—and week after week every last one of 'em would show up in church to worship the Virgin Mary. And then one day the priest had the altar taken up, so as to make some repairs, and underneath it he discovered another altar, with an idol much older than his, a cruel-looking thing with a snake head and teeth."

"And that's what they'd really been worshiping all along?"

Poroth nodded. "But the point is, they were all just fooling themselves. The Catholics thought they were praying to one god and the Indians thought they were praying to another, but they were really praying to the same. It's as if below both the Virgin and the snake was still another god—the true one."

"The one with the capital G," said Freirs. Privately he had drawn a different conclusion from the story: something about older, darker gods, and rites in which the blood wasn't just a symbol.

"It's the same with the Feast of the Lamb," Poroth was saying. "Actually, it's got another celebration buried underneath, though folks around here wouldn't have heard of it."

"What kind of celebration?"

Poroth shrugged. "Pagan. Your standard harvest festival." He held open the screen door. "Come on, I'll show you."

Deborah was standing at the sink as they passed through the kitchen but didn't look up from her washing. A glowing lantern made the night beyond the windows look darker than it had from the porch. Sarr lit another and they went into the living room, where he stooped before his little cache of books in the corner, peering at the names on the spines.

"Sometimes," he said, "the Christians took a pagan day and made it their own—like Easter, which, as I expect you've heard, was a planting festival long before Christ." He pulled out a battered grey volume from the bottom shelf and began thumbing through it. "Sometimes they changed the name a little, to disguise the origin. That's what we Brethren did with the Feast of the Lamb, which sounds so proper and Christian."

"It wasn't originally?"

Poroth looked up from the book. "No," he said in a low voice. "And I'm probably the only one who knows."

"What's that you're looking at? Some rival to the Bible?"

The other laughed uneasily. "No, just an almanac, something I haven't opened for years." He squinted at the cover, but the name had long since worn away, and he turned instead to the title page. *"By-field's Newly Revised Agricultural Almanack and Celestial Guide for 1947,"* he read. "I found it at a church bazaar in Trenton for fifteen cents." Looking down, he flipped through several more pages, then paused. "Ah, here's what I've been searching for." He handed the open book to Freirs, pointing to a line in the middle of what appeared to be a chart. "See? Right there."

The book itself smelled faintly of mildew, its covers warped and faded. Freirs scanned the opened page. *Festivals of the Ancients,* it said at the top; below it lay a complicated-looking calendar. He found the indicated line. *August 1,* it said. *Lammas.*

"It's got nought to do with lambs," said Poroth. "Nor does the night before."

Freirs checked the previous column. *July 31,* he read. *Lammas Eve.* "Hmmm, sounds sinister!"

"It can be. Black magic's always powerful on Lammas Eve. There'll probably be some odd doings somewhere in the world that night."

"Why's that?"

Instead of answering, Poroth merely pointed back to the calendar in the book. There was something called Roodmas on May third, and Mid-summer on the twenty-fourth of June, and the day Deborah had spoken of, St. Swithin's, on the fifteenth of July. Several dates, he noticed now, were marked with tiny asterisks—dates like the first of May and the last day of October. So was Lammas Eve, the last day of July.

He looked down at the bottom of the page. There beside an asterisk was the footnote, a simple one, just two words long:
Sabbats likely.

Moonlight slanted through the misty air of the place known as McKinney's Neck, through motes of dust and dancing insects, through the latticework of ancient roots that spread from the column of a fallen cottonwood, down through the roots, down to the freshly built little altar of rock and mud and bone.

The altar was smaller than the first but considerably more colorful. Between each of the tiny standing pebbles that encircled the mound like a miniature Stonehenge lay freshly plucked rose blossoms that shone, by day, like red beacons in the mud, and at night looked like small knots of darkness. And stuck at the top of the mound, like a comical little pompom atop a clown's hat, there now lay a single round head, eye sockets empty but ears and whiskers intact—and with black fur still soft enough to pet.

Night. The crescent moon is hidden by trees as the animal creeps out upon the lawn and sits gazing at the farmhouse. Singing comes from a dimly lit room on the second floor where the farmer and his woman are at their evening devotions.

> *"Watchman of Zion, herald the story,*
> *Sin and death His kingdom shall destroy . . ."*

It moves closer, to crouch below the window. Forty miles away and twelve floors up, a wrinkled shape upon a bed hears the closing verses of their song.

> *"All the earth shall sing of His glory;*
> *Praise Him, ye angels, ye who behold Him,*
> *Great is Jehovah, King over all."*

The voices die away. Briefly the man is heard again, reciting a short prayer; the woman joins him, echoing his words. Then, as always, the light goes out. Soon the room will echo to the sounds of their lovemaking. The animal moves on.

Around the front of the house, lights are still burning on the first floor. There he sits again tonight, the visitor from the city, absorbed in a book, his plump white face glowing like a full moon in the lamplight. The animal watches, and the Old One watches, as he turns another page.

Momentarily, as if aware he is observed, the visitor sets down the book and goes to the window. His troubled eyes peer blindly through the screen, unable to see past the lamplight. Seven feet away, the animal sits watching him, shielded by the darkness.

The man returns to his chair and, moments later, to the thick grey book he has been reading. The animal turns and pads briskly around the side of the house to the porch steps in the back. There, in the darkness beneath the stairway, two metal garbage cans stand reeking of death and corruption. On one of them the scent is old, but the other has accumulated a full week's stock of tiny mangled corpses, a choice supply of putrefying meat.

And this very putrefaction has its uses.

With the easy swipe of a paw and a clank of metal the can is overturned, the lid tumbling noisily off to roll several feet away upon the grass.

Upstairs, in the darkness, the woman's grip tightens on the man's shoulder. "Honey, wait," she whispers. "Did you hear that?"

He makes a low sound of assent. "Coon," he says, and enters her again.

Downstairs, in the living room, the visitor puts down the book and walks around the room, carefully shutting each window.

The animal, untroubled, creeps into the darkness of the overturned can. The fragrance of death fills its lungs. Before it lies the little mound of bodies, the field mice, frogs, and snakes. Delicately, methodically, it runs its razor claws through the soft and rotting flesh—first the front claws, then the rear, shredding the flesh with machinelike efficiency, working the corruption into the fur and deep beneath each gracefully hooked nail.

Forty miles away the Old One watches, smells the death smell, feels the decay beneath the nails of his own fingers. Yes, it is good: it may be helpful in tomorrow evening's enterprise. A little poison never hurts.

JULY TWENTY-SECOND

Amos Reid had a bag of Bordeaux dust under his arm for the leaf blight on his cukes, young Abram Sturtevant was about to buy his third can of Malathion for a sudden invasion of aphids, and Rupert Lindt was stocking up on Gurney's patented worm powder for the cutworms and snails that had already slaughtered a third of his tomato plants. None of them had any moral qualms about using chemicals on their crops; what qualms they had were purely economic. Pesticides were expensive, but under the circumstances they were going to have to rely on them and salvage whatever they could. It was suddenly turning out to be a bad year. You could see it in their faces; you could hear it in their talk.

Not even Bert Steegler was happy, though business had been brisk today. He and his wife worked mainly on salary; the profit or loss they derived from the store hardly differed from anyone else's. Besides, Bert's married daughter, Irma, had just had an entire plot of pattypan squash wiped out, almost overnight, by a particularly voracious breed of corpulent grey slug that had never been seen in the area before.

"You heard about what happened at the Verdocks'?" asked Steegler, as he rang up Abram Sturtevant's purchase.

"I've been too busy tryin' to save my crops to worry myself about other folks' affairs," said Sturtevant.

"*I'll* tell you," said Rupert Lindt, from halfway across the store. "Lise got herself kicked in the head by one of Adam's cows, tryin' to squeeze a bit of milk from it."

"You don't say! Lord's mercy on her, how's she bearin' up?"

"Pretty bad," said Lindt. "They think she may not live till Sunday."

"We've been prayin' for her regular," added Amos Reid. "'Tis all we can do."

"I'll be sure to do the same," said Sturtevant. "Does my brother know of this?"

"You can ask him yourself," said Steegler, who'd been looking out the screen door. "That's him comin' now."

They heard Joram's heavy footsteps on the porch outside. He was a tall, formidable-looking figure with eyebrows black and heavy as his beard, but as he entered the store he appeared pale and unwell. "Aye," he said, of the news about Lise, "I'll be headin' over there this evenin' to pray with Brother Adam and their girl." He sounded troubled, but from the briefness of his response it was clear that it was some other trouble that occupied his mind.

"And how's Sister Lotte bearin' up," said Amos Reid, "in *her* time of trial?"

"As well as a man can expect," said Joram gloomily. "I'd thought her a stronger woman than she's turnin' out to be, but—" He shrugged. "The child's a large one, I guess. The labor's goin' to be hard. But we're resigned to it, Lotte and I. If that's God's will, so be it."

He moved off down the aisle, peering through the shelves of household goods, obviously somewhat unfamiliar with an aspect of the shopping that, before her pregnancy, his wife would have seen to. As he crossed to the adjoining aisle, he found himself face to face with Lindt, the only man there as tall as he was.

"Greetings to you, Brother Joram," Lindt said. "Anna and me, we've been includin' Sister Lotte in our prayers."

Joram nodded curtly. "That's good of you, Brother Rupert. 'Tis a time for prayin' now, if ever there was one."

"Ain't that the gospel truth," the other said. "You heard 'bout the trouble Ham Stoudemire suffered yesterday? Well, the same thing's been happenin' up the road from me, over at Bethuel Reid's. 'Tis like the Land o' Tophet—never saw so many serpents in one place. Old Bethuel don't even want to set foot outdoors no more."

"'Twill pass," said Joram. "All things must." He did not sound very hopeful.

"Of course," said Lindt, following the other as he continued up the aisle. "The Lord takes care of His own. But when you start to add up what's been goin' on—" He enumerated on his thick fingers. "They say there's a pack of dogs runnin' wild now up by the Annandale road, runnin' wild the way the Fenchels' did just yesterday, I'm told. And what happened to poor Sister Lise, well . . ." He shook his head. "The same thing's agoin' to happen again, you mark my words, 'cause *all* the Verdocks' cows have been actin' up."

"Matthew Geisel's too," said Steegler, from the counter in front. "He says they're like to kick the barn door right down."

"Fact is," said Lindt, "we've all of us got our tribulations—"

"Werner Klapp was in earlier this mornin'," Steegler cut in, "and he says he's havin' troubles with his fowl. Sold four of 'em to Sarr Poroth and his woman just the other day, and now he's afraid they'll be askin' for their money back when they find out that the critters just ain't layin'."

"We were of a mind to ask you what you thought, Brother Joram," Lindt continued. "When people's got troubles like this—"

"Man is born to trouble," said Joram, "and 'tis through tribulation that we enter the kingdom of God. You know that, Brother Rupert. The Lord is testin' us."

"Aye," said Lindt, "but mightn't He be warnin' us as well? I'm talkin' about the one who's come amongst us this season—the one from the city, who's took the prophet's name as his own."

"I'm aware of how you feel," said Joram. "You don't have to lay these snares for me. I knew what was in your heart from the beginnin', for 'twas in mine as well. I'll be wantin' to hear what Brother Sarr has to say for himself when next we meet—don't forget, the worship's at his farm this week—and I'll also be lookin' at the stranger come Sunday, lookin' real hard. Then we'll see what the Lord commands of us. But till that time there's nothin' more to be done. Remember, now, 'Blessed is he that watcheth . . .' "

"Amen," they said mechanically, little satisfied, as Joram continued his distracted way down the aisle, thinking of a pregnant wife back home.

Sarr Poroth, too, knew trouble now, as if clouds that had once loomed on the horizon were gathering dark and thunderous overhead. He was plagued by a host of small afflictions; he despaired of the fate of his farm. Though the surviving hen from the original four had once more begun to lay eggs, they had proved to be hideously soft things, almost transparent, that shook like jelly when you held them in your hand. He reminded himself repeatedly that, for poultry, this was not so uncommon an ailment—it might be cured within a week or two by adding calcium to their feed, normally in the form of the ground-up eggshells of healthier birds—but for now the thought of a nestful of eggs as soft as his own testicles filled him with disgust; they were obscene, against nature, an abomination unto the Lord. Deborah had sworn they could be eaten, that there was no harm in them at all, but Sarr had done a different kind of swearing and had hurled the eggs against the barren ground east of the barn. He had acted, he realized, like a spoiled child and felt shame for it now, but it was already too late to apologize.

Yet even soft eggs were better than nothing, and nothing was what they'd had so far from the four hens they'd purchased Wednesday morning. Perhaps it was just a question of their new surroundings, he was too inexperienced a farmer to know for sure; perhaps they simply needed time to grow used to the place. Nevertheless he'd already decided that, if they weren't laying regularly by the end of the month, he'd go to Brother Werner and demand his money back.

Money—that was the real trouble, the one that stung the most. For just this morning the thing he'd been dreading had happened: Freirs had come to them and told them he was leaving—Freirs, whom they'd sheltered for the last two nights beneath their very roof and whom they'd treated, at all times, like a guest rather than a paying tenant. Freirs had cleared his throat this morning, after helping himself to his usual oversized breakfast, and, obviously shamefaced, had announced that he'd be pulling out on Saturday.

And why? All because he was frightened of that damned infernal cat.

"You told me yourself that the devil's in her," Freirs had said. "And maybe I'm beginning to believe it. At any rate, I don't particularly relish sleeping back in the outbuilding with a thing that likes to claw its way through screens."

"You don't run from the devil," Poroth had argued, "not when it's your own land. You stand and fight him."

"It's *your* land," said Freirs, "not mine. You fight the devil. I'm going home."

Well, he'd seen it coming, this betrayal; he'd discussed it with Deborah just the night before last. He had warned her that city people turned tail and fled at the first sign of adversity. After all, they had no God to call upon, no certitude of heavenly support. Even the best of them were faithless.

At any rate, he hadn't made a scene; he hadn't argued with Freirs and he hadn't pleaded with him either. "I expect you know what's best for you," he'd said, reaching across the breakfast table to shake Freirs' chubby hand. "I wish you all the luck a man can have." He had comported himself gently, like a true Christian should; though inside he'd been crushed—panicked, even, for a moment—and haunted by a mocking little voice that echoed *All the luck a man can have* and then whispered *You're ruined!*

"Honey," Deborah had said, when Freirs had gone back to his room, "this means we'll be out nearly five hundred dollars. Do you think it'll be—"

"None of that matters!" he had said, more roughly than he'd intended. "We'll just find the money somewhere else. God watches out for His own."

Still brooding over Freirs' announcement, he had gone stalking down the slope toward the cornfields when his eye had fallen on the old wooden smokehouse that stood between the barn and the stream. He had always avoided it because of the wasps' nest somewhere inside, but now he saw it as a challenge, an outlet for his frustrated energies: something he might do to cleanse the land. Seizing a broom from the barn and prepared at any moment to flee, he had peered inside the little building through the hanging-open door. To his surprise he had seen no sign of a nest until, looking upward through a smokehole in the ceiling—a hole that now led nowhere, for the roof above it had long since been sealed over—he glimpsed in the darkness a pale grey clay-like thing the size and shape of a human brain, plastered to the underside of the roofbeams.

There would be no knocking the nest down, he realized; it was too inaccessible. The only way of reaching it was by the circuitous route the insects themselves used, flying in and out the open doorway and up through the passage in the ceiling. It would have been a great place to hide money, if he'd had any, but in truth he had nothing worth stealing. Halfheartedly he had jabbed the broom up through the smokehole, and had been rewarded for his effort with a painful sting on his right hand just beneath the thumb.

Grimly he had hurried off to the abandoned field and, despite the pain, had busied himself clearing rocks when, like a messenger come to see Job, worried Amos Reid had come bumping down the road in his car with the news that Poroth's aunt, Lise Verdock, had been kicked by a cow last night as she tried to coax some milk from it and now lay at death's door. So he and Deborah, both sorely troubled, had piled into the truck and had followed Amos back toward town and up the hill to the Verdocks' farm. Aunt Lise had been lying pale and unconscious on the bed with a horrible purple swelling curved across one temple like a hungry living thing, while Minna, her daughter, had been sitting exhausted nearby, and poor Adam Verdock—who'd known trouble enough the past week, God knows, what with his cattle having ceased to give milk—was almost too distraught to speak. Poroth had looked down at the unconscious woman and a terrible dread seized him; he had thought for just an instant, *She'll die if they don't get her to a hospital* . . . But that had been the devil's solution, not his own, a remnant of the years he'd passed in the wicked world outside. Prayer, he knew for sure now, worked just as well as surgeons' polished steel.

And prayer was what they'd raised. They had gotten on their knees, all five of them together by the bed, and had prayed silently for what seemed close to an hour. And here he had discovered the most terrible secret of all: for while the others had been praying, he'd been wrestling with visions of losing the farm; and that mocking little voice had kept whispering *Money* . . . *ruined* . . . *damned!*

And so, because of him, what should have been a holy occasion, filled with the devotion a man owes his father's only sister, had been blighted. The guilt was his alone; he had discovered sin, not under his roof but in his own heart.

He stood leaning by himself against the pickup truck parked just beside the barn. He surveyed the straggly rows of cornstalks, prey to all manner of vermin and not half so high as they should have been by this time of year, and he wondered, for the first time in his life, what the future held in store for him, for Deborah, for the Brethren. Had they been abandoned by God? Did the devil have his claws around their ankles? And was he somehow to blame, if this was so?

He kicked gloomily at the earth at his feet. How ironic, that the Brethren should be coming here this Sunday to hold their worship! This was no place for blessings. This earth was damned.

The student checked his watch—two P.M. exactly—and opened the door marked AUTHORIZED PERSONNEL ONLY. Switching on the light, he crossed the small cluttered room and unlocked a cabinet where the rolls of lined paper were stored. Taking a fresh roll, he returned to the main room; here the geology department's recording instrument stood on permanent display, connected by cables to a Sprengnether vertical seismograph in the basement. With another key he unlocked the large glass-and-steel case and slid back the heavy glass lid that protected the device from dust and disturbances in the room. The paper on the drum was changed daily at this hour, and the task had to be done quickly; back in 1979 the department had missed recording one of the largest earthquakes in central New Jersey history because a student had been caught between rolls.

Carefully he lifted the delicate metal stylus from the paper, the ink at its tip leaving a jagged little squiggle as if the vicinity had suffered some small disturbance. Slowly turning the metal drum, he pulled off the old paper roll and slipped the new one in its place, fitting the ends into slots in the metal. He relocated the stylus and, taking a pen from his pocket, scribbled a few words on the new paper: the date, time, attenuation, or signal power of the machine, and the name of this seismographic station—PRIN for Princeton. Closing the glass lid, he locked it in place.

Turning to the previous day's record, the student scanned the thin black line that rose and fell across the paper as if tracing the contours of a mountain range. Yes, the pattern had been holding all this week, as it had been for most of the month, and even without triangulating the data with the other stations in the Lamont network, he knew exactly what it represented: minor seismic disturbances in the north central part of the state.

For the next half hour, he transcribed the data onto a series of U.S. Geological Survey record forms; the paper roll was filed in a closet. Still calculating mentally to himself, he carried the forms across the corridor to an office marked "Prof. J. Lewalski—Director." He knocked twice and went in.

The young man inside was not Professor Lewalski; he was a graduate student in geology employed by the department for the summer. He took the forms and ran his eye over the data.

"Hmm, one point four, eh? That's up a little, isn't it?"

The younger student nodded. "Yes, it was one point two on Wednesday. It's been climbing all week. Are we supposed to inform someone about this?"

The other rubbed his chin. "Well, according to policy, we're not supposed to issue reports unless disturbances get above three, when they may start doing some damage. Otherwise, all you do is scare people." He looked down at the data once again and frowned. "Of course, this trend is rather interesting . . . But with things like this, you never know. It could stay at one point four all year or die away tomorrow. Anyhow, Lewalski won't be coming back till August, and I don't want to make it seem like I'm out to get publicity while he's gone." Opening a desk drawer, he filed the forms inside. "Besides," he added, before turning back to his work, "people aren't even aware of readings below three. The only things that feel them are animals."

Back in the outbuilding tonight—my last night here on the farm. Can't help wishing I'd stayed in the farmhouse again, but felt so guilty about cutting short my stay that I wanted to get as far away from the Poroths as possible, & now it's too late to change my mind. I don't intend to set foot outside, & I'll keep the lights on in here till dawn.

Deborah seemed really disappointed to hear I was leaving. Wonder if I've read her wrong; maybe she's fonder of me than I realized. Sarr didn't seem at all surprised, & though he may have been hurt, he's much too proud to ever show it. In fact, he's been extremely nice about the whole thing. Refused to accept the extra week's rent I offered him by way of apology, though I'm sure he's strapped for funds right now. He even lent me his sickle for the night, knowing it would make me feel less nervous. It's certainly better than the axe I had here last time. Hope to hell I won't have to use it.

Immobile in the silence of the apartment, heedless of the streetlights outside, he lies watching through the animal's eyes as, behind the encircling screens, the man sits writing.

He is up late tonight. So far he has shown no signs of ever going to sleep. He is alert, edgy, obviously nervous, jerking his head at every sound. The sickle lies well within his reach.

It will have to be done quickly. There is going to be blood. And even now, with the new strength and speed the animal has gained, even with its infinitely sharper senses and the extra sting it carries in its poisoned claws, killing the man is going to be difficult.

Lying on his bed, the Old One tenses his limbs and ever so slightly trembles.

It will be difficult indeed. It is going to require all his concentration, all the animal's strength, all the ferocity of their combined wills.

But the twitching of the old man's limbs has also been a tremor of exultation. This is, after all, the moment he's prepared for . . .

Taking a deep breath, feeling in his city lungs the cool moist country night, he begins.

I suppose that, in one way or another, I'm going to miss this place. It's certainly more peaceful than New York, at least it was in the beginning, & I imagine the city's going to seem pretty dirty, hot, & sticky when I get back. And for all my rural fears, of course, it'll probably be a lot more dangerous. It would be just my luck to flee in terror from what's really no more than a nasty little house cat, only to get brutally mugged a few minutes after I step off the bus.

Another irony: Just today got a really offensive letter from the folks, reminding me that I'm "not cut out to be a woodsman" (maybe they think I'm cooking on campfires & sleeping in a tent!), with a typically derisive little comment at the end, chiding me for wanting to do "the old Thoreau bit."

I'd almost be tempted to stay here for the rest of the summer, just to spite those two. Hate to give them the satisfaction of learning they were right, that I couldn't make it out here . . .

Still, no sense jeopardizing my safety. And besides, it's impossible to have a good time anymore, with all this Bwada nonsense going on.

I suppose if I'm really going to stay awake I ought to try doing something a bit more useful & continue going through the source material. Probably I ought to choose a book that won't—

Think I hear something in the bushes. Am turning off the light.

Leaves stirring, insect noises, touch of breeze on fur. The animal leaps nimbly from the tree; feet claw the night air, then soft earth as it lands in the undergrowth beneath one of the windows and begins a slow, cautious circle of the building, searching for an opening.

Inside, the man rises and hurriedly snaps off the lamps. Apparently the fool believes that the darkness will make him less vulnerable.

That is his mistake. The darkness will, in fact, make it easier to catch him unawares.

Silent as a shadow now, on velvet paws, it continues to circle the building.

Freirs stood frozen in the center of the room, ears straining for a sound. For a moment he thought he heard the stealthy, irregular crackling of leaves from the direction of the woods . . . or was it coming from the side that faced the lawn? He turned, trying in vain to follow it. His hand reached out gingerly in the darkness, felt the smooth metallic curve of the sickle, and passed on, grasping the flashlight.

Blindly, eyes not yet adjusted to the moonlight outside, he groped toward the screens facing the woods and stood looking out, seeing, hearing nothing.

Hadn't that been a new sound from the lawn side? He tiptoed across the room, the linoleum cool beneath his bare feet, and paused beside the closest window, listening, feeling against his cheek the faintest hint of breeze.

Was that the sound again? Was it his imagination? He held his breath and listened, pressing his face close to the screen . . .

Silence. No, there it was again, a tiny rustling in the ivy, not far below him. Silence again. He stood there frozen, still hardly daring to breathe, straining to hear.

A minute passed. At last, patience exhausted, he brought the flashlight to the screen and switched it on.

With a cry he fell back, dropping the flashlight; there was a shattering of glass, then darkness. For an instant, in its beam, he had seen the animal's wide grey face just inches from his own, the yellow gleaming fangs, the two eyes blazing like coals in the light.

Blindly he groped for the sickle, hearing, behind him, a sound that made his blood freeze. It was the slow, methodical tearing of the screen.

It can see the man perfectly now. He is blundering through the darkened room, fingers scrabbling frantically for a weapon.

Beneath its claws the screen wires tear like thinnest silk, strand after strand . . .

The aged figure on the bed feels the pressure of the wire beneath his fingertips, the successive individual strands giving way, his claws widening the gash . . .

Suddenly there is another sound. The clank of metal echoes through the halls. At the other end of the apartment, up and down the front door, the locks are being turned.

Feverishly he throws himself back to the countryside. Hurriedly his claws push aside the flaps of screen.

A crash out by the doorway; the sound of the door swinging open; and voices. Voices here in his apartment.

He cannot remain in the country. He must return at once. In an instant they will discover him naked here on the bed . . .

Looking one last time through the eyes of the animal, he comes to a decision. The animal, alone, may still be no match for the man. The risk of failure is too great. Too much is at stake.

Voices in the hallway. A heavy voice calls out, "Mistah Rosebottom?"

He has time for just a single thought, one final command before contact is broken.

Leave the man for now! he screams silently. *Go for the easier kill!*

A softer voice. "Hello? Hello? Is anybody—Oh, my God, Rosie!"

It knows itself to be alone now, on its own once more, but it feels neither loss nor regret. There will not be time to kill the man till later, but it is not impatient. All its strength and cunning will be turned, with cold precision, to its new task.

Withdrawing a paw from the rent in the screen, it drops silently to the ground beneath the window. Within seconds it is racing across the moonlit lawn in the direction of the farmhouse.

Quick as a spider it scurries up the gnarled trunk of the apple tree that grows at the rear of the house, pale claws sinking deep into the bark. Reaching the upper portion of the tree, it darts along one of the limbs and springs lightly to the nearby windowsill. The window is open; the room within stands empty, nursery figures grinning from the wall. All that blocks the window is a screen. With a touch delicate as a surgeon's it rends the wire, then slips inside and drops soundlessly to the braided rug beside the bed.

A new darkness now, new smells. Padding stealthily through the hall, it passes an open doorway and looks in. It is the bedroom. Moonlight falls upon two sleeping forms, the man and the woman entwined in one another's arms, and on the eight wide, watchful eyes of the cats that crowd beside them on the bed.

Deep in the orange one's throat a warning sound begins, a growl of anger and alarm . . .

Before the sound grows louder the intruder is gone, racing onward through the hall and down the stairs. It remembers the house perfectly; it knows where it must go.

Turning at the foot of the stairs, it passes through the lower hall and stops before a doorway. Then it is gone once more, vanished down the steps into the darkness of the cellar.

JULY TWENTY-THIRD

Freirs fell asleep just before dawn and dreamed he was fleeing down an endless dark passageway from something small and silent and untiring, but that was also huge, bigger than he was, bigger than the labyrinth he struggled through. In the distance someone called his name. He awoke with sunlight in his eyes—and had a moment of terror. A face was studying him through the gash in the screen.

It was Poroth, standing outside on the lawn, a rake in one hand.

"It's almost eleven," he said softly. "You asked me to wake you today." He pointed to the torn screen. "What's this? Has she been back?"

Freirs nodded sleepily, sitting up in bed. "It was her, all right. She tried to get in here last night, but for some reason she gave up. I haven't seen her since."

Rubbing his eyes, he slipped on his glasses and peered through the screen, wondering if the animal might still be nearby. By daylight the farm seemed a completely different place; it was impossible amid the tranquilizing warmth, the singing of the birds, the bright green canopy of maple leaves dancing in the sunshine, that anything terrible could ever happen here.

Poroth gazed gloomily at the damaged screen. Shaking his head, he pulled the two sides closed. "The animal is cursed," he muttered, "or else I am." He looked down at Freirs. "Well, maybe she'll stop her mischief once you're gone. I don't pretend to understand the devil." Shouldering the rake, he turned to leave. "I'll be out by the barn, for now. Let me know when you're ready and I'll drive you into town." He nodded toward the farmhouse. "Deborah'll have some lunch for you before you go."

Yawning, Freirs watched him move off toward the barn and disappear around the back, returning moments later with a tall ladder. Raising it against one side and hoisting the rake, he began to climb. As Freirs turned to dress, he saw Poroth poking morosely at a network of gypsy moth nests that bulged like white hammocks beneath the eaves.

The bus would be leaving at a quarter to one. Freirs would not have time to dawdle. The thought of leaving prompted an unexpected wave of sadness, but he forced it down. *That's just dumb,* he thought. *In-*

*stant nostalgia! You always feel bad about leaving a place you know
you'll never see again.* Throwing a towel around his neck and buttoning his shirt, he walked outside and headed for the farmhouse.

The kitchen smelled of baking bread. Deborah seemed in a better
mood this morning than she'd been in yesterday. The disappointment
at his leaving was still apparent, but it was with her usual energy that
she hurried around the kitchen, kneading a yellowy mass of dough, pe-
riodically checking a second loaf in the oven. "If I'd had more time,"
she said, "I'd've cooked you up a big fat blueberry pie for you to take
back to New York. Do you do your own cooking?"

"Some," said Freirs. "I eat a lot of my meals out. But none of it's as
good as I've had here."

She smiled broadly, wiping her hands on her apron. "I sure wish I
had time to make you something nice for lunch, but there's a million
things I've got to do before tomorrow morning." Taking a loaf of brown
bread from the shelf, she sliced off several pieces with the bread knife.
"It's a shame you won't be able to come to worship." She shrugged.
"But then, you'd probably be bored by it anyway."

Freirs watched her pour him a small glass of milk. "I'd give you
more," she said, "but there isn't much left. There's that trouble at the
Verdocks' with poor Lise, and Sarr says Brother Matthew didn't have
anything to sell this morning either. His cows haven't been right." She
set a plate before him. The sandwich she'd made was enormous—ham
and cheese on thick slices of brown bread. Freirs ate it with a twinge of
regret: it was the same as the first meal she'd ever served him.

When he got back outside, he saw that Poroth had abandoned the
ladder and was crouched precariously on the lower edge of the barn
roof. Freirs winced as the other reached beneath the eaves with his
bare hand and hurled down a writhing clump of caterpillars.

Eventually Poroth looked up, noticed him watching, and nodded in
the direction of the road. He called, "You about ready to go?"

"In a minute. I just have to get the rest of my things together."

A few bugs, having found their way into his room through the tear
in the screen, were now buzzing against the wire trying vainly to find a
way out. *Nature!* he said to himself. He fastened the clasp of his suitcase and strapped on his watch. It was an automatic, supposed to wind
itself from the movement of his wrist, but he'd worn it so seldom out
here that he now had to wind it by hand. Taking his wallet from the
dresser drawer, he slipped it into his pocket, followed by the unfamiliar bulge of his apartment keys, a handful of loose change, and a New
York subway token.

Briefly a sound reached him from the farmhouse, a single muffled
wail, but it died away in the air. He was tying twine around a final
stack of books when, from across the lawn, he heard the thump of something hitting the ground. He looked outside in time to see Poroth

stumbling to his feet; in an instant he was off and running toward the farmhouse. Freirs saw him dash up the back steps and disappear inside, and moments later heard him shouting Deborah's name. Knocking aside the books, Freirs hurried after him.

He entered the house just as the other, with pounding feet, was coming down the stairway from the second floor. "She's here somewhere," Poroth said. "I heard her scream." Suddenly his gaze fell upon the peg high on the wall where the extra lantern usually hung. The lantern was gone. "The cellar!" he cried. Rounding the hallway, he paused at the top of the steps and peered worriedly into the darkness. "There's another lantern in the kitchen," he called over his shoulder. "Get it and follow me." Putting out his hand to feel his way, he started down.

"Wait!"

The voice had come from below them, up through the cracks in the floor. It was feeble, a mere croaking, nothing at all like the voice they knew. "Wait," they heard again. "I'm . . . all right now. Give me just—" It paused. "Just one moment."

There was a slow, unsteady shuffling from within the cellar, then the clump of footfalls on the wooden steps. Gradually the outline of a dark form appeared, advancing slowly toward them up the stairs. Sarr reached down and grasped her arm, and moments later Deborah staggered out into the light. She was clutching her bunched-up apron to her throat. The apron had been white; now it was sticky and red where the patches of blood had seeped through.

Suddenly her eyes rolled up, her legs buckled, and she tilted forward. Sarr caught her before she hit the floor. Lifting her as lightly as if she were a rag doll, he carried her upstairs, two steps at a time, and laid her gently on the bed in their room.

Freirs followed them up. Deborah seemed to be still conscious—her eyes were open and she was staring dully at the ceiling—but her always pale skin was now deathly white save for dark skull-like rings beneath her eyes. Her breathing was labored, rasping deep in her throat, and her head lay like a stone upon the pillow, yet she resisted Sarr's efforts to pry away the bloody apron she held pressed to her neck. "No," she whispered hoarsely. "Not yet."

"What happened?" said Sarr. "Can you tell me?"

Her eyes rolled slowly around to look at them both, but she remained silent. At last, very feebly, she shook her head. Removing a hand from her throat, she pointed to the floor. "Bwada," she whispered.

Sarr, who had been leaning over the bed, straightened up, eyes blazing. "That devil's down there now?" He started for the door.

Deborah grasped his wrist, holding him back. She managed to get out one word.

"Dead."

We raced downstairs & down the cellar steps, Sarr grabbing the lantern from the upstairs hall. Even with the light it was hard to see down there, & the ceiling was so low he had to duck his head. Near the foot of the stairs, on the hard dirt floor, we saw an overturned milk pitcher, the lantern Deborah must have dropped, & what at first looked like a clump of matted grey fur. It was Bwada. She looked, in death, amazingly small. How could a creature that size have inspired such terror?

She seemed frozen in the middle of an attack: eyes wide & glassy, filthy-looking claws extended, mouth agape, the rubbery-looking grey lips pulled back & exposing a row of yellow fangs. Even though it was obvious she was dead, I still couldn't hold back a shudder; in the glare of that lantern she looked just the way I'd seen her last night in the beam of my flashlight, her face pressed to the screen.

I saw a small round hole in her side—a puncture wound, from the look of it—bordered by pinkish grey flaps of skin. Nearby, at the foot of one of the shelves, we saw the gleam of Deborah's long thin bread knife & began to figure out what had happened . . .

Later, after she'd had a bit of sleep, Deborah was able to stammer out the rest, though it was clear she still found it painful to speak. Apparently she'd come down to the cellar, after I'd gone out, to see how much milk was left & to bring up some things for tomorrow. She'd already been down there several times before, during the course of the morning, but she hadn't noticed anything wrong; the animal must have remained hidden. This time, though, there was no one else in the house upstairs; maybe that's what made the difference. She says she heard a sound just above eye level & was suddenly looking at the cat, crouched on one of the shelves. No sooner did she see it than it sprang for her throat.

This is when God, or luck, or something, seems to have saved Deborah's life: for all this time she'd had the bread knife by her side, hanging from a loop of her apron; she had carried it downstairs, she said, to cut off a slab of bacon for tonight's meal. Somehow, when she was attacked, she had the presence of mind to grab for the knife. She managed to wrench the animal off her neck & with the other hand was able to impale it on the sharp end of the blade.

Judging from the nature & position of the wound, I'd say she had even more luck than she & Sarr realize, because the tip of the knife must have caught the animal precisely in its old wound, reopening it—to the extent that, when the blade was withdrawn, the flesh bulged out just the way it had before. Naturally I couldn't mention this to Sarr.

It seems somehow poetically appropriate, when you stop to think of it: that murderous creature finally dispatched—& efficiently, too—by the smallest & weakest among us. Maybe there is a God after all.

Deborah was weak from shock throughout the afternoon & lay upstairs on the bed. When we finally persuaded her to take the cloth away, we were relieved to find that the gashes in her neck were relatively small, the claw marks already clotting. (Thank God that thing didn't get the chance to sink its teeth in.) Sarr was so glad to have her alive that he couldn't do enough for her. He said he heard "heavenly choruses." Kept kneeling at odd moments in the corner of their bedroom, thanking the Lord for delivering Deborah safely & for ridding him of his curse. For the rest of the afternoon he & I took turns bringing things up to her from the kitchen—towels soaked in cold water, etc. At one point, while he was downstairs, she reached out & took my hand as I was standing by the bed. "Thank you," she said in a hoarse whisper, giving my hand a squeeze. "Thank you for staying."

That jolted me. In all the commotion I'd completely forgotten about catching the bus home. I glanced down at my watch; it was already half past one. I'd missed my chance to leave today.

"Well," I said, as if I'd actually planned it this way, "I couldn't leave you at a moment like this. I'll think about leaving tomorrow."

She was still gripping my hand. "Please," she whispered, looking up at me, her eyes wide & somehow even more beautiful in that pale, bruised face. "Please stay."

I hadn't thought of staying; I hadn't even considered it. But it occurred to me now that with Bwada gone—gone for good, this time—the reason for my leaving had been eliminated.

"Well," I said, still doubtful, "maybe I can stay a while longer. At least till you're well again."

She smiled & squeezed my hand tighter. "Good," she whispered. We stared at one another for a moment or two more, & then, hearing Sarr's footsteps on the stairs, we dropped our hands.

He fixed dinner for us tonight—little more than soup, actually, because he thought that it was best for Deborah. She stayed upstairs, resting. Her voice sounded so bad—breath so rasping, words so slurred—that he told her not to strain herself any more by talking.

We had left Bwada's body in the cellar; it's the coolest spot in the house. After dinner I sat with Deborah again while Sarr drove the cat's body into Flemington to have it checked for rabies. (For once he spared us the expected diatribe about veterinarian bills; apparently when it's something as serious as this, his faith in God isn't quite enough to rely on.) He was away for almost two hours, during which time, as Deborah was too overwrought to fall asleep, I did my best to entertain her by reading aloud from one of the books of inspirational verse I'd found downstairs. I could see, from the notes in the margins, that it had belonged to Sarr in college. (Typical that he'd favor humorless old bores like Milton, Vaughan, & Herbert.) Most of the poems were dark, somber things, perfect for a Puritan's funeral; the rest were rosily optimistic—Sunday school stuff. Deborah just lay there on the bed listening, watching me rather dreamily (& appreciatively, I hope), smiling but saying nothing, not stirring at all, barely even blinking.

Sarr got back long after dark, looking quite exhausted. He said Bwada's body had begun to stink even before he got into Flemington, & now the whole truck smells of her. The vet was surprised at how quickly she'd started to decompose; the dampness, apparently. He took scrapings from her teeth & will know by tomorrow if there's any sign of rabies. It'll give the Poroths something extra to pray about tonight.

They were, in fact, doing just that when I left them: Sarr on his knees in his accustomed spot, praying aloud, Deborah watching him silently from the bed but, in her heart, I'm sure, praying along with him.

I can still hear him, more faintly now, as I sit out here. No, he's stopped now; the night is silent again. We'd had some faraway thunder before, but now that too has stopped. When I think of how nervous I was about staying out here alone last night, I feel a tremendous sense of relief; God knows how many times I've lain here thinking every sound I heard was Bwada. Nice to have that reign of terror over.

Hmm, I'm still a wee bit hungry—that soup we had for dinner didn't really fill me up. I'll probably dream of hamburgers & chocolate cake tonight.

I've unpacked all my books & things; New York will just have to wait. Looks like I'll be doing "the old Thoreau bit" a while longer . . .

Dear Jeremy,

I was so glad to hear from you again. How awful about those two cats. Hope that grey one's gone for good. I never did like her.

I wish the Poroths had a telephone; there are so many things I'd like to tell you, my head's still spinning. I suppose they'll have to wait—but only till next weekend, fortunately, because, taking you up on your invitation, I do hope to come out again and see you. The weekend of the thirtieth, I mean. And I want to bring Rosie. I think the trip would be good for him (and besides, it's his car). He's been ill and is badly in need of a vacation. After not hearing from him all week, I got very worried and last night I got the super to let me into his apartment. The two of us found poor Rosie in a really terrible state, naked on his bed, and I swear we both thought he was dead. And the way he looked—I just hope I never have to see anything like that again. It really gave me quite a shock. I'm convinced that if I hadn't taken a chance and come in when I did, we would have lost him.

He apologized later—said this had happened to him before, it's just a kind of nervous condition he gets—and I must say he's recovered nicely. You've met him, Jeremy, so you know how easy he is to get along with. I'm sure he won't give the Poroths any trouble at all. He'll sleep anywhere there's room for him, even a living room chair will be all right (he *claims* he needs only an hour or two a night), and we'll be bringing out extra food with us so that no one will have to go to any added expense.

He's really amazing, in fact, for a man his age. (My guess is he's eighty if he's a day.) He was up and around in less than an hour, after we got some food in him, just as cheerful and energetic as ever and, as you can imagine, *very* grateful to me. He rested most of the day, but this afternoon he called to say he was sick of being cooped up and wanted to get out; and earlier tonight, though I kept asking him if he really felt up to it, he insisted on taking me to the ballet, just as he'd promised—the Royal Ballet's on tour here now—even though I'd have been perfectly willing to forgo it. I'm glad I went, though; we had great seats, first row dress circle (leave it to Rosie!), and saw, among other things, a beautiful Antony Tudor ballet called *Shadowplay*, a sort of pagan piece with wood spirits and all, and so continually inventive and lively that I'm sure even you would have liked it.

Afterward we went and had dessert across the street at one of those cafes, the kind I never could afford on my own—they charge $5.95 for a little dish of ice cream—and then he insisted on seeing me home. You can never get a cab around here, so we ended up on the IRT. It was really crowded on a Saturday night, but Rosie somehow manages to turn everything into a game. He had us sit up front where we could watch the tunnel ahead of us through the little window. As we sped along, he told me about some scene in the old *King Kong* in which the gorilla sticks his head up through an elevated track and derails an entire train. I never saw the movie, you know I hardly ever had a chance to see *anything* before I came to New York, but I tried to imagine what the scene must be like and pictured a huge snarling head filling the subway tunnel. And then Rosie said, Okay, but what if it wasn't a head, what if it was just a *hand* big enough to stop the train? (That's one of the games he plays, the What If game, also called the Riya Mogu or something like that. Whatever the other person says, no matter how outrageous, you have to force yourself to really totally believe in it with all your heart.) I could picture a huge clawed hand sticking up in the middle of the tunnel. And then he said, What if it was just a single finger big enough to fill the tunnel? And I said, How about the *claw* of such a finger? The *tip* of the claw? A thing so big it filled the whole tunnel? . . . Rosie laughed and said, Yes, that's the idea.

But maybe I have too vivid an imagination, because somehow I managed to make myself sick that way, picturing those huge things in front of us; or maybe it was the heat on the train after all that ice cream, and the crowd, and the roaring. I started feeling very weak, all of a sudden, and someone nice got up for me so I could sit down. And just then the train came screeching horribly to a stop, right in the middle of the tunnel, all the lights went out and the air got hot and stopped moving, and I got a sudden icy feeling up and down my spine, so bad I thought I'd throw up. Someone said, Don't you see it, there's something blocking us, and Rosie went up and tried to see if there was another train up ahead, but he couldn't see through the crowd; he'd been standing next to me and we'd lost our place by the window.

A few moments later the lights came on and the train began creeping forward. Then suddenly it stopped again, and again the lights went out. This jerking, starting, and stopping made me feel even worse. It happened several more times, and each time we ground to a stop I felt my stomach heave like I was going to be sick, even though Rosie was right there beside me with his hand on my shoulder.

The train kept rocking and jerking all the way downtown; it was really nightmarish. I know it was the movement that was making me sick, though the odd thing was that each time I seemed to get this wave of nausea just *before* we stopped, as if it was the train that was somehow affected by what was happening inside me, rather than the other way around. I told Rosie I was afraid I was going to be sick, and he said, Try to keep it down, we'll be there in a minute or two; and I managed to control myself all the way, fighting down the nausea while the whole world seemed to twist and heave inside me. Keep it down, Rosie kept saying, and it seemed to work; and just as he was helping me off the train he turned to me, smiling, and gripped my hand, and said, Congratulations, Carol, you've passed the test . . .

BOOK NINE

McKINNEY'S NECK

There were black terrible woods hanging from the hill all round; it was like seeing a large room hung with black curtains, and the shape of the trees seemed quite different from any I had ever seen before.

   —Machen, *The White People*

JULY TWENTY-FOURTH

Sunday dawned grey and gloomy, mammoth clouds rising on all sides like the smoke from distant fires. Freirs got up early, awakened by voices up at the farmhouse, followed by the slamming of the screen door. Sleepily he remembered: this was Sunday, the morning that the Poroths were to play host to the assembled Brethren. He sat up in bed and looked out. A shiny navy blue station wagon was already parked beside the house. He reached for his eyeglasses, then took his wristwatch from the night table. Seven fifteen—an ungodly hour to be thinking about God. He wondered if plans were being changed in light of Deborah's injury, but probably it was too late for that now.

Slipping on shorts and a T-shirt, he left his building and crossed the damp grass to the house. As he climbed the steps to the back porch, he could hear a gruff voice saying, in a slightly defensive tone, "We'd planned on walkin' here, but with Lotte's condition—"

As Freirs opened the screen door, the man who'd been speaking fell silent. He was seated at the kitchen table with Sarr Poroth and a slim grey hard-faced woman whom Freirs recognized as Poroth's mother. The two men had mugs of coffee before them. All turned as he came in. Freirs felt like a child who'd blundered into a party where he didn't belong; only Poroth's face showed friendliness.

"Ah," he said, getting to his feet, "you've risen early this morning!" He turned to the other man, who was also standing now. "Brother Joram, this is our guest, Jeremy Freirs. Jeremy, this is Joram Sturtevant."

"Good morning," said Freirs.

The man nodded stiffly. "A good morning to you." So this was the leader of the sect; Freirs had heard much about him. He was bearded like Poroth, with eyes as dark and piercing, but his face looked older and even more severe. The formal-looking black jacket he wore lent him an air of authority. Freirs waited to see if he would extend his hand, but the man made no further sign of greeting. In the silence Freirs heard voices coming from the living room—children's voices and a woman's. The guests were here early.

"And I know you two have met," Poroth was saying, with a nod to his mother.

"Yes indeed," said Freirs. "Under rather unpleasant conditions."

He turned to the woman, who sat regarding him silently, with no trace of recognition. There were still a pair of thin red lines across her cheek. "You look as if you're healing nicely."

She arched her brows. "If that's God's will."

Poroth heaved a sigh as he sat down. "Ah, well, 'tis all in the past now, thank the Lord."

"The past?" The woman gave a skeptical shrug. "That's hardly for the likes of us to say."

Sturtevant cleared his throat. "With the Lord's help we'll put the wickedness behind us this very morning." He shifted his gaze to Freirs. "I'm told the accursed creature had a special . . . interest in you."

"Yes," said Freirs, still standing in the doorway; no one had invited him to sit down. "I'm not sure why, but it seemed to bear me a particular hatred."

"And yet for all that, you were never actually harmed by the beast."

Sturtevant's eyes were subtly accusing; Freirs decided to end the conversation. "I guess even us infidels have someone watching over us." He turned to Sarr. "How's Deborah this morning?"

"Healing well," said Sarr. "She's upstairs taking her rest now, but she'll be down. Why don't you have yourself some breakfast while we three move into the living room and wait for the others?"

There was a sliding of chairs, and they filed out of the kitchen. Freirs could see a boy around nine or ten already in the living room, and a large, flushed young woman, obviously very pregnant, who sat slumped in the rocker as if exhausted.

Heating some coffee, he took from one of the cabinets a box of cold cereal he'd bought on his first trip to town. The milk pitcher on the table was almost empty. Picking it up, he took the lantern that hung by the top of the steps and went down to the cellar in search of more.

There was still an inch or two of milk at the base of the metal storage container, but it had gone decidedly sour. The smell pervaded the entire cellar—or was that, perhaps, another smell, the odor of decay? Could the smell of Bwada's body have lingered so long? Passing the farthest shelf as he headed back upstairs, he looked in vain for eggs. The egg rack was empty; the hens still weren't laying. *What the hell is this place coming to?* he thought. *Everything's falling apart.*

Upstairs more people were beginning to arrive, some of them pulling up in cars or pickup trucks, others who lived closer arriving on foot. The later arrivals headed directly for the back lawn; those who'd been seated in the living room moved outside to join them, leaving the house to Freirs. He watched black-garbed families congregate outside as he attempted, stomach growling, to make a breakfast for himself out of burnt toast and coffee. He recognized some of the faces that passed beneath the window and noticed family resemblances in others. Matthew

Geisel had arrived with a beaming grey-haired woman Freirs guessed to be his wife, and now he recognized Geisel's brother Werner from their long-ago meeting at the Co-op. He saw Bert and Amelia Steegler, the store's managers, and Rupert Lindt, whom he recalled disliking, flanked by a wife and two daughters. One of them, the younger, looked familiar; he stared at her a long time, increasingly convinced that she'd been the girl in the truck that had tried to run him down. *Mustn't jump to conclusions,* he told himself. *With all the inbreeding around here, everyone looks a little bit alike.*

In fact, the people assembling on the lawn were hard to tell apart; they were dressed and groomed alike, as well. He felt, more than ever now, like an outsider. He didn't belong here. Better to be back on Bank Street, with the radio playing and the traffic outside. Briefly he considered retreating to the privacy of his outbuilding, but in his incongruously bright clothing he knew he'd feel even more conspicuous crossing the lawn; and then, too, he'd be trapped in his room like an animal in a cage. He decided to stay where he was.

The screen door burst open and Poroth hurried in, looking distracted. He headed for the stairs but called over his shoulder, "Aren't you coming out?"

"I'm not really dressed for it," said Freirs. "I think I'll just watch from in here."

Sarr paused. "You'll have to come out eventually," he said. "We're performing a Cleansing."

"A what?"

But the other was already hurrying up the stairs. Freirs could hear him tramping overhead, then the creak of floorboards as he helped Deborah off the bed. Their footsteps as they descended were slow and unsteady. Moments later Sarr appeared with Deborah leaning on his arm. She looked as pale as before, with the same dark rings beneath her eyes, and her pallor was further accentuated by a black scarf wrapped around her throat, concealing her up to the chin. She smiled weakly at Freirs as they passed.

"Sarr, what's this Cleansing you spoke of?"

"Something special," said Poroth, busy helping Deborah out the door. "You'll see. Best just to stay inside here till the singing's over."

The screen door slammed, and Freirs could see the assembled Brethren turn to watch as the two of them stiffly descended the back steps, like the last and most important arrivals at a ball. There were by now nearly a hundred people in the yard. Among them he recognized the leathery old farmer who'd given him a lift and the elderly couple who'd refused him one. He even thought he recognized, from the skimpiness of his beard, the teenage boy who, with the girl, had almost run him down. He wished once again that he'd gotten a better look at them.

Abruptly the elderly couple turned their backs on one another like figures in a dance, and, as he watched, the woman appeared to walk away without a word of goodbye. In fact, he noticed now, all the women, old and young alike, had begun to move off to the side of the lawn nearer the barn, leaving the major portion of it to the males. He realized that the sexes were once again being segregated, just as they'd been in the Bible school yearbook. *Like Orthodox Jews*, he decided. *Crazy*.

Freirs had expected Joram Sturtevant to lead the worship, but apparently the man's position was more social than theological, for when the services finally began it was neither he nor Poroth, the host, who strode to the front of the group and asked for silence, but rather a short, older man whom Freirs had never seen before. Clasping a large, worn-looking black Bible before him, he called upon the assembled Brethren to pray with him for Sister Lise Verdock, who, along with her family, could not be with them this morning owing to her tragic accident. All eyes were downcast as the man led the invocation, quoting at length from Jeremiah—"O Lord, my strength and my fortress and my refuge in the day of affliction"—the Bible open in his hands now but never actually looked at, as if the mere act of holding it affirmed the truth of what he said.

After the prayer the man stepped back, handing the book ceremoniously to a younger man who took his place. Gradually, as the morning progressed and new speakers, women as well as men, replaced the old, each of them holding the Bible while addressing the congregation, Freirs began to realize that what had seemed, at first, to be an unstructured occasion was in fact highly formalized. People seemed to know just when to take their turns as speaker; when, as happened but seldom, two Brethren found themselves approaching the front of the congregation at the same time, one would hold back and wait, as if by some prearranged system of dominance.

Nearly a dozen people, mostly men, had addressed the group, with further prayers for everything from more rain to the smiting of idolaters, along with another prayer for Lise Verdock, when, after a pause in which no others had volunteered to speak, Sarr Poroth pushed his way to the front. Watching from his seat by the window, Freirs saw him scan the congregation and smile at Deborah, who was supported by two of the women—and closely observed, at the same time, by Mrs. Poroth.

Holding the Bible open before him, Sarr began to speak. Freirs leaned closer to the screen to hear better.

" 'And all flesh died that moved upon the earth, both of fowl, and of cattle, and of beast, and of every creeping thing that creepeth upon the earth, and every man . . .' "

It took Freirs a moment to recognize the passage. Though most of the others had spoken from Jeremiah, Sarr was telling of the Flood, of great cataclysmic events that at last, under God's goodness, had had an end. " 'And Noah builded an altar,' " he said, not once looking down at the text, " 'and offered burnt offerings on the altar. And the Lord smelled a sweet savor; and the Lord said in his heart, I will not again curse the ground any more for man's sake; for the imagination of man's heart is evil from his youth; neither will I again smite any more every thing living, as I have done. While the earth remaineth, seedtime and harvest, and cold and heat, and summer and winter, and day and night shall not cease.' "

Freirs found the singsong rhythm of the passage unexpectedly comforting, easily as much so as the words themselves, though for hours afterward something in him would repeat, troubled, that final qualifying phrase:

"While the earth remaineth."

Joram Sturtevant stood ramrod straight, defying the heat and staring intently at each successive speaker, but he found it hard to concentrate on what was being said. His thoughts were on the stranger back there in the house.

He had not liked what he'd seen. Granted, the man bore a name hearkening back to the prophet, yet he himself was, by his own admission, an infidel. That had been his very word, in fact; he'd spoken it with pride.

There'd have been danger enough if the stranger had been of a rival faith, one of the numerous Christian or Hebrew or mongrel sects that schemed and struggled and vied for men's souls in the vast benighted world beyond the borders of the town; they were all the same, those sects, all greedy and, when the Last Judgment sounded, all damned. But to have so bluntly declared himself an infidel, an enemy of faith itself—surely this was a hundred times worse. Maybe Brother Rupert had been right about him.

And to call this infidel a "guest," as Poroth had this morning—surely that was the flimsiest of lies.

Poroth himself was speaking now, drawing laborious parallels, in a low and earnest voice, between the tribulations of Noah and the Brethren's current difficulties. The young man had a good mind, Joram conceded, but he was clearly nervous in groups and made a poor speaker. And it seemed he made an even worse farmer. Joram cast his eye over the cornfields in the distance, the small, sickly-looking stalks already prey to all manner of weeds and pests. He could see, even now, that Poroth's first crop would be accounted a failure.

The image struck him as an apt one: for wasn't Gilead itself a kind of garden, carefully cultivated, nourished and protected, its families as varied as the crops of a well-managed farm, its young like tender

shoots? Yes, here was the stuff of some future sermon! And admitting a
stranger entrance, as Poroth had, was akin to opening a garden's gates
to predators. The shoots would be corrupted, seeds trampled, the soil
itself tainted.

Perhaps, though, as with the first Fall, a woman was to blame.
Young Poroth, lacking as he did a father's guidance, seemed inclined
to let Deborah order him about, and it was said that taking in the
stranger had been her idea.

There she was now, amongst the women near the barn, staring dully
at the proceedings. What had happened to her yesterday had been no
surprise to Joram. He had been convinced for some time that the devil
was in that cat; his right hand still smarted from his encounter with
her earlier in the year. Sister Deborah should have foreseen the tragedy. Like as not it had been a judgment upon her. She was, Joram allowed, a handsome woman; he admired the slimness of her form and
her dark, wanton-looking eyes, though he suspected she'd be capable of
all manner of sin.

Lotte, his own wife, had once been just as slim, but after three sons
her figure had thickened. And now, of course, the woman was almost
unrecognizable, her belly grown so enormous it pained her constantly.
Joram thought of her as Sarr came to the end of his talk. He had left
her in the Poroths' living room, her sweating form filling their little
rocker in a way he'd found faintly disagreeable. Somewhere in him was
the vague suspicion that he'd been wrong to bring her here today, but
this he'd long since repressed, and what he felt instead was, for the
most part, a mixture of irritation at her feminine frailty—the other
children hadn't been such trouble—and concern at her appearance. If
he felt any guilt, it was for not having insisted that she come outside
here with him for the services, to stand, just like Deborah, with the
other women. They couldn't allow themselves to grow soft, he and
Lotte. They had an example to set for the community.

Freirs had expected the services would be over when Poroth finished
speaking; he hadn't counted on the hymns. There were more than a
dozen of them, from "Blue Galilee" to "Christ the Harvester," growing
in volume and fervor until he felt sure some of the Brethren would wilt
beneath the steadily advancing sun, which, having risen above the low
wall of clouds, now shone down fiercely.

Toward the end, growing weary of the songs, he thought he heard,
from the living room, a low, agonized moan. Leaving his seat by the
window, he walked to the doorway and looked in. There, still sunken in
the rocker where he'd seen her before, was the pregnant woman, alone
now and looking barely conscious, sweating terribly in her heavy black

dress and obviously in great discomfort. She looked up dully as he entered, blinking at him through great trusting cow eyes that showed neither recognition nor fear.

Freirs approached the chair and stood staring down at her, thinking, *Christ, she shouldn't be out of bed looking as pregnant as this.* As she raised her head to look at him, he forced his face into a smile. "Hello," he said softly. As the morning sunlight touched it, he saw her swollen belly squirm.

He was the first man to smile at her all morning. Joram only glowered at her these days, as if her condition were somehow not a blessing but a curse. She hadn't wanted to come to the worship, she'd felt so tired, so filled up inside she could scarcely breathe. It had never been like this before, not with the others; sometimes, when the child inside her moved, it felt as if the child were rearranging all her insides to suit itself, so strong-willed was it, like Joram. It was surely bound to be another boy. She wished that just this once the Lord would let her have a daughter, but it wasn't for her to question His ways. Joram would be angry with her if he knew she'd even thought of it.

She wanted this pregnancy to end. It was becoming too much for her to bear. And it was so hot today; she'd have liked to sit out upon the back porch and watch the services, she knew they'd be a comfort to her, but Joram wouldn't hear of it. He'd said that either his woman stood out there in the sun with the rest of the congregation or else hid herself away; he'd not be shamed by having her sit while the others stood. So she'd been condemned to this airless little living room. She had been feeling dizzy from the heat and the discomfort when the stranger approached her.

She envied the way he was dressed; he looked so much more comfortable, and you could see his plump arms and legs, like a baby's. The colors of his clothing reminded her of the flowers in her garden. He had a kind face, and his hands looked soft, like healing hands; they stirred vague memories of Joram's own hands long ago, before the children came, and memories of the soft hands of the midwives.

"How are you feeling?" he was asking, smiling down at her like the sun.

"Oh, my," she said, "just look at me!" And she shook her head, almost ready to laugh, as if the two of them were sharing a joke, one that people like her husband would never understand.

"I *am* looking," he was saying, and his smile was so sympathetic she was almost able to forget the ache inside her. She smoothed back a strand of hair from her sweating brow, wishing he could see her at her best, and realized, suddenly, that her thighs were parted more than was proper for a married woman with a strange man, the heavy black material dipping like a damp trough between her legs. But it was all right, the stranger was comfortable in his way and she was comfortable in hers. He looked as though he would understand.

"How much longer do you have?" he was asking, nodding at her stomach. She could see he was impressed. She was proud of her condition once again and remembered that she didn't have to be ashamed at all, the way Joram tried to make her feel. She thrust her belly upward even more.

"'Twill be any day now," she confided, with a little shiver of excitement. "I feel it movin' all the time."

The stranger smiled. "I guess the poor kid's getting impatient!"

She giggled; the sound felt funny, she hadn't laughed in so long. "It's movin' now," she said, but not alarmed for once; she was pleased at the stranger's interest. She ran a hand over her belly, feeling the child kick but also feeling how good her own hand felt. His would feel even better.

"You can touch it if you want," she said, smiling up at him, her body so huge and so sensitive. The stranger reached toward her, then hesitated.

"Go ahead," she said breathlessly. "Touch it . . . Touch it . . ."

They were all looking at Sturtevant now, waiting for him to give the word. He turned to the assembled group. "Brothers and Sisters, as you know, the Lord has given us a special task to perform today. These good people fear they've been sheltering malign spirits under their roof. It is for us, their brethren and neighbors, to purify the house and all within it. Let us, then, have a Cleansing. Join with me now in divesting their home of its worldly goods so that we may better fill it with the Holy Spirit."

The sun was hot on his head. He wiped the sweat off his forehead with the back of his hand. While the others formed themselves into a line and made ready for heavy labor, the men laying aside their vests and rolling up their sleeves, Joram walked round the side of the house and, slipping off his heavy black jacket, left it folded on the front seat of his car. In a moment or two the others would be filing into the house, with Lotte still seated there fat and sweating in the living room. He hated the thought of them seeing his wife like that; better to rouse her and get her outside, maybe have her sit in the car. He hoped she would not attempt to argue with him; with a determined stride he hurried up the front steps and through the open door.

The short hallway was dim, but sunlight streamed from the living room, through whose doorway, as if within a frame, he saw the figure of his seated wife—and of Jeremy Freirs bending over her, murmuring soft words as he stroked her rounded stomach.

It took the others several minutes to calm Joram down. The first group of Brethren had entered the house just as the yelling began, and in the end what they remembered were Joram's wild expression, the way the veins stood out in his forehead, and the admirable way that, in consideration of Freirs' relations with the Poroths, he restrained himself from physically attacking their guest.

His greatest fury was directed at his wife—though this, too, was held in check before the eyes of the community. Choking out a "Woman! Remember yourself!" he seized her arm and dragged her roughly past the others, down the porch steps, and out to the navy blue station wagon parked beside the house. And what he said to the quaking woman once they were inside the car with the windows rolled up tight, no one in Gilead ever learned.

Meanwhile, politely ignoring the contretemps, if not oblivious to it, the others were continuing to file inside for the Cleansing, the crowd streaming through the back door and spreading throughout the house, each person taking as many objects as his or her arms could hold and carrying them out onto the lawn behind the house. It was like an old-fashioned moving day, Freirs decided, with the entire community there to help. He had stoutly maintained his innocence throughout Sturtevant's harangue, and now, reluctant to venture outside where the two of them were parked, he remained on the first floor watching the activity and lending a hand when he could. He saw men carry out chairs, shelves, a picture of the Holy Land from the living-room wall, even the andirons from the fireplace; two men struggled down the narrow wooden stairway with a chest of drawers; Rupert Lindt picked up the heavy wooden kitchen table all by himself and bore it outside. Women moved through the house, their arms laden with stacks of plates, clocks, rugs, or jars from the cellar. Even the smallest children worked, one with a handful of silverware, another with a flat, hard pillow from the bed, another with the little weather house from the living room. Cats darted excitedly beneath everyone's feet.

Gradually they were stripping the house of everything but the walls. Corah Geisel carefully untied the red glass witch ball from the lintel above the window in the nursery. Joram's brother Abram helped Poroth and Galen Trudel as they struggled to haul the Poroths' huge, heavy bed down the narrow stairs. Deborah, ill as she was, tried to

carry out the Bible from the night table in the bedroom, but in her
weakness dropped it to the floor, so that old Sister Corah, muttering
a hurried prayer, had to carry it for her, Freirs helping Deborah
herself downstairs. He was pleased at how tightly she gripped his
arm.

The Poroths did not have a great many possessions, but the collection on the lawn grew huge, encompassing as it did all their worldly
goods, even to the tiniest thimble. Freirs, when he wasn't actually
helping, stood in the living room watching the furniture and objects
being taken away around him with bemusement, like a homeowner
surrounded by moving men—nearly a hundred moving men, to be
exact, and clearly familiar with the requirements of the occasion. In
little more than half an hour the lawn outside, like the scene of some
desperate everything-must-go tag sale, lay covered with household be-
longings and a mob of milling people.

The barn was next. Poroth released the hand brake in the truck and
the assembled men pushed it out of the building and into the yard,
with no need to start its engine and break the holy silence of the service. Following the truck, men hauled out the rusted old farm implements and, from the attic, the tools and removable furnishings from
Sarr's workshop. The five hens and the rooster, cocking their heads as
they looked down curiously on all the activity through the wire of their
cage, were left inside to be blessed.

Poroth stood by the barn with hands on hips, overlooking the accumulation on his lawn with a gaze that appeared transported. Freirs
realized that he must be seeing, in all this, proof that his luck would
surely turn. What Deborah felt was impossible to make out.

Freirs moved beside him and looked dubiously at the clouds. In a
clearing to the east a smoke-white half-moon hung suspended in the
sky. "Let's hope it doesn't rain," he said.

Poroth glanced up but, surprisingly, showed no concern. "No matter," he said with a shrug. "'Twould simply be a cleansing sign from
the Lord."

Freirs nodded, privately recalling twin sayings about the weather at
funerals: sunshine was a sign that heaven loved the deceased; rain was
a sign that heaven was weeping for him. It was impossible to lose.

He looked back down at the lawn in time to see that a group of
nearly twenty young women had joined hands in a ring and were staring in their direction.

"Who are they?" he whispered.

"Unmarried women," said Poroth. "I'll explain in a minute." Smiling, he strode off into the center of the circle. One of the girls brandished a large black kerchief and, as Freirs watched, bound it around
Poroth's eyes like a blindfold. Suddenly the group began singing, their
high, girlish voices carrying eerily across the lawn:

> *"Make the choosing, round about,*
> *Choose the one and draw her out.*
> *First her willing hand you take,*
> *Then the Cleansing she will make."*

As they sang, they began turning slowly around Sarr, watching him intently. They had circled three times and had finished three complete choruses of the song when suddenly Sarr's hand shot out and tapped one of them, a thin young blond girl, on the shoulder.

"Eve Buckhalter," someone called.

"Draw her out!"

It was Joram Sturtevant who'd spoken. He was standing straight and tall on the back steps of the farmhouse, still grim-faced from the encounter and careful, it seemed, not to glance in Freirs' direction. Freirs assumed that, by this time, he'd settled the matter with his wife, for she was no longer in the car. Perhaps he was even ashamed now of having gotten so hot under the collar.

The Buckhalter girl was led outside the ring, where a woman Freirs didn't recognize handed her a small white feather. Grinning broadly, she stood waiting, awkward as all teenagers but clearly pleased at the attention.

"She will lead the Cleansing of the barn," called Sturtevant. "Now choose for the house."

Once more the girls in the ring began revolving, raising their voices in song. They had sung for three more revolutions of the circle when Sarr's hand shot out again, touching another girl, this time just below her breast, which made her squeal.

"Sarah Lindt," Brother Joram called. "Draw her out!"

It was Rupert's daughter; Freirs studied her closely as she was led from the circle, recognizing the wide face and snub nose. He felt even more certain now that she had been the girl in the truck.

Sarr, his task completed, had returned to Deborah's side, while in the center of the yard two women—the girls' mothers, he guessed, recognizing the woman he'd seen arrive with Lindt—proceeded to twine corn leaves in their daughters' hair. The leaves in place, the pair of girls, each grasping a white feather, were led before the group, where they stood waiting nervously. The second girl, young Sarah, he saw, looked *very* nervous.

Sturtevant, on the back steps, raised his hand. Turning to the girls, the congregation murmured an invocation:

"May the Lord be with you as you carry out your holy task."

"They're the ones who'll cleanse the buildings," whispered Poroth, his arm around his wife. He looked pleased, though Deborah's face was blank. "They're robed in innocence, you see, and are fit for such holy work."

"Oh, so that's the object," said Freirs. "Yes, I guess it makes sense." *Virgins,* he said to himself, as, in silence, the Buckhalter girl began walking past the company toward the barn while the Lindt girl proceeded toward the house.

For all the awkwardness of it—the round self-conscious teen-aged shoulders and the determinedly stately pace, the silly white feathers and the corn leaves in their hair—it was a curiously solemn moment. He scanned the assembled crowd. Parents were nodding and murmuring silent prayers; Poroth was gazing at two girls like a proud papa at graduation. Only one face made Freirs pause: that of Poroth's mother. For the first time that he could remember, the woman looked surprised and uneasy. Freirs followed her gaze. She was staring hard at the Lindt girl as the latter walked slowly toward the house, her girlish face grave, eyes directly before her, clutching the white feather as reverently as if it had been plucked from an angel wing.

"What's troubling your mother?" whispered Freirs.

"Sshh!" said Poroth, not looking at him. He did, however, turn to look at the woman, and, seeing her expression, his own face grew puzzled.

All this time the Lindt girl had been advancing slowly toward the house past the rows of assembled men and women. Suddenly Freirs saw her pause and, for the briefest moment, gaze wide-eyed with terror and misery at a white-faced young man who stood in the midst of the crowd. It was him once again, the one from the truck; Freirs had no doubt of it now. For an instant the young man returned the girl's gaze; then he looked guiltily away.

The eye contact between the two teenagers had been brief, and only someone who'd been watching for it could possibly have noticed. But it had lasted long enough for Freirs to see the look that passed between them, and he almost burst out laughing. *Hah!* he thought, *she's not really a virgin! And the only ones who know it are her, the boy, and me!* Scanning the crowd again, he saw the shock on the face of Sarr's mother. *And maybe,* he added, *Mrs. Poroth.*

No one else had seen. Sarah Lindt continued moving toward the house, Eve Buckhalter toward the barn. At last the two disappeared into the buildings, the Lindt girl hesitating a moment before entering, and there was an audible sigh from the assembled Brethren. As if suddenly released from a spell, they broke ranks and milled around the yard while Freirs and Poroth looked on, the crowd eventually spreading over the lawn so that each person was left standing before a small clump of household objects.

"What's going on?" whispered Freirs.

Sarr, too, seemed more relaxed. "Well, the girls are inside now. Sarah will go through every room of the house, from attic to cellar, blessing each room with a prayer, and Eve will do the same with the barn. Meanwhile, the others are going to bless our possessions out here. Deborah and I aren't allowed to participate."

The blessing he'd spoken of had already begun, Freirs saw; Brethren with waving hands were making signs and passes in the air, murmuring strings of prayers like people at some ancient bazaar.

"This does my heart real good," said Sarr, taking it all in.

Obviously size didn't matter. Freirs saw a little boy who looked all of seven standing solemnly before the grandfather clock, which dwarfed him, while hulking Rupert Lindt, his younger daughter in the house, stood mumbling a prayer over several lanterns and a rolled-up rug. Corah Geisel stood before a table piled high with jugs and jars and bowls; nearby stood her husband, blessing two of the implements from the barn, a broken plow and a rusted vehicle with wicked-looking prongs around the wheels. Brother Joram gravely blessed the pickup truck, whose cab, Sarr had said, still smelled of decay. Freirs wondered if the smell would disappear now.

Watching Geisel at his prayers, he realized that an item had been overlooked. He slipped into the outbuilding and emerged with Poroth's shiny little sickle, which had been lying on his night table. "I wouldn't want anything to escape your blessing, Matthew!" he said, tossing the sickle on the ground beside the plow. The old man nodded distractedly and continued praying.

At last Eve Buckhalter appeared in the doorway of the barn. Sticking the white feather like a talisman into a chink in the wood by her head, she gazed around her, smiling. Moments later Sarah Lindt appeared and forced a smile too, though she looked somewhat drawn and pale. Pausing at the back door, she struggled for a moment and finally managed to fit the white feather into a crack in the wood. She descended the back steps to a host of smiling faces; the praying had stopped. The Cleansing was completed.

"Brothers, Sisters," said Poroth solemnly, climbing onto the porch, "I thank you all for the service you've performed and the kindness you've done me and Deborah. Now let us thank the Lord for allowing us all to be here together."

He bowed his head; they all prayed silently for more than a minute. Freirs bowed his head, too, but only briefly; looking around, he saw that all other heads were bowed. Deborah was gazing at her feet, seemingly either deep in thought or not thinking at all. Sarr's eyes were shut tight, as if with profound concentration. Joram glared severely at his clasped hands, obviously with weighty matters on his mind. But Sarr's mother was staring intently at Deborah.

Moments later Joram raised his head. "Amen," he said.

There was a further easing of tension, a loosening of posture. A faint breeze had sprung up, tempering the force of the afternoon sun. Across the dome of sky a white half-moon hung just over the horizon like a smoke wisp. One by one, as if a film had been reversed, the Brethren picked up the objects on the lawn and carried them back inside. The bed and bureau were hauled up to the Poroths' bedroom; the truck was rolled into the barn.

Freirs checked his watch. It was just after one P.M. Deborah was standing silently on the porch. Sarr was supervising the moving in, pointing out where objects were to go, but was obviously not worrying much about exactness. "'Tis fine, 'tis fine," he was saying, as the women replaced the dishes in the cupboards. "Deborah and I can arrange it all later."

"Are you going to have to feed all these people?" asked Freirs, during a moment when the other was not distracted.

"No, thank the Lord." Poroth smiled. "We Brethren know how to control our hungers."

"It's clear you do," said Freirs, but he was thinking of the Lindt girl.

People, as he spoke, were beginning to leave: making their goodbyes, blessing one another, and drifting off up the road in little groups or, more frequently, piling into cars parked near the front of the house. On their way out, many of the Brethren stopped to thank Poroth and wish him well.

"I think the Cleansing went splendidly," said Abram Sturtevant, a dutiful brother, "and I know Joram thinks so as well." In fact, the latter and his family had been among the first to depart.

"I just hope it proves a help to us all," said Amos Reid. And old Jacob van Meer stopped to offer wishes from himself and his wife that Deborah, who had long since retired to her room, would make a speedy recovery.

Moments later Freirs saw Poroth talking in urgent whispers to his mother. The farmer looked annoyed. "I will," he kept saying. "Don't worry, I'll be there." At last the woman left, but Freirs could see she was dissatisfied and troubled.

The Geisels appeared reluctant to go. "Please," said Poroth, "stay and share our Sunday meal. We'd like you to, Deborah and I."

Corah Geisel elected to stay, but it was with the express purpose of caring for Deborah. "I'd like to stay too, Sarr," said Matthew. "I know your woman's in no fit way to cook or fix the house after today. But I'm sorry, I have to go. There's been a mess of trouble at our place too—in fact, we may call for a Cleansing of our own, if we can get the Brethren together before next Sunday. Our hens and cows haven't been right all week."

After the old man had bid goodbye to Sarr, Freirs accompanied him out past the front yard and onto the dusty road. "What's the matter with your animals?" he asked. "I've been drinking your cows' milk all summer. It's tasted fine."

They walked a little way in silence, till the Poroths' farmhouse was well behind them. "Most of the livestock in the area's been acting strange lately," said Geisel. "I don't rightly know what's behind it all. Some folks think—well, I don't mind telling you, there's those who say all sorts of things. Some even maintain the trouble comes from you."

"Me?" Freirs' laughter felt a little forced. "Why in the world would anyone think that? I've got nothing to do with this place."

"That's just the point," said Geisel. "You're an outsider. You're livin' here amongst us, but you ain't one of us. But don't you go worrying yourself over it. Some folks around here just get scared and look to all *kinds* of excuses."

"And what do you think the cause is?"

But the old man never got a chance to reply, for at that moment the earth tremors began.

Bert Steegler and Amelia had already gotten back to the store. They were invariably among the first to leave worship so that they could get the merchandise out and open up for business on Sunday afternoon. They sensed that something was wrong when all the lanterns, hanging sausages, wires, auto clips, and fishing rods hanging from the overhead beams began to tremble. As they stood there in terror, gripping the counter at the front of the store as if it were a life raft, they felt a deep, very low rumbling beneath their feet. Before the vibrations ceased ten seconds later, three heavy glass lanterns had crashed to the floor, and all the items on their shelves had crept mysteriously toward the north, as if magnetized.

Most of the Brethren were still on the road—the Poroths' dirt road or the paved ones nearer town—when the tremors hit. Those who were walking felt themselves rocked and came close to losing their balance. "It was like setting foot in a tippy boat," Galen Trudel would say later. He felt the ground shift, and the simple phrase "the solid earth" came mockingly to mind. Those in cars had to fight to keep their vehicles on the road. Driving close to town, Amos and Rachel Reid saw the pavement ahead slowly undulate as if it were a black ribbon floating on waves.

Many Brethren, true to their natures, were driven to recall warnings from the Bible. Klaus and Wilma Buckhalter, driving Eve home after an already exciting day, were reminded of Matthew: "And behold, the veil of the temple was rent in twain from the top to the bottom; and the

earth did quake, and the rocks rent; And the graves were opened . . ."
Eve herself felt witness to a God "whose voice shook the earth." Others
remembered the book of Revelation or, like Bethuel Reid, thought of
Isaiah: "Thou shalt be visited of the Lord of hosts with thunder, and
with earthquake, and great noise, with storm and tempest, and the
flame of devouring fire."

And twenty-five miles to the south, graduate students in the geology
department at Princeton, responding to a call from the Lamont-
Doherty Geological Observatory in Palisades, New York, checked their
instruments and verified the findings from Lamont: that north central
New Jersey had just suffered a minor earthquake measuring four
point nine on the Richter scale.

The excitement only lasted a few seconds, though it gave us all something to talk about over lunch. And it'll give me something to talk
about when I get back to New York. Never experienced one of these
things before; hope they're all as mild as this one proved to be.

Corah Geisel stayed upstairs with Deborah & left soon afterward,
reporting that Deborah's reflexes seemed a little off, but that otherwise
the wounds were superficial & were healing well.

It was grey the rest of the day & I sat in my room reading Robert W.
Chambers & half waiting for another earth tremor, which fortunately
never came. Most of Chambers' tales begin with marvelously ominous
quotations from a mythical book called *The King in Yellow*. However,
that single gimmick—masterful, I admit—seems to have been his sole
inspiration.

I was sorry that old Corah left & that dinner was again made by
Sarr; Deborah was still upstairs resting, he said. He sounded a trifle
concerned, despite all the good things that had happened to this place
today. He alluded to things wrong with her that Corah & the rest
hadn't noticed or had overlooked. He & I ate a forlorn bachelor meal of
cheese & bacon from the cellar (which, despite the Lindt girl's visit,
still smells—went past the doorway tonight & got a strong whiff of
decay). To keep Sarr company I stuck around the farmhouse a while,
after washing the dishes, but felt very drowsy & for some reason rather
depressed. Hardly the appropriate mood for what's supposed to be a
new beginning for this farm & my renewed decision to stay on. May be
the gloomy weather; we are, after all, just animals, more affected by the

sun & the season than we care to admit. Most likely, though, it was the absence of Deborah. Hope she feels better soon. We depend on her.

After Freirs went out, Sarr blew out one of the lamps. Taking the other, he walked softly upstairs, keeping to the edges of the old wooden steps so that they'd creak less. As he tiptoed into the bedroom, the light fell on Deborah's pale form. She was lying in bed on her back, staring into the darkness.

"Oh, you're awake."

She nodded. "Lots . . . to think about." Her voice, a croaking whisper, still disturbed him.

He patted her head. "I was going to pray silently, but I'm glad I won't have to. Just let me pray for both of us, okay? No talking now."

"All right."

He knelt in the corner, his knees upon the wooden planks. "O Lord, hear me in Heaven thy resting place . . ."

She watched him levelly until he was done. He was smiling as he came toward her. "And no singing tonight either," he said, climbing into the bed. He brought the lamp closer on the night table and gently touched the bruises on her neck. "These look even better now than they did this afternoon," he whispered. "God loves you, honey, and so do I." Slowly he leaned over and kissed the raw places at her throat. She stirred slightly; he took it for a response, hoping that, after this weekend's events, she'd want to make love as badly as he did. Leaning farther, he kissed her lips. She kissed him back only halfheartedly, her lips clamped closed. He kissed her again, waiting for her to open her mouth; she did not. Well, perhaps she still hurt there; he pulled away, feeling foolish.

Later, as they lay together in the darkness, he reached out and touched her shoulder. He felt her stir. Running his hand over the nightgown, he moved down her breasts toward her stomach and belly, sensing himself grow aroused. She stirred again and rolled away, turning her back to him. Guiltily he withdrew his hand and, with a sigh, turned over and tried to go to sleep.

JULY TWENTY-FIFTH

The Poroths had been up for hours when he awoke. He rolled over in bed and looked out. The first thing that caught his eye was a garden spider just outside the screen, clutching the tattered remnants of a moth. *Nature!* he thought, as he had in days past. The animal was grey and hairy, as large as some of the mice the cats had killed. It was clinging to the dark green ivy that grew over the outside of the sill; obviously it had had good hunting this summer, preying on the insects that lived among the leaves. Almost as if it sensed Freirs' revulsion, the thing suddenly began to move, climbing purposefully up the screen and, as he watched, horrified, making straight for the rent in the wire. Hurriedly he seized the spray can from the shelf by his bed, held its nozzle against the screens, and inaugurated the new week at the farm by dousing the creature with poison. It struggled to within several inches of the gap, then stopped, arched its legs, and dropped backward into the ivy.

Darkly the nursery rhyme came back to him:

> *If you wish to live and thrive,*
> *Let the Spider walk alive.*

He tried to shrug it off, reminding himself that he had already killed so many that he was living, even now, on borrowed time.

A rather quiet day, after the weekend's excitement. No visitors, no accidents, no noise or movements in the earth. Read some de la Mare in the morning—horrifying story of a little boy who sees a crouching demon each time he turns his eyes to the left—but his writing's so tentative & subtle & the day was so quiet & muggy that I somehow couldn't keep reading. Sarr was scattering some sort of white powder in the cornfield that's supposed to keep cutworms away, but he was also making sure to keep an eye on Deborah. She in turn sat watching him from a rocking chair on the back porch, rocking slowly back & forth but not otherwise moving, like a silent old woman more dead than alive.

Seeing Sarr's labors, I felt I ought to get some physical activity myself; but the thought of starting my exercises again after being out of practice so long seemed just too unpleasant. I took a walk down the road a little way, up to the first bend where the house is lost from sight. Perhaps I was hoping that the driver from the gas company would happen by again & offer me a lift . . . Somehow, though, I didn't want to get out of sight of the house, as if it might not be the same—or there at all—when I got back. Like the way Sarr keeps one eye on Deborah . . . I was bored, & walking to town sounded tempting, but Gilead had so little to offer & just seemed too far away.

Was going to cut the ivy away from my windows when I got back, as it's become a haven for all sorts of bugs, but decided the place looks more artistic covered in vines.

Deborah made dinner tonight—meat loaf, string beans, & potatoes—but I found it a bit disappointing, probably because I'd been looking forward to it all day. The meat was underdone, somehow, & the beans were cold. Though she still seems tired & stiff, she seems otherwise normal now, & at least was able to talk over dinner—more than Sarr, in fact, who said almost nothing, except that he'd been unable to find out anything about the McKinneys (if in fact there *are* any). Deborah's voice is still hoarse, though, & she ate very little, as she has trouble swallowing. I persuaded her to let me do the dishes again. I've been doing them a lot lately.

I didn't have much interest in reading tonight & would have preferred sitting around their living room, like we used to do in the past, listening to the radio—Deborah, I'm sure, would have been up for it—but Sarr's gotten into one of his religious kicks lately & began mumbling prayers to himself immediately after dinner. Guess he's still worked up after the services here yesterday. Absorbed in his chanting, he made me uncomfortable—I didn't like his face—& so after doing the dishes I left, borrowing the radio for the night.

Walked back here with some rock music playing. It sounded pretty obscene, here in this rural quiet beneath the stars, but somehow once I got inside it seemed to keep the night at bay. Listened to the ads between each song—plugs for car stereos & acne cream & roadside disco lounges. It all sounded terribly alien out here; what must people like the Brethren make of such stuff? Next I listened to a bit of the news (no mention, alas, of our pathetic little earthquake). Lots of heavy international power politics, crime & corruption in New York, blacks & Libyans demanding this & that, bus drivers threatening a walkout . . . No wonder the people here despise the outside world; judging from the picture of it you get on the radio, it's as wicked as Sarr claims.

*

Have been listening to the radio for the past hour or so. Recall the days, not so long ago, when I'd have gotten uptight at having wasted an hour, but out here I'm slowing down, more & more, the longer I remain.

. . . Can't find that goddamned new can of bug spray. I usually keep it right by this table, close at hand, and play Search & Destroy each night before turning in. Annoying to think that one of the Poroths took it & didn't return it; don't like the idea of their entering my room. The other can's almost empty, but by judiciously using it & an old rolled-up *Sight & Sound* (whose cover I'll now have to throw away) I managed to give the place a good going over. Now the room smells of spray & I'm exhausted.

Just shut the radio off. I'd be tempted to leave it on all night as I go to sleep, but then you can't hear what's happening outside, and I don't like to be at that sort of disadvantage.

Now that it's quiet, I can hear Sarr praying & singing hymns. Odd to think of him doing so alone. I imagine that Deborah must be up there with him, mouthing the words.

JULY TWENTY-SIXTH

Writing this, breaking habit, in early morning. Was awakened around two or so last night by sounds coming from the woods. A wailing—deeper this time than anything I've heard before—followed by what sounded like a low, guttural monologue, except there seemed to be no words, at least none I could distinguish. Maybe it was another whippoorwill, or a large bullfrog, or even some local poacher on a nightly sortie through the swamp. If frogs could talk . . . For some reason I fell asleep again before the sounds ended, so I don't know what followed.

This morning's paper had a brief piece about our "earthquake." Also had a letter from Carol today. She'll be coming out this weekend—unfortunately with that creepy old Rosie. Don't like the way he's cozied up to her; she practically lives for the guy. Still, it'll be great to see her again. Despite what they say about Lammas Eve, this weekend shouldn't be so unpleasant after all . . .

From the *Hunterdon County Home News,* Tuesday, July 26:

QUAKE CAUSE STILL UNDETERMINED

Gilead, July 25.—Though this tiny farming community is located less than ten miles from the Ramapo Fault believed to run from Somerset County to the Hudson, a research team of Princeton University geologists reports that the causes of Sunday afternoon's earth tremor here appear to have been "independent of the fault." According to the group's findings, released early today and based upon data collated with other seismographic laboratories in the region, the quake's epicenter was somewhere north of the town. Damage was slight, confined to broken windows and household articles, though farmers report some panicking of herds. The disturbance appears to have been highly localized, affecting only the town and its surroundings; neighboring communities were not aware of it.

Contacted by telephone in Connecticut, vacationing department staffer Dr. James Lewalski, director of laboratory facilities, noted that no place on the continent is totally free from such quakes; even New England, he noted, has had "at least one recorded earth tremor of sizable proportions every year since the founding of the colonies." Lewalski pooh-poohed the notion that the state might be entering a new earthquake phase not associated with the Ramapo Fault. "There will always be a few freak quakes whose cause is difficult to pinpoint," he said, "but there is at this point no cause for alarm."

Deborah was able to walk around today & spent most of it in the woods, picking berries. She came back & made us dinner, but it was nothing special. The four new chickens have begun to lay, but we've only had around half a dozen eggs from them since they were purchased; the old hen, after a week of laying soft eggs, has responded to her new high-calcium feed by not laying anything at all. Deborah made us a vegetable omelet using all six eggs, but it was surprisingly poor. Odd medicinal taste; Sarr didn't even finish his. Deborah herself barely ate, which also seemed to annoy Sarr. "Eat something," he kept saying. "You don't even open your mouth." He's been in a bad mood lately.

Dessert not much good either: cheese & early apples which Sarr had bought in town last week. He'd been keeping them down in the root cellar; now most of them have gone bad. I took a few steps down to the cellar & could smell that the food down there has started to spoil.

Probably it's just as well I ate so little tonight; I'm definitely getting heavier out here, despite all my good intentions. Or flabbier, if not heavier. Really ought to do my exercises. Maybe tomorrow. Looked in the bathroom mirror after dinner, before coming out here, & wasn't too pleased with the sight. Maybe I can try to get a better suntan before Carol arrives, & I could also really use a haircut. Must shave, too.

As I left the Poroths, they didn't seem to be getting along. Deborah, still hoarse, announced that she was tired & went upstairs alone. I left Sarr praying in the living room.

While I was outside, just before entering this room, I chanced to turn around & look at the farmhouse. The lamp was burning in the Poroths' bedroom, & to my amazement I saw, in silhouette, Deborah slipping off her long black dress. She was right in front of the window. Then she turned & stood there a moment, looking out. Sarr must have come upstairs right after that, because I heard him call to her & she quickly moved away . . . But until she did I had the distinct feeling that, as she stood there, she knew she was being watched, & that she, in turn, was looking right at me.

Later they would talk about it often. The good people of Gilead would talk and speculate and argue, gathered around Bert Steegler's cash register at the Co-operative, or sipping tea or lemonade on the van Meers' front porch, or on their way to Sunday worship: how, on the night of July twenty-sixth, just before the strange culmination of the events at Poroth Farm, Shem and Orin Fenchel saw the light dancing in the woods.

Neither father nor son was the kind to show up at Sunday worship, and the past Sunday, while their fellows were congregating at the Poroths, the younger, more enterprising Fenchel had been helping himself to a basketful of tomatoes from Hershel Reimer's garden (taking care to leave no tracks), and old Shem had been fast asleep and snoring. As to the events of the twenty-sixth, they would claim, later, that they'd been searching for a favorite hound that had wandered from the yard and lost itself in the swamp outside of town; but those who knew them best would suspect, always, that they'd been hunting out of season, the Fenchel larder being surprisingly well stocked with meat despite the annual failure of that family's crop.

It was safe to say, too, that the pair had drained a bottle or two that night; as one of the town's rare jokes had it, the elder Fenchel had brought up young Orin on the words of Jeremiah 25:27—"Thus saith the Lord of hosts, the God of Israel: Drink ye, and be drunken, and spue, and fall."

Their testimony, therefore, was not the most convincing, and there were those in Gilead who would deny that the two had seen anything at all. But there were others who, noting the son's wide-eyed amazement, the older man's obvious confusion, the discrepancies in their stories, and reflecting that the two had nothing to gain from lying—for indeed, the incident could only increase their notoriety in the town—would be inclined to believe all or much of what they said.

The moon was gibbous that night, casting a cold, sluglike face at the trees and rivulets and fallen logs over which they'd been stumbling. They were nearing the marshy region along the northwest border of the old Baber place—Sarr Poroth had bought the property last fall, and Fenchel agreed with those in town who held that he'd been cheated—and walking had become difficult; their boots made a wet, sucking sound with each step, and to remain too long in one place gave them the feeling of sinking into the earth.

The younger man was the first to hear it. Initially he took it for an animal caught, struggling, in some remote trap, but then he began to pick out what sounded like words—foreign words. The father heard it too, by now, and was thereafter to maintain that the language was Hebrew; his son, less dogmatic, would never venture to guess.

It was shortly afterward that they saw, far in the distance, the dancing light. It was bobbing up and down out there in the swamp, over land so treacherous that neither man dared approach too closely. Sometimes it would dip below a shrub or rotting log and would be lost from sight; at other times it seemed to float above the surface of the groundwater, as if playing with its own reflection. Occasionally it winked, flickered, and dimmed; most often it burned with a small, steady flame. Both men would later agree that it had been moving ever deeper into the woods, away from Poroth Farm.

But subsequently their reports would differ. Orin, who had the sharper eyes of the two, was to describe the light as that of a single candle. His father would deny this with a queer vehemence; though in his sorry life he'd been accused, by his more pious brethren, of every form of blasphemy, he would shudder, even months afterward, at the notion of a burning candle, as if at something unnatural and obscene. He would never explain his reasons, however, except to say that no candle could have cast so strong a glow; he'd claim that what they'd seen had, in fact, been a hand-held lantern, or even a flashlight.

As to just what sort of hand held the lantern, it was still too far away to tell, and a low midsummer mist obscured their view. They stood awhile in uneasy silence, squinting at the light. It seemed, slowly, to be drawing closer. Occasionally the faint singsong voice would reach them from over the swamp. Shem, at this point, observed that whoever was carrying the lantern must be small indeed, because it appeared to be swinging only inches from the ground. Perhaps it was a child . . . The two peered into the darkness ahead, wondering how any being could make its way through that mud and looking in vain for a face they might recognize above the approaching light.

In fact, they looked in vain for any face at all.

It was here that Orin broke and ran. Later, when asked to account for his uncharacteristic faintheartedness, he would mutter something about that light's having been "too damned close to the ground. No man could carry a candle that low," he'd say, crossing himself. "Least-wise not in his hand."

Shem Fenchel didn't remain there much beyond his son, but he lingered long enough to form an opinion—or, rather, several opinions—of what might have been out there. "Some kinda animal," he told his wife, when he woke her that night. "A dog or monkey or"—his eye fell on young Lavinia's picture book—"or a trained seal. Like in the circus. Carryin' the lantern in its teeth."

It was only later, when in his cups at the roadhouse up near Lebanon, that he was heard to brag that what he'd really seen crawling through the swamp that night had been a naked woman.

JULY TWENTY-SEVENTH

Feeling tired & on edge today. I was up most of the night, thanks to the sounds outside—like distant thunder . . . And when I finally slept, woke up wishing I hadn't. If only there were some way of warding off these bad dreams. They're soon forgotten, of course, & seldom repeated; but while you're living through them they're all the reality you've got.

How does that line from the Cabala go? Reality hangs by—a thread?

Closing his journal, Freirs strolled outside and wandered toward the farmhouse. He felt grubby and was sure he needed a bath, but he'd forgotten to bring his towel and was too enervated to go back and get it. Heating the water for a bath was too complicated anyway.

Deborah was nowhere around, but there was a hot fresh blueberry pie cooling by the window. He was still aroused, in memory, from the sight of her disrobing in her room last night and was eager to see her again. From Sarr's workroom in the attic of the barn came the sound of steady hammering, echoing through the yard. He found some lukewarm milk left in the pitcher on the counter, enough for a shallow bowl of cereal, but he felt like something more; lighting the lantern, he climbed down the narrow steps to the cellar. The entire room now smelled of spoiled food; had the weather really gotten so much hotter lately that the perishables had . . . perished? He stayed down there as short a time as he could: just long enough to assure himself that the milk in the container was sour and that there were no eggs on the shelf. He was glad to get back upstairs.

Wandering out to the back porch, he heard Poroth in the barn give a yell of exultation. It was the first time in days that the farmer had shown such emotion; lately he had grown morose and moody. Freirs hurried to the barn to see what had produced the change.

Poroth was crouching on the platform that supported the chicken coop, peering into the nest with the smile of a brand-new father looking through the glass of the maternity ward. Freirs climbed up the ladder to join him.

"Look," said Poroth, "look what they've done." He pointed to a pair of pristine-looking white eggs lying on the platform by his feet. "I found them under two of the new birds."

"About time they got the hang of it."

"And look at this." Leaning into the coop and digging beneath the one surviving hen from the previous flock, who scattered, squawking, as he reached toward her, Poroth pulled out another egg.

"See? The calcium's working! This one's back to normal."

Indeed, when held up to the light, the egg seemed plump and healthy and the shell hard.

"A welcome sight," said Freirs, "I've missed my morning omelets."

"Yes," said Poroth, "I have too." He was staring pensively at the egg.

"Should we take them up to the house?"

"Those two," said Poroth, indicating the pair at his feet, "but not this. It's already fertilized—I just felt it tremble in my hand. Here, feel." Without warning he thrust it into Freirs' unwilling hand.

Freirs hefted it gingerly, thinking of Lotte Sturtevant's stomach. The egg was warmer than he'd expected. Soft, impatient movements came from within it. Hurriedly he returned it to the other, who slipped it back into the eldest hen's nest.

"We'll let her sit on it awhile," said Poroth, "and soon we'll have ourselves another bird."

Each with an egg, the two strolled toward the farmhouse, their spirits high. Nature, in the end, would not be denied; the sun was out, the corn was ripening, and the hens were laying again.

For several minutes after the two figures had gone, the old bird continued to pace round and round in the dust and odor of the coop, at last settling herself back onto the remaining egg. The barn was still. Shafts of sunlight crept steadily across the wooden floor; a trio of bluebottles buzzed in contentment.

Suddenly she jerked her head erect, her round eyes staring wide. With a flurry of feathers she hopped off the nest and scrambled to the far corner of the coop, where she stood quivering against the wire, claws raking the straw.

Behind her, in the filthy down-lined nest, the egg twitched, rocked back and forth, and jerked to a series of invisible blows, looking more like a living thing than the container of one. A split appeared in the

side. The four new hens and the rooster left their perches and gathered
to watch, cocking their heads and twitching as a dark, jagged hole appeared in the side of the egg and a tiny pink arm slipped through. At
last a head appeared, and as the squawking of the adult birds rose
higher, the child hatched, scattering bits of shattered eggshell.

With frenzied cries, the surrounding chickens pecked to death the
glistening pink reptilian thing that emerged.

The house, by this time, had a kind of shabby hominess for Freirs, as if
the depressions in the sofa in the living room had come from him, the
worn spots on the wooden armrests from his hands. He sat back in the
rocker that stood near the fireplace and waited idly for lunch to be
ready. Deborah had returned; he could hear her now in the kitchen but
didn't have the energy to get up and go in.

Poroth emerged from the cellar, a look of satisfaction on his face. He
joined Freirs in the living room, ducking his head as he passed
through the doorway.

"Well," he said, "we've made a new start. By next week I'll bet the
whole shelf's full of eggs again." He stood thinking, arm propped on
the mantel. "And maybe by fall we'll have enough birds to eat."

Freirs imagined living beings trapped inside smothering shells, bent
almost double with beaks between legs, struggling insanely to burst
free. "You know," he said, "until today I never held a fertilized egg,
and I'm not sure I ever want to hold one again. It felt really weird. Reminded me of those earth tremors we had on Sunday."

Poroth smiled. "A little milder, surely."

"Oh, I don't know," said Freirs. "It's all a matter of scale. If that egg
were the size of the earth, those movements we felt would have been
worse than any quake in history."

"You may have a point." Rubbing his chin, Poroth stared speculatively at the books occupying the lower half of the writing desk in the
corner. "Seems to me I've heard something like that before—the idea
that the earth is one big egg. 'Twas a tale my mother told me when I
was small. A kind of fairy tale. Or maybe it was just a dream she'd
had."

"They say that myths and fairy tales are public dreams."

"Well, maybe so. In this one, I recall, a girl believes the earth is a
dragon's egg—a dragon's egg just waiting to be hatched. 'Tis all symbolic, of course. A parable, just like in the Bible."

"Yes, I can see that," said Freirs. "And then what happens?"

The other shrugged resignedly. "What else? The world ends with the roar of a dragon."

Just beyond the doorway of the kitchen, Deborah added a dash more pepper to the pork patties sizzling on the gas range, then threw in another pinch of salt. Two spoonfuls of flour went into the mix, followed by a fresh patty glistening here and there with fat. It hissed as it settled in the pan, scattering drops of burning grease upon her fingers. She did not flinch. Taking an onion from the wicker basket on the counter, she carefully peeled off the larger leaves and dropped them in. There were no tears.

In a shallow bowl she mixed the salad dressing, compounded of oil, lemon juice, vinegar, and garlic. Tasting the result from a finger dipped into it, she picked up the pepper mill once more and gave it three firm shakes over the mixture, then paused and tilted her head, almost catlike now, listening. Outside, the stillness of the yard was broken by the distant crowing of a rooster. From the next room came the sound of the two men in earnest conversation.

Silently she crouched, reached beneath the counter, and drew forth a squat silver can. Prying off the heavy plastic top, she poured a measured amount of pale liquid into the bowl, adding a dash more of the liquid directly onto the sizzling meat. It smoked fiercely for a moment, bubbling with a new and shriller noise. Quickly pressing back the top, she slipped the can back into its hiding place, so that no one except her could possibly have seen the directions on it, or the brand name, or the warning, *For Outdoor Use Only.*

Only four cats are left from the original seven, yet none of these survivors seem to feel the slightest sense of loss. Played with them for a while after lunch—or, rather, watched them chase insects, climb trees, doze in the sun. Spectator sport.

Speaking of which, finally got around to going "birding," something

I'd been meaning to do ever since I got here. Armed myself with Peterson guide & marched off into the fields. Saw a redwing blackbird, three starlings, & what may have been a grackle, then called it a day. Whole thing seems as pointless as tallying out-of-state license plate on a road trip.

Came back in here, opened my notebook, & sat down to reread "Supernatural Horror in Literature" in the Lovecraft collection. Sort of a Poetics of the Horror Tale, & a marvelous guide; I've been using it as a summer reading list, trying to cover the material Lovecraft recommends. But it worries me to see how little I've actually accomplished this summer, and how far I still have to go. So many obscure authors I couldn't find at Voorhis, so many books I've never even heard of . . . Left me feeling depressed & tired. Took a nap for the rest of the afternoon.

Deborah looked much better at dinner. Though she still did little talking, her features were more animated, she had good color—she's been spending time berry-picking in the woods, she says—& she seemed energetic & cheerful. Sarr, by contrast, was moody again. He picked at his food (beef stew, & like the pork at lunch, actually quite poor, though I was too polite to say anything) & kept asking her why *she* didn't eat more. When she brought out the blueberry pie he flatly declined to have any. "How do I know the berries aren't poison?" he demanded. Both Deborah & I were scandalized that he'd even think such a thing, & I could see that, after all her work, the poor girl was very upset, so I had a huge extra slice. Deborah ate a lot too, no doubt just to show Sarr up.

Sometimes I stay with them & talk, but didn't want to hang around tonight; can't get used to the changes in Sarr. He barely said a civil thing all evening. One exception, though: he told me he'd found out, in answer to my question, that there never *were* any McKinneys. Seems McKinney's Neck is actually taken from some old Indian word.

Felt like rain when I came back out here; clouds massing in the night sky & the woods echoing with thunder. Little Absolom Troet seemed to smile at me from his photo when I turned on the light, as if glad to have me back.

Still no rain. Read most of John Christopher's *The Possessors*. Pretty effective, drawing horror from the most fundamental question of human relations: How can we know that the person next to us is as human as we are? Then played a little game with myself for most of the evening, until I—

Jesus! I just had one hell of a shock. While writing the above I heard a soft tapping, like nervous fingers drumming on a table, & discovered an enormous spider, biggest of the summer, crawling only a few inches from my ankle. It must have been living behind the bureau next to this table.

When you can hear a spider walk across the floor, you *know* it's time to keep your socks on! If only I could find the damned bug spray. Had to kill the thing by swatting it with my shoe, & think I'll just leave the shoe there on the floor until tomorrow morning, covering the grisly crushed remains. Don't feel like seeing what's underneath tonight, or checking to see if the shoe's still moving . . . Must get more insecticide.

Oh, yeah, that game—the What If game. The one Carol says Rosie taught her. For some reason I've been playing it ever since I got her letter. It's catching. (Vain attempt to enlarge the realm of the possible? Heighten my own sensitivity? Or merely work myself into an icy sweat?) I invent the most unlikely situations, then try to think of them as real. *Really* real. E.g., what if this glorified chicken coop I live in is sinking into quicksand? (Maybe not so unlikely.) What if the Poroths are getting tired of me? What if, as Poe was said to fear, I woke up inside my own coffin?

What if Carol, right this minute, is falling in love with another man? What if her visit here this weekend proves an unmitigated disaster?

What if I never see New York again?

What if some stories in the horror books aren't fiction? If Machen told the truth? If there *are* White People out there, malevolent little faces grinning in the moonlight? Whispers in the grass? Poisonous things in the woods? Unsuspected evil in the world?

Enough of this foolishness. Time for bed.

Adrift—afloat—adream—he was spinning down the river on a narrow wooden raft, speeding toward the falls. He heard them ahead, a monstrous cataract of mist and white smoke and a rumbling deeper than thunder. He was almost upon them now, the raft was tilting forward, he felt it rock frenziedly as the raging current caught it.

And suddenly the raft tipped over and flipped him out of bed. He landed on the floor.

And the floor itself was moving.

Two miles down the road and a mile nearer town, Ham Stoudemire fought his way to the window and peered out, muttering snatches of prayer. His jaw fell. Outside in the moonlight the cornfield was rising, the land tilting as if from giant limbs beneath a patchwork quilt. "Dear Lord," he gasped, "is it the Final Judgment?"

Adam Verdock had been sleeping on a cot beside his wife's bed. He dreamed his daughter Minna was shaking him, and felt a sudden half-formed hope, he was to say afterward, that she had good news of Lise. But Minna was nowhere about when he awoke, and Lise's eyes were closed, and he felt himself tossed around the little bedroom—"like a terrier shaking a rat" was how he'd put it later. And still his wife's eyes failed to open.

Deborah's eyes were open. Sarr awakened with a start to find her shoved roughly against him in the bed. He heard the sound of glass breaking somewhere below. The walls of the house were bending and creaking like the masts of a ship in a storm. "Honey," he said, "come on, we've got to get out!"

She stared at him glassy-eyed; perhaps she was dreaming with her eyes open. She seemed not to hear.

"Honey," he said, voice rising now, "come on, 'tis another quake." He lifted her from the bed, the two of them in their nightgowns, and started toward the stairs.

Shem Fenchel, dead drunk, slept through it all.

In the darkness of the woods, by the tiny mud-packed altar at the margins of the swamp, the thundering vibrations tore the forest floor and threw up great jagged chunks of rock. Part of the ground trembled and gave way, swallowing up all that remained of the fire-blackened cottonwood and the tiny mound of mud. Animals fled the area in terror. Trees still standing bent as from a violent storm. With an awesome cracking sound the earth split, bulged, and lifted, as if from some immense form pressing upward from beneath, straining toward the moon.

Gradually the trembling subsided, the land settling back upon itself. Ham Stoudemire saw his field grow still, the giant asleep again beneath its coverlet. Sarr, carrying Deborah's stiff form down the stairs, felt the tremors stop; Freirs picked himself nervously from the floor. They walked out to the yard and stood with relief upon the firm ground, and the two men talked until the rain came.

And in the forest a gigantic shape, furred with foliage and humped like the back of some huge animal, stood upreared against the stars.

The next morning, in the drizzle, they picked up the pieces. Bert and Amelia Steegler walked up and down the aisles of their store sweeping up the broken shards of bottles. A grieving Adam Verdock roamed through the countryside rounding up his cattle, which had kicked down their already damaged stalls. Old Bethuel Reid, summoning his courage, brandished a rake and chased the snakes that swarmed over his land into the forest.

And young Raymond Trudel, while searching the swampy region of the woods for an escaped hog, came upon the scene of the worst devastation and went running back to his family's farm, screaming in terror about the monstrous hill that had risen in McKinney's Neck during the night.

BOOK TEN

THE SCARLET CEREMONY

There are the White Ceremonies and the Green Ceremonies, and the Scarlet Ceremonies. The Scarlet Ceremonies are the best. —Machen, *The White People*

JULY TWENTY-EIGHTH

Rain spatters the sidewalk; the morning sun glows dimly behind a veil of cloud. Poised between the twin spires of a cathedral, the gibbous moon, just three days short of full, is a blob of smoke against the greying sky. As he wanders through the city, peering from beneath his black umbrella as he catalogues all that will be gone, the Old One perceives the moon's true meaning:

It is a portent of imminent completion.

The two initial Ceremonies are behind him, the woman has been tested and found ready, the Dhol lives clothed in human form . . . Yet a single step remains now, one last transformation, and the final act, the Voola'teine, can be performed.

All that's needed now is one more body, that of the man; and watching the fall of rainwater from a spout shaped like a gargoyle's mouth above him to an oil-rainbowed puddle at his feet, he is suddenly filled with certainty that the man will meet his end this very day—and with a vision of how that end will come about.

He can see it. It is as real as the rain upon the grimy streets around him.

Death by water.

He awoke to the patter of rain on the already wet grass, as if last night's cataclysm had been, in truth, just thunder and a vivid, violent dream. But no, he recalled, it had been more than that; there really had been a quake of some sort . . . The memory made this morning's rain seem a kind of absolution, something that would turn the earth into mud which, like mortar, would seal all last night's cracks.

He lay on his bed for a few more minutes, lulled by the sound, but gradually became aware that he was cold. The air was damp today, and a cool wind had sprung up. Across the lawn the house looked dry and cheerful. His watch said ten thirty. He roused himself and hurried out, keeping beneath the nearest line of trees for as much of the way as he could.

Worms had crawled out of the grass and were wriggling like drunken things on the flagstones as he dashed up the walk toward the porch. To his left the cornfield looked drenched, the thinner stalks drooping wearily in the mud. Hard to believe, on such a day as this, that the sky above the farm had ever been sunny.

The radio in the kitchen was tuned to a religious station. Sarr and Deborah were sitting across the table glaring into one another's eyes, like two card players suspecting each other of cheating and waiting to see who would draw first. Freirs could feel the tension break as he came in. Deborah smiled with obvious relief. Rising, she switched off the radio and went to the stove. "We've no milk today," she said—her voice had improved dramatically overnight—"and no new eggs from any of the hens, and the two downstairs were broken when the shelf collapsed last night. So unless my husband—"

"I'm going," Sarr said loudly. "I'm going into town this afternoon, to see about the damage and how Aunt Lise is doing, and when I'm there, I told you, I'll stop at the Co-op and buy whatever we need."

"Why don't you go now? Before it's all gone?"

He snorted with annoyance. "I told you, I'll not be panicked by what happened last night, and I'll not have it look to the community, when I march into the store and ask for credit to buy powdered milk and eggs and other provisions, that I tried to get there first. Besides, I want to get that broken glass cleared from the cellar."

"Well, why don't you?"

"I am." He stood and headed for the cellar.

"Let me know when you're going into town," said Freirs, "and I'll come along."

The other looked dubious. "You're sure you want to come and see Aunt Lise? I don't think that would be wise."

Freirs shrugged. "Maybe, but there are a few things I'd like to pick up before Carol and her friend come out—and I'll be glad to chip in on the rest."

Sarr nodded morosely. "I'll not say no to help like that," he said. "Thanks." He left the room; they heard him descending the cellar steps, and then the clatter of broken glass.

"It's a shambles down there," said Deborah. "An unholy shambles. Even the things that weren't in jars got spoiled somehow. I did manage to save the bacon and potatoes, though. Why don't I add some to last night's stew—there was a lot left over. Sarr's been off his feed lately."

"Great. Never let it be said that I require milk and cereal for breakfast." He ate heartily, not minding that, like last night, it didn't taste up to Deborah's usual standard. She, too, must be a little off her feed.

Afterward, he went to the living room and watched the cats at play; the four had moved inside this morning, away from the cold drizzle and the breeze. But the animals and their ceaseless quest for amusement now depressed him. A moving sock, the sound of a slither or scrape—anything seemed to excite them for a moment, then ultimately bore them. He, too, felt bored. Borrowing the radio and holding it under his shirt, he walked back to his room. He reopened *The Possessors* and came close to completing it, but soon his mind began to wander to all the books he hadn't yet read that summer, and the thought of them all so depressed and tired him that he laid aside the novel and turned on the radio. He found a New York news station, but though he listened for half an hour, there was once again no mention of the previous night's earthquake. *We're too small to count out here,* he decided. He felt abandoned. He switched to a local station, but it was the old religious bit. Maybe, though, they would give the news; weren't they required by law to do so every hour?

He listened for a few minutes, trying sporadically to read amid the usual half-heard biblical injunctions, but his mind drifted. "There is none beside me," the radio was thundering. "I am the Lord, and there is none else. I form the light, and create darkness: I make peace, and create evil. I the Lord do all these things."

In that case, Freirs thought dully, *you certainly aren't much use to anyone*—and drifted off to sleep.

The rain, for the moment, had let up. Tiptoeing down the back steps, Poroth slogged through the drenched grass and peered in the window of the outbuilding. Freirs was asleep. Just as well; he hadn't wanted anyone to come with him. His plans today were secret. Silently he moved toward the barn.

Slamming the door of the truck, he twisted the ignition key and jammed his foot on the gas pedal. The engine kicked over once, twice, three times, and died. The next time, it caught. He pulled out of the barn and over the swampy grass, circling around the side of the house and down the dirt road now turned to mud, truck wheels sinking into the water-lined ruts.

He had told Freirs the truth; he was going to stop at the store and to pay a prayerful visit to poor Aunt Lise. But there was another reason for his haste, and for the trip itself. He had an additional appointment—with someone whose advice he craved.

It is a most extraordinary vision. Distractedly he seats himself on the steps of the nearest building, oblivious to the wet concrete or the rain that falls around him like a cage, and from beneath his umbrella he stares at the swirling puddle in the gutter, watching the scene that has taken control of his fancy.

There is the farmwife standing pink and naked in her bath, and the man fully clothed and nervous by her side, and now she has seized his arm in an iron grip and is pulling him into the tub with her. He struggles, off balance, the bathroom rug sliding beneath his shoes; he reaches out blindly to steady himself, but his groping hand encounters only space, then her warm and slippery flesh, and there is nothing to lean against, nothing to break his fall as his knees strike the hard white side of the tub, echoing, and he tumbles head first into the warm water.

He splashes wildly, the water drowning his screams. It is clear, even as she drags his head down and holds it jerking beneath the soapy surface and settles her knees on his heaving chest, that he still cannot believe this is happening.

Deborah on his mind, he trudged grimly up the sloping lawn toward the little stone cottage. Rainwater ran down the back of his collar and flowed in rivulets through the terraced flower beds toward the stream far below, beside the road where his green pickup stood parked. Before him, like three guard towers, rose the boxlike wooden beehives; he gave them a wide berth as he passed, shielding his face when, despite the rain, several insects circled buzzing round his head. *The usual welcoming committee,* he thought. He waited till they were gone, then hurried onward, arriving at last before the front door. He knocked three times, pounding his fist against the dark wood, then stepped back.

"Mother?" he called, his voice reverberating from the stony walls, the vines that, with thorns and blossoms, climbed in profusion up the sides of the house, toward the little second-story window in the peak of the roof.

The door swung open. "Good," she said briskly. "I've been waiting for you."

The wind had picked up again, and the rain had come back, a dull monotonous drizzle. Freirs roused himself and looked at his watch. Though it looked like early evening, it was just after two; Sarr would be leaving soon. He forced himself to his feet and hurried toward the house. Halfway there, shielding himself against the rain, he came to a bare patch in the yard and saw tire tracks filling with water. *Shit!* he thought. *I'll bet he left without me.* He looked back to where the barn stood. There was no sign of the truck, but perhaps it was hidden inside. Rather than run all the way back, he continued up the walk to the house.

The kitchen was deserted. "Sarr?" he called.

"Gone."

The voice was hoarse, nearly inaudible. It had come from the bathroom, just off the kitchen. The door stood partly open, outlined in light from within.

"Deborah?" He drew closer. "Sarr left already?"

"Yes."

Freirs stopped awkwardly several feet away. Through the crack in the door he could see a little slice of bathroom. It looked steamy in the lantern light.

"Jeremy?" Her voice was softer now.

"What is it?"

"Come here, Jeremy." He didn't move. "I have something to tell you."

Slowly he pushed the door open. The room inside was misty; warm moist air bathed his face, smelling of rose-scented soap.

She was lying back in the tub with just her head above the surface of the water. Through swirls of steam his darting glance took in the pale pink length of her body, the dark nipples of her breasts blurred beneath the soapsuds, the widening dark shadow where the black hair curled between her legs.

She lay content beneath his gaze. "Do you remember," she said, after a pause, "how you offered to scrub my back?"

"Yes." He stood hesitantly in the doorway, wondering if he dared take a step closer.

"And do you remember what I said?"

"Uh, I'm not sure. Something about 'some other time.'"

She nodded, half smiling. "Some other time when my husband wasn't here."

"Uh-huh." He swallowed nervously.

"He's not here now."

Slowly she began sitting up. Her shoulders rose above the surface, milky water lapping at the tops of her breasts. Soon, unsupported, they hung heavy and full, water dripping from them, while her glistening black hair fell wetly down her shoulders like a shawl.

She was seated upright now, the water about her waist like a nightgown she'd sloughed off; and still she continued to rise, tucking her legs beneath her and getting to her feet.

"Come on, Jeremy," she said, standing before him. "You're just the one I need."

Rain pounded against the cottage's stone walls and rattled the windows of the parlor. Inside, in the dim light, listening to his mother's words, the farmer felt a chill. The woman seemed farther away than ever. The room, like the entire house, was hers alone and held no place for him. It was the refuge of her widowhood, she'd moved in while he'd been away. He had visited her here many times since his return, but he always felt like a stranger.

"You've come to find out about Deborah," she was saying. "You feel a change in her. A distance."

He nodded, too old to be surprised by the woman's ability to read his mind.

But he was surprised by what she told him.

She told him of virgins and dragons and Dhols, of the rarity of months with two full moons, and of an old man who, if he got his way, would bring this green spinning world to an end. She contradicted everything he'd ever known, and swore to things that couldn't be. He didn't believe a word she said—and yet he trembled.

She showed him the Pictures, and told him where they came from, and his horror grew; for he recognized the figures from the Dynnod, and wondered if they might somehow be real. He sensed things pressing in on him, and knew his life would never be the same.

And when she was done she told him, "Remember, come to me when your visitors arrive. Come to me in secret that night. And bring the virgin with you." She leaned toward him, eyes glittering; talonlike fingers gripped his arm. "That's the most important thing, son. You mustn't forget to bring her. The Lord and I will see to the rest."

Suddenly she cocked her head and looked toward the rain-smeared window. When she turned back to him, her expression had changed.

"Go now," she said. Her voice held a new urgency. "Go and speed home, if you want to prevent a drowning."

She hurried him out the door, not even saying goodbye.

... And I'd have climbed right in there with her, if Sarr hadn't come driving up the road just then, truck wheels splashing through the puddles. I dashed from the room like a thief, cursing my own stupidity; if he'd found us together I swear he's the kind who'd have killed us both. I fled to the living room & snatched up the first thing I came across, that book of inspirational poems I'd been reading from, so that by the time he'd put the truck away in the barn & had come running through the rain back up to the house, I was sitting in the rocking chair with his book on my lap, open to the dryest-looking Milton I could find. I was still nervous as he came in—I could feel my heart pounding—but I don't think his mind was on me.

"Where's Deborah?" he said, looking very troubled.

"I'm not sure," I said vaguely. "She may be in the bathroom."

He stood there for a minute, not saying anything, and eventually settled himself on the stool. Only then did he seem to notice me. He cleared his throat a couple of times, as if there were something he was dying to ask but afraid to. Finally he said, "Jeremy, I don't want to seem like prying, & you don't have to answer this, but—" And I thought, *Oh, Jesus, I'm in for it now, he suspects!* But then, of all things, he asked his question: was Carol still a virgin?

That really caught me by surprise. "I don't know," I think I said. "I doubt it. She's obviously not very experienced—she's a good Catholic & all—but she's an attractive girl, & I'd assume that somewhere along the line she's had a guy or two." He looked skeptical. "If you're asking whether *I've* ever slept with her," I added, "the answer's no, I haven't."

I would have thought that was what he'd want to hear; I assumed he was asking because, with Carol coming for another visit the day after tomorrow & probably staying again under his roof, he wanted to be certain she was pure. But instead of looking cheerful, he looked even more troubled. I asked him what the matter was, but he said he'd explain it all this weekend.

Sausage & rice for dinner tonight, both courtesy of the Co-op. String beans from a can & powdered milk for our coffee: what's the world coming to? Deborah was cool as can be—didn't look at me once, just concentrated on dishing out the food and smiling at Sarr—but he wasn't having any of it. He just kept staring at her, saying nothing. I got very uncomfortable by the end, certain he suspected. Hope he's not giving Deborah hell tonight.

Back here after dinner, escaping as fast as I could. Should be cleaning this place up before Carol & Rosie get here, but with this drizzle & the sudden, lonely wind, I somehow have little energy for anything but reading; even keeping up this journal seems a chore. Tomorrow I've got to clip that ivy; it's beginning to cover the windows again, & the mildew's been climbing steadily up the walls. It's like I'm sinking into a pool of dark-green water.

Odd that I'm so tired, esp. considering that between getting up late & my afternoon nap, I must have slept half the day. Alas, old & worn out at thirty!

At least tonight it's quiet in the woods.

He is back in his apartment, the shades drawn and his umbrella drying in the tub, when it comes to him that the man is still alive. Something has interfered.

No, not something. Someone.

And suddenly he knows who it is.

Water hemlock, amanita, hellebore . . .

As she sat in her kitchen, Mrs. Poroth contemplated the enormity of what she was going to do: the killing of the red-haired girl.

It would be easily accomplished; she had more than enough materials here at hand.

Monkshood, lambkill, death camas . . .

And she saw no other way. The necessity was clear. The girl must not be allowed to play her destined role.

Banewort, mayapple, fly agaric . . .

But oh! it was a wicked thing that she was considering, to raise her hand against so innocent a child! A sudden terror seized her, as if from outside herself, like a thin chilly finger of breeze sent to search for her through the open window. Someone far away was thinking about her, had sought her . . . and had found her.

No, it was from within *herself* that the fear had come; she must not yield to despair. No doubt what she'd felt had only been the dread of her own imminent sin. She had to guard such selfish thoughts; a world hung in the balance. She said a prayer to the cruel Lord and continued with her preparations.

Dogbane, greyana, deadly nightshade . . .

Sarr turned the lamp down in the kitchen and climbed the stairs to bed. Deborah was gazing out the window as he came into the room, the moon hanging just beyond her head. He heard wind stir the apple tree beside the house, a wind that rose and died and rose again, blowing stronger, tossing the tops of the distant pines. Seating himself on the edge of the bed, he began removing his shoes. "We'll have to get a new lock for that bathroom door," he said. "The one there now doesn't even close any more."

"You can pick one up in town."

"Right. And I'd better do it soon, too. Otherwise you know what's going to happen?" He watched her closely. "One day Jeremy's going to come walking in and catch you in your bath."

She turned and stood up from the bed. "We can't have that, can we?"

"No," he said slowly. "We can't." He watched her as she walked to the closet in the corner. Opening the door, she stepped out of his sight. He heard the rustle of cloth, and moments later she reappeared, dressed in her nightgown. Seating herself before a small oval mirror, she began unfastening her hair.

"Time was," he said, "when you got undressed in front of me." Standing and throwing off his shirt, he approached her. Tentatively he reached out and touched her shoulder. "Time was when things were better between us."

He thought he saw her stiffen, and something ached inside him—but then she reached up and pressed his hand, and he felt a surge of relief.

"I know, honey," she said. She was still slightly hoarse. "It's just that I haven't been well. Give me a few more days . . ."

"Of course," he said. He bent and, pushing aside the length of hair, kissed the back of her neck. "I'm sorry, I've been on edge lately myself."

He walked back to the bed and continued undressing, while she reached for her brush and began to comb her hair. He watched her out of the corner of his eye as he took his own nightgown from the hook in the closet. This was the same woman, he was sure of it. The graceful way she brushed her hair, the softness of her skin—this was the woman he had always loved. For once his mother was wrong. She'd never liked Deborah; she'd never even made an attempt to get to know her. How could she expect, then, to recognize a change in her character? Perhaps she even hoped to turn him against Deborah—to harden his heart—to blight his marriage . . .

"Tonight," he said, "maybe we can pray together again. Your voice sounds like it's coming back."

"I don't know, honey," she said. "I'm feeling awful tired." Yawning, she laid aside the brush.

"Well, if you'd rather not, I can—What's that?"

She turned to look at him, her eyes wide. "What?"

"There. Inside your mouth." He pointed, half conscious that his hand was trembling. "I saw it in the mirror, when you yawned. There was something there."

"Nonsense!" She tossed her head and turned away. "It's just the light."

"Don't try to fool me, woman! I know what I saw!" He crossed the room in two steps, grabbed her by the shoulders, and whirled her around to face him. He could feel his heart pounding in his chest. "Now open your mouth!"

She shook her head, glaring at him. Her jaw was clamped shut.

"Deborah, open your mouth! If something's the matter, I want to know about it."

"Get your hands off me," she hissed through clenched teeth.

"Open your mouth or I'll pull it open myself."

She tried to yank her shoulders away; he held on, dragging her toward the lamp, amazed at how strong she was as she struggled in his arms. Her hands reached clawlike for his face; nails like a cat's raked his cheek. He pulled back, grabbing at her wrists. She spat as he forced her backward, away from him, toward the light. Suddenly she yielded and went limp; caught off balance, he stumbled forward, falling against her and knocking over the table on which the lantern stood. It crashed to the floor and rolled under the bed, still burning. With a yell he released her and lunged for the lantern, fingers groping blindly beneath the bed while she stood above him, not moving, in the darkness. Reaching out, he touched something hard, and screamed as the glass burned his fingers. Ignoring the pain, he grasped the lantern and drew it forth from beneath the bed. It was still flickering; he set it down and checked beneath the bed. It had not caught fire.

"Fool!" Deborah hissed. She was looking down at him, her hands curled into fists. He had never seen her so angry. "You could set this place aflame."

Panting, he picked up the lantern by the handle and got to his feet. "All right," he said. "Let's see."

He brought the lantern close to her face. She hesitated a moment, then opened her mouth wide. He peered into it in the glowing light.

"See?" she said at last. "Was I lying?"

"No." He hung his head. There had been nothing there. "No, you weren't lying. I'm just seeing visions, that's all." Sighing, he righted the overturned table, set down the lantern, and turning his face to the corner, knelt to say his prayers. She was right; he was a fool. Yet earlier he could have sworn he'd seen something there, small, black, and convoluted, on the back of her tongue.

Hours later he lay staring at the ceiling, unable to fall asleep. He felt her there beside him, felt her weight on the mattress, heard the regular, slow rhythm of her breathing, and wondered what he lay with in the bed.

Outside, in the moonlight, where trees whispered urgently, the wind had begun to sound to him like the rise and fall of breathing, sometimes even coinciding eerily with the breathing beside him; but the breathing outside was of something huge and monstrous, something so big that, with each breath, the trees shook.

Finally, when the sky had grown purple before the next dawn, he was able to drift into sleep. And perhaps it was already the beginning of a dream, but the last thing he recalled, as he turned in sleep toward her, was his wife's face lying on the pillow next to him, her eyes as wide as the moon.

JULY TWENTY-NINTH

From the *Hunterdon County Home News*, Friday, July 29:

VOLCANOES IN HUNTERDON COUNTY???
VOLCANOES IN HUNTERDON COUNTY???
by *News* Science Writer Mike Aldano

The Mexican volcano Paricutín, it's said, appeared one morning in a farmer's cornfield. Now New Jerseyans may have a similar surprise in their own back yard: a 40-foot hill in the woods outside Gilead in the heart of Hunterdon County—a hill that, townspeople believe, wasn't there a few days before.

"It just grew up during the night," said Galen Trudel, whose son Raymond, 12, claims credit for discovering the formation yesterday. "You could hear the sound for miles, like a roaring. We had our pigpen blow down and we still haven't recovered all the animals."

The little farming community of Gilead (pop. 187) has already had its share of disasters this week. Sunday it was rocked by a minor earth tremor that measured 4.9 on the Richter scale. Wednesday night it suffered an even greater shock, 6.1 on the scale, causing an estimated $50,000 in damage. (A spokesman for the Governor's office says that to date no claims have been filed with the state.)

The second quake may also have had an additional result: the strange new hill in the woods three miles north of town.

The cone-shaped dirt-and-basalt structure has drawn geologists from all over the state—and some worried comments from townspeople. "I don't want my children going near it," says Hannelore Reid, a housewife and mother of six. "Everybody knows the swamp around there is unsafe."

Bert Steegler, manager of the Gilead Town Co-operative, is more blunt. "The woods around there are haunted," he maintains. "They always were."

BUBBLE IN THE EARTH?

Authorities, however, paint a less romantic picture. Describing the formation as the result of "an immense bubble of methane"—commonly known as "swamp gas"—Dr. James Lewalski of Princeton Univerity's department of geology, contacted by phone, noted that north central New Jersey lies over a recognized geological fault area, the so-called Ramapo Fault, and dismissed the mound as "a perfectly explainable natural phenomenon," although he admitted that few such mounds are created with such rapidity and suddenness . . .

There were other reports, too, that day, in the local press. The tombstone of one Rachel van Meer, who'd died in 1912, had been toppled by the quake and had rolled down the hill to the road, where John and Willy Baber, young men of the town, had hit it the next morning in their pickup truck. The nine-foot-tall granite monument to the Troet family had cracked in two, and a number of graves had been so shaken that at least three wooden coffins were actually left jutting above the ground. "'Tis like the Day of Judgment," remarked Jacob van Meer, whose house adjoined the cemetery.

A man in nearby Annandale had commented that it was "lucky that the quake hit Gilead," as it was the only town around without a steeple. A Lebanon man had added, "It's a good thing those people don't have electricity." A state legislator for the district had suggested, in a meeting at the local schoolhouse, that the town apply for federal disaster aid and had almost been run out on a rail.

And according to another item, a representative of the U.S. Geological Survey, after visiting the site, had concluded: "Recent reports of unusual animal behavior in Gilead and the surrounding area may be attributable to preliminary earth tremors leading to this week's disturbances."

But the people of Gilead didn't see it that way.

To Abram Sturtevant, whose German shepherd had gone wild and had had to be shot; to Klaus and Wilma Buckhalter, whose cow had miscarried; to Adam Verdock, checking the splint on his cow's rear leg, broken when, Wednesday, it had clambered out of its collapsed stall; to Hershel Reimer, repairing the stable door that his horse had kicked down; to Galen Trudel and his son, still searching through the swamp for their missing hogs; to Werner Klapp, burying thirty-seven chickens that had been pecked to death by their fellows on the night of the quake; to old Bethuel Reid, who refused to go outside now without a rake in his hands for fear of serpents; to all of them, the earthquake itself and the animals' unusual behavior were merely two symptoms of the same fundamental disturbance. The one was not the cause of the other; rather, both were portents, signals from above, warnings of divine displeasure.

But what, they asked, was He displeased about?

Sunlight & grasshoppers: the woods are quiet now. Slept long into the morning, then walked up to the house, scratching groggily. Sounds of Sarr's axe echoing from across the stream. Kitchen deserted; splashed some cold water on my face in the bathroom, gazing longingly at the tub & thinking of Deborah's pale lovely body, almost mine for the asking. Over a solitary lunch—mostly store-bought cookies—thumbed through today's *Home News*. There's some kind of volcanic thing out there in the woods. Must visit.

Felt fat from lunch, & angry at the breakdown of my discipline. Ambled down to the stream. Deborah was kneeling in front of it, daydreaming, & I was embarrassed because I'd come upon her talking to herself. I asked her if Sarr had shown any suspicion about yesterday. "No," she assured me, "not even a hint." She didn't dwell on the subject & went back to the house without mentioning it again. I suspect she feels guilty about the whole thing.

Sat by some rocks on the bank of the stream, throwing blades of grass into the water & playing word games with myself. *The shrill twitter of the birds,* I would say, *the white birds singing in the sun ...* And inexorably I'd continue with *the sun dying in the moonlight, the moonlight falling on the floor ...* The sun's heat on my head felt almost painful, as if my brain were growing too large for my skull. *The floor sagging to the cellar, the cellar filling with water, the water seeping into the ground ...* I turned & looked at the farmhouse. In the distance it looked like a picture at the other end of a large room; the carpet was grass, the ceiling was an endless great blue sky. Deborah, in the distance, was stroking one of the cats, then seemed to grow angry when it struggled from her arms; I could hear the screen door slam as she went into the kitchen, but the sound reached me so long after the visual image that the whole scene struck me as somehow fake. *The ground twisting into smoke, the smoke staining the sky ...* I gazed up at the oaks behind me & they seemed trees out of a cheap postcard, the kind in which thinly colored paint is dabbed over a black-&-white photo-

graph; if you looked closely at them you could see that the green was
not merely in the leaves, but rather floated as a vapor over leaves,
branches, parts of the sky . . . *The sky burning in the sun, the sun
dying in the moonlight, the moonlight falling on the floor* . . . endless
progressions that held my mind like a whirlpool. The trees behind me
seemed the productions of a poor painter, the color & shape not quite
meshing. Parts of the sky were green, & pieces of it kept floating away
from my vision, no matter how hard I tried to follow them.

  Reality hangs by a thread . . .

  Far down the stream I could see something small & kicking, a black
beetle, legs in the air, borne swiftly along in the current. Then it was
swept around a bend & was gone.

  By a thread . . .

Sarr woke me for dinner; I had dozed off, there by the water, & my
clothes were damp from the grass. I saw scratches on his cheek. As we
walked up to the house together he whispered that, earlier in the day,
he'd come upon his wife bending over me, peering into my sleeping
face. "Her eyes were wide," he said. "Like Bwada's. Like the moon."

  Could he be drinking? No, he didn't smell of alcohol. I said I didn't
understand why he was telling me this.

  "Because," he recited in a whisper, gripping my arm, " 'the heart is
deceitful above all things, & desperately wicked: who can know it?' "

  Dinner was especially uncomfortable; the two of them sat picking at
their food, occasionally raising their eyes to one another like children
in a staring contest. I longed for the conversations of our early days,
inconsequential though they must have been, & wondered where things
had first gone wrong.

  The meal was dry & unappetizing, but the dessert looked delicious—chocolate mousse, a rather fancy dish for people like the
Poroths, but which Deborah considers one of her specialties. She took
none for herself, explaining that her stomach was upset.

  "Then we'll not eat any!" Sarr shouted, & with that he snatched my
dish from in front of me, grabbed his own, & hurled them both against
the wall, where they splattered like mud balls.

  Deborah was very still; she said nothing, just sat there watching us.
She didn't look particularly afraid of this madman—but *I* was. He
may have read my thoughts, because as I got up from my seat he said
much more gently, in the normal soft voice he has, "Sorry, Jeremy. I
know you hate scenes. We'll pray for each other, all right?"

  "Are you okay?" I asked, turning to Deborah. "I'm going out now,
but I'll stay if you think you'll be needing me." She stared at me with a
slight smile & shook her head; when I glanced pointedly at her husband, she just shrugged.

"Things will work out," she said. I could hear Sarr mumbling one of his insane prayers as I shut the door.

I walked back here through a cloud of fireflies, like stars, the stars themselves frosting the sky like bubbles in a water glass. Inside here the bubbles in my water glass, left unemptied by my bed all week, were like the stars . . .

I realized I was shaking. If I have to tangle with him, big as he is, I'm ready. I took off my shirt & stood in front of the little mirror. How could Deborah have allowed me to touch her yesterday? How can I face Carol tomorrow? It has been days since I've bathed, & I've become used to the smell of my body. My hair has wound itself into greasy brown curls, my beard is at least a week old, & my eyes . . . well, the eyes that stared back at me were those of an old man, the whites turning yellow as rotten teeth. I looked at my chest & arms, plump & flabby at thirty, & I thought of the frightening alterations in Sarr, & I thought, *What the hell is going on?* I smoothed back my hair & got out my roll of dental floss & began running the thread through my teeth, but it had been so long since I'd done it that my gums began to bleed, & when I looked back into the mirror I had blood dripping down my lips like a vampire.

I made a resolution as I stood there. When Carol and Rosie leave after this weekend, I'm going back with them.

Poroth stood on the back porch, lost in imaginary arguments with himself as he stared out at the night, the cats miaowing plaintively at his feet. He felt an angel perched on his right shoulder, a demon on his left. *Lord,* he whispered from time to time, *give me strength.* He had erred, losing his temper like that over dinner; he'd been a fool. He had yielded to despair, and that, his mother had always said, was the devil's oldest weapon. But he hadn't lost his faith, he reminded himself; God watched and loved him, just as before; there was still hope. If only he wouldn't tremble so . . .

He regretted that he'd ever lent an ear to his mother's bizarre notions about dragons and ceremonies and intruders from outside, and that he'd ever allowed her to show him those hellish pictures: that small black shapeless thing like the one he had seen on the cards, and that black face peering from the tree, and the squat unnatural contours of that mound . . . The myth was just too alien to take seriously, of course; it conflicted with everything he'd been brought up to believe. And yet its power was undeniable.

By rights these visions should have meant no more to him than a

half-heard fairy tale from some country far away. His mother's gods
and demons were, after all, not his; her virgin was nothing like the
Virgin. To think that poor prim little red-haired Carol, who'd be here
from the city tomorrow, could have any mythological significance! And
that her cosmically decreed counterpart might be right here on this
farm in the person of Jeremy Freirs! Preposterous! He would have
laughed—and someday, perhaps, he might be able to. He gazed out
over the lawn, where the light was on in Freirs' room. He could see the
plump little figure scribbling away at his studies or meditations or letters or whatever they were. Well, God would set his mother right soon
enough . . .

A jet passed overhead, the customary Friday night visitation, a me-
mento of the modern world he'd rejected. Straightening his shoulders,
he turned and walked back into the house.

The house was silent, except for the ticking of the clock. Shutting the
kitchen door, he paused after turning down the lamp. He hated to
think about going upstairs. Up there was Deborah, with whom he'd
taken holy vows to share his life, and if the devil was hiding in her
somewhere—*his* devil, Satan, the devil he knew—well, one didn't flee,
one stood and fought, cleansing the woman the way he'd seen his house
and barn cleansed last Sunday.

Why, then, did he hesitate? Had his mother's stories really gotten to
him: her talk of eggs and dragons, and beings that changed shape? Had
those pictures of hers had their intended effect? Maybe not; but he
knew he wasn't ready to face his wife yet, not after that scene tonight
in the kitchen. To lie so close to someone and know that in her heart she
was your enemy . . . It took more courage than he had right now. *Lord,*
he said again, *give me strength.*

If only he could prove his mother wrong. If only she'd said something
that might actually be verified.

There was one thing, perhaps . . .

In the living room he lit the lamp and crouched before his little
cache of books. Byfield's almanac was still on the top of the pile from
the evening Freirs had asked him about Lammas. Sure enough, in the
back of the volume was a section of lunar tables, page after page of
spidery fine print. Taking both book and lamp over to the rocker, he
settled back to read.

His mother had said yesterday that there'd be two full moons this
month; well, that much he'd known already, as any farmer would—any
farmer, at least, here in Gilead. But she'd also said that the occurrence
was a rare one, at least when the second moon in question turned full
on Lammas Eve. This happened more seldom, she had hinted, than
mere chance might have led one to expect.

Running his finger down the columns, he squinted at the listings for July thirty-first. The tables were difficult to follow; there were footnotes to refer to, quantities for leap years to be added or subtracted, and rows of tiny figures that seemed to swim together in the flickering light. But as near as he could make out, his mother had been right. In fact, he saw now, if the tables were correct, in the past hundred years there'd been only two occurrences of the full moon on the final night of July: in 1890 and again in 1939 . . .

The wide plank floorboards echoed as he paced back and forth. He was still reluctant to go upstairs—more so than ever, in fact, considering how his mother's words had just found some small measure of scientific support. And those crudely drawn images she'd shown him were still buzzing around in his head like a horde of insects that, once inside his skull, had no way of ever getting out. The luridly colored figures seemed less alien now, the more he thought about them, and no longer quite so impossible: the rose with lips and teeth; the black shape called the Dhol; the odd two-ringed design . . .

If only he could turn his mind to some passage from the Bible, he would be comforted, he was sure. But the Bible was upstairs, next to Deborah, and though he knew all the words in it perfectly, he needed before him the reality of print.

His eye fell on the ornate binding of the poetry collection Freirs had been reading, still lying out upon the desk. Sighing, he sat back in the rocking chair and opened the book. He remembered how he'd struggled through it years ago, underlining passages, writing comments in the margins, as if these words of mere men deserved the scrutiny he'd given to the words of God.

Still, there was a kind of comfort here in the old familiar religion of his childhood. The volume fell open to a poem he'd studied at the Bible school in town. *Christmas meditation,* he'd written in careful schoolboy script at the top. It was Milton, he saw, good, dark, steady, pious Milton: "On the Morning of Christ's Nativity," a celebration of the birth of the Savior. He read it through, lips moving with the words, barely thinking about what they said, soothed just as he'd hoped to be—until with a jolt he saw what he'd been reading. He went through the stanza a second time.

> *. . . from this happy day*
> *Th'old Dragon under ground,*
> *In straiter limits bound,*
> > *Not half so far casts his usurped sway,*
> *And wrath to see his Kingdom fail,*
> *Swinges the scaly Horror of his folded tail.*

Why was he trembling so again? The poem, at least, was perfectly confident: Christ had banished the dragon, the ancient evil kingdom had been overthrown . . . But still, something told him, still it waits—waits, like that other poet had said, for the cycle to come round again; waits for another Christmas, maybe thousands of years hence, when it will find release once more.

He closed the book and sat there bolt upright, the planks creaking beneath him as he rocked back and forth. But as fast as he rocked and as hard as he tried, he couldn't shake off the feeling, the terrible conviction that had suddenly seized him. *God's Lord now*, he said to himself, *but the Other waits below. And sooner or later, his turn will come*

She came to him that night, long after the moon had gone down and the fireflies had vanished from the fields. He awoke to find her crouching over him like a succubus, gazing urgently into his face.

Blinking up at her groggily, trying to understand, he began to form a question, but she pressed a hand over his mouth and shook her head. Her eyes burned into his as she sat herself beside him on the bed. She was in her nightgown, her nipples prominent beneath the cloth. Instinctively he embraced her; he was naked and already aroused, the aftermath of a dream now forgotten, as he pushed the sheets away with his foot and drew her down beside him. She wriggled like a cat as he ran his hand down her body, slipping the nightgown up over her hips. He felt her own hands on his penis, guiding him into her as she lay beside him. She was bone-dry; he could not go in. He slipped his hand down to touch the thick patch of hair that, yesterday, had been dripping from the bath, and found it dry as brambles.

"Wait," she hissed, pushing his hand away, "let me." She brought her fingers to her mouth. "Damn it to hell, I haven't any spit!"

"No need for hurry—"

She hushed him by cupping her hand over his mouth, but kept it there.

"Wet me with your tongue."

Obediently he licked her hand, then felt it withdrawn, leaving a smear of saliva on his chin. She stared into her hand with what seemed, at first, a grimace of distaste, but then he saw her mouth working fiercely, cheeks sucking inward, and with a harsh little sound she spat into her palm. Once more he felt her hands on his penis, moistening it. He raised himself on one elbow, preparing to mount her from above, but she shook her head and pushed his shoulder flat against the bed. Straddling him, she slipped him inside her. She was dry inside as well, he could feel it, but she spread herself wider and settled farther down, her nightgown slipping back below her waist, concealing the place where the two of them were joined. Tensing her leg muscles, she slowly moved herself up and down. He felt himself gripped as by a fist; there was a roughness in her, something that abraded. *God,* he thought, *she's so dry.*

"Don't rush it," he whispered, drawing her mouth down to his and covering it with his lips. Her own lips remained clamped shut, and moments later he felt her resist. He held her tightly. Without warning her mouth opened under his, but barely, and she got out the name "Sarr" before his tongue had found its way between her lips.

The name jolted him back to his senses. He felt a twinge of guilt, felt himself shrink and withdraw from her; but it hadn't just been the name, he'd felt something, too, with the tip of his tongue: a roughness at the back of her mouth, a lump of flesh he'd never felt before.

He was out of her now; she had swung herself off him and was sitting on the edge of the bed, smoothing down her nightgown.

"I've got to leave," she whispered, getting to her feet.

"Couldn't you just—"

She shook her head. "There isn't time. Not now. I'll come back to you tomorrow night."

Tomorrow, he wanted to say, *Carol will be here, she may be in this bed with me . . .*

But with a final fierce look she had slipped out the door and was hurrying ghostlike across the moonless lawn.

And in the city, silent in the darkness of his apartment, staring straight ahead at nothing, the Old One contemplates tomorrow's trip—and the past he'll be returning to.

He will be coming home at last, for the first time in over a century. He has been near the place more recently—as recently as 1939—but he hasn't seen the farm itself since when he was a boy. It will probably not be much different now, though. Things do not change much in those parts.

He will also be returning to Maquineanok, where the two previous women met their peculiar deaths. Now the moon has called for the third and final woman, the third and final death . . .

Of course, the place will be transformed. The tree will be gone now, swallowed up in the earth: the tree that had seen so much blood and sacrifice will not be there, replaced, though, by something far more wonderful and terrible, the great mound, before which he will stand and perform the final Ceremony.

He laughs his old man's high-pitched cackle. The poor little fools!

JULY THIRTIETH

The woman on the bed groaned. Joram stroked his beard and stared worriedly at her swollen belly. None of her previous children, not even her first, had given her as much pain as this. He bit his lip, wishing that labor would start so that he could in good conscience summon Sister Nettie Stoudemire, the midwife.

Lotte's belly seemed so *large*. He'd been told that there were signs for twins or triplets, omens he could watch for, but he'd watched and prayed and called on God for advice, and nothing had suggested that his wife had anything more than a single child in her belly. He was frankly scared, and he craved an explanation. He could find only one: the fat, interfering stranger at the Poroths' who'd had the temerity to place his hand on his wife's belly during last Sunday's worship at their farm. If he was really a cursed being, as some of his neighbors were hinting, then couldn't his touch be in itself a curse, to blight the child within?

Joram stood awkwardly by the bedside, brooding about what he should do. He would simply have to wait—and pray, of course—pray that nothing went wrong when the birth came. He hoped it would not come tomorrow, on the Lammas Eve; he hoped, for Freirs' sake, that the birth proved a successful one.

At the farmhouse farther up the road, Adam Verdock gazed mournfully down at his wife on the bed. She had never regained consciousness; she was losing strength fast. Their daughter, Minna, had been wonderful, she'd been there to tend Lise day and night, but the woman had shown no signs of recovery, and this morning he'd been forced to tell old Brother Flinders the carpenter to set aside the pine boards for a coffin. Their prayers, all of them, had been in vain.

Poroth, too, was praying, kneeling as he faced the corner of his room, eyes tightly shut. He had been there all afternoon, unmindful of the heat, the Bible beside him turned to Judges 6 ("And Gideon said unto him, Oh my Lord, if the Lord be with us, why then is all this befallen us?"). But nothing brought him peace today. The Lord was unforgiving. How empty the phrases of the Scriptures seemed, how barren the rituals of his religion. Whom was he calling upon, anyway? He felt as if he were kneeling here speaking only to himself. Was anyone listening?

"O Lord," he prayed, "let me know that we, thy children, still merit thy love. Vouchsafe me a sign of thy presence . . ."

He was chilled to hear, as if in answer, a low, malicious laugh. Opening his eyes, he gazed around the room in horror; the sound had seemed to come from just beside his ear. But now he heard voices and more laughter—a man's, a woman's—and realized they were coming from outside. He went to the window and looked out. Down in the yard a dusty white Chevrolet was parked near the house, and beside it stood Freirs, alternately embracing a red-haired young woman, whom Poroth recognized as Carol, and pumping the hand of a short white-haired old man who looked damnably familiar and who, as Poroth watched, threw back his head and laughed.

So they had arrived. He would slip away with Carol tonight, as promised, and report back to his mother.

Below him he heard the screen door swing open; slow footsteps descended the back stairs. The old man turned, suddenly no longer laughing, and for a moment Poroth saw his eyes narrow and a new look enter them, a kind of guarded excitement. All at once he beamed. "Ah, yes," Poroth heard him say, his little frame now shaking once again with laughter, "yes, indeed, and this must be Deborah!"

At last Deborah herself stepped into view. Gravely she advanced across the yard to meet them, a smile spreading slowly across her face as she extended to both visitors, but especially to the little old man, a hand of welcome.

Aside from the contact he's established, there is no particular joy in being back. Everything is much as he's remembered it, despite the passage of a century. In size, shape, even the weathering of its shingles, the little farmhouse looks almost the same as the first one that stood on this site. The apple tree behind it is new, of course, and so is the line of rosebushes he saw as he climbed from the car. But he recognizes the broad unpainted barn farther down the slope, where he'd drawn his secret pictures and practiced secret chants; its roof is sagging now, and, for all its rusted body, the battered old pickup truck parked within the doorway seems alien and new. So does the little wooden smokehouse at the edge of the property, another addition since his time, though for all he knows its door has been hanging open that way for the past eighty years.

The black willow rising by the barn is new to him, gnarled and ancient as it seems. But the acres of cornfield (looking stragglier than those he remembers), the vine-encrusted ruins of the outhouse that the woods have all but reclaimed, the brook where he'd performed those preliminary sacrifices, the dense surrounding forest and the hot, doomed country air—all these are familiar. Yet the memories mean little to him.

He notices, with no more than the faintest curiosity, that some things are gone: the woodshed and the stables and the old chicken coop, replaced by the squat grey structure that the Poroths have converted into a guest house; the elms that lined the roadside (victims, no doubt, of that Dutch disease); and the tall, slender oak that once stood beside the house, shading the living room. But of course, he's almost forgotten: the tree, like the house itself, perished in the fire . . .

The fire: how far away that night seems now, in the present afternoon sunlight—and yet how close! He can still remember standing in the back yard, beside the barn, watching as the roof caved in and the walls collapsed and the house folded in upon itself and all it contained like a clenching fist . . .

Just as the Master had said.

That same night, at the Master's instructions, he had burned the Master's body and ground the ashes to a black powder—the powder he'd used, as the Ceremony required, to mark the two sacrificial women.

But he'd been careful to save a part of the Master's body from the flames—a single part which, as the Master had decreed, he had buried at the base of the tree.

And now this fragment of the Master is free once more, risen from the earth. It has survived. He has just seen it looking at him through the eyes of the one called Deborah.

Carol had had strong misgivings about bringing Rosie with her to the farm—she knew it was sure to preclude her going to bed with Jeremy, who'd probably resented the old man from the start, and she worried that the Poroths might find him too effete, compared to the crusty old-timers they probably associated with—but now she was glad he'd come along. Good God, he was practically the only one with any animation tonight, and her respect for him grew as she listened to him recount stories of his travels, and poke fun at his own fussy driving, and tell amusing anecdotes, with actual beginnings, middles, and ends, about their adventures together in the subway and the park; and all the while, as he talked, the fat red rose that Deborah had given him kept wobbling absurdly in his buttonhole, as if he were the father at a wedding, come to give away the bride. Without him, dinner would have been a real struggle to get through.

The two of them had "shot the works," as Rosie'd put it. They'd brought out cold pasta from the city, and four pounds of flank steak—not for her, of course—and half a cheddar wheel that Rosie had picked up at Zabar's, and along the way they'd stopped off at a sun-baked little roadside stand outside Morristown for a dozen ears of deliciously sweet fresh corn. She hoped Sarr hadn't been offended by it; his own crop looked terrible.

So did Sarr himself. He had been silent and morose all evening—so different from the first time she'd seen him, when he'd spoken so freely—and there were deep rings of worry beneath his eyes. Clearly he was going through some kind of crisis: whether marital or spiritual, she couldn't say.

Jeremy wasn't much better; he looked positively awful, in fact, his complexion blotchy, his hair long, unkempt, and none too clean-looking. And he didn't seem to have lost any weight at all so far this summer; he looked more out of shape than ever. She wondered if this was a preview of what he'd be like ten years from now and was vaguely troubled at the fantasies he'd inspired.

Deborah, too, seemed out of sorts, and it was clear from her hoarseness and her uncommunicativeness that she hadn't yet gotten her voice back—but then, at least she had an excuse; she was still getting over that horrible incident with the cat, Jeremy had told her about it earlier. Carol noticed with uneasiness, not for the first time tonight, that he kept eyeing Deborah surreptitiously across the dinner table, though Deborah herself seemed unaware of it; the woman had eyes only for her guests.

God, what if there'd been something between them, Jeremy and Deborah? And what if Sarr suspected? Certainly the farmer had been giving the two of them a lot of funny looks all evening.

Most of his attention, though, seemed to be focused on, of all people, Rosie. In fact, Sarr had been sneaking glances at the old man all through the meal, even during grace, as if hoping to catch him out in the midst of a prayer. Maybe, after all, it *was* religion that was on his mind. Serenely oblivious to all this, poor little Rosie had clasped his hands and smiled and uttered a heartfelt *amen* at the end, right along with everyone else. Carol had actually felt relieved. Yet afterward Sarr had continued to stare at Rosie—and at her too—in the most peculiar way, as if he expected one of them to suddenly do something outrageous. It was disconcerting, to say the least. What in the world had gone wrong with these people? She felt sure that she herself had grown stronger and more confident this summer—had positively blossomed, in fact, out from beneath Rochelle's shadow and under Rosie's kindly tutelage—while here at the farm they were falling apart.

At the end of the meal, Rosie yawned, gave his lips a prissy wipe with the napkin, and informed them all that, thanks to this afternoon's hours on the road, he was "weary unto death." Pushing his chair back, he shuffled off to the bathroom and, on his return, announced that he was going to bed. "I'll leave the night to you youngsters," he said, chuckling. "I'm sure you can make better use of it. Now if someone here can just provide me with a blanket . . ."

"I'll bring you everything you'll need," said Deborah. She stood, a trifle unsteadily, and moved toward the stairs. They heard her rummaging in the linen closet in the hallway.

It had already been agreed that Rosie would spend the night on a spare cot in Jeremy's room—an arrangement suggested, to Carol's surprise, by Jeremy himself. Even with Rosie along she'd had a faint, stubborn hope that maybe somehow she'd be able to stay with Jeremy tonight, and she'd at least expected him to ask her. But he hadn't even made an attempt; didn't he realize that it might be weeks before he saw her again? The summer already seemed drearier without him.

Maybe this was simply further proof that he preferred Deborah to her—or even, however unlikely, that something had gone on between the two of them, a possibility she preferred not to think about.

Deborah came downstairs with an armload of sheets, blankets, towels, and a pillow. "Splendid!" said Rosie. "My dear, I can't thank you enough." And bidding the others a cordial goodnight, he followed her out the back door.

Sarr kept his eyes on the screen door as if waiting to see that they were gone. At last, clearing his throat, he turned to Carol. "I'm a little curious," he said lightly, as if in fact he wasn't curious at all, "just how did you and Rosie come to meet?"

"Well," said Carol, surprised, "it's a rather long story—"

"And rather too long to tell now," Jeremy cut in. "Why don't we save it for morning?" To Carol, caught off guard, he added, "Look, let's you and I take advantage of the moonlight and go for a walk, okay?"

It was only a tiny hint of pleading in his voice that prevented her from scolding him. She still felt embarrassed and was not about to abandon Sarr. "Jeremy, I really don't think it's very nice to go off and leave your host like this."

"No, it's all right," said Poroth, "you two go ahead. You deserve some time together." He dismissed them both by getting up from the table with a contented stretch and wandering into the living room.

"Jeremy," Carol snapped, when they got outside, "how could you be so rude to him?"

He did not immediately reply, but put his arm around her. "Let's just walk," he said. Lightning bugs made the lawn look like a convocation of souls, winking silently as they hurried back and forth. The crickets were louder tonight than she'd ever heard before, with a distant chorus of frogs keeping statelier rhythms at the brook. The two of them were passing the side of the farmhouse now; ahead of them a nearly full moon hung low above the ribbon of dirt road. Freirs nodded in the direction of the house, where, through the unlit living room window, outlined in the faint rays of lamplight still streaming from the kitchen, Poroth could be seen pacing up and down in the darkness.

"He's been acting really weird lately," said Freirs. "Almost like he's hitting the bottle. Maybe it's financial problems, maybe some kind of religious mania."

"I *thought* it might be that."

"Whatever it is, I want to go back to New York with you tomorrow. If it's okay with you, I'd even like to stay for a few days in your apartment—sleeping on the couch, of course—till I figure out what to do."

"Do the Poroths know?"

"No."

"When do you plan on telling them?"

"Tomorrow, I guess."

She felt a little thrill of excitement. He was asking her to rescue him; she was now a fellow conspirator. "So this means we won't have to say goodbye tomorrow after all."

"That's right. We can be together—if you're willing."

"I am." She turned to face him. "And you won't have to use the couch, either."

They kissed, and she let him kiss her breasts, and she knew that the summer was saved.

Moist air. Scent of roses. Bats fluttering by the barn roof. Silently the two figures—the slim, dark-haired woman and the short, white-haired man—emerge from the outbuilding and make their way toward the barn. Their voices are hushed, their faces indistinct blobs of white.

The one now called Deborah pauses and turns to the Old One. For an instant her eyes flash in the moonlight.

"He knows."

"Yes, I saw it every time he looked at you. And he suspects me, too."

"His mother told him."

The old man nods. "She's a Troet, like I was. She has the gift. But there are things she doesn't know."

The woman turns her eyes briefly toward the moon. "She will be visited tonight."

They pause in the darkness of the doorway to the barn, beside the broad form of the pickup truck parked inside. The one called Deborah runs her hand lovingly over something unseen in the shadows on the wall.

"They're weak," she says, "both of them. I've been poisoning them." There is something like pride in her voice.

"In that case," says the Old One, "we'll be able to make a tiny alteration in our cast. I'd been grooming our chubby friend from the city for this, but under the circumstances—since he's potentially more dangerous—the farmer will serve just as well."

He watches as the one called Deborah nods in agreement, her hand still caressing the thing hanging in the shadows. It swings gently on its hook; moonlight catches a length of wooden handle, an edge of steel blade.

"So," the Old One continues, "he's the one you kill."

Things going wonderfully with Carol. Suspect she may really be the one. Can't wait till I get back to the city.

Have been talking about her to myself.

"I'm in love with her."

"Yeah? And what's that supposed to mean?"

"You know—the works. The whole hog. I like spending time with her, want to fuck her, marry her, give her presents. Want to have kids with her, share my old age with her, have her around when I die. All that stuff."

Poroth lay awake, deliberately keeping his breathing deep and regular. waiting till the others were asleep. Carefully he turned to look at his wife. For once her eyes were shut tight.

Sitting up in bed, he placed a bare foot tentatively on the floor, then the other, knowing that Deborah usually woke when he went downstairs to the bathroom and not wanting to waken her on this of all nights.

His clothes and shoes were where he'd left them, in the closet; he put them on in the hall. Tiptoeing to Carol's room, he stood looking in at her, asleep there on her back beneath the nursery cutouts on the wall: the moon, the bearded old men, the fire. One arm, unseen, cradled the pillow; the other, exposed to view, was lightly freckled and slim as a reed, her wrist a fragile piece of china, her face unclouded by anything but dreams, slack but for slightly pursed lips. He felt an innocence all about her, the innocence of a little child, and he wondered, for the first time since coming home to Gilead, if the room would ever hold a real child, born of him and Deborah.

Better not to brood on that now. God would reward him as He saw fit. Buttoning his shirt, he stepped into the room.

Just before waking her, he hesitated. It might not be so easy to convince her to come with him; there might be an argument—a struggle, even. Embarrassing, under his roof. How could his mother have failed to realized that?

She's crazy, said a mocking little voice inside his head. *Why take orders from a crazy woman?*

Better to let Carol sleep, he decided. He would bring his mother out here to the farm; she would just have to be content with that. Backing out of the doorway, he continued down the stairs.

He didn't see the thing that sat upright in the bed and crept down the stairs after him.

The moon was higher now, a beacon at the center of the sky so bright it hurt his eyes to look as he hurried across the lawn toward the barn. He knew that, when he started the truck, the sound of the engine might wake the others, but that couldn't be helped; surely in a moment they'd fall back asleep, and by then he'd be gone. As he tiptoed past the dark outbuilding where Jeremy and Rosie lay sleeping, he heard the throbbing rhythm of the frogs, but he didn't hear the pale, naked figure that followed on his heels like a shadow.

Rounding the corner of the barn and slipping inside, he opened the door of the truck and was about to step up to the driver's seat when,

with a cry, he swore and jumped back, away from the form already
crouched there directly before his face, little pink hands and plump
red lips and wrinkles around eyes that were like razors now. Poroth
recognized him at last.

"'Twas you in the park ten years ago," he said. "I remember now.
What business have you here?"

The old man grinned. "Waiting for you, Sarr Poroth."

Poroth saw the eyes look past him briefly, to a place just behind his
shoulder, and he would have whirled around, but the figure wielding
the axe was too swift. Its blade caught him square in the back of the
skull and buried itself in his brain.

This is the part he likes. This is what he's waited for. The farmer has
toppled like a dying tree and now lies sprawled lifeless at his feet,
blood soaking into the dusty floor of the barn. Grasping an arm, the
Old One turns the body over onto its back, then watches raptly as the
thing that was the farmwife climbs naked astride the farmer and,
crouching there, places her open mouth directly over his. A minute
passes.

Suddenly an old wound opens in her throat; her body crumples and
goes limp, sagging in upon itself just as the corpse's eyes flash open.
With an impatient swipe of its arm the thing that was the farmer
shoves aside her stiffening body and gets to its feet. Blood continues
flowing down its head from the gaping red crack in its skull. It looks at
the Old One and smiles.

The man returns its smile. What a moment this has been! The being
itself remains hidden from view—it's been more than a hundred years
since he's seen it—but he's sensed the thing's presence tonight and has
charted its progress as it made its blind way from mouth to mouth. He
has seen the farmwife's cheeks bulge, then grow slack; he has seen the
wriggling at the farmer's throat. It is lodged there now, just beneath
the flesh, already accustoming itself to its new home. He still cannot
see it, but he knows it is there, nearly close enough to touch: the one
thing left alive after the Master's death; the part he'd left unburned;
the organ with no clear human analogue, but corresponding roughly to
a phallus, instrument of regeneration; the black thing, undying and
unkillable; the Dhol.

*

Silence within the darkened barn. Beneath the smell of straw, a faint whiff of decay. He grasps the farmwife's body by the ankles.

"I'm good at hiding bodies," he says, dragging the thing away from the truck. "You have your own work to do tonight."

The corpse, heavy, comes to a stop at the doorway. He tugs on the ankles. Slowly it begins to move, then stops again.

He gets a better grip and is about to pull further when the figure of the farmer steps forward, bends stiffly toward the floor, and picks up the corpse as if it weighed nothing. Slinging it roughly over one shoulder like a sack of grain, it strides into the night.

It feels strong now. It flexes its great hands, heaves its massive shoulders, gazes down with pleasure at its lean, untiring form. The burden it carries is a minor one, so light that it might well be made of straw.

Shortly before dawn a tall, shambling figure, the head still bloody from some recent injury, wanders along the borders of the property with the already stiffening carcass of a naked female slung carelessly over its shoulder, the black hair hanging almost to the ground. Making at last for the line of pine trees on the far side of the brook, it strides briskly downhill and, without pausing, steps into the shallow water, scattering the frogs. As if it were walking on dry land, it starts across.

Just beyond the center of the stream, it comes to a sudden halt and stands immobile, the frigid water swirling unnoticed over shoes and ankles. Finally, after nearly a minute in the water, the figure turns and strides back onto the land, heading toward the old abandoned smokehouse by the edge of the woods.

Umindful of a few unsleeping wasps that still circle the building and are already stirred up, the figure yanks the sagging wooden door open wide and clumsily thrusts its burden into the darkness. Wasps, like bees, go for the eyes. Unlike bees, they can sting many times without dying. Maddened by the intrusion, insects circle the figure's head like attacking warplanes, dealing sting after death-dealing sting.

But venom, however deadly, has no effect on things already dead. The hulking figure feels no pain, no more than it feels from the split down the center of its skull. Heedless of the tiny swarm and the needle-sharp spears that pierce the flesh of its face, the figure grasps the carcass by the legs and shoves it upward into the round hole in the smokehouse ceiling, as if to jam the thing into the tiny attic. But the body cannot fit; the legs wedge tightly in the hole, ridges of flesh bulging up around them. The body hangs head downward like a slaughtered animal, the long black hair swinging like Spanish moss.

Dawn approaches. Leaving the carcass dangling behind it, the thing shambles toward the truck.

Freirs stirred and woke at the sound of the engine, in time to see the broad, dark shape of Poroth's truck roll past the outbuilding and head out to the road. Dimly he could make out Poroth at the wheel. Without his glasses Freirs could not be sure, but the farmer appeared to be wearing a red skullcap.

Rosie's bed, he noticed, was empty. Seconds later Rosie entered, wiping his hands and smiling. "Had to obey the call of nature!" he said, winking.

"Where's Sarr gone off to? That was him in the truck."

Rosie shrugged. "You got me, partner. He said something about keeping an appointment."

The moon stares down as the truck pulls up at the foot of the grassy slope, just down the road from the little stone bridge. Heavily a tall, ungainly figure drops from the cab and lumbers up the slope toward the cottage, heedless of the darkness, trampling upon a bed of flowers as if they weren't there. Thorns tear at its clothing, but it doesn't slow; clumsily it blunders into the beehives standing on the lawn, knocking one of them over.

The insects emerge in an angry swarm and attack the face and eyes. The shambling figure pays them no mind as it moves up the hill toward the house.

At last it turns its shattered face toward the door. Clenching its huge fist, it knocks three times, the noise echoing hollowly in the night.

"Mother," it calls hoarsely. "Mother . . ."

JULY THIRTY-FIRST

Ten A.M. now. Woke up feeling weak & disoriented. Dead spider floating in my water glass. Rosie was already awake & bustling energetically about, humming some tuneless little song. Said he'd be making Carol & me breakfast, as it's Sunday (I'd totally forgotten) and the Poroths have already gone to worship . . .

But the Poroths were not at the worship that morning, and their absence excited much comment. "I can't understand it," muttered Amos Reid, waiting for the opening prayers to begin. "For Brother Sarr not to be here at a time like this . . ." He shook his head despairingly.

Joram Sturtevant and his family were not there either—they were home, all five of them, in the sprawling white farmhouse over on the next hill—but at least they had a good excuse: Lotte Sturtevant had gone into labor this morning.

Lise Verdock, too, was absent; yet in another sense her presence was felt deeply by everyone in attendance. The worship was being held in her front yard, in fact, right beneath her window. It was a memorial service in her honor. She had died during the night.

She had slipped away just after midnight without ever having regained consciousness, watched over by her grieving husband and daughter. In testament to the high regard with which she'd been held in the town, this morning's worship, originally scheduled for the home of Frederick and Hildegarde Troet, just across the road, had been hastily reconvened here at the Verdocks' dairy farm, where, in a moment or two, Jacob van Meer would be leading them all in a prayer.

"It just ain't *like* Sarr," muttered Amos. "That woman of his, now, I wouldn't go countin' on her, but for Sarr to be late when it's his own poor aunt we're honorin' . . . it don't make sense." He looked around. "And where in blazes is his ma?"

Matthew Geisel was standing next to him, thinking sadly of the departed woman while gazing with unconscious envy at the tall, newly painted cattle barn to their left, the lush fields and rich pasturage, and, in the distance ahead of them, the broad, imposing vista of the Sturtevant homestead.

"Well," he said, scratching his chin, "maybe they're all over at Fred Troet's right now, lookin' for the rest of us."

A low burst of laughter came from Rupert Lindt, standing with folded arms behind them. "That would probably suit 'em just fine," he said. "I don't know as those three.ever had much use for the rest of us."

"I'm sure there's a good reason," said Amos, half to himself. He stared down at his clasped hands as, with a burst of Jeremiah, the service began.

"Therefore they shall come and sing in the height of Zion, and shall flow together to the goodness of the Lord, for wheat, and for wine, and for oil, and for the young of the flock and of the herd: and their soul shall be as a watered garden; and they shall not sorrow any more at all . . ."

It wasn't till all the prayers were over and the Brethren were deep into the hymn-singing that Amos, nudged by Matthew Geisel, looked up and saw what many others there on the lawn had already noticed: the thin black tentacle of smoke twisting toward the sky from the Sturtevant back yard.

The egg in Rosie's hand was large, smooth, glistening white; and if it was a trifle heavier than any normal egg of that size had a right to be, no one was the wiser. Eyes twinkling with the contentment of a mother who knows no children in the world are better fed than her own, he cracked the egg on the rim of the already half-full bowl, let the yolk drop inside, and whipped the liquid to a yellow froth. "Hungry?" he called gaily over his shoulder.

"I'm always hungry," said Freirs, slouched unshaven and tousle-haired over the table, and Carol, across from him, added, "It's that famous country air."

Rosie chuckled. "That's just what I like to hear." He poured the liquid into the heated frying pan, where it hissed and bubbled like hellfire.

Breakfast left them feeling heavy and overfull. While Rosie fussed about the kitchen, the two stumbled groggily from the house and down the back steps, kicking off their shoes in the grass. It was nearly eleven, the sun high overhead. The Poroths still had not returned.

Reaching out a sleepy hand for Carol's, Jeremy pulled her after him, and together they wandered downhill toward the brook, the unmown grass dry beneath their feet. The day was warm, and by the time they'd passed the smokehouse and the barn, Carol was finding it hard to keep her balance; the lawn seemed to slope more steeply as she neared the water, tilting in ways that didn't seem right at all, and she had to stop herself from falling forward into the weeds that grew along the bank. The greenness seemed to spin around her; she felt Jeremy's hand slip from her own, and then she was floating, blue sky underfoot, green overhead, or was it the other way around? . . . Carol blinked and shook her head, trying to clear her thoughts. The sunlight from the flashing brook was dazzling, almost blinding. There was a rushing of water in her ears, and she couldn't tell if it was the brook or her own lifeblood.

"I feel as if I haven't slept in weeks," Jeremy was saying, yawning. She saw him remove his glasses and sink beside her to his knees by the bank of the stream, then lie back, and as she bent to kiss him she saw his eyes close in sleep. She lay beside him on the grass, feet toward the water, and just before her head fell back against the soft ground she thought, with a brief and terrible clarity, *He's drugged us . . .*

They slept.

But in the smokehouse, other things were awake—and angry.

The wasps that inhabited the small, enclosed area just beneath the peaked roof had seen their tranquil world rocked shortly before dawn by the intrusion of a pair of human legs, naked and female, thrust roughly upward into their domain through the hole in the ceiling boards. A few of the insects had been away from the nest at the time; others, during the course of the morning, had by sheer chance managed to slip through a small crevice in the boards, the one small portion of the hole that the legs did not fill. But like dwellers in an attic who have found their trapdoor sealed, hundreds more of the insects were still imprisoned, bottled up amid the darkness and the heat, their passage to the outside world effectively cut off by a stopper of decaying human flesh.

They were angry now, and frantic to escape, their frenzy mounting with each passing minute as the sun climbed higher in the sky and the air within the tiny chamber grew even hotter. In furious circles they swarmed around the grey, brainlike nest, blind things, maddened, stinging one another in their madness.

The morning passed, gave way to noon. Shadows of clouds swept over their bodies, then a sun so fierce it would have wakened any normal sleepers. Insects circled buzzing around their faces, settled on their eyes; a dragonfly hovered as if with evil intent above Carol's half-open lips. Freirs' plump belly rose and fell without a break in rhythm as flies crawled over his skin and mosquitoes feasted on his sun-warmed blood. Two cats crept forward to peer inquisitively at him, and a pale, glistening slug crept in stately slowness over his wrist and down the other side into the grass. His glasses gleamed beside him in the sunlight. The glimmering brook murmured unheard at their feet.

In the distance, up the sloping lawn, the screen door swung open, then shut with a bang. The old man approached them softly, peering at their sleeping forms. Briefly he knelt beside Carol, making curious passes over her face. Getting to his feet, he stood gazing down at them again, his eyes darting back and forth between a heavy-looking rock and Freirs' head.

Suddenly he froze, listening; his expression changed, face hardening into a smile as his eyes scanned the edge of the woods along the far side of the brook. Casually, almost as an afterthought, he brought his foot down on Freirs' glasses, crushing them into the ground. Then, finding a series of stepping stones, he stepped delicately across the brook and disappeared among the trees.

It was a mark of the Brethren's restraint, their sense of decorum and protocol, as much as of their religious devotion that, though all of them were soon staring with curiosity and alarm at the twisting thread of black smoke in the distance, they continued singing as if nothing were wrong, pressing on through the traditional sixteen hymns. Even when the service was over and the Bible shut, few of them made any move in the direction of the Sturtevants' house, preferring to stay and give Adam Verdock and his daughter (who, of late grown used to death, seemed to be bearing up better than her father) what small comfort they could. Too much curiosity wasn't seemly; there were those among them who'd even objected to the presence of the local newspaper in their homes, arguing, with considerable zeal, that what God intended men to know was already set down in the Bible and that other printed words were mere distractions.

And so, in the end, when the assembly at last began to break up, it was only the more avidly curious among them—those such as Bert and Amelia Steegler, Galen Trudel, Rupert Lindt, and Jan and Hannah Kraft—as well as those closest to the Sturtevants—Joram's brother Abram and his wife, the van Meers and the Klapps, Matthew Geisel, Klaus Buckhalter, and a dozen or so more, including Ham Stoudemire, whose wife, Nettie, would be in attendance as midwife—who actually walked, in a party, toward the Sturtevant farm.

The house itself, a broad, white-shingled Colonial with low single-story wings on each side, was set well back from the main road at the end of a pathway bordered by tall shrubbery. The first things the party encountered, after ascending the path, were the Sturtevants' three young boys, normally a rowdy, outspoken bunch, standing in uneasy silence by the front of the house. "Father won't let us inside," the oldest boy explained somewhat fearfully. "We have to stay here in front. Aunt Wilma's in there, though. So's Sister Nettie."

This last had been addressed to Klaus Buckhalter, whose wife, Wilma—Lotte Sturtevant's older sister—was already inside, helping Nettie Stoudemire with the birth.

Buckhalter conferred briefly with his nephews, then turned back to the group. "I think Abram and I had best go up alone."

The others hung back as the two men climbed the front steps and knocked, almost timidly, at the door. After some moments, it was opened by Buckhalter's wife. She looked as if she'd been weeping.

"You can all come in," she said. "It's done now . . . She's alive."

"And the child?" asked Abram.

She shuddered and shook her head.

Frowning, the two men entered the house, Wilma standing at the door as the rest filed nervously in behind them. Ahead of them, at the top of the stairs, the midwife stood wringing her hands.

"Is my brother up there?" asked Abram.

Wilma pointed, trembling, in the direction of the yard. "Back there." She turned and started up the staircase; as if by unspoken agreement the women in the group filed upstairs behind her, continuing toward a doorway at the right, from which issued a series of low moans. Left to themselves, the men stood awkwardly in the downstairs hall, then followed Abram toward the back of the house.

They found Joram seated in a rocking chair in the middle of the glassed-in back porch. He was rocking furiously, as if possessed, and seemed barely to notice them. His face, they saw, was drawn, weary, but his eyes, which stared at nothing, had a wild look. Behind him, outside in the yard, they could see a round pit filled with ashes from which a few dark tendrils of smoke still rose.

At first it seemed that Joram was addressing them, but then they all saw that he was in fact talking to himself. "God is merciful," he was saying as he rocked back and forth, over and over like a litany of comfort. "God is merciful, merciful . . ."

Abram grasped him by the shoulder. "What is it, brother?"

Slowly the man in the chair looked up, and recognition dawned in his face. "He touched her belly," he said, "and she gave birth to—" A fit of trembling seized him. He shook his head. "Thank the Lord it didn't live!"

Rupert Lindt stepped forward. "Joram, what are you talkin' about? Who touched Lotte's belly?"

Joram turned to look at him. He was silent a moment, as if trying to recollect. "'Twas the one from the city. The one livin' out at Poroth Farm."

The men eyed one another in silence, the same dark look growing on all their faces.

"I think it was the *air*," Joram was saying. "'Twas the Lord's pure, holy air that killed it. It wasn't meant to breathe as we do . . ."

And the men looked at one another, and nodded, there on the porch with the ashes just outside, while upstairs, at the other end of the house, out of Lotte's hearing, Wilma Buckhalter sat huddled with the womenfolk and told them, weeping, of the terrible thing that had been born a few hours before and that Joram and the midwife had burned in the back yard—a thing with tiny yellow claws and the beginnings of a tail . . .

The two men were working in the shadow of the hill. The younger, still in his teens, was crouching over a small grey box-shaped instrument, an emanometer, used to measure radon gas. From a strap by his side hung a similar device for the measurement of methane. The older of the two, a tall, stoop-shouldered man with thinning black hair, was pacing around the base of the hill taking readings on radiation with a scintillation counter. A camera and a light meter dangled round his neck.

"No," he said, sounding far from surprised, "it's the same over here. Just background count." Squinting, he peered up along the length of the cone. It towered forty feet above the forest floor—not so high as most of the older trees, but in this section, where the trees were short and vegetation sparse, its top protruded well above them all. "Think I'd better get a couple more pictures."

He backed into the sunlight, holding the light meter before him. Checking the dial, he raised the camera and focused on the top of the mound. The younger man stood watching him. Moments later he called out, "Dr. Lewalski? We've got a visitor."

The other lowered his camera and turned where the younger man was pointing. At the far side of the mound stood a short, somewhat paunchy old man with glowing pink skin and a halo of fine white hair.

"Oh, don't mind me!" the old man cried. "I'm just passing through." He stood staring at them for a moment and made no move to go. "You two prospecting for uranium or something?"

The one named Lewalski smiled and shook his head. "Just taking a few measurements, that's all." He indicated the mound. "We're trying to find out how this thing was formed."

"Seems like quite a lot of fellows have been around here lately asking that same question."

The other laughed. "Yes, I know. We're a little behind. I cut short my vacation just to come down here. It's quite an unusual formation."

"We're going to drill a hole right through to the center," added the younger man, "and see what's inside."

The old man's eyes widened respectfully. "Drill a *hole?*" He looked around. "With what?"

Lewalski laughed. "Oh, we're not going to do that now. We'll have to come back tomorrow with the right equipment."

"Oh, yes, I see. Tomorrow." He nodded to himself. "I take it you fellows aren't from around here."

"We're from Princeton," said the younger man. "From the geology department."

"Really?" The old man seemed impressed. "And so you drove out here today, did you?"

"That's right," said Lewalski. "Why, what's the matter?"—because the other had suddenly frowned and now looked troubled, as if he'd just remembered something particularly unfortunate.

"Oh, it's nothing," said the old man. "It's just that—tell me, where are you parked?"

Lewalski nodded toward the north. "An old dirt road about a mile, mile and a half from here. It runs past what must be the town dump."

The old man shook his head glumly. "That's just what I thought."

"Is something wrong?"

"Probably not. It's just that there's some fool law in this town about parking on that road on a Sunday, and—well, there've been some incidents. Quite a few out-of-towners have had their cars towed away."

"On a Sunday?" said Lewalski. "That's absurd! I'm not even on the road, I pulled way over."

The old man shrugged. "I'm sure you're completely in the right. I just wish the people of this town had a little more respect for state laws. They have some funny ideas around here about Sunday driving . . ."

"Hold on a minute!" said Lewalski. "We saw people driving around here today—at least I think so."

The old man nodded, looking sorry he'd ever brought up the subject. "Of course you did. They were probably on their way to Sunday worship. Out-of-towners they regard a bit differently."

"But we're from *Princeton,*" said the younger man.

"You're saying they tow away people's cars?" asked Lewalski. He was beginning to look nervous. "It makes no sense. This is practically official business."

"Well, that road to the dump is town property, you see—so are these woods—and, well . . ." He shrugged and looked away.

"Aw, come on, Dr. Lewalski," said the younger man, "nobody's going to touch your car."

The other looked dubious. He scratched his chin. "No, I guess not." He stepped back and brought the camera up to his face. "We'll just—Jesus, what was that?"

A thick brown snake had slid past his feet. He saw it disappear into the bushes out of the corner of his eye.

"Been a lot of snakes around here lately," said the old man. "I suppose you read about it. Some folks say it was the quake that stirred them up. We've had quite a few people bitten this year—more than in the past twelve years combined. Copperheads, mostly. Hope you brought your snakebite kit along."

The younger man turned to Lewalski. *"Did* you?"

Lewalski grimaced. "No, of course not. I know these woods. There's no danger at all, if you don't go around—Jesus, there's another!" He stepped back, then stared up at the hill, frowning. "You know, maybe this isn't such a good idea today after all."

The younger man shrugged. "Whatever you say."

The old man cleared his throat. "Do you, uh, know your way out of here all right? I only ask because I'm heading up that way myself. I can show you the right path, take you back to your car without your getting lost."

Lewalski was fitting his camera back into its case. "You know, mister, we'd really appreciate that." He turned to the other. "Come on, let's go—we can do a really thorough job tomorrow."

They followed the old man down the path that wound northward. He was whistling.

"You seem to know these woods pretty well," said Lewalski.

The old man smiled but didn't look back. "Yes, known 'em since I was a boy. Grew up around here."

They were passing a tall clump of bushes. For just an instant the old man's eyes darted to the side, toward where the leaves and brambles grew thickest, and he gave a nearly imperceptible shake of his head.

"Stay with me now," he added, "I don't want to lose anybody."

It wasn't till the three had continued down the path and were almost lost from sight amid the foliage that the bushes stirred, then shook, and the hulking form of the farmer pushed its way out onto the path.

It stood for a moment, watching their retreating forms; then it turned to face the mound. Pressing its shoulder to a massive grey rock, larger than any living man could move, it wrested the thing from the earth and rolled it toward the base of the hill. Another boulder followed, and another. Soon the structure rose against the hillside.

It was building an altar.

"You know we've got to do something . . ."

"No doubt *of* it!"

The men had walked down the path from the Sturtevants' house in silence, each lost in his own thoughts. Now the group stood huddled together by the roadside.

"I ain't never seen old Joram so upset."

"Well, and don't he have a right to be?"

"Seems to me we got to act now. Let's get our trucks and head on out to Sarr's."

"Now just a minute, Rupert, we can't none of us be sure—"

"I ain't takin' no chances!" Lindt smacked his fist into his palm. "I was at the Poroths' place last Sunday, and I watched that boy. I saw the way he was lookin' at my little Sarah."

"We're not gonna do him any harm now, that wouldn't be right."

"Course not, Matt. We're just gonna *call* on him, that's all. We're just gonna see that he leaves—"

"Before tonight."

"Before dark!"

"Yeah, leaves before dark and never comes back."

"No weapons now, mind you."

"No, o' *course* not! We don't need weapons against a little worm like that! Why, did you see how soft his hands are?"

There was a pause.

"And if he knows spells," said Abram Sturtevant, touching on what was in all their minds, "you know that weapons ain't gonna help us anyways. We got to trust in the Lord."

"Now wait a minute," said Geisel. "The Lord councils patience, you all know that, and maybe we should talk this out with Joram first, when he's come 'round again. Ain't no need to rush into things."

"Don't forget what day this is, Matt. We don't want that sort of person around here tonight. He could get himself into all *kinds* of mischief."

"But there's no sign he even knows what tonight is."

"Listen, brother." It was a leathery-faced old farmer who spoke up. "I gave that boy a ride in my car just the other week, and do you know what he kept askin' me? All about this very day—the thirty-first of July—and whether we get many killin's on this date." He glared at Geisel. "Now what do you say to that?"

The other was silent.

"That settles it," said Lindt. "Come on!"

Walking through this part of the woods with the two scientists, he feels a tug of memory almost akin to nostalgia.

He remembers, even now, with perfect clarity, how a century ago he stood here while the Master still lived to command him. He remembers that day in the woods, that chilly Christmas afternoon, and how, as a boy, he first saw the black form in the tree . . .

And he remembers exactly what it told him that day—remembers because his entire life, since that moment, has been lived in accordance with its words. He remembers how the black thing's eye glared at him with its eye and opened up its black fleshless mouth.

He remembers what it said.

I have been waiting for you.

"How long?" the boy had stammered, breathless.

Long.

"What do you want of me?"

Much.

"What must I do?"

You shall perform Ceremonies in my honor.

"Ceremonies for what?"

To bring me back as my Son.

"Where is he now?" the boy had asked, and he remembers today the Master's answer.

He isn't born yet.

The planet rolled through the afternoon with only a scattering of clouds. A soft breeze sprang up, tropical in its warmth; the pine trees stirred among themselves on the other side of the brook. Where small birds had hopped and chirped among the branches, there was now only the whisper of the wind, the most solemn of stillnesses. The branches stretched yearningly toward the two sleeping figures on the farther bank; the shadows of the trees grew longer, reaching across the water where they lay. Slanting rays of sunlight hung like curtains before the bases of the trees, shifting with each movement of the branches. The sun seemed to die a little.

Still prisoner of some all-enveloping dream, Carol shifted in her sleep as if in response to a call. Slowly she stretched and sat up. She gazed across the water into the darkness of the woods; and if she saw the figure there standing veiled in yellow curtains of sunlight, as unmoving as the trees, and if she was surprised, and if she saw it was a man, tall, bearded, nearly naked, his clothing in ribbons, his hands black with dirt, and if she saw the thing that had happened to his skull, she made no sign. She stared at him a moment and said nothing.

Gazing at her from across the water, the figure raised its hand and beckoned.

She stood, paying no attention to Freirs sleeping obliviously beside her among the weeds. Hesitating but a moment, she stepped slowly into the stream, the water swirling round her bare ankles. Heedless of the chill, looking neither left nor right, she walked across, stepped onto the other side, and joined him where he waited for her. His hand reached out for hers, took it imperatively in his grasp. For a moment, as his hand touched hers, she turned to cast a single, half-regretful backward glance at the man still sleeping on the other bank. Then the figure pulled her toward him, and the darkness of the woods closed over them both.

The day is waning at last, and he is glad of it. It is the night that concerns him. He watches impatiently as the professor and student climb into their car and drive off. They wave one more time in thanks. He nods, waves back, smiles till the car has disappeared. They will not return today, and tomorrow—tomorrow will be too late.

For a moment back there on the trail he had contemplated ordering the Dhol to kill the two of them—it would have been far simpler and wasted less precious time—but there is always a chance that the men might have been missed and that others might have come looking for them: others who might interfere with the events planned for tonight. No, he decides, there's no use taking chances. Not with so much at stake.

Which is why he must dispose of the extra man. There is no more need for him; the woman, by now, must be in their hands, and the role Freirs was to play has already fallen to another. It will be well, for safety's sake, to make sure he cannot threaten the proceedings. It will be simpler this way. Cleaner. He has the necessary straps in his pocket, and though they'll eventually be needed for the woman, they may also prove useful for the man.

Hands tingling with anticipation, the Old One turns his back on the road and sets off once more up the trail.

There were less than a dozen of them now: Bert Steegler had had to go back and open the store, Jacob van Meer was feeling poorly, and others had dropped out for reasons of their own. They had crowded into three trucks, Rupert Lindt's in the lead, and had raced along the main road from town, over the bridge and past the silent stone cottage beside it, then up the winding roads into the backcountry. Now they had reduced their speed and were moving up the Poroths' road like a convoy, maneuvering slowly over the ruts and gaps and potholes, yet still stirring up enough dust so that the rear truck, Abram Sturtevant's, was covered with a reddish film, making visibility difficult for the three men inside.

It was old Matthew Geisel, sitting up beside Lindt, who saw it first, at the bend before the Poroth farm. He pointed toward the side of the road. There, tilted forward in a ditch, its right rear tire lifted in the air, was the battered form of Poroth's pickup truck.

"Appears he's had himself an accident," said Ham Stoudemire, "and left the truck where it stopped."

Lindt pulled over to the side; the other two trucks behind him slowed to a halt. The men dismounted and hurried to the truck.

It was empty. Along the upper rim of the steering wheel was a suspicious-looking smear of dried blood.

"Suppose he may be hurt," said Geisel, "and crawled off into the woods?" He surveyed the dense vegetation before him.

"It may be so," said Abram Sturtevant. "We'd best look for him."

The men fanned out from the ditched truck, searching for signs: a broken branch, a tatter of cloth, more blood. Lindt, Stoudemire, and Geisel continued on foot now toward the house several hundred yards ahead.

Geisel glanced back at the Poroths' truck; he was troubled. 'Twasn't like Sarr to go off the road like that; the man knew every twist and turn of its length. No, 'twasn't like him at all.

Frowning, he followed the two younger men toward the farmhouse.

Shadows. Evening coming on.

He emerges from the woods, slightly winded, to stand a moment on the narrow strip of level ground that, just ahead, dips downward toward the brook. In the distance the farmhouse, barn, and outbuildings have caught the dying sunlight and glow as if aflame; the sky behind the cornfield is a wall of red, turning the field into a battleground where stunted cornstalks stand silhouetted against the sky like doomed men. Just across the brook Freirs' plump form lies defenseless in sleep, his stomach rising and falling among the weeds. As if sensing the other's presence, he stirs.

For most of his journey through the woods the Old One has been considering Freirs' death. It will be what it should have been three days ago: death by water. His vivid dream of Deborah in the bathtub has been thwarted, chance has saved Freirs from the clutches of the Dhol, but now he will be able to do the job himself. In Freirs' insensible condition, it will be easy; he feels as if he has already done the deed, so detailed and real is the picture. He sees himself turn Freirs onto his belly for the precautionary tying of the wrists, then haul him by the ankles to the stream and shove his face beneath the rushing water. He sees a tremor shake the sleeper's frame, sees his arms twist and strain against the leather in an instinctive, futile effort to escape. The body jerks and thrashes as the Old One bends his full weight upon it. Once, twice, three times Freirs' dazed face, streaming water, lifts above the surface as he wrenches his neck back, legs kicking. But the Old One's grip is like iron, and the joy of what he's feeling now, savoring the final moments of a human life communicated through the spasmodic twitching of the flesh, gives him a tenfold strength. Just another minute to be sure all breathing's stopped . . .

The reality will be even better. Stepping nimbly from stone to stone, the Old One crosses the stream.

It takes him but a moment to bind the wrists. He is dragging Freirs' inert form roughly toward the brook, scanning the property one more time to make sure there are no witnesses to what's about to happen, when his gaze comes to rest on the smokehouse and the pale thing hanging upside down inside it, clearly visible through the wide-open door and outlined in the final rays of sunlight.

The fool! He moves quickly, cursing. This must not be discovered. Left like this, the body can be seen by anyone who chances to visit the farm. And anyone searching for the Poroths will find it within minutes. Better to hide the thing deep in the woods, where it will be safe until tonight.

Abandoning Freirs for the moment, he hurries to the smokehouse. The little wooden structure already reeks of decay, the smell of something that's been dead more than a week. He does not find it disagreeable; he steps inside, brushing away swarms of flies, and finds himself face to face with Deborah Poroth's earthly remains. Her upside-down eyes, hanging level with his own, are shrunken in their sockets like old apples. His glance takes in her dangling arms, the hands even with his belt, and the crumpled black torn place in her throat, pulled wider by the weight of the head and gaping like a second mouth. The sight inspires in his breast precisely nothing. Reaching up, he grasps the rib cage and pulls.

The body does not give. From somewhere above him comes a muffled buzzing sound, easily confused with the buzzing of the flies that continue to swarm around his head.

He pulls harder, but without success. The two kinds of buzzing blend together in an irritating song.

Grabbing the limp arms, he yanks with all his might. Still the body doesn't move.

Embracing the thing now, he puts all his weight on it, hangs grimacing with his own feet in the air. Vertebrae snap, some strands of long black hair shake loose and drift slowly toward the floor, but the legs remain stuck fast.

Wiping away a drop of sweat that has formed on his brow, he stands on tiptoe, reaches up as high as he is able, and grasps the legs nearer the ceiling, tugging on each one individually, trying to dislodge them from the wood. There is a cracking sound; the body starts to give a little. The buzzing overhead is growing angrier, and loud enough for him to distinguish it from the flies.

But now there is a more urgent sound.

"Sarr! Deborah!"

Voices ring out from up the slope, by the farmhouse and the road.

Instinctively he pulls the door closed and turns the catch, concealing himself within the tiny shack. It is hot inside, airless, dark and crowded as a coffin. He is pressed against the wall by the loose, ungainly bulk of the corpse. But he is still confident. There is still time. Distracted, he shoves the corpse aside.

With a splintering of wood it tears loose, crashing to the floor of the smokehouse—and behind it, like a demon from a bottle, rushes a torrent of invisible wings and legs and death-dealing stingers, buzzing, stinging again and again, as if it is the sound itself that brings the pain. They take their venomous revenge, as wasps will, upon the only living thing at hand; and as wasps will, they go first for the eyes.

Blindly he batters at the closed door. The tiny building echoes with his screams.

For nearly a minute they grow louder, higher-pitched, the screaming of a thing no longer human, carrying across the farm, the fields, the woods. The smokehouse trembles, rocks on its foundation, shivers with the pounding from within.

Then at last it is silent.

His sleep was invaded by screaming, high and womanish and just out of reach. He dreamed of Carol. He willed himself to go to her, to help her, but his body was a thing of rock and would not move.

At last the screams ended, and there was silence. And then that ended too. Dimly he heard voices, men this time, confused, frightened, shouting out to one another in their fear—and then screams again, and running, and a great inhuman buzzing . . .

He didn't see Rupert Lindt throw wide the smokehouse door, or the cloud of maddened wasps that spilled out, scattering the men and leaving the two who'd been the closest, Lindt and Stoudemire, with painfully stung arms, necks, and faces. He didn't see the horrible swollen red thing that came tumbling out after the wasps to lie twitching and oozing upon the grass, a thing almost unrecognizable as human, puffed up as it was to nearly twice its size. And he didn't see what lay behind it on the smokehouse floor, a moldering corpse easily identifiable as human, female, young . . .

"Oh, my God—Deborah!"

"Matt's right. It's Deborah Poroth."

"How long's she been dead?"

"Looks like a long time."

He heard the cries of horror and dismay, the babble of unanswered questions, and a voice that demanded, "Where's Sarr Poroth?"

He didn't see or hear the rest: how the thing lay there looking up at them with what was left of its eyes, and how, before dying, it smiled. "Too late," it whispered toothlessly through cracked lips, as its eyes rolled toward the darkening sky. "Too late."

It stands above the expectant earth, its feet planted wide upon the topmost boulder of the great spiked thing it has built against the side of the hill. In the dying light it surveys the scene below.

Twenty feet down, the forest floor lies streaked by shadow, except for a flickering light at the base of the hill where, within a tiny ring of stones, a fire burns. Higher, midway up the altar, on a flat outcropping of granite some ten feet from its perch, it can see the body of the woman, her nakedness pale against the dark grey stone, her hair an obscene splash of red. Her body has not yet been painted. Her eyes, it sees, are shut tight now, her breathing slow; she is dreaming again, lost once more in a drugged slumber. By her hands and feet lie curled the lengths of rugged cloth ripped from the farmer's shirt and trousers, crude substitutes for the straps the Ceremony requires, but sufficient.

The Old One, it remembers, had brought leather straps from the city, but he has not returned. He may not arrive in time to help it shave its head clean for the Marriage, to light the fire, to sing the words. But this absence is of no importance; it can perform the Ceremony without the old man. It knows what to do.

The great hill towers at its back like an immense dark hood. Along the ground the encircling trees make black, twisted patterns in the twilight, the visible veins of some vast invisible being. Shadowy forms shift like woodsmoke in the air overhead. The altar stone trembles at its feet.

It is time. Reaching up past its farmer's face and running its fingers through the shattered remnants of its scalp, it proceeds with its grooming for the Marriage, yanking out clumps of the farmer's black hair, ignoring the swatches of flesh that come loose and the sluggish gouts of blood. No assistance is needed; it puts the old man from its mind. Before the final rays of sunlight have faded from the summit of the hill, its skull is as smooth as a freshly cracked egg. Tearing open the tattered remains of its shirt, it lifts its long pale arms in invocation. Above it, as if a monstrous hand has thrown the switch, the sky darkens.

The mound beneath its feet is trembling more violently now. It can hear the frightened cries of animals in the woods below; black hunched shapes are racing back and forth among the trees.

Carefully, dropping on all fours, it picks its way past the girl and down the slope. Seizing a burning brand, it touches it three times to the ring of wood, undergrowth, and debris it has piled at the base of the hill. The pile smokes, flickers, catches: like a moat that makes of them an island, cutting them off from the surrounding forest, a line of fire leaps outward in a great circle, sweeping out of sight around the far side of the hill, the flames seeming to speed the advancing darkness.

The woman moans, stirs. Firelight glistens in her hair; in the farmer's shattered skull the spaces glow a deeper red. The two of them are like a pair of brands: pale slim bodies, smooth limbs, heads of flame. The trees beyond the firelight are almost invisible now, dim skeletal shapes half hidden by the smoke. The dark hill rears malignly toward the empty sky; the stars are not out, the moon not yet risen. Screaming shapes wheel unseen overhead.

At the foot of the altar it throws the brand aside, stretches up on tiptoe, fingertips reaching toward the ledge, and, like some long pale lizard, climbs laboriously up the rock face toward the woman. Crouching above her, in the absence of the Old One, it opens wide its corpse's mouth, tilts its face skyward, and starts to sing the words.

" 'Too late,' " Abram Sturtevant repeated, for at least the sixth time. He fingered his coffee-colored beard. "'Twas exactly what the man said, wasn't it?"

Galen Trudel nodded. "His very words." He and Matthew Geisel had gone up to the house and had found nothing but four cats who'd followed them back down here, where the others were standing in an awkward, puzzled group around the sleeping form of Freirs. The wasps had missed him; he lay in the grass on his belly, his wrists freed from the straps, arms thrown forward as if to embrace the earth.

"And we were too late, weren't we?" said Sturtevant. "Too late for him. That would be what he meant. Had we arrived any sooner, we could've saved the poor old man's life."

It made sense to them. It was just about the only thing that did.

All the rest was questions. Why had the stranger, so monstrously transformed by the venom and clearly in pain, died with a smile on his lips? And who was he, anyway? The men had come dashing down the slope from the road, hurrying toward his screams ringing like a woman's from the smokehouse, and had stumbled into a morass of questions—along with swarms of deadly insects, a pair of ruined corpses, and a sleeper who wouldn't wake up no matter what they did, even when Brother Rupert, his own arms and neck aching horribly from the stings, brought a hatful of cold water from the brook and threw it in Freirs' face. Freirs had simply turned back onto his belly, pressing his ear to the ground as if listening.

Questions. So many things they didn't understand . . .

They had prayed, all of them, over the bodies of the stranger and Deborah Poroth, and afterward had contented themselves with sending Klaus Buckhalter off to Flemington in his truck to summon the county police; on his way he would take the suffering Ham Stoudemire home, where Nettie could tend to his swellings. Rupert Lindt decided he would stay around, stings or no stings. "I ain't leavin' till I get some answers," he'd declared, nodding toward Freirs. "Unless Klaus wants to drive him into Flemington."

"Best not to move him," said Sturtevant.

Freirs slept on. At least, now, he was freed from suspicion; the bound wrists had convinced them that here was no malefactor, just another victim.

But were they all victims? Even the stranger they'd seen die, red and swollen, at their very feet? And what had killed poor Sister Deborah, her (they remembered) so lately recovered from the attack of that demon-ridden cat? And where had Brother Sarr disappeared to? And who had tied up Freirs?

Questions. A sea of questions lapping at their ankles . . .

Silent and uneasy, the men shifted from foot to foot and looked at Freirs lying motionless on the grass, the deserted farm, the frozen ranks of pines across the brook. They avoided looking at the two ruined corpses by the smokehouse; they avoided one another's eyes. This was not turning out as they'd expected; they had come, nursing their anger and their fear, to usher this intruder from their midst . . . and had found, instead, a mystery.

A breeze traveled up the slope toward the farmhouse, fluttering the leaves in the garden. Roses shook like fists in the waning light; the dark pines stirred. Night was coming on. At their feet the churning waters of the brook seemed strangely hushed. Somewhere in the forest a jay screamed, once, twice, three times, then fell silent. It was like the signal to begin.

Suddenly, overhead, the sky darkened. Beneath their feet, the ground shook. The land around them trembled with a deep, distant, almost inaudible rumbling.

"Oh, my God," said Matthew, "it's startin' again."

He felt the planet pounding with the beating of his heart, the land beneath him rocking, blood squeezing once again through his veins. *I'm alive!* he thought dimly. But it was much too slow, too vast, and he realized it was coming from beneath him, and there were voices.

And darkness all around him.

"Looks like he's woke up."

Sound of footsteps.

"Son, listen to me." Someone was standing above him. "Listen, you've got to tell us—"

"His name's Freirs. Jeremiah Freirs."

"No—" another voice "—it's Jeremy."

Someone was shaking him. "Listen . . . Jeremy. Tell us what's happened here. Where's Sarr Poroth?"

"Sarr?" He sat up, rubbed his eyes, searched in vain for his glasses. "Ask—" He looked around him in the darkness, gripped by a sudden panic. "Where's Carol?"

"Carol?"

"That's that girl o' his," he heard someone say. "'Twas her car we saw in the drive." Rupert Lindt, it sounded like. But then another voice, much louder, demanded, "What's she gone and done with Brother Sarr?"

He was confused. "You mean—" he stammered, "you mean the Poroths still aren't back?"

"Deborah's dead, son," said Matt Geisel.

And over the sound the earth was making, punctuated by tremors whose effects came more regularly now, they told him of the old man's death, and the body in the smokehouse, and the wasps.

"Rosie," whispered Freirs, "Deborah . . ." He shook his head. It wasn't real, none of it, they were lying to him, and as soon as he found his glasses he would show them they were wrong. The world was a dark place, blurred and confusing. He felt the ground tremble. "I don't know what's happened," he said, raising his voice to compete with a rumbling that had grown progressively more insistent. "All I know is I'm worried about the girl who came out here yesterday. We've got to find her."

He heard someone cry out and saw the others turn to look. Behind them one of the men was pointing into the darkness, where several small grey shapes were racing madly round the lawn in endless circles.

"The cats!" said Geisel. "My Lord, just look at 'em, they're chasin' one another's tails . . ."

Freirs remembered the Uroborus, the dragon with its tail gripped in its teeth. A full circle, that's what it signaled. Completion. The rolling year come around again to this most special day . . .

"What we ought to do," one of them was saying, "is try Shem Fenchel's dogs. I hear they're real good trackers."

"We should head back to the trucks," said someone else, "and split up when we get to town." They began moving back toward the road.

In the east, like a great cyclopean beast lifting its huge head, the moon rose majestically above the treetops, casting long gigantic shadows across the lawn. It was full tonight, the second full moon of the month, and very bright. To Freirs, without his glasses, there seemed something new in its face, something baleful and malign. Yet at its rising he felt a surge of sudden, unlikely hope: maybe in the moonlight they would be able to search for Carol . . . like those searchers in the moonlight, on the two other nights, for the two other girls. The memory flooded back to him.

"Bloodhounds," another was saying, as they drifted off, "that's what we need. We ought to go back to town and get those two pups Jacob's son's been raisin' out behind his house—"

"Wait," Freirs called after them. "Listen to me!" He stumbled to his feet.

The men paused, turned to face him. "What is it?" came a voice.

"I know where they are."

Several figures left the group and approached him in the darkness. "Yeah?" said one. "Where's that?"

He nodded toward the woods. "McKinney's Neck."

The night has deepened and the sky has turned a velvet black when the thing on the hillside finishes its song. Tiny crow's- feet of blood mark the corners of its mouth where, stretched taut by widening jaws, the skin has torn like old paper. Beneath its feet the land is shaking rhythmically now, throwing up small clouds of dust, as if the entire world, wilderness and cities and seas, were echoing to an immense heartbeat.

Poised naked on a rock above the altar, it lifts its face to the sky. It spreads its arms like angel wings and dances like a serpent in the moonlight. It spins, leaps, crouches, stands, spits blood into its mutilated hands. It gestures toward the earth.

It speaks the final Name.

Around it birds fall to the ground and crawl among the rocks like lizards. They open their razor beaks, and the air is filled with a great roaring.

Spiderlike it turns and clambers down the wall of boulders, pointing its face toward the woman.

Miles to the south, the farmhouse stands trembling in the moonlight. Beneath its darkened windows, one by one, the roses in the garden lift their heads, point their faces toward the moon, and open wide their secret mouths; while in the night sky overhead, one by one, the stars come out of hiding.

It is Lammas Eve.

They ran noisily through the woods, crashing through the underbrush like a pack of dogs, dodging brambles and tree trunks, a few of the men in the rear armed with weapons they'd seized from the Poroths' barn—pitchforks, a rake, a long-handled axe with a smeared, discolored blade—mumbling snatches of prayer as they ran and shouting directions and encouragement to one another. Freirs followed blindly behind them, relying mainly on sound, able to see only dimly without his glasses and still unsteady on his feet. In his right hand he gripped the sickle that he'd lifted from the wall of the barn, holding it before him as he stumbled forward through the darkness, trying to block the invisible branches that snapped painfully at his face. Amid the shouting and confusion he remembered how, at last Sunday's worship, the sickle had been blessed in the Cleansing; maybe it would bring him luck tonight.

They had charged heedlessly over the stream, all of them but Lindt who was hurt and Geisel who was old and Freirs who was sightless; these three had picked their way more slowly, fearful of losing their footing. Freirs had been the last. As he stumbled across, the air ringing with shouts and splashing and the subterranean rumbling that still hadn't ceased, he was sure that he'd heard singing behind him, a thin unearthly wailing, rising from the direction of the farmhouse. He had felt, in that sound, dark heads turn and tiny mouths gape wide, and he'd thought automatically, *the cats*—but he'd shuddered, for the voices he'd heard hadn't sounded like cats, or anything that crept upon the earth. He heard them no longer, but he couldn't get them out of his mind. *Just the cats,* he told himself, and hurried on.

They were well past the stream now, heading north through the swampy sections of the woods, where their progress was slowed as their feet were sucked down by the mud. Yet even here the ground was quivering as if alive, and below it thunder rolled, as if echoing from caverns deep within the earth.

There were other voices too, filling the darkness with sound. Occasionally he could hear the weird night cries of woodland creatures and, far off, a low, indistinct roaring as from a thousand animal throats; and once a great pale round shape had come hurtling toward them out of a clump of bushes like some boulder come to life, squealing in terror.

"Brother Galen," someone had called, "'twas one o' your hogs."

And there was still another sound now, far in the distance, a vast and wrathful buzzing. It was like the warning growl that cats make just before they strike, only amplified a million times, or like the buzzing of a million bees.

Panting, Freirs pushed onward, desperate to keep up with the others and afraid of losing them in the darkness. The sporadic shafts of moonlight illuminating the spaces between the trees were of little help and only confused him, like panels in a hall of mirrors. Branches seemed to reach out toward him, as if to hold him back. Thorns and brambles tore at him as he passed. Once, at the edge of the swamp, he tripped over a root and fell headlong in the mud, nearly losing the sickle. Floundering to his feet, he stumbled onward. The roaring was all around him now, rising and falling in time with the beating of the earth, and the buzzing had grown louder.

They had emerged from the swamp and were passing through a stretch of slightly drier ground where the foliage was thinner, when they saw the fire. It was impossible to tell how large it was, or how far away. All of them were tired now, but seeing the flames through the skeletal forms of the trees, and with an objective at last in sight, they broke into a run, though not without a certain wariness lest the blaze prove so large they be forced to turn and flee.

They ran with a new urgency as it became more apparent, the nearer they drew to it, that the fire had been man-made. And suddenly they were running over rocks and debris, the forest had fallen away, and they found themselves facing a wall of leaping flames as tall as they were, and waves of scorching heat, and blinding smoke that blotted out the sky. And beyond the flames, like a great dark presence at the end of a dream, stood the hill.

It rose black and obscene in the moonlight, thrusting itself above the tops of the dwarfed trees like some huge squatting animal, its great humped back furred with clumps of vegetation. Freirs, racing up behind the others, saw them silhouetted against the fire at its base as they stumbled into the clearing with arms or weapons raised, and heard the screams of those who'd blundered too close to the flames. And above the screams a roaring split the night, and a buzzing as of insects, as loud as all the insects in the world; and the roaring came from all around them, from the land and the trees and the darkness itself, but the buzzing came only from the hill.

Beneath the sound he heard a higher, rhythmic cry, the moaning of a woman in pain.

"Carol!"

She was somewhere above him on the hill. Freirs pushed through the crowd of men and hurried forward, but the heat was too intense; he fell back wincing with pain, gasping, eyes smarting.

"She's up there!" He was shouting to anyone who could hear him over the deafening noise. No one turned. Several dim figures were poking feebly at the fire with pitchforks, keeping well back from the flames. He reached for the man who was closest, grabbing him roughly by the shoulder.

"We've got to reach her!"

The other turned, face glowing redly in the firelight, the eyes wide and frightened as a rabbit's, and Freirs saw that it was the leathery old farmer who'd given him a ride from town; he didn't even know the man's name. The farmer shook his head, said something unintelligible, pointed to his ear. *He can't hear me,* Freirs realized. *And he doesn't hear Carol.*

Freirs shielded his eyes and looked for the others. Amid the smoke they seemed a crowd of milling shadows, their figures black against the flames, blurred and distorted by the rising waves of heat. None of them seemed to hear.

The moaning came again.

She was just behind the wall of fire, he was sure of it; she sounded almost close enough to touch. And she was hurt, hurt badly; he could hear it in her voice. In despair he stared down at his body, with the fleeting realization that, for all its weight, it was a fragile and sensitive thing, easily pained, easy to damage irreparably, and knowing nonetheless that *someone* was going to have to do it, *someone* had to go. Fate, it seemed, had painted him into a corner; he had no choice. Throwing his left arm before his face and brandishing the sickle as if the flames were a curtain he could slice through, he thought of Carol as he wanted to remember her, so sweetly, trustingly naked that evening on the couch in her apartment, and leaped.

And as he did so, just as his feet left the ground, a final thought struck him: what if this was *not* a wall of fire? What if it was thicker than a wall, or had no end at all? What if—

He felt his feet drag against timber stacked too high for him to clear, felt some of it give way as he crashed through. He was suddenly surrounded by flames. They licked at his legs and his feet, and he screamed and kicked out as his skin burned beneath his shoes and clothing, his lungs were bursting from the heat, he was breathing fire . . . and then he had passed through, he had tumbled among the rocks at the base of the hill and was dragging himself weakly to safety. Clutching the sickle, he staggered to his aching feet and looked up.

The world was a blur, a roaring, earsplitting blur aglow with flame. In its wavering red light he saw the huge mound looming blackly overhead, throbbing as if it were alive, with steady even beats that shook the ground like thunder; he saw the crude truncated pyramid of boulders piled against its sloping side; he saw the narrow ledge some ten feet above him to his left, midway up the rockpile, with a figure that must be Carol still moaning, lying up there on her back so that he could see a pale slice of her body—a leg, an arm, an edge of naked breast—in a travesty of the way he'd just remembered her; and he saw the slender white form, supple as a milk snake, that curled over her in an arch no human should have made, a white rainbow of flesh with ends at Carol's head and feet. This final figure looked barely human; an emaciated naked man, perhaps, with an abnormally elongated body and a shaved head . . .

He was no longer sure what he was seeing. Shapes were indistinct without his glasses, and the figures on the ledge seemed far away. He was sure the serpentine figure was a man, but he couldn't tell just where the face might be, or how a man could stretch like that, or what was happening to Carol; for all Freirs could see, the two might be enacting some strange solemn theorem of geometry. He noticed now that, in two places, slim white sticklike shapes hung down beneath the man's arched form like twin supports, pointing toward Carol's horizontal body, which now seemed to struggle and heave, her cries rising in pitch. Frantically he hauled himself up onto one of the lower boulders and climbed higher, drawing several yards closer to the level of the pair, and discerned at last the strips of black and white cloth binding Carol's wrists and ankles. He saw the sticks for what they were and realized, with a shock of disbelief, that what he was seeing was a rape.

But the rapist's head and face, he saw now, were not where he'd expected to find them: the act occurring up there on the rocks was a reverse one, a living yin and yang, a mystical obscenity as smooth as a symbol of the zodiac. The white rod of the man's sex, a long, preternaturally thin phallus, exaggerated like the things the satyrs bore in old pagan images, hovered expectantly above the girl's mouth, a mouth still open wide and moaning, while from the rapist's own mouth hung what Freirs at first took, crazily, for a long pale twisted horn, an instrument of bone or wood, but which he now perceived was a living appendage that curled and quested toward her open legs like a great blind worm, prodding them softly and irregularly with its tip. There was a tiger stripe across one thigh· he saw as he climbed closer, that her legs had been painted at their juncture with a black design of two concentric rings.

Suddenly, like some hungry predator that's sensed the prey at last, the appendage stiffened with a life of its own, stretched taut, and seemed to bury itself deeper between her legs. The girl's struggles ceased, and at the same moment her cries were silenced as the man's sex slipped between her lips.

With the touch of these two organs it was as if a circuit had been forged, a switch thrown, the completion of a white circle there upon the altar, body linked to body, end to end, a double serpent swallowing its tail. Carol's body jerked as if touched with electricity, a great flash of red fire glowed up and down the length of the hill, and with it came the sound of the rending of earth.

Clinging to the trembling rock, Freirs craned his neck, squinted upward through the smoke, and gasped. A crack had appeared in the dark slope above him. The hill was beginning to open. Inside, fires glowed a molten red, smoke belched forth into the night, and he could see, dimly within, a great bunched shape begin to stir, coiling and uncoiling, like a giant worm curled within a apple.

He hung frozen to the rock face, watching as the fissure grew. The opening in the giant mound gaped wider like the jaws of some immense beast, and the buzzing that came from within it grew ever more shrill, as if the sound itself might force open the portals still further.

It was the sound that shook him free. He struggled forward now with a new urgency, ignoring the pain of his burned feet, clawing his way feverishly up the rocks that shook and heaved as if to throw him off, pulling himself at last to the ledge by his hands, one hand still gripping his weapon. Before him lay the spread form of Carol and the long white body arching above her, the face turned away, the torso like an immense white artery throbbing in time with the throbbing of the earth.

Even in the darkness he could see that it looked barely human. And what had happened to the head? Once, as a boy, he had chanced to drop a giant jar of peanut butter onto a stone floor; the container had shattered, but the shards of glass had remained clinging loosely in place, held by the substance inside. So it was, he thought suddenly, crazily, of this creature's hairless skull: shattered like crockery, yet all the pieces still intact.

The other took no notice as Freirs dragged himself onto the rock shelf beside them. Suddenly the white arc of the body tautened, the face, once hidden, turned toward Freirs, the tube filling the mouth, and in the moonlight Freirs recognized the farmer, his host and friend Sarr Poroth.

The face stared past him with no more recognition than a scarecrow, the eyes unseeing. There was nothing behind them. Carol's body quaked, her legs sprawled open in the moonlight, and it dawned on Freirs what the concentric rings on them were for: a signpost for something unfamiliar with the human female body. A target.

Slowly, as if it had read the revulsion in Freirs' mind, the farmer's eyes turned toward him, and the corners of the mouth stretched in a smile.

In terror Freirs lashed out with the sickle, the metal flashing in the firelight. The thing before him barely quivered at the blows, as unyielding as a slab of dead meat. Idly it raised a ravaged hand and groped toward Freirs' face. With the next blow Freirs struck home, the sharpened blade sweeping cleanly through the appendage that snaked from the farmer's open mouth.

Severed, the thing twisted and shriveled like a sliced-open worm, streaming obscene milky fluid. The farmer's body jerked twice, then fell limp upon Carol's. Above them the buzzing grew higher in pitch, became a scream as the thing within the mound thrust once more toward the stars, rising coil upon coil, then subsided. The seam began to close. Freirs saw the line of fire grow thinner as the massive blocks of earth slid together again, the great portals shutting. Miles to the south, the singing ceased as roses turned black and withered on their stems.

The mound sank inward on itself, settling back to its original shape, the cracks closing completely and blocking the fire inside, the tremors subsiding. The white appendage hung limply from the corpse's mouth like a severed umbilical cord. Freirs looked down in time to see a tiny charcoal-black creature slip from the hollow tube and scurry down the rocks, a rodent fleeing the collapse of its home. Poroth's tale came back to him, the mouse within the dead man's gaping mouth. Before he could cry out, the creature had leaped nimbly down the wall of rocks and the dark earth had swallowed it up.

The roaring was stilled, the vibrations had stopped. Around him now he could hear the innocent crackling of the flames and the voices of men pushing their way through to the hillside. Once again the sound of crickets filled the night.

Carol lay dazed upon the altar, eyes shut, her mouth still hanging open. Freirs rolled the farmer's body off her; it was already stiffening, the appendage dry and withered. Gently he closed Carol's mouth as one would the mouth of a corpse, not daring to peer inside, and covered her nakedness with his torn and sweaty shirt, thinking how different the moaning, heaving woman he'd seen below the farmer had been from the Carol he'd known, and wondering, reluctantly, how much pain there'd really been in those sounds she'd made, and how much pleasure.

Embracing her, he promised himself not to think too hard about it.

The moon gazed silently upon his kiss, the stars stared coldly down; and if they heard his vow, they made no sign.

CHRISTMAS

Those same stars looked coldly down that winter upon the teeming city.

The stores were open late that night for last-minute shopping. Crowds hurried through the frozen streets, arms laden with packages. Salvation Army bands competed with the sounds of the traffic. Steam rose from holes in the pavement.

He walked with her, hand in hand, through the crowd. She was smiling at the shop windows, the Santas in the street, the excited, rosy faces of the children, but something in her gaze seemed far away, and always would be.

He, too, was distracted. He was musing upon the holy birth now being celebrated, and upon the unholy one so narrowly averted that very summer. He reminded himself for the thousandth time that nothing, that night, had been born.

And yet the monstrous thing itself, the thing the old man had given his life for, had not been destroyed. Might it not be living still, waiting in its egg of earth? Had he interrupted the Ceremony in time?

The stars trembled unseen beyond the lights of the city. He felt his wife's hand in his. Surrounded by the throng, he paused, listened a moment, then walked on.

"What is it, Jeremy?" she asked. "Is something wrong?"

"It's nothing, honey," he said. He smiled at her and clutched her hand more tightly. She hadn't heard it.

But he had—he was almost sure of it. Above the sounds of the city, the taxi horns, the music, and the laughter, he had heard the roar of the dragon.